SELECT EDITIONS

Selected and Edited by Reader's Digest

SELECT EDITIONS

Selected and Edited by
Reader's Digest

 New York · Montreal

FROM THE EDITORS

We usually use this space to give you a bit of background on the books in the volume. But this time we have something different to share. To put it bluntly, this is the end of an era for Select Editions. Longtime deputy editor Jim Menick has finally tossed in the bookmark and is retiring after nearly forty years at Select Editions.

Jim started out as a senior editor in 1981 and worked his way up to head honcho in 2008. He knows a thing or two because he's seen a thing or two. When he started at SE, we had a staff of dozens. We were called Condensed Books. We edited on (gasp!) paper. But we've changed along with the rest of the world. We're now called Select Editions. We do all our editing on computers. We're a much leaner staff that relies in part on our team of excellent freelance editors.

Jim has been at the helm for much of this transition and has been an outstanding example of embracing change while maintaining the core values that really matter. And what really matters is simple: finding great books for SE and editing them with care, skill, and respect. We still seek stories that entertain, inspire, and open our minds to new worlds. That will never change, no matter who's in charge. We've hired some terrific new employees—senior editor Meredith Hale and associate production editor Julia Bullock. I'll be taking over the helm after twenty-nine years at Reader's Digest, and I promise to honor the Select Editions legacy and to do my best to always find books that you'll love. So thank you, Jim, and here's looking forward to a bright future.

—*Amy Reilly*, EXECUTIVE EDITOR

Inside
SELECT EDITIONS

"Breathtaking—brightly written, scalpel-sharp, and altogether inspired."
—A. J. FINN, #1 New York Times Bestselling Author of THE WOMAN IN THE WINDOW
THE LAST TIME I LIED
National Bestselling Author of FINAL GIRLS
RILEY SAGER
A Novel

This is how it begins.

You wake to sunlight whispering through the trees just outside the window. It's a faint light, weak and gray at the edges. Dawn still shedding the skin of night. Yet it's bright enough to make you roll over and face the wall, the mattress creaking beneath you. Within that roll is a moment of disorientation, a split second when you don't know where you are. It happens sometimes after a deep, dreamless slumber. A temporary amnesia. You see the fine grains of the pine-plank wall, smell the traces of campfire smoke in your hair, and know exactly where you are.

Camp Nightingale.

You close your eyes and try to drop back into sleep, doing your best to ignore the nature noise outside. You catch the drumroll of insects, the chirp of birds, a solitary loon letting out one last ghostly call. The racket of the outdoors temporarily masks the silence inside. But then you realize how quiet it is. Your eyes dart open again as you strain to hear something else—anything else—coming from inside the cabin. There's nothing.

It's a small space. Just enough room for two sets of bunk beds, a night table topped by a lantern, and four hickory trunks near the door for storage. You fling your gaze to the bunks across from you. The top one is neatly made. The bottom is the opposite, a tangle of blankets.

You check your watch in the early half-light. It's a few minutes past five a.m. Almost an hour until reveille. The revelation brings panic.

Emergency scenarios trot through your brain. A sudden illness. A frantic call from home. You even try to tell yourself it's possible the girls had to leave so quickly they couldn't be bothered to wake you. Or maybe they tried but you couldn't be roused. Or maybe they did and you can't remember.

You kneel before the hickory trunks by the door and fling open all of them but yours. The inside of each satin-lined box is stuffed to the brim with clothes and magazines and simple camp crafts. Two of them hold cell phones, turned off, unused for days. Only one of them took her phone. You have no idea what that could mean.

The first place you think the girls can be is the latrine, a cedar-walled rectangle just beyond the cabins, planted right at the threshold of the forest. You open the cabin door and step outside. It's a gray, chilly morning. Inside the latrine, you check every stall and shower. They're all empty.

You head back to the cabins, circling them quietly. There are twenty cabins in all, each named after a tree. Yours is Dogwood. You squint into windows, scanning the double-decker rows of sleeping girls for signs of additional campers.

You make your way to the other side of the camp. The mess hall is locked. It's the same at the arts-and-crafts building next door. Locked.

You head into the center of camp, where a mammoth, log-frame building sits at the end of a circular drive. The Lodge. Right now, it's silent. Dark. You can barely make out its red door.

Part of you wants to run to that door and pound on it until Franny answers. She needs to know that three girls are gone. She's the camp director, after all. The girls are her responsibility.

You resist because you could be wrong. That you overlooked some important place where the girls might have stashed themselves. Then there's the fact that you're reluctant to tell Franny until you absolutely must. You've already disappointed her once. You don't want to do it again.

Something behind the Lodge catches your eye. A strip of orange light beyond its sloped back lawn. Lake Midnight, reflecting sky.

The girls aren't there, of course. There's no rational reason they would be. It feels like a nightmare come true. Maybe that's why you don't stop walking once you reach the lake's edge. You keep going, into the lake itself.

You rotate in the water, examining your surroundings. Behind you is the Lodge. The lakeshore stretches away from you on both sides, rocky coast and leaning trees. The opposite shore is just a dark streak faintly visible in the mist. All of it—the camp, the lake, the forest—is private property, owned by Franny's family, passed down through generations.

The girls could be anywhere. You imagine them stumbling through the woods, hungry and scared and shivering. You picture them under the water, sinking into the muck, trying to grasp their way to the surface.

You think of all these things and begin to scream.

PART ONE

Two Truths

Chapter 1

I PAINT THE GIRLS in the same order.

Vivian first. Then Natalie. Allison is last, even though she was first to leave the cabin and therefore the first to disappear.

My paintings are typically large. Massive, really. Yet the girls are always small. Their arrival heralds the second stage of a painting, after I've laid down a background of earth and sky in hues with appropriately dark names. Spider black. Shadow gray. Midnight blue.

Then come the girls. I put them in white dresses that flare at the hems, as if they're running from something, their hair trailing behind them as they flee.

I create the woods last, using a putty knife to slather paint onto the canvas in wide, unwieldy strokes. I glob on layer upon layer, each wall-size canvas slowly succumbing to the forest of my imagination. Thick. Forbidding. Crowded with danger.

I paint until there's not a bare patch left on the canvas and the girls have been consumed by the forest, rendered invisible. Only then do I swirl my name into the lower right-hand corner.

Emma Davis.

That same name, in that same borderline-illegible script, now graces a wall of the gallery. Every other wall is filled with paintings. *My* paintings. Twenty-seven of them. My first gallery show.

It's a week until St. Patrick's Day. The gallery is packed. Collectors and critics, champagne in hand, reaching for the mushroom-and-goat-cheese croquettes that float by. I've been introduced to dozens of people important enough for Randall, the gallery owner, to whisper who they are in my ear as I shake their hands.

"From the *Times*," he says of a woman dressed head to toe in shades of purple. Of a man in an impeccably tailored suit and bright red sneakers, he simply whispers, "Christie's."

"Very impressive work," Mr. Christie's says. "They're so bold."

In person, I'm anything but bold. Tonight's little black dress and black pumps are as fancy as I get. My only jewelry is the silver charm bracelet always wrapped around my left wrist. Hanging from it are three charms—tiny birds made of brushed pewter. In truth, boldness in one's personality seems futile to me. Vivian was bold in every way. It didn't keep her from disappearing.

Once Randall has exhausted his supply of strangers to introduce, I hang back from the crowd, nursing a glass of champagne. I perk up once Marc arrives. He fits in perfectly. Bearded with adorably mussed hair. A plaid sport coat thrown over his worn Mickey Mouse T-shirt. Marc snags a glass of champagne and one of the croquettes, which he pops into his mouth and chews thoughtfully.

"The cheese saves it," he informs me. "But those watery mushrooms are a major infraction."

"I haven't tried one yet," I say. "Too nervous."

Marc puts a hand on my shoulder, steadying me. Marc Stewart. My voice of reason. My best friend.

"You're allowed to enjoy this, you know," he says.

"I know."

"You can be proud of yourself. There's no need to feel guilty. Artists are supposed to be inspired by life experiences. That's what creativity is all about." Marc's talking about the girls, of course. Buried inside every painting. Other than me, only he knows about their existence. The only thing I haven't told him is why.

I never intended to paint this way. In art school, I was drawn to simplicity in both color and form. Then came an assignment to paint a portrait of someone I knew who had died. I chose the girls.

I painted Vivian first, because she burned brightest in my memory. That blond hair right out of a shampoo ad. Those incongruously dark eyes that looked black in the right light. The pert nose sprayed with freckles brought out by the sun.

Natalie came next. High forehead. Square chin. Hair pulled tight in a ponytail. Her white dress got a dainty lace collar that downplayed her thick neck and broad shoulders.

Finally, there was Allison, with her wholesome look. Apple cheeks and slender nose. Brows darker than her flaxen hair. I painted an Elizabethan ruff around her neck, frilly and regal.

Yet there was something wrong with the finished painting. Something that gnawed at me until the night before the project was due, when I awoke at two a.m. and saw the three of them staring at me from across the room.

Seeing them. That was the problem.

I crept out of bed and approached the canvas. I grabbed a brush, dabbed it in some brown paint, and smeared a line over their eyes. A tree branch, blinding them. More branches followed. Then plants and vines and whole trees. By dawn, most of the canvas had been besieged by forest. All that remained of Vivian, Natalie, and Allison were shreds of white dresses, patches of skin, locks of hair.

That became No. 1. The first in my forest series. The only one where even a fraction of the girls is visible. That piece, which got the highest grade in the class, is absent from the gallery show. It hangs in my loft, not for sale.

Most of the others are here, though. Seeing them together like this makes me realize how obsessive the whole endeavor is.

"I *am* proud," I tell Marc before taking a sip of champagne.

"Then what's up? You seem *vexed*."

"It's just weird. I never expected any of this."

It's the truth. If I had expected a gallery show, I would have actually named my work. Instead, I simply numbered them in the order they were painted. No. 1 through No. 33.

Those thirty-three canvases are the only things I've painted outside my duties as house artist at an ad agency. I've attempted other things, of course, but I return to the girls every damn time. I know I can't keep painting them, losing them in the woods again and again. To that end, I've vowed not to paint another.

When Marc leaves my side, it gives Randall the perfect moment to clutch my wrist and drag me to a slender woman studying No. 30, my largest work to date.

"Here she is, darling," Randall announces. "The artist herself."

The woman whirls around, fixing me with a friendly, green-eyed gaze I haven't seen in fifteen years. "Hello, Emma," she says.

I freeze. I had assumed Francesca Harris-White wanted nothing to do with me. Yet she smiles warmly before pulling me close. A semi-embrace that Randall witnesses with palpable jealousy.

"You already know each other?"

"Yes," I say, still stunned by her presence.

"It was ages ago. Emma was a mere slip of a girl. And I couldn't be more proud of the woman she's become."

I realize how happy I am to see her. "Thank you, Mrs. Harris-White," I tell her. "That's very kind of you to say."

She mock-frowns. "What's with this 'Mrs. Harris-White' nonsense? It's Franny. Always Franny."

I remember that, too. Her standing before us in her khaki shorts and blue polo shirt. *Call me Franny. In the great outdoors, we're all equals.*

It didn't last. Afterward, when what happened was in newspapers across the country, it was her full name that was used. Francesca Harris-White. Net worth estimated to be almost a billion.

Now she stands before me, seemingly untouched by time, even though she must be in her late seventies. Her skin is tan and radiant. Her sleeveless blue dress emphasizes her trim figure. Her hair, a shade balanced between blond and gray, has been pulled back in a chignon, showing off a single strand of pearls around her neck.

She turns to the painting again, her gaze scanning its formidable width. "It's really quite marvelous," she says. "All of them are." There's a catch in her voice. Something tremulous and uncertain.

"I must confess that I came here under false pretenses," she says, still staring at the painting. "I have what you might call an interesting proposition." She fixes those green eyes on me. "I'd love to discuss it with you, when you have the time."

Randall, standing behind Franny at a discreet distance, mouths the word *commission*. The idea prompts me to say, "Of course."

"Then join me for lunch tomorrow. Let's say twelve thirty? At my place? It will give us a chance to catch up."

I find myself nodding. "Of course," I say again.

Franny beams. "Wonderful."

She presses a card into my hand. Navy print on heavy white vellum. Simple but elegant. It bears her name, a phone number, and a Park Avenue address. Before leaving, she pulls me into another half hug. Then she turns to Randall and gestures toward No. 30.

"I'll take it," she says.

FRANNY'S building is easy to find. It's the one that bears her family's name. The Harris is understated architecture rising high over Park Avenue. Above the doorway is the Harris family crest carved in marble. It depicts two tall pines crossed together to form an X, surrounded by an ivy laurel. The family's initial fortune came from the culling of such trees.

The inside of the Harris is as somber and hushed as a cathedral. The doorman smiles and greets me by name. The warm welcome continues when I'm directed to the elevator. Standing inside is another familiar face from Camp Nightingale.

"Lottie?" I say.

Unlike Franny, she's changed quite a bit in the past fifteen years. The shorts and plaid shirt have been replaced with a charcoal pantsuit over a crisp white blouse. Her hair, once long and the color of mahogany, is now jet-black and cut into a sleek bob that frames her pale face. But the warm, friendly smile is the same.

"Emma," she says, pulling me into a hug. "It's nice to see you."

I hug her back. "You too, Lottie. I wondered if you still worked for Franny."

"She couldn't get rid of me if she tried. Not that she'd want to."

Indeed, the two of them were rarely seen apart. Franny the master of the camp, and Lottie the devoted assistant. Their benevolent patience never strained, even when surprised by a latecomer like myself. I can still picture the moment I met Lottie. The unhurried way she emerged from the Lodge after my parents and I arrived hours later than expected. She greeted us with a smile and a sincere "Welcome to Camp Nightingale."

Now she ushers me into the elevator and presses the top button. As we're whisked upward, she says, "You and Franny will be lunching in the greenhouse. Just wait until you see it."

I nod, feigning excitement. Lottie sees right through me.

"Don't be nervous," she says. "Franny's forgiven you a hundred times over."

The elevator doors open, and I find myself looking at the entrance foyer to Franny's penthouse. To my surprise, the wall already bears the painting she purchased the night before.

Lottie leads me down a short hallway to the left, past a formal dining room and through a sunken sitting room.

"Here we are. The greenhouse."

Franny's greenhouse is a two-story conservatory built on what was once the penthouse terrace. Panes of heavy glass rise from floor to vaulted ceiling. Contained within this fanciful structure is a miniature forest. There are squat pines, flowering cherry trees, and rosebushes aflame with red blooms. In the center of this fairy-tale forest is a redbrick patio. That's where I find Franny, seated at a wrought iron table already set for lunch.

"Here she is," Lottie announces. "And probably famished. Which means I better start serving."

Franny greets me with another semi-embrace. "How wonderful to see you again, Emma. What do you think of my greenhouse?"

"It's marvelous," I say. "Too beautiful for words."

"It's my oasis in the big city. I decided that if I couldn't live outdoors, then I'd have to bring the outdoors inside to live with me."

Lunch is trout amandine and arugula salad, washed down with a crisp Riesling. The first glass of wine calms my nerves. The second lets me lower my guard. By the third, when Franny asks me about my job, my personal life, my family, I answer honestly—hate it, still single, parents retired to Boca Raton.

"Everything was delicious," I say when we finish a dessert of lemon tart so tasty I'm tempted to lick the plate.

"I'm so pleased," Franny says. "The trout came from Lake Midnight, you know." Franny notices my surprise and says, "We can still think fondly of a place where bad things have occurred."

It's understandable that Franny feels this way in spite of everything that happened. It is, after all, her family's property. Four thousand acres at the southern base of the Adirondacks, all preserved by her grandfather after he spent a lifetime deforesting land five times that size. I suppose Buchanan Harris thought saving those four thousand acres made up for it. Disappointed he couldn't find a tract of land that contained a large body of water, Franny's grandfather decided to create one himself. He dammed the tributary of a nearby river, slamming the gates shut with the push of a button at the stroke of midnight on New Year's Eve in 1902. Within days, what was once a quiet valley became a lake.

"It hasn't changed one bit," Franny continues. "The Lodge is still there, my home away from home. The boys hate that I go so often. Especially when it's just Lottie and myself. Theo worries that there's no one around to help if something terrible befalls us."

Hearing about Franny's sons gives me another uneasy jolt.

Theodore and Chester Harris-White—Theo and Chet. The younger, Chet, is hazy in my memory. He was just a boy when I was at Camp Nightingale, no more than ten. The product of a surprise, late-in-life adoption. Theo was also adopted. Years before Chet. I remember a lot about him. Maybe too much.

"How are they?" I ask, even though I have no right to know.

"They're both well. Theo is spending the year in Africa, working with Doctors Without Borders. Chet will be getting his master's from Yale in the spring. He's engaged to a lovely girl."

She pauses, allowing the information to settle over me. The

silence speaks volumes. It tells me that her family is thriving, in spite of what I did to them.

"I suppose it's time I reveal why I've asked you here today," Franny finally says.

"I'll admit I'm curious," I say, the understatement of the year.

"I'm going to reopen Camp Nightingale," Franny announces.

"Are you sure that's a good idea?" The words tumble forth, unplanned. "I'm sorry," I say. "That came out wrong."

"You're not the first person to have that reaction. But I feel like it's the right time. The camp has been quiet long enough."

Fifteen years. That's how long it's been. The camp closed early that summer, shutting down after only two weeks.

Camp Nightingale wasn't just any summer camp. It was *the* summer camp. At my school, it was known as Camp Rich Bitch. We said it with scorn, trying to hide our disappointment that our parents couldn't afford to send us there. Except, in my case, for one summer. The same summer that shattered the camp's reputation.

The people involved were all notable enough to keep the story in the news. Natalie, the daughter of the city's top orthopedic surgeon. Allison, the child of a prominent Broadway actress. And Vivian, the Senator's daughter. The press mostly left me alone. I was a nobody, a gangly thirteen-year-old whose grandmother had recently died, leaving her with enough money to spend six weeks at one of the nation's most exclusive summer camps.

It was Franny who received the bulk of the media's scorn. Articles about how Lake Midnight was unsafe, especially considering that Franny's husband had drowned there the year before Camp Nightingale opened. Claims that the camp was understaffed and unsupervised. Think pieces blaming Franny for standing by her son when suspicion swirled around him. Yet Franny shows no ill will as she outlines her vision for the new Camp Nightingale.

"It won't be the same, of course," she says. "I'm going to do things differently this time. I've set up a charitable trust. No one will have to pay a penny to stay there. The camp will be completely free, serving girls from around the tristate area."

"That's very generous," I say.

"I don't want anyone's money. I certainly don't need it. All I need is to see the place filled again with girls enjoying the outdoors. And I'd truly love it if you would join me."

I gulp. Me? Spend the summer at Camp Nightingale?

"It's not that strange of an idea," Franny says. "Yes, the girls there will swim and hike and do all the usual camp activities. But I also want them to learn about writing, photography, painting."

I don't get why Franny wants me, of all people, to be there.

"I understand your trepidation," she says. "But it's my great wish to have some former campers there. To show everyone that it's a safe, happy place again. Rebecca Schoenfeld has agreed to do it."

Becca Schoenfeld. Notable photojournalist. Becca's also a veteran of Camp Nightingale's final summer. Becca was quiet, often alone, content to view the world through the lens of the camera that always hung around her neck.

"I'm not sure I can go back," I say. "Not after what happened."

"Maybe that's precisely why you *should* go back," Franny says. "Nature heals, Emma. I firmly believe that."

I say nothing. Franny's green-eyed gaze is fixed on me.

"Tell me you'll at least give it some thought," she says.

"I will," I tell her. "I'll think about it."

THE next day, I stand before a blank canvas in my loft. I haven't painted a thing in the past six months.

It's pathetic. *I'm* pathetic. The girls are always in my thoughts and on my canvases. After fifteen long years, I know as much about what happened now as I did the night they left the cabin. In the days following the disappearance, I only made things worse. For Franny. For her family. For myself. I could finally change that. Just one small hint about what happened could make a difference.

I grab my phone and dial the number printed so elegantly on the calling card Franny gave me. The call goes straight to voice mail.

"This is Emma Davis. I've given more thought about the offer to spend the summer at Camp Nightingale." I pause, not quite believing what I'm about to say next. "My answer is yes. I'll do it."

I hang up before I change my mind. Even so, I'm struck with the urge to call and take it back. Instead, I call Marc. "I'm going back to Camp Nightingale," I announce. "I want to try to find them."

Fifteen Years Ago
"WAKE up, sunshine." It was just past eight when my mother crept into my bedroom, her eyes already glazed from her morning Bloody Mary. "You all ready to go?" she said.

"Go where?"

My mother stared at me. "Camp, of course."

"What camp? You never told me about any camp."

"I did, Emma. I told you weeks ago. Don't tell me you forgot. Where's your suitcase? We need to be on the road in an hour."

"An *hour*?" My stomach clenched. "Where are we going?"

"Camp Nightingale."

That changed things. For two years I had begged my parents to send me, only to be told no. Now I was suddenly going. In an hour.

My mother started to root through my closet. "You'll love it there. It'll be a summer you'll remember for the rest of your life."

A shiver ran through me. Camp Nightingale. "Whatever," I say with an indignant huff. "I'll go, even though I don't want to."

It was a lie. My first in a summer filled with them.

Chapter 2

THE DRIVE TO CAMP NIGHTINGALE takes up most of the afternoon. The driver of the town car Franny hired for me hardly says a word. My nervousness is the same as my first visit. Back then, it was because I didn't quite know what the camp would be like. Now I know exactly where I'm going.

In the months leading to my departure, I applied for a leave of absence from the ad agency and found someone to sublet the loft while I'm gone. I received weekly e-mails from Lottie that filled in various details of my stay. The debut summer of the new Camp Nightingale planned to have roughly fifty-five campers, five counselors, and five specialized instructors made up of camp alumni.

When I was thirteen, the sudden notice about going to camp delayed our departure for hours, necessitating a trip to Nordstrom's to pick up the things I lacked. This time around, I went overboard in the sporting goods store. Several pairs of shorts. Heavy-duty socks and a sturdy pair of hiking boots. An LED flashlight with a wrist strap. A waterproof case for my iPhone.

Now as we drive there is nothing left for me to do but quell my growing anxiety by sorting through all the things I thought I'd need to help my search. There's a map of Lake Midnight and the surrounding area; a satellite view of the same thing, courtesy of Google Maps; and a stack of old newspaper articles about the disappearance collected from the library and printed off the Internet.

I examine the map and satellite view first. From above, the lake resembles a giant comma that's been tipped over. More than two miles from end to end, with a width ranging from a half mile to five hundred yards. The narrowest area is the eastern point, the location of the dam Buchanan Harris used to create the lake. Camp Nightingale sits to the south, a rectangle of fern green, speckled with buildings in variations of brown.

The newspaper clippings and Internet articles offer nothing new. Vivian, Natalie, and Allison vanished in the early morning hours of July 5. They were reported missing by yours truly a little before six a.m. A camp-wide search that morning turned up nothing. By the afternoon, the camp's director, Francesca Harris-White, had contacted the New York State Police, and an official search began. Because of the girls' high-profile parents—Vivian's, especially—the Secret Service and the FBI joined the fray.

The only trace of the girls anyone ever found was Vivian's sweatshirt, white with PRINCETON spelled out in orange across the chest. But here's the weird part. Vivian wasn't wearing the sweatshirt when I saw her leave the cabin. I'm certain of it.

The only person ever considered a suspect was Franny's oldest son, Theo Harris-White. Nothing came of it. With no evidence that a crime had actually taken place, Theo wasn't charged. Which meant he also wasn't officially exonerated. The hunt for the girls didn't officially end so much as it lost steam. News coverage also evaporated as reporters moved on to newer, flashier stories.

Filling that void were darker theories found on conspiracy websites. Rumors swirled that the girls had been murdered by a savage madman who lived in the woods. That they had been abducted by aliens. That something even more mystically sinister happened to them. Witches. Werewolves. Spontaneous cellular disintegration.

The truth is that what happened to Vivian, Natalie, and Allison wasn't an accident. Although their eventual fate remains a mystery, I'm certain that what happened to those girls is all my fault.

THE driver announces, "Almost there, Miss Davis."

The car starts to bump down a gravel road. Soon we're at the wrought iron gate that serves as the only way into Camp Nightingale. It's wide-open—an invitation to enter. An ornate archway, also wrought iron, curves over the road, giving the impression that we're about to enter a cemetery.

The camp reveals itself in increments, remnants from when the land was a private retreat for the Harris family. The arts-and-crafts building, low-slung and quaint, used to be a horse stable. Next is the mess hall, a former hay barn. In the distance to my right are the cabins, barely visible through the trees.

Atop the arts-and-crafts building, a handyman nails shingles to the roof. I recognize him from my first visit. I remember seeing him quite a bit around camp, constantly tinkering and fixing. He was younger then, of course. Better-looking. Possessed a brooding intensity that intimidated some, intrigued others. He raises his hammer, pounds a shingle into place.

The town car whips around the circular drive in front of the Lodge. Franny's home away from home, as she calls it. There's a heaviness to the Lodge, a somberness. I think of all the years it's witnessed. All those seasons and storms and secrets.

"We've arrived," the driver says as he stops the car in front of the Lodge's red front door. "I'll get your bags from the trunk."

I exit the car, and I'm immediately engulfed by fresh air. It's a smell I'd forgotten. Clean and pine-scented. It beckons me, pulling me forward. I start walking, unsure of where I'm headed.

"I'll be right back," I tell the driver. "I need to stretch my legs."

I keep walking, around the Lodge to the grassy slope behind it. There I see what the fresh air has led me to. Lake Midnight.

It's larger than I remember, a vast, sparkling presence that dominates the landscape. I start down the sloping lawn, continuing until I reach the tidy dock that juts over the water. Two motorboats are moored to it. On the shore nearby are two racks upon which upside-down canoes have been stacked like firewood.

I walk the length of the dock. At its edge, I stop to look across the lake to the far shore. The forest there is a dense wall of foliage shimmering in the sunlight, at once inviting and forbidding.

A voice rises behind me like a bird chirp. "There you are!"

The voice belongs to a twentysomething woman who rushes down the dock. Behind her, still on land, is a man roughly the same age. Both are young and tan and fit in their official Camp Nightingale polos. They have the same outdoorsy, sun-kissed glow.

"Emma, right?" the woman says. "Hooray! You're here!"

I reach out to shake her hand but wind up getting pulled into an enthusiastically tight embrace.

"I'm Mindy," she says. "Chet's fiancée."

She gestures to the man onshore, and it takes me a moment to realize she's referring to Chester, Franny's younger son. He's grown into a handsome man, lean and tall, a far cry from the short, skinny kid I had seen flitting around camp. Yet hints of that boyishness remain. In the sandy hair that flops over one eye. In the shy smile that flickers across his lips as he calls out, "Hey there."

"I was just getting reacquainted with the lake," I say to Mindy.

"Of course you were," she says. "It's nice, right? Although the weather isn't doing it any favors. It hasn't rained in weeks, and the lake is looking a little ragged, if you ask me."

It's only after she's pointed it out that I notice the telltale signs of drought around the lake. The plants on its bank bear several inches of browned stem—areas that had once been submerged.

Mindy grabs my hand and leads me off the dock. "We're thrilled to have you back, Emma," she says. "Franny especially. This summer is going to be awesome. I just know it."

Back onshore, I go to Chet and shake his hand.

"Emma Davis," I say. "You probably don't remember me."

"Oh, I remember you well," he says, not elaborating.

"Before you get settled in, Franny needs to see you," Mindy says.

"About what?"

"There's a problem with the rooming situation. But don't worry. Franny's going to sort it all out." Leaving Chet behind, she loops an arm through mine, guiding me up the slope and into the Lodge.

It's the first time I've ever been inside. It's musty and dim, the air tinged with a century's worth of wood-fed blazes in the fireplace. The entrance hall we stand in leads to a living area stuffed with worn furniture. Covering the walls are antlers, animal skins, and an assortment of antique weapons. Rifles. Bowie knives. A spear.

"Everything's so old, right?" Mindy says. "The first time Chet brought me here, it felt like sleeping in a museum."

When we pass a small office on the left, I ask, "What's in there?"

"The study."

One wall is filled with framed photos. Another contains a bookshelf. As we pass, I glimpse the corner of a desk.

"I use the electrical outlet in there to charge my phone," Mindy says. "You're welcome to do the same. Just don't let Franny catch you. She wants all of us to disconnect and commune with nature."

"How's service up here?"

Mindy makes a gagging sound. "Horrible. Like, one bar most of the time. I honestly don't know how these girls are going to cope."

"The campers can't use their phones?"

"They can until their batteries run out. No electricity in the cabins, remember? Franny's orders."

We move on. Soon we're at the back deck, which spans the entire width of the Lodge. Scattered around the deck are several small tables and Adirondack chairs, all painted as red as the front door. Two of the chairs are occupied by Franny and Lottie. Both are dressed in the same khaki shorts and camp polo ensemble as Chet and Mindy. Franny surveys Lake Midnight from the heightened view provided by the deck. Lottie, meanwhile, taps the screen of an iPad, looking up when Mindy and I step outside.

"Emma," she says, her face brightening as she pulls me into a hug. "You have no idea how nice it is to see you back here."

"It is," Franny agrees. "It's wonderful."

I clear my throat. "You needed to see me about something?"

"Yes. I'm afraid there's a bit of a problem." Franny frowns slightly. It's an echo of the half frown she gave me upon my first arrival at camp, when the family Volvo finally pulled up to the Lodge at the cusp of eleven. *I wasn't expecting you,* she said. *When you didn't arrive with the others, I thought you had canceled.*

"A problem?" I say, trepidation thickening my voice.

"I suppose it's more of a complication. About where to put you."

"Oh," I say. Franny told me something similar fifteen years ago.

Back then, my lateness was to blame. They had already gotten all the girls settled into their cabins, grouped together that morning by age. Since there was no more room available with girls my own age, I was forced to bunk with ones who were several years older. That's how I ended up with Vivian, Natalie, and Allison.

Now Franny tells me it's the opposite problem. "My intention was to give the instructors some privacy. Let you have a cabin all to yourselves. But there was a bit of a mix-up with planning, and we find ourselves with more girls than we initially expected. All our instructors will have to share lodgings with some of the campers."

"Why can't the instructors bunk together?"

"That's a fine idea in theory, but there are five of you and only four bunks in each cabin. One person would have to bunk with the campers anyway. Which wouldn't be fair to that single person."

"Couldn't we stay in the Lodge instead?"

"There aren't enough bedrooms," Franny says. "I do apologize."

"It's fine," I say, when in fact it isn't. I'm a twenty-eight-year-old woman being forced to spend the next six weeks living with strangers half my age. "Can I at least choose my cabin?"

"What did you have in mind?"

I touch my charm bracelet, giving it a quick twirl. "I want to stay in Dogwood." The same cabin I stayed in fifteen years ago.

Franny turns to Lottie and says, "Please arrange it so that Emma can stay in Dogwood." To me, she says, "You're either very brave or very foolish, Emma. I can't decide which one it is."

I can't, either. I suppose I'm a little bit of both.

Fifteen Years Ago

As THE sound of my parents' Volvo faded into the night, Francesca Harris-White's green eyes latched on to me like twin spotlights.

"I must admit, dear, I have absolutely no idea where to put you," Franny said, turning to Lottie, who stood behind her. "Is there any room left in a cabin reserved for our junior campers?"

"The only open spot is in a senior cabin. Dogwood."

Franny turned back to me, smiling. "Then Dogwood it shall be. Lottie, be a dear and fetch Theo to take Miss Davis's bags."

Lottie vanished into the massive house behind us. A minute later, a young man emerged. Dressed in baggy shorts and a tight T-shirt, he had sleepy eyes and tousled brown hair. On his feet were flip-flops that clapped against the ground as he approached.

"Theo, this is Emma Davis, our latecomer," Franny told him. "She's headed to Dogwood."

Theo was unlike any boy I had ever seen. Not cute. Handsome. With wide brown eyes, a prominent nose, a slightly crooked smile that slanted when he said, "Hey, latecomer. Welcome to Camp Nightingale. Let's get you to your cabin."

Franny bade me good-night as I followed Theo deeper into the camp. I couldn't take my eyes off him as he walked a few paces ahead of me. His tall frame; the long, steady stride of his legs; the spread of his back and shoulders under his threadbare shirt. It didn't hurt that he was friendly, calling over his shoulder to ask me where I was from, what music I liked, if I had been to camp before.

When we reached the cabin, he rapped on the door, prompting a response from inside. "Who is it?"

"Theo. Are you awake and decent?"

"Awake, yes," the same voice replied. "Decent, never."

Theo handed me the suitcase and gave an encouraging nod. "Go on in. And remember, their bark is worse than their bite."

He walked away, flip-flops clopping, as I turned the doorknob and stepped inside. The cabin's interior was dim, lit only by a lantern placed beside a window opposite the door. In that golden half-light, I saw two sets of bunk beds and three girls occupying them.

"I'm Vivian," announced the one sprawled on the top bunk to my right. She gestured to the bunk directly across from her. "That's Allison. Below is Natalie."

"Hi," I said, clutching my suitcase just inside the cabin, too frightened to enter farther.

"Your trunk is by the door," said the girl identified as Natalie. "You can put your clothes there."

"Thanks." I opened the hickory trunk and started transferring all my clothes into it. Everything except my nightgown, which I kept out before sliding the suitcase under the bed.

Vivian slipped from the top bunk in a cropped T-shirt and a pair of panties, her exposure making me even more self-conscious as I stripped off my clothes under the protection of the nightgown.

"You're a little young. Are you sure you're supposed to be here?" She turned to the others in the cabin, both still ensconced in their bunks. "Isn't there a cabin for babies we can send her to?"

"I'm thirteen," I said. "Clearly not a baby."

Vivian terrified and dazzled me in equal measure. All three of them did. They seemed like women. I was just a girl.

"You're not going to cry, are you?" Vivian said. "All newbies cry their first night. It's so damned predictable."

I faced Vivian head-on. "If I cry, it's because I've been put in here with you bitches."

Vivian grinned and shook her head. "Well played, kid."

"Don't call me kid," I said, feigning toughness despite the fact that I wanted to cry with relief. "My name is Emma."

Vivian reached out and tousled my hair. "Well, Em, welcome to Camp Nightingale. You ready to help us rule this place?"

Chapter 3

FROM THE OUTSIDE, Dogwood looks exactly the way I left it. Same rough brown walls. Same green-shingled roof speckled with pinecones. Same tidy sign announcing its name. When I twist the doorknob, I don't know what I'm expecting. Ghosts, I suppose.

Instead, I find three different girls, all of them very much alive as they lounge on their respective bunks.

"Hi," I say. My voice is meek, as if I'm sorry to be invading their space, dragging my suitcase behind me. "I'm Emma."

"Hi, Emma. I'm Sasha." This is spoken by the youngest, a girl of about thirteen who's perched on the top bunk to my left. She's got a friendly face—huge smile, rounded cheeks, bright eyes made even more prominent by a pair of red-framed glasses.

"Nice to meet you, Sasha."

"I'm Krystal," says the girl sprawled on the bunk below her. "Spelled with a K."

A few years older and several pounds heavier than Sasha, she's practically hidden inside an oversize hoodie and baggy shorts. In her lap sits a comic book. Captain America.

"Krystal with a K. Got it."

I turn to the other girl in the room, who lies on her side on the top bunk. She appraises me in silence, her almond-shaped eyes flashing a combination of disdain and curiosity. A diamond stud adorns her nose. She looks to be about sixteen.

"Miranda," she says. "I took the top bunk. Hope you don't mind."

"Bottom bunk is fine," I say as I hoist my suitcase onto the bed.

The girls stare at me expectantly. Well, Sasha and Krystal do. Miranda spreads herself across her bed with a dramatic sigh.

"Are you our camp counselor?" Sasha asks.

"More like babysitter," Krystal adds.

Miranda does her one better. "More like warden."

"I'm an artist," I tell them. "I'm here to teach you how to paint."

"What if we don't want to paint?" Sasha says.

"You don't have to, if you don't want to."

"I like to draw." This comes from Krystal, already leaning off the bed to reach beneath it, where several tattered notebooks sit. She pulls one from the pile and opens it up. "See?"

On the page is a sketch of a superhero. A woman with fiery eyes and bulging muscles. Her uniform is blue and skintight, with a green skull emblazoned across the chest. The skull's eyes glow red.

"You did this?" I say, sincerely impressed. "It's really good."

"Her name is Skull Crusher. She can kill with her bare hands."

"I wouldn't want it any other way," I say. "Since you're already an artist, I'll let you draw while the others paint."

Krystal accepts the deal with a smile. "Cool."

She and Sasha continue to stare as I unpack. Feeling awkward, I ask, "So why did you want to come to camp?"

"My guidance counselor at school suggested it," Sasha says. "She said it would be a good learning experience for me, seeing how I'm inquisitive."

"Oh?" I say. "About what?"

"Um, everything."

"It was either this or get a job flipping burgers," Krystal says.

"I think you made the right choice."

"I didn't want to come," Miranda says. "My grandmother said I'd only get in trouble if I stayed home this summer."

I look up at her. "And would you?"

Miranda shrugs. "Probably."

"Listen," I say, "I need to be clear about something. I'm not here to be your den mother. Or babysitter." I flick my gaze up at Miranda. "Or warden. I'm here to help you learn, if you want. Or, if you'd like, we can just talk. Basically, think of me as your big sister for the summer. I just want you to enjoy yourselves."

"I have a question," Sasha says. "Are there bears here?"

"I guess so," I reply. "But they're more afraid of us than we are of them."

"I did some research before I left home and read that that's not true. What about snakes? How many do you think are in the woods? And how many of those are venomous?"

I look at Sasha, her eyes wide behind her glasses.

"I don't know," I say. "But honestly, the only thing you need to worry about is poison ivy."

"And getting lost in the woods," Sasha says. "According to Wikipedia, it's very common. People disappear all the time."

I nod. Finally, a fact I can confirm. And one that I can't forget.

WHEN it's time for dinner, I stay behind. I stand in the middle of the cabin, wondering what the girls of Dogwood would look like today. Allison would probably still be cute and petite like her mother, whom I saw a few years ago in a revival of *Sweeney Todd*. I suspect Natalie would have remained physically formidable, thanks to sports in college. And Vivian? I'm certain she'd be the same. Slim. Stylish. A beauty that bordered on haughtiness.

I open my suitcase. Quickly I change into a pair of shorts and one of the official camp polos that arrived in the mail two weeks ago. The rest go into my assigned trunk by the door. It's the same trunk from my previous stay here. I run my hands across the lid, feeling the bumps and grooves of all the names that have been carved into the hickory. Another memory prods my thoughts. Me kneeling before this very trunk with a dull pocketknife in my hand, carving my name. Two letters in all caps: EM.

Vivian stood behind me as I did it. *Make your mark. Let future generations know you were here. That you existed.*

I then move to the trunk next to mine. Vivian's. She had carved her name in the center of the lid, larger than all the others: VIV.

I crack open her trunk, even though I know it's Miranda's now and that inside aren't Vivian's clothes and crafts. In their place are Miranda's clothes and a surprisingly high stack of paperbacks. *Gone Girl, Rosemary's Baby,* a few Agatha Christie mysteries.

The lining inside the lid is burgundy satin. Just like mine. The only difference is a six-inch tear in the fabric. It sits on the left side of the lid, running vertically. Vivian's hiding place, used to store the pendant necklace she took off only when she slept. I know of the hiding place only because I saw Vivian use it on the first full day of camp. She unclasped the necklace and held it for a moment in her cupped hands.

That's pretty, I said. *An heirloom?*

It belonged to my sister. She died.

Sorry. I'd never met someone with a dead sibling before and didn't know how to act. *I didn't mean to bring it up.*

You didn't, Vivian said. *I did. And it's healthy to talk about it. That's what my therapist says.*

I felt another flutter. A dead sister *and* therapy?

How'd she die?

She drowned.

Oh, I said, too surprised to say more.

Now I stare at the slash in the fabric, fingering my own piece of jewelry. Unlike Vivian's necklace, I never remove the charm bracelet. Not to sleep. Not to shower. Not even when painting.

I plunge my right hand through the tear in the lining. I'm not expecting to find anything. Certainly not the necklace, which Vivian had been wearing when she left the cabin for the very last time. I do it because once I check, I'll know there's no trace of Vivian left.

Only there is. Something is inside the lid, wedged between wood and fabric. A piece of paper, folded in half. I slide it from the lining. Age has given the paper a yellowish tint that reminds me of dried egg yolk. The page crackles when I unfold it, revealing an even older-looking photograph.

I study the photo first. Sepia-toned and worn along the edges, it depicts a young woman in a plain dress, long dark hair cascading down her back and out of frame. Clutched in the woman's hands is a large silver hairbrush. Her eyes, wild and dark, convey sadness, loneliness, and something else. An emotion I know well. Distress.

I flip over the photo and see a name scrawled in faded ink.

Eleanor Auburn.

Who is this woman? When was this picture taken? And, above all, where did Vivian get it, and why was it hidden in her trunk?

The contents of the unfolded page don't provide any answers. Instead, I see a drawing crudely scratched onto a ruled piece of paper torn from some sort of notebook. The focal point of the drawing is a blob that resembles a paisley, strange and formless. Surrounding it are hundreds of dark slashes. Beneath the paisley are several shapes. Messy ones. Not quite circles, not quite squares. Off to their left is another, bigger circle-square.

I realize what it is and gasp. The paisley is Lake Midnight, dominating the landscape. The slashes are an abstract version of the woods surrounding it. The series of shapes are the cabins. The big splotch is the Lodge. Vivian had drawn another cabin-size shape on the other side of the lake, almost directly across from camp. It sits next to the water, all alone. Only there aren't any structures on the other side of the lake. At least, none that I'm aware of.

I bring the page closer to my face. A short distance behind the mystery structure is something barely distinguishable from the slashes that surround it. An X. Small but noticeable, it sits near a cluster of ragged triangles that resemble tiny mountains drawn by a kindergartner. Something of interest was located there.

I fold the photograph inside the map and secure them both inside my own hickory trunk. It strikes me that if Vivian had taken such great care to hide them, then I should do the same.

Fifteen Years Ago

"THERE'S one thing you need to know about this place," Vivian said. "Never arrive to anything on time. Either be first or last."

"Even meals?" I asked.

"*Especially* meals."

It was my first morning at camp, and Vivian and I had just left the latrine on the way to the mess hall. Although the mealtime bell rang fifteen minutes earlier, Vivian showed no sign of hurry as she looped her arm through mine, forcing me to slow as well.

When we eventually did reach the mess hall, I noticed a girl with frizzy hair standing outside the arts-and-crafts building with a camera around her neck. She aimed the camera our way.

"Who was that taking our picture?" I asked.

"Becca?" Vivian said. "Don't mind her. She's a nobody."

Taking my hand, Vivian pulled me toward the front of the room, where a handful of kitchen workers in hairnets stood before steaming trays of food. Because we were among the last to arrive, there was no wait. Vivian was right, not that I ever doubted her.

The only person later than us was a smiling redheaded counselor with the name CASEY stitched onto her camp polo. She was short—practically my height—and had a pear-shaped frame made more pronounced by the pockets of her cargo shorts.

"Well, if it isn't Vivian Hawthorne," she said. "You told me last summer that you were done with this place. Couldn't stay away?"

"And miss out on a chance to torment you for another summer?" Vivian said as she grabbed two bananas, placing one of them on my tray. "No way."

The counselor gave me an appraising look. "You're new, right?"

Vivian ordered two bowls of oatmeal, again giving one to me. "Emma, this is Casey. Former camper, current counselor, forever bane of my existence. Casey, meet Emma. She's my protégé."

"That's a scary thought." Casey put a hand on my shoulder. "Come see me if she starts to corrupt you too much. I'm in Birch."

She passed us on her way to a decanter of coffee and the platter of doughnuts next to it. Before leaving the food line, I also ordered what I really wanted for breakfast—toast and a plate of bacon. Vivian eyed the extra side dishes but said nothing.

Vivian led me to the side of the mess hall populated by older girls. She waved to some and ignored others before sitting me down with Allison and Natalie.

"Morning, bitches," she said to the others. "Sleep well?"

"The usual," Allison said as she picked at a bowl of fruit salad. "You, Emma?"

"Great," I said. It was a lie. The cabin was too stuffy, too quiet. I missed air-conditioning and the sounds of Manhattan.

"Thank God you don't snore, Em," Vivian said. "We had a snorer last year. Sounded like a dying cow."

"It wasn't that bad," said Natalie. On her tray sat two servings of bacon and the syrupy remains of flapjacks. "You're just being mean because you don't like her anymore."

Already I had noticed the weird dynamic between the three of them. Vivian was the ringleader. Obviously. Natalie, athletic and a little bit gruff, was the resistance. Pretty, subdued Allison was the peacekeeper, a role she assumed that very morning. "Tell us about yourself, Emma," she said.

"I go to Douglas Academy."

"Do you like it there?"

"It's nice, I guess. For an all-girls school."

"Ours is, too," Vivian said. "And I'd honestly kill to spend a summer away from some of these sluts."

"Why?" Natalie asked. "You pretend half of them don't exist when we're here."

"Just like I'm pretending right now that you're not stuffing your face with bacon," Vivian shot back. "Keep eating like that, and next year it'll be fat camp for you."

Natalie sighed and dropped the half-eaten bacon onto her plate.

"I was just joking," Vivian said. "I'm sorry, Nat. Really. You look . . . fine." She smiled, the word lingering like the insult it was.

I spent the rest of the meal eyeing Vivian's plate, taking a bite of oatmeal only when she did. I didn't touch the banana until she did. The bacon remained untouched. I told myself it would be worth it.

VIVIAN, Natalie, and Allison left the mess hall before me, preparing for an advanced archery lesson. Senior campers only. I was scheduled to take part in an activity with girls my own age. On my way there, I passed the girl with the camera. She veered into my path, halting me. "What are you doing?"

"Warning you," she said. "About Vivian."

"What do you mean?"

"Don't be fooled. She'll turn on you eventually."

I took a step toward her. "How so?"

"You'll find out," she said.

Chapter 4

ARRIVING AT THE MESS HALL for dinner, I find Franny standing at the head of the room, already halfway through her welcome speech. It sounds just like the one I heard fifteen years ago. She's already recited the part about how the lake was formed by her grandfather and is now delving into the history of the camp itself.

"For years, this land served as a private retreat for my family. When my parents passed away, it was left to me. So, in 1973, I decided to turn it into a camp for girls. Camp Nightingale opened a year later, where it welcomed generations of young women."

She pauses. Contained in that brief silence are years of omitted history. About my friends, the camp's subsequent closure.

"Today, the camp welcomes all of you," Franny says. "Camp Nightingale isn't about cliques or popularity contests or feeling superior. It's about you. All of you. Giving each and every one of you an experience to cherish long after the summer is over. So if you need anything at all, don't hesitate to ask Lottie, my sons, or Mindy, the newest member of our family."

She gestures to her left, where Chet stands against the wall, pretending not to notice the adoring gazes of half the girls in the room. Next to him, Mindy smiles and gives a beauty pageant wave. I scan the room, looking for Theo. There's no sign of him.

"One last thing," Franny says, pretending to think of it just now. "I don't want to hear a single one of you call me Mrs. Harris-White. Call me Franny. In the great outdoors, we're all equals."

From her spot along the wall, Mindy starts clapping. Soon the whole room is applauding as Franny, their benefactor, skirts out of the mess hall via a side door opened by Lottie.

I make my way to the food stations, where a small crew of

white-uniformed cooks dishes out greasy hamburgers, fries, and coleslaw so runny that milky liquid sloshes around the bottom of the plate.

I head to a table near the door where eight women are seated. Five of them are young, definitely college age. The camp counselors. The other three range in age from mid-thirties to pushing sixty. My fellow instructors. Minus Rebecca Schoenfeld.

I recognize only one—Casey Anderson. She's still got that pear-shaped frame and red hair that grazes her shoulders. "It's good to see you back here, Emma."

Casey introduces me to the other instructors. Teaching creative writing is Roberta Wright-Smith, who attended Camp Nightingale for three summers, beginning with its inaugural season. She's plump and jolly and peers at me through a pair of glasses perched on her nose. Paige McAdams, who went here in the late '80s, is gray-haired and willowy. She's here to teach pottery.

Casey informs me she's been assigned to arts and crafts. She's an eighth-grade English teacher during the school year, available to help out here because her two kids are away at their own camp and it's her first summer alone since she divorced her husband.

The counselors are college juniors, pretty and bland and basically interchangeable. Hair pulled into ponytails. Pink lip gloss. Their names leave my memory five seconds after I am introduced to them.

"Don't you think it's weird?" Casey says. "I mean, Franny's decision to open the camp again after all these years."

"I don't think it's necessarily weird," I say. "Surprising, maybe."

"I vote for weird," Paige says. "I mean, why now?"

"Why not now?" This comes from Mindy, who's swooped up to the table without notice. "I didn't know it was wrong to give a new generation of girls the same experiences the four of you had."

Mindy's tone is so sweetly sanctimonious that I can't help but say, "I wouldn't wish my experience here on anyone."

Mindy gives a sad shake of her head. "I expected more from you, Emma. Franny showed a great deal of courage inviting you back."

"And Emma showed courage by agreeing to come," Casey says.

"She did," Mindy replies. "Which is why I thought she'd show a little bit more Camp Nightingale spirit." She plops into an empty chair and lets out a sigh. "I've been told by Lottie that we need to make a cabin check schedule."

Ah, cabin check. The nightly examination of the cabins by counselors to make sure everyone is present and staying out of trouble.

"Each night, we need two people to check on the cabins that don't have counselors or instructors staying in them," Mindy says. "Who wants to volunteer first? And where's Rebecca?"

"Sleeping, I think," Casey says. "I saw her earlier, and she said she needed a nap or the jet lag was going to kill her. She was on assignment in London and came straight here from the airport."

"I guess we'll have to pencil her in later," Mindy says. "Who wants to do it tonight?"

As the others wrangle over the schedule, I see the mess hall's double doors open and watch as Rebecca Schoenfeld steps inside. Unlike Casey, she's changed quite a bit. She's become harder, compact, with a worldly style. Her hair, once a frizzy mass kept in place with a scrunchie, is now sleek and short. She's accented her shorts-and-polo ensemble with a brightly colored scarf. Beneath it hangs her camera. She crosses the mess hall to the food station and grabs an apple. She takes a bite on her way out, stopping only when she spots me on the other side of the room. The look she gives me is unreadable. After another bite of apple, she exits the mess hall.

"I need to go," I say.

Mindy emits another sigh. "What about cabin check?"

"Sign me up for whenever."

Outside the mess hall, I search in every direction for signs of Becca. But she's nowhere to be found. I start to head back to the cabins when someone says my name.

"Emma?"

I freeze, knowing exactly who the voice belongs to. Theo Harris-White. He calls to me from the open door of the arts-and-crafts building. I turn around slowly, unsure what to expect. He's aged, of course. No longer the strapping nineteen-year-old I remember him being. That youthful glow has dimmed into something darker, more intense. There's more bulk than before, but it's all muscle.

The flecks of gray in his dark hair and five o'clock shadow suit him. So does the slight weathering of his face. When he smiles at me, a few faint wrinkles crepe the skin around his mouth and eyes.

"Hi." It's the best I can manage. I'm being blindsided by the memory of Theo standing in front of the Lodge, looking exhausted and disheveled after a day spent searching the woods. Me rushing at him, crying as I pound his chest and scream, *Where are they? What did you do to them?*

I expect him to be angry or bitter. I stay completely still as Theo steps forward and, shockingly, gives me a hug.

"I can't believe you're here. I didn't think it would happen."

"Here I am."

"And it looks like life is treating you well. You look great."

He's being kind. I know how I look.

"So do you," I say.

"I hear you're a painter now. Mom told me she bought one of your works. I haven't had a chance to see it yet. I just got back from Africa two days ago."

"Franny mentioned that. You're a doctor?"

Theo gives a shrug, scratches his beard. "Yeah. A pediatrician. I've spent the past year working with Doctors Without Borders. But for the next six weeks, I've been demoted to camp nurse."

"I guess that makes me the camp painter," I say.

"Speaking of which, I was just working on your studio for the summer. Care to take a peek?"

"Sure," I say. "Lead the way."

I follow him inside, finding myself in the middle of an airy, open room. The walls have been painted a cheerful sky blue. The carpet and baseboard are as green as grass. The three support columns that rise from the floor to the ceiling in equal intervals have been painted to resemble trees. It's happy and bright.

To our left is a little photo studio for Becca, complete with brand-new digital cameras, charging stations, and a handful of sleek computers used for processing pictures. The center of the room is an elaborate crafts station, full of circular tables, cubbyholes, and cabinets filled with string, beads, leather bands the color of saddles.

I spot several dozen laptops for Roberta's writing classes and a pair of pottery wheels for Paige.

Theo leads me to the far end of the room, where a semicircle of easels has been set up. Along one wall is a shelf holding tubes of oil paints and brushes clustered in mason jars. Clean palettes hang next to windows that let in natural light.

"I put your supplies over there," Theo says, gesturing to the box I brought with me. "I figured you'd want to unpack them yourself."

Honestly, there's no need. Everything I could possibly want is already here. Yet I go to the box anyway and start pulling out my personal supplies. The well-worn brushes. The squished tubes of paint. The palette thoroughly speckled with color.

Theo stands on the other side of the box, watching me unpack. Fading light from the window falls across his face, highlighting something I didn't notice until just now. A scar. Located on his left cheek, it's an inch-long line that slants toward his mouth. I'm about to ask Theo how he got it, when he checks his watch and says, "I need to go help Chet with the campfire. Will I see you there?"

"Of course. I never turn down an opportunity to have s'mores."

"Good. That you're coming, I mean." Theo ambles to the door. When he reaches it, he turns and says, "I'm glad you're here. It means a lot to my mother. It means a lot to me, too."

Then he's gone, leaving me alone to wonder what, exactly, he meant by that.

APPARENTLY, to Mindy, *whenever* meant *tonight*, because after the campfire I find myself on cabin check duty with Casey as my co-checker. Together we go from cabin to cabin, peeking inside to do a head count and ask if any of the campers need anything.

After the cabins have all been checked, Casey and I walk to the patch of grass behind the latrine. Casey pulls a cigarette from a pack hidden in her cargo shorts and lights up.

"I can't believe I'm sneaking cigarettes. I feel like I'm fourteen."

"Better this than face the wrath of Mindy."

"Her real name is Melinda," Casey says. "She goes by Mindy to be more like Franny." She blows out a stream of smoke and watches it languidly float in the night air. "Honestly, though, it's probably for the best that she's here. Without her, it would be open season on poor Chet. These girls would eat him alive."

"But they're all so young."

"Girls that age are just as full of raging hormones as boys. Remember how you were back then. I saw the way you fawned over Theo. Not that I blamed you. He was a fine-looking young man."

"Have you seen him now?"

Casey gives a slow, knowing nod. "Why is it that men only look better with age? It's completely unfair."

"But he's still just as friendly," I say. "I didn't expect that."

"Because of what you said last time you were here?"

"And because of what people are saying now. I saw some posts on the Internet. A few of them mentioned some legend."

"It's just a silly campfire tale. You never heard it?"

"I guess I wasn't here long enough."

Casey looks at me, the cigarette held between her lips, its trail of smoke making her squint. "The story is that there was a village here," she says. "Before the lake was made. Some will say it was full of deaf people. I heard it was a leper colony."

"A leper colony?"

"I didn't make up the story," Casey snaps. "Now, do you want to hear it or not?"

I do, no matter how ridiculous it seems. I nod for her to continue.

"Deaf village and leper colony aside, the rest of the story is the same," Casey says. "It's that Franny's grandfather saw this valley and decided on the spot it was where he was going to create his lake. But there was one problem. The village sat right in the middle of it. When Buchanan Harris approached the villagers and offered to buy their land, they refused. This made Mr. Harris angry. He was a man accustomed to getting what he wanted. So when he increased his offer and the villagers again refused, he bought all the land surrounding them instead. Then he built his dam and flooded the valley, knowing the water would wash away the village and that everyone who lived there would drown."

She lowers her voice, speaking slowly. Full storyteller mode.

"The village is still there, deep below Lake Midnight. And the people who drowned now roam the forest. Anyone unlucky enough to encounter them gets dragged into the lake and pulled to the bottom. Then they become ghosts, cursed to search the woods for all eternity looking for more victims."

I give her an incredulous look. "And that's what people think happened to Vivian, Natalie, and Allison?"

"No one truly believes that," Casey says. "But bad things have happened here, with no explanation. Franny's husband, for example. He was a champion swimmer. Almost made it to the Olympics. Yet he drowned. Franny's grandmother also drowned here. So when Vivian and the others disappeared, some people said it was the ghosts of Lake Midnight. Or else the survivors."

"Survivors?"

"It's been said that a handful of villagers escaped the rising waters and fled into the hills. There they stayed, where no one could find them. And on nights when the moon is full, their ancestors sneak down to exact their revenge. Vivian, Natalie, and Allison were just three of their victims."

"What do you really think happened to them?" I say.

"I think they got lost in the woods. Vivian was always wandering off." Casey drops her cigarette and grinds it out with the toe of her sneaker. "I was a camp counselor. It was my job to make sure all of you were safe. I regret not paying more attention to you and what was going on in that cabin."

"Were there things going on I didn't know about?"

"I don't know," Casey says. "Maybe."

"Like what? You were friends with Vivian. Surely you noticed something."

"I wouldn't say the two of us were friends. I was a senior camper her first summer and then came back to work as a counselor the two years after that. She was always a troublemaker, but charming enough to get away with it. But something about her seemed off that last summer. She seemed distracted."

I think of the strange map Vivian had drawn and the even stranger photo of the woman with long hair.

"By what?"

"I don't know, Emma. Like I said, we weren't that close. I noticed her walking alone around camp a few times. Maybe . . ." Her voice trails off.

"Maybe what?"

"She was up to no good," Casey says. "On the second day of camp, I caught her trying to sneak into the Lodge. She said she was looking for Franny, but I didn't buy it."

"Why would she want to break into the Lodge?"

Casey shrugs. "Your guess is as good as mine," she says.

My FINAL stop on cabin check is Dogwood, where I find all three girls on their beds, phones in hand. Sasha is under the covers, her glasses perched on her nose as she plays a game. In the bunk below her, Krystal has changed into baggy sweats. She watches a Marvel movie on her phone, the soundtrack leaking out of her earbuds. On the other side of the cabin, Miranda reclines on the top bunk, now dressed in a tank top and black shorts. She holds her phone close to her face, doing a faux pout as she takes several pictures.

"You shouldn't use your phones," I say. "Save your batteries."

Krystal tugs off her earbuds. "What else are we going to do?"

"We could, you know, talk," I suggest. "People actually did that before everyone spent all their time squinting at screens."

"I saw you talking to Theo," Miranda says, her voice wavering between innocence and accusation. "Is he, like, your boyfriend?"

"No. He's a . . . an acquaintance," I say.

"How do you know him?" Krystal says.

"From when I was a camper here."

A wicked grin widens across Miranda's face. "You were at Camp Nightingale before?" she says. "Must have been a long time ago."

I smile, impressed by the stealthiness of her insult. She's a sly one. Vivian would have loved her.

"It was," I say.

"Did you like it here?" Sasha says.

"At first. Then not so much."

"What happened?" Miranda says. "Something horrible?"

She leans forward, her phone temporarily discarded as she waits for my answer. It gives me an idea.

"Phones off," I say. "I mean it."

All three of them groan. Miranda's is the most dramatic as she, like the others, switches off her phone. I sit cross-legged on the floor, my back pressed against the edge of my bunk. I pat the spaces on either side of me until the girls do the same.

"What are we doing?" Sasha asks.

"Playing a game. It's called Two Truths and a Lie. You say three things about yourself. Two of them must be true. One is false. The rest of us have to guess the lie."

We played it a lot during my time in Dogwood, including the night of my arrival. The four of us were lying on our bunks in the darkness when Vivian suddenly said, *Two Truths and a Lie. I'll start.* She began to utter three statements, assuming we already knew how the game was played.

One: I once met the President. His palm was sweaty. Two: My parents were going to get a divorce but then decided not to when my dad got elected. Three: Once, on vacation in Australia, I got pooped on by a koala.

Three, Natalie said. *You used it last year.*

No, I didn't.

You totally did, Allison said. *You told us the koala peed on you.*

That's how it went every night. The four of us in the dark, sharing things we'd never reveal in the light of day. Constructing lies so they'd sound real. The game was Vivian's favorite. She said you could learn more about a person from their lies than their truths.

"I'll start," Miranda says. "Number one: I once made out with an altar boy in the confessional during Christmas mass. Number two: I read a hundred books a year, mostly mysteries. Number three: I once threw up after riding the Cyclone at Coney Island."

"The second one," Krystal says.

"Definitely," Sasha adds.

Miranda pretends to be annoyed. "Just because I'm smoking hot doesn't make me illiterate. Hot girls read."

"Then what's the lie?" Sasha says.

"I'm not telling." Miranda gives an impish grin. "Let's just say I've never been to Coney Island, but I go to mass all the time."

Krystal goes next, telling us that her favorite superhero is Spider-Man; that her middle name is also Crystal, although spelled with a C; and that she, too, threw up after riding the Cyclone.

"Second one," we all say in unison.

"Was it that obvious?"

"I'm sorry," Miranda says, "but Krystal Crystal? No parent would be that cruel."

When it's time for her turn, Sasha wrinkles her brow in concentration. "Um, my favorite food is pizza," she says. "That's number one. Number two: My favorite animal is the pygmy hippopotamus. Three: I don't think I can do this. Lying's wrong, you guys."

"It's okay," I tell her. "Your honesty is noble."

"She's lying," Miranda says. "Right, Sasha? The third is the lie?"

Sasha shrugs broadly, feigning innocence.

"Your turn, Emma," Krystal says. "Two truths and one lie."

I take a deep breath. "One: My favorite color is periwinkle blue," I announce. "Two: I have been to the Louvre. Twice."

"You still need to give us a third one," Miranda says.

"During my thirteenth year, I did something terrible."

"Totally the last one," Miranda says to nods of agreement from the others. "I mean, if you truly had done something terrible, you're not going to admit it during a game."

I smile, pretending that they're right. What none of them understand is that the point of the game isn't to fool others with a lie. The goal is to trick them by telling the truth.

Fifteen Years Ago

My SECOND night at Camp Nightingale was as sleepless as the first. Possibly worse. I awoke before dawn, sweaty and uncomfortable, a patch of warm moisture between my legs. When I dipped an index finger into my underwear to investigate, it came back stained with blood. I knew about menstruation, of course. The girls in my class had been given "the talk" the year before, but my clueless gym teacher had neglected to tell us what to do when it happened.

Ignorant and fearful, I crawled out of bed and awkwardly climbed the ladder to the bunk above mine. By the time I reached the top, Vivian was already half awake. Her eyes fluttered beneath a swath of blond hair. "What the hell are you doing?"

"I'm bleeding," I whispered.

Vivian's eyes opened fully. "You mean—"

I nodded.

"Is this your first time?"

"Yes."

"Come on. There are tampons in the latrine."

I followed Vivian. Inside the latrine, she led me to the nearest stall. Along the way, she grabbed a tampon from the dispenser attached to the wall. I sequestered myself inside the stall, Vivian whispering instructions from the other side of the door.

"I think I did it right," I whispered back. "I'm not sure."

"You'd know if you did it wrong."

I remained in the stall, humiliated, humbled. I began to cry. Vivian, of course, heard me and said, "Are you crying?"

"No."

"You totally are. I'm coming in."

Before I could protest, she was in the stall, nudging me aside with her hips so she could join me on the toilet seat.

"Come on," she said. "It's not that bad."

"How would you know? You're, like, three years older than me."

"Which is a lifetime. Trust me. Just ask your older sister."

"I'm an only child," I said.

"That's a shame. Big sisters are awesome. At least mine was."

"I always wanted a sister," I said.

"Since I've already gone above and beyond the call of duty here, I am offering up my services as surrogate big sister. For the next six weeks, you can talk to me about anything you want."

"Like boys?"

"Oh, I happen to have lots of experience in that area."

I thought of Theo just then. How handsome he was. How looking at him made me feel deliciously unbalanced. In that cramped stall with Vivian I understood that I had experienced the first flush of desire. The realization almost made me start to cry again. The only thing that stopped me was the sound of the latrine door squeaking open, followed by the slap of flip-flops on the tile floor. Vivian peeked through the crack in the stall door. She turned back to me with wide eyes. *Who is it?* I mouthed.

Vivian answered in an excited whisper, "Theo!"

Water began to blast inside a shower stall. The one in the far corner of the latrine.

"What do we do?" I whispered to Vivian.

She didn't answer. Instead, she moved. Out of the stall. Toward the door. Dragging me with her, the two of us incapable of making a silent retreat. Vivian giggled madly.

"Halt!" Theo called from the shower stall. "Who goes there?"

Vivian and I exchanged looks. "It's *Vivian*," she said coyly, drawing out the end of her name into an extra syllable.

"Hey, Viv."

Theo said it so casually that jealousy bloomed in my chest. Vivian noticed the envy in my eyes and added, "Emma's here, too."

"Emma who?"

"Emma Davis. She's new."

"Oh, that Emma. Cool, fashionably late Emma."

I let out a squeak, shocked and elated that Theo remembered leading me to Dogwood in the dark of night. Vivian elbowed me in the ribs, prompting me to meekly reply, "Hi, Theo."

"Why are you two up so early?" he asked.

"The real question," Vivian replied, "is why you're here. Isn't there a shower in the Lodge?"

"The water pressure there sucks," Theo said. "Which is why I shower here extra early before any of you girls can stumble in."

"We were here first," Vivian said.

"And I'd be grateful if you'd leave so I can shower in peace."

"Fine," Vivian called back. "We're gone."

We departed in a torrent of giggles, me clutching Vivian's wrist, the two of us twirling each other in the predawn. We spun until I grew dizzy and everything became a glorious, happy blur.

Chapter 5

IT TAKES ME HOURS to fall asleep. When I finally do manage to drift off, my sleep is stormy with bad dreams. In one of them—the most vivid—I see the long-haired woman from the photo in Vivian's trunk. I stare into those distressed eyes until it dawns on me that it's not a picture I'm looking at but a mirror. It's *my* absurdly long hair trailing to the floor, *my* dark-cloud eyes staring back at me.

The realization jolts me from sleep. I sit up, my breath heavy and my skin coated in a thin sheen of sweat. I'm also struck by the need to pee, which tugs me reluctantly from bed.

Inside the latrine, I head to the nearest stall. The same stall where Vivian led me on that fraught, frightening night.

As I prepare to leave the stall, I'm stopped by the sound of the latrine door being opened. When I peek through the crack in the stall door, I see a girl. Long, bare limbs. A flash of blond hair. I push out of the stall, calling her name. *"Vivian?"*

I know I'm wrong even before the girl at the sink spins around.

"Who the hell is Vivian?" Miranda asks.

"No one," I start to say, stopping myself mid-lie. "A camper I knew."

"Can't sleep?"

I shake my head. "You?"

"Same." She says it with forced casualness, which instantly tips me off that it's a lie.

"Is everything okay?"

Miranda gives me a slow shake of her head. "I was just dumped."

I go to the sink next to her and turn on the tap. "You want to talk about it?"

"No," Miranda says, but then adds, "it's not like we were serious. We'd only dated for, like, a month."

"But . . ."

"But he dumped me by text. What kind of jackass does that?" Tears glisten at the edges of her eyes.

"By the time you get back from camp, you'll wonder why you even liked him in the first place," I tell her.

"And he'll regret dumping me." Miranda checks her reflection in the mirror. "Because I'm going to look so hot with my camp tan."

"That's the spirit," I say. "Now go back to the cabin. I'll be there in a minute."

Miranda heads to the door, giving me a wiggle-finger wave as she goes. I stay behind to splash cold water on my face and compose myself. I can't believe I'd momentarily thought she was Vivian. Not a road I want to go down again.

When I step outside, the sky is a shade of grayish blue that I've used often in my paintings. It was that same color when Vivian and I bolted from the latrine in the wee hours of the morning, laughing with abandon, the rest of camp sleepy and silent.

Come here, Vivian whispered, standing by the latrine, her elbow bent against its cedar wall. *There's something you'll want to see.*

With a grin, she gestured to two planks in the latrine's exterior wall. One was slightly crooked, leaving a crack big enough for light to trickle through it. Occasionally the light would blink out a moment, blocked by someone on the other side of the wall.

That someone was Theo. Still in the shower.

Vivian grinned from ear to ear. *I found it last year. No one knows about it but me.*

And you want me to spy on Theo?

No, Vivian replied. *I dare* you *to spy on him.*

I edged closer to the wall. Even though I knew it was wrong. I placed an eye to the crack, at first seeing nothing but steam and the water-specked shower wall. Then Theo appeared. I didn't watch him for very long. After a few seconds, the wrongness of the situation crashed over me and I turned away, red-faced.

Now, as I reach Dogwood, I notice something out of the ordinary. A light. Tiny and red. It glows from the back wall of the cabin in front of ours. I aim my flashlight at it and see a black rectangle tucked into the nook where the two sides of the roof connect.

A surveillance camera.

I turn off the flashlight and stare at the camera's lens. I don't move a muscle. The red light snaps off.

I wait five seconds before waving the flashlight over my head. The red light flicks on again, triggered by the motion.

Fifteen years later, I'm the one being watched.

INSIDE, I'm unable to go back to sleep. I change into my bathing suit and robe. I then grab a towel from my trunk and slip quietly out of the cabin. I will myself not to look at the camera.

As I make my way to the lake, I sneak glances at the other cabins, checking for cameras on those as well. I don't see any.

At the edge of Lake Midnight, I place the towel on the cracked dirt of the shore, drop the robe, and step gingerly into the water. The lake is cold, bracing. And murky. When I scoop some water into my cupped hands, I see swirling specks of feathery algae.

Steeling myself with a deep breath, I dive under, kicking, arms extended in front of me. I emerge only when my chest starts to tighten, lungs swelling. I then start to cut my way across the lake.

I stop once I reach the middle—probably a quarter mile from shore. I think about how everything below me used to be dry land. I think of the story Casey told me. The village still at the bottom of the lake, its skeletal inhabitants tucked in their beds.

I turn back toward camp. It's quiet and still, bathed in pinkish light from the rising sun. A solitary figure is standing at the dock's edge. Even from this distance, I know the figure is Becca Schoenfeld. I see the splash of color from the scarf circling her neck and can make out the shape of her camera as she lifts it to her face.

I get to my feet a few yards from shore and wade the rest of the way. Becca has left the dock and is now directly in front of me, gesturing for me to stop. I indulge her, standing shin-deep in the water as she clicks off a few more shots.

"Sorry," she says once she's finished. "The light was so perfect, I couldn't resist. Such a beautiful sunrise."

She holds the camera in front of me as I dry off, scrolling through the photos. Of the last one, she says, "This one's the keeper."

In the picture, I've risen from the lake, water streaming down my body, backlit by the sunrise. I think Becca was going for something fierce, a woman emerging victorious from the surf, now determined to conquer land. But instead of fierce, I simply look lost.

We settle onto the grass and stare out at the water. "So you're an artist," Becca says. "I read about your gallery show."

"And I've seen your photographs."

Having stated the obvious, we settle into an awkward silence.

"I can't believe I'm back here," Becca eventually says. "I can't believe *you're* back here."

"You and me both."

"Listen, I'm sorry for acting weird yesterday. I saw you in the mess hall and momentarily freaked out. I don't know why."

"I do," I say. "Seeing me brought back a hundred different memories you weren't prepared to face. It happens all the time to me."

"I'm assuming Franny lured you back," Becca says.

I nod, even though it's not entirely the truth.

"I volunteered," Becca says. "For the past three years, I've been living out of a suitcase. Staying in one place for six weeks definitely had its appeal."

She lifts her chin to the sunrise and closes her eyes. In that light clenching of her eyelids, I can see that she, too, is haunted by the unknown. The only difference between us is that she's returned to Camp Nightingale to forget. I'm here to remember.

"Yesterday when I saw you in the mess hall, I wanted to ask you something."

"Let me guess," Becca says. "It's about that summer."

I give a curt nod. "The disappearance. Did you notice anything strange the night before it happened? Or maybe the morning I realized they were gone?"

A memory arrives. A bad one. Me at the lake, telling Franny that the girls were missing as other campers gathered around. Becca watching it all through her camera, the shutter clicking away.

"I remember you," she says. "How frantic and scared you were."

"Other than that, you don't recall anything out of the ordinary?"

"Nope." The word comes out too fast. Like a chirp. "Nothing."

"How well did you know the girls in my cabin? You all spent the previous summer here. I thought you might have known them."

"I didn't. Not really."

"Not even Vivian?" I think of Becca's warning my first morning at camp. *Don't be fooled. She'll turn on you eventually.* "I thought the two of you might have been friends."

"I mean, I knew her," Becca says. "Everyone here knew Vivian. And everyone had an opinion."

"What was the general consensus?"

"Honestly? That she was kind of a bitch."

I flinch at her tone.

Squaring her shoulders, she says, "Come on, Emma. Vivian doesn't automatically become a good person just because of what happened to her. You of all people should know that."

She stands and brushes dirt from her shorts. Then she walks away, slowly, silently, not looking back. I remain where I am, contemplating the two truths Becca just revealed to me. The first is that she's right. Vivian wasn't a good person. The second is that Becca remembers much more than she'd like to admit.

Fifteen Years Ago

THE beach at Camp Nightingale—a combination of sand and pebbles—felt as uncomfortable as it looked. Still, I grinned and tried to bear it as I watched waves of campers tiptoe into the water.

Although all four of us had changed into our bathing suits, only Natalie and Allison joined the others in the lake. Natalie swam like the natural athlete she was, using hard, long strokes to easily make it to the string of foam buoys marking the area no one was allowed to swim past. Allison was more of a show-off, somersaulting in the water like a synchronized swimmer.

I remained onshore. Vivian sat behind me, coating my shoulders with Coppertone, its coconut scent sickeningly sweet.

"It's criminal how pretty you are," she said.

"I don't feel pretty."

"But you are. Hasn't your mother ever told you that?"

"My mother gives me as little attention as possible. Same thing with my dad."

Vivian clucked with sympathy. "That sounds just like my parents. My sister's the one who made me realize how pretty I was. Now I'll do the same for you."

"I'm far from pretty."

"You *are*," Vivian insisted. "And in a year or two, you'll be gorgeous. I can tell. You'll snag yourself a hottie like Theo." She gestured to the lifeguard stand a few feet away, where Theo sat in red swim trunks, the whistle roped around his neck.

"Why aren't you in the water?" he called down to us.

"I don't know how to swim," I said.

A grin spread across Theo's face. "That's quite a coincidence. One of my goals today is to teach someone."

He hopped down from the lifeguard stand and, before I could protest, took my hand and led me to the dirty-looking water. Bits of brown stuff floated just below the surface. When some touched my ankle, I recoiled. Theo tightened his grip around my hand.

"Relax. A little algae never hurt anyone."

He guided me deeper into the lake, the water rising against me in increments. Soon I was up to my waist.

"Awesome, Em," he said. "You're doing great. But you need to relax more. The water is your friend. Let it hold you up."

Without warning, he slid behind me and scooped me up in his arms. One wrapped around my back. The other behind my knees.

"Close your eyes," he said.

I closed them as he lowered me into the lake until I couldn't tell the difference between his arms and the water. When I opened my eyes, I saw him standing next to me, arms crossed. I was on my own, letting the water hold me up.

Theo grinned, his eyes sparkling. "You, my dear, are floating."

Just then, noise rippled across the lake. Splashing. Urgent and panicked. A couple of girls in the deep end began to shriek. Beyond them, I saw a pair of hands rising and falling from the lake's surface, waving frantically. A face poked out of the drink, gasped, slipped back under. Vivian.

Theo left my side and surged toward her. Without him near me, I sank into the water. I began to paddle, guided by instinct more than anything else, until my nose and mouth broke the surface. I continued to paddle and kick until, lo and behold, I was swimming.

I kept at it, looking across the water first to Vivian, still flailing, and then to Natalie and Allison, who bobbed in place, frozen with fear. I watched them watch Theo as he reached Vivian and clamped an arm around her waist. He swam to shore that way, not stopping until both of their backs were on the beach.

Vivian coughed once, and a bubble of lake water spurted from her throat. Tears streamed down her crimson cheeks.

"I—I don't know what happened," she said, gasping.

"Hell, Viv," Theo said angrily, "I thought you could swim."

Vivian sat up and shook her head, still crying. "I thought I'd try after watching you teach Emma. You made it look so easy."

Standing a few yards away from them was Becca. She clicked off a picture of Vivian sprawled onshore. Then she turned to the lake, picking me out of the crowd of still-stunned campers paddling in the water. She smiled and mouthed four words. *I told you so.*

Chapter 6

I REMAIN ON THE BEACH until reveille blasts from the ancient speaker atop the mess hall. The first full day of camp has begun.

I shuffle to the mess hall. It's mostly empty. Nobody but the kitchen workers. One of them—a guy with dark hair and a goatee—checks me out for half a second before turning away.

I grab a doughnut, a banana, and a cup of coffee. The banana is consumed quickly. The doughnut not so much. Each bite brings a flash of Vivian squinting, her lips pursed. Her disapproving look.

In the latrine, all but one of the shower stalls are in use. The empty stall is the last one in the row. Like the others, it's a cubicle of cedar walls and a door of smoked glass. A pinpoint of white light glows in the center of that door. Behind me, a similar light peeks through a crack in the cedar wall. The same crack I peered through to spy on Theo fifteen years ago.

I shower as fast as possible. I give my hair a quick shampoo and rinse, closing my eyes as the soapy water cascades down my face. When I open my eyes, the point of light on the door is gone.

I spin around, frantically checking the shower wall behind me. No light peeks through the crack. It's gone, eclipsed by something outside. No, not something. *Someone.* Right on the other side of the wall. Watching me.

I push my way out of the stall, yanking on my robe and clutching it tight around me. I rush through the now empty latrine, bursting through the door.

No one is outside. The entire vicinity is deserted.

By the time I'm back at Dogwood, I've concluded that it was a trick of the light. A brief optical illusion.

Lying to myself. It's the only falsehood I allow.

The first painting lesson of the summer is held outside. A dozen girls stand at their easels facing the lake, palettes in hand. The girls from Dogwood are here, including Krystal with her promised sketch pad and a set of charcoal pencils.

"The assignment this morning is to paint what you see," I announce. "Just look out at the lake and paint it as only you see it. Use whatever colors you want. Use any techniques you want. The only person you need to please is you."

As the girls paint, I walk behind them, checking their progress. Some—such as Sasha and her meticulously clean lines—even show promise. Others, like Miranda's defiantly blue brushstrokes, do not. When I reach Krystal, I see that she's sketched a superhero in tight spandex and a flowing cape standing before an easel.

"I think I'm going to name her Monet," Krystal says. "Painter by day, crime fighter by night."

Class ends when a bell clangs from the mess hall, signaling lunchtime. The girls put down their brushes and scurry off, leaving me alone to gather up their canvases and easels. I move the canvases first, carrying them back to the arts-and-crafts building two by two so as not to smudge the still-wet paint. Then I return for the easels, finding them already in the process of being collected.

The gatherer is the maintenance man I saw fixing the roof of the arts-and-crafts building when I arrived. He's come from the tool-shed on the edge of the lawn. Its door sits open, offering a glimpse of a lawn mower, a handsaw, chains hanging on the wall.

"I figured you could use some help," he says. His voice is gruff.

"Thanks." I hold out my hand. "I'm Emma, by the way."

Instead of shaking my hand, the man nods and says, "I know."

"You were here before, right? I recognized you when I arrived."

The man drops another easel onto a growing pile of them. "Yep."

Not wanting to feel useless, I collapse the last remaining easel and hand it to him. He adds it to the stack and scoops up all of them at once, carrying six under each arm. Then he's off, carting away the easels as if they weigh nothing at all.

BEFORE heading to lunch, I return to the arts-and-crafts building. I find what I'm looking for at Paige's pottery station, a dime-size chunk of wet clay. Perfect for what I have planned.

I make my way to the latrine. I head to the side of the building, seeking out the crack on the exterior wall. Once I find it, I stuff a bit of clay between the two planks, covering the crack.

When I finally do reach the mess hall, I find Theo waiting for me outside, a wicker basket at his feet. He announces, "I'm going on a picnic. And I thought you might like to come along."

"What's the occasion?"

He nods toward the mess hall doors. "Does one need a special occasion to skip the horror of whatever's being served in there?"

He says it with his brows arched, aiming for levity. There's no doubt he's forgiven me. What I don't understand is why.

Still, a picnic lunch does sound appealing. "Count me in," I say. "My taste buds thank you."

Theo lifts the basket and leads me away from the mess hall. He guides me past the cabins and latrine and into the woods.

Although there's no path for us to follow, he walks with purpose, as if he knows exactly where he's going. Eventually we come to a small circle cleared of dead leaves and underbrush. In its place is a patch of soft grass punctuated in spots by clusters of wildflowers. A halo of sunlight pours through the gap in the trees. A round table sits in the middle of the clearing, similar to the one where Franny and I had lunch in her fantastical greenhouse. And just like at that months-ago meal, Franny is present, already seated at the table.

"There you are," she says with a warm smile.

"Hi," I say, hoping I don't sound as surprised as I feel.

Six marble statues are arranged on the outskirts of the space, almost tucked into the trees, like silent witnesses. Each statue is of a woman in artful stages of half dress.

"Welcome to the sculpture garden," Franny says. "One of my grandfather's more fanciful ideas."

"It's lovely," I say, even though the opposite is true. The statues bear the scars of years exposed to the elements. All have blank eyes, as if they've been blinded.

"You don't need to be polite," Theo says as he places the picnic basket on the table and starts to unpack it. "It's creepy as hell."

"I'll admit it's not to everyone's taste," Franny says. "But my grandfather was proud of it. And so it must remain." She shrugs.

"Lunch is served," Theo announces. A plate bearing an open-faced sandwich of smoked salmon heaped with crème fraîche, capers, and dill now sits in front of me. When Theo pours me a glass of prosecco, I take a long sip in an effort to calm my nerves.

"Now that we're all cozy," Franny says, "I think it's time to reveal why we've brought you here. There's an important matter Theo and I would like to discuss with you."

Apprehension clings to my insides. "What is it?"

"The camera outside your cabin," Franny says.

I freeze, a forkful of salmon poised halfway to my mouth.

"We know you've seen it," Theo says. "We watched the footage this morning."

"To be completely frank, we were hoping it wouldn't be noticed," Franny adds. "But now that it has, I do hope you'll give us the chance to explain why it's there."

I set my fork on my plate. "I'd certainly appreciate one. I didn't see any others around the camp."

"That's because it's the only one, dear," Franny says.

"How long has it been there?"

"Since last evening," Theo says. "Ben the handyman installed it during the campfire."

"Why? Are you spying on me?"

"That's putting it a bit harshly. *Spying.*" Franny takes a tiny sip of prosecco. "I like to think it's there for your own protection."

"From what?"

"Yourself." It's Theo who answers.

"Back when I was getting ready to reopen the camp, we did background checks on everyone staying here for the summer," Franny says, a pained expression crossing her face. "We know what happened to you after you left Camp Nightingale."

I DON'T talk about those horrible six months when I was fourteen.

It began during a class trip to the Metropolitan Museum of Art. A hundred schoolgirls tittering through the halls in a parade of plaid skirts. I had broken off from the group in the wing of nineteenth-century European paintings.

One of the galleries was empty, save for three girls standing in front of a massive landscape. The girls wore white dresses. Plain and subdued. They stood straight-backed and completely still.

It's beautiful, one of the girls said. *Don't you think so, Em?*

She didn't turn around. She didn't need to. It was Vivian. The other two were Natalie and Allison.

You seem surprised, Vivian said.

It took all the strength I could muster to take a step backward, trying to put some distance between us. Vivian, Natalie, and

Allison were now facing me. Before I could run away completely, Vivian winked and said, *See you soon.*

And I did. A few days later during a matinee of *Jersey Boys*, when my mother had ducked out to the lobby bar, Vivian took her place, once again in the white dress. *This show sucks,* she said.

I stayed frozen in my seat, eyes fixed to the distant stage in front of me. *You're not real.* My voice was a murmur. *You don't exist.*

Come on, Em. You and I both know you don't believe that.

Why are you doing this?

You know exactly why.

Then she was gone.

The girls appeared frequently after that. On the opposite side of the street, across the cafeteria, roaming the lingerie department at Macy's. I woke up one night to find Vivian sitting on the edge of my bed. *I'm curious, Em,* she said. *Did you really think you could get away with it?*

After that, I refused to leave the apartment. My parents had no choice but to take me to a psychiatrist, who declared that the sightings of the girls were in fact hallucinations.

I was diagnosed with schizophreniform disorder, a kissing cousin to schizophrenia itself. What happened at Camp Nightingale didn't cause the disorder. That particular chemical imbalance had always been there, lightly percolating in the recesses of my brain. All the girls' disappearance did was set it free.

The doctor also stressed that schizophreniform disorder was mostly temporary. Those who suffered from it usually got better with the right treatment. Which is how I came to spend six months in a mental health facility that specialized in treating teenage girls.

The place was clean, comfortable, professional. There was no raving insanity on display. It was just a bunch of girls my age trying their best to get better. And I did, thanks to a combination of therapy, medication, and old-fashioned patience.

On my last day there, the kind, infinitely patient Dr. Shively presented me with a charm bracelet. Dangling from it were three delicate birds. *Consider it a talisman,* she said as she clasped it around my wrist. *Never underestimate the power of positive thinking. If you*

ever experience another hallucination, I want you to touch this bracelet
and tell yourself that what you're seeing isn't real, that it has no power
over you, that you're stronger than everyone realizes.

I never saw the girls again. Except in my paintings.

I had thought that information was private. Yet somehow Franny
was able to find out. "It was a long time ago," I say.

"Of course it was," Theo says.

Franny adds, "The last thing we want is for you to feel ostracized
or punished in any way. Which is why we should have told you
about the camera in the first place."

"I understand," I say, my voice clipped. "Better safe than sorry.
After all, we don't want another mess on our hands, do we?"

I excuse myself from the table and make my escape.

Theo follows me into the woods. "Emma, don't be mad."

"I don't want to talk to you," I say.

"Listen, you have every right to be angry. We should have just
told you what we were doing. We handled it the wrong way."

"If you don't trust me, then why did you invite me back here?"

"Because my mother wanted you here," Theo says. "We just had
no idea what you'd be like. It was a matter of safety, not trust."

"Safety? What do you think I'm going to do to these girls?"

"Maybe the same thing you said I did to Vivian, Allison, and
Natalie."

"It's because of that, isn't it? The camera. Digging up my health
records. It's because I accused you of hurting them all those years ago."

Theo runs a hand through his hair, exasperated. "That couldn't
be further from the truth. But since you brought it up, I have to say
it was a lousy thing you did back then."

"It was," I admit. "And I've spent years beating myself up over it.
But I was young and confused and scared."

"You think I wasn't?" Theo shoots back. "You should have seen
the way the police grilled me. They made me take a lie detector
test. They made Chet do it, too. A ten-year-old kid hooked up to
a polygraph. Because of what you accused me of doing." He's mad
now, piling it on to make it clear how much I had wronged him.

"I didn't know any better," I say.

"We were friends, Em," Theo says. "Why did you think I had anything to do with what happened to them?"

I stare at him, dumbfounded. "You know exactly why," I say.

Then I'm off again, leaving Theo behind. After a few wrong turns, I find my way back to camp, seething all the way.

Back at Dogwood, I throw open the door. Inside, something springs from the floor, taking flight. I see dark shapes at the window, hear the flap of wings. Birds. Three of them. Crows.

They fly in a frenzy, smacking against the ceiling, squawking. One of them swoops toward me. Claws skim my hair. Another heads straight for my face. Black eyes staring. Sharp beak gaping.

I drop to the floor and cover my head. The crows keep flapping. Keep squawking. I reach for the door, opening it wide. The movement sends the birds in the opposite direction. Toward the window, where they strike glass in a series of sickening thuds.

I crawl toward them, my right hand over my eyes, my left one shooing them the other way. The bracelet slides up and down my wrist. Three more birds in motion. It does the trick. One crow spies the open door and darts through it, followed immediately by the others, leaving the cabin suddenly silent.

I remain on the floor, catching my breath. I assume they came in through the window, curious and hungry. But then I remember the birds thudding against the glass. Such a dreadful sound.

The window was closed the entire time.

IT TAKES me ten minutes to gather all the feathers the crows have left behind. Someone caught the birds and released them inside on purpose. Who would do such a thing? And why?

I feel the need to get out of the cabin for a little bit. I throw open my hickory trunk, looking for my hiking boots. The first thing I see is the folded piece of paper Vivian had hidden. I pick it up. The photograph of Eleanor Auburn once again slides from its fold.

Setting the picture aside, I make another examination of the map Vivian had drawn. The camp. The lake. The forest on the far shore. My gaze lingers on the small X. Something is located there.

There's no way to know for certain until I go there myself. I begin to gather supplies and stuff them into my backpack. On my way out, I give the camera a defiant stare.

Before departing camp, I stop by the mess hall to fill up my water bottle and grab a banana and granola bar. Two women and a man are outside. Kitchen workers spending the lull between lunch and dinner smoking in the shade of the overhanging roof. The man is the same guy who briefly checked me out this morning. The tag affixed to his apron strap says his name is Marvin.

Now Marvin stares past me to the lake in the distance. Afternoon swimming lessons are taking place, the shore and water dotted with young women in bathing suits of varying degrees of modesty. He catches me watching him and displays a slimy grin.

"It's not illegal to look," he says.

"Those girls are young enough to be your daughters."

Marvin drops his cigarette, stubs it out, goes back inside. The women chuckle. One of them nods my way. A silent thank-you.

I continue toward the lake, my backpack slung over my shoulder. I spot Miranda in a bikini lingering by the lifeguard station. The lifeguard for the afternoon is Chet. He's undeniably handsome up there on his perch, with his Ray-Bans and whistle. Miranda stares up at him, a finger twirling in her hair. Apparently she's already gotten over the texter who broke her heart.

Nearby, Sasha and Krystal share a beach blanket. They sprawl across it, still in shorts and camp polos, flipping through comic books. I walk over to them, my shadow falling across the blanket.

"Where are you going?" Krystal asks, eyeing my backpack.

"Canoe trip."

"Alone?" Sasha says. "Each year, an average of eighty-seven people die in canoe and kayak accidents. I looked it up."

"I'm a good swimmer. I think I'll be okay."

"It's probably safer if someone is with you."

Next to her, Krystal slaps her comic book shut and sighs. "What Miss Wikipedia here is trying to say is that we want to come along. We're bored, and we've never been canoeing."

"It's a long trip. And there'll be hiking involved."

"I've never hiked, either," Krystal says. "Please, can we come?"

Sasha bats her eyes at me behind her glasses. "Pretty please?"

A sense of duty tugs at me. Franny told me the purpose of reopening Camp Nightingale was to give the campers new experiences.

"Fine," I say. "Put on life vests and help me with the canoe."

The girls do as they're told, grabbing dirty life vests that hang from the sides of the canoe racks. They slip them on and help me lift a canoe off one of the racks.

Miranda trots over to us and says, "Where are you going?"

"Canoeing," Sasha says.

Miranda frowns. "Without me?"

"Go get changed," I tell her. "We'll wait for you."

Another person means another canoe. So while Miranda runs back to the cabin to fetch shorts and a pair of sneakers, Krystal, Sasha, and I wrangle a second canoe to the water's edge. When Miranda returns, we climb in, she and Krystal in one canoe, Sasha and me in the other. We push off.

It takes us a half hour to cross the lake. We slow when the water's surface is darkened by tall pines along the shoreline, their reflections jagged and unwelcoming. Just beneath the surface are the remnants of trees submerged when the valley was flooded. Because the lake's been lowered by drought, the farthest-reaching branches scrape the bottoms of the canoes, sounding like fingernails trying to scratch their way out of a coffin.

More trees jut out of the lake in front of us. They're bare and sun-bleached. Gone are their bark, their leaves, their limbs.

After passing through the graveyard of trees, we come to the shore itself. The landscape rises sharply—an ascent that eventually leads to the rounded peaks in the distance. The trees here tower over the water, forming a pale green wall.

To our right, a heap of boulders sits partway out of the water. Beyond them is a cliff where the land has been chipped away by the elements. Trees line the ridge atop the cliff.

"I see something," Miranda says, pointing to a ragged-looking structure sitting farther down the shore.

I see it, too. It's a gazebo. Rather, it used to be. Now it's a leaning structure of splintered wood slowly being overtaken by weeds. I think it might be the cabin-like structure marked on Vivian's map.

We row toward it. Onshore, we step out of the canoes, life vests discarded. I grab my backpack and pull out the map.

"What's that?" Sasha asks.

"A map."

"What does it lead to?"

"I don't know yet."

I run my finger from the spot that is probably the gazebo to the ragged triangles nearby. I assume those are rocks. Which means we need to make our way northeast until we reach them. After that, it looks to be a short walk north until I find the X.

Our route now set, I open the compass app downloaded to my phone the morning I left for camp, rotating until it points northeast. Then I snag a handful of wildflowers and, with Miranda, Sasha, and Krystal in tow, march into the forest.

Fifteen Years Ago

"LET'S GO," Vivian said.

"Go where?" I was curled up in my bunk, reading. Vivian stood by the cabin door. Allison's floppy straw hat sat atop her head.

"On an adventure," she said. "To search for buried treasure."

I closed my book and crawled out of bed. As if there was any doubt I wouldn't. What Vivian wanted, she got.

"Allison's going to need her hat," I told her. "You know how she is about UV rays."

"Allison's not coming. Neither's Natalie. Just you and me, kid."

She didn't tell me where, exactly, we were going. I simply let her lead the way. First to the canoes near the dock, then across Lake Midnight itself. We came ashore alongside a grassy area aflame with tiger lilies. Vivian picked enough lilies to make a bouquet. When we entered the woods, she began to pluck their petals and drop them to the ground.

"Always leave a trail of bread crumbs," she said. "So you know how to find your way back."

Vivian dropped another petal, and I turned around to look at the long line of them stretching away from us, marking our progress. It was a comforting sight. Like tiny, tangerine-colored footprints we had left behind that would eventually guide us home.

"Two Truths and a Lie," Vivian said. "I'll go first. One: A guy once flashed me in the subway. Two: I have a flask of whiskey hidden under my mattress. Three: I don't know how to swim."

"The second one," I said. "I'd have noticed if you were drinking."

"Aren't you the observant one," Vivian said. "That's why I thought you'd like to see this."

We had come to a large oak tree, its sturdy branches spread wide to create a canopy over the surrounding ground. An X had been carved into the bark. At the base of the tree sat a pile of leaves that camouflaged something beneath it.

Vivian pushed the leaves out of the way, exposing an old and rotting wooden box. Time had stripped the veneer from the lid, which allowed water and sunlight to do their damage, staining the wood in some spots, bleaching it in others.

"It's cool, right?" Vivian said. "It's, like, ancient."

I ran a finger over the lid, feeling a series of grooves in the wood. When I looked closer, I noticed two faint letters etched into the wood. Only when I leaned in close could I read them: CC.

"Where did you find it?"

"Washed up on the shore last summer. I brought it here for safekeeping. Go ahead and open it."

I lifted the lid, the wood so soft and waterlogged I feared it might disintegrate. The inside was lined with a fabric that was in tatters—nothing but dark, leathery strips.

Inside the box lay several pairs of scissors. Antique ones with ornate circles for finger holes and thin blades tapered like stork legs. They'd been tarnished the same color as motor oil.

"Who do you think they belonged to?"

"A hospital or something. There's a name on the bottom." Vivian took the box and shut the lid, holding it closed. When she flipped it over, the scissors inside rattled together. "See?"

Engraved on the bottom of the box, in tiny letters dulled by time, were four words: PROPERTY OF PEACEFUL VALLEY.

"I wonder how it got here."

Vivian shrugged. "Tossed into the lake, probably. Decades ago. No one else knows about it but me. And now you."

"Why are you showing me this?"

"I'm your big sister for the summer, remember? This is what big sisters do. We share things. Things no one else knows."

Chapter 7

I TAKE THE LEAD in the woods. Krystal and Sasha walk behind me. Every so often, Sasha calls out the names of trees she recognizes. "Sugar maple. American beech. White pine. Birch."

Behind them is Miranda, who peels off petals from the flowers I'd picked and drops them to the ground at regular intervals.

"Why do I have to do this again?" she asks.

"Always leave a trail of bread crumbs," I tell her. "It'll help us find our way back."

The ground slants upward as we walk, slightly at first, but soon the landscape becomes more obviously steep. We press on, shoulders hunched, legs bent.

The incline finally levels off into less wearying terrain. We pause to catch our breath and take in the scenery. On our right, slivers of blue sky peek through the trees. I move instinctively toward them, following the light, emerging from the trees onto a thin strip of craggy ground. Beyond it, the land drops away. When the girls reach my side, Miranda whistles with appreciation.

We're atop the ridge I'd spotted from the canoe, overlooking the stone-walled cliff. The view it affords us is stunning. Lake Midnight spreads out below, the water dappled with sunlight. Across from us, hazy in the distance, sits Camp Nightingale.

I dig the map from my pocket. From what I can gather from Vivian's crude markings, we're close to the raggedly triangular rocks. Sure enough, when I turn and point north, I get a glimpse of rocks through the thick forest. These are boulders. Dozens of them. Massive and unwieldy. They sit in a line running up a sharp rise similar to the one we've just climbed. The girls spread out among them, scaling the boulders like kids in a playground.

"I bet these rocks used to be part of the mountain's peak," Sasha says as she clambers up a boulder twice her height. "They froze and broke apart; then glaciers took them down the hill."

I check the compass and the map. "Hey, girls," I call out. "We should keep moving."

I squeeze between two boulders and edge around another. That's when I get a view of another rock farther up the incline. One bigger than the others. A monolith. Nearly two stories tall, it rises from the ground like an enormous tombstone. The side facing me is mostly flat. A sheer wall of rock. A large fissure runs diagonally through it, widening at the top. A tree grows inside the crack, its roots curling along the rock face, seeking soil. Standing beside the tree, looking up into its branches, is Sasha.

Krystal is up there, too. She takes a step toward the boulder's edge and peers down at me. "Hey," she says.

"What are you doing up there?"

"Exploring," Sasha says.

"I'd prefer it if you stayed on the ground. Where's Miranda?"

"Right here."

Miranda's voice emanates from the northwestern side of the giant rock. It sounds watery, akin to an echo. I follow it as Sasha and Krystal scramble down the boulder's opposite side. I work my way around, seeing another large crack in the rock's side. This one runs in a straight line, widening at the bottom. It opens up completely about a foot from the ground, creating a hole large enough for a person to crawl into. Or, in Miranda's case, crawl out of. She climbs to her feet, circles of mud dotting her knees and elbows.

"I wanted to see what was in there."

"Bears or snakes, probably," Sasha says.

"Exactly," I say. "So no more exploring. Understood?"

Miranda stands with her hand on her hip, annoyed. "Isn't that why we're out here?"

I say nothing. I'm too busy looking past her. In the distance are what appear to be ruins. I can make out a crumbled stone wall and one jagged wooden beam pointing skyward. When we get closer, I see that it's the remains of what might have been a barn or farmhouse. The walls are mostly now a pile of rocks, but enough are intact to be able to make out the building's rectangular foundation. Inside are several pines that have sprouted from what's left of the building's roof and floor.

In much better shape is a nearby root cellar built into the slope of the land. There's no roof—just a slightly rounded mound of earth. A fieldstone wall forms the front. In the center is a wooden door, shut tight, its rusted slide bolt firmly in place.

"Creepy," says Sasha.

"Cool," says Miranda.

"It looks like something from *Lord of the Rings*," says Krystal.

But I'm thinking of another, more ominous tale. One about a flooded valley, a clan of survivors hiding in the woods, a thirst for revenge. Someone used to live in these hills. The foundation and root cellar make that abundantly clear. "We should—"

Go. That's what I intended to say. But I'm stopped by the sight of a large oak sitting fifty yards away. The tree is large, its thick branches spread wide. In its trunk is a familiar letter. X.

It's not the same tree Vivian led me to fifteen years ago. I would have remembered the crumbled foundation and creepy-cool root cellar. No, this is a different tree and a different X.

"Stay here," I tell the girls. "I'll be right back."

"Can we look inside that hobbit house?" Miranda asks.

"No. Don't go anywhere."

They mill about the crumbled foundation while I dash to the tree and search around its trunk. I take a step, and the ground beneath me thumps. A muffled, hollow sound. Something is down there.

I drop to my knees and start scraping away years' worth of weeds and dead leaves until I reach soil. I swipe my hands back and forth, clearing the dirt. Something brown and moist appears.

Wood. I sweep away more dirt before burrowing my fingers into the soil underneath it, prying the plank loose. Beneath the plank someone has dug a hole the size of a shoebox. Inside the hole is a yellow grocery bag wrapped tightly around a rectangular object.

I unfurl the bag and reach into it, feeling more plastic. A freezer bag. The kind that can be zipped shut. Through the plastic, I see a splash of green, the stubble of leather, the edges of pages kept dry by the double layers of protection. A book. Auspiciously fancy.

I carefully open the bag, letting the book slip out of it. It's floppy in my hands, yet I'm able to peel back the cover to the first page, where I see the swirl of someone's handwriting.

Vivian's handwriting, to be exact.

"What are you doing over there?" Miranda calls.

I slam the book shut and shove it into my backpack. "Nothing," I reply. "It's not what I was looking for. Let's head back."

I place the now empty bag back in the hole and cover it with the plank. I kick some dirt and leaves over the wood. I want to keep Vivian's secret safe. Because whatever's inside this book, she thought it important enough to hide it on the other side of the lake, as far away from prying eyes and Camp Nightingale as possible.

Fifteen Years Ago

"Two Truths and a Lie," Vivian said as we rowed back to camp. "Your turn."

I dipped my paddle into the lake. "One: My mother once got so drunk that she passed out in our building's elevator," I said. "Two: I've never kissed a boy. Three: I think Theo is the most handsome man I've ever seen."

"You're *cheating*," Vivian said. "None of those are a lie."

She was almost right. My mother had passed out *waiting* for our building's elevator. I'd found her facedown in the hallway.

"But I'll allow it," Vivian said as she pulled her oar from the water and set it aside. "Just this once. Mostly because of your incorrect guess during my turn."

"I don't think so," I said. "I totally know you don't have a flask. Besides, I saw that you can't swim."

"Guess again." Vivian stood suddenly, the canoe rocking as

she shed her clothes. There was no bathing suit underneath, just matching pearl-colored bra and panties. Before I could utter a word of protest, she dove into the lake.

Vivian sliced the water like a knife through butter. Her strokes were quick, powerful, elegant. Feet flicking in short, strong kicks. Hair billowing behind her. A mermaid.

When she came up for air, she was ten feet from the canoe.

"Wait," I said. "You really can swim?"

She grinned. "Duh," she said.

"I thought you were drowning," I said. "We all did. Why would you lie about something like that?"

"Why not?"

"Because it wasn't one of your stupid games!"

Vivian sighed. "Everything is a game, Em. Whether you know it or not. Which means that sometimes a lie is more than just a lie. Sometimes it's the only way to win."

Chapter 8

THAT NIGHT, I WAIT until the girls leave for the campfire before reclining in my bunk with the book Vivian had left behind.

On the first page, I see a date written in her hand. The first day of camp. Fifteen years ago. This is a diary. Vivian's diary.

June 22

Well, here I am, back at Camp Nightmare for another six weeks. I can't say I'm thrilled to be back, unlike the Senator and Mrs. Senator, who were ECSTATIC when I told them I wanted to spend the summer here. This place creeps me out. There's something not right about it.

But here is where I need to be. Just for one more summer. As they say, I've got unfinished business. But will I finish it? That's the big question hanging over this whole summer. Before I left, I asked it to Katherine's stupid Magic 8 Ball that she loved so much. All signs pointed to yes.

Nat and Ali are here, of course. Fourth camper to be announced. I hope that bottom bunk stays empty. It'll make things easier. If not, I'll settle for Theodore. I'd sleep on top of him any damn day of the week. He is looking FINE!!!!

Pull it together, Viv. Don't get distracted by all that fineness. You're on a mission. Theo isn't part of it.

Update: The fourth camper just came in. A new girl. Time to either terrorize her or befriend her.

June 23

Today I showed New Girl the ropes. Someone had to. This place is not for the faint of heart.

New Girl has a name, by the way. It's Emma. Cute, right? And she is. So young and innocent. Underneath that My Little Pony exterior, I think she might actually be a bitch in training. She stood up to me last night, which took major ovaries. I was duly impressed. No one has stood up to me since Katherine died.

But, like Theo's divine handsomeness, I can't let New Girl distract me too much. Mission first. Friendship second.

At least I got to roam a bit after archery. I scoped out all the places I haven't looked yet, including the Big L. I almost made it inside before Casey caught me sniffing around. She's weirdly devoted to this place. I mean, a former camper coming back as a counselor for two summers in a row? Pathetic.

June 24

On her second night at camp, poor Emma had her VERY. FIRST. PERIOD. I felt so bad for her. I remember my first period. It was awful. I swear, the only thing that kept me sane was Katherine. So I did for Em what Kath did for me.

She survived.

June 26

I almost drowned this afternoon.

Well, pretended to drown. It wasn't planned. I just spontaneously decided to do it. Still, I deserve an Oscar. Best Performance of Drowning by a Regional Champion in the 100-Meter Butterfly. The gulping-down-lake-water part sucked, but it was worth it. I got the reaction I was looking for.

June 28

I made it into the Big L. At last! I went during lunch when I knew F and her entourage would be dining on the back deck. That gave me enough time to slip in through the front door without anyone noticing. And wow, was it worth the wait. I knew F was hiding something in there. And, sure enough, she was. Several somethings. I managed to steal one before Lottie caught me in the study. And now I'm freaking out because she's going to tell F. I just know it. Not good, diary.

My reading is interrupted by a sudden, startling rap on the cabin door. I look up from the page and call out, "Who is it?"

"Emma, it's Chet. Is everything okay?"

I stuff the diary under my pillow before saying, "Yeah, I'm fine."

The door opens a crack, and Chet peers inside, his hair a swoosh over his eyes. He pushes it away and says, "Can I come in?"

"Make yourself at home."

He steps inside and takes a seat on my hickory trunk, his long legs extended, arms crossed. Although he and Theo aren't biologically related, the two nevertheless share some traits. Both have the height and physique that makes everything they wear seem perfectly tailored. Both move with athletic grace. And both radiate that laid-back, carefree vibe that comes from being to the manor born. Or, in their case, adopted.

"I noticed you weren't at the campfire," Chet says. "I wondered if something was wrong."

"Which one of them sent you? Your mother or your brother?"

"Neither, actually. I came on my own. I wanted to clear up a few things. About the camera and why my mother invited you back here. Both were my idea."

I sit up in surprise. "I had assumed both were Franny's idea."

"Technically, they were. But I'm the one who instigated them." Chet gives me a grin. It's a great smile. Another thing he and his brother have in common. "The camera was just a precaution. Theo and my mother had nothing to do with it."

It's a polite way of saying that he, too, knows about my fragile mental state after my first stay here. At this rate, it'll be common knowledge by the end of the week.

"Please don't be offended," Chet says. "I understand why you felt unfairly targeted, and I'm sorry. We all are. If you want it taken down, I'll get Ben to do it first thing tomorrow morning."

After what happened in the shower this morning, it's not a bad idea to monitor the camp.

"It can stay," I tell him. "For now. And only if you tell me why it was your idea to invite me back here."

"Because of what you said back then," Chet says. "About Theo."

He's referring to how I told police Theo had something to do with the girls' disappearance.

"I can't change what I did back then," I say. "All I can do is tell you that I regret it and that I'm sorry."

Chet raises a hand to stop me. "Getting an apology isn't why I told my mother she should invite you back here. I did it because your presence says more than any apology ever could."

"Because I'm here again, it means I think Theo is innocent."

"Exactly," Chet says. "But it's more than that. I thought having you here would be a chance to make amends. That it would do Theo some good. God knows, he needs it."

"Why?" It's the only thing I can think to say. Theo is handsome, wealthy, successful. What else could he possibly need?

"He had a rough time after what happened here," Chet says. "The police kept questioning him. Vivian's father said some awful stuff about him, as did the press. And Theo couldn't take it. Dropped out of school. Went heavy on the drugs and alcohol. Rock bottom came on the Fourth of July. A year after the disappearance. Theo went to a party in Newport, got lit, borrowed someone's Ferrari, and smashed it into a tree a mile down the road."

I shudder, recalling the scar on Theo's cheek.

"It's a miracle he survived," Chet continues. "He's never come out and admitted he was trying to kill himself, but that's my theory.

Things got better after that. My mother made sure of it. Theo spent six months in rehab, went back to Harvard, finally became a doctor. It's hard to forget watching your only brother go through something like that." He lets out a long, sad sigh.

"I'm so sorry," I say, even though it's meaningless. It can't erase the pale line that now runs down Theo's cheek.

"I don't know why you accused him," Chet says. "What matters is that you don't believe it now; otherwise you wouldn't be here."

I stare at the floor, mute and guilt-ridden.

"Don't beat yourself up over it," Chet says as he stands to leave. "That's the last thing any of us want. It's time to let go of the past. That's why we're all here. And I hope it'll do everyone some good."

I WAIT a full five minutes after Chet leaves before diving back into Vivian's diary, to decompress after what he said about Theo. Theo spent six months in rehab. Probably at the same time I was being treated for my own problems. Our first years after Camp Nightingale were almost identical. The only difference was the demons we faced. Mine looked like Vivian. Theo's looked like me.

I know I can't repair the damage I've caused him. But I can prevent further damage if I find out more about what happened to Vivian, Natalie, and Allison. He'll no longer have suspicion trailing after him like a shadow. He'll be free. And if it happens to him, it could also happen to me.

I remove Vivian's diary from under my pillow and dive in.

June 29

It turns out I was right. Lottie told F, who pulled me aside and basically went ape on me. She threatened to call the Senator, as if he'd care. She also said I needed to respect personal boundaries. I felt like telling her to shove those personal boundaries. I didn't because I need to keep my head down. I can't rock that boat until it must be capsized.

So, to recap:

Bad news: She definitely suspects something.

Good news: I'm close to finding out her dirty little secret.

July 1

I'm thinking about telling Emma. Someone needs to know in case something happens to me.

July 2

Well, that sucked.

I decided not to tell Em the whole truth about what I'm doing. It's safer for her that way. Instead, I opted to hint at it by taking her to my secret stash in the woods. You guessed it, THE BOX. The thing that started this whole investigation.

I thought showing it to Emma would spark her interest, just in case the Magic 8 Ball lied and all signs actually point to getting booted from camp. That way she can continue what I started, if she's so inclined.

But then the bad stuff had to take place. Yep, I showed her that I could swim. I thought she should know, for several reasons. One: If, God forbid, my body washes up on the beach one morning, she'll be able to tell police that I'm an expert swimmer. Two: She needs to learn not to trust everything everyone tells her. Two Truths and a Lie isn't just a game. For most people, it's a lifestyle. Three: I'll need to break her heart eventually. Might as well put a crack in it now.

So now she's pissed at me. And there's so much I want to tell her. That life is hard. That you need to punch it before it punches you. Hopefully Em will only pout a day. I'll give her flowers tomorrow, and she'll love me again.

July 3

Fun fact: In the 1800s, women could be sent to asylums for hysteria, egotism, immoral life, jealousy, bad company, novel reading (!), or kicked in the head by a horse.

Other than the horse kicking, every single woman I've ever met could have been declared insane back then. That's the lesson I learned today. Every woman is crazy. The ones who can't hide it well enough are out of luck.

150.97768 WEST

164

Update: I forgot I left you out, dear diary. Came back from the campfire to find Natalie and Allison reading you.

I've decided it's best to hide you. You're no longer safe here, baby. The less they know, the better.

Update #2: Welcome to your new home, little book. Drawing a map so I don't forget where you are.

July 4

I. Found. It. That clichéd missing piece that ties everything together. Everything makes sense now. I know the truth. All I need to do is expose it.

But there's a hitch. After reading you, dear diary, Natalie and Allison want in on it. And I've decided I'm going to tell them everything. Because I can't do this without their help. I thought I could, but that's no longer an option.

Yes, I know I could just drop it, forget the whole thing, spend my summer, my year, the rest of my life pretending it never happened. A sane person would do that.

But here's the thing: Some wrongs are so terrible that the people responsible must be held accountable. Call it justice. Call it revenge. Call it whatever. All I care about is this particular wrong. It can't be ignored. It must be righted.

I'm scared.

That's it. The rest of the pages are blank.

I close the diary and exhale. Vivian was looking for something, that much is clear. What it was—and what she eventually found—remain frustratingly out of reach. Honestly, the only thing I'm certain about is that the paper on which Vivian drew her map was torn from the journal. There's a page missing before the one she made on the fourth of July. I hold the map against the ragged remnants of the missing page. It's a match.

I'm scared. That entry confounds me the most. Of all the emotions Vivian displayed when I knew her, fear wasn't one of them.

"What did you learn, Viv?" I murmur.

Judging by the entry dates, I assume she buried the book sometime during the night of July 3. My guess is that she snuck out while the rest of us were asleep. She had also done it the night before. I remember because I was still mad that she had lied to me about her swimming skills. I was especially livid about the reason she lied—because Theo had been paying too much attention to me. She faked drowning just to become the center of attention again.

I went to bed early that night. Later I woke to find Vivian tiptoeing into the cabin. I sat up, bleary-eyed. *Where did you go?*

I had to pee, Vivian said.

She said nothing else as she climbed up to her bunk. But in the morning, a handful of tiny flowers were sitting on my pillow, right beside my head. Forget-me-nots. Their petals were a delicate blue. In the center of each was a yellow starburst. I knew they were from Vivian. Just as she thought, I loved her again.

I turn to the page with Vivian's musings about insanity. Of all the things she had written, this one shakes me to my core. Reading it feels as though she's speaking directly to me, as if she foresaw my slide into madness a year before it would happen.

But why did she seek out that information? And where?

I vividly remember the day she made that entry. Riding to town in the camp's mint-green Ford, me squeezed tight between Vivian and Theo at the wheel. I didn't mind at all when Vivian said she was going shopping and left me alone with Theo.

I flip to the next page, where she had jotted down that strange set of numbers.

150.97768 WEST
164

I'm taking a picture of the numbers with my phone when the door to Dogwood opens and Miranda, Krystal, and Sasha burst inside. Their sudden presence sends me once again scrambling to close the book and shove it under my pillow.

"What are you doing?" Sasha asks, eyeing first the corner of the book poking from beneath my pillow and then my phone, which remains clutched in my hand.

I tell them the truth, minus any context. "I'm trying to decipher something. A code."

Miranda's face lights up. "What kind of code?"

I glance at the picture on my phone, reading off the number. "What does 150.97768 WEST mean to you?"

"Easy," Miranda says. "It's the Dewey decimal system. Some book has that call number."

"You positive?"

She gives me a disbelieving look. "Um, yeah. I've spent, like, half my life at the library."

The library. Maybe that's where Vivian went when she claimed to be shopping. While there, she found a book important enough to note its call number in her diary.

I recall her entry about getting somewhere she wasn't supposed to be. The Big L is the Lodge. F is Franny. Simple enough. But Vivian frustratingly failed to mention exactly what she found there and what she managed to steal. Franny's reaction to her snooping sends a chill through me. It doesn't sound like Franny at all.

I'm close to finding out her dirty little secret.

It turns out something bad did happen, only there's no proof it had anything to do with Franny or a deep, dark secret. Yet some events are too connected to be mere coincidence.

I know the truth.

The idea that I might be closer to learning what happened to the girls should excite me. Instead, a hard ball of pain forms in the pit of my stomach. I assume Vivian experienced this exact feeling when she scribbled those last two words in her diary.

I'm scared.

So am I. Because it's possible I've stumbled upon something sinister, even dangerous. Above all, I'm scared that if I keep digging I might not like what I'll find.

THAT night, my dreams are haunted by Vivian. First running through a forest. Then on a barren island, holding a pair of scissors. Finally in a canoe, rowing mightily into a rolling fog bank that whooshes over her, swirling and hungry, ultimately consuming her.

I wake clutching my charm bracelet as reveille blasts through camp. Even before my eyes are fully open, I can make out something at Dogwood's front window. A shape, dark as a shadow.

A gasp catches in my throat as whoever's at the window flees. I can't tell who it is. All I see is a dark figure streaking away.

I bolt outside to see if I can spot whoever was at the window. Already dozens of girls are spilling out of their cabins, roused by reveille. Their gazes are fixed on the cabin behind me.

I turn around. The door of Dogwood has been smeared with paint. Red. Still wet. Sliding down the wood in rivulets that resemble streaks of blood. The paint forms a word in all caps: LIAR.

FRANNY again stands before a mess hall filled with campers, although this time it's to give a different kind of speech.

"To say I'm disappointed is an understatement," she says. "I'm devastated. Vandalism of any sort will not be tolerated at Camp Nightingale. Under normal circumstances, the culprit would be asked to leave immediately. But since you all have only been here a few days and may not yet understand the rules, whoever painted on the door of Dogwood will be allowed to stay if you come forward now. So, please, if any of you are responsible, speak up now, apologize, and we'll put the entire incident behind us."

Silence follows. No girls stand to confess. Most of the girls have their heads bowed in collective shame. Standing along the wall are Lottie, Theo, Chet, and Mindy.

"Well then," Franny says. "After breakfast, you will return to your cabins. Morning classes are canceled."

She makes her way out of the mess hall with the rest of the Lodge denizens in tow. When they pass, Lottie taps my shoulder and says, "Emma, please come with us."

I follow them to the arts-and-crafts building next door. Once everyone's inside, Lottie closes the door.

"Well, this is a fine mess," Franny says. "Emma, do you have any idea who could have done this?"

The obvious answer would be someone in this room. Other than Mindy, I've lied to all of them in the past.

"I don't know. I only knew about it once I left the cabin."

Franny turns to Chet. "Did you check the camera?"

"Yeah," he says. "There's nothing. Which is a big red flag. The slightest motion triggers that camera."

"Is the camera working now?" Franny asks.

"Yes," Chet says. "Which means either it malfunctioned overnight or someone tampered with it. I imagine it wouldn't be too hard to climb up there on a ladder and put tape over the sensor."

"Wouldn't there be video of that?" Theo says.

Chet answers with a shake of his head. "Not necessarily. The camera is programmed to automatically turn on at nine p.m. and turn off at six in the morning. Someone could have tampered with it before nine and removed the tape right at six."

"Let's talk about the paint," Theo says. "If we can figure out where it came from, maybe it'll give us an idea of who did it."

"Emma's the painter," Mindy pipes up.

"Oil paint," I say, shooting her an angry look. "And that's not what was on the door. It doesn't run like that. If I had to guess, I'd say it was acrylic paint."

"What's it used for?" Theo says.

I look to where Casey's workstation sits. "Crafts," I say.

I edge around one of the crafting tables and head to the cabinet against the wall. Flinging it open, I see rows of plastic paint bottles. They're translucent, giving a glimpse of the colors contained within them. All the bottles are full, save for one. Basic red.

Sitting nearby is a trash can. I go to it and spot a medium-sized paintbrush at the bottom. Red paint clings to the bristles, still wet.

"See?" I say. "Not my paint. Not my brush."

"So someone snuck in here early this morning and used the paint," Theo says.

"The door is locked overnight," Lottie replies. "Maybe whoever was last to leave yesterday forgot to lock it."

"Or has a key," Chet adds.

Lottie shakes her head. "The only people with keys are me, Franny, and Ben."

"Neither Lottie nor I would do such a thing," Franny says. "And Ben was only just arriving when the paint was discovered."

"So that means the door was left unlocked," Theo says.

All eyes turn to me. "You honestly think I'm the one who did this?" I say. "Why would I vandalize my own door?"

"Why have you done a lot of things?" Mindy says. I assume that question has occurred to everyone in the room at some point.

"If Emma says she didn't do it, then I believe her," Theo says. "We should be asking why someone would do this to her."

I know the answer. It's because someone at camp knows.

That's why I was watched in the shower. Why those three birds were released into the cabin. Why someone was at the window and smeared paint across the door. It was their way of telling me that they know. Not what I did to Theo. What I did to the girls.

Everyone starts to leave. Before exiting, Theo looks at me with concern. "Are you okay?" he says.

"No. I need to get out of here. Just for a little bit."

"Where do you want to go?" Theo says.

I think of Vivian's diary. "Town," I say.

Fifteen Years Ago

"So why are we doing this again?" Theo asked as the truck passed under the camp's entrance arch.

"Because I'm in need of some hygiene products," Vivian said. "Personal, lady ones."

Theo shook his head, amused. "What about you, Em?"

"I'm just along for the ride."

And I was. Quite unexpectedly. I had been waiting for the others outside the mess hall when Natalie and Allison arrived.

"Vivian needs you," Allison said.

"Why?"

"She didn't say."

"Where is she?"

Natalie jerked her head toward the arts-and-crafts building.

That's where I found Vivian, Theo, and the mint-green pickup. I squeezed between them, their bodies warm against me as the truck bucked along the pothole-riddled road. Theo's legs continually bumped mine, making my stomach flutter and heart ache.

The town could have been any small town. There was a main drag; quaint storefronts; red, white, and blue bunting on porches. A sign promised a parade the next morning and fireworks at night. Theo parked the truck, and Vivian and I hopped out. Vivian started to cross the street, heading toward an old-timey drugstore on the corner. "I'll see you losers in an hour," she said. "You and Emma go get lunch or something."

She strode into the pharmacy without another word. Through the window, I watched her pause at a rack of cheap sunglasses by the door and try on a pair shaped like hearts.

"Well, I guess it's just us," Theo said.

We walked to a diner and settled into a booth by the window. Theo ordered a cheeseburger, fries, and a vanilla milkshake. I did the same, minus the milkshake, which Vivian never would have approved of in a million years.

As I sat there with Theo, listening to oldies drift from a juke-box, I understood that the whole trip was Vivian's ruse to let me spend time alone with him. Another apology. One better than flowers.

"How are you liking Camp Nightingale?" Theo asked once the food had arrived.

"I love it," I said, taking a rabbitlike nibble on a french fry.

"My mother will be pleased to hear that."

"Do you like it there?"

Theo took a bite of burger. "I love it, too. Unfortunately, this looks like it'll be my last summer before internships take over my life. College certainly keeps you busy when you're premed."

"You're going to be a doctor?"

"That's the plan. A pediatrician. And what do you want to be?"

"I think I want to be a painter." I don't know why I said it. I certainly had no artistic ambitions. It just sounded like the kind of profession Theo would want a woman to have.

"Emma Davis, famous painter." Theo gave me a smile that made my legs quiver. "Maybe I'll come to one of your gallery openings."

Within seconds, I had my entire future mapped out. We'd keep in touch after the summer, exchanging letters that would become more meaningful as time passed. Love would eventually be declared. Plans would be made. We'd stay devoted as I went to art school and he completed his residency. Then we'd marry and be the kind of couple other people envied.

As outlandish as it seemed, I told myself it could come true. I was mature for my age, or so I thought. Smart. Cool. Like Vivian. And I knew exactly what she would have done in that situation.

So when Theo attempted to take a sip of his milkshake, I beat him to it, leaning in and sucking from his straw. The move was bold, so utterly unlike me. Yet there was more boldness in store. I closed my eyes and tilted my mouth toward Theo's, the vanilla taste on my tongue spreading to my lips as I kissed him. A sweet, fluttery sensation filled my body.

I pulled away quickly, my eyes still closed. I didn't want to bring an end to the magic spell I was under. He ended it anyway, softly saying, "I'm flattered, Emma. I really am. But—"

"I was just kidding," I blurted out. "It was a joke. That's all."

Theo said nothing, which is why I turned to the window. Vivian was on the other side of the glass on the sidewalk, wearing the drugstore sunglasses. Heart-shaped frames. The smile that played across her lips made it clear she'd witnessed everything.

Chapter 9

MY EXCUSE FOR GOING into town was to fill a prescription for allergy medicine I'd forgotten to bring with me. Yet another lie. I returned to Dogwood to grab my backpack and Vivian's diary. By then the paint on the door had been completely wiped away.

Now Theo and I ride in the same mint-green pickup that had whisked us out of camp fifteen years ago. I'm not sure how to act. Silence seems to be the best choice.

It becomes too much for Theo, for he suddenly says, "Can we start over?"

I wrinkle my brow, confused. "You mean go back to camp?"

"I mean go back to the beginning. Let's start fresh. Pretend it's fifteen years ago and you're just arriving at camp." Theo flashes the same crooked smile he gave when we first met. "Hi, I'm Theo."

Once again, I'm amazed by his forgiveness.

"Feel free to play along," he urges.

I'd love nothing more than to erase much of what's happened. But the past clings to the present.

"Thank you for doing this," I say instead. "I know it's an inconvenience."

Theo keeps his eyes on the road, trying to hide how I've disappointed him yet again. "It's nothing. I needed to go into town anyway. Lottie gave me a list of things to pick up."

When we reach town, I see it's more or less the same. The drugstore remains, although it's now part of a chain.

"After this, I might make a quick stop at the library. I need a place with good Wi-Fi to catch up on work e-mails," I say.

"Sure, I'll meet you there in an hour."

I hurry into the drugstore. Since I know it'll look suspicious on the return trip if I'm not carrying a bag from the place, I spend a few minutes browsing the shelves for something small to buy. I settle on a four-pack of disposable phone chargers. One for me and each girl in Dogwood.

At the cash register, I notice a rotating rack of sunglasses. I give it a spin, barely eyeing the knockoff Ray-Bans and cheap aviators when a familiar pair whirls by. Red plastic. Heart-shaped frames. I snatch the sunglasses from the rack, remembering the pair Vivian wore the entire ride back to camp that long-ago summer. I try on the sunglasses and lift my face to the rack's mirror. Vivian wore them better, that's for damn sure. On me, they're just silly.

I toss the sunglasses onto the counter anyway. I pay with cash and stuff the chargers into my backpack. The sunglasses are worn out of the store, slid high up to keep my hair in place.

Next, it's on to the library. Soon I'm scanning the stacks for

150.97768 WEST. Astonishingly, it's still there. *Dark Ages: Women and Mental Illness in the 1800s* by Amanda West.

I take the book to a secluded cubicle in the corner. Vivian held this book in her hands mere days before she disappeared. I fling it open, seeing on the first page a vintage photo of a young woman confined in a straitjacket. Below the photo is a caption as sad as it is vague. *Unknown asylum patient, 1887.*

Skimming through the book is an exercise in masochism. There are more photos, more infuriating captions. Had I been born a hundred years earlier, I would have become one of these women.

I finally come to page 164. The one Vivian noted in her diary. It contains another photo, one that fills most of the page. This photograph shows a man standing in front of an ornate, Victorian structure. The man is young, tall, thick of chest and stomach. He boasts an impeccably waxed mustache and a distinct darkness to his eyes. One hand grips the lapel of his morning coat. The other is slid into a vest pocket. Such a pompous pose.

The building behind him is three stories tall, made of brick, with dormer windows on the top floor and a chimneylike turret gracing the roof. The windows are tall and arched. A weather vane in the shape of a rooster rises from the turret's peaked roof. Beneath the photo is a caption—*Dr. Charles Cutler poses outside Peaceful Valley Asylum, circa 1898.* The name summons a memory, the tiny name engraved on the bottom of a rotting box. *Peaceful Valley.*

Peaceful Valley had been an insane asylum.

I look at the text on the page opposite the photo.

By the end of the nineteenth century, a growing divide had formed regarding the treatment of mentally ill women. In the nation's cities, asylums remained crowded with the poor and indigent. It was quite a different story for the wealthy, who turned to small, for-profit asylums on country estates in remote areas.

A few progressive doctors attempted to bridge the gap by opening the doors of their bucolic retreats to those less fortunate. For a time, Dr. Charles Cutler was a common sight in the asylums of New York and Boston, where he sought out patients in the most unfortunate of situations, became their legal guardian, and whisked them away to Peaceful Valley Asylum, a small retreat in upstate New York.

I have no idea what this has to do with Franny. There seems to be only one way to find out—I need to search the Lodge. Vivian discovered something in the study. Whatever she found led her here, to this same book in this same library.

Always leave a trail of bread crumbs. That's what Vivian told me. *So you know how to find your way back.*

Only the trail she left for me won't be enough. I grab my phone and FaceTime my friend Marc at his bistro.

"It's a bad time, I know," I tell him.

"The lunch rush," Marc says. "I've got exactly one minute."

I dive right in. "Remember that reference librarian at the New York Public Library? Are the two of you still friendly?"

"He follows me on Twitter," Marc says.

"Do you think he'd help you do some research for your best friend in the entire world?"

"Possibly. What will we be researching?"

"Peaceful Valley Asylum." I quickly tell him about Vivian, her diary of cryptic clues, the fact that an insane asylum might be involved. "I need to know more about that asylum," I say.

Marc pulls his phone closer to his face. "Where are you?"

"The local library."

"Well, someone there is watching you."

My eyes dart to the lower corner of my screen, where my own image rests in a tiny rectangle. A man stands roughly ten feet behind me, his arms folded across his chest. Theo.

"I need to go," I tell Marc before ending the call.

When I turn around to face Theo, his face is a placid surface, unreadable. "All done," I say.

I gather my things, leaving the book where it is. On our way out of the library, I pull the sunglasses over my eyes, shielding them from Theo's inquisitive gaze.

Then we're off, heading back to camp in a fresh cocoon of

silence. It's only when the camp's gate slides into view that Theo says, "I need to ask you something. About that summer. About that day we drove into town."

"What about it?"

"Well, we had lunch at that diner and—"

"I kissed you."

Theo chuckles at the memory. I don't. It's hard to laugh at one of the most humiliating moments of your adolescence.

"Yes, that. Were you lying then? About it being a joke?"

Rather than continue the lie, I say, "Why?"

"Because, at the time, I didn't think it was." Theo pauses. "But I was flattered. And I want you to know that, had you been older, I probably would have kissed you back."

"And now?" I say.

Theo steers the truck to its spot behind the arts-and-crafts building. As it shudders to a stop, he says, "What about now?"

"I'm older. If I kissed you now, would you kiss me back?"

A grin spreads across Theo's face. "You'll have to try it again sometime and see for yourself," he says.

I step out of the car. Theo—and the prospect of kissing him—is a distraction. And I can't be distracted. Not by Theo. Not by what I did to him. And especially not by the lies both of us have told but aren't yet brave enough to admit.

THAT evening, I present the girls with their disposable chargers. "For emergencies only," I say, even though I know all that extended battery life will be wasted on Snapchat, Candy Crush, and Krystal's beloved superhero movies. Still, it puts the girls in a good mood as we head off to the nightly campfire.

The firepit is located on the outskirts of camp. It sits in a round meadow that looks carved from the forest like a crop circle. In its center is the firepit itself—a circle within the circle ringed by rocks. The fire is already burning when we arrive.

The four of us sit together on one of the sagging benches placed near the blaze. We roast marshmallows on twigs.

"You went here when you were our age, right?" Sasha asks.

"I did."

"Did you have campfires?"

"Of course," I say, pulling a freshly roasted marshmallow off my stick and popping it into my mouth.

"Why didn't you like this place, again?" Miranda says.

"It's not the place I didn't like," I tell her. "It's what happened while I was here."

"Someone vandalized the cabin back then, too?"

"No," I say.

"Did you see ghosts?" Sasha asks, her eyes shiny and wide behind her glasses. "Because Lake Midnight is haunted, you know. A lot of people really believe it. Especially once those girls vanished."

My body tenses. The girls. I had hoped their disappearance would somehow elude this new group of campers.

"Disappeared from where?" Krystal says.

"Right here," Sasha replies. "It's why Camp Nightingale closed in the first place. Three campers snuck out of their cabin, got lost in the woods, and died or something. Now their spirits roam the forest, trying to find the way back to their cabin."

"That's just a dumb story to frighten people from going into the woods," Krystal says.

Miranda, not to be outdone, pulls out her phone and holds it to her ear, pretending to answer it. "It's the creepy ghost girls calling," she announces to Sasha. "They said you're a terrible liar."

LATER in the night, after the girls have gone to sleep, I remain awake in my bottom bunk, irritated and restless. I stare out the window at heat lightning flashing in the distance. Each flash brightens the cabin in throbbing intervals—a strobe light painting the walls an incandescent white.

During one blinding burst, I see someone at the window.

A girl. Vivian. I'm sure of it. It's the Vivian I knew fifteen years ago, unchanged. Held in her fist is a bouquet of forget-me-nots.

My right hand drops to my left arm. I give the bracelet around my wrist a sharp tug. "I know you're not real," I whisper.

The bird charms clatter together—a muted, clicking sound.

"You have no power over me."

More tugging. More clicking.

"I'm stronger than everyone realizes."

The bracelet breaks. I hear a snap of the clasp, followed by the sensation of the chain slithering off my wrist. Lightning flashes again. All I see outside are a smattering of trees and a sliver of lake in the distance. No one is at the window.

I'm not going crazy. I'm not going crazy. I'm not going crazy.

Fifteen Years Ago

IN THE morning, instead of reveille blaring from the speakers on the mess hall roof, I was yanked from sleep by "The Star-Spangled Banner" in honor of Independence Day. Vivian slept right through it.

I spent the morning separated from the others in Dogwood, relegated to the arts-and-crafts building, where the camp's other thirteen-year-olds and I used leather presses to decorate rawhide bracelets. After that, I headed to Dogwood to look for them. The roar of voices inside told me all three were there.

"Don't lecture us about secrets!" I heard Natalie yell. "Especially when you refuse to tell us where you were this morning."

"It doesn't matter where I went!" Vivian shouted back. "What matters is that you lied."

"We're *sorry*," Allison said. "We told you a hundred times."

"That's not good enough!"

I opened the door to see Natalie sitting shoulder to shoulder with Allison on the edge of her bunk. Vivian stood before them, her face flushed, hair stringy and unwashed.

"What's going on?" I asked.

"Emma," Vivian replied, "we're in the middle of something that needs to be sorted out. Come back later, okay?"

I backed out of the cabin, closing the door behind me. I turned to head back to the center of camp. There was Lottie, standing right behind me. She wore a plaid shirt over a white tee. Her long hair was pulled back in a braid that ran down her back.

"First time living with a group of girls?"

I nodded.

"It takes some getting used to. Each summer there's always a fight or two. It comes from being together in such close quarters."

"This one sounds pretty bad," I said.

"Well, I know of a friendlier place we can go."

Lottie put a hand on my shoulder, steering me away from the cabin. To my surprise, we headed to the Lodge, to the steps that led to the back deck. At the top stood Franny, looking at the lake.

"Emma," she said. "What a pleasant surprise."

"There's some drama in Dogwood," Lottie explained.

Franny shook her head. "It'll pass. It always does."

She waved me to her side, and the two of us stared at the water, Lake Midnight spread before us in all its sun-dappled glory.

"Gorgeous view," she said. "Makes you feel a little bit better, doesn't it? This place makes everything better."

I looked across the lake, finding it hard to believe the entire body of water hadn't existed a hundred years earlier.

"Did your grandfather really make the lake?"

"He did indeed." Franny inhaled deeply. "And now it's yours to enjoy. You do enjoy it here, don't you, Emma?"

I thought I did. I loved it here before Vivian took me out in the canoe to her secret spot. Since then, my impression of the place had been chipped away by things I didn't quite understand. Vivian and her moods. Natalie and Allison's blind acceptance. Why the thought of Theo continued to make my knees weak.

Unable to let Franny know any of this, I simply nodded.

"Wonderful," Franny said, beaming at my answer. "Now try to forget about the unpleasantness in your cabin. Don't let anything spoil this place for you. I certainly don't. I won't let it."

Chapter 10

I WAKE WITH THE DAWN, my fingers curled around the broken bracelet. I slide out of bed, shuffle to my trunk, and dig out my bathing suit, towel, trusty robe, and drugstore sunglasses. I shuffle to the latrine, where I change into the bathing suit, then to the lake and finally into the water.

I lean back, floating the way Theo taught me. I shouldn't have been surprised by Vivian's appearance. Honestly, I should have expected it after three days of nonstop thinking about her.

I take a deep breath and slip beneath the lake's surface. When I emerge, someone is sitting onshore near the water's edge. It's Franny. She still wears her nightgown, a Navajo blanket wrapped around her shoulders. She waves to me as I swim back to shore.

"You're up early," she calls out.

I say nothing as I dry myself with the towel, put on the robe, and slip on the sunglasses.

"I know you're still upset about yesterday. With good reason, I suppose. But I hope that doesn't mean you can't sit with an old woman looking for a little company." She pats the grass next to her—a gesture that squeezes my heart a little. I sit. Franny talks.

"I used to spend so much time in that lake. As a girl, you couldn't get me to leave the water. Not anymore, though. Not after what happened to Douglas." She's referring to Douglas White. Her much older husband. The man who died years before she adopted Theo and Chet.

"Now," she says, "instead of being in the lake, I watch everything going on around it. Gives you a new perspective on things. For instance, this morning I've been keeping an eye on that hawk."

Franny points to a hawk lazily circling over the lake.

"Looks like an osprey," she says. "I suspect he sees something he likes in the water. Once, years ago, two peregrine falcons made their nest right outside our living room window at the Harris. Chet was just a boy at the time. My word, was he fascinated by those birds. He'd stare out that window for hours, just watching, waiting for them to hatch. Soon enough, they did. Three eyases. That's what falcon chicks are called. They were so small. Like squawking, wriggling cotton balls. Chet was overjoyed. It didn't last long. Nature can disappoint as easily as it entrances."

The osprey overhead suddenly dives toward the lake and, wings spread wide, slices its feet through the water. When it rises again, there's a fish gripped in its talons. The osprey swoops away.

"Why did you reopen the camp?" I blurt it out, surprising myself.

"Because it was time, Emma. Fifteen years is too long for a place to stay empty."

"What do you think happened to Vivian and the others?"

"I don't know, Emma. I really don't."

"You must have some theory. Everyone else does."

"Theories don't matter," Franny says. "What's done is done. Besides, I don't like being reminded of how much that disappearance cost me in so many ways. That's why I reopened the camp. I thought if I could do that successfully, with a new mission, then it might ease the pain of what happened fifteen years ago. It would certainly be a shame if something happened to spoil it."

"I'm sure it won't. Everyone I've talked to is having a great time."

"And what about you, Emma? Are you enjoying your time here?"

"I am," I say. "Very much."

"Good," Franny says. "I'm so pleased."

Her voice contains not a hint of pleasure. It's as chilly as the slight breeze that gusts across the lake and ripples the water.

"But I haven't finished my story about Chet and the falcons," Franny says. "It ends not long after those birds emerged from their eggs. Chet spent all his free time watching them. But then something happened that he wasn't prepared for. Those eyases got hungry. So the mother falcon did what mother falcons are known to do. She fed them. Chet watched her leave her perch outside our window and fly into the sky, circling, until prey appeared. It was a poor, unsuspecting pigeon. That mama falcon swooped down and snatched it in midair. She brought it back to the nest by our window, and as Chet watched, she used that sharp, curved beak to tear that pigeon apart and feed it to her babies, piece by piece."

I shudder as she talks.

"You can't blame that mother falcon," Franny says matter-of-factly. "She was simply doing what she needed to do. Taking care of her children. But it broke Chet's heart. Some of his innocence was taken away that day." Franny climbs to her feet, pulling the blanket around herself. "You have a good morning, Emma."

She shuffles away, leaving me alone to contemplate the story of Chet and the falcons. It might have been, I realize, a threat.

THE morning painting class is spent in a state of distraction. The girls arrange their easels in a circle around the usual still-life fodder. Table. Vase. Flowers. I monitor their progress with disinterest, more concerned with the bracelet that's once again around my wrist. I'd managed to fix the clasp with some colored string from Casey's craft station—a stopgap measure.

I'm made nervous by all the activity drifting through the building like a tide. Becca and her budding photographers. Casey and her crafters. All these girls. All these prying eyes.

And one of them knows what I did fifteen years ago.

From the arts-and-crafts building, I see Mindy and Chet as they head to the mess hall, followed by Theo trotting past on a morning jog. A minute later, I spot Lottie guiding Franny toward the lake. Right now, the Lodge is empty. This is my only chance.

"I need to take care of something," I tell the class. "I'll be right back. Keep painting."

Outside, I slip away to Dogwood and retrieve my phone and charger. I then make my way to the Lodge. I knock on the red front door. When no one answers, I give the doorknob a twist. It's unlocked. Quickly I tiptoe inside and close the door behind me. Then it's through the entrance hall and living room to the study.

The room is roughly the same size as Dogwood, with a desk in the center and floor-to-ceiling bookshelves where our bunk beds would be. The wall behind the desk is covered with photographs. I lower myself onto my hands and knees, searching for an outlet. I find one behind the desk and plug in the phone charger. Then I stand in the middle of the study, wondering where to look first.

I head to the bookshelf on my left, which holds dozens of musty volumes about nature. Darwin's *On the Origin of Species*. Audubon's *Birds of America*. *Walden* by Thoreau. *Poisonous Plants of North America*. I doubt these are what Vivian was referring to.

I turn next to the desk, reaching for the three drawers stacked from floor to desktop. The first drawer is the usual menagerie of pen caps and paper clips. Inside the middle one is a stack of folders. They bulge with documents, their edges brittle with age. Most appear to be receipts. None contain a hint of scandal.

In the bottom drawer, I find a wooden box. It's just like the one Vivian showed me during our outing to the other side of the lake, only better preserved. Same size. Same surprising heft. Even the initials carved into the lid are the same: CC.

Charles Cutler. I lift the box and carefully turn it over. On the bottom are four familiar words. PROPERTY OF PEACEFUL VALLEY.

I turn the box back over and open it, revealing a green velvet interior. Nestled inside are photographs. Old ones. Of women in gray with long hair draped down their backs. Each one assumes the same pose as Eleanor Auburn, minus the clutched hairbrush.

This is where Vivian got that picture. I'm certain of it. It's merely one of what appears to be two dozen. I sort through them, unnerved by their uniformity. Same clothes. Same bare-wall background. Same eyes made dark by despair and hopelessness. Just like the one of Eleanor, the back of each photo has been marked with a name. *Henrietta Golden. Lucille Tawny. Anya Flaxen.*

A chill settles over me. Auburn. Golden. Tawny. Flaxen. Those aren't last names. They're hair colors. I'm struck by a dozen different thoughts, all clashing together in my brain. Scissors in that crumbling box. The broken-glass sound they made when Vivian turned it over. Watching Allison's mother in *Sweeney Todd*, a character sent to bedlam, at the mercy of wardens who sold their hair to wigmakers.

That's what Charles Cutler was doing. It explains these women's long locks and why the only important aspect of their identity was the color of their hair. They weren't patients but commodities. The idea is so distractingly sad that I don't realize someone has entered the Lodge until a voice rings out from the entrance hall.

"Hello?"

I drop the photos back into the box and quickly replace the lid.

"Is someone in here?" the voice calls.

"I am," I say, closing the desk drawer. "Emma Davis."

Springing to my feet behind the desk, I find Lottie in the doorway. She's surprised to see me. The feeling is mutual.

"I'm charging my phone. Mindy told me I could if I needed to."

"You're lucky Franny's not here to see you. She's a stickler about such things." Lottie joins me at the desk, focusing on the framed photographs cramming the wall. Color photos mingle with black-and-white ones, a collage of images. I spot a grainy picture of an imposing man in front of what I presume to be Lake Midnight. A date has been scrawled in the picture's lower right corner: 1903.

"That's Franny's grandfather," Lottie says. "Buchanan Harris."

He has a hugeness so many important men of that age possessed. Big shoulders. Big belly. Lottie points to a birdlike woman also in the photo, dwarfed by her husband. "Franny's grandmother."

"I heard she drowned," I say.

"Childbirth," Lottie replies. "It was Franny's husband who drowned."

"How did it happen?"

"The drowning? That was before my time. What I heard is that Franny and Douglas went for a late-night swim together like they did every day. Nothing strange about that. Only on that particular night, Franny came back alone. She was hysterical. Carrying on about how Douglas went under and never came back up. His body wasn't found until the next morning. Washed up onshore."

Lottie moves on to another one showing a young girl leaning against a tree. Clearly Franny. Below it is another photo of her, taken at the lake. Another girl stands beside her, smiling.

"There she is," Lottie says. "My mother."

I take a step closer to the photo. "Your mother knew Franny?"

"Oh, yes," Lottie says. "They grew up together. My grandmother was the personal secretary to Franny's mother. Before that, my great-grandfather was Buchanan Harris's right-hand man. In fact, he helped create Lake Midnight. When Franny turned eighteen, my mother became her secretary. When she passed away, Franny offered the job to me."

"Is this what you wanted to do?"

"Not exactly. I was going to be an actress. Which meant I was a waitress. When my mother died and Franny offered me the job, I was in my thirties, barely scraping by. And the Harris-Whites have been so kind to me. I think of them as family. So I accepted Franny's offer and have been with them ever since."

There's so much more I want to ask. If she's happy doing the same thing her mother did. If the family treats her well. If she knows why Franny keeps photos of asylum patients in her desk.

"I think I see Casey in this one," Lottie says farther down the wall. "Right here. With Theo." She points to a photo of the two of them swimming in the lake. Theo stands waist-deep in the water, the lifeguard whistle around his neck. Cradled in his arms—in the exact way he cradled me during my swimming lesson—is Casey. She's slimmer in the picture, with a happy, youthful glow.

Just above that picture is one of two girls in polo shirts. One of the girls in the photograph is Vivian. The other is Rebecca Schoenfeld. The realization stops my heart cold. I stare at the two of them and their easy familiarity. Wide, unforced smiles. Skinny arms tossed over shoulders. Keds touching. It's a picture of friends.

"I should go," I say as I quickly gather my phone and charger. "You won't tell Franny about this, will you?"

"Some things Franny's better off not knowing."

She also starts to leave, skirting around the desk and giving me roughly two seconds to lift my phone and snap a picture of Vivian and Becca's photo. I then hurry out of the room, exiting the Lodge the same the way I came.

The morning lessons have ended, and when I reach Dogwood, I find the girls inside, indulging in some reading time. A comic book for Krystal and an Agatha Christie paperback for

Miranda. Sasha flips through a battered copy of *National Geographic*.
"Where did you go?" Krystal says. "You never came back."
"Sorry. I got tied up with something." I kneel in front of my hickory trunk and run my hands over the lid, feeling the ridges of all the names that had been carved before mine.
"What are you doing?" Miranda asks.
"Looking for something."
"What?" Sasha says.
I lean to my right, my fingers tripping down the side of the trunk. That's where I find it. Five tiny letters scratched into the hickory, a mere inch from the floor. BECCA.
"A liar," I say.

Fifteen Years Ago

CAMPFIRE. Fourth of July.

There was a charge in the air that night. A combination of heat, freedom, and the holiday. The campfire seemed higher, hotter. The girls were louder and happier. Even my group of girls. Whatever had caused the earlier drama in Dogwood was resolved. Franny was right. The storm passed. Now they surrounded me beside the fire, basking in the orange warmth of the leaping flames.
"We're sorry about earlier," Vivian told me. "It was nothing."
"Nothing," echoed Allison.
"Nothing at all," added Natalie.
All that mattered was that they were with me now, at the end of my lonely day. "You're best friends," I said. "I understand."
The counselors handed out sparklers, which we lowered into the campfire until they ignited into starbursts. Sizzling. White-hot.
A distant boom drew our attention to the sky, where golden tendrils of fireworks painted the night red, then yellow, then green. The fireworks promised in the nearby town. Vivian embraced me from behind and whispered in my ear, "Awesome, right?"
I knew she was referring to us. This place. This moment.
"I want you to always remember this," she said as another bloom of color streaked through the sky. "Promise me you will, Em. Promise me you'll never forget."

"I promise."

"That's my little sister." She kissed the top of my head and let me go. I kept my eyes on the sky, enthralled by the colors, how they shimmered and blended before fading away.

"So pretty," I said, turning around to see if Vivian agreed.

But there was no one behind me. Vivian was gone.

Chapter 11

I SKIP THE CAMPFIRE AGAIN, using tiredness as an excuse. When the girls leave Dogwood, I'm back outside and heading to another cabin. Golden Oak. I wait by the door until a trio of campers scurry out, on their way to the campfire. Becca is the last to emerge. Her body goes rigid when she sees me. "Need something, Emma?"

"The truth would be nice." I hold up my phone, revealing a photo of a photo. Her and Vivian, their arms entangled, inseparable.

Becca nods, her lips pursed, and retreats back into the cabin. She comes out with a leather satchel slung over her shoulder.

"Supplies," she says. "I think we're going to need them."

We cut through the cabins and head to the lake. It's the thick of twilight, the sky tilting ever closer from day to night.

Becca and I each take a seat on rocks near the water's edge. She opens the satchel, removing a bottle of whiskey and a large folder. She opens the bottle and takes a gulp before passing it to me. I do the same, wincing at the whiskey's sharp burn. Becca takes the bottle from my hands and replaces it with the folder.

"What's this?"

"Memories," she says.

I open the folder, and a stack of photographs spills onto my lap. "You took these?"

"Fifteen years ago."

I sort through the photos, marveling at how talented she was. The pictures are in black-and-white. Two girls hugging in front of the campfire. The bare legs of someone playing tennis. A girl swimming in Lake Midnight. Allison, I realize. The last photograph is of Vivian, a lit sparkler in her blurred hand. Fourth of July.

"My God," I say. "This could be—"

"The last picture ever taken of her? I think it is."

The realization makes me reach for the whiskey. "What happened between you and Vivian? I know you stayed with them in Dogwood the year before I came to camp."

"The four of us had a complicated history. We went to school together. Vivian and I were best friends. Then it stopped."

"Why?"

"The short answer? Because Vivian wanted it to."

"And the long answer?"

"I think it was because she went through some kind of identity crisis after her sister died. She ever tell you about it?"

"Once," I say. "I got the sense she didn't like to talk about it."

Becca takes another swig from the bottle. "One night in the dead of winter, Katherine decided to get drunk and go to Central Park. The reservoir was frozen over. Katherine walked out onto it. The ice broke, she fell in, never came back up."

I'm struck by the memory of Vivian pretending to be drowning. Her sister had to have crossed her mind as she flailed in the water.

"Katherine's death absolutely crushed her," Becca says. "That was the beginning of the end of us. I did the best-friend thing and was by her side when she came back to school. But she was pulling away from me and being drawn to Allison and Natalie. They were Katherine's best friends. All three were in the same class."

"I always thought they were the same age as Vivian," I say.

"She was a year younger. Although you couldn't tell from the way she acted. They found comfort in one another. I assume that was the appeal. Honestly, before Katherine died, Viv wanted nothing to do with them. You should have heard the way she made fun of them whenever all five of us were at her apartment. We were like warring factions, even when playing something as innocuous as Truth or Dare."

"Two Truths and a Lie. That was Vivian's game of choice."

"Not when we were friends," Becca says. "I think she joined in because Katherine liked to play it. She idolized her sister. And when she died, I think she transferred those same feelings to Natalie and Allison. I wasn't surprised when I found out we'd all be bunking here together in the summer. What I wasn't ready for was how much I'd be left out. Around them, Vivian acted like she hardly knew me. By the time camp was over, we were barely speaking to each other. It was the same way back at school. When summer came around again, I was banished from Dogwood."

It's fully dark now. Night settles over us, as does a prolonged silence in which Becca and I simply pass the bottle back and forth.

"Why didn't you tell me all this the other morning?" I say.

"Because I didn't want to go into it. And I was surprised *you* did. I mean, Vivian treated you the same way, right?"

"No," I say. "It wasn't the same."

"I think we're past lying to each other, Em," Becca says. "I know what happened right before the three of them disappeared. I was in the cabin next to Dogwood, remember? The windows were open. I heard every word."

My heart falters in my chest, skipping like a scratched record.

"I'm not judging you for what you told Vivian that night. In fact, I wish I'd said some of it myself. She definitely had it coming."

"What I said to Vivian that night, it wasn't what it sounded like."

It was so much worse than Becca could ever imagine.

Fifteen Years Ago

"WHERE'S VIV?" I asked Natalie, who merely shrugged in response.

Allison did the same. "I don't know."

"I'm going to look for her," I announced.

I headed to the latrine, which was the only logical place I thought she could be. When I tried the door, I found it locked. Strange. I took a walk around the side of the building. When I reached the gap in the planks, I heard the sound of running water coming from inside. The shower. Just beneath it was another noise. Moaning.

I couldn't resist taking a peek. I leaned toward the gap.

What I saw was Vivian. Facing the shower wall, her palms flat against it. Theo stood behind her. Hands over hers. Face buried against her neck and muffling his grunts. The sight of the two of them cleaved my heart in two.

I ran to the lake, where I stood so close that water lapped at my sneakers. Then I cried. I had no idea for how long. I just wept and wept, the tears falling directly from my eyes into Lake Midnight.

AFTER my tears ran dry, I returned to Dogwood, finding Vivian, Natalie, and Allison in a circle on the floor, smack in the middle of a game of Two Truths and a Lie. In Vivian's hand was the flask she had told me about. Its existence wasn't a lie.

"There you are," she said, holding out the flask. "Want a swig?"

I stared at her. And at that moment I despised her. "No," I said.

Allison continued with the turn I had interrupted. "One: I met Sir Andrew Lloyd Webber. Two: I haven't consumed bread in a year. Three: I think Madonna's version of 'Don't Cry for Me Argentina' is better than Patti LuPone's."

"The second one," Vivian said, taking a hit of the flask.

Allison flashed a smile. "Correct. I had pancakes this morning."

"My turn," I announced. "One: My name is Emma Davis. Two: I am spending the summer at Camp Nightingale." I paused. "Three: I didn't just see Vivian and Theo screwing in the latrine showers."

Allison shrieked, "Oh my God, Viv! Is that true?"

Vivian looked at me calmly. "Clearly that upsets you."

I turned away, unable to endure her stare.

Vivian kept talking. "I'm the one who should be upset by this situation. Knowing that you were spying on me. Watching me like some pervert. Is that what you are, Emma? A pervert?"

Her calmness lit the fuse that made me explode. "You knew I liked him!" I screamed. "You knew and couldn't stand the thought of having someone pay more attention to me than to you."

"Theo?" Vivian laughed. A single short, disbelieving burst. "You actually think Theo is interested in you? Em, you're just a baby."

"That's still better than being a bitch like you."

"I'm a bitch, but you're delusional. Truly delusional."

Had any tears been left in my body, I'm certain I would have started crying. But I'd used them all up. All I could do was crawl into bed. I lay on my side, knees pulled to my chest.

The three of them didn't say anything else after that. They went to the latrine to do their gossiping, sparing me the humiliation of having to listen. I fell asleep not long after they left.

When I woke, it was the middle of the night. Light from the full moon outside slanted through the window in a gray-white beam. Each girl passed through it, shimmering a moment on her way out the door. First Allison. Then Natalie. And finally Vivian, who froze when she saw me awake and watching.

"Where are you going?" I asked.

Vivian smiled, although no amusement could be found in that slight upturn of her lips. Instead, I sensed sadness, regret, the hint of an apology. "You're too young for this, Em," she said.

She raised an index finger and pressed it to her lips. Shushing me. Conspiring with me. Requesting my silence.

I refused. I needed to have the last word. Only after it was uttered, its sour echo lingering in the air, did Vivian leave the cabin, closing the door behind her, vanishing forever.

Chapter 12

I'M DRUNK BY THE TIME I'm walking among the cabins. Rather than head straight to Dogwood, I keep walking, pulled subconsciously in another direction. To the latrine. But I don't go inside. Instead, I lean against it, wondering why I've come here in the first place.

On the edge of my vision I see someone round the corner. Casey. Sneaking a cigarette like a high school sophomore.

"You startled me," she says before a languid puff. "I thought you were Mindy." She drops the cigarette, stubs it out. "Are you okay?"

"I'm fine," I say, stifling a giggle. "Just fine."

"Are you drunk?"

"I'm not," I say, the words slurred into one. *Imnot.*

"You better not let Mindy see you like this."

Casey leaves. I stay, roaming the perimeter of the building, an index finger sliding along the cedar shingles. Then I see the crack. That gap between planks now stuffed with clay. And I remember why I'm here—I'm retracing my steps. Going to the same spot I went after Vivian disappeared from the campfire. Fifteen years later, I can still see her and Theo together in the shower stall. I can still feel the heartache that caused. A muted memory pain.

I also feel something else. A shiver of awareness jumping along the skin of my arms, the back of my neck. I look up. I see Vivian.

Not all of her. Just a glimpse as she rounds the corner of the latrine. A spray of blond hair. A slip of white dress scraping the cedar wall. I instinctively reach for my bracelet. It's not there.

I flick my gaze to the corner of the latrine. Vivian is there, peering at me. I want to tell her that she's not real, that she has no power over me, that I'm stronger than everyone realizes. But I can't.

So I run away from the latrine. Back to Dogwood.

My run is really a combination of swaying and lurching that ultimately lands me at the cabin door. I fling it open, push inside, slam it shut. I collapse against the door, breathless and frightened.

Sasha, Krystal, and Miranda sit on the floor, hunched over a book. My presence makes them look up in surprise. Miranda slams the book shut and tries to slide it under my bunk. But she's too slow, the gesture too obvious. They were reading Vivian's diary.

"So all of you know," I say, still out of breath. It's not a question.

"We googled you," Sasha says.

"I'm sorry," Miranda says. "You were acting so weird the past two days that we had to find out why."

"It's okay. Really, it's fine." I plop down onto the lid of my hickory trunk. "You probably have questions," I say.

Sasha's the first to ask one. Of course. "What were they like?"

"Like the three of you but also very, very different."

"Where did they go?" Krystal asks.

"I don't know," I say. "But that's not the whole story. There's more. Things no one but me knows." Seeing Vivian again has messed with my emotions. "Two Truths and a Lie. Let's play."

I slip off the trunk, joining them. It's a sudden, ungainly slump that makes the three of them recoil when I hit the floor.

"One: I have been to the Louvre. Twice. Two: Fifteen years ago, three of my friends left this cabin. No one saw them again." Guilt compels me to keep talking. "Three: Right before they left, I said something I regret. Something that's haunted me ever since."

I hope you never come back.

The memory of that moment feels like a sharpened sword swooping toward me, slicing me open, exposing my cold heart.

"I told them I hoped they'd never come back," I say. "Right to Vivian's face. It was the last thing I ever said to her."

"That doesn't mean what happened is your fault," Miranda says. "Those were words, Emma. You didn't make them disappear."

I stare at the floor. There's still more to confess. "But they *did* come back. Later that night. Only they couldn't get back in."

"Why?" Miranda asks.

"Because I locked the door behind them."

Miranda sucks in air. A muted gasp. "You locked them out?"

I nod, a tear falling. "I refused to let them back in. Even after they knocked. And jiggled the doorknob. And pleaded with me."

I look to the cabin door, picturing it the way it appeared that night. Pale in the darkness, doorknob rattling back and forth. I hear the sharp rapping on the wood and someone calling my name on the other side. *Emma.* It was Vivian. *Come on, Em. Let me in.*

I shrank into my bunk, squeezing myself into the corner.

Emma, please.

I slid under the covers, lost in the darkness within, staying there until the knocking, the rattling, Vivian herself faded away.

"I could have let them in," I say. "I should have. But I didn't. Because I was young and stupid and angry. But if I *had* let them in, all three would still be here. And I wouldn't be carrying around this awful feeling that I killed them."

More tears. I wipe them away with the back of my hand.

"I paint them. All three of them. Every painting I've finished for years has included them. Only no one knows they're there. I cover them up. And I don't know why. It's crazy. *I'm* crazy. But now I think that if I can somehow find out what happened, then maybe I'll be able to stop painting them. Which means that maybe I've finally forgiven myself."

Sasha, Krystal, and Miranda stare at me, silent and motionless.

"I'm sorry," I say. "I'm not feeling well. I'll be fine in the morning." I stand, woozy. "Don't let me spoil your night. Keep playing."

They do. Because they're nervous. Because they're scared.

"One more round," Miranda says. "I'll go."

I close my eyes before crawling into bed. I'm too tired. Too drunk. I curl into a ball, back turned to the girls.

"One: I once got sick after riding the Cyclone at Coney Island." Miranda's voice slows, cautious, pausing to hear if I'm asleep yet. "Two: I read about a hundred books a year."

Sleep overwhelms me immediately. It's like a trapdoor, opening up beneath me. I willingly fall, plummeting into unconsciousness. As I tumble, I still hear Miranda, her voice faint and fading fast.

"Three: I'm worried about Emma."

THIS is how it continues.

You scream again. And again.

You do it even though you don't know why. Yet you also sort of do. Because no matter how much you try, you can't rid your mind of those too-terrible-to-think thoughts.

So you scream one more time, waking the rest of the camp.

The first person you see is Franny. She bursts onto the back deck of the Lodge. She flies down the wooden steps, the hem of her white nightgown fluttering. Chet is next, all sleepy eyes and bedhead. He stays on the deck, his hands gripping the railing. After that comes Theo, not even pausing, racing down the steps. You see that he's clad only in a pair of boxer shorts. You look away, queasy.

Others have gathered along the shore, campers and counselors alike,

*standing motionless in the mist. Becca Schoenfeld stands among them,
her camera raised. She clicks off a few shots.*

*But it's only Franny who comes forward. She stands at the edge of the
lake, her bare toes this close from the water. "Emma?" she says. "What
are you doing out here? Are you hurt?"*

You don't answer. You're unsure how.

"Em?" It's Theo. "Come out of the water."

"Go back to the Lodge," Franny snaps at him. "I can handle this."

*She marches into the lake. Knees lifting. Arms pumping. Nightgown
darkening at the hem as it sucks up water. She stops a few feet from you,
her voice calm. "Emma, what's the matter?"*

"They're gone," you say.

"Who's gone?"

"The other girls in the cabin."

*Things move quickly after that. Everyone spreads out across the camp,
going to places you've already looked. The firepit. The latrine. The hunt
turns up nothing.*

*A search party is organized. You insist on tagging along, even though
you're in no condition to be roaming the woods, calling out the names of
girls who may or may not be missing. You march behind Theo, trying
hard to keep up. You search the woods that flank the camp. First one side,
then the other.*

*No girls appear, alive or dead. There's no trace of them. It's as if they
had never existed at all.*

*You return to Camp Nightingale during lunch, with all the remaining
campers in the mess hall. You make your way to Franny's table. "Anything?" Franny asks.*

Theo shakes his head. A few of the campers begin to weep.

"I think it's time I call the police," Franny says.

*A half hour later, you're still in the mess hall. The place is empty except
for you and a state police detective whose name you've already forgotten.*

"Now then," he says, "how many girls seem to be missing?"

"I thought Franny already told you everything."

*"I'd like to hear it from you." He leans back in his chair, crosses his
arms. "If you don't mind."*

"Three," you say.

"All staying in the same cabin?"

"Yes."

The detective reaches into his suit coat and removes a pen and a notebook. "Let's start by telling me their names."

You hesitate, because to identify them is to make it real.

"Miss Davis?"

"Right," you say. "Their names."

You take a deep breath. Your heart does several little flips in your chest. "Their names are Sasha, Krystal, and Miranda."

PART TWO

And a Lie

Chapter 13

THE DETECTIVE WRITES their names in his notebook, making the situation official. My heart completes another sorrowful flip-flop.

"Let's go back to the beginning," he says. "Back to the moment you realized the girls were missing from the cabin."

An awkward moment passes. *Which ones?* I almost say.

I can't help but feel like that thirteen-year-old cowering in the presence of a different detective asking me about a different set of missing girls. Everything is so similar. The empty mess hall and the slightly impatient lawman and my simmering panic. The detective's name suddenly comes to me. Flynn. Detective Nathan Flynn.

This isn't happening. Not again.

"Miss Davis, I need you to focus, okay?" Flynn's voice slices through my thoughts. "I understand your shock. I really do. But every minute you spend not answering these questions means another minute goes by that those girls are still out there."

"What was the question again?"

"When did you realize the girls were missing?"

"When I woke up. A little past five."

"You always such an early riser?"

"Not usually," I say. "But I am here."

Flynn makes a note of this. I'm not sure why. "So you woke up and saw they were gone," he says. "Then what?"

"I went to look for them."

"Where?"

"All over the camp. Latrine. Mess hall. Arts-and-crafts building."

Flynn flips to a new page in his notebook.

"Mrs. Harris-White told me they found you standing in the lake this morning. After you realized the girls were missing. Did you have some reason to think the girls had gone swimming?"

"I just thought they might be there," I say. "Standing in the lake."

"The way *you* were standing in the lake?"

"I don't know why I did that."

"Mrs. Harris-White also said you were screaming. Why?"

"Because I was scared," I say. "Wouldn't you be? If you woke up and everyone else in your cabin was gone?"

Detective Flynn flips to a fresh page. "Is there a chance you screamed for another reason? Maybe out of guilt."

I shift in my seat, discomfited by Flynn's tone.

"Guilt?" I say.

"You know, for losing them when they were under your care."

"I didn't *lose* them."

"But they *were* under your care, right? You were their counselor."

"Instructor," I say. "I told them when I first arrived that I was here to be a friend and not some authority figure."

"And you had no issues with them? No disagreements or fights?"

"*No,*" I say, stressing the word. "I liked them." I glance out the mess hall window and see a couple of police cruisers and a smattering of state troopers milling about outside. "Is someone looking for them?" I ask. "There's going to be a search party, right?"

"There will be. We just need some more information from you."

"How much more?"

"Well, for starters, is there anything about the girls you think I should know? Something that might aid in the search?"

A realization pops into my head. "Miranda took her phone. It wasn't among her things. Could that be used to find her?"

Flynn suddenly perks up. "Yes, it definitely could. All cell phones come with a GPS. Do you know the carrier?"

"I don't."

"I'll have someone contact her family and ask," Flynn says. Seeing his pen scurry over the paper pleases me. It means I'm helping. "Let's talk about fifteen years ago. You were here when three other girls went missing. Is that correct?"

I stare at him. "I assume you already know that it is."

"You were staying in the same cabin, were you not?"

"Yes," I say, buzzing with defensiveness.

Flynn plows ahead. "Back then, a fellow camper said she heard you and one of the girls who vanished fighting earlier that night."

Becca. "It was an argument," I say weakly. "Not a fight."

"What was this argument about?"

"I honestly can't remember," I say, when of course I can. Me screaming at Vivian about Theo.

"None of those girls were seen or heard from again," Flynn says. "Why do you think that is?"

"What are you implying?" I say.

"I'm just being thorough, Miss Davis."

"Maybe you should start searching for Miranda, Krystal, and Sasha instead. Be thorough with that."

A grim understanding settles over me. I now know the reason no one seems to be searching for the girls. I should have seen it coming. I'm a suspect. The *only* suspect.

"I didn't touch those girls. Then or now."

"You have to admit, it's an awfully big coincidence," Flynn says. "Fifteen years ago, all the girls from your cabin vanished in the night. All of them but you. Now here we are, with all the girls from your cabin once again vanishing in the night. All of them but you."

"I'm not the only one who was here back then," I say. "There are plenty of others." Vivian's diary slides into my thoughts. *I'm close to finding out her dirty little secret. . . . I know the truth. . . . I'm scared.* "I think you should talk to Franny."

"Why?"

"Vivian—she's one of the girls who vanished fifteen years ago—was poking around camp. Investigating."

"Investigating what?" Flynn asks, his impatience pronounced.

I wish I knew. "Something Franny wanted to keep secret."

"Are you saying you think Mrs. Harris-White did something to the girls in your cabin? Not just now, but also fifteen years ago?"

It sounds ridiculous. But it's the only reason I can think of to explain a situation that defies easy explanation. Vivian was looking for something, possibly related to Peaceful Valley Asylum. She found it and enlisted the help of Natalie and Allison. All three promptly vanished. Now I'm looking for what Vivian was after, and Miranda, Krystal, and Sasha also go missing. Maybe I'm on the verge of finding it out, and this is another warning from Franny.

Her story about the falcons shoots into my brain. Is that why she told it? To make me frightened enough to stop searching?

"All I know is that it wasn't me," I say. "It was never me. Something strange is going on here."

"Would you care to elaborate?"

There's no choice. I have to tell him. "Someone's been watching me all week," I say. "I was spied on in the shower. Someone put birds in the cabin."

"Birds?" Flynn says, once again reaching for his notebook.

"Crows. Three of them. And someone vandalized the outside of the cabin two days ago."

"What was the vandalism?"

"Someone had painted the door." I hesitate before saying the rest. "They wrote the word *liar.*"

"Interesting word choice. Any reason behind it?"

"Maybe to preemptively make sure no one believes me."

"Or maybe you did it to deflect suspicion from yourself."

"You think I *planned* to abduct those girls?"

"That makes about as much sense as everything else you've told me," Flynn says.

"Someone was watching us," I say. "Someone was *there*."

"It's hard to believe you without any proof," Flynn says. "And right now, there's nothing to back up your story."

Another realization swerves into my head. One that will prove to Flynn he's wrong about me.

"There is," I say. "A camera. Pointed right at the cabin door."

THE cabin glows green on the monitor, thanks to its night-vision feature. It's angled downward into a bird's-eye view.

"The camera is motion sensitive," Chet explains. "It starts recording only when movement is detected. It stops when whatever it's recording also stops moving. Each time the camera records something, a digital file is automatically saved. For instance, this is a paused shot from the night it was installed." On-screen, the cabin door is ajar. The motion that triggered the camera. In that sliver of darkness, I can make out a foot and a green-tinted glimpse of leg.

Chet moves to a second monitor—one of three that sit side by side in the Lodge's basement. While most of the space is filled with boxes and cobwebbed furniture, one corner has been outfitted with unpainted drywall and a floor of white linoleum. This is where the monitors reside on a metal desk with two PC towers.

Chet occupies a chair in front of the desk. The rest of us—Theo, Franny, Detective Flynn, and myself—stand behind him.

"This all seems pretty elaborate for one camera," Flynn says.

"It's just a test camera," Chet replies. "We're going to install more throughout the camp. For security reasons."

Behind him, Franny flinches.

"The camera can also be set to a constant live feed. That's what this is." Chet points to the third monitor, a daytime view of Dogwood. "Usually the live feed is turned off because there's no one to constantly monitor it. I turned it on while we're all down here, just in case the girls return."

I stare at the screen. I see Casey pass by, leading a group of crying girls to their cabins.

"The recordings are stored here," Chet says, using a mouse to open a file folder on the monitor. "The file names correspond to the day, hour, minute, and second each recording was made."

"Are there files from last night?" Flynn asks Chet.

"Several. There's one file from between midnight and four. There are three between four thirty and five thirty."

"Let's see them," Flynn says.

"This is from a little after one."

Chet clicks the first file, and Dogwood appears. A mother deer and two fawns cross carefully in front of the cabin. Twenty seconds tick by as they make their way past. The camera shuts off.

"This one is about five minutes before five," Chet says.

He clicks, and the first monitor lights up again. The cabin door slowly opens. Miranda is the first to emerge. She tiptoes out of the cabin, followed by Sasha and Krystal, sticking close together. Krystal carries a flashlight and a rolled-up comic book stuffed into the back pocket of her cargo shorts. Sasha carries a water bottle. They go right, toward the heart of camp, vanishing one by one.

"This is five minutes later." Chet opens the next file.

The monitor shows me emerging from the cabin in bare feet and the T-shirt and boxer shorts I wore to bed the night before. I walk away in the opposite direction of the girls, toward the latrine. Five minutes. That's how little time had passed between the girls' leaving the cabin and my realizing they were gone. If only I had awakened earlier, I might have been able to stop them.

Even worse is how guilty it makes me look. Stepping outside mere minutes after the girls departed. It looks intentional, like I was waiting to follow them at a discreet distance. It doesn't matter that I went in the opposite direction. Because the next video—the final one from that highly trafficked predawn hour—shows me walking past Dogwood during my wander around the cabins. I unwittingly followed the same path the girls had taken.

"I was looking for them," I say.

"All this video does is confirm that you left the cabin not long after the girls did," Detective Flynn says.

Instead of coming to my defense, Franny says, "Normally, I wouldn't feel comfortable sharing this. But under these circumstances, I feel I must. Emma, please forgive me." She offers a look that's half apology, half pity. "Years ago, Miss Davis was under psychiatric care for an undisclosed mental illness. We discovered this during a background check. We didn't think she was a threat to herself or the campers. Nonetheless, precautions were taken."

Flynn says, "Hence the camera."

"Yes," Franny says. "I just thought you should know."

On the screen, a girl edges into view, her back straight, her steps precise. Then I see the blond hair, the white dress, the locket around her neck. It's Vivian. I gasp in shock.

Chet's the first to notice and says, "Emma? What's wrong?"

I point to the monitor. Vivian is still there. "You see that, right?"

"See what?" It's Theo this time.

"*Her*," I say. "In front of Dogwood."

"There's nothing there," Theo says.

"Vivian. I saw Vivian."

On the monitor, Vivian's no longer there. Nor is anyone else.

I tell myself, *This isn't happening. I'm not going crazy.*

It's no use. A fuzzy blackness encroaches on the edge of my vision. I fall, crashing onto the cellar floor and fainting dead away.

Fifteen Years Ago

THE sweatshirt sat on a table in the arts-and-crafts building, sleeves spread wide. "Do you recognize it?" asked a female state trooper.

I stared at the sweatshirt—white with PRINCETON spelled across the front in proud Tiger orange—and nodded. "It's Vivian's."

The trooper shot a glance at a colleague on the other side of the table. He nodded and quickly folded the sweatshirt. Latex gloves covered his hands. I had no idea why.

"Was Vivian wearing that sweatshirt when you saw her leave the cabin?" the female trooper asked.

"No." The girls had been missing for more than a day, and everyone was running out of hope. "Where did you find that?"

"I'm not at liberty to say," the female trooper said.

The sweatshirt was being placed into a cardboard evidence box.

"Did any of the girls have secrets they might have shared with you but not with others?" the trooper said.

"I don't know."

"Most times teenage girls run away, they do so because they're meeting someone," she said. "A boyfriend. Or a lover. It's usually someone others don't approve of. A forbidden romance. Did any of the girls mention anything like that?"

I wasn't sure how much I should say. "Vivian *was* seeing someone." My heart thundered. "Theodore Harris-White."

I didn't believe it, not even as I said it. Yet I wanted to. I wanted to think Theo had something to do with the girls' disappearance, that he was capable of hurting them. Because he already *had* hurt me. This was my chance to hurt him back.

"Are you sure?" the trooper said.

I tried to convince myself that it made sense Theo would be involved. Once Vivian, Natalie, and Allison returned to the locked cabin, the first thing they would have done was find a counselor. They didn't because they had been out after hours, not to mention drinking. So they had gone to the one person of authority they could trust—Theo. Now they were missing, likely presumed dead. That couldn't be a coincidence.

At least that's the lie I told myself. "I'm certain," I said.

A few minutes later, I was allowed to leave the arts-and-crafts building. The area outside hummed with activity. There were cops and reporters and the bray of bloodhounds in the distance. A search party was just returning from a trek through the woods. I spotted a few familiar faces in the crowd. A kitchen worker. The handyman. Then there was Theo, looking haggard in jeans and a T-shirt darkened by sweat. His hair was a shambles.

I flung myself toward him, not knowing what I intended to do. I was both mad at Vivian and terrified for her, furious at Theo and in love with him. My hands curled into fists. I pounded his chest.

"Where are they?" I cried. "What did you do to them?"

Chapter 14

THIS ISN'T HAPPENING. *I'm not going crazy.*

The words crash into my brain the moment I regain conscious-ness, making me sit up with a start. My head slams into something hard above me. Pain pulses along my hairline, joining another, pre-viously unnoticed pain at the back of my head.

"Whoa," someone says. "Easy."

I realize where I am. Camp Nightingale. Dogwood. Ensconced in a bunk bed, the top of which I just introduced to my forehead. The person who spoke is Theo, sitting on my hickory trunk.

I rub my head, my palm alternating between the two points of pain. The one in the front is already fading. The one in the back is the opposite. It grows in intensity.

"You took quite a tumble in the cellar," Theo says. "I broke some of your fall, but you still banged your head pretty bad."

I slide out of bed and stand. My legs are rubbery but strong enough to keep me upright. "They're still missing, aren't they?"

Theo confirms it with a solemn nod.

"Did Flynn talk to the kitchen staff?"

"He did. No one stayed behind last night, and no one came in early this morning. Not even Marvin."

Disappointment swells in my chest, tight against my rib cage.

Theo says, "Do you want to talk about what happened back at the Lodge? You said you saw Vivian."

My mouth goes dry, making it hard to speak. A bottle of water sits next to Theo. He gives it to me, and I swallow all but a few drops. "I did," I say after clearing my throat. "On the live feed of the cabin. It was . . ." A hallucination? My imagination?

"Stress," Theo says. "You're under a tremendous amount."

"But I've seen her before. When I was much younger. It's why I was sent away. I thought she was gone. But she's here. Now."

Theo cocks his head. "I had a conversation with my mother," he says. "We both agree it was wrong to invite you back here."

"Are you telling me to leave?"

"Yes," Theo says. "I think it's for the best."

"But what about the girls?"

"There's a search party looking for them right now."

"I need to join it," I say, making a move toward the door.

Theo blocks my path. "You're in no condition to go trampling through the woods."

"But I need to find them."

"They'll be found," Theo says as he holds me in place. "Every square foot of this property will be thoroughly searched."

A similar search did little good fifteen years ago. "I'm staying," I insist. "I'm not leaving until they're found."

A rumble sounds in the distance—a helicopter joining the search. The sound is familiar to me. I heard it a lot fifteen years ago. The cabin rattles as the chopper roars overhead.

"My mother doesn't trust you, Em," he says, raising his voice so it can compete with the helicopter. "I'm not sure I do, either."

I get louder, too. "I swear to you, I didn't hurt those girls."

"How can you be so sure? You were so messed up last night that I doubt you'd remember it if you did."

The helicopter zooms out over the lake. Its departure leaves the cabin draped in silence. "What are you talking about?"

"Casey said she saw you last night. She said you seemed drunk. Becca admitted the two of you shared a bottle of whiskey."

"It doesn't mean I did something to those girls." I stare into his brown eyes. "Please believe me," I whisper.

A moment passes. Then Theo whispers back. "I do."

I nod, overwhelmingly grateful. Then I kiss him.

It's a surprise to both of us. Just like the last time I kissed him. This time, it's not boldness that makes me do it. It's desperation. I need something to take my mind off what's happening. Soon he's kissing me back. But I can't let this go any further.

"Theo, stop. I can't do this." I move to the other side of the cabin.
"Not until I tell you something. I know. About you and Vivian."

"There was no me and Vivian."

"I saw you in the shower. I saw, and it broke my heart."

"When was this?" Theo says.

"The night they vanished."

I don't need to say anything else. Theo understands the rest.
Why I accused him. How that accusation has followed him since.

"I'm so, so sorry," I say. "I was young and stupid and heartbroken.
So when that state trooper asked me if any of them had a boyfriend, I told her that you were secretly seeing Vivian."

"But I wasn't," he replies.

"Theo, I saw you."

"You saw someone. Just not me. I was never interested."

I replay that moment in my mind. Hearing the moans muffled
by the rush of the shower. Peering through the space between the
planks. Seeing Vivian shoved against the wall, Theo behind her,
face buried against her neck.

His face. I never actually saw it. I had just assumed it was Theo
because I had seen him in the shower before.

"It had to be you," I say. "There's no one else it could be."

Even as the words emerge, I know I'm wrong. There was someone else here close to Theo's age. Hiding in plain sight.

"The groundskeeper," I say.

"Ben," Theo says with a huff of disgust. "And if he did something like that back then, who knows what he's been up to now."

"Tell me about the girls," Detective Flynn says. "The ones who
are missing. Did you have any interactions with them?"

"I might have seen them. Don't remember, but probably."

"Did you have any interactions with *any* of the girls in camp?"

"Not on purpose. Maybe if I needed to get somewhere and they
were in my way, I'd say excuse me. Other than that, I keep to myself." He looks up at us from a chair built for someone half his age,
his gaze resting a moment on each of our faces. First me. Then
Theo. And finally Detective Flynn.

We're all in the arts-and-crafts building. I stand next to Theo. For now, we're uncomfortable allies, united in our suspicion of a man whose full name I've only recently learned.

Ben Schumacher. The groundskeeper. The man who had sex with Vivian. He certainly appears capable of doing harm. He's got a hard look about him, and there's a noticeable bulk hidden beneath his flannel shirt and white tee.

"Where were you at five this morning?" Detective Flynn asks.

"Probably in my kitchen. About to get ready for work."

Flynn nods toward the gold wedding band on Ben's left hand. "Can your wife confirm that?"

"I hope so, seeing how she was in the kitchen with me. Why are you asking me this stuff?"

"What's your job here?" Flynn says, ignoring the question.

"Groundskeeper. I told you that already."

"I know, but what specifically do you do?"

"Whatever needs doing. Mowing the lawn. Working on the buildings."

"And how long have you worked for Camp Nightingale?"

"I don't. I work for the family. Sometimes that means doing some things for the camp. Sometimes it doesn't."

"Then how long have you worked for the Harris-Whites?"

"About fifteen years."

Flynn makes a note of it. "Back to your interactions with the girls in camp. Are you certain there wasn't any contact with them? Maybe you had to do some work in their cabin."

"He installed the camera outside Dogwood," Theo says.

Flynn writes that down in his notebook. "Did you happen to see the missing girls when you were putting up the camera?"

"No. None of this camp stuff is my business."

"What about fifteen years ago? One of the girls who disappeared back then was named Vivian Hawthorne. I was told you might have had a relationship with Miss Hawthorne. Which would be the complete opposite of minding your own business. So is it true? Was there a relationship?"

I expect a denial. Ben gives us all a defiant look, but then he says,

"Yeah. Although it wasn't much of what you'd call a relationship. A one-and-done kind of deal."

I can't stop myself from saying, "She was only sixteen."

"And I was only nineteen," Ben says. "It wasn't illegal."

"But you knew it was a bad idea," Flynn tells him. "Otherwise you would have told someone about it after Miss Hawthorne and two other girls from her cabin went missing."

"I knew the cops would think I had something to do with it."

"How did it start?"

"I don't know. It just kind of happened."

"Did you find her attractive?" Flynn asks.

"Sure. She was hot, and she knew it. But there was something else about her. She was different."

"Different how?"

"Most of those girls were stuck-up. Snooty. Vivian wasn't like that. She asked me about my job, how long I'd been here. Just friendly. It felt nice having someone like her pay attention to me."

That sounds like the Vivian I knew. A master at seduction.

"How many times did the two of you engage in intercourse?"

"Once," Ben says. "The Fourth of July. All the girls were at the campfire. She just came right up to me and kissed me. Then she walked away, looking over her shoulder to make sure I followed."

"That was the night Miss Hawthorne and the others disappeared," Flynn says. "Was that the last time you saw her?"

"Yes, sir, it was." Ben scratches the back of his neck. "Sort of."

"So you did see her again after that?"

"Not her," Ben clarified. "Something she left behind."

"I don't follow," Flynn says, speaking for all of us.

"On the drive home, I realized my keys were missing. The ones I use for camp. I thought they might have fallen out of my pocket in the latrine. When I got to work the next morning, I went looking for them. I ended up finding them at the toolshed behind the Lodge. The door was open. The keys were still in the lock."

"And you think Miss Hawthorne left them there?"

"I do. I think she took them out of my pocket when we were in the latrine."

"Why would she need to go to the toolshed?"

The question elicits a shrug from Ben. "Damned if I know."

But I do. Vivian went there to retrieve a shovel. The same one she used to dig a hole that would eventually conceal her diary.

A noise rises suddenly from outside. Someone shouting. The voice echoes off the water. "I see something!"

Theo turns to me, panicked. "That's Chet."

We rush out of the arts-and-crafts building. At the mess hall, a bunch of girls are pushing out of the door, clutching one another. Chet stands at the lake's edge, pointing to something in the water.

A canoe. Unmoored. Adrift, a hundred yards from shore.

I race into the lake until the water reaches my thighs. I fall forward, swimming now, taking quick, forceful strokes toward the errant canoe. Behind me, others do the same thing. Theo and Chet.

We each grip the edge of the boat with one hand and start the swim ashore with the other. Once in shallow water, the three of us stand and drag the canoe to shore. A crowd has gathered by then.

The boat is empty. No oars. No life vests. Certainly no people. The only thing inside is a pair of glasses, twisted like a wrung-out washcloth, one of the lenses spiderwebbed with cracks.

Flynn uses a handkerchief to lift the glasses from the canoe. "Does anyone recognize these?"

I manage to nod. "They belong to Sasha," I say, my voice weak.

BACK in Dogwood, I lie in the bottom bunk, trying to keep it together. After the canoe was found, I spent a half hour crying in the shower before changing into dry clothes. Now Detective Flynn graces me with another disbelieving stare.

"That's an interesting thing you did back there," he says. "Swimming out to the canoe like that. I would have preferred for you to let the police retrieve it."

"Sorry," I say, only because it's what he obviously wants to hear.

"Maybe. Or maybe you did it on purpose. Covering up evidence you'd left behind." He reaches into his pocket and pulls out a clear plastic bag. Inside is a curl of silver chain on which hang three pewter birds. My charm bracelet. "I know it's yours," Flynn says. "Three people confirmed they saw you wearing it."

"Where did you find it?"

"In the canoe. Would you like to explain how it got there?"

"I—I lost it." Shock makes it a struggle to utter even the simplest words. "Yesterday."

"Lost it," Flynn says. "That's convenient. So how do you think it got into the canoe?"

"Maybe one of the girls found it and picked it up, intending to return it to me later."

The only other possible explanation is that it was found by the same person responsible for the girls' disappearance.

"What if I'm being framed? Talk about convenient. What if whoever took the girls put it there to make me look guilty?"

"I think you're doing a pretty good job of that all by yourself."

"I didn't touch those girls! How many times do I have to say it before you believe me?"

"I'd love to believe you," Detective Flynn says. "But it turns out you're a difficult woman to believe, Miss Davis."

My face gets hot with anger. "Are you going to charge me with something?"

"Not yet," Flynn replies.

"Then get the hell out of this cabin until you do."

Flynn moves to the door. "We're done, for now," he says. "But I'll be watching you, Miss Davis."

When Detective Flynn leaves, his exit lets in the sound of police boats out on the lake. They arrived shortly after the discovery of the canoe. Meanwhile, the helicopter is still going, rattling the cabin with each pass.

I can't remember if the helicopter fifteen years ago showed up the first day or the second. By then, Franny had decided to close the camp, and campers were hustled onto buses or pulled into SUVs with dazed parents behind the wheels. I wasn't so lucky. I had to spend another day here, for investigative purposes.

Fifteen Years Ago

AFTER lashing out at Theo, I spent the rest of the day weeping in my bottom bunk. When the cabin door opened, it was Lottie, solemnly bearing a tray from the mess hall. Pizza. Salad. Bottle of Snapple.

"You need to eat something, honey," she said.

"I'm not hungry," I told her.

"Starving yourself won't help anyone," Lottie said as she placed the tray on my hickory trunk. "You need a good meal to be ready for when your friends return."

"Do you really think they're coming back?"

"Of course they will."

"Then I won't eat until they do."

Lottie gave me a patient smile. "I'll leave the tray here in case you change your mind."

IN THE morning, it was Lottie who knocked on Dogwood's door to tell me my parents had arrived to take me home. I carried my suitcase out of the cabin and into a camp that had become a ghost town. Silence hung over the darkened buildings—an eerie hush broken only by the sound of my parents' Volvo idling near the mess hall. My mother got out of the car and opened the trunk. She then flashed Lottie an embarrassed smile.

"Franny apologizes for not being able to say good-bye," Lottie told me, pretending that neither of us knew it was a lie.

In the distance, the door to the Lodge opened and Theo stepped outside, flanked by two detectives. They walked him to the arts-and-crafts building, likely for another interrogation. Theo caught sight of me and gave me a look, silently begging me to intervene.

It was my last chance to tell the truth. Instead, I climbed into the Volvo's backseat and said, "Please, Dad. Just go."

As my father started to drive away, the Lodge door opened yet again. This time, Chet ran out, his face tear-stained, legs a blur. He sprinted to the arts-and-crafts building, calling out Theo's name. Lottie rushed to intercept him and dragged him back to the Lodge.

I continued to watch out the window as Lottie, Chet, and the quiet remains of Camp Nightingale faded from view.

Chapter 15

I REMAIN CURLED UP in my bunk, staring out the window, watching the evening sky succumb to darkness. The search crew in the helicopter has started using a spotlight, sweeping it across the water.

I'm watching the play of the light in the leaves, when there's a knock on the door. It opens a second later, revealing Mindy bearing a tray. "I brought dinner," she announces.

This is dinner straight from the Lodge. Filet mignon swirling with steam and roasted potatoes seasoned with rosemary.

"I'm not hungry," I say. Anxiety has knotted my stomach.

"I also brought wine." Mindy holds up a bottle of pinot noir.

"That I'll take."

"I get half," Mindy says. "I'm telling you, it's been a day."

She sets the tray on the hickory trunk that was once Allison's and is now Sasha's. From the way Mindy simply plucks the cork from the wine, I can tell the bottle had been opened back in the Lodge. Probably to prevent me from having access to a corkscrew. On the tray, I see that the fork and knife are plastic. When Mindy pours the wine, it's into plastic cups.

"Cheers," Mindy says as she hands me a cup and taps it with her own. "Drink up."

That I do, draining the entire cup before coming up for air and asking, "Why the special treatment?"

Mindy sits on Krystal's bed, facing me. "It was Franny's idea for us to share this wine and get comfortable with each other, seeing how I've been ordered to spend the night here."

"Why?" I ask.

"To keep an eye on you, I guess."

There's no need for her to elaborate. No one trusts me. Hence the flimsy knife and plastic cup, into which I pour more wine.

"The way I see it, we have two choices here," I say. "We can either ignore each other and sit in silence. Or we could chat."

"The second one," Mindy says. "I hate too much quiet."

It's exactly the answer I expected. Which is the reason I gave her the choice—to make it feel like it was her idea to gossip.

"How's the mood in the Lodge?" I ask.

"They're worried sick. Especially Franny."

"What about Lottie? I bet she's good in a time of crisis."

"I don't know. She seems just as worried as the rest of us."

"That doesn't surprise me," I say. "I imagine she must be pretty devoted to Franny after working for her all these years."

"You'd think," Mindy says. "But I also get the sense that Lottie considers it just a job, you know? She gets to Franny's penthouse in the morning and leaves in the evening like any employee. I don't think she's too happy about having to spend the summer here. Neither am I, but here I am, doing my best to impress Franny."

"And how's that working out for you?"

Mindy pours herself some more wine. After taking a hearty sip, she says, "You don't like me very much, do you?"

I say nothing. Which, in its own way, is an answer.

"I knew it. I could tell," Mindy says. "Let me guess: You probably took one look at me and thought I was some spoiled sorority girl who screwed her way into the Harris-White family."

"Aren't you?"

"A sorority girl? Yes. And proud of it. Just like I'm proud of the fact that I was pretty enough and charming enough to catch the attention of someone like Chet Harris-White."

"I agree you're pretty," I say, shedding any pretense of civility.

"For the record, Chet pursued me. And it took a lot of convincing. I had no interest in dating the spoiled rich kid."

"But aren't you spoiled and rich?"

"Far from it," Mindy says. "I grew up on a dairy farm in Pennsylvania. Every morning I was up before dawn, feeding and milking the cows. I hated it. But I knew I was smart, and I knew I was pretty. I studied hard and socialized and tried my best to pretend that my hands didn't always stink of raw milk and cow manure. And it paid off. Class president. Homecoming queen. When I got to Yale, the pretending continued, even after I started dating Chet."

Mindy leans back on the bed, swirling the wine in her cup.

"I was so nervous the first time Chet took me to meet Franny. I thought she'd see right through me. But the nerves went away when I learned the truth." She takes a gulp of wine. "They're not nearly as rich as they look. Franny sold the Harris years ago. All she owns now is the penthouse and Lake Midnight."

"That still sounds pretty rich to me."

"Oh, it is. But now it's only a few million and not, like, a billion."

"How'd Franny lose so much money?"

"Because of this place. Restoring a bad reputation can get expensive. For Franny that meant settlements to the families of those missing girls. She did the same thing to a bunch of charities, trying to get back in people's good graces. And don't get me started on what she spent to get Harvard to take Theo back. They weren't keen on inviting an accused killer onto campus. No offense."

I nod, grudgingly respecting Mindy for giving as good as she gets. "None taken."

"Chet told me Franny had to pay for a new lab building before they'd consider letting Theo return. Anyway, that's their money situation. There's still plenty, but it's less intimidating. The more money there is, the more I feel the need to pretend. Which means I'll keep worrying that my hands still smell like a dairy farm."

"I'm sorry for judging you," I say.

"Thank you. And for the record, I don't think you did anything to those girls. You all liked one another. I could tell."

"I hope they're okay," I say. "I need them to be."

"I do, too." Mindy drains her cup. "Otherwise the Harris-White name is going to be dragged through the mud again. And I've got a feeling that this time it's going to stick."

AFTER the bottle of wine has been emptied and the steak and potatoes have long gone cold, Mindy falls asleep.

I don't. Whenever I close my eyes, I see Sasha's mangled glasses and think of her alone, stumbling blindly, possibly bleeding. So I keep them open.

It's almost midnight when my phone springs to life. My friend Marc has sent a text: FOUND SOMETHING. CALL ME!

I slide out of bed and tiptoe to the door. Then I realize that I can't go outside. Not with a camera aimed at the door. Rather than risk raising all kinds of red flags, I climb out the back window.

To avoid the camera completely, I have to cut behind the other cabins on my way to the latrine. I move in a crouch, trying not to be noticed by anyone inside the cabins or roaming about outside.

When I get to the empty latrine, I pull out my phone and call Marc. When he answers, I ask, "What did you find?"

"Billy ended up looking everywhere," Marc tells me. "Books. Newspapers. Historical records. I'm going to e-mail everything he found. Some of it couldn't be scanned because it was too old or in bad condition. But I wrote those down."

The sound of rustling paper bursts from the phone.

"Billy found a few mentions of a Mr. C. Cutler of Peaceful Valley in the ledger of Hardiman Brothers, a wig company on the Lower East Side. Do any of those names sound familiar?"

"Charles Cutler," I say. "He was the owner. He sold his patients' hair to wigmakers."

"That's Dickensian," Marc says. "And it would explain why the Hardiman brothers paid him fifty dollars on three different occasions. Once in 1901. Twice in 1902."

"That lines up with what I saw in the book Vivian found at the library. There was a picture of the place from 1898."

"Did the book mention when it closed?" Marc asks.

"No. Why?"

"Because something strange happened after that." There's more rustling on Marc's end. "Billy found a newspaper article from 1904. It's about a man named Helmut Schmidt of Yonkers. Helmut was a German immigrant who spent ten years out west. When he returned to New York, he sought out his sister, Anya."

There was a photograph of someone named Anya tucked into the box I found in the Lodge. I remember her hair color. Flaxen.

"Helmut described her as 'often confused and prone to nervous exasperation,'" Marc says. "It appears that while Helmut was gone, Anya's condition worsened until she was committed to Blackwell's Island. He looked for her there and was told she had been put into the care of Dr. Cutler and taken to—"

"Peaceful Valley," I say.

"Bingo. Which is why Helmut Schmidt then traveled upstate to Peaceful Valley to retrieve his sister. Only he couldn't find it, which is why he spoke to the press about it. It vanished."

"How does an insane asylum just disappear?"

"No one knew. Or, more likely, no one cared," Marc says. I hear a click. "I just e-mailed the files."

My phone vibrates in my hand. An e-mail alert. "Got them."

"I hope it helps." Concern creeps into Marc's voice. "I'm worried about you, Em. Promise me you'll be careful."

"I will," I say, smiling. "Pinkie swear."

I end the call and check my e-mail. The first item Marc sent is scans of two pages from the same book I found in the library. The next few files are all text—pages from psychology books, psychiatric journals, a master's thesis that makes a cursory mention of Peaceful Valley. The final file holds an assortment of images. The first picture is the familiar one of Charles Cutler outside Peaceful Valley. The second photo is a shot of just the asylum itself.

But it's the third picture that makes my heart thrum. Identified merely as the entrance to Peaceful Valley, it shows a low stone wall broken by a wrought iron gate and ornate archway. They're the same gate and arch I passed through the other day in Theo's truck. The very same ones that now grace Camp Nightingale.

The blood freezes in my veins. Peaceful Valley Asylum was here. Right on this very piece of land. Which explains why Helmut Schmidt couldn't find it. By the time he came looking for his sister, Buchanan Harris had already turned the area into Lake Midnight.

That, I realize, is the information Vivian was looking for. It's why she snuck into the Lodge and went to the library. It's why she was so worried about her diary getting into the wrong hands that she rowed across the lake to hide it. And it's why she was so scared.

Because she learned that there's a ring of truth to the stories surrounding Lake Midnight. Only it wasn't a deaf village or a leper colony that got buried beneath the water.

It was an insane asylum.

DESPITE the late hour, Camp Nightingale still crawls with cops. They linger in the arts-and-crafts building, visible through the lit windows. More stand outside, chatting as they smoke cigarettes.

At the Lodge, I pound on the front door, not even trying to be discreet about my arrival. I want the whole place to know I'm here. The pounding continues for a full minute before the door swings open, revealing Chet. "You shouldn't be out of your cabin, Emma."

"I don't care. Where's your mother?"

Franny's voice drifts to the door. "In here, dear. Do you need something?"

I push past Chet into the entrance hall and then the living room. Franny is there, cocooned in her Navajo blanket.

"This is a pleasant surprise," she says with faked hospitality.

"We need to talk," I say.

"About what?"

"Peaceful Valley Asylum. I know it was on this land. Vivian knew it, too."

It's easy to see why she went looking for it. She'd heard the story about Lake Midnight. Then she found that old box by the water's edge, filled with scissors. She did some digging. Searching the Lodge. Sneaking off to the library. Eventually she realized the campfire tale was partially true.

And she needed to expose it. I suspect she felt a kinship with those women from the asylum, all of them likely drowned, just like her sister. Keeping that secret must have made Vivian so lonely and scared. She hinted at it in her diary when referring to Natalie and Allison. *The less they know, the better.*

Vivian wasn't able to save them. Just like her, they had learned too much after finding her diary. But she had managed to keep me safe. I understand that now. Her mistreatment of me wasn't an act of cruelty but one of mercy. It was her way of trying to protect me from any danger her discovery created. To save me, she forced me to hate her. It worked.

"The only people she told were Natalie and Allison," I say. "Then all three of them disappeared. I doubt that was a coincidence."

"I don't know what you want me to say."

"You can tell me what happened to that asylum. Something bad, right? And all those poor girls there, they suffered, too. I know those women existed. I saw their pictures."

I march to the study, heading for the desk and its bottom drawer. I yank it open and see the familiar wooden box. I carry it into the living room and slam it down on the coffee table.

"These girls right here." I open the box and grab a handful of photos, holding them up. "Charles Cutler made them grow their hair. Then he chopped it off and sold it. And then they vanished."

Franny's expression softens. "Oh, Emma. You poor thing. Now I know why you've been so distressed."

"Just tell me what happened to them!"

"Nothing," Franny says. "Nothing at all."

"I don't understand," I say.

"I think perhaps I should explain."

It's Lottie who says it. She emerges from the kitchen wearing a silk robe over a nightgown. A mug of coffee rests in her hands. She sits down next to Franny and reaches for the wooden box.

"It just occurred to me, Emma, that you might not know my given name."

"It's not Lottie?"

"That's just a nickname," Lottie says. "My real name is Charlotte. I was named after my great-grandfather. Charles Cutler."

I falter a moment, buzzing with confusion.

"His mother was insane," Lottie says. "My great-great-grandmother. Charles saw what madness did to her and decided to devote his life to helping others who suffered the same way. First at an asylum in New York City. A terrible place. The women forced to endure horrible conditions. They didn't get better. So he got the idea to create Peaceful Valley on a large parcel of land owned by my great-grandmother's family. A small private retreat for a dozen women. Charles chose the worst cases he observed in that filthy, overcrowded asylum. He took them in."

Lottie rifles through the open box, smiling at the photographs as if they were pictures of old friends. She pulls one out and looks at it. On the back, I see the words *Juliet Irish Red*.

"From the very beginning, it was a struggle. The asylum required so much money. The patients needed food, clothing, medicine. To make ends meet, he came up with the idea to sell the patients' hair—with their permission, of course. That kept things afloat for another year or so, but Charles knew Peaceful Valley would eventually have to close. His noble experiment had failed."

She pulls out more photos. *Lucille Tawny* and *Henrietta Golden*.

"But he was smart, Emma," Lottie says. "In that failure, he saw opportunity. He knew an old friend was looking to buy a large parcel of land for a private retreat. Buchanan Harris. My great-grandfather offered the land at a discounted price. That was the start of a relationship between our families that continues today."

"But what happened to Peaceful Valley?"

"It stayed open while my grandfather went about building the dam that would create Lake Midnight," Franny says.

"During that time, Charles Cutler found new situations for the women in his care," Lottie adds. "None of them returned to those brutal asylums in the city. My great-grandfather made sure of it. He cared deeply about those women. Which is why I still have their photographs. They're my family's most prized possession."

"So it had nothing to do with what happened to Vivian and the others?"

"Not a thing," Franny says.

"Then why did you keep it a secret?"

"We didn't," Lottie says. "It's no secret. Just ancient history, which has been warped over the years."

"If Vivian had wanted to know more about it," Franny adds, "all she needed to do was ask."

I nod, feeling suddenly humiliated. "I'm sorry," I say, knowing that a simple apology isn't nearly adequate. "I'm going to go now."

I edge out of the room. In the entrance hall, I break into a run, fleeing out the front door. I keep running. Past the cops outside the arts-and-crafts building. Past the cluster of dark cabins. I stop when I notice a girl standing outside the latrine. Her stillness catches my attention. That and her white dress aglow in the moonlight.

Vivian. I'm not surprised to see her. Not after the day I've had.

Rather than speak, Vivian merely turns and walks into the forest, the hem of her white dress scraping the underbrush. I start walking, too, pulled along against my will by Vivian's reemergence.

"I'm not going crazy," I whisper. "I'm not going crazy."

Oh, but I am. Of course I am.

I FOLLOW Vivian to the sculpture garden, where she sits in the same chair Franny occupied days earlier. The statues around us watch with their blank eyes.

"Long time, no see, Em," Vivian says. "Miss me?"

I find my voice. "You're not real. You have no power over me."

Vivian leans back in her chair. "Then why are you here? I didn't ask you to follow me. You're still trailing after me like a lost puppy."

"Why did you come back?" I say. "I was doing fine without you."

"Oh, you mean painting us then covering us up? Is that the *fine* you're talking about?"

"I don't do that anymore. I've stopped. That's why you're here, isn't it? Because I stopped painting you."

"This has nothing to do with me," Vivian says. "It's all you."

"Then why am I only seeing you and not—"

"Natalie and Allison? I'm the puzzle you're still trying to figure out." Vivian stands and winds her way around the statues. "That's why you came back, right? To find out what happened. Snooping around. As a result, look what happened to your new best friends."

Her mention of the new girls catches me off guard. I spend a second wondering how she knows about them. Then it dawns on me. Vivian isn't a ghost. Nor a hallucination. She's *me*. A fragment of my distressed brain trying to help me figure out what's happening.

Which is why I stare her down and say, "You know where they are, don't you? You know where I can find them."

Vivian moves on to another statue. "Let's play a game, Emma. Two Truths and a Lie. One: Everything you need to know is already in your possession."

"Just tell me where they are."

"Two: The question isn't where to find them but where to find *us*. As in me and Natalie and Allison."

"Vivian, please."

"Three," she says. "As for where we are, I can tell you this: *If* you find us, maybe—just maybe—I'll go away and never come back."

She slips behind the statue, temporarily eclipsed. I wait for her to pop into view again. When a minute passes and she doesn't appear, I take a few weak steps toward the statue. Vivian is gone.

Yet her parting words remain. Those three statements. Two true, one a lie. I have no idea about the first two. As for her third statement, I hope it isn't a lie. I want it to be the truth. Every word of it.

Chapter 16

I SLIP TO THE BACK OF THE CABIN and hoist myself inside through the open window. Mindy's snores tell me she's still asleep. Good. I get to avoid having to explain both where I've been and where I plan on going next. To find the girls. Both sets of them.

The question isn't where to find them but where to find us.

Something Miranda said comes back to me. *I'm worried about Emma.* That worry might have led her to action. Brash, confident, mystery-lover Miranda. Like Vivian, leading another set of girls into the woods for answers.

I tiptoe across the cabin, the memory of something else Vivian said fresh in my mind. *Everything you need to know is already in your possession.* I know what she's referring to. The map.

It's why they came back to the cabin, only to discover the door locked. Vivian needed her hand-drawn map to help her find the spot where her diary was hidden.

I quietly open my trunk and remove my flashlight. Then I reach inside and feel around, searching for the map. It's not there. The girls must have taken it with them.

As Mindy keeps on snoring, I take another trip out the window. Five minutes later, I'm out on the lake in a canoe. I row in strong, fast strokes, my phone in my lap, set to the compass app. I glance at it every few seconds, keeping myself on track, making sure I'm cutting across the lake in a straight line.

I know I'm near the far shore when I start to hear eerie scraping along the bottom of the canoe. Underwater tree branches, making their presence known. Flicking on the flashlight, I'm greeted by dozens of dead trees rising from the lake. They're a ghostly gray in the flashlight's beam. The same color as bones.

Soon I'm past the trees and close to the other side of the lake. The flashlight's beam skims the shore. Finally, it illuminates a wooden structure rotted beyond repair. The gazebo.

I guide the canoe onto shore and hop out. I shove my phone back into my pocket and aim the flashlight toward the woods. I breathe deeply, trying to focus, rewinding to that earlier trip and how we got from here to the X marking Vivian's diary.

I sweep the flashlight's beam back and forth over the ground, looking for any footprints we might have left behind. The beam catches something that glows dull-white. Stepping closer, I see splashes of color—vibrant yellows, blues, and reds. It's a page from a comic book. Captain America. A small rock rests atop the page, keeping it in place. The girls were here. Just recently. It's their trail of bread crumbs, marking the way back to the lake and their canoe.

I step over the paper, tighten my grip around the flashlight, and, like the girls before me, vanish into the woods.

THE forest at night is alive with noise as I move deeper through the woods. Crickets screech and frogs belch, competing with the calls of night birds rustling the pines. I sweep my flashlight back and forth, looking for another page ripped from Krystal's comic book. I spot one where the ground begins to slant upward.

I pass five more pages as the incline sharpens. Captain America, leading me higher. Another page waits at the top of the incline. I'm now mere yards from the cliff that drops away into the lake. I turn left, approaching the boulders that punctuate yet another steep rise.

Captain America is there as well, placed atop several boulders, held in place with small rocks. I scramble among them until I reach the massive rock. The monolith. There's still no sign of the girls.

The forest around me continues to hum. I close my eyes, trying to tune out the noise and really listen. That's when I hear something—a dull thud that sounds once, twice.

"Girls?" I shout out, the echo of my voice booming back at me. "Is that you?"

The forest noise ceases. In that blessed moment of silence, I hear a muted reply. "Emma?"

Miranda. I'm sure of it. And she sounds close.

"It's me," I call back. "Where are you?"

"The hobbit house."

"We're trapped," someone else says. Krystal, I think.

Miranda adds one more desperate word: *"Hurry."*

I rush onward, my flashlight gripped in my hand. I leap over tree roots. I dodge boulders. I don't slow down, not even when the crumbling stone foundation comes into view. Instead, I run toward the root cellar cut into the earth. At the door, someone has pushed the ancient slide bolt into place, locking the girls inside. A knee-high boulder has been rolled in front of it for good measure.

Another thump arrives from inside the root cellar. "Are you here yet?" Miranda calls. "We need to get out of here."

"In a second!"

I give the slide bolt a mighty shove. It rasps past the door itself, allowing Miranda to open it a crack before being stopped by the boulder. She presses her face to the crack. I see one bloodshot eye, a red-rimmed nostril, her parted lips sucking in fresh air.

"Help us," she says with a gasp, giving the door another desperate rattle. "Why aren't you opening it?"

"It's still blocked," I say. "How are Krystal and Sasha?"

"Awful. We all are. Now *please* let us out."

I crouch and give the boulder a push. It doesn't budge.

Using the flashlight, I scan the ground for anything that can help. I grab a rounded rock that had chipped off the crumbled wall nearby. Then I spot a fat branch on the ground that's almost as long as I am. It looks sturdy enough to be used as a lever. I hope.

I shove one end of the branch as far under the boulder as it can go and place the rock under it a few feet away before grasping the other end of the branch and pushing down. It does the trick, setting the rock rolling a bit. I drop the branch and run to the boulder, pushing, continuing the momentum until it's past the door.

"All clear!"

The door flies open, and the girls burst out. Sweaty and dirt-smeared, they suck in fresh air, stretch their limbs, give dazed looks to the sky. Without her glasses, Sasha is forced to squint. Her nose is swollen and colored a brutal shade of purple. Rust-colored flecks run from her nose all the way to her neck. Dried blood. I use the hem of my T-shirt to wipe some of the blood from her face.

"How long were we in there?" Miranda says as she spreads out on the ground, panting with relief. "My phone died before noon."

"Almost a full day."

Krystal plops down next to Miranda. "Damn."

"Tell me what happened," I say. "From the moment you left the cabin."

"We came here to look for your friends," Krystal says. "It was Miranda's idea."

Miranda sits up, too spent to be ashamed. "I only wanted to help. You were so upset last night. I could tell you needed to know what happened. And since this is where you found that diary, I thought there might be more clues here."

"You came here, and then what?"

"Someone jumped us," Miranda says, fear peeking through her exhaustion. Tears cling to the corners of her eyes.

"Who?"

"None of us got a good look."

"Miranda and Krystal went inside," Sasha says, nodding toward the root cellar. "I didn't want to, so I stayed out here. But then someone came out of nowhere. They punched me and my glasses fell off and I couldn't see who it was, and then they shoved me inside and slammed the door."

Someone followed them here, attacked, trapped them rather than outright killing them. It makes no sense. Unless whoever did it wanted them alive. Which means they might be coming back.

Fear zips through me. I yank my phone from my pocket to see if I can call the police. There's no signal.

"We need to go," I tell the girls. "Right now. I know you're tired, but do you think you can run?"

Miranda climbs to her feet. "Why do we need to run?"

"Because you're still in danger. We all are."

A beam of light hits my face. A flashlight. I put my hand over my eyes, shielding them from the glare. Behind the flashlight, I can make out Theo, flashlight in hand, taking a step toward us.

"Emma?" he says. "What are you doing here?"

Seeing Theo here feels like a minor earthquake. His presence can't be an accident. He's come back for the girls.

He attacked them, locked them away, waited until the dead of night to return. A chain of events I suspect happened fifteen years ago with a different trio. My accusation, as misguided as it was, might have been correct. Truth disguised as a lie.

I edge in front of the girls, shielding them from Theo. I slip a trembling hand through my flashlight's wrist strap, securing it. Although not much of a weapon, it'll do in a pinch.

"Miranda," I say with as much calm as I can muster, "there's a canoe onshore in the same place we landed the other day. Take Sasha and Krystal there as fast you can. If Sasha has trouble, you might need to carry her. Do you think you can do that?"

Miranda's reply is streaked with fear. "Yes."

"Good. When you get to the canoe, row across the lake. Don't wait for me. Just row as fast as you can back to camp."

Theo aims his flashlight at my face again. "Emma, maybe you should step away from the girls. Let me see if they're hurt."

I ignore him. "Miranda, do you understand?"

"Yes," she says again, more forceful this time.

"Good. Now go. *Hurry!*"

That last word gets the girls moving. Miranda bolts away, all but dragging Sasha behind her. Krystal follows, slow but determined.

Theo makes a move to stop them, but I lunge forward, flashlight raised, threatening to strike. He freezes when I'm two feet away and drops his flashlight. He raises his hands, palms open.

"Don't you dare go after them," I warn.

"Emma, I don't know what's going on."

"Stop lying!" I shout. "You know exactly what's happening. What did you plan to do with those girls?"

Theo's eyes go wide. "Me? What were *you* going to do with them? I followed you here, Em. I watched from the Lodge as you got into that canoe and rowed across the lake."

It's another lie. It has to be.

"I need to know why you did it," I say. "Both now and back then."

"I didn't—"

I lift the flashlight higher. Theo flinches. "I think you had the hots for Vivian," I tell him. "You wanted her, and she rejected you. You got mad. You made her disappear. Natalie and Allison, too."

"You're wrong, Emma. About everything."

Theo takes a step toward me. I stay put, trying not to show fear.

"Since you got away with it once, I guess you thought you could do it again. Only this time you tried to make me look guilty. My bracelet in the canoe was insurance."

"You're troubled, Emma. You need help. So how about you drop the flashlight and come with me. I won't hurt you. I promise."

Theo risks another step closer. This time, I take a step back.

"I'm done being lied to by you," I say.

"It's not a lie. I want to help you."

"You could have helped me fifteen years ago by admitting what you did. Instead, I spent fifteen years blaming myself for what happened to them. And I blamed myself for causing you pain."

"I don't blame you, Emma. This isn't your fault. You're sick."

"Stop saying that!"

Theo takes two steps forward. I move backward, first shuffling, then turning around and running. Theo chases after me, catching up within seconds. He grabs my arm and jerks me toward him. I raise the flashlight and swing it against Theo's skull.

It's a weak blow. Just enough to shock him into letting me go. Then I run again. Back the way I came. Toward the lake.

"Emma!" Theo shouts at my back. "Don't!"

I keep running. Heart pounding. Pulse loud in my ears. Trees and rocks seem to lurch at me from all sides. Theo's also running. His footfalls echo through the woods behind me, outpacing my own. He'll catch up sooner rather than later. I need to hide.

Something looms before me in the darkness. The monolith. I run to it, swerving right until I'm at its northwestern edge. I shine my light over the rock wall, seeing the fissure that opens up a foot from the ground. The cave Miranda had crawled into.

I drop to my hands and knees in front of it and shine the flashlight inside. I see rock walls, dirt floor, a dark recess that runs into the ground. I flick off my light, drop to my stomach, and back into the cave, worried I might not fit. I do. Barely.

The sky outside the cave brightens. Theo's flashlight. I slide back even more. I'm on a slant, edging downhill.

"Emma?" he says. "Are you here?"

I move back even farther, wondering how deep the cave goes.

"Emma, please come out."

Theo's right outside the cave. I see his shoes. I continue to slide backward, faster now, praying he can't hear me. I feel water dripping down the cave walls. Mud starts to squish beneath me.

I'm still sliding, although now it's not by choice. The tunnel turns sharply steeper. Soon I'm sliding fast, out of control, my chin leaving a groove in the mud. When I flick on the flashlight still around my wrist, all I see are gray walls, brown mud, the shockingly long path I've just traveled. Then the ground below me vanishes, and I'm plummeting into nothingness.

Water breaks my fall.

I drop right into it, caught by surprise, unable to close my mouth before plunging under. Liquid pours in, choking me as I keep falling, somersaulting in the depths.

When I finally do touch bottom, it's a gentle bump and not the life-ending crash against hard stone I expected. I push off from the bottom as water continues to tickle the back of my throat. Then I'm at the surface, my head emerging and water unplugging from my nostrils. I cough a few times, spitting up water. Then I breathe. Long and slow inhalations of dank, subterranean air.

With the flashlight miraculously still dangling from my arm, I paddle in place. I'm in a cavern roughly the same size as Camp Nightingale's mess hall. The beam of the flashlight stretches over black water, damp rock, a strip of dryish land surrounding the pool in a crescent shape. The water itself takes up about half the cave, no larger than a backyard swimming pool. I see a dome of rock above me dripping with stalactites. A dark hollow sits in a corner where rock wall meets cave ceiling. The spot from which I fell. It looks to be about a ten-foot drop.

I swim forward, heading to the land that partially rings the water. I pull myself onto it.

The stretch of cave wall rising to the hole above me is steep. Not quite a ninety-degree angle, but mighty close. Before trying to climb it, I scan the rest of the cavern, looking for another way out, seeing nothing. Scaling that wall is my only option.

In desperation, I run to it, not pausing to look for places to grip. Instead, I leap onto the wall, clawing at rock, scrambling for outcroppings. I get about three feet before I lose my grip and fly backward, landing hard on the cave floor.

I try again, this time making it four feet off the ground before getting bucked off. I make a third attempt, slowing down, puzzling together the best places to grip. It works. I find myself rising higher. Six feet. Seven. When I'm about a foot from the tunnel that leads outside, I realize there's nothing left to grasp. For a second, I dangle against the cave wall. Then I plummet back to earth, landing feetfirst, my right ankle twisting beneath me before buckling. I think I hear something snap. There'll be no more climbing for me.

That's when reality sets in. I'm trapped here. No one knows where I am. I'm now as lost as Vivian, Natalie, and Allison.

THE FLASHLIGHT DIES SHORTLY after four a.m. I sit in darkness so complete it feels like death. Nothing but black emptiness.

I huddle against the side of the cave. I sleep. For how long, I have no idea. When I awake, it's with a pain-filled jolt, my sleep-blurred gaze landing on Vivian right in front of me. She reclines on the cave floor, her elbow bent, head propped up. It's how she liked to play Two Truths and a Lie.

"You're awake," she says. "Finally."

"How long was I asleep?" I say.

"An hour or so."

"Have you been here that whole time?"

"Off and on. I guess you thought you were rid of me. Well, you're not." Vivian spreads her arms wide in mock delight. "Surprise!"

"You must find this amusing," I say as I sit up and roll my neck until it cracks. "I'm a lost girl, too."

"You think you're going to die down here?"

"Probably."

"I guess it makes us even, then."

"I wanted you to come back," I say. "I didn't mean it. And I'm sorry. Just like I'm sorry for locking the cabin door. It was a horrible thing to do, and I regret it every day. That's all truth. No lies."

"I would have done the same thing," Vivian admits. "That's why I liked you, Em. We were both bitches when we had to be." She smiles at me. Her kind smile. The one from the Vivian I thought of as a potential big sister.

"Viv, what happened to you guys that night? Was it Theo?"

"This is something you have to figure out on your own," Vivian says. "Everything you need to know is right there in front of you. All you need to do is look." She points to the other side of the cavern, where a snake of light crawls along the rock wall. Several more surround it, undulating like waves.

Then it hits me. I can *see*. The darkness is gone, replaced by a warm light radiating through the entire cave. It comes, improbably, from the pool in the middle of the cavern. Sunrise. The presence of light means one thing—there's another way out of the cave.

"Vivian, I think I can get out!"

She's no longer there. Not that she ever truly was.

I limp to the water's edge. The light seems brightest to my right. Its glow suggests a straight path from the cave to the outside world. Most likely an underwater tunnel connecting cave to lake.

I slide back into the pool and face the light. Through the water, I see a glowing circle roughly the same size as the tunnel I entered through. I line my body up with the tunnel entrance. I start shivering, more from nerves than the chill of the water.

I take a deep breath. I slip under the water. I stare at that gold-and-pink light and start to swim toward it.

Swim. That's all I need to do. Swim and try not to think about how much my ankle hurts.

I swim straight into the light, blinded by it, the glare forcing my eyes shut. My lungs scream. My ankle screams. I'm on the verge of screaming myself. But then the tunnel falls away. My eyes open to the sight of water everywhere. No cave. No walls. Just blessed open lake glowing yellow in the ever-brightening dawn.

I shoot to the surface and gasp, gulping down precious air until the ache in my lungs subsides. My ankle still hurts. As do my exhausted, limp-rag arms. Yet I have enough strength to stay afloat and keep my head above water.

I hear the hum of a motorboat in the distance. I rotate in the water until I can see it—a white skiff, one of two normally moored to Camp Nightingale's dock. Chet sits by the outboard motor, steering the boat across the lake. With what little air I have in my lungs, I scream his name. "Chet!"

He spots me, his face bright with surprise. He cuts the motor, grabs a wooden oar, and paddles my way.

"Emma? My God, we've been looking everywhere for you."

I resume swimming. He keeps paddling. Together we finally meet, and I latch on to the side of the boat. With Chet's help, I climb aboard and collapse inside, panting, too tired to move.

"Did you find the girls?" I ask, panting out the words.

"Early this morning. They're dehydrated, hungry, and in shock, but they'll be fine. Theo was going to take them to the hospital."

I sit up, buzzing with alarm. "Theo's back at camp?"

"Yes," Chet says. "He said he found you with the girls and that you attacked him before vanishing in the woods."

"He's lying. He hurt those girls, Chet. He can't be near them. We have to call the police."

I reach for my phone, amazingly still in my pocket and in working order. There's even a bit of battery left. I start to dial 911 but am halted by a shadow crossing the screen. Chet's reflection, as warped as a funhouse mirror. Gripped in his hand is the oar. I see that reflection, too. A faint glimpse of wood swiping across my screen right before Chet swings it into the back of my head.

For a slice of a second, everything stops. My heart. My brain. My lungs and ears and eyes. Then the pain arrives. A screaming, nerve-jolting pain that floods every part of me. My vision blurs. My head rings. I collapse to the bottom of the boat.

I COME to on the floor of the boat. The outboard motor hums like white noise. Occasional sprays of lake water mist my face.

I've landed on my side, my left arm pinned beneath me, my right one twitching slightly. My left eye is closed, smushed as it is against the floor. The lid of my right eye keeps blinking, the sky and clouds above flickering like an old movie.

I'm still in pain, but it's no longer all-consuming. I can move, if I really put my mind to it. That twitching right arm bends. Both legs stretch. I wiggle my fingers, marveling at the accomplishment.

When the sound of the motor ceases and the boat slows, I'm able to flip onto my back, pleased to learn that my left eye also works. I see Chet standing over me. The oar is back in his hands.

"I can't believe you had the nerve to come back here, Emma," he says. "Even though it was my idea, it still surprised me. I just didn't think you'd be that stupid."

"Why . . ." I pause to take a dry-mouthed swallow, hoping it will help get the words out. "Why ask me back?"

"Because I thought it would be fun," Chet says. "I knew you were crazy. Theo told me all about that. And I wanted to see just how crazy you'd get. You know, trap a few birds and put them in the cabin. A little paint on the door. A little peek in the shower." Chet pauses to give me a wink that makes my stomach roil. "I totally didn't expect you to run with it, though. But all that talk about seeing Vivian? That alone made everyone think you'd snapped."

"But *why?*"

"Because of the real reason I wanted you back here. Girls from your cabin go missing, and to put you at the scene of the crime, I drop something of yours into an empty canoe with a broken pair of glasses and set it adrift. That bracelet of yours worked wonders, by the way. When I snapped it off your wrist outside the Lodge, I knew it would be perfect." He flashes me a twisted smile. It's the grin of a madman. Someone far more insane than I ever was. "After that, all I needed to do was delete any surveillance video of me near your cabin and change the file name of the one showing you leaving Dogwood yesterday morning. I'll let you in on a little secret, Em. The girls didn't sneak out five minutes before you woke up. They'd been gone at least an hour."

I sit up. "All that effort. I don't understand."

"Because you almost ruined our lives," Chet says with a snarl. "Especially Theo's. So much that he tried to kill himself. When you destroyed his reputation, you destroyed ours as well. When I got to Yale, half the school wouldn't even talk to me. They saw me as the kid whose brother got away with murder because we're filthy rich. And we're not. Not anymore. All we have left is my mother's apartment and this godforsaken lake."

I finally understand. This is his revenge. An attempt to make me look as guilty as I had made Theo look. He wants me to live under the same cloud of suspicion. To lose everything.

"I didn't want to kill you, Emma," he says. "I would have much rather watched you suffer for the next fifteen years. But the plan has changed. You made sure of that when you freed those girls."

Chet grabs me by the shirt collar and hoists me off the floor. I don't struggle. I can't. All I can do is wobble precariously as he plops me onto the edge of the boat.

We're in a part of the lake I don't recognize. A cove of sorts. Trees crowd the shore, ringing the water like walls of a fortress. Muted light seeps through them, doing little to burn away the fog that rolls across the water. Something sits in the mist, jutting out of the water a few feet from the boat. A rooster weather vane.

It's the same weather vane I've seen in pictures, perched atop Peaceful Valley Asylum. And the asylum it sits upon rests deep beneath Lake Midnight. I peer into the water, getting shimmery glimpses of its mud-caked roof. It's still here. Right where it's always been. Only now covered by the lake.

"I had a feeling you'd recognize it," Chet says. "Little nosy Emma has really been doing her homework."

Judging from the ring of dried mud along the shore, I suspect the lake is usually high enough to completely cover the weather vane. It can be seen now only because of the current drought.

"I found it when I was a teenager," Chet says. "No one will know to look for you here."

My heart gallops. "Don't do this, Chet. It's not too late."

"I think it is, Em."

"The girls didn't see you. They told me so. If you want me to tell the cops I did it, I will. I'll take the blame. I'll plead guilty."

Chet transfers the oar from one hand to the other.

"You want to see me suffer, right? Then imagine me in prison. Think how much I'll suffer then."

I'm hit by a flash of memory. Me leaving Camp Nightingale fifteen years ago. Chet was there, calling after his brother, his face tear-streaked. Maybe that was the moment he decided he needed to get revenge. I need to remind him of the boy he was before that.

"You're not a killer," I tell him. "You're too good of a person for that. I'm the one who did something bad. Don't be like me. Don't become someone you're not."

Chet raises the oar, ready to bring it down once more. I lurch forward, slamming myself into him. The strength comes out of nowhere. A coiled energy ignited by terror and desperation. It sends Chet stumbling against one of the boat's seats. His legs catch on it, and he tumbles backward. The oar leaves his hands, clatters to the floor. I reach for it, but Chet's faster. He grabs the oar with one hand and slaps me with the back of the other.

Spikes of pain sting my cheek. But the blow also zaps one last bit of adrenaline into me. Enough to let me scramble to the front of the boat and crawl onto the bow.

Behind me, Chet's on his feet, oar in hand. He lifts it. He swings.

I close my eyes, screaming, waiting for the blow to connect with my skull. Instead, a shot rings out, the sound careening across the cove. My eyes fly open in time to see the oar explode into a thousand splinters. I shut them again as wood sprays my face.

The boat tips. I tip with it, tumbling into Lake Midnight.

My fall through the water is brief. Just a quick, disorienting drop before I slam into something a few feet from the surface. A roof.

As I'm realizing this, the wood beneath me buckles, giving way. Soon I'm falling again. Still underwater but now also surrounded by walls, encased within them. Peaceful Valley Asylum.

I'm inside it, dropping from the ceiling to the floor below. Faint light trickles through algae-streaked windows. It's enough brightness for me to see an empty room taken over by mud. Everything is tilted—walls, ceiling, door frame. The door itself has come off its hinges and now sits askew, revealing a short hall, stairs, more light. I swim toward them, struggling to make it through the doorway, across the hall, down the steps.

At the bottom, the front door gapes open. I swim out the open door, passing from inside to outside, even though it's all part of the same watery landscape. Pain pulses through my body. My lungs burn. I need air. I need sleep. I start to swim upward, heading to the surface, when something catches my eye.

A skull. Bleached white. Eye sockets aimed at the sky. Scattered around it are more bones. A dozen, at least. I glimpse the arch of ribs, the curl of fingers, a second skull a few yards from the first.

The girls. I know because nestled among the bones, shining faintly in the muck, is a length of gold chain and a locket in the shape of a heart. A tiny emerald sits in its center.

Something enters the water behind me. An arm reaches out and wraps around my waist. Then I'm tugged upward, away from the girls, toward the water's surface.

Soon we're breaking through Lake Midnight. I see sky, trees, the camp's other motorboat bobbing on the water a few yards away. Within it stands Detective Flynn, his gun trained on Chet.

And I see Theo. Swimming next to me. Arm still around my waist. Lake water sloshing against his chin.

"Are you okay?" he says.

I think of Vivian, Natalie, and Allison lying below us. I think of all the years they spent down there, waiting for me to find them.

So when Theo asks again if I'm okay, I can only nod, choke out a sob, and let the tears flow.

I SIT in the front seat of Detective Flynn's police-issued sedan, the hospital in the rearview mirror. I ended up spending two days there. The girls were there for one of them. I shared a room with Miranda, and we spent that time complaining about our sorry states, giggling over the ridiculousness of it all and gossiping about the handsome male nurse who worked the morning shift.

I plan to head back to Manhattan later this afternoon. For now, though, I have unfinished business to attend to, as Detective Flynn reminds me.

"Here's what probably happened," he says. "Based on what she wrote in her diary, Vivian, like you, assumed the worst about Peaceful Valley. She found the location of the asylum and took Allison and Natalie with her to get proof of its existence. From the way you described it, it's probably very easy to get disoriented down there. They went into the water, swam around the wreckage, never came back up. Accidental drowning."

I now know that Vivian died the same way her sister did.

"There's still quite a few bones at the bottom of that lake. It'll take a while to find them all. Until then, we won't know for certain it's your friends down there. As for the second group of girls from Dogwood, Chet said he had no plans to hurt them. Seems like he was just running on anger, not thinking about the consequences."

"Where is he now?"

"County jail for the time being. He'll probably be transferred to a mental health facility."

I'm relieved to hear it. I want Chet to get the help he needs. Because I know a thing or two about seeking vengeance.

"And I guess I owe you an apology," Flynn says. "I should have listened to you more. I was so quick to think you did it because it was the easiest explanation. For that, I'm sorry."

"Apology accepted."

We reach the wrought iron gate of Camp Nightingale. Flynn steers the car into the heart of camp. It feels empty and silent. All the campers, counselors, and instructors have been sent home. Camp Nightingale has closed early. This time for good.

Lottie is outside waiting for me when the sedan pulls up to the Lodge. Because my ankle is wrapped with an Ace bandage, she helps me from the car. Before letting go of my hand, she gives it a squeeze. A signal that she has no hard feelings about what I've said.

Flynn honks the horn and gives me a wave. Then he's off, as Lottie guides me to the Lodge. I'm led to the back deck, where Franny rests in an Adirondack chair tilted to face the sun. She greets me warmly, clasping my hand and smiling as if accusations and misdeeds between us mean nothing. Maybe now they don't.

"Dear Emma. How nice to see you up and about again." She gestures to the floor next to her chair, where my suitcase and box of painting supplies have been placed. "It's all there. I made sure Lottie packed everything. The only things missing are Vivian's diary, which the police took, and the photograph she removed from the Lodge. That deserves to stay with Lottie, don't you think?"

"I couldn't agree more."

"I'm sorry I didn't visit you in the hospital. Under the circumstances, I thought it best to stay away."

"You have nothing to feel sorry about," I tell her.

"But I do. What Chet did is inexcusable. I'm deeply sorry for whatever pain he caused. And please believe me when I say that I didn't know what he had planned."

"I believe you," I say. "You've been nothing but kind to me, Franny. It's me who should be begging for your forgiveness."

"I already gave it. Long, long ago."

"But I didn't deserve it."

"You did," Franny says. "And speaking of forgiveness, there's someone else who has a thing or two to say about that."

She stretches out her hand. Sitting on the lawn, staring out at the water, is Theo.

"Go on," Franny urges. "You two have a lot to talk about."

AT FIRST, I say nothing to Theo. I simply join him on the lawn, my eyes on the lake. Theo is silent in return, for obvious reasons. I've now accused him twice. He has every right to hate me.

Yet Theo still made sure I made it out of the lake alive. Detective Flynn talked at length about how quick Theo was to dive into the water after me. I could sit here and thank Theo for hours, beg for his forgiveness, or apologize so many times I lose count. But I don't. Instead, I hold out my hand and say, "Hi, I'm Emma."

Theo at last acknowledges my presence with a turn of his head. Shaking my hand, he replies, "I'm Theo. Nice to meet you."

It's all he needs to say.

Theo shifts beside me and pulls something out of his pocket, which he drops into my hand. I don't need to look to know it's my charm bracelet. "I thought you'd like it back," Theo says, adding with a grin, "even though we've only just met."

I cup the bracelet in my hand. I've had it for more than half my life. But I won't be needing it anymore. "Thank you. But . . ."

"But what?"

"I think I've outgrown it. Besides, I know a better place for it."

Without a second thought, I toss the bracelet into the air, the three birds taking flight at last. I close my eyes before it lands. I don't want the memory of seeing it vanish from view. Instead, I listen, reaching for Theo's hand as the bracelet drops with a light splash into the depths of Lake Midnight.

THIS is how it ends.

Franny passes in late September. You attend her funeral on a Monday that's been kissed by Indian summer. After the service, you and Theo go for a walk in Central Park. You haven't seen him since leaving Camp Nightingale. A host of unspoken emotions hangs over the reunion. You don't know what kind of relationship the two of you will have going forward. Especially when halfway into your walk, Theo says, "I'm going away next week."

You come to a sudden stop. "Where?"

"Africa," Theo says. "I signed on for another tour with Doctors Without Borders. One year. I need time to sort things out."

You understand. You wish him well.

"When I get back, I'd love to have dinner," Theo says.

"You mean like a date?"

"It could just be a casual meal between two friends who have a habit of accusing each other of doing terrible things," Theo replies. "But I kind of like the date idea better."

"I do, too," you say.

That night, you begin to paint again. You paint the girls in the same order. Vivian first. Then Natalie. Then Allison. You cover them with sinuous shapes in shades of blue and green and brown. You fill the canvas with algae, pondweed, underwater trees with branches twisting toward the surface. You paint a weather vane–topped building submerged in the chilly depths, dark and empty, waiting for someone to find it.

When that canvas is complete, you paint another. Then another. And another. You paint nonstop for weeks.

By January, you have completed twenty-one paintings. Your underwater series. A new gallery show is set for March.

The morning of the opening, you get a phone call from Detective Nathan Flynn. He tells you what you've known all along—the bones discovered in the water belong to Natalie and Allison.

"What about Vivian?" you ask.

He tells you that none of the bones are a match. He tells you that both Natalie's and Allison's skulls were fractured in a way that suggests they were struck in the head, possibly with a shovel found near the bones. He tells you that chains and bricks had also been discovered, indicating both bodies might have been weighed down.

"What are you suggesting?" you ask.

"Exactly what you're thinking," he says.

What you're thinking about are Vivian's last words to you, when she knocked on Dogwood's locked door. Come on, Em. Let me in.

Me. That's what she had said. Not us. *Meaning that she was alone.*

At the gallery, you sip wine and watch shrimp canapés float by on silver trays. Sasha, Krystal, and Miranda attend. Marc takes a picture of the four of you standing in front of your largest painting, No. 6, which seems as massive as Lake Midnight itself.

Later that night, you're at that very same work when a woman comes up beside you. "This is lovely," she says, her eyes on the painting. "So beautifully strange. Are you the artist?"

"I am."

You glance her way, getting a glimpse of red hair, a striking frame, regal bearing. Her clothes are effortlessly cool. Black dress. Black gloves. Floppy black hat and a Burberry trench. Then you recognize her pert nose and cruel smile, and your legs buckle.

"Vivian?"

She continues to stare at the painting. "Two Truths and a Lie, Emma," she says. "You ready to play?"

You want to say no. You have to say yes.

"One: Allison and Natalie were with my sister the night she died," she says. "They dared her to go out on that ice. They saw her fall in and drown. Yet they told no one. But I had my suspicions. I knew Katherine wouldn't do something so dangerous unless she'd been coerced. So I befriended them, earned their trust, pretended to trust them in return. It's how I learned the truth, teasing it out of them on the Fourth of July. They swore they tried to help Katherine. I knew they were lying. After all, I pretended to drown in front of everyone. As I flailed in that water, only Theo made a move to help me. Natalie and Allison did nothing. They simply watched, just as they had watched Katherine drown."

You think about the day you found the girls fighting. You realize now that you had walked into their confession.

"Two: I spent a year planning. I learned about the history of Lake Midnight. I found a place no one knew about—a flooded insane asylum. I placed a sweatshirt in the woods to confuse searchers. I stole the key to the toolshed. Then I led Allison and Natalie to that spot on the lake where no one would look. I did to them what they had done to my sister."

She didn't look for Peaceful Valley to expose its existence. She sought it out because it was the best place to hide her crime.

You think about the shovel stolen from the toolshed. You think about fractured skulls resting on the lake bed. You think about the locket, which you now know Vivian dropped into the water because just like you and your bracelet, she no longer needed it.

"Three: Vivian is dead."

You manage to croak out, "The third one."

"Wrong. Vivian died fifteen years ago. Let her rest in peace."

She leaves the gallery quickly, her boots clicking against the floor. You follow her. Out on the street, you see a town car streak away.

Back in the gallery, you murmur your good-byes. At home in your studio, you paint all night. You paint until the sun peeks over the buildings on the other side of the street. When you stop, you stand before the finished canvas. It's a portrait of Vivian.

Not how she looked back then but how she looks now. Her nose. Her chin. Her eyes, which you've painted midnight blue. She stares back at you with a coy smile playing across her lips.

It's the last time you'll ever paint her.

In a few hours, when the post office opens, you'll ship the painting to Detective Flynn. You'll include a note telling him that Vivian is alive and was last seen in Manhattan. You'll ask that the painting be released to the media, who can use it any way they want.

You will expose who she is, how she looks, what she's done.

You won't hide her beneath layers of paint.

You will refuse to cover her up.

The time for lies is over.

AfterWords

Despite his vivid depiction of Camp Nightingale, Riley Sager's latest thriller is not based in any way on his own summer camp experience.

In an online interview, Sager explains that *The Last Time I Lied* was actually inspired by a book he read called *Picnic at Hanging Rock* by Joan Lindsay. In that novel, several students from an Australian boarding school go missing. "I was drawn to the idea of a group of girls simply disappearing," he says, "and how something like that could traumatize the people left behind."

Sager admits his own summer camp days at age ten were considerably less dramatic. "I was not a fan, to say the least," he says. While everyone else was lining up to swim, "all I really wanted to do was sit by the lake and read."

As a bestselling author, Sager's aim is to write books that sweep readers up in the story. "If readers keep turning those pages, then I'm doing something right," he says. His readers may soon get to see his page-turners on screen. Universal Pictures has optioned the film rights to Sager's previous thriller, *Final Girls*, and Amazon Studios has picked up *The Last Time I Lied*, with the idea of adapting the book into a limited series for television.

Riley Sager is the pseudonym of Todd Ritter, a former journalist, editor, and graphic designer. A native of Pennsylvania, the author currently lives in Princeton, New Jersey.

A BORROWING OF BONES

OF

A MYSTERY

BONES

"A one-sit read!"
—LISA GARDNER,
#1 *New York Times*
Bestselling Author

PAULA
MUNIER

Chapter 1

GRIEF AND GUILT are the ghosts that haunt you when you survive what others do not. Mercy Carr survived, and so did Sergeant Martinez's dog. Nearly a year after her best friend died in Afghanistan, she rose at dawn and took Elvis on another long hike through the Vermont woods. A tired dog was a good dog. At least, that's what the sergeant used to say.

Good was a relative term. Mercy was not Martinez, and Elvis knew it. The bomb-sniffing Belgian shepherd missed his handler and his mission. Just as she did. Every morning, they marched off their grief mile after mile in the mountains, where the cool greens of the forest could chase away the dark ghosts of the desert, at least until night fell.

But today the wilderness held a hush that unnerved her, the same sort of hush Martinez always called a disturbance in the force when they went on patrol. Bad things usually followed.

The dog didn't seem to notice. He raced ahead of her and plunged through a stream, a streak of damp camel-colored fur disappearing into a thicket of small spruce. Mercy hoped he'd circle back to her shortly, as he'd been trained to do. And would have done for his sergeant, no problem.

She sighed. The woods were blessedly calm and empty of people so early in the day. Towering birches, beeches, and maples in full leaf draped the trail in shade. A downpour the night before had left muddy puddles in its wake. She tramped on, her eyes on the slick stone-ridden path and her mind off her future, which loomed ahead of her with no clear goal in sight.

After that last deployment, the one where Martinez got killed and she got shot and Elvis got depressed, Mercy and the dog were sent home. Martinez's last words to her had been "Take care of Elvis," so they entered retirement together. Two former military police—one twenty-nine-year-old two-legged female Vermonter with an exit-wound scar blighting her ass, and one handsome five-year-old four-legged male Malinois with canine PTSD—reclaiming themselves in the woods one hike at a time.

The terrain grew rougher, steeper. She adjusted her pack, which at fifteen pounds barely registered on her body. She whistled.

Nothing.

In Afghanistan, Elvis's job had been to walk in front of his sergeant and their unit, scouting ahead and alerting them to danger. The only dangers here in the southern Green Mountains were clouds of biting deerflies and the occasional bear. Still, she paused to listen for the sound of a lively dog diving into the scrub. All she heard was the rush of the nearby brook.

Too quiet. Mercy whistled again and waited.

The Belgian shepherd darted onto the path, his fawn fur stippled with dark splotches of sludge, his black muzzle muddy. Elvis skidded to a stop in front of her and jangled his head. In his mouth he held what looked like one of his squeaky toys.

"Drop it." She held out her hand, and the dog released the canary-yellow object into her open palm. "I think it's a baby teether," she told him. It was shaped like a plastic daisy, with a thick stem for a baby's grip. Apart from dog drool, the little toy was clean, so it wasn't something abandoned in the woods for long. She bent over toward Elvis, holding the teether out. "Where did you get this?"

Elvis pushed at her hand with a cold nose and whined. With another quick yelp, he leaped back into the underbrush. Mercy followed the dog, as he obviously meant her to do.

He barreled through the tangle of bracken and brushwood to a stream that paralleled the trail. He jumped, clearing the six-foot-wide current easily. Mercy splashed after him.

She clambered out of the brook and stumbled over the stones into a copse of birch trees. There Elvis dropped down on his haunches in the middle of a blowdown area littered with tree limbs. This was his alert position—the posture he assumed when he sniffed out weapons or explosives. IEDs were his specialty.

"What you got there?" She squatted next to him. He looked at her as if to say, *My job here is done. Where's my reward?*

But Mercy wasn't sure if he'd earned it. The forest floor was thick with dead leaves and twigs. No evidence of trespass. No evidence of explosives. As far as she knew, Elvis wasn't trained to alert for babies—not that there was evidence of a baby here, either. On the other hand, Elvis had rarely been wrong before. What were the odds he was wrong now?

"Good boy." She slipped a treat out, and Elvis licked it up.

If they'd been on a mission, the sergeant would've called in the team for bomb disposal. But here there was no team trailing them. Mercy wasn't even sure Elvis had alerted to explosives.

Mercy rose to her feet, wondering what to do. Elvis leaped ahead of her and darted into the brush. She headed after him.

And that's when she heard it. A thin cry. Followed by another. And another, growing in volume with each wail. Sounded like her mother's cat back in Boston, meowing for breakfast.

But she knew it was no cat.

ELVIS bellowed. Mercy broke through the leatherleaf and bog laurel and came into a small glade. There in the middle sat a squalling baby in a blue backpack-style infant carrier.

A baby girl, if her pink cap and Hello Kitty onesie were any indication. A red-faced, cherub-cheeked baby girl, chubby arms and legs flailing against an assault of deerflies.

Mercy hurried over and fell to her knees, swatting away at the swarm. The baby appeared to be about six months old. Mercy unbuckled the straps on the carrier and pulled out the wailing child.

The baby lifted up her small head. Mercy stared into round slate-blue eyes rimmed in tears and deerfly bites.

"'Though she be but little, she is fierce,'" Mercy quoted, and the baby scrunched up her face as if to screech again, but hiccupped instead. Maybe Shakespeare calms her the way he calms me, Mercy thought. She cradled the little girl in her arms and stood, holding her against her chest. She bobbed her up and down until her sobs subsided. Within minutes the baby was asleep.

"Where's your mom?" she asked the sleeping child. Maybe she'd gone off behind some bushes to pee. "Hello," she called.

No answer.

The last time she'd held a baby over there, the child had died in her arms. She shook off the memory and kept on rocking the baby and calling for her mother. Maybe her mom had hurt herself. Mercy walked around the clearing, eyes on the ground.

She could see the trail they'd left behind as she and Elvis had barreled into the glade. But leading out in the opposite direction, she saw broken branches and faint boot prints. Mercy and Elvis followed the markings into a denser area of forest and hiked through the wood. The traces ended abruptly at a rushing stream. Too fast-moving to ford holding a baby.

She yelled again. Elvis barked. She listened for the sounds of humans, but all she heard was the sound of the water. The baby would be hungry soon and tired and cold.

"We're going back." Holding the baby tightly with her left arm, she pulled her cell out of her pocket with her right hand.

No bars. She'd try again when they were closer to the trail.

Mercy and Elvis retraced their steps. When they reached the baby carrier, Mercy carefully strapped the dozing child into it. There was a large zippered compartment on the back; she rifled through the baby bottles and formula and diapers to pull out a blanket, covering the infant in an effort to keep away the flies.

Mercy slipped off her small pack, tying it to the big one with the baby. She hoisted the carrier up onto her shoulders.

"Home," she told Elvis.

She never had to tell him twice to go where his bowl and bed were. He set the pace, blazing back the way they came. When they came to the blowdown, he trotted over to the same place where he'd alerted before and dropped into his alert position.

Mercy didn't know why he seemed fixated on this spot. Maybe he detected explosives, or maybe he was just confused, his PTSD kicking in. Either way, she couldn't bet against Elvis and his nose. Martinez would never forgive her.

Mercy unhooked her pack from the carrier and pulled out the duct tape and her Swiss Army knife, the two tools she never left home without. She used the duct tape to rope off a crescent around the area Elvis had targeted, using saplings as posts.

"Better safe than sorry," she told him.

Elvis vaulted ahead, steering them out of the forest. When they reached the trail, Mercy taped the spot where they'd gone into the woods. She checked her phone again. Still no bars. They'd have to trek down to the trailhead for a stronger signal.

"Back to civilization," Mercy said with a sigh.

VERMONT Fish and Wildlife game warden Troy Warner hated national holidays. Holidays brought the most uninformed nature lovers to the southern Green Mountains. If the term "nature lovers" could *really* be applied to city people, whose idea of a hike was stumbling inebriated through the woods in the hope of finding a bear to pose with them for a quick selfie.

So when the dispatcher Delphine Dupree called him about an abandoned baby, Troy was intrigued as well as concerned. He expected the lost hikers (usually found), the snakebites (usually nonlethal), the poachers (usually long gone), but a baby . . .

"The hiker found the child off-trail," she said. "So she's carrying her to the trail to meet you. There's a big pileup on Route three thirteen. Most everyone who's available has gone down there. That, plus all the holiday nonsense, means you're on your own."

"I'm on it." He signed off and jogged back along the shoreline of Branch Pond, where an enthusiastic troupe of ten-year-old Boy Scouts hankering for a fishing badge waited for him.

The boys were playing with Susie Bear. The big black shaggy

dog was leaping in and out of the lake, splashing the Scouts. She was a Newfoundland retriever mix he'd adopted a few years ago and named for the character in John Irving's *The Hotel New Hampshire*. One hundred pounds of muscle and shiny obsidian fur punctuated by a thick pink tongue that hung out of the side of her mouth. Everybody loved her. Which was good for Troy, who relied on his sidekick for comic relief as well as search and rescue. Troy was not a big talker. When he struggled to find the right words, Susie Bear stepped in and won over the crowd every time.

"Sorry, guys." He whistled for the dog. "We've got to go."

The Newfie mutt did her canine version of the twist, and water flew from her fur, spraying the laughing boys. She bounded over and slid to a stop at Troy's side. Together they hustled back to the government-issued dark green Ford F-150 truck, which served as his mobile office as well as his transportation.

Nothing like the smell of wet dog, thought Troy as they bumped along on the rough logging road that ran through the national forest, bordering the Lye Brook Wilderness. There were no roads inside the wilderness, so he parked at the trailhead. They got out, and he added the deluxe first-aid kit and an extra blanket to his pack, pulling it onto his back, then stocked Susie Bear's pack with more water and slipped it onto the dog.

Troy shouldered his rifle. "Let's go get that baby."

HALF an hour of huffing up the mountain later, Troy sighted a huddle of living creatures up the trail. He pulled out his binoculars for a closer look and zeroed in on an attractive young woman, a sleeping baby, and a good-looking Belgian shepherd.

"Heel," he said to Susie Bear, and jogged up to them, stopping about ten feet away on account of the dog.

The woman had seen him coming and put the baby in a carrier and slung it onto her back. She was about five feet eight inches, with a lean build and an erect carriage that spelled military. Her chin-length hair was as red as a burning bush in October, framing a freckled, finely boned face that looked upon him with a mixture of relief and reserve. She did not smile.

"Stay," she said to the Malinois at her side, and walked over to Troy. "Mercy Carr." She held out a long-fingered hand, and he shook it. A firm and forceful handshake. Definitely military.

"Troy Warner, state game warden. This is Susie Bear."

"'We need a good, smart bear,'" she quoted from the John Irving novel so softly he almost didn't hear her. But loud enough so that he'd know she got the reference.

Troy smiled. She was a genuine New Englander.

"That's Elvis." She tossed her head in the direction of her dog. "Baby Doe has got some deerfly bites that need attending to, and she's probably dehydrated. I did give her a bottle."

"Let me get her to the hospital," said Troy.

"We're coming with you."

"That won't be necessary, Ms. Carr."

"Call me Mercy."

"Troy."

"We found her, Troy, and we'll see it through."

Troy realized she was talking about herself and her dog. He nearly grinned, as he was often guilty of the same thing.

"Besides, you'll need to take my statement and come back to check out the scene. We can show you where we found her."

Military police, he thought. "My truck's down at the trailhead." He waved her ahead with his arm. "After you."

"Come," she said to Elvis.

Troy stood there with the Newfie mutt at his side and watched the trio of woman, baby, and dog waltz by them single file down the narrow trail. He and Susie Bear took up the rear.

THEY made good time. Mercy Carr was tough and fast and used to a quick march. Troy was impressed.

When the trail widened enough to allow him to step up beside her, he quickened his gait and then matched hers, stride for stride. She turned and smiled at him for the first time—and her pretty pale face brightened into a fine beauty. Troy was struck by the feeling that he knew her, but he could not place her. His confusion must have registered on his face, because she laughed.

"You don't remember me," she said.

"I'm trying. Are you from Northshire?"

"I was born here and spent my summers here as a child." She ducked to avoid a low-hanging branch. "You were a lifeguard at the town pool. You and your friend Hunter Boggs."

A murky memory of a long-legged red-haired kid diving into the pool over and over again drifted in and out of his mind.

"I was fourteen. I had the biggest crush on you."

"Me?" He and his best bud had scored jobs as lifeguards the summer after graduation. "Most of you girls went for Hunter."

"Not all of us." She looked at him, her blue eyes lit with mischief. "He was full of himself. Always checking himself in every rearview mirror when he walked across the parking lot."

He laughed. "You were a very observant fourteen-year-old."

"Nothing to do but swim and read and watch the cool kids."

Troy shook his head. "I was not so cool. But Hunter was."

"Only in his own mind."

He frowned. She sounded like his estranged wife, Madeline, the prettiest girl at the pool. Hell, the prettiest girl in the county. Who shocked everyone when she chose him over Hunter.

"Didn't you marry Madeline Renard?" Mercy asked, as if she could read his mind.

"Yes," he said, not trusting himself to say any more.

They approached the trailhead.

"Mine's the red Jeep." She pointed to the vehicle parked a few spaces beyond his Ford. "I don't have a car seat. Do you?"

"No. We'll all have to go together in the truck." Troy rearranged the stuff in his backseat to make room for her, the baby, and the Malinois. Then he settled in front with Susie Bear.

The medical center was only three miles down the road in Northshire. When they arrived, Mercy hurried out of the vehicle with the baby; Troy brought along the carrier.

Once inside the hospital, Mercy turned Baby Doe over to the ER nurse with reluctance. The baby cried for her. She insisted on waiting close by while the doctor examined the infant.

Dr. Sharma was a young physician with a faint Indian accent

who cooed at the little girl as he gently examined her. "Very odd to be finding a baby in the woods. Especially one who, apart from this disturbing incident, is seeming well cared for."

"That's what I thought," Mercy said.

"She seems to be all right," said Dr. Sharma. "We will be treating the bites and keeping her overnight for observation."

"What will happen to her after that?"

"We will be contacting Child Protective Services," Dr. Sharma said. "If no one is coming forward to claim the child."

"CPS. Right." She turned to Troy. "Here's hoping that you find her family before that happens."

"I'm sure law enforcement will do everything possible to track down her next of kin," Troy said to both of them.

But unless someone had put out an Amber Alert, odds were they wouldn't know who the baby was until he found the mother himself. "I need to get back to the scene. And I'll be keeping this." He pointed to the baby's blanket by the carrier.

"Of course." The doctor nodded.

"Thank you," said Mercy, looking back at the baby before she walked away. "Bye, baby," she said.

"Come on," Troy said softly, touching her shoulder gently. He led Mercy down the corridor and out of the building.

Without a word, Mercy headed right for his truck. This time she sat in front, and the dogs shared the backseat amicably.

The quick ride was a quiet one. He didn't want to push her; he'd save his questions for the scene.

"Do you have any children?" Mercy asked.

He looked at the fourth finger of his left hand, still showing the faint circle of lighter skin left by the wedding ring he'd worn for nine years. The removal made him feel like a quitter, even though he knew his marriage was over. And kids were one of the reasons for that. He wanted them. His wife didn't.

"No," he said, careful to keep his eyes on the road. "No kids. Not yet." That was the only good thing about his wife leaving. The possibility of children. Someday, with someone else.

"Not yet," repeated Mercy, a catch in her voice.

Troy eased the truck into the parking lot at the trailhead. And for the second time that day, he and Susie Bear took up the rear as Mercy and Elvis led them up the trail.

It was almost noon, the sun nearly straight above their heads. Mercy wore a blue Red Sox cap now, shading her eyes. She stopped about ten feet beyond where he'd found her and the baby. "This is where Elvis took me off-trail."

"Is it marked?"

"Yep."

This time Troy and Susie Bear led the way. Apart from their own footfalls and the panting of the dogs, the only sounds were the rushing of Lye Brook and birds chattering in the trees.

"Is this it?" he asked when they came to a clearing marked by the same duct tape Mercy had used along the trail.

"Uh, no." Mercy stopped at the edge of the tape. She removed her cap. Her face shone with sweat, and she wiped her brow.

"But you taped it off anyway. Why?"

She sighed and put her cap back on. "Explosives."

"Explosives?" He stood very still and stared at the area she'd marked off. The earth before him revealed nothing: no raised patches or subtle variations in the color of the soil.

"Elvis alerted to explosives." She said this casually, as if it happened every day. Maybe it did for her and Elvis. "Two tours in Afghanistan. Elvis is an EDD extraordinaire."

"Explosive detection dog." Troy regarded the Malinois with a new respect. He'd done a tour in Afghanistan himself and knew what important work these K-9 soldiers did. "And you?"

"U.S. Army corporal, retired. We're both retired now."

"Retired," he repeated. "But you just happened to be searching for explosives in the Lye Brook Wilderness."

"No, we were just out for a walk. I don't know what set him off. I got worried. So I taped it off."

"So you're not sure about the possibility of explosives."

"I don't know. Back in Afghanistan, Elvis would do what he was supposed to do. When he got the right command."

"But you gave him no such order here today."

"Of course not," she said. "We left all that behind us. It's been a long time since Elvis got that order. Maybe he's rusty."

"But you're not convinced."

"No," she admitted.

"Because?"

"Because he was the best," she said, her voice thick and her eyes shining with pride or tears or both. "The very best."

He considered this. "Maybe somebody buried fireworks or lost a gun or— What's this got to do with our Baby Doe?"

"I don't know. Nothing, maybe."

"Okay, I'll have a team come check it out. Let's move on."

She led them through the bramble. Ten minutes later, they entered the glade where Mercy and Elvis had found the child.

Troy scoured the ground. "Not much here." But on the other side of the opening in the trees, there were footmarks.

"I followed those tracks to the stream, where they ended."

"Show me."

She took him through a scrub of birch to the stream. He waded across, Susie Bear on his heels. There were no traces of any human traffic here. Susie Bear ran up and down the banks trying to pick up the scent where someone may have exited the water. But she found nothing. He and his dog splashed back, and she repeated the exercise along this side. Nothing.

"Only one more thing to try." Troy pulled the baby's blanket out of his pack. "Here's hoping that the scent of whoever brought her out here is still on this."

"The baby's scent is on it, as is mine. And yours."

"It's a long shot. But if any dog can do it, Susie Bear can."

He held the blanket under the Newfie mutt's nose for a long moment. Then he pulled it away and said simply, "Search."

She went to work, nose sniffing, clumping up to Mercy and then over to Troy.

"Search," he said again, and gave the dog another opportunity to smell the blanket.

Broad snout twitching, she lumbered along the edge of the stream for a hundred yards, then turned into another blowdown area littered with fallen limbs. Elvis bounded after Susie Bear.

"Call him back," Troy told Mercy.

"Sorry." She whistled for the shepherd, but he ignored her.

Troy ran after the two dogs. He could hear Mercy jogging after him. By the time he caught up to them, the canines were playing together in a corner of the blowdown area. Susie Bear was kicking at a pile of debris. Elvis was clawing at the earth.

At the sound of his approach, the Newfie mutt dropped to all fours. She looked at him, her black feathery tail whacking the forest floor. Elvis ignored Troy, intent on his burrowing.

He realized that they might not be playing.

"What are they doing?" Mercy appeared at his side, slightly out of breath. "Your dog seems to be alerting to something."

They stepped forward together. He grabbed a stick and pushed around the loose soil, scraping away bark and brush. "I don't see anything." He looked at the dog. "Nothing here, girl."

She whined and wagged her long tail even harder.

"Always trust your dog," Mercy said as she turned her attention to Elvis. Troy followed her gaze and watched the sleek shepherd nose a long bone from a mound of dirt.

"That looks like . . ." She hesitated.

"A femur bone." He finished the observation for her.

"Come," said Mercy in a stern voice.

Elvis trotted over to her.

"Drop it," they ordered in unison.

To his credit, the shepherd dropped the bone.

"Let's take a closer look." Troy retrieved a pair of plastic gloves from his pack and slipped them on. Then he picked up the femur bone gingerly. He raised it up in front of him.

The bone was more than twenty inches long.

"That's a tall person," Mercy said.

Susie Bear barked. She still lay at the edge of what Troy now suspected could be a shallow grave.

"Good job, girl." Troy gave her a treat from his pocket.

"Always trust your dog," Mercy repeated.

Troy tossed a treat at Elvis, too, and he caught it easily.

Mercy leaned in close to examine the bone more carefully. She pointed to a clear marking on the bone, her forefinger fractions of an inch from the femur. "Looks like an old break."

"Don't touch it." He stepped away from her.

Mercy snorted. "I wasn't going to touch it."

Elvis growled at him.

"Quiet," she told the Malinois. He settled down but still appeared ready to pounce at any moment. "Sorry. He can be a little high-strung sometimes."

"PTSD?" It would explain why Mercy was so protective of the shepherd and why he alerted to explosives in a forest halfway around the world from the battlefield.

"Yeah." Mercy stiffened. "But he's doing much better."

Troy wondered if Mercy suffered from PTSD, too. He'd seen a lot of soldiers fall apart both on and off the battlefield.

"That break might help us identify the victim," she said, changing the subject.

There was no us here, he thought. There was just him and his congenial dog in the woods with this woman and her unpredictable dog. He sighed.

"Babies, bombs, bones." Troy looked at Mercy. "You and your dog have had a very busy day."

Chapter 2

MERCY STOOD WITH ELVIS at the edge of the crime scene behind the tape as the crime-scene search team sorted through the detritus of the forest floor for evidence.

"Bone fragments everywhere," Troy was saying to the medical examiner, a short, cheerful woman of about fifty named Dr. Darling. "A bear must have gotten to the body fairly early on."

"We may not find many more of the large bones left intact. You know how much black bears love their marrow."

Mercy knew they were probably right. The question was, how did the victim die? Did the bear kill the victim, or was the victim already dead when the bear came along for a snack?

"The remains are strewn all over. Maybe we'll get lucky."

"We'll keep on looking." Dr. Darling squatted on the ground, sorting contentedly through the remains.

"This must be a fairly old burial site," Troy told her, "given the state of the remains."

"What we've found so far has been picked pretty clean, so they've probably been here a while," she conceded.

Dr. Darling reminded Mercy of a pug. The game warden, on the other hand, was your classic Labrador, good-hearted and good-looking in the earnest and energetic way of retrievers.

She remembered the first day she'd seen him at the Northshire pool all those years ago. He'd filled out a little but still had the athletic build, that outdoorsy tan, those warm brown eyes. Although there was a hint of sadness around them now.

Elvis sat leashed at her side, ears up, watching Susie Bear, also banished to the far side of the clearing. The Newfie mutt's eyes— like Mercy's—were on the game warden.

The doctor and the techs kept on sifting and sorting. Troy nodded at Dr. Darling, then strode over to Mercy.

"You should go on home," he told her.

"I don't think so." She didn't want to go. This was the most interesting thing that had happened to her since coming home.

"You've got to be exhausted."

"Not really." She petted Elvis's head. "We're fine."

"I could order you off the scene."

She smiled at him. "Are you going to arrest me?"

He smiled back. "Okay, don't say I didn't try."

"Victory!" Dr. Darling's shout boomed across the clearing.

Troy strode quickly over to the doctor. "What is it?"

She held up a dusty, roundish pale object in her gloved hands. "An intact skull. More or less."

Troy said something in reply, but Mercy missed most of it. His back was to her now, and she couldn't hear what he was saying to the doctor. She leaned forward across the tape. "Warden Warner!"

He turned to look her way.

"Come on!" Mercy yelled.

The medical examiner grinned at Mercy and raised her already resounding voice. "An adult male shot in the head."

Troy held up his hands in mock surrender. "Okay, but watch your step."

"Stay," Mercy said to Elvis, and joined them in the circle.

Dr. Darling was on her feet now. "You can see the entrance wound here." She pointed to a round hole in the crown of the skull. Long fissures radiated out from its center in a starburst pattern.

"I guess the black bears are off the hook," Mercy said.

"Yep." She smiled at Mercy and tipped the skull forward to reveal its back side.

"No exit wound?" asked Troy.

"No." She tipped the skull forward again. "Hear that scraping sound? The bullet is inside. A stroke of luck for us."

"Maybe," said Troy. "If we can find the weapon or casing."

A tall, skinny man in a Tyvek suit approached them from the crime scene in a seemingly purposeful slow and steady gait that Mercy suspected drove the game warden crazy. She smiled.

"What do you have for us?" asked Troy, failing to hide the note of impatience in his voice.

"Bob," said the doctor pointedly, "this is Mercy Carr. Mercy, meet Bob, head of the crime-scene search team."

"Hi," Mercy said.

Bob dismissed her and addressed Dr. Darling. "Not much left of the victim's clothes, and the boots are so common as to be useless in terms of identification."

"Any teeth?" asked the medical examiner.

"Just fragments. Any left in the skull?"

"A few."

"You didn't walk all the way over here to tell us about teeth fragments," said the game warden.

Bob held out his gloved hands. There, revealed in his cupped fingers, was what appeared to be a tarnished pewter belt buckle.

In unison, the three of them leaned toward the ornament.

"Is that a pine tree?" asked Dr. Darling.

"Yes, set against the mountains," Mercy said. "One of the classic symbols of Vermont."

Troy peered at the buckle and read the words that ran underneath the pine tree. "'Freedom and Unity.'"

"Interesting," said Dr. Darling.

"That it?" asked Troy.

"For now," said Bob. "I'll bag this and get on with it."

They watched him amble back across the crime scene.

"I'll be wrapping up soon," Dr. Darling told them.

Troy ushered Mercy back to Elvis. "Now you really do have to go home."

She didn't say anything. But she didn't move, either.

"Look, there's nothing more to do here." He frowned. "And the bomb squad says they haven't found any explosives."

"Nothing?" She stared at him. "I find that hard to believe."

"Look, I've already crossed over the line here. Besides, it's out of my hands. The state police are running this show now."

"But you're still here."

"I'm not a civilian."

You're not a detective, either, thought Mercy. They'd found these bones, and there was a responsibility that came along with that. Whether you were a game warden or a civilian.

"'Blessed be the man that spares these stones,'" she quoted quietly. "'And cursed be he that moves my bones.'"

"What's that supposed to mean?"

"Shakespeare."

"What's Shakespeare got to do with anything?"

"Somebody killed this man and then abandoned his body in the woods. Robbed him of the dignity of a decent burial. In effect, failing to spare his stones and honor his bones."

"And cursing himself in the process. I get it."

"That curse begins with us." She stood taller and leaned forward. Elvis growled softly. "What aren't you telling me?"

"What's wrong with your dog?"

"He's just being protective." The fierce Belgian shepherd had always stood ready to defend his sergeant, but today he'd indicated he was prepared to defend her as well.

"Are you hungry?" Troy grinned at her. "How about we go grab something to eat? For us and the dogs. My treat."

She knew he was changing the subject, but she also knew an olive branch when she saw it. "Sure."

"I've got to drop by the hospital later, anyway," he said. "And we can go over your statement."

And she could drill him over dinner.

MERCY started going to the Vermonter Drive-In when she was just a kid. Famous for its sandwiches and milkshakes, the popular joint drew people every day rain or shine. Calling it a drive-in was a glamorous misnomer; the restaurant was really just a glorified lean-to with a large window fronting the parking lot, where she stood in line with Troy. The dogs waited in their respective vehicles.

"Come on up, Warden." Lillian Jenkins, the owner, waved Troy up to the window. Everyone knew the effusive petite brunette who ran the drive-in during the summer and the book club the rest of the year. She also served on every committee in town, from the Friends of the Library to the historical society.

"Hi, Lillian." Troy smiled.

"Who's your friend?"

"Mercy Carr," he said.

"I know you." She gave her a long look. "You're a Fleury."

"Patience Fleury O'Sullivan is my grandmother."

"The veterinarian?" asked Troy.

"One and the same," answered Lillian, her eyes still on Mercy. "I went to school with Patience. You got your grandmother's good looks. But that red hair is all your granddaddy. I hope you didn't get the O'Sullivan temper to go with it."

Mercy's grandfather had been the sheriff in Lamoille County for decades, and as many people loved him as hated him.

"No, ma'am." She could see Troy holding back a laugh.

Lillian tapped her pencil against her pad. "Two cheeseburgers, fries, and chocolate shakes?"

"Make that four cheeseburgers, fully dressed," said Troy. "We got a couple of dogs to feed."

Lillian looked out into the parking lot and spotted Elvis. "That sweet shepherd yours?"

"Yes, ma'am."

"Now that's a Fleury for you." She bestowed a warm smile on her. "Have a seat out back. And feel free to bring the dogs."

TEN minutes later all four of them were gathered around the lone picnic table behind the burger shack. The weathered table sat at the edge of Lillian's potager garden, a beauty of raised beds that produced a bounty of vegetables and herbs.

"How's the baby?" Mercy knew Troy had received several texts, and she assumed at least one of them concerned the infant.

"She's doing well. But they're still keeping her overnight."

"And then she goes into the system." She sipped at the chocolate shake. "Will you even try to find her mother?"

"They've got volunteers doing a grid search. We'll find her."

"Alive?"

"There was no sign of foul play."

"Except for the corpse and explosives."

"Alleged explosives."

"So you think it's all a big coincidence?" She refused to believe that was even a possibility. And his believing it angered her.

"I don't believe in coincidence," Troy said.

"Neither do I." Mercy tapped the surface of the table with her index finger. "Someone took good care of that baby."

"Right up until they left her in the woods to die."

"Maybe they didn't leave her to die but to be found."

"By you?"

"By somebody. It is a holiday week. Maybe they figured someone was bound to come by sooner or later."

"Seems risky. The Lye Brook Wilderness is not as popular as the national forest. Why not pick a well-traveled route?"

"I don't know. But some of us hike there regularly, anyway. Maybe they knew that. And they left diapers and bottles and formula—everything she'd need, at least in the short term."

"Yeah."

"Elvis and I have hiked up to those falls nearly every morning since spring. We don't see many people on the way up, because it's so early. But we glimpse more people on the way down. Sometimes with babies. Not often. But it does happen."

"Just because you don't see them doesn't mean they don't see you. Especially if they're off-trail." He seemed to be warming to her theory. "We've got the baby clothes and carrier. Maybe that will give us something."

"I could take her," she said. "I mean, instead of her going to Child Protective Services."

He eyed her with surprise. "That's not really how it works."

"I did keep this baby alive until you came along."

"You saved her life," he said. "No question about that. And maybe her mother was counting on that."

They both fell silent at that.

Finally Mercy spoke. "If her mother left her there for me and Elvis to find, then she must be in trouble."

"Which leads us right back to the bones and bombs."

"But you said there were no bombs."

"I said they didn't find any explosives."

"But they did find something."

"You never give up, do you?"

She didn't say anything. Just waited him out.

"I couldn't tell you at the crime scene. Too many people around." He paused. "I probably shouldn't be telling you now."

She leaned toward him. "You know you want to."

He stiffened, and she laughed. To his credit he laughed, too. "They found traces of PETN, a chemical compound often found in—"

"In explosives," Mercy interrupted. "Yeah, I know."

More important, Elvis knew. As a sniffer dog, he was trained to find weapons and to detect a number of explosives' odors.

Troy looked over at Elvis. "That explains why he found the PETN. But it doesn't explain why he found the bones."

"Susie Bear found the bones."

"But Elvis was there, too. Is he trained to find cadavers?"

"Not exactly. That is, I don't know." Like all military dogs, Elvis was trained to secure bases and apprehend suspects. Beyond that, most military dogs were specialists. For Elvis it was all about explosives. At least, that's what Martinez told her.

"What does that mean, exactly?"

"It means that I don't know. Not for sure."

"What kind of dog handler are you?"

"I'm not a dog handler," Mercy said.

"But you said you were an MP." He looked confused.

"Let me explain." She'd have to tell him everything, like it or not. She didn't want him to lose confidence in her. Or Elvis.

Troy waited. The dogs waited. All three pairs of brown eyes on her now.

Mercy looked past them all, out over Lillian's potager garden. "I was an MP stationed in Afghanistan. Elvis was one of the sniffer dogs attached to our unit. Martinez was his handler."

At the sound of his handler's name, Elvis sat back up again, ears up. Troy noticed, and Mercy noticed his noticing.

"Sgt. Juan Miguel Pedro Martinez," she said.

"What happened to the sergeant?" Troy's voice was quiet.

"He died in action." She reached down and placed her hand on Elvis's fine head. "One year ago tomorrow."

"I'm sorry."

"Our team was en route to a nest of high-value targets. As soon as we breached the perimeter, we came under fire. A sniper took him out. They dragged him to safety, but there was only so much the medics could do. They had to get him out of there. Elvis helped the team establish a safe zone where the helicopter bound for the hospital unit could land."

She hesitated and removed her hand from Elvis's head. She folded her arms around herself, suddenly cold. "They got him out of there, but it was too late. He died on the operating table."

"And then you and the dog came home." There was a question in his voice.

"I was sent home to recuperate from my own injury." At the look on Troy's face, she was quick to reassure him. "I'm fine."

"And Elvis?"

"He was never really the same again. They sent him back to the defense contractor, but I'd promised Martinez I'd take care of him myself. So I bullied them until they let me have him."

"You were obviously very close. I'm so sorry for your loss."

"We weren't supposed to be together. Non-fraternization policy. So we kept our feelings to ourselves." Mercy willed away the un-shed tears gathering in the corners of her eyes. "As long as we were deployed together."

Elvis moved his nose onto her lap. Mercy cupped his dark muzzle in her hands and looked into the dog's deep brown eyes. "We were going to be married as soon as our assignments changed. He put in for a transfer to train dog handlers at Lackland. It was just a matter of time before they sent him to Texas. He insisted we wait until we could do it right." Mercy released the shepherd and looked up at Troy. "And now he's dead. Nothing right about that."

"I'm sorry," he said again.

"So I'm no dog handler." She stood up abruptly. "Elvis is stuck with me, and I'm learning as fast as I can."

Troy came to his feet. "It's not easy to take on a dog who's already bonded so tightly with his handler. He's a lucky dog."

"It's the least I could do. I've been working with him one on one, the way Martinez used to."

"That's great. Do you do agility training with him?"

"Not beyond the usual obstacles on the trail. You know, jumping over logs, streams, whatever's in the way."

"You might want to try Two Swords K-9 Training. Jake over there works with a lot of dogs like Elvis. Susie Bear loves it."

Mercy knew that agility training had been part of the Malinois's training at Lackland. "I'll think about it."

"We'd be happy to take you guys over there anytime."

"Thanks. He might like that."

Susie Bear barked as if she knew what they were saying—and maybe she did, or maybe she just wanted more fries. They both laughed. Mercy divvied up the rest of her french fries between the two dogs while Troy checked his messages.

"Time to go," he said, his face hard with an emotion she couldn't quite name. But whatever it was, it wasn't good.

"What's wrong?"

"The baby's gone."

THE children's wing of the medical center was on the third floor. Troy and Mercy stood in a small office decorated with the same bright, cheerful jungle murals as the rest of the ward, interviewing head pediatric nurse Anne Dougherty. So far they'd gotten nowhere. No one knew anything or saw anything.

Troy was frustrated, but he hoped it didn't show on his face as clearly as it did on Mercy's. Even her freckles looked angry now, dark dots against pale skin flushed with impatience.

"There's a security code to get into the ward," she was saying to the nurse. "How could anyone get in?"

He cleared his throat, a signal to Mercy to back off.

"Yes," said Anne. "There is a security code. But we had to admit several young people injured in that big accident on Route three thirteen. Much more coming and going than usual. Whoever took her must have slipped in then. We were focused on getting everyone in and evaluated and treated as quickly as possible."

Troy nodded. "Let's see the room where the baby was staying."

"Of course." Anne led them out of her office and down a long hall lined with patient rooms.

The baby's room held a white metal adjustable crib and the usual medical paraphernalia. The crib was empty and unmade.

"Everything here looks like hospital issue," he said.

"Yes," confirmed Anne.

"What happened to the backpack carrier?" asked Mercy. "And the baby's clothes? The teethers?"

"Whoever took the baby must have taken those things, too."

"Sounds like a domestic snatch," said Troy. "So she's probably physically safe, at least."

"We've got to find her," said Mercy.

"We will," he said. "Starting with an Amber Alert."

MERCY was not happy when Troy sent them home. He'd told her to get some sleep and they'd touch base in the morning, which was cop code for "You're a civilian; let us pros handle it." She didn't expect to hear from him anytime soon. So she'd have to carry on herself, with Elvis as her right-hand canine.

She turned the Jeep into the long drive that led up to the old log cabin on the hill. The small house sat on fifty acres of forest land fronted by a stream that ran along the back of the barn. She'd bought the property when she came home from Afghanistan, drawn to its Lincoln Log charm and desolate isolation.

She pulled up to the side of the cabin, parking by the old stone wall. She grabbed their packs and opened the hatchback for a very animated Elvis. The dog leaped out and streaked straight for the front door. He seemed as happy to be home as she was. It had been a long day, and they were both tired.

She followed him through the weathered rose arbor and up the granite path that led to the wide south-facing front porch, where you could watch the sun rise over the mountains to the east at dawn and set over them to the west at dusk. Her only enhancement to the splendid view was a flagpole and an American flag, which flew half mast in honor of her fallen comrades.

She paused for a quick salute. "Martinez."

Mercy always saluted when coming and going—her way of including him in her life here. It was not the life they planned. They were going to get a ranch out on the south Texas plains and raise dogs and kids and roses. He loved roses.

Her parents wouldn't be pleased. They'd abandoned their rural upbringing for the city life, going to law school and setting up their own firm in Boston, which she was expected to join.

She never wanted to do that. She'd only ever been interested in two things: literature and law enforcement. When she dropped out of Boston College, she'd joined up right away.

Then she met Martinez. She loved him as widely and deeply as she did poetry and police work. When she lost him, she lost two of her three anchors. She was no longer a lover, no longer a soldier. She had nothing but the cold consolation of words to comfort her. Even Shakespeare came up short now.

Her parents saw her fiancé's death as an opening and resumed their campaign to bring her back to Boston to finish college and go on to law school. Sometimes she wondered if it just might be easier to follow the path they'd already laid out for her rather than try to blaze a new one on her own. But then, she wasn't really alone.

Elvis sat patiently at the door, ears perked, waiting for her. She plodded up the porch steps to his side, unlocking the door and shouldering her way in, dropping their packs onto the oak hall tree, and kicking off her boots. "Come on in," she said.

The Malinois bounded in. The cabin's wide windows were full of late-afternoon shadows. A northwest wind shuddered through the tall white pines and sugar maples. With the approach of sunset came the slow quieting of the forest.

The growing silence unsettled Mercy. She shook off her unease and padded to the kitchen, where the dog waited.

She grabbed a peanut-butter chew treat from the cookie jar and tossed it his way. "This should keep you busy for a while."

He caught it easily and retreated to his bed. Which was really Mercy's couch. A deluxe dog bed occupied a corner of the kitchen, but Elvis never slept there. He preferred her sofa, with its soft butter-colored leather, preferably nested in the quilts she kept at each end. A maroon one for her, a teal one for him.

When she moved in here, she'd brought her great-grandmother's cherry four-poster bed that she and Martinez had intended to share. But she couldn't bear to sleep there alone. So she usually slept on the couch with Elvis.

Mercy left him there chomping away. She took a long, hot

shower, scrubbing away the dirt and sweat of the day. Then she slipped into her favorite moose-print flannel pajamas.

She went back to the couch, but Elvis wasn't there. She looked around the great room and over into the kitchen, but no dog. He hadn't had supper, so he should be at her feet, bowl in his mouth. The fact that he wasn't meant he was stressed out.

She knew how he felt—and where she'd find him. She went to the far side of the cabin to the workout room that had been a screened-in porch. She'd furnished it with a heavy bag and weights, but the reason she and Elvis loved it was the yoga mat and candles and soft music. It was here that they came when the stress of the outside world threatened to overwhelm them.

The shepherd was there, curled up on the orange mat. He looked up at her as if to say, *What took you so long?*

She lit a candle, sweetening the air with lavender and sage, and turned on her playlist, a mix of Gregorian chant and kirtan. She settled cross-legged on the mat, and Elvis scooted over to her, dropping his head in her lap. She closed her eyes as he did.

As the haunting intonations enveloped them, she breathed in and out, stroking the dog's dark muzzle. She could hear his quick panting slow and deepen as her own breathing slowed and deepened, and they fell into a synchronized rhythm.

They sat together like this for a long time, until Elvis nudged her hands with a cold, wet nose. A signal that he was feeling better and ready for dinner. Funny how he was always quicker than she to know when they needed to sit and breathe and when they were ready to move on.

She followed him into the kitchen and poured herself a glass of Big Barn Red and made a roast beef and Vermont cheddar sandwich. Slicing it in half, she placed one side in his bowl and laid the bowl on the coffee table before him. She carried her wine and her half of the sandwich to her side of the couch.

"Bon appétit!" She lifted her glass to him, and he devoured his dinner on cue.

Mercy nibbled at her sandwich and gave the rest to Elvis. He gobbled it down, then stretched out on the sofa. Within minutes he was asleep. She knew that she should sleep, too. But her head was crowded with the mysteries of the day: the missing baby, the corpse, the buried explosives—or lack thereof. And Troy Warner, the lifeguard who grew up to be a game warden.

She grabbed her glass of wine and went out to the porch, settling into a rocker. She watched the stars blink into view and reminded herself to notice how beautiful it was here and how lucky she was to be home when so many others were not.

Even if it was lonely sometimes.

TROY spent a couple of hours at the regional office filing reports. He put out an Amber Alert on Baby Doe, while Susie Bear slept at his feet. Troy, who could use some shut-eye himself, whistled for the slumbering dog to wake up. Together they trudged to the truck, and Troy drove home to the fire tower on the Battenkill River.

He had refashioned the forty-seven-foot tower—an open fifteen-by-fifteen-foot room on stilts—into a three-story home by enclosing the lower portion and keeping the original lookout at the top. The ground floor housed the kitchen; his living space, which doubled as a bedroom, was on the second floor.

He loved this place. He opened the red door—the only painted surface in the all-wood structure—and Susie Bear lumbered up the steep wooden stairs that flanked the far wall. She was as eager to hit the sheets as he was. And he was right behind her.

But first he climbed a final flight of stairs to the top of the tower. He opened the sliding-glass door and stepped onto the deck. The outlook provided a 360-degree vista of the surrounding area, a splendor of forest, river, and sky. Gazing out always reassured him that life was bigger than his own problems. Even after his wife ran off with that flatlander from Florida.

Tonight the jagged tapestry of treetops against the sweep of stars moved him more than he could say. He stared at the North Star for a long time before going back inside and down the stairs. Pulling the Murphy bed out of the wall seemed like too much trouble, so he crashed on the sectional with his dog, still in his uniform, and dozed off to the comforting sound of canine snoring.

Chapter 3

Captain Floyd Thrasher stood in the reception area and waved Troy into the small office. He scratched Susie Bear's head and led the way to the operations room. They were the only people there today, which was the way Troy liked it when he had to be in the office at all. Most of his time was spent in the field. One of the many reasons he loved this job.

Thrasher, on the other hand, seemed completely at home in every environment. With the punctilious bearing of an officer and the gravelly voice of a blues baritone, he seemed much taller than his five-ten frame, due to his super-erect carriage and salt-and-pepper buzz cut. His eyes were the kind of blue-green that could melt a woman's heart or nail a grown man to the floor.

"Dr. Darling has narrowed the time of death of the victim in the woods to about three years," Thrasher said. "Still no ID."

"I can check the missing-persons files from that time."

"Do it. But make it fast. It's really not our problem. And the unlicensed fishermen and drunk ATVers and pirate rafters will be waking up soon, and you'll need to get back in the field."

"Yes, sir." Troy knew that the captain didn't like the idea of people dying in their woods any more than he did.

"You've got an hour," Thrasher said. "I'll be in my office."

Troy logged on to the computer and began checking missing-persons reports filed around the time of the victim's death. Three adult males had been reported missing during the specified time period: Gary Bowles, Jack Hess, and Wayne Herbert.

There was a story behind each of the missing individuals. Bowles turned out to be on a bender in Portsmouth and spent a few nights in jail before taking off and showing up months later in Glastonbury. Hess ran off with his sister-in-law and sent his brother a postcard from Cabo featuring the happy couple on the beach. As far as anyone knew, he was still in Mexico.

Wayne Herbert, the last guy on the list, had never been heard from again. He was known to be an avid hunter and was suspected of poaching time and again, but the game warden's predecessors had never been able to catch him in the act.

Troy printed out the case files, missing-persons report, and photos of the victim and the belt buckle and then whistled for the dog. She padded along behind him as he knocked on the captain's door and then filled him in on Wayne Herbert.

"Oh, yes, the Herberts," said Thrasher. "Quite the family. Drinking, disturbing the peace, poaching." They both hated poachers. Game wardens were pledged to protect wildlife—and poaching was one of the premier crimes against wildlife.

"Sneaky, though."

"Yeah. We've only caught them at it once. Before your time. But I'm surprised Wayne might be our vic. I always thought he hightailed it to Canada to get away from his mother."

Troy knew that since he'd joined up, the Herberts had been suspected of running dogfights. "Queen of the Pit Bulls."

"Exactly. But we've never been able to prove anything."

"We will." The only thing Troy hated more than poaching was dogfighting. He found himself clenching his fists.

Thrasher grinned. "Give her my regards."

It sounded like the captain wanted Troy to check out the Herberts on his own. The state police wouldn't like that. The game wardens were supposed to stick to fish and wildlife. But the captain didn't trust state police to handle what went wrong in his woods. Neither did Troy. He nodded in understanding.

"Watch your back. And your dog," Thrasher said.

"Yes, sir."

"And then get on to the fishing-license checks."

WAYNE Herbert's mother, Florence "Flo" Herbert, lived with her two younger sons in a double-wide on twenty acres in southwestern

Rutland County. A six-foot-high chain-link fence surrounded the vinyl-sided manufactured home and its outbuildings on about a square acre of the family's land.

NO TRESPASSING signs were posted along this rusted barricade. A new lock hung on the big gate fronting the road entering the compound, but the smaller lock on the people-wide gate was busted. Troy let himself in, Susie Bear on his heels.

All was quiet at the house. The yard was cluttered with junk, and the path to the front door was strewn with timber. They'd picked their way about halfway through the wreckage, when the door swung open and two enormous pit bulls charged out.

"Truck!" Troy yelled at Susie Bear. The pit bulls stumbled among the junk in the yard, slowing down long enough for him and his dog to retreat behind the fence. He slammed the gate shut just as the beasts flew at him.

A sharp whistle stopped the dogs cold. They barreled back to the house, disappearing inside. Troy hightailed it to his vehicle, and he and Susie Bear took cover. He needed to calm the situation down before the Herbert boys did something even stupider than setting dogs on him. He pulled the megaphone from the back of the cab as the first rock cracked his headlight. Too late, he thought, looking up at the open window from where he believed the rock had come.

"Down," he ordered his dog. He pointed under the vehicle, and she reluctantly squirmed under its bed.

"Mrs. Herbert, this is Game Warden Troy Warner." He kept his voice calm and deep. That sureness echoed through the megaphone. "I am here to talk to you about your son Wayne."

A sudden movement at the window. Troy glimpsed a slingshot appear and disappear. Another stone flew through the air.

"Tell your boys to put away those slingshots before I lose my patience and arrest them for assault," he warned. "Do you want to know what happened to your firstborn or not?"

The barking and the rock slinging stopped. Troy waited.

The front door opened again, and a small, wiry woman in her mid-fifties stepped out, wearing camouflage cargo pants and an army-green T-shirt. Her gunmetal-gray hair was chopped off at her chin, and rattlesnake tattoos roiled up her sinewy arms. On her heels followed two enormous young men. But the square-built boys with arms the size of their mother's thighs were just the window dressing. She was the one in charge.

"Come on in," she called to him. "We don't bite."

"Yes, ma'am." Troy allowed himself a small smile. "I'm going to bring in documentation for your review." He opened the truck door and retrieved his folder. "Don't hurt my dog."

He snapped his fingers, and Susie Bear crawled out from under the truck. He pointed to the backseat, and she whined. She didn't like being left behind. But she did as she was told.

"Stay," he said. "Good girl."

He closed the door quietly and strode through the yard.

Mrs. Herbert stepped forward at his approach and shook the hand he offered her with a grip worthy of a wrestler.

"Mrs. Herbert," Troy said formally.

"Warden." She nodded to the young behemoths behind her. "My boys, Louis and Paul."

Troy shook her boys' hands as well, each the size of hams.

"Come on in." She waved a serpent arm at him and marched through the front door into the living room.

He trailed after her, taking his time to note the position of the dogs and the sons. The dogs ran to greet Mrs. Herbert, snarling at him. The sons sat in two matching supersized recliners the color of dried blood. Troy didn't trust the dogs or the sons.

"Down," Mrs. Herbert ordered, and the pit bulls fell back. She sat on the large couch that sat between the recliners. It was the same oxblood color as the rest of the furniture. The only ornaments adorning the walls were impressively antlered buck and moose heads. The other decoration of note was a black-skirted round table, which served as a shrine to the lost son.

Troy stepped over to the table to take a closer look. A sentimental tableau telling the story of a young man's life: smiling baby pictures, surly middle school portraits, photographs of Wayne as a full-grown man—longer and leaner than his brothers, but with the same short sandy brown hair and brown eyes—posing with his mother, his brothers, his dogs, and his guns.

"He's a good boy, my Wayne." She joined him at the shrine.

"Yes, ma'am."

"Why did you come here?" Her voice betrayed her fear. "You're just a fish cop. What could you know about Wayne?"

"Please sit." Troy ushered her back to the sofa. "Remains of an adult male have been found in the Lye Brook Wilderness."

"And you think it might be my Wayne."

"We're trying to determine the identity of the deceased at this time." Troy paused. "He died around the same time that your son disappeared three years ago."

"That could be just coincidence." Mrs. Herbert lifted her chin. She straightened on her seat, her pale lips a thin, hard line.

"Maybe," he said gently. This was the worst part of his job. The part that made him feel inadequate. The part that broke his heart. "But preliminary forensics indicate that when the victim died, he was about the same size and age of your son."

"Victim?"

"The deceased was the victim of foul play."

"How?" The woman closed her eyes against the news she'd hoped never to hear.

"The victim died of a gunshot wound."

Her eyes snapped open. "How, exactly?"

"A bullet to the brain." He plowed on. "There was evidence that the victim suffered a broken femur earlier in his life."

Mrs. Herbert gripped her hands together. "Which leg?"

"The left," he said.

She looked down, away from him. "Wayne broke his left leg playing hockey when he was ten years old."

"I'd like to show you a picture of an object found among the remains." Troy pulled the photograph of the pewter belt buckle from his folder and held it out in front of her.

A sharp intake of breath, and she sagged, body crumpling.

Her sons, who had remained apart and silent, came and sat beside her then on the sofa, one on each side.

"He was very proud of that buckle," she said, her voice ragged.

"Said it was specially made by a master jeweler. Can't recall his name. But Wayne told me the buckle was one of the last ones the jeweler made before he retired and went back to Ireland."

Troy drew a pen and notebook out. "And when was that?"

"Three, four years ago. Maybe five. I don't know. When can we bring our boy home?" Her voice was thick with resignation.

"We'll need to confirm that the remains are Wayne's." Troy paused, considering the evidence: the timing, the broken femur, the belt buckle. Odds were that the victim was indeed Wayne Herbert. "Compare dental records, conduct DNA testing."

"The police asked for his dental records and his hairbrush for DNA when he went missing. In case . . ." She trailed off.

"Good. That should help facilitate things."

"I never thought they'd really need them."

Troy realized that she'd never believed that her son was dead. Like Thrasher, she thought he'd simply up and left. "Where did you think your son had gone?"

"I don't know. Canada, maybe. Or someplace warm. Mexico. He was always talking about making a fresh start."

She closed her eyes again. Troy was wearing out his welcome. But there were still a few things he'd like to ask about.

As if she'd read his mind, she opened her eyes, now dark with sorrow. "What else do you need to know?"

"Did your son have any enemies?"

"Everyone loved Wayne," she said.

Paul and Louis didn't say anything, but he could see by the way they glanced at each other over her head that they knew more about their brother's activities than their mother did. Or at least more than she was willing to acknowledge.

Troy addressed the sons. "So, guys, can you think of anyone who might want to hurt your brother?"

"Everyone loved Wayne," she repeated.

"Not everyone, Ma," said Paul.

"The tree huggers hated him," said Louis.

"Tree huggers?"

"Losers always talking about saving the trees," said Paul.

Mrs. Herbert rolled her eyes. "They're all about 'reducing their footprint' and living 'off the grid.'"

"That Adam dude hated Wayne," said Paul.

"Adam?"

"I don't know his last name. But he's the worst of them. Always sneaking around in the woods, looking for trouble."

Mrs. Herbert shook her head. "They don't like outdoorsmen like Wayne. But they're basically harmless."

Troy knew that to people like the Herberts, *outdoorsman* was code for *poacher*.

"Wayne had been in trouble with the law from time to time," he said. "Poaching, drug dealing, gambling."

"No one ever proved anything. My Wayne was a good boy."

She shrank back against the couch. Her sons leaned over her in a tunnel of protection. A closing of the ranks. Time to go.

"Thank you for your time. I'm so sorry for your loss."

"You'll find him, then." It was an order, not a request. "The man who killed my Wayne. You'll find him."

He nodded. "If you think of anything else . . ." he said, looking directly at Paul and Louis. They said nothing.

He left them there, the surviving brothers flanking their mother, her shuttered face as solid and impenetrable as stone.

As soon as he shut the door quietly behind him, the keening began. Mrs. Herbert's terrible wails followed him all the way to the truck and echoed in his ears long after he'd turned down the rutted dirt road and driven away.

MERCY had slept late, hours past her usual rise-and-shine routine. Elvis raised his head and looked at her, dark eyes bright, eager to start the day. Martinez's dog was always eager to start the day.

"Coffee first." She groaned and dragged herself upright.

The shepherd padded to the kitchen ahead of her, waltzing on his feet as she filled the pot with water and ground the beans. As soon as she finished her prep, he soared for the back door. Mercy slipped on her Wellies and let the dog out.

She stepped onto the wide deck. The sun shone brightly in

a cloudless blue sky. The unnamed anxiety that had plagued her yesterday was gone, replaced by the dull pain of prolonged sorrow. Today was the anniversary of her fiancé's death. She'd mourn later, she thought. After she found that missing baby.

Usually she'd pull weeds in the garden while she waited for Elvis to do his business. But rather than head for the deep end of the lawn, Elvis shot toward the barn, barking all the way.

Mercy scrambled after him. He was scratching at the wagon doors of the barn. She ignored him, spotting footprints in the mud leading to the small door to the left. "Quiet," she ordered.

He stopped mid-bark, trotting over to her. Noiselessly, she opened the door, the shepherd at her side. They crept across the floor. There were three horse stalls on the right side and a tack room in the far corner. All signs and smells, apparently, pointed to the tack room, but she checked each stall anyway. Empty.

Slowly, she and the dog approached the opening of the tack room. She knew Elvis could smell intruders on the other side of the jamb by the way he stood, every muscle tense, his carriage proud.

She flattened against the wall and whipped her head around in a quick surveillance of the room. Empty.

Except for a pile of horse blankets along the wall. Just sizable enough to cover someone small.

"Okay," she said quietly. "Go."

Elvis barreled through the tack room, halting at the stack of stable covers. He turned back to Mercy and wagged his tail.

Friend not foe, she thought, and quickly strode across the space and tugged the sheets away from the wall. Baby Doe looked up at her and smiled, even as the teenage girl holding her hid her face.

"Peekaboo," said Mercy.

The baby laughed, and the girl lifted her face. She was about eighteen, slim and fair and scared.

"Are you her mother?"

The girl nodded.

Mercy fought the urge to lambaste the girl for leaving the baby in the woods. "Would you like a cup of tea?"

The girl nodded again.

"Come on inside, then." She held out her hand.

The girl looked at the dog, who pounded his tail on the floor and licked Baby Doe's tiny bare foot. The infant giggled again.

Mercy grinned. "Elvis loves babies."

THE girl's name was Amy Walker. She was very hungry and, once Mercy served up her famous blueberry pancakes, very chatty. In a stream-of-consciousness, nonlinear way.

"I named her Helena, after the character in *A Midsummer Night's Dream*." Amy cut a piece of pancake for her girl, whom she held on her lap with one hand. "That's Shakespeare."

"Yes." Mercy pushed the Corse Maple Farm syrup a little closer to Amy. "It's a beautiful name for a beautiful baby."

"Yeah." Amy swapped her fork for the syrup. "Dad took us to the Corse Farm sugarhouse when I was little." She drenched the stack in the sweet amber liquid. "It was so much fun. Even Mom had a good time." She swirled her finger in the syrup and lifted it to the baby's lips. Helena tested it with her tongue, then beamed. Amy beamed back at her, showing deep dimples in a heart-shaped face framed by choppily cut light brown hair.

The young mother looked even younger than her eighteen years when she smiled. At least she claimed to be eighteen, as of Valentine's Day, her favorite day of the year until Helena was born on Thanksgiving. Now Amy liked Thanksgiving best.

Mercy doubted she had made that up. Or anything else. Only an accomplished liar could talk so much and so fast and so randomly and make it up as she went along all at the same time.

"Where are your parents now?"

Amy frowned. "Dad died when I was ten years old."

"I'm so sorry."

"He was the best, you know. The best." Her dark blue eyes filled with tears. "I still miss him every day."

The baby, sensing her mother's distress, started to wail. Elvis leaped from the couch, skirting the table to check on Helena.

Amy bounced her crying baby on her knee, and the little one settled down. "I think she'll take a nap now." She stood up.

Amy was a good mother. So why did she leave her alone in the woods? Mercy cleared the table, one eye on Amy, who wandered around the great room snuggling Helena until she fell asleep. The young mother spread a quilt on the couch and laid the baby down. Elvis curled up on his side, his dark eyes on the infant.

Amy backed away softly. Drawn to the floor-to-ceiling bookcases, she fingered the spines of the many leather-bound copies of the Bard's plays, then pulled down a cheap paperback copy of *Othello* and studied it. "I guess you like Shakespeare."

"Yes, I studied him in college."

Amy opened the book and started reading, somewhere in the middle, as far as Mercy could see. After a couple of minutes, the girl seemed to sense Mercy watching her and looked up.

"I thought you were a soldier." She put down *Othello*, still open as if not to lose her place, and pointed to the photograph of a smiling Mercy and Martinez in uniform in Afghanistan.

"I was." She smiled. "Soldiers like Shakespeare, too, you know. He wrote a lot about the military."

"Is that why you like his plays so much?"

"Partly. But mostly I like him because he makes me feel better about being human."

Amy stared at her, then tapped the silver frame with her fingers. "You look happy in this picture." She regarded her carefully, as if searching for that same happiness in her face now. "Is that your boyfriend?"

She nodded. "My fiancé."

"Cute. He looks like a good guy."

"He was." Mercy glanced away. "He died."

"I'm so sorry." Amy sighed. "The good guys are always dying on you. Like my dad. And your fiancé." She turned back to the wall of books and tapped the spine of a slim paperback of *A Midsummer Night's Dream*. "We did this one junior year. In Mrs. Berentz's English lit class. I played Helena."

"I bet you were good." Mercy could see her in the role of the devoted, thoughtful romantic.

"I was. Mrs. Berentz said so." Amy smiled. "She liked me. She said I was college material. Like that was ever going to happen."

"It's not too late." Mercy climbed up the ladder and retrieved a stunning limited edition of the Bard's most beloved comedy.

"I never graduated. Quit when I got pregnant senior year." Amy paused. "But it's cool. I'm a mama now."

Mercy climbed back down and handed the girl the book.

Amy held the old volume carefully and slowly flipped through the pages. "These illustrations are so pretty. I still think it's weird. A soldier who likes Shakespeare."

"You sound like my parents." Mercy grinned. "They wanted me to be a lawyer, like them."

"Boring."

"You have no idea." She laughed at that, then sobered. "But speaking of mothers, would you like to call yours?"

"No, thanks." For the first time, the girl looked scared.

"Are you all right?"

The baby fussed a little. Amy shut the old book and picked Helena up. "You can't tell my mother I was here."

"Okay."

"Or my stepfather." She shot to her feet. "Especially him."

The bitterness in her voice told Mercy everything she needed to know. "Okay."

"Promise." She bounced the startled baby against her chest. Up and down. Up and down. Up and down.

"I promise." Mercy fought the urge to reach for the child. "I'm sorry. I didn't mean to upset you."

Amy wound down the bouncing to a slow swaying.

"What about the father?" Mercy asked gently.

"No." The girl's voice was firm.

"Not a good guy?"

"He's not a bad guy. I mean, I love him. And he loves Helena." She shook her head. "But he's all stage-five clinger now."

"How's that?"

"It started out fine." She settled onto the sofa, holding Helena on her lap. "Adam is an artist. Real creative. Real smart. A genius, you know?.." She paused. "You should see the sculptures he makes.

Out of stones and salvage and wood. Recycled art, it's called."

"Art trouvé," said Mercy.

"Yeah. He only uses reclaimed wood. He loves trees."

Mercy sat on the arm of the couch. "Trees?"

"He's totally into saving the woods." Amy smiled. "We held rallies, planted disease-resistant elm trees. To save the forest."

"That sounds like good work."

"It was." Amy's smile faded. "But after Helena was born, Adam wanted to do more. He said we had to live off the grid. Deep into nowhere. He wouldn't let us leave."

"Stage-five clinger."

"Yeah." Amy kissed the top of her baby's head. "It's so not fair. He gets all jealous, when he's the one with the crazy exes."

"What do you mean?"

"Groupies. They're the worst."

"Adam has groupies?"

"Art lovers, he said." Amy rolled her eyes. "Always hanging around. When we got together, he stopped hooking up with them. They weren't happy about it. They all hated me."

"That must have been hard."

"Yeah. But eventually they all went away. I was glad at first. I wanted him all to myself. He was so sweet. But then we had Helena and he changed. It started getting really weird. I just had to get us out of there."

"Is that why you left the baby in the woods?" Mercy held her breath, hoping for an answer that she—and Child Protective Services—could accept.

"I thought we could slip away from Adam on our bird-watching walk. Lately that's the only time he lets us out of the compound. He says walks are good for the baby. We stay off-trail, where hikers don't usually go." She looked at Mercy. "But we see you and Elvis every morning. Like clockwork."

"Really? I never realized . . ." Some investigator she was.

"We keep out of sight." Amy laughed. "But Elvis finds us off-trail and comes and says hello. He likes the baby."

Mercy smiled. "Yes, he does." She suspected Elvis was better than she was at practically everything. "How did you get away from Adam?"

"Sometimes he gets inspired with his art and tells us to go back to the compound on our own. He's very secretive about his work. Doesn't like anybody to see it before it's finished. I figured the next time that happened, we just wouldn't go back."

"But something went wrong."

"Max came with us."

"Max?"

"He's Adam's best friend. An artist like him, only creepier. I don't think he likes me. Or Helena. He calls us a distraction."

"Back to what happened in the woods," Mercy said gently.

"Adam told me to take the baby and go back to the camp. I headed off that way, then doubled back and started for Route Seven. I heard Max and Adam fighting. Max was yelling something about me and the baby. I got scared and cut through the blowdown to get away from Max. I heard someone behind me and figured it was him. I saw Elvis on the other side of the blowdown and knew Helena would be safe with him. I put her in the clearing and ran the other way. I didn't know what else to do."

"It sounds like you did the right thing." That was all Mercy needed to know. Now she could text Troy and tell him Amy was here and that the baby was safe.

Elvis sat up, ears perked. He bolted for the door, barking.

"What's wrong?" The young mother shrunk back.

"Stay here." Mercy went to the front window and saw a forest-green truck making its way up the long drive to the cabin.

"Who is it?" Amy was right behind her.

"Troy Warner. The game warden."

"Adam says cops are bad news." Amy backed away from the window. "Don't let him in. Please."

"There's an Amber Alert out on the baby. You could get in big trouble if we don't talk to him. I could get in big trouble."

"I don't know."

"I know Troy Warner. He's a good guy. With a good dog. We can trust him. You'll see."

Amy frowned. "Whatever."

TROY PULLED THE TRUCK UP next to Mercy's red Jeep. On his way to Stratton Pond, he'd stopped by the office and told the captain about his encounter with the Herberts.

"So Wayne Herbert might well be our victim, after all," said Thrasher. "Of course, we'll have to wait for DNA analysis to confirm. Good work."

"Thank you, sir."

"The Amber Alert has attracted a couple of good leads. A Canadian bird-watcher named Rufus Flanigan reported seeing a teenage girl hiking in the woods with an infant. He claimed to have seen the two walking through the forest many times over the past few weeks. Another witness, Mabel Hennessy, gave a young female hitchhiker and a baby a ride from a gas station not far from the hospital to a convenience store in East Dorset."

"That's on my way."

"Your new girlfriend lives right near there."

"Sir?"

"Mercy Carr."

"She's, uh, a little young, sir," he said, remembering that summer long ago.

Thrasher raised an eyebrow. "How so?"

"When I was in high school, she was just a kid."

"High school is over. She's all grown up now." He checked his watch. "Better get to East Dorset. Start with Mercy Carr."

Which is how Troy found himself here with Susie Bear at the Mercy Carr residence. Before he could knock on the orange door, it opened. Just by a couple of inches.

"Hi," Mercy said. "Can you give me just a minute?"

"Sure."

She disappeared behind the door, but Elvis shot out before it closed behind her. The dogs raced off for the barn. Susie Bear started to bark, her trademark "I've found something" howl. Elvis joined in, aggressive intruder–alert mode kicking in.

Troy jogged after the dogs, wondering what had them so fired up. Maybe there was a baby hiding in the barn. He skidded to a stop just as Susie Bear began to paw at the handle on the side door of the barn.

A simple latch she'd figure out in no time. "Down!" he ordered.

Susie Bear shook her pumpkin head at him but did drop back away from the door. She didn't stop barking. Neither did Elvis.

He heard footfalls behind him and turned to see Mercy running toward him.

"What are you doing down here?" She seemed confused.

"What's in the barn?"

"We need to talk. Come on up to the house."

"What's in the barn?" He repeated. "The dogs are alerting."

"There's nothing in there. Tools, hay, snowmobile—the usual." She spoke loudly to be heard over the bellowing. "Let's go back up to the house. I need to show you something."

"I'm going into that barn." He didn't know why she was trying to keep him out of there.

"Fine." She opened the side door. "But it's a waste of time."

Susie Bear shot into the barn, Elvis on her heels.

Troy marched after the dogs into the tack room. Susie Bear lay on the floor, her nose within an inch of a pink baby blanket.

"Good girl." Troy pulled a treat from his pocket and tossed it to her. He gave Elvis one, too. Then he turned to Mercy and held out the blanket. "What's the meaning of this?"

"I've been trying to tell you. I found the baby and her mother in the barn this morning. Well, Elvis found them. I was going to call you right after I got them something to eat."

"Right."

"They're in the house. I was going to let you in, I was just reassuring her that you were, you know, good people."

"Let's go." He whistled for Susie Bear and headed out of the barn. Mercy and Elvis kept up with them.

"Look, she's just a kid. A scared kid."

"Maybe. But she did leave her baby alone in the woods."

"She had a good reason. She loves that child. You'll see."

She let them all into the cabin. Once inside, he stepped aside and allowed her to lead him into the great room, a towering space with a stone fireplace and an impressive wall of books.

The living room was separated from the open-style kitchen by an antique oak dining table and chairs. Beyond was an island topped with reclaimed wood and three steel barstools.

But no baby. And no mother.

"She was right here with the baby, I swear." Mercy looked around. "Amy," she called. "Come on out. Everything's fine."

They searched the rest of the small house—a neat master bedroom in blue and white; a small yellow guest room; and an odd workout room, equipped with a heavy bag, a yoga mat and meditation pillow, and a small altar with candles and family photos. Mercy Carr, he was beginning to realize, was a complicated woman. And as the captain said, all grown up now.

"I think it's safe to say they're not in the house," she said.

Troy spotted *A Midsummer Night's Dream* on the table. A yellow scrap of paper stuck out of it. He retrieved the paper. The note read, "Thanks for breakfast." He handed it to Mercy.

She shook her head. "I thought I was getting somewhere with her. I guess she just panicked when you pulled up."

Rain was falling now, and the skies were gray outside the big windows that ran along the back of the cabin.

"I'm sorry. I was going to text you."

"When?"

"Right before you showed up. Really."

"Look, I understand. But you interfered with an ongoing investigation and failed to report on an Amber Alert."

"I thought I could help. She needs help." She told him about the child's possessive father and Amy's abusive stepfather.

"Susie Bear and I will find her. We'll start with the woods."

"We'll come with you."

"You've done quite enough for one day." Troy's cell phone beeped. A text from Thrasher: MISSING BOATER. "I've got to go."

"What are you going to do? Amy and Helena are in trouble."

"We can't help her unless she files a complaint."

"But if she comes in, what will Child Protective Services do? Amy's only eighteen. A kid with a baby."

"She's an adult in the eyes of the law." Amy Walker could possibly be charged with child endangerment.

"Yes, but she's got nowhere to go." Mercy gave him a pleading look. "Don't call CPS. I can find her."

Troy hesitated. By law he had twenty-four hours to report suspicion of child endangerment. So technically he would not be breaking the law if he waited a few hours.

"I'll think about it." He whistled for Susie Bear, who leaped to his side. He hurried out of the cabin with the dog and went to his truck. He could hear Mercy and Elvis on their heels.

"Good-bye," she yelled after him.

Troy waved his hand without looking back. He hustled Susie Bear into the Ford F-150, slamming the door in his haste. They had a missing boater to find and a murder to solve.

And the day had barely begun.

Chapter 4

"THAT WENT WELL," Mercy said to Elvis as they stood together on the porch and watched them drive away.

She felt energized. Today the mountains and the woods and the sky spoke to her—not calling her to escape, but calling her to act. Elvis felt this sense of mission, too; she could see that in the way he nudged her with his cold nose, bullying her to get moving. She felt useful for the first time since Martinez died.

This is what it felt like to engage with the world, to care what happened next. This was dangerous. But this was living.

The Malinois cocked his dark triangular ears.

"I know, you're right. We'd better go find them before they get into any more trouble."

Within minutes they were on the move. The rainfall had stopped as quickly as it had begun, making tracking easy. She found disturbed debris and footprints in the mud leading into the forest.

The morning shower made the work easier for Elvis, too, because cool, moist air kept the scent closer to the ground.

They traced the young mother and child northwest through the woods to the county road. There the trail ended abruptly.

"Probably hitched a ride," she told the dog.

There was another place to look.

"Home." She trudged back through the forest, Elvis bounding ahead. When they arrived at the cabin, the shepherd dozed while she Googled "Amy Walker." What came up confirmed what Amy had told her. She'd been a student at Northshire Regional High School and a member of the drama club. The baby's birth announcement was reported in the *Northshire Review-Journal*. And Karen Walker, Amy's mother, had posted photos of her daughter and her granddaughter on Facebook.

"Bingo." She researched the mother and found that she lived with her husband, Donald Walker, northwest of Sunderland. She knew her mother's house wouldn't be Amy's first choice, but if she felt she'd nowhere else to go . . . it was worth a shot.

Mercy snapped her computer shut. "Wake up, soldier." At the sound of her voice, the dog awoke. "Time for a ride."

THE Walkers' residence was more dilapidated than Mercy had expected. There was nothing but dirt where the front yard should be. The tin-roofed farmhouse had seen better days, its gray paint peeling. The porch sagged under the weight of years of wear and tear, neglect, and three abandoned sofas.

But what struck her the most were the cats. She sat in the Jeep, stunned by dozens of tabbies, torties, and calicos peeking out from under the house and cuddling on the couches.

Other than the cats on the porch, the place seemed deserted.

"Stay," she told Elvis, but she left the hatchback open so she could call for him if she needed him.

She stepped carefully around the cats, few of whom bothered to move. Many were lethargic. At the front door she paused, then rapped sharply on the faded wood. The door creaked open.

"Hello," she called. "Mrs. Walker? Mr. Walker?" She could

hear the muted broadcast of a soccer game on television.

A black cat slipped through her legs. Her nose was smudged with red. A sudden roar from the TV signaled a goal, and the little pussy sprang off the porch. Still no sign of the Walkers.

Mercy whistled for Elvis, and he tore up to the house and halted at her hip. At her nod they entered the house together.

The front room was cluttered with empty Bud Light cans and old newspapers. In the middle of the room, a few feet from the television, loomed a faux-leather recliner, its back tilted toward Mercy. She could see a pale hairy hand spilling off to one side.

"Mr. Walker?" she asked as she circled the recliner to get a better look.

Splayed in the seat was a thick-bellied middle-aged man with white spindly legs sticking out of Hawaiian-print shorts and a white sleeveless T-shirt that partially revealed a colorful tattoo wrapping around his left bicep and disappearing over his shoulder. He had a broad, jowly face and dyed jet-black hair.

But the most striking thing about him was the Buck hunting knife that stuck out of his chest, the fatal bull's-eye of a dark red blood blotch that stained his T-shirt with death.

SHE didn't think the man had been dead very long, so she and Elvis were careful as they checked the remaining rooms, but there was no one around. They checked the back of the house, too, but there was nothing out there but a weed-choked strip of concrete.

Nothing to do but contact the authorities. She texted Troy, and he texted her back right away to say that he was out in the field and that she should call the police and let them handle it.

She called 911, and while she waited for the authorities, she snapped photos of the scene with her cell while Elvis amused himself in the yard chasing cats. When she heard the sirens, she whistled for him. He trotted up to her, nose in the air. His way of bragging. That's when she realized he had something in his mouth.

"Drop it," she said, holding out her open palm. He opened his mug and let a purple pacifier fall into it.

She stared at the binky. A car door slammed. She slipped the pacifier into her pocket. By the time footfalls sounded on the porch, she and Elvis were standing quietly in the front room.

The young deputy who walked in the front door had rookie written all over him. His name was Josh Becker, and this was obviously his first violent death. He secured the crime scene—all by the book, with a careful, if nervous, thoroughness. Then he excused himself to throw up behind the house. After a couple of minutes, she could hear him call in the major crime unit before rejoining her inside.

"Detective Kai Harrington, the crime-scene search team, and Dr. Darling will be here shortly," he told her. "I'll take your statement, but he'll want to talk to you, too."

He took her name and address and phone number and asked her what happened. She told him and answered all his questions truthfully. Which was easy, because he was not a skilled investigator yet. She didn't say anything about the pacifier.

Before he could drill down more deeply, she was saved by the arrival of the medical examiner. The ever cheerful Dr. Darling gave her a smile. "Didn't expect to see you again so soon."

Mercy smiled back. "An unexpected pleasure."

"Indeed." The doctor leaned in conspiratorially. "We've got to stop meeting like this. Harrington won't like it."

"Detective Harrington didn't come to the other crime scene."

"He likes them fresh." Dr. Darling laughed as she began her examination of the dead man. "No glory in a cold case."

"I see."

Dr. Darling stared past Mercy. "Speak of the devil."

Harrington nodded at the medical examiner. He was tall and dark and slickly handsome, and he carried himself like he knew it in his way-beyond-his-pay-grade custom-tailored gray suit.

He introduced himself to Mercy with a quick, firm handshake and a frank once-over that infuriated her.

"I understand you discovered the body."

"Yes. I dropped by to see Mrs. Walker."

"And you just let yourself in?"

"The door was open. Nobody answered me when I called out. I knew something wasn't right."

"So you went in to check it out. Alone."

"I had my dog, Elvis, with me." She felt Elvis stiffen at her side as he stared down the detective.

"Right." Harrington stepped back under the shepherd's glare. "I understand this is your second crime scene in as many days."

"Just lucky, I guess." Mercy smiled, her equilibrium restored, thanks to Elvis.

"You say you were here to see Mrs. Walker. We're trying to locate her. Do you have any idea where she might be?"

"No." She stopped at the sound of a ruckus on the porch. A distraught woman burst into the room, Becker hot on her heels.

"I'm sorry, sir. She just barged right by me," said Becker.

"Don? What's happened?" The plump blonde rushed into the room, right smack into Harrington. Her resemblance to Amy Walker was striking: the daughter's same heart-shaped face and narrow build burdened and bloated with age in the mother.

"Where's my husband?" Her voice was shrill now.

"Karen Walker?" asked the detective. He turned a practiced look of compassion on the hysterical woman. "Let's talk on the porch," he said quietly, and ushered her out of the house, looking over his shoulder to tell Becker to take Mercy's statement.

"I already did," said Becker.

"Then do it again."

Becker turned to her. "I'm sorry, but . . ."

"It's fine." She walked him patiently through her discovery of the body again, then said, "You have all my information. If you need anything else, you know where to find me."

"You can't leave yet."

"I'm just in the way here." Mercy waved a hand at the team working the scene behind them. Through the front-room window, she could see Harrington talking to Mrs. Walker.

"Let her go." Dr. Darling was standing now, backing up from the victim. "Not much more to do here."

Becker relented, and Mercy mouthed a thank-you to the medical examiner. She whistled for Elvis. "Come on," she said, and took the long way around the house to the Jeep, hoping to eavesdrop on the detective. But all she heard was an angry Karen Walker.

"Amy hated him. If anyone killed my Donald, she did."

Mercy stopped to listen, hoping to hear more. Elvis heeled.

"Ms. Carr," yelled the detective. "Don't leave town."

Not trusting herself to turn and face them, she held up a hand and wiggled her fingers in reply, then strode toward the Jeep.

Elvis beat her there. He stretched himself out along the passenger door, his long nose pointed at the front tire.

"You are full of surprises today." She peered under the Jeep. A thin, straggly tiger-striped cat was curled under the wheel.

Elvis pushed at the cat's belly with his nose. The little feline only meowed faintly, winding herself more tightly into a ball.

"She must be sick." Mercy gathered the poor thing into her arms, intending to take it back to the house.

Elvis whined his disapproval.

"They're probably all sick. I'm going to call animal rescue."

The Belgian shepherd whimpered again. The cat lifted her tiny head and licked Mercy's hand with a scratchy pink tongue.

"Oh, all right." With a sigh, she deposited the too-quiet kitty on the floor in the back. "Now let's go, boy."

He jumped in, settling on the backseat to keep watch over his new charge, while Mercy drove them all home.

When she pulled into the long drive that led up to the cabin, Elvis alerted. She let him out of the Jeep, and he barged up the path to the cabin, barking so wildly that there was only one explanation Mercy could think of: Someone was in the house.

MERCY called Elvis back to her. "Quiet," she said, and they approached the door. She waved Elvis down into a sit and flattened herself against the wall. Peeking inside the window, she caught sight of a tall figure in dark clothes wearing gloves and a ski mask. He was running through the great room.

She hesitated, not wanting to go in, especially unarmed. But the dog was braver than she was. He broke away and raced for the front door. She scrambled after him and threw open the door. Elvis tore after the intruder in a blur of fur and fury.

Mercy dashed after the shepherd into the cabin and tripped, plunging to the floor. Elvis circled back to make sure she was all right. She hauled herself to her feet and stepped over the objects strewn across the floor. This guy had tossed the place—her closets emptied, her drawers dumped, her bookshelves cleared.

She heard the back door slam and hurried its way, Elvis bounding ahead. He scratched at the wood furiously, barking wildly, until she let him out. He sped across the lawn just as the man slipped into the woods. The shepherd was within yards of overtaking the prowler when a shot rang out. Elvis yelped.

"Down!" shouted Mercy, her voice echoing across the lawn. She dropped to the ground herself and crawled to cover.

Another shot, this one wide of both Elvis and Mercy. But it spooked the shepherd, and he hightailed it for the barn.

Out of her sight—and the shooter's. This was the hardest part, waiting and listening, and deciding whether to advance or retreat. Elvis had chosen retreat. Even though he was trained to wait for that order, Mercy was glad he was out of harm's way.

No more bullets. Just the sound of the man withdrawing into the forest. Mercy wanted to follow him. Martinez was whispering into her ear. *The dog comes first. Revenge will wait.*

As soon as she dared, Mercy ran for the barn. She let herself in, calling for Elvis. He didn't answer, and she couldn't see him. She listened hard. His heavy breathing led her to the first horse stall. The dog lay there, a tense ball of trembling fur. He lifted his head and strained to lick his left hindquarter.

Mercy knelt down beside the distressed dog. She gently separated the soft hair that ran along his backside. Elvis whined, and now Mercy could see why. A bullet had grazed his haunch.

"Poor baby," she cooed, stroking the shepherd's fine head. "We've got to get you checked out. Can you get up? Up?"

He lifted his heavy head, ears soft. His dark eyes were clouded with a pain she hadn't seen in them since Afghanistan.

She retrieved a horse blanket from the tack room. Folding it lengthwise, she made a sling for his hips. "Up," she said.

He moved forward easily on his front legs as she held his

backside aloft. She steered him slowly through the barn and across the yard to the Jeep, helping him into the backseat.

The kitten she'd rescued was still there on the floor, curled up tight. Patience should probably look her over, too. She texted her grandmother to let her know they were on the way.

She kept one hand on the wheel and the other on Elvis's head as she drove down the road. Patience Fleury O'Sullivan was a big-animal vet. She treated horses, goats, sheep, and, of course, cows in a fully equipped bright yellow mobile unit.

She also treated cats and dogs and other small animals here in the oversized Victorian farmhouse, with its attached barn that served as the hospital. She'd opened the Sterling Animal Hospital twenty years ago. Naming it in honor of her late husband, Sheriff Sterling O'Sullivan. Mercy spent her childhood summers here helping Patience—and she still helped out from time to time, now that she was back home in Vermont.

Her grandmother was outside waiting for them when they drove up in the Jeep. "My darling girl."

"Hi, Patience." She leaned in to give the lively gray-streaked blonde a kiss, struck as always by the energy and optimism that radiated from this woman she was lucky enough to call her grandmother. Not that Patience would allow that. She insisted everyone call her by her given name. A useful name, she said. One that reminded people of one of the great unsung virtues.

"I'll help you carry him inside." But when she opened the door, Elvis backed away from her, curling up in a tight ball. "Go around to the other side of the Jeep and open that door. I'll try on this side. Between the two of us, we'll get him out."

Mercy did as she was told, while her grandmother leaned in toward Elvis. "There's a sick cat on the floor here."

"Long story," said Mercy.

"One animal at a time." Patience laughed, and the shepherd's triangular ears perked up. She had a great laugh—one that lifted the spirits of all two-legged and four-legged creatures within its range. "Let's get you checked out." She held out a treat.

Elvis crawled across the seat and licked the treat out of her hand.

She backed up slowly. He followed, jumping out of the Jeep, even though he winced as his back legs hit the pavement.

They ushered the whimpering dog inside and laid him on the examination table. While Patience checked him out, Mercy told her all about Amy and Helena, Elvis and the game warden, the bones and maybe bombs in the woods, the sick cat, dead Donald Walker, the intruder, everything.

Finally Patience spoke. "You've both been through a lot during the past thirty-six hours."

Mercy nodded. She stroked the dog's dark, silky ears while Patience administered local anesthesia, then cleaned the gash.

"No stitches needed," said Patience. "Best possible outcome. But I'd like to give him a sedative and monitor him."

"Okay."

"You know it's not as bad as it looks."

"I know." Mercy knew exactly what it was like to get shot in the ass. Painful but not fatal. And embarrassing.

"You actually do." Patience laughed.

She laughed, too. Her grandmother was the rock in her life. Whenever she was with her, she felt both safe and hopeful.

Patience bandaged the injury and slipped Elvis a tranquilizer treat, then secured a cone around his neck. "Just to keep him from licking." She flipped the switch to lower the exam table.

As soon as the table began to move, Elvis stumbled off and ran out of the room.

"Let him go," said her grandmother. "He'll sleep it off. Promise." Patience squeezed her shoulder. "Now what about that cat?"

"I'll go get her." She went out to the Jeep and carried the kitten back. She could feel its tiny ribs right under the matted fur.

"Poor little thing." Patience took the bag of bones from her.

"I know. There are a lot more where she came from." Mercy described the abomination of abused cats at the Walkers'.

"I'll let the animal-rescue folks know." She sighed. "We'll organize an evacuation. This one is a cutie. What's her name?"

Mercy shrugged. "I don't know."

"She'll need a name."

"Okay."

"You're distracted. And it's not this tiger tabby you're worried about. It's the prowler. You're itching to go after him."

"Yeah." She looked away from Patience's sharp blue eyes.

"Without backup." Patience examined the cat. The kitty just stood there, body trembling, tail twitching, whiskers twiddling.

Mercy's grandfather never waited for backup, either. It had killed him in the end.

"Everyone's working overtime. The holiday."

"Call Troy Warner."

"He's a game warden. He's busy writing up drunk boaters."

"Troy Warner is a good man with a good dog." High praise from her grandmother. "He adopted Susie Bear, you know."

"Nice dog," Mercy said evenly.

"Great dog. She was a rescue from Alabama. Left to die in the woods down there. Half-starved, full of parasites."

"That's terrible." Mercy shook her head. "Seems fine now."

"Thanks to that handsome young man." She injected the cat with a slew of vaccines. "I'll have to keep her here for a couple days until those parasites are cleared up. And get her spayed."

"Whatever she needs. You know best."

"Remember that." Patience retrieved a cat carrier and slipped the kitty inside. "Let's go into the kitchen for a cup of tea."

"I should get going."

"You need to eat before you head off after an armed robber."

She knew there was no point in arguing. Patience had an infuriatingly gracious way of making you feel like an unreasonable boor if you disagreed with her.

They walked through the French doors that separated the clinic from the house. The kitchen was her favorite room—a large, welcoming space dominated by a big island topped with white marble. The yellow walls glowed in the natural light pouring in from the windows. And there on the long pine table, just where she hoped to see it, was a freshly baked carrot cake.

Her grandmother turned on the electric teapot.

"You cut the cake and I'll pour the tea," Patience said.

Time for a chat, thought Mercy. Tea and cake was how her grandmother always began delicate conversations.

"And how are you?" Patience handed her an orange mug filled with spicy chai.

"Fine." She sipped. "Tastes as good as it smells."

"Fine? Really?"

"Why wouldn't I be? I'm in your kitchen eating your cake."

"You found and lost a baby, then found and lost her mother; you discovered a corpse and maybe explosives; your house got tossed; your dog got shot . . . Have I missed anything?"

"When you put it that way . . ."

"And you met a man." Her grandmother snapped her fingers. "I knew I forgot something."

"What?" Mercy laughed. "Who?"

"Troy."

"Not my type," Mercy said, her mouth full of cake. "Besides, he's married to the most beautiful girl in the county."

"She ran off with a doctor from Orlando."

Mercy nearly choked. "Seriously? When?"

"Christmas before last." Patience sighed. "It hit him hard."

"I bet."

"It was inevitable. That lightweight was never right for him."

"And the game warden is no lightweight." Mercy smiled.

"He's a good man with a good dog."

"So you've said."

"I've been a widow for twenty years. I'm not lonely, mind you, but we women do have needs. That's why I have Claude."

Claude Renault was an animal surgeon from Quebec, a congenial man who kept her grandmother company.

"Don't look at me that way. I got married, I raised my children, and now I can play. With Claude." Patience reached for her hand and squeezed it. "Maybe you need a Plan B. Just as I did. You're young. You need to get married, have a family. You owe it to yourself."

"I can't do that now."

"Maybe not. But you will. You must."

That was enough grandmotherly advice for one day. Mercy pulled her hand away gently. "I have to go."

"I know. You want to catch your masked man."

"He's long gone by now."

"But you won't rest until you know that for sure."

"I should sit with Elvis."

"It's not like he's going to die," she said gently. "Promise."

Mercy hesitated.

"Go on. I'll take good care of the wonder dog."

Patience gathered Mercy in her arms, just as she had done when she was a little girl. There were few things more comforting than this kitchen, this carrot cake, this woman hugging her.

Chapter 5

AS SOON AS SHE GOT HOME, Mercy slipped her Beretta into her belt and went out to track the intruder. She followed his boot prints across the lawn to the tree line. She looked for shell casings but didn't find any. This guy knew what he was doing.

She continued through the bramble into the forest. The damp leaves and mud readily revealed the man's trail. Too easily.

She realized he hadn't cared if she could track him. He must have known he could get away. She pushed on through a long thicket. On the other side was an ATV trail. The prints ended there, where disturbed ground indicated that a large object had recently occupied the spot, leaving behind tread marks in a tangle of tread marks left by the heavy traffic of the holiday.

Most of the land out here was owned by a flatlander from Boston, an investment banker named Daniel Feinberg who'd bought a big estate named Nemeton. They say he'd bought the land to preserve it from logging and had mostly done just that, apart from weekend parties. She was sure Feinberg would not welcome trespassing ATVers on his land.

Nothing more she could do here, for Feinberg or for herself. At least, not today. It was late afternoon now, and she was tired. She trudged back through the woods, missing Elvis. She'd grown more attached to him than she'd thought possible.

Back at the cabin she began the time-consuming job of cleanup. She reshelved books, replaced pillows, restocked her desk, and repacked clothes in drawers and closets.

A mess, to be sure, but nothing seemed to be missing. What she most valued—her books and her pictures—were mostly no worse for the violation. But the bastard had broken the frame of the photograph of her and Martinez. The one Amy said she looked so happy in. She did look happy, her face alive with a luminosity that occurred in rare moments of true contentment. She wondered if that happy woman was lost to her forever.

Mercy dumped the glass and the frame into the trash and hung the photo on her fridge. She stared at the man she loved, his handsome features animated. *Time to get with the program*, he seemed to be saying, *get on with your life*. She loved to look at the photo, even when it hurt. But at this eye-to-eye level, it suddenly seemed like a rebuke. She turned the picture over and placed it back on the fridge. Nothing but an empty white space now, dated with a time stamp long expired.

It was nearly suppertime, and she was hungry and thirsty. Mercy poured herself some Big Barn Red and pulled a lamb shepherd's pie out of the freezer. She popped it in the oven.

While the frozen dinner heated up, Mercy curled up on the couch and sipped her wine and thought about Elvis's close call. She closed her eyes and tried to breathe through the fear that she'd failed him and Martinez. Just as she'd been breathing through her grief for the past year. Never mind step by step—breath by breath was how she'd made it this far.

She kept breathing, and eventually her inhalations and exhalations allowed her to surrender to her exhaustion. She dozed off, dreaming of masked men and crying babies and lost lovers.

THE TIMER WAS CHIMING AND the doorbell was ringing when she awoke with a start, the name of her lost soldier on her lips.

"Coming!" Jogging for the front door, she checked the peephole. There on her porch stood her grandmother and Elvis.

"Elvis!" Careful to avoid the cone and bandage on his butt, she body-hugged the dog, burying her head in his soft coat.

"He's fine." Patience pushed her way into the cabin.

Elvis shook Mercy off. She stepped aside and watched as they passed by. Elvis looked back at her as if to say, *Come on, Carr. Move it!* Just like his sergeant would have done.

She traipsed after them into the kitchen. Her grandmother snapped off the timer and retrieved the shepherd's pie.

"Eat," Patience ordered, handing Mercy an empty dish.

Mercy spooned some shepherd's pie onto the plate. "How's the kitty?"

"She's fine. Still no name?"

"Not yet."

"Maybe tomorrow's cat rescue will inspire you. The Cat Ladies have gotten the clear to go over to the Walker place in the morning." Her grandmother gave her an expectant look.

"I don't know. Elvis needs to rest." The Cat Ladies was a rescue group funded by the estate of a local heiress. She knew she should help, but she wanted to look for Amy and the baby.

"He'll be fine." Patience raised her eyebrows. "Like it or not, you are a civilian. You need to stay out of this investigation."

"I know." She looked down, away from Patience's scrutiny.

Patience sighed. "But if you need a legitimate reason to revisit the crime scene, this would be it."

"Well, when you put it that way . . . count me in." Mercy raised her head and grinned at Patience. "Always glad to help."

"I thought so. Tell me what happened to your masked man."

Mercy recounted her unsuccessful trek through the Feinberg property to the ATV trail and the cleanup effort of her cabin.

"I don't get it," Patience said. "What was he looking for?"

"Nothing that I can tell. But I feel I'm missing something."

"Want to talk it through? I used to do that with your grand-father. He always said it helped."

"Okay." She retrieved her cell, flipping through photos of the crime scene for her grandmother, including close-ups of Donald Walker. In one photo the tattoo that inked his arm was more vis-ible. Something familiar about it drew her attention.

The art was crudely drawn, but the faded black-and-white im-ages clearly revealed a pine tree against the mountains, bundles of grain, and a stick-figure cow.

"What is it?"

"This tattoo." Mercy enlarged the image on her phone and handed it to her grandmother. "What does it remind you of?"

"It looks like the Vermont coat of arms."

Patience pointed to the poorly printed word *Vermont* and the state motto, "Freedom and Unity," that ran along the bottom of the tattoo. She drew her finger upward. "But are these crossed rifles? They're supposed to be evergreen branches."

"You're a real Vermonter. This adaptation is the same image that appears on the belt buckle we found with the bones."

"So the two deaths may be connected."

"Looks like it."

"You knew it." Patience beamed at her. "Clever girl." She gave her back the phone. "Aren't you going to tell Troy?"

"I want to check a few things first."

"Of course you do." Patience stood up. "You have work to do. I'll let myself out."

"What about Elvis?"

"I'll be back tomorrow. Don't go anywhere tonight. Because if you do, he'll want to go with you. And while he's not badly hurt physically, emotionally he could use a rest. So could you."

"If I do go out, he'll stay right here on the couch."

"No, he won't. Would he stay put if it were Martinez?"

"No."

"What he needs more than anything is you. You're his Martinez now." She kissed her forehead, then headed out the door.

Mercy poured herself more wine and moved to the couch. She logged on to her laptop to research symbols of Vermont. Some of the information confirmed what she already knew: the scene depicted on both the belt buckle and tattoo was very much like the coat of arms, which dated back to the time of the Vermont Republic, when Vermont was an independent state.

That explained the motto, but not the rifles that replaced the evergreen branches. She kept on Googling and hit on several articles on the Vermont Republic's latter-day imitations. The so-called Second Vermont Republic was a secession movement dedicated to the reestablishment of an independent Vermont.

A man called Adam Wolfe was mentioned briefly in one of the pieces, and a search on his name revealed a couple of profiles of the self-proclaimed "Vermont Firster," an artist activist dedicated to "saving the authentic Vermont."

Amy's Adam. He certainly looked the part of the wild creator, with his wire-rimmed glasses and shoulder-length brown hair and full, unkempt beard.

One essay in an academic journal expounded on the relationship between art and politics and featured Wolfe and his sculptures, a series of big and bold abstract bronzes. The author was one Candace Winters, Ph.D., professor at Bennington College.

Did politics and art equal explosives? Mercy wasn't sure, so she'd just have to track this woman down and find out.

Elvis twitched in his sleep, paws moving as if he were running. He yipped and yapped. A nightmare.

Mercy cuddled up to the shivering dog. "Just a bad dream." She stroked his back. "You're okay, big guy. We're okay."

She couldn't leave Elvis. Not like this.

She texted Troy, filling him in on all that she'd discovered about Wolfe, Donald Walker, Wayne Herbert, and Dr. Winters.

She told him they'd have to follow up, and he told her he was out on patrols but that he'd pass it all along to Captain Thrasher. She asked about Amy and Helena, but there was no news there.

She hoped Troy and Thrasher could do what she could not.

Because she had a dog who needed her. She would stay right

here, watching over her poor suffering shepherd and hoping that Amy and Helena were safe and on their way back to her.

Mercy's mind raced with random thoughts and associations just out of reach. She knew she should try to get a good night's rest. Her grandmother and her animal rescue friends were early morning people. She reached for her wineglass. If deep breathing didn't help her sleep, more Big Barn Red might.

Her Beretta was still under her pillow. In case the masked man returned for whatever he was looking for—and had obviously failed to find.

TROY and Susie Bear had spent hours checking fishing and boating licenses and chasing down those driving under the influence. He was looking forward to a hot shower and a cold beer. But by the time they got home, there was a text from Thrasher telling him to call him. He answered on the first ring.

"We followed up on that information your girlfriend sent."

"Sir."

"We ran Adam Wolfe by the local PD and the Feds. They say he's in Quebec. Hobnobbing with secessionists up there."

"What about his activities down here?"

"They suspected him of setting fire to a few logging trucks, but they couldn't prove anything. They did cite him for putting in art installations on private property without permission."

"Art installations?"

"Apparently he's a sculptor. He gave up doing bronzes and switched to creating works of natural materials."

"So no one's going to move on this."

"He's in Quebec. We've got our hands full with the holiday. Stay out of it."

"Right." He knew how territorial law enforcement could be. But he didn't see how he could stay out of it as long as Mercy wouldn't stay out of it. And she was nothing if not stubborn.

"You like her." Thrasher laughed.

Troy ignored that. "Sir."

Thrasher was still laughing when he hung up.

THIS TIME MERCY LET HIM IN right away. She seemed surprised to see him. Her eyes were sleepy, and she held a glass of wine.

"I'm sorry to disturb you," Troy said, sounding stiff.

"No problem." She scratched Susie Bear between her shaggy ears, then let the black dog rumble in to say hello to Elvis, who lay forlornly on the couch, embarrassed by his condition.

"The Cone of Humiliation," Troy said. "What happened?"

She told him about the intruder.

"This is the first I've heard of this." He was not happy.

"He's long gone."

"For now. He could be connected to this investigation. We should at least dust for prints."

"He wore gloves. He knew what he was doing. And I don't think anything is missing. Besides, Elvis is my first priority."

"Understood." Troy looked over at Elvis, seemingly content to hang with Susie Bear, cone and all.

"Patience says he's fine. Just a little rattled."

"If she says so, then it must be true. She's the best."

"She is," Mercy said. "So I took some photos and did some checking." She showed him the cell phone pictures of the deceased Donald Walker and the research she found online.

"Good work." The truth was, he really was impressed. He told her what Thrasher had given him on Adam Wolfe.

"I'd like to talk to this Dr. Winters."

"I don't know about that. Way out of our jurisdiction."

"Law enforcement is not going to do anything. They're busy with the fireworks and parades and drunk and disorderlies."

"Not true. Now that there could be a connection between the cold case and Walker, Harrington's going to be all over this." Troy sighed. "Captain Thrasher told me to stay out of it."

"But this professor is our best lead to Wolfe and these Vermont Firsters," she said. "Who knows what they're up to."

"It's Detective Harrington's turf. He hates the captain. He doesn't need an excuse to make his life miserable. Or mine."

"But it doesn't change anything. We've still got a missing mother and baby, bones in the woods, and a dead Donald Walker. Not to mention evidence of explosives and an armed intruder. And the one common denominator is Adam Wolfe."

"Who's in Quebec."

"Maybe. Maybe not. Dr. Winters might know where he is."

She wasn't going to give up.

"You're going to go see her whether I go with you or not."

Mercy planted her fists on her hips. "He shot my dog."

There was really no arguing with that.

"Okay. But I do all the talking."

"Understood."

"We're on second shift tonight. We'll be by in the morning."

Mercy frowned. "I promised I'd help Patience rescue the cats at the Walker place. Dozens. Half-starved and sick."

"The Cat Ladies?" Troy grinned. "Susie Bear loves the Cat Ladies. I'll text you when we come off patrol."

He whistled softly, and the Newfie mutt slowly shambled to her feet. Mercy walked them to the door. "See you tomorrow."

Troy thought a trip to Bennington was probably a wild-goose chase. But he wasn't going to let her go off on her own. Dead bodies turned up whenever she and Elvis ventured out alone.

SATURDAY, JULY 3

Chapter 6

BY THE TIME TROY and Susie Bear got to the Walker place, there were no cats or Cat Ladies to be seen. But he did see Mercy with her grandmother and Denise Boudreaux, the Northshire Animal Control officer.

"Got 'em all?" Troy looked around the Walker homestead.

"We were going to have Elvis search for any stragglers," said Mercy, who managed to look good even in this heat.

He smiled. "I'm sure Susie Bear would be happy to help."

"Troy!" The veterinarian gave him a quick hug.

"Warner." Denise nodded smartly at Troy, saving her enthusiasm for Susie Bear, who greeted her with unreserved joy.

"Hey, Boudreaux." He'd worked with her many times, repatriating black bears and capturing rabies-infected raccoons.

"I guess we all know each other," said Mercy.

"How many cats did you get?" Troy asked.

"Thirty-three," said Patience. "Most should make it."

"That's great." He knew it didn't always work out that way.

"Let's wrap this up," said Denise.

"Sure." Mercy turned to Elvis, who'd been prancing in place, desperate to be released.

"Search," said Troy and Mercy in unison.

At the sound of the call to work, both dogs bounded off.

"Yin and yang," said Patience. At what must have been the blank look on Troy's face, she added, "Male and female energies. Opposite and yet complementary."

"Right." He loved the vet, but when she went all woo-woo, he tuned out. "Excuse us," Troy said, and followed Mercy.

Elvis yelped and circled around the house, Susie Bear lumbering right after him, apparently all yin to his yang.

Mercy and Troy trailed after them. The backyard was just a narrow slab of concrete flanked by the forest.

Elvis loped across the patio and around the far end of the home. Susie Bear crisscrossed the concrete slab in a more leisurely fashion. Then she disappeared around the corner.

Troy heard her bark. "She's alerting to something."

They sprinted around the house and found the dogs sniffing around at the edge of a pile of broken flowerpots.

"What you got there, guys?" Mercy squatted down and peered between two of the largest shards of terra-cotta. She pulled the pieces away. "There's a cat in here." She reached to pick it up, but the sly little thing leaped past her long fingers.

Troy dropped to his knees and opened his arms just in time to catch it in his hands, like an errant football. "Gotcha!"

"Good save," she said, laughing.

Like a fool he grinned in pleasure for having amused her. He held out the orange kitten so she could get a better look at him.

"A Munchkin." Due to a gene mutation, Munchkins' legs are far shorter than the average cat's legs.

Susie Bear and Elvis gave the little guy a good snuffling, as the kitty meowed wildly and waved his legs around.

Patience appeared with a carrier. "He's a lively thing."

Mercy opened the top, and Troy put the kitty inside. Closing the kitty in, she handed the carrier back to Patience.

Troy looked back down into the pile of terra-cotta. "There's more stuff here."

"They also call Munchkins magpies, because they love shiny objects," Patience said. "They steal pretty things and hide them."

Denise walked toward them. "We'll take the Munchkin back. Unless there's anything else."

"Sure," Troy said, but he didn't move. Neither did Mercy.

"Are you two coming?" asked Patience.

"Not yet." Mercy looked at Troy. "I'd like to go through the Munchkin's stash first."

"Technically, this is a crime scene," he reminded her.

"Maybe the crime-scene techs missed something."

"Will we see you back at the Cat House?" asked Patience.

"Maybe later," said Mercy.

"Uh-huh." The vet wrapped an arm around Denise's shoulder. "I guess it's just you and me and the Cajun mutant thief."

"Don't you kids stay out too late," yelled Denise over her shoulder as she and Patience walked away with the Munchkin.

"She can't be any older than you are," said Troy.

"Pay no attention to them. Got any more plastic gloves?"

Troy pulled a pair from his pocket and gave her them. He stood there as she picked through the jumble of stolen goods.

Mercy opened her fist, and he spotted a couple of mismatched earrings. "There's more where that came from."

Troy opened one of the evidence bags he had on him, and Mercy dropped in the earrings. He doubted anything a cat dragged in could bear much relevance to the case. But he kept that to himself as he held out more bags as Mercy dropped the items inside: a couple of thin silver bracelets, four old keys, a brass shell casing, two gold barrettes, and a few necklaces.

"This is the last one." Mercy held up a delicate if dirty silver chain with a silver pendant. "A mountain range with pines."

"Like the Vermont coat of arms."

"Not exactly. But definitely inspired by a landscape like ours." She squinted at the piece. "And close enough in style that it could have been made by the same jewelry designer."

"Coincidence or tied to the belt buckles?"

"I don't believe in coincidence," they said at the same time.

She smiled at him. "It looks handmade, which means there may be a maker's mark. The best jewelers stamp their work."

"The belt buckles didn't have a mark."

"But they were definitely handmade. Maybe whoever made them didn't want to be associated with the Vermont Firsters."

"I'll have them take a good look when they clean them up."

Mercy frowned. "You're going to be in trouble for removing evidence. Harrington won't like it."

"But I didn't do anything." He grinned at her as she handed him the pendant. "You found the Munchkin and removed the kitty's favorite things as part of an animal rescue."

"Having first received permission from local authorities." She grinned back at him.

"Unfortunately, the cat's stash was found right after the Northshire Animal Control officer left the scene."

"Unfortunately."

"Okay, let me take in this evidence. And then we'll go see Dr. Winters, as promised."

THEY took both dogs and both vehicles, in case Troy got called in to work, which was likely. He could sleep next week.

After he dropped off the evidence, he led the way, careful to keep Mercy in his rearview mirror. Thirty minutes later down Route 7, he turned into a quiet old neighborhood. Nineteenth-century houses lined the wide street under a canopy of trees.

The professor lived in the most imposing of these Victorian piles, an enormous painted lady done in dark purples, reds, and blues. Troy parked across the street, and Mercy pulled up behind him. Susie Bear whimpered when he told her to stay put and stepped out of the truck without her. Mercy followed suit.

"Creepy house," she said.

"Yeah."

They walked up a long stone path and up a half-dozen steps onto a wraparound porch, crowded with dark wicker furniture.

"That's one angry gargoyle." Mercy pointed to the knocker.

"Go ahead," said Troy.

Mercy banged the brass knocker, then stepped back, allowing him to take the lead. So far, so good.

The small woman who answered the door seemed every bit the mousy professor, with her messy brown hair, pale skin, and gray eyes huge behind nerdy black glasses. But her lips shone with red lipstick, and her white blouse and navy pants fit so snugly it was obvious she wasn't wearing anything underneath.

"And you are?" Dr. Winters slipped her thick glasses down her thin nose and peered up at him with those myopic eyes.

"Warden Troy Warner."

"A man in uniform." She ran those expressive eyes over him once more before turning her attention to Mercy.

"This is Corporal Mercy Carr," he said.

"Not in uniform," said the professor.

"We're here to talk about Adam Wolfe," said Mercy.

"Oh, Adam." Dr. Winters walked away from them, down a wide marble-tiled hall. She stopped and turned, her tousled hair falling around her face, framing her red mouth. "Come on."

He caught Mercy rolling her eyes behind the professor's back as they followed her into a parlor. Heavily curtained mullioned windows ran the length of the room, which was decorated within an inch of its life with antique furniture.

Dr. Winters curled up in a love seat as neatly as a cat. "What's Adam done now?"

"We understand that he's active in the Vermont First movement."

The professor laughed. "Adam is an artist, not an activist." She dismissed the thought with a flutter of her hands. "No matter what he says."

"You seemed to take him seriously when you wrote that article about him in the arts and politics journal," said Mercy.

"When it comes to politics, Adam is a poseur. But when it comes to art, he's the real deal." She pointed to a two-foot bronze sculpture that sat on an ornately carved stand. The striking piece was of a vaguely female form, all curves and whirls and hollows, all strength and softness and shine.

"It's lovely," said Mercy.

"It's brilliant," corrected the professor. "That piece is one of the last of his series of bronze nudes."

"He sold the rest?" said Troy. "He must be very successful."

"He would have been." She shook her head. "He sold a couple pieces and kept the remainder in a warehouse. Thieves stole them all. The suspicion is that the pieces were sold for scrap." She unwound her lithe body slowly. "Such a waste. Criminal."

"You were the model," said Mercy with a small smile.

"Yes." She licked her red-stained lips. "I'm grateful that in recognition of my contribution as his muse, he gifted me with my first choice of the series. This one is my favorite."

"No more modeling, then?" asked Mercy.

"Alas, no. Adam abandoned his work in metals to create natural sculptures. He gathers material he finds in nature—stones, sticks, feathers, bones—and creates sculptures there on site, integrating the art into the natural landscape."

"How can it last?" Troy asked.

"It's not meant to last. It's meant to be ephemeral. Like life."

"Like a sand painting?" asked Mercy.

"Adam does not create work only to have it blown away with the first strong wind. He designs it to last, with the understanding that Mother Nature will have the last word."

Troy wanted to steer the conversation back to the matter at hand. "He's been accused of setting fire to logging trucks, trespassing, and creating his art on private property."

"Absurd." The professor slid over to the sculpture. "Adam only wants to preserve the gallery that houses his art now."

"The woods?" asked Mercy.

"Exactly." She ran her slender fingers along the curves of the artwork, which modeled her own. "It's called *Candy*."

"So you were close."

"We were more than close." The professor regarded Mercy. "We met at a party. Then we went to the south of France. The French understand love. Or, at least, lovers." She smiled at them. "I spend every summer there. With a lover."

"It's July," said Mercy. "You're late."

"It's un-American to leave before the Fourth of July," the professor said, her eyes still on Troy. "I'm leaving for Provence on Tuesday. And I have an extra ticket."

He heard Mercy stifle a laugh. "Back to Adam Wolfe."

"These things run their course, don't they?" Dr. Winters smiled. "I had other interests. Tramping around in the wilderness . . . Let's just say that's not my natural habitat. Adam became a hermit of sorts, living out in the woods, creating his art. We lost touch. The last I heard, he was in Canada."

"Lots of secessionists up there," Troy said.

"Lots of wilderness, too."

"Anything else you can tell us about his whereabouts?"

"I'm afraid not."

He handed her a card. "If you think of anything . . ."

"You know where I live." She smiled at him.

"Yes, ma'am."

"You never told me what this was about."

"Adam is wanted in connection with a possible murder."

She laughed again. "Impossible."

They left her there in the parlor. Troy felt a surge of relief as he stepped out of that woman's hothouse into the cool shade of the oaks and maples.

"Wow." Mercy inhaled deeply and exhaled slowly. "Some woman. 'Love is all truth, Lust full of forged lies.'"

"What do you mean?"

"I mean that I didn't believe a word of it. Except the part about her being the model for that sculpture."

"Why would she lie?"

"You don't know much about women, do you?"

Troy shrugged. "Maybe not." He checked his phone for messages. "I've got to get back to my patrols."

They crossed the street to their vehicles.

"Thanks for doing this," she said.

"I'm not sure what we've accomplished here."

"We've learned that everyone wants us to believe that Wolfe is in Canada."

"You think the Feds and local PD are lying?"

"I think they're mistaken. Amy says he's here."

Troy shook his head. "He's long gone. And so is she."

"You don't really think she killed her stepfather." Mercy shook her head. "Her mother is not to be believed."

"Agreed," he said. "But Amy remains a person of interest."

"So you are looking for her."

"Yes. But she's probably in Canada by now. With him."

"She was serious about leaving him." Mercy shook her head again, a flurry of loose curls. "I've met her. I can't believe she's capable of killing anyone."

"Amy isn't capable of murder, Wolfe isn't capable of murder, none of our suspects is capable, yet two men are dead."

Troy walked Mercy to her Jeep. Elvis was sitting up, cone in place, alert as ever. "You should go home. Get some rest."

"Sure," she said. "But first I'm going to get me and Elvis a creemee. Do you want to join us?"

"Thanks, but we've got to get back."

He could feel her eyes on his back as he jumped in the truck, scratched Susie Bear's ears, and took off down the road. He watched her in the rearview mirror as long as he could, then tried to put her and her dog and the Vermont Firsters out of his mind. Back to his real job.

MERCY drove around the block, coming back to the street where the professor lived and parking several houses away. She bided her time. She was used to waiting. The army taught you patience. A patient soldier was a smart soldier.

Elvis was a smart soldier, too. Martinez had seen to that. The high-energy shepherd could stay perfectly still, quiet, and alert as long as needed. She smiled and patted the dog's head.

Nearly two hours passed before the heavy oak door opened and Dr. Winters came out, now dressed in cargo pants, hiking boots, a white T-shirt, and a camouflage-colored fanny pack.

Mercy watched as the woman drove off in a forest-green SUV. Her Vermont vanity license plate read DR ART.

"Let's see where Dr. Art goes," she told Elvis. "Ten bucks says she takes us right to Adam Wolfe."

When the professor was a couple of blocks away, Mercy began to follow her. She headed onto Route 7 going north.

An hour later the SUV exited Route 7 and navigated a number of increasingly remote, rugged roads. Mercy pursued her at a discreet distance, thankful for the twists and turns of these roads, which afforded her red Jeep some much needed cover.

The SUV jostled down an old logging road. The more slowly Dr. Winters went, the greater the risk of Mercy being spotted. She let the Jeep fall back. If the woman drove any more slowly, she'd have to pull over and pursue Dr. Winters on foot.

Elvis was agitated now, banging the cone against the door.

"Settle down," she ordered.

He ignored her, bashing the cone harder. He began to bark.

"Okay." She unsnapped her seat belt. "You're going to hurt yourself if you keep this up." She released him from the cone.

Elvis shook his head, his dark eyes shining with triumph.

"Show-off." She tried not to laugh as she parked the Jeep in a little clearing behind a thin copse of young birch.

"Let's go," she said sternly, slipping her pack onto her back and pushing the door open for him. He leaped along the pitted path, overjoyed to be free of impediments and on the job again.

The SUV was out of sight, but she could still hear it caroming farther into the wilderness. The sun hung lower in the sky now. Only a few hours of daylight left. She and Elvis kept to the tree line. The logging road wove in and out of the national forest, thick with pine, maples, beech, and birch.

When the SUV finally came to a full stop before a clumsily fenced encampment, Mercy and Elvis ducked deeper into the forest. The barbwire rolls that comprised the barrier were standard-issue military-grade perimeter controls.

The compound was a squatters colony of three tent cabins on raised logs and a long Quonset hut, cuddled together in a clearing shaped like a baseball diamond. A truck was parked in front, its back door rolled up. She couldn't see what was inside.

She watched as a tall man in running pants and a dark T-shirt talked to Dr. Winters across the fence. She couldn't hear them well, but from the look on his face, he was not happy to see her. She thought she heard the professor call him Max as her voice raised in protest over something he said. He shook his shaved head, opening the gate and letting Dr. Winters drive inside.

The man offered the professor a hand to help her out of the SUV, but she shook him off, jumping down to the ground as gracefully as a lynx. She strode off to the tent cabin in the middle.

Mercy wanted to get a closer look. She made her way with Elvis around the colony. The woods were dense here, the forest floor thick with brambles. Elvis stepped through the chaos carefully. She followed in his wake. He alerted, whether to the tall man or to Dr. Winters or to the truck, Mercy wasn't sure.

There was something familiar about the way the man held his shoulders, but she couldn't say for sure whether he was the masked man she'd seen running from her house or not. As she studied him, he raised his head and looked their way. She didn't think he saw them, but she wasn't taking any chances.

"Come on," she whispered to Elvis. Together they melted back into the forest and proceeded around the perimeter from the safe perspective of at least twenty feet deep under the leafy cover of maples and beeches and birches.

If the entrance to the compound was home plate, then the tent cabin where Dr. Winters had gone was about second base. They were somewhere between first and second base when they came upon an art installation. The work was so cleverly woven into the natural landscape that Mercy nearly missed it.

Secreted among the logs of a small blowdown area was a stone structure seemingly suspended between two granite outcroppings. The arch was made of smooth granite stones chiseled into rough bricks. The artfully shaped crescent seemed to grow right out of the boulders that served as its abutments. Along its archivolt, there were faint, fairly shallow markings that looked like Greek letters. She snapped cell photos.

A dry riverbed of rocks ran underneath. When she squatted down to examine the stone current, she realized this, too, was part of the sculpture. The spirals of stone were too perfect to be natural. Fractal patterns of swirls echoed the curve of the arch.

The materials and settings of the two art pieces she had seen today—the bronze sculpture at Dr. Winters's and this natural sculpture—were very different, but she could see the hand of the same artist in each piece. The feminine curves and whorls of the bronze were echoed here in this piece, expanded and enlightened in the wilderness. Adam Wolfe, thought Mercy.

She tried to use her phone to text Troy, but of course she got no signal. Elvis sniffed at a hiking trail. Mercy figured the trail must lead back through the northwestern corner of the forest. She thought they'd stumbled upon it on one of their hikes last fall but wasn't sure. Elvis would know. He never forgot a trail.

She was glad to see it; if the way back around the compound and out to the Jeep was blocked and they needed to escape quickly, they'd need an alternate route. And here it was.

"Good job," she whispered to Elvis.

She heard a snap behind her. The shepherd growled, a guttural utterance from deep within his chest.

She spun around. A man of medium height and weight stepped

forward. A bird-watcher, if the birding binoculars and field bag and safari hat were any indication. He wore a blue plaid shirt, khaki trousers, and hiking boots. He was about thirty-five years old, with tired hazel eyes and short brown hair.

"It's a little late in the day for birding, isn't it?" Mercy said.

"I was hoping for a close-up glimpse of black-throated warblers. If you listen carefully, you can hear their zoo-zee song."

She listened, and followed the buzzy birdsong to a nest woven of bark strips. A little gray bird perched inside, while its brighter blue mate darted among the leaves, looking for dinner.

"Beautiful, aren't they?"

"Yes."

"They're making a comeback, at least for now."

Elvis growled again.

Enough about birds, thought Mercy.

"What do you know about that compound?" Her voice held a command in it, and the bird-watcher looked startled.

"Rufus Flanigan," he said, putting out his hand with caution, one anxious eye on the dog.

"Mercy Carr," she said, and shook his hand.

"Are you a police officer? You act like a police officer."

She didn't say anything. Just let him ramble on as Elvis snarled.

"I was on my way home. Then I saw the girl and baby. The one in the Amber Alert. I reported seeing them yesterday."

She nodded. "Were they all right?"

"They were in the company of a man who looked . . . I don't know . . . sketchy. The girl seemed unhappy about it."

"Where are they now?"

"I think they're in one of the tent cabins. I was going to hike out and call for help, and then I saw you. And your dog."

"I don't think she's here because she wants to be."

"Me, either. I see the mother with her baby on my hikes. When the Amber Alert went out, I thought I should come forward. I was worried they might be in trouble. Then I see them with this creepy guy."

"I'm retired law enforcement. We sometimes assist. Hike out of here and get help." She handed Troy's card to the guy.

"What are you going to do?"

"We'll see."

He glanced toward the compound. "Be careful."

"I've got Elvis."

"Okay." He backed up. "This trail leads back around through the Lye Brook Wilderness. I'll call as soon as I get a signal."

He turned to go. She wasn't sure what she thought of him, and it was clear Elvis didn't much like him.

"He's all we got," she told the dog as they watched him hike away. She hoped she could trust him.

Together Mercy and Elvis circled the compound. She needed a spot out of the line of sight that she could snip the razor-sharp wire and wiggle through. She patted her pocket, reassuring herself that her trusty knife was still there as always. The Swiss Champ boasted thirty-three functions, including a wire cutter.

They stayed hidden in the forest a dozen feet within the perimeter of the compound. They didn't see anyone, other than the tall man. He was back, loading the truck with boxes. Whoever else was in the clearing—the professor, Amy and Helena, the elusive Adam Wolfe—was apparently in a tent cabin.

It was slow going. The forest floor was cluttered with vegetation and downed branches. Dusk was falling now, and soon the forest would be cloaked in darkness.

Fifteen minutes later they came around to the back of the last tent cabin. She sneaked up toward the barbwire barrier. Elvis dropped to his haunches, scooting beside her and alerting.

She didn't see anyone. The truck was still there, its cargo now secured behind the closed door. Mercy pulled out the wire-cutting tool. She was about halfway through the triple rolls of metal when Elvis perked up and pawed at the ground.

Then she heard it, too. The faint cry of an infant. Helena.

"Stay," she ordered, and hurried to cut through the remainder of the wires. Once it was cut, she pulled the fence apart cautiously. As soon as she'd managed a foot-wide opening, Elvis slipped past her, bounding toward the sound of the crying baby.

Cursing, she scrambled in through the barbwire after him. She stood up, ready to follow the dog. The snap of a twig behind her stopped her cold. She heard Elvis snarl just as she sensed someone behind her and the blow to come. She couldn't let anything happen to him again. "No, Elvis!" She needed him to be safe. "Go home. Home to Patience!"

The last sounds that registered in her brain were those of a dog barking and a baby crying and a shot firing. Or was it a truck backfiring? Her brain wouldn't work. She stood there, suspended in time, while the inside of her head exploded. "Patience," she said again, her voice a squeak, and she went down.

TROY and Susie Bear spent half the night tracking down drunk boaters and issuing citations for speeding. By the time they got home, it was after eleven. They were both exhausted.

He took a quick shower, pulled down the Murphy bed, and tumbled into it. Susie Bear joined him.

By midnight the phone was ringing. He reached for his cell, and to his surprise it wasn't Thrasher or Mercy Carr calling.

It was Patience O'Sullivan.

Fifteen minutes later he and the Newfie mutt were in the vet's kitchen rich with the smell of freshly brewed coffee. Patience poured him a cup while she told him what had happened.

"Elvis showed up at my back door. Dirty and dehydrated and completely stressed out."

Susie Bear sniffed her canine friend all over, from tail to nose. Finally she licked his snout and banked up next to him.

Troy petted the shepherd's fine head. "He seems okay."

"He's fine now. Watered and fed and somewhat rested."

"Where's Mercy?"

"She's not answering her cell or landline. I drove over there, and she's not at home. The Jeep's not there, either. No sign of forced entry." Her voice was steady, but her hand shook slightly as she sipped her coffee. "She was going after the intruder."

He shook his head. "I left her at the professor's house. She was on her way home."

"Was she?"

"My fault." Troy felt stupid and, worse, incompetent. "She asked me if we wanted to join them for a creemee."

"And you declined."

"Patrols."

"Uh-huh." Patience looked at him. The same look her grand-daughter had given him when she told him he didn't know any-thing about women. "Elvis knows where she is."

"I'll get Thrasher to put a trace on her cell." Troy texted his boss, then stood up. Susie Bear scrambled to her feet. "Don't worry. We'll find her."

"What about Elvis?"

Troy looked down at the dog, resting quietly. "He should prob-ably stay here."

"But you'll need him. Mercy will need him."

"If you're sure . . . I don't want to be responsible for anything happening to her dog."

"I don't, either. But I'm not sure you could stop him. He came here to me for a reason."

"I'm not sure what you mean."

"Mercy sent him. Otherwise he would never have left her."

As if to prove her right, the shepherd leaped to his feet, barking and nudging Troy's hands with his nose. "Okay, okay."

With both dogs ready to roll, he snapped on the tracking leads Patience provided.

Thrasher called him back. "Signal ends at the northwest end of the national forest. I'll text you the coordinates."

"Thank you, sir."

"Probably a wild-goose chase." Thrasher paused.

"She'd never leave the dog." As soon as he said it, he realized that it was not just an argument, it was the truth.

"If you need backup, it may take a while."

"What else is new?"

"Be careful."

"I'll be fine. These are my woods."

SEVEN MILES UP ROUTE 7, Troy pulled into a dirt road, the first of many unpaved roads that led to the coordinates that the captain had given him. They were deep in the forest.

Troy parked on an old logging road. He slipped his headlamp, red light shining, around his head. He slid on his pack, the dog leads tight in one hand, his flashlight in the other. He let Elvis and Susie Bear out. They bounded down the road, Elvis in front, straining at the leash. Troy jogged to keep up.

A mile down the trail, they came upon Mercy's Jeep. Its tires were all flat, thanks to long cuts made by a knife.

The Malinois ignored the Jeep and danced at the end of the leash, pressing onward and nearly toppling him.

"Stay," he ordered, and to his surprise the dog stayed.

He examined the area around the vehicle and saw where Mercy had tracked someone. Her Jeep's tread marks stopped where it was parked, but another set continued down the road.

"Go on," he told the dogs. "Search."

Elvis leaped for the tracks she had left behind, and Troy and Susie Bear charged after him. He thought about Mercy, out here all alone but for the beasts of the woods and the dark of the night and whoever slashed her tires.

He had a bad feeling. He picked up his pace. Elvis felt his increase in speed and ran faster, faster, faster. Susie Bear lumbered along, the steady metronome between the wired shepherd and his own anxious self. Troy hoped they weren't too late.

Chapter 7

MERCY'S HEAD HURT. She was cold and lying on the forest floor within the compound. Her Red Sox cap was still clamped over her curls. She raised her hands and tentatively touched the back of her skull, felt around with her fingers. No blood, just a whopper of a bump.

She had to stay awake, but every time she tried to stand up, her head swam and her knees buckled. So she crawled over to a beech tree, fighting down the bile that rose in her throat. She leaned against the thick trunk for support, breathing heavily.

There was no sign of activity in the compound. All was quiet. The darkness was so complete that she could not even make out the shapes of the tent cabins. Her phone and her gun were gone, but her pack remained. She had a flashlight in her pack.

She retrieved the flashlight and turned it on. She waved the flashlight at the darkness, and images appeared. Trees and tarps and abandoned tent cabins. No vehicles. No people. No Elvis.

She hoped that meant that he had gotten away and gone home to Patience. That's what she'd told him to do.

A rustling at her feet. A cawing in her ears. Slowly, deliberately, painfully, she rotated her head toward the commotion and shined the light on its source. As her battered brain cleared and her focus sharpened, she spotted the body.

A man, she thought. A dead man. Prone. With a Buck hunting knife in his chest, buried right up to the hilt. The same type of blade she'd seen piercing Donald Walker's chest.

This was getting to be a bad habit, Mercy thought. Still unsure that she could stand upright, she crept over to the corpse, waving her arms at the critters feeding on what was the newly deceased form of the bird-watcher Rufus Flanigan.

Mercy struggled to her feet and covered the bird-watcher's mottled face with his safari hat, and his torso with her hoodie, in a mostly ineffective effort to keep away the scavengers.

She trudged over to the tent cabins. The first two were empty. Nothing but discarded water bottles and stacks of fliers urging the people of Northshire to save the trees on one side and join the town's Fourth of July festivities on the other.

She stuffed a flier in a back pocket; maybe she could find out who printed them and that would lead to something. Or not.

In the third cabin, she found a baby bottle among the litter. Amy and Helena had been here. But where were they now?

There was no sign of the man loading the truck or the professor or Adam Wolfe. The place was deserted.

The only secured dwelling appeared to be the Quonset hut, locked up tight, a new padlock in its roll-up door. She pulled out her knife, grateful that whoever tried to crush her skull did not pocket it, and found its thinnest tool. She slipped the tool into the lock mechanism. A trick Martinez had taught her.

She wiggled the tool to trip the lock and pulled the shackle out. She rolled up the door far enough so she could step inside.

She shuffled around the edge of the hut. At the back of the building, a line of steel trunks hugged the wall. They were secured with padlocks like the one on the roll-up door, just as easy to open. Nothing here but packing material—bubble wrap, rolling tubes, folded boxes—and a short length of what looked like clothesline. Barely an inch long, but she knew det cord when she saw it. Maybe that's all the explosives they'd ever find. But it was enough to prove Elvis right.

She replaced all the padlocks on the trunks as well as the one on the Quonset door. Time to think about getting out of here. But first she made her way back to the corpse so she could examine him more thoroughly. She removed her hoodie from his body. As she pulled it away, the victim's shirttails parted, revealing a leather belt with a pewter belt buckle. She leaned in for a closer look. It was the same belt buckle with the same gun-toting adaptation of the Vermont coat of arms that was found with the bones. Not your average bird-watcher, after all.

So who was this guy, really? Mercy searched his pockets and found his wallet, thirty bucks in cash, a burner phone, a Canadian passport in the name of Rufus Flanigan, and a flier like the one she'd found in the tent cabin.

Mercy sighed. The Feds and the staties agreed that Adam Wolfe had gone to Canada to work with secessionists in Quebec. And here was this bird-watching Vermont First belt buckle–wearing corpse from across the northern border. Surely not a coincidence. She thought about what that might mean, but her skull was drumming again. She needed to get home.

She started the long hike back to her Jeep, going through the gate at the front of the compound, which they hadn't bothered to lock in their hurry to leave. An odd oversight, given the fact that they'd remembered to lock up the Quonset hut and trunks.

She worried over what that meant, but it hurt her head too much. So she focused on moving down the trail. She proceeded slowly, and every hundred yards or so she paused, leaning against a tree to beat back the dizziness.

She'd gone about a quarter mile when she heard sounds of movement up ahead. She ducked behind some pines. The quick action rattled her brain, and she closed her eyes, sinking down on her knees. She felt the darkness spinning in on her again.

IN HER dream she was rolling, rolling, rolling on the forest floor, a dead soldier unfurled from a Stars and Stripes shroud. She came to a stop on her back, blind to the light. The darkness was a living, pulsating thing, and it enveloped her. Sucked the soul right out of her. And left the remains to the feeders.

A slap of cold and wet hit her chin. She opened her eyes to a blur of tawny fur and a dark muzzle nuzzling her face. Elvis.

She threw her arms around him and hugged him hard. He seemed as happy to see her as she was to see him, licking her nose and cheeks and ears thoroughly.

Troy was behind him, a headlamp bathing her in red light.

"How did you find me?"

"Patience sent us." He held a flashlight with one hand and held back Susie Bear with the other. The Newfie mutt strained at her lead. He told her to sit, and she did so reluctantly.

"Is Elvis okay?"

"He's fine. Your grandmother says so. But what about you?" Troy squatted down to get a good look at her.

"Someone hit me from behind. Knocked me out. But I'm good now." Which was at least mostly true. She was feeling much better now that the canine cavalry had arrived.

"I'm taking a look," he said. He slowly removed the Red Sox cap. Still, that gentle movement brought tears to her eyes.

He brushed away her hair gently and examined her skull. "Some bump you got there. No blood that I can see." He pulled an ice pack out of his first-aid pack. "Here. That should help."

She smiled at him. The cold felt good against her sore skull.

"Did you see who hit you?"

"No. They came up behind me." She told him about the baby wailing and Elvis running toward the cries. "They're all gone now," she said. "But there's something I need to show you."

"Of course there is."

She started to rise and fell against him.

"Whoa." Troy caught her and helped her up, his strong forearms supporting her as she wobbled to her feet. "Take it easy."

"You have to see this." She led them back down the logging road to the compound. Elvis and Susie Bear danced around, eager to search, but as instructed, they accompanied Mercy and Troy as they walked over to where the dead body lay.

Troy shook his head. "What is it with you and the woods?"

She chose to ignore that remark. "Rufus Flanigan."

"The bird-watcher who called in on the Amber Alert?"

"If that's what he really is." She pointed her flashlight at the belt buckle. "Same as the one we found buried with the bones."

"And the tattoo. I'd better get this called in. It'll be a while until the techs can get here. Will you be okay while I secure the scene?"

"I'm fine. I can shine the flashlight for you."

Troy snapped photos with his phone. Then he shooed away the scavengers and covered the corpse with a plastic tarp from his pack. He roped off the scene with duct tape, then turned to her. "Anything else you'd like to show me?"

"The rest of the compound. I took a look around, but I wasn't too steady on my feet. I might have missed something."

"I need to examine the area, anyway," he said. "Even if we miss something in the dark, odds are our sniffer dogs won't."

They let the dogs go, and they bounded ahead. She and Troy made their way around the encampment and in and out of the first two tent cabins. As they explored, she briefed him on the activity she'd witnessed before she'd been knocked out.

Susie Bear loped around with her usual good cheer. Elvis circled the compound in his own aggressive fashion. He headed for the Quonset hut, while his Newfie companion settled in front of the third cabin, which had housed Amy and the baby.

Mercy and Troy checked out the tent cabin. They congratulated Susie Bear on finding the baby bottle, slipped her a treat, then joined the shepherd at the Quonset hut.

"This is where the steel trunks are?" he asked. "It's locked."

Uh-oh. She didn't know whether to lie and say the lock wasn't there earlier when she went in or to come clean.

"There weren't any locks on the tent cabin doors," Troy went on. "There must be a reason they locked this one. What do you think?" He regarded her with amusement.

"Huh?" She had a feeling playing dumb wouldn't work.

"You picked the lock, didn't you?"

She flushed. "Maybe."

"Two working dogs have alerted to this building." He grinned. "That's probable cause. Let's see you in action."

Mercy picked the lock quickly and handed him the padlock.

"Outstanding," he said.

The dogs barreled into the building, heading straight for the trunks. Troy nodded toward the locks. She picked those, too, and showed Troy the packing material and piece of det cord.

"Is that our explosives alert?" He looked at Elvis, who sat at attention at her side. "It's not much."

"They could have more with them."

"Or they could have used it to take down trees to clear the area. Loggers use it out here all the time."

"Maybe."

"I need to get to a place where my sat phone will work." He took her arm gently. "Think you can make it to my truck?"

"I can drive myself."

"Not a good idea. Besides, someone slashed your tires."

"Seriously?" In her frustration Mercy shook her head, then winced. Her skull still ached when she moved too fast.

"You need to get that injury checked out. I'll arrange a tow for you as soon as the crime-scene techs have come and gone."

They put the dogs on their leads and left the compound through the entry gate, setting off down the logging road.

"This case is getting crazier by the minute," Mercy said. "So many pieces to the puzzle."

"That's assuming it's just one puzzle."

"It's got to be connected. In the past couple of days, Amy ran away with the baby from a Vermont Firster's compound and three guys with Vermont Firster sympathies turn up dead."

"Another piece: The police found twenty grand in Donald Walker's recliner. And there's the guy who broke into your house."

"And what's Dr. Winters got to do with it?" Mercy asked.

"Maybe she's a Vermont Firster, too."

"The only Vermonter she's putting first is herself. We've got the activist and artist Adam Wolfe, the lowlife Donald Walker with the tattoo, and the belt-buckle guys."

"The body in the woods—aka Wayne Herbert—and the bird-watcher from Canada," said Troy.

"Right. And that guy Max, who was at the compound. And who might be the guy who broke into my house."

"So far, the compound is the common denominator." Troy held her arm, helping her over the roughest patches.

"I'm fine," she said, even though she wasn't. "The compound is where Elvis alerted and we found the det cord."

"Wolfe has been in trouble for blowing up logging trucks. Maybe he's planning on blowing up more."

"That doesn't explain Max or the truck that Elvis alerted to. We need to figure out where that truck was going. It can't be a coincidence that all this has happened in the past few days."

"Things do appear to be coming to a head."

They reached her Jeep, and Mercy leaned against the hood to rest for a moment. Troy excused himself to call Thrasher.

She waited, brooding over the evidence they'd found so far: the explosives, the truck, the timing.

The timing.

Timing was everything.

Make use of time, let not advantage slip.

SHE PULLED THE "SAVE THE TREES" flier from her pocket and scanned the Northshire Fourth of July activities listed on its B side: fun run, parade, concert, fireworks, and so forth. By the time Troy got off the phone, she knew what they had to do.

"Maybe there's a reason it's coming to a head right now." She handed the flier to him. "Independence Day. The perfect time for the Vermont Firsters to make their move."

Troy nodded. "I can see that."

"It's got to be the parade. Lots of hotshots will be there, including the senator."

"If the senator's going to be there, they've already got people in place. Besides, you need to go to the hospital."

"I'm fine."

"Sure. That's why you're so eager to go the last mile here."

Mercy stood up straight. "I was just taking a little breather. Let's go. The sooner we get back, the sooner we can check on the parade." She barreled down the trail, trying not to let her fatigue show. Elvis and Susie Bear ran past her to take the lead.

"It's mostly speculation, you know." Troy strode beside her. "But I'll let Thrasher know."

"You need us," she told Troy. "I'm the only person who's seen Amy and that guy Max. And you're going to need all the bomb-sniffing dogs you can get."

"Even I'm not really supposed to be there," said Troy. "It's the local PD and staties' show. The Feds could be there, too."

"The parade is open to the public. Elvis and I are the public. We're going, even if we have to steal my grandmother's car to get there."

They argued all the way back to Troy's truck. She was determined to wear him down, concussion or no concussion. "I know that Amy and Helena are in trouble."

"Not your problem. None of this is your problem. You've done enough. Time to let the professionals take over."

She knew what he was thinking: She was just another civilian now. But she couldn't accept that. Not as long as Amy and Helena were unaccounted for.

"You nearly got yourself and your dog killed. I don't understand why you are doing this." He leaned in toward her. "What aren't you telling me?"

Mercy backed away and climbed into the passenger seat. She listened to the sound of the dogs scrambling into the backseat, followed by the slam of that door, then another as Troy took his place behind the wheel. But he did not turn on the engine.

"Tell me," he said.

He was more perceptive than she thought. What's more, she knew he was right; she was holding back.

"We were doing a house-to-house in a village. We'd built a school there, the first in decades. The Taliban torched it. The teacher—just a teenager herself—and her baby had gone missing the morning of the fire." She stopped, her head pounding.

"I take it back. You don't have to tell me," Troy said gently.

"You should know. Maybe then you'll understand."

He took her hand in his and squeezed it gently. "Go on."

"We found the teacher, beaten, her baby left to die beside her. But they were alive. Just barely. The mother was scared for her little girl. I told her everything would be okay. We got them to the hospital. I held her hand, like you're holding mine. She begged me to stay, but I had to go. Another mission."

"You did what you had to do."

"By the time I got back, it was too late. The baby was dying, and the mother was so upset, they had to sedate her. I held the baby for her, and she died in my arms. The mother survived, but a week after she left the hospital, she hanged herself."

They fell into silence for a moment.

Mercy squeezed Troy's fingers and pulled her hand away. "Maybe you're right and nothing's going to happen at the parade and this is all overkill," she said. "But better that than something terrible happening and knowing we could've stopped it."

"Okay." Troy turned the key in the ignition, and the Ford F-150 roared to life. "The parade isn't until noon. It's nearly three now. We all need to get some rest. Then, if Patience agrees that you can go, I will drive you there myself."

Chapter 8

MERCY AND ELVIS ENDED UP spending the night at Patience's house. Mercy had refused to go to the hospital, and Patience had finally agreed, provided they stayed where she could keep an eye on them.

The next morning, true to his word, Troy showed up with Susie Bear for breakfast.

"How's her head?" Troy asked Patience between bites of bacon and eggs and biscuits.

"Contusion, certainly. Concussed, most likely."

"I'm fine," said Mercy.

Troy raised his eyebrows at Patience. "Do you think she's really up to this?"

"I think she should get a CT scan just to be safe and, failing that, at least get some rest today." Patience offered him another biscuit. "But she's as stubborn as her grandfather."

"I'm sitting right here, guys," Mercy said.

"I reported the det cord you found," Troy said to Mercy. "Everyone's on alert. They can handle it."

"We're good to go," insisted Mercy.

"If the senator's there, Harrington will be, too. The captain says he likes the limelight. Thrasher warned me to steer clear."

"Understood." She grinned. "But he's not the boss of me."

Patience sighed. "There's really no stopping her."

"Okay, but you keep a low profile." Troy slathered a last bite of biscuit with honey. He popped it into his mouth.

"Deal."

Mercy and Troy both looked at her grandmother.

"Oh, all right." Patience frowned. "But when you get back, you go in for that CT scan."

"Promise."

SHE and Troy and the dogs piled into his truck for the short ride to the village. Most of the Fourth of July festivities were held in the town center, which dated from the 1700s. Many of the buildings and houses throughout the village were vintage.

"The crowd is bigger than I expected," said Mercy.

"Usually triple the population in summer," said Troy, parking on a side street. "Maybe more, since they're rededicating the Fountain of the Muses on the village green tomorrow."

"I'd forgotten all about that." The Fountain of the Muses was a lovely Beaux-Arts fountain featuring the three original Muses of Greek myth: Melete, the Muse of meditation; Mneme, the Muse of memory; and Aoide, the Muse of song.

A century of harsh weather had taken its toll on the grand centerpiece. It had been decades since water had flowed through the fountain. But tomorrow, a year after it had been shipped off for restoration, the fountain would return. Art aficionados from the world over were here for the rededication.

"More people, more crowd cover," said Troy.

"Makes it even harder to find them. Good thing we have the dogs." She slipped the body armor onto Elvis while Troy prepped Susie Bear. Mercy was worried about Elvis; this was the first time he'd worn the protective gear since Afghanistan. He seemed okay, standing still if alert while she snapped on his lead. He licked her hand and then danced against the door until she let him out of the truck. He knew he was here to work.

"Put this on." Troy handed her a covert vest.

She hunkered down in the cab to take off her T-shirt. She put the vest over her cami, then slipped her shirt back on. "Ready."

"The 5K Fun Run is nearly over." He pointed to the middle of Main Street, which was blocked off from all motor vehicle traffic and flanked with crushes of men, women, kids, and pets. "That means the parade will be under way shortly."

"Right." She held Elvis's lead firmly. Both he and Susie Bear were excited, tails wagging, paws prancing, as they waited for instructions. She hoped that the shepherd's high-energy level reflected his anticipation of a fine reward for a job well done—and not anxiety triggered by the noise and the people.

Troy led them through the crowd, weaving around bystanders to the starting point of the parade. Most everyone smiled at the working dogs, waving their Stars and Stripes flags.

"The logical mark is the grandstand," Troy said over his shoulder. "That's where the big shots will be."

They stood behind a barricade. The Northshire High School marching band at the front of the parade struck up a blaring rendition of "Yankee Doodle Dandy," signaling the kickoff.

"I'll take that side of the route; you take this one. Text me if you see anything." Troy gave her a hard look. "Don't try anything on your own. And keep that dog of yours under control."

He waited for her to say something, but she didn't. No point in making promises she might not keep.

Troy shrugged and trotted away, Susie Bear at his hip. Mercy turned her attention to her and Elvis's side of the street. She had Patience's phone so she could contact Troy if necessary.

"We're here to work." She scratched the shepherd's dark, triangular ears, then scanned the crowd. "Search, Elvis."

The shepherd launched ahead, and they were off. A young mother with a baby caught her eye. Fair-haired, but too short. Not Amy. Not Helena. She also scrutinized every tall man, every curvy brunette, and every wild-haired hippie, thinking she might be looking at the tall man called Max or the elusive professor Dr. Winters or the activist artist Adam Wolfe.

Ceremonial cannons fired on the common, and Elvis stopped short. Mercy nearly fell over him. The dog was nervous. The drummers in another marching band banged out the rhythm to "The Army Goes Rolling Along." Mercy and Elvis winced, she at the memory of Martinez and he at the bursts of percussion.

The crowds grew thicker as they approached the grandstand, where the local and state dignitaries were sitting. Mercy recognized the senator, the mayor, the governor, and a congressman. Detective Harrington was there, too, chatting up the mayor. And Lillian Jenkins, the owner of the Vermonter Drive-In, who was probably running this whole show.

Calmer now, Elvis plowed on, tail high. Mercy held on and navigated the throngs of energetic revelers as best she could. On the village green a small group of Revolutionary soldiers fired their muskets. To Elvis's credit and her pride, he remained poised and focused despite the bedlam all around him. She wished his sergeant could see him now. She wished he were here with them now. She wished she could get past this wishing.

They were directly in front of the grandstand now. She surveyed the scene again. The easiest way anyone could get close enough to endanger one of the dignitaries without detection would be on a float. She sent Troy a text saying that she was going back to where the floats were lined up.

Elvis did not protest when she turned around and indicated she wanted to move back toward the beginning of the parade.

"Search," she told him again, looking herself for anything out of the ordinary. The theme of this year's parade was "Arts in America," a nod to the return of the Fountain of the Muses. There was a Grandma Moses float and a Vermont folk art float.

Next in line was the Vermont Republic float, festooned with a living diorama of the coat of arms against a green mountain backdrop. And the Green Mountain Boys band, featuring a girl singer and two beefy male fiddlers dressed like minutemen accompanying her on the "Ballad of the Green Mountain Boys."

> *Hurrah for Vermont! For the land that we till*
> *Must have sons to defend her from valley and hill*
> *Our vow is recorded—our banner unfurled,*
> *In the name of Vermont we defy all the world!*
> *Then cheer, cheer, the green mountaineer,*
> *Then cheer, cheer, the green mountaineer.*

As she listened, she realized that this float could hold the key to these murders. She sent a text to Troy about her suspicions. She looked at Elvis, but the dog did not alert. She hustled him through the crowd, following the Green Mountain Boys.

"Search, boy, search!"

Again the bomb-sniffing dog did not alert. Mercy was so sure that he would find something of interest on that float—so sure that she had been right. But nothing happened.

Elvis zoomed on, intent on his search, indifferent to the band and the Vermont Republic float on which they continued to play.

Her head ached; her vest was hot; her confidence lagged. She stopped in front of the Ben & Jerry's storefront where a girl was handing out free samples of ice cream. The sugar rush helped, and she turned away from the shop to view the parade.

A guy dressed like a minuteman broke through the crowd and ran alongside the Vermont Republic float, jumping onto the back as the float continued to move down the street.

"Better late than never!" he yelled. The crowd laughed.

His militia tricorn hat hid most of his face, but he was tall and moved gracefully, as had the intruder at her cabin. He carried a musket; a hunting cartridge, haversack, and fife case were slung over his shoulder. A canteen was belted to his hip.

Why a musket and a musical instrument? Mercy wondered. The assumption was that if he were going to join the Vermont Republic float, he was a member of the band. She took a harder look at his hunting cartridge and haversack. Both seemed out of place. Something was off with this guy, she thought, even as he pulled out the fife and began to play.

Elvis didn't like him, either. The shepherd's ears perked up, and he pulled at the lead. They pushed past several rows of parade-goers to get to the curb. They jogged by the Friends of the Library, pushing their book carts decorated with art posters.

Elvis pulled away from her, gaining on the Vermont Republic float. A posse of farmers steering bright green John Deere tractors and a contingent of cadets clad in navy-and-white uniforms were the marchers separating them from the float.

No sign of Troy yet. He'd warned her against going it alone, but she'd have to if he didn't show up soon. Elvis shot through the tractors and cadets. Mercy struggled to keep up. She stumbled, dropping the leash. A cadet helped her to her feet.

"Elvis!" Mercy panted, and kept on running.

But the Malinois didn't even slow down. He caught up to the Vermont Republic float, keeping pace alongside it.

And then Elvis soared.

Mercy saw the sleek shepherd sail after the moving target that was the minuteman on the Vermont Republic float. He landed lightly on all paws, barking like the hound of Hades.

The music stopped, and the girl singer screamed, and the tall man turned. He dropped his haversack and hunting cartridge to the floor of the float and raised his musket against the dog.

"No!" Mercy pumped her legs and lunged for the float. The flatbed hit her at the hip. She pulled herself up onto the platform and threw herself forward toward the minuteman's legs, clamping her fingers around his ankles. He tried to escape her grip, and his hat fell off, exposing his shaved head. She recognized him at once as the man Dr. Winters had called Max.

He pounded the musket butt on the float, just missing her hands. Mercy rolled away before the musket struck again.

"Get him," she ordered.

Elvis tackled the guy, chomping down on his wrist. Max cursed, dropping the rifle, trying to shake off the dog. But the ferocious shepherd hung on, forcing his perp to the floor.

Mercy kicked the musket away, sending it flying off of the float. The fiddle players moved in to help Max but thought better of it as Susie Bear bounded onto the float, bellowing.

Troy heaved himself onto the float after his Newfie mutt, nodding at Mercy as he cornered the fiddlers. "I've notified Thrasher," Troy said. "Backup is on the way."

The float rumbled on past the grandstand. Behind them the cadets marched on and the tractors chugged along.

Mercy kept her eye on Max and Elvis as police officers flanked the float. They removed the barriers, diverted the onlookers, then guided the float onto a side street.

She called off Elvis, and the police officers arrested the tall man, who identified himself as Max Skinner from Provo, Utah.

"I don't know what you're talking about," he was telling the cops. "I'm an artist." She heard him ask for a lawyer as they took him off to the station.

Troy and Susie Bear joined Mercy and Elvis, and together they left the float, giving the bomb squad room to clear the vehicle. They sat on a fence and watched as the rest of the band were escorted away for questioning. The dogs sat at their feet.

"The fiddlers are Paul and Louis Herbert," Troy told her. "Wayne Herbert's little brothers."

"They're wearing the same belt buckles as the one we found with the bones. Who's the girl?"

"Sarah Lavery, a sous chef from Bennington. Not sure what she's got to do with this yet."

Together they watched as the bomb squad checked the float and found no evidence of explosives. Or of anything else criminal. The hunting cartridge Skinner had carried was empty. The knapsack held a tambourine. The canteen was filled with water.

"I don't understand," said Mercy. "Elvis is a bomb-sniffing dog. He's trained to alert to explosives. That's what he does."

"They didn't find anything. Maybe it was Skinner himself. If he was your intruder, Elvis may have alerted to him."

Mercy tossed her head, not caring that it still hurt like hell whenever she did that. "Look, can we go now?"

"You'll have to make a statement."

"I really don't feel up to hanging around the station for hours." She touched her crown gently. "And it looks like rain."

"Of course." Troy stood up. "Stupid of me. You should be home in bed. I'll explain to the captain."

"I don't want to get you in trouble." Mercy stood, too.

"Don't worry about it." He offered her his arm, and she took it. The dogs followed them as he led her to his truck. Troy ushered them all into his vehicle just as the downpour began.

"I was so sure." Mercy couldn't understand how she could be so wrong. About the parade. About Elvis. About herself.

"You may have been wrong about the parade, but you aren't

wrong about the case. Something is going on here." He pulled out onto the road. "We've got the dead bodies to prove it."

"And a missing mother and child."

"Yeah," he said. "Still no word on them." He looked over at her with concern. "But the evidence team did clean up that pendant. I'll text you the images."

She knew he was just trying to make her feel better. Not that it was working. "If I don't figure it out soon, Amy and Helena may be the next—" She stopped. She couldn't say it out loud.

"It's not all on you. We'll figure it out."

Mercy leaned her head back and closed her eyes. "It's been a long day. I just want to go home."

"Not to your grandmother's?"

"Home."

If there was one thing Mercy hated, it was going home in defeat. But retreat was not always defeat. So she'd retreat . . . for now.

MERCY texted her grandmother, and by the time Troy dropped them off at the cabin, Patience was waiting for her at the dining table. As the storm raged on, Patience listened to her sad story of humiliation and defeat at the parade with generous offerings of sympathy and red velvet cake.

"What are you going to do now?"

"I don't know."

"The proper answer would be 'CT scan.'"

"Not in this weather."

"The storm will be gone by morning. It's just going to last long enough to postpone the fireworks until tomorrow night."

"My pride may be hurting, but my head is fine."

"Your grandfather used to say that eliminating possible solutions was as important as nailing the right one."

"I eliminated one solution in high style today."

"And now which are left to investigate?"

Mercy reached for her borrowed phone. "Troy was going to text me photos of the pendant we found at the crime scene. We think the jeweler who made the belt buckles made this, too."

"Why don't you take a look while I clean up?"

"Thanks." Mercy abandoned the table for the couch. She pulled up the photos and looked at the maker's mark on the pendant. She read off the letters and numbers that ran along the back: POM 925, followed by an image of a calla lily.

"What did you find?" Her grandmother stood behind her, looking over her shoulder.

She pointed to the symbols. "POM should be the designer's initials; nine twenty-five means it's sterling silver—that is, ninety-two point five percent pure silver. And the calla lily is probably the designer's logo. I need to track down this artist."

"Of course you do. But don't spend too long on that computer. Not good for your head. Half an hour; then it's lights out."

"Okay." She waited until Patience had gone back into the kitchen, then texted Troy. He told her Flo Herbert claimed that the artist who made the buckles had retired to Ireland, and the police were trying to trace the maker's mark. Then he signed off.

Ireland, thought Mercy. Ireland of the Easter Rising, the famous rebellion that kicked off the Irish revolutionary period during Easter week in 1926. Calla lilies, long the symbol of Easter, had become one of the symbols of a free Irish Republic as well.

She grabbed her laptop and went to work. After dozens of searches, she found a pendant on eBay just like the one the Munchkin found, designed by one Patrick O'Malley.

"Time's up," said Patience, looming over her.

Mercy jumped. "You startled me."

"You need to go to bed so I can go home."

"You're leaving?" She wanted her grandmother to stay.

"I've got to get back to the sick kitties."

"What about tomorrow? Will you need help?"

"Thanks, but I've already arranged for help." Patience waved her arms in the air. "I'm going out," she said grandly.

"Going out where?"

"I've wrangled an invite to the poshest affair this town has seen in years. The Northshire Historical Society and Museum is hosting an exhibit in honor of the return of the Fountain of the Muses. Your neighbor Daniel Feinberg is the grand master."

"I didn't take him for the committee type." Not that she knew much about the billionaire whose land cozied up to hers.

"He's not. But he's a serious art collector and has been very generous to the museum. He underwrote the restoration of the fountain. And he's donating the famous Grandma Moses painting of our village green to the museum. You know the one."

"Yes." The acclaimed primitive artist had painted the village green—with the Fountain of the Muses center stage—in the spring of 1954 and called it, simply, *Northshire*.

"The viewing is tomorrow morning, and they're having a fancy reception. Anyone who's anyone in the New England art world will be there. I'm surprised you haven't heard about it."

"I'm not big on the news." She avoided all manner of media, since as far as she was concerned, no news was good news.

"You really need to rejoin the human race sometime soon."

Mercy remembered the flier that had led her to the parade—and disaster. She'd posted it on the fridge to remind her of her hubris, right next to the facedown photo of Martinez.

She got up and snatched it off the fridge and carried it back to the couch. She looked at the activities for the day after the Fourth, which she'd ignored in her obsession with the parade.

Monday, July 5
10 a.m. *Northshire Historical Society and Museum Reception (limited tickets available, contact society)*
Noon *The Unveiling of the Fountain of the Muses*
Noon to 5 p.m. *Art Fete on the Green (music, food, face painting, arts & crafts fair, open to the public)*

Her grandmother tapped the reception entry. "That's it."

"Are you going to get all dolled up?" asked Mercy.

"It is a semiformal affair. One should make an effort."

"You'll want to hold your own with the beautiful people," Mercy said, thinking that if all the artists in Vermont were there, Dr. Winters and Adam Wolfe could be, too. "Do you think you could wrangle me an invitation?"

"Are you serious?"

"You know, something to do. To rejoin the human race."

Patience wasn't fooled. "You hate functions like this."

"I'm very supportive of the arts."

"Sure you are. What about the CT scan?"

"I could go right after the reception."

"Your parents will be there."

Mercy sighed. "Let me guess. They're Feinberg's attorneys."

"Yep. Of course, you should get that CT scan. Or at least stay home and rest." Her grandmother smiled, a smile of collusion. "But I do happen to have an extra ticket."

"I couldn't let you go all alone. I'll be your plus one."

"I can think of a million reasons why you wouldn't want to go— and only one why you would. You think you might learn something. You're going as a spy."

Mercy demurred, but her grandmother laughed her off. "At least this way I can keep an eye on you. Do us all a favor and wear something your mother would like."

MONDAY, JULY 5

Chapter 9

THE NEXT MORNING, Mercy laid out the gifts her mother had given her since she'd come back from Afghanistan: at least a dozen outfits, due to her insistence that her only daughter needed an entire new wardrobe now that she was a civilian again and would be applying to law schools in big cities soon.

The gifts were mostly work clothes, what her mother liked to call "power suits," featuring tailored jackets paired with skirts. For "after hours" wear she'd curated four little black dresses. They all showed either too much leg or too much décolletage.

One shopping bag left. Mercy prayed for something normal. She pulled out a navy jumpsuit made of light cotton jersey, with wide palazzo-style pants and a cold-shouldered top.

She could definitely move in this without showing too much skin. And she could add the Chanel fanny pack—a little quilted black purse on a gold chain belt. Plenty of room to carry a cell, her Swiss Army knife, and whatever else she might need.

She showered, then slipped on the jumpsuit. She secured the Chanel purse around her waist and added gold hoop earrings and low-heeled gold sandals that she could run in if needed.

A glance in the mirror told her that she should add a little blush and mascara and lip gloss. She didn't cover up her freckles with foundation, as her mother always advised her to do.

The only thing her mother hated more than her freckles was her hair. But there was no containing it in this humidity. She ran some styling mousse through her damp frizz. Au naturel would have to suffice, whether her mother liked it or not.

PATIENCE whistled when she saw Mercy.

"You look pretty good yourself," Mercy said, admiring her grandmother's turquoise silk tunic, which she wore with black silk pants and silver ballet slippers.

"Too bad your game warden is on patrol," said Patience.

"He's not my game warden," she said.

"Oh, but he could be. Especially if he saw you right now."

"Come on, let's go."

Elvis jumped up.

"Sorry." Mercy patted his head. "You're staying home."

She locked the door as she followed Patience to her "fun" car, the little red Mustang convertible that spent most of the year in the garage. Except for beautiful sunny days like this.

"Your mother will be pleased," Patience said as she peeled down the drive and out to Route 7A. When unencumbered by four-legged passengers, she liked to drive fast.

"I live to serve," said Mercy, holding on to her seat.

"She loves you."

"I know."

"Be nice," her grandmother admonished her.

"I'm always nice."

"You're always polite. Polite is not the same as nice."

Mercy closed her eyes and leaned her head back, letting the wind rush over her face as they sped down the road.

THE Northshire Historical Society and Museum sat on the edge of the village green. The large white building was built in the Greek Revival style, with a long front porch supported by graceful fluted columns. The gracious lady was festooned with red-white-and-blue bunting for the Fourth, and a long banner topped the porch, proclaiming ARTS OF AMERICA EXHIBITION.

Lillian Jenkins, chairperson of the society's Arts in America Committee, stood just inside the entrance at the head of the reception line. The restaurateur had abandoned her Vermonter Drive-In apron for a dazzling sparkly gold dress.

Lillian embraced her and her grandmother in turn.

"You look very pretty," she said. "Did you bring that handsome Troy Warner with you?"

"Uh, no."

"I think they're having a thing," said Lillian to Patience.

"We're just friends," said Mercy.

"I thought you were smarter than that." Lillian frowned.

Mercy capitulated. "He's on patrol."

"Then you'll have to settle for his yummy captain." Lillian waved her golden arm across the room at Captain Thrasher.

He was resplendent in his dress uniform, with its tailored scarlet jacket and distinctive black trim and black leather belt.

Then the captain shifted on his feet, and she saw that he was talking to her parents.

"Chin up," said Patience as they nodded good-bye to Lillian.

"Let's get this over with."

Her grandmother took her arm in solidarity and marched her over to the distinguished couple and the dashing captain.

"Darling, how wonderful to see you," said her mother.

"Hi, Mom." Mercy kissed her cheek dutifully.

"Let me look at you." She grabbed her shoulders and stepped back to inspect her. "I knew that color would flatter you."

Her mother was a slim, pale blonde impeccably dressed in a little black dress. Her father stood beside her, a tall, stooped man who looked more like a professor than an attorney.

"This is my daughter, Mercy Carr," her father told the captain. "And my mother-in-law, Patience O'Sullivan."

"I know the captain," said her grandmother. "He's the fine human to a magnificent Maine coon cat."

"May I steal your granddaughter for a moment?" Thrasher asked. "I'd like to show her something."

Before Patience could protest, the captain guided Mercy over to a finely rendered pen-and-ink drawing of Shakespeare's *Dark Lady*. She hoped there was no hidden meaning in that.

"We have a mutual friend," he said.

"Yes." She waited to see what he would say next.

"You've distracted him," he said. "And not in a good way."

"I'm sorry." So much for hidden meanings.

"Are you?" He frowned. "You keep turning up at our crime scenes. And now you see criminal activity wherever you go."

"Elvis was alerted to something, sir."

"The dog." Thrasher crossed his arms. "You and your dog caused the service some considerable embarrassment."

"I am sorry about that. But three people are dead. A young mother and her baby are missing. And Max Skinner is involved somehow. I think he's the man who broke into my house."

"Understood. But he and the Herbert brothers have been released for lack of evidence. Calling out the bomb squad is an expensive proposition for a false alarm."

"Better a false alarm than an unfortunate outcome."

"Harrington is not happy," said Thrasher, lowering his voice. "And when he's not happy, our mutual friend is at risk."

"I wouldn't want to hurt our mutual friend in any way." She caught sight of her mother coming toward her and for once was glad of it. "I must get back to my family." She turned her back on him and went to join her mother.

"Let's take a look at the exhibition, shall we?" Her mother squeezed her arm. "There are people I'd love for you to meet."

Which Mercy knew meant "Have I got a man for you!" But if the alternative was another warning from Thrasher, she'd sooner make the rounds with her overzealous mother.

THE gala was now in full swing. People wandered from room to room of the graceful mansion, taking in the art that represented the best of the Green Mountain state.

The prized *Grandma Moses* painting stood on an easel, covered with a midnight-blue silk cloth, in the middle of the Grand Gallery, set off by red velvet rope. With the viewing an hour away, partygoers focused on drinking champagne, eating hors d'oeuvres, and networking, networking, networking. Mercy's idea of hell.

But she had a job to do.

While her mother trotted her around to meet potential sons-in-law in situ—a tax attorney, an intellectual property attorney, a mergers-and-acquisitions attorney—Mercy smiled sweetly at the men and surreptitiously checked out the artwork and the security measures in place to protect it. She spotted motion sensors in the corners and video cameras hanging from the ceiling.

Patience rescued her just as her mother was introducing her to a personal-injury attorney, whom she knew could not be her parents' first choice.

"They must be getting desperate," she whispered to Patience.

"They just want you to be happy."

"They have no idea who I am."

"It's nearly time for the viewing of *Northshire*. Come on."

Everyone started gravitating toward the roped-off area in the Grand Gallery, clustering in a crescent in front of the easel.

Daniel Feinberg, the billionaire landowner, stepped up with the mayor to begin their presentation. All eyes were on the prize now, except for Mercy's, who scanned the crowd.

No Adam Wolfe. No Max Skinner. No Herbert brothers. No Dr. Candace Winters. And no Amy and Helena.

The speeches began, and Mercy tuned out. She grabbed a flute of champagne and downed it. What a waste of time this had been. The bubbly rushed to her head, and her skull started to pulsate. She should have known better. Sparkling wine gave her a headache even when she didn't have a concussion.

Head pounding, she went in search of a ladies' room, which was in the back of the building. Mercy walked in, and there she was, preening in front of the long mirror: Dr. Candace Winters, dressed in a tea-length blue dress with a white Peter Pan collar that seemed prim and proper when seen from the front but was completely backless, revealing a sexy stretch of creamy skin.

"Dr. Winters," she said, acknowledging her with a nod.

The professor finished applying her red lipstick before she spoke. "Corporal Carr." She turned and regarded her with those huge gray eyes, magnified through her nerdy black glasses.

"What do you think of the exhibit?" Mercy asked.

"It's not the best curation, is it? But it does have its moments. Have you made it to the West Gallery yet?"

She shook her head. "I don't think so."

"You won't want to miss it." Dr. Winters pursed her red lips. "I hardly recognized you. You look so presentable." With that, she swept out of the ladies' room, her bare back glistening.

What a piece of work is woman, Mercy thought, paraphrasing the Bard. She ran a paper towel under the faucet and wrung it out before patting her forehead and cheeks and collarbone. The damp cloth felt cool against her face, and the throbbing in her head subsided.

She made her way back to the viewing area, where Dr. Winters had joined the crowd, which was far larger now that the moment they'd all been waiting for approached. There must have been at least three hundred people. Standing room only.

The mayor stepped forward to pull the covering from the easel with a flourish, revealing the work. Painted with oils, the naïve work pictured the village green in summer, children in their

Sunday best playing around the Fountain of the Muses, their parents looking on under a canopy of trees and a blue sky.

The crowd oohed and aahed and surged forward. Mercy lost sight of the professor, then spotted her again by the entrance, on the arm of the mergers-and-acquisitions attorney her mother liked so much. They seemed enthralled by one another, if the way he ran his hand down her bare back was any indication.

By the time she made her way through the throngs of gala guests, Dr. Winters was out the front door. So was the attorney.

Mercy considered going after them, but she wasn't sure what that could achieve. Besides, she had no car and no plan, and Detective Harrington was blocking her way.

"Ms. Carr?"

Harrington took her by surprise. She blinked. "Yes?"

"Daniel Feinberg would like a proper introduction."

Another surprise. "Sure."

He grabbed her harshly by the elbow and hustled her along to within a foot of Feinberg. But before he let go, he whispered in her ear: "Watch yourself. Because I am watching you."

She didn't say anything. Just shook the man off and smiled at the billionaire.

"Thank you, Harrington," said Feinberg in a dismissive tone.

Harrington nodded at Feinberg and glared at her before falling back into the crowd. Out of sight. But still watching her.

"It's a pleasure to meet you, Ms. Carr," said Feinberg.

"Please call me Mercy."

"Mercy." He smiled at her, and she was struck by the aura of power emanating from him. He made a strong impression, with his full head of wavy salt-and-pepper hair and dark brown eyes that went from warm to wary to warm again in a split second.

They walked together toward the elegant staircase that led to the second floor of the museum. Two bodyguards in black suits and earpieces followed at a discreet distance. They reached the second-floor landing, and he escorted her into the West Gallery, a large, graceful space with an inlaid hardwood floor.

This gallery was devoted to sculpture. There was a nineteenth-century figurehead of an exotic raven-haired beauty that reminded Mercy of Cleopatra. "'Eternity was in our lips . . .'"

"Pardon?" asked Feinberg.

Mercy flushed, realizing to her embarrassment that she'd quoted *Antony and Cleopatra* out loud to herself. "Sorry, sculpture always brings out the worst in me. Shakespeare."

"Interesting." He gave her a shrewd look. "And unexpected."

Mercy was barely listening. She walked away from her host toward the back of the room, where a striking bronze glowed like fire in the afternoon sun that poured in from the windows.

Another one of Wolfe's pieces. This sculpture was much like the one she'd seen in Dr. Winters's parlor, only far larger. The massive curves seemed to fall into themselves, repeating in sensuous waves that reminded her of the professor's bare back.

Feinberg came up behind her and smiled at her obvious appreciation of the sculpture. "Do you know Adam Wolfe's work?"

"I've only recently discovered it. It's beautiful."

"Yes, he's very talented." Feinberg cleared his throat. "You found a dead body at Adam's compound in the woods."

"Yes, I did." There was no point in denying it.

He nodded. "The dead man was a Canadian, they tell me."

"Rufus Flanigan. I met him hiking the day before."

"But Adam was not there."

"No. Everyone was gone. Most everything was cleared out."

Feinberg's dark eyes grew wary again. "I own that land."

"Squatters?"

"No. I gave him permission to set up a studio there. I admire his work, and we share a commitment to preserving the land."

"Did you know him well?"

"As an artist, yes. As a man, that's harder to say." Feinberg gazed at the bronze. "I met him in Quebec."

"Quebec?"

"I was in the market for a piece by Paul-Émile Borduas, one of Canada's foremost abstract painters. Leader of the Automatistes movement and author of *Le Refus global* manifesto."

"Manifesto? So he was an activist as well as an artist."

"Very antiestablishment. That's why Adam likes his work so much. He fancies himself an activist as well."

"You sound skeptical."

"Adam is a wild man, given to enthusiasms." Feinberg shrugged. "His so-called activism is one of those enthusiasms."

"He's been hanging out with a lot of Vermont Firsters."

Feinberg laughed. "He's not really a Vermont Firster. He's not even from here. He's from Quebec. He left there to revitalize his career, just as his hero Borduas did. I encouraged him."

"You're his friend as well as his patron."

"We bonded over Borduas. I thought he had talent."

"Do you know Amy Walker and the baby Helena?"

"I've met them a few times at the art colony. I don't go to the compound often. Usually Adam comes to the house."

"You don't think he was keeping her there against her will?"

"I've never seen anything that would lead me to believe that." He shook his head. "Artists live by their own rules."

"Amy and the baby are missing. She came to me for help. And now she's gone."

"I'd like to know what's really going on myself."

"I thought he might be here today."

"So did I. He was supposed to be here."

"When did you see him last?"

"Oh, it's been several weeks. He's off creating."

"You must have been disappointed when he abandoned the bronzes for natural sculpture."

"Not at all. Do you know what a folly is?"

"As in foolishness?"

"No. I'm talking about the decorative Greek ruins built on the grounds of old estates in Britain. Just for the hell of it."

"What do you mean, just for the hell of it?"

"That was the point of follies, that they served no purpose."

"No purpose but art," she said.

"Art is its own purpose. I commissioned Adam to create natural-sculpture follies on my land."

"He was cited for putting installations on private property."

"I know. It was my land and my complaint. But when I realized what wonderful work he was doing, I paid the fines for him myself and commissioned the follies."

"I think I found one not far from the compound." Mercy smiled. "A beautifully crafted arch made of chiseled stones."

"That was his first." He smiled back. "He's finished two—the one you found and another somewhere closer to my house."

"I'd love to see the other one."

"Then you'll have to find it, just like I have to do." He laughed. "He says he's working on ideas for the third. There will be nine in total, scattered through the woods like jewels."

"Nine. As in nine circles of hell. Nine Supreme Court justices. Nine Worthies." Mercy snapped her fingers. "Nine Muses."

"You got it." Feinberg's smile faded. "If he comes back."

"That's why you thought he'd be here today. For the return of the Fountain of the Muses."

The three original Muses—the meditation Muse, Melete; the memory Muse, Mneme; and the song Muse, Aoide—were the ancient ones featured on the Fountain of the Muses. Over time these three became the Nine Muses—from Calliope, the Muse of epic poetry, to Urania, the Muse of astronomy—who together embodied all of the arts and inspired artists of all kinds.

"Yes," said Feinberg. "Shall we go have a look?"

THE black suits trailed Mercy and Feinberg back down the staircase to the ground floor of the museum. The galleries were empty now, the guests having retreated outside to the village green. Only the cleanup crew and the security guards remained.

"Heavy security," she said as they stepped out onto the porch and the guards shut the doors behind them.

"Art theft is on the rise statewide. So we've put in the very latest in alarms, infrared motion detection, scanners, twenty-four-hour video surveillance, staffing vetting and security."

The village green looked much like it did in the *Northshire* painting: young couples picnicking on the grass, vendors selling balloons and cotton candy, children playing by the three-tiered fountain. They walked down the middle path for a closer look. Now cast in durable aluminum and painted in a burnished dark antique copper, the three Muses glistened in their diaphanous gowns as they sat in contemplation of the arts, crowned by curls of water spraying forth from the mouths of cherubs.

"You've done a good thing here," she said. "I imagine your own private collection is quite impressive."

"I've been collecting art for more than twenty-five years."

"Did you ever meet Max Skinner or the Herbert brothers?"

"I know of the Herbert brothers because my groundskeeper caught them poaching on our land. Adam talks a lot about his buddy Max, but we've never met. He did arrange for me to see some of his art in Quebec. But I didn't connect with it."

"Why not?"

"I found Skinner's work too dark and disturbing. While I consider my art an investment, I also have to like what I buy."

They circled the fountain. Feinberg's presence was beginning to attract notice, and several people came up to greet him, Harrington among them. He glared at her, and she glared back.

"I'm sorry," Feinberg said, shaking her hand. "Do come to the house. I'll arrange a tour."

"I'd like that." She turned to go, then thought better of it. "Did you ever buy that Borduas?"

"It's hanging over the fireplace," Feinberg said. "You'll like it. It's called *Chinoiserie*, aka *Birches: Winter*."

"Two names?"

"Yes. Two names, like Paul-Émile Borduas. Adam says it's the nature of duality."

"Duality," she repeated. "Opposite sides of the same coin. Like light and dark. Good and evil. Artist and activist."

Feinberg smiled. "That's one way to look at it."

Well-wishers converged on the billionaire, under the watchful eye of Harrington and his bodyguards. Mercy waved good-bye and went in search of a snack. The green was lined with vendors: the American Legion grilling hot dogs and burgers, Friends of the

Library hosting a bake sale, Animal Rescue selling fried dough.

Lured by the sweet scent of crispy crust and powdered sugar, she asked for a double order. She caught sight of her mother talking to Lillian Jenkins. Her mother did not look happy. She had a terrible feeling the ebullient Lillian had said something that upset her. Probably about a certain game warden.

Mercy watched as her mother scanned the crowd for her. She darted into the arts-and-crafts tent, where she'd be safe. Her mother wouldn't be caught dead buying anything in here.

She walked up and down the aisles, glancing at the paintings and wood carvings. She stopped at a booth with silk-screened T-shirts emblazoned with endangered species. Bats and butterflies, wolves and wolverines, whipsnakes and sea turtles.

She thought about buying a T-shirt for her grandmother. Mercy was partial to the wolves, but maybe that was just because she had another wild Wolfe in mind.

Wolves. Wolfe. Wolf.

He's mad that trusts in the tameness of a wolf.

She ran out of the arts tent. Past her mother and Lillian. Past Feinberg and his fans. Past Harrington and his dark looks.

Chapter 10

THERE WAS NOTHING like a hot shower after long patrols in the woods and a dressing-down by Harrington. Troy washed away the dirt and sweat and humiliation of the past twenty-four hours. He'd have time for a quick nap before going back out.

From now on he'd stick to what he was good at: patrolling the wilderness and protecting the wildlife.

No more parades. No more goose chases. He knew he should say no more Mercy Carr, too, but he wasn't sure he could.

As he shut off the water, he heard Susie Bear lumber to the front door, barking all the way. He tied a towel around his waist and followed her. Through the front window, he saw a red Mustang convertible he didn't recognize. So much for that nap.

There was a pounding on the door.

"Sit," he told Susie Bear, and she sat, tail thumping. Which meant she liked whoever was on the other side of the door.

He opened it—and found Mercy and Elvis. She was all dressed up, as if she'd been to a party.

"What are you doing here?" He was stunned to see her so decked out. She looked pretty great. Girly, even.

"Sorry for just dropping by like this, but it couldn't wait. Something amazing has happened."

"Uh-huh." She was all worked up. Her pale skin was so flushed with exhilaration, she was practically luminescent.

"I figured it out," she said, her voice high with excitement. "Adam Wolfe and Rufus Flanigan are the same person."

Troy stared at her. This might be her craziest idea yet.

"Has his next of kin identified him?" she said. There was a challenge in her blue eyes.

"I'm not sure they've even had time to find his next of kin."

"You should run his prints."

"You'd better come in." He stood aside and waved Mercy inside.

"I think Max Skinner killed him."

"Like he blew up the parade."

"I know I was wrong about that," she said in a low voice. "And I'm so sorry. But this is different. I'm not wrong now."

"We've just come off patrol, and we have to go back soon."

"I can prove they're one and the same person."

Troy hesitated. She'd been right about everything else . . . well, except for the explosives. "Why don't you have a seat and tell me all about it." He pointed her to a chair at the table.

"Okay." But she didn't sit down.

"I was just about to make us some supper. Are you hungry?"

Both dogs barked at the sound of one of their favorite words: *supper.*

"Why don't you feed them while I change? The Crock-Pot on

the counter has Susie Bear's stew in it. You're welcome to share it with Elvis. There should be plenty."

"Smells good."

"If Elvis likes it, I'll give you the recipe." He headed across the room. "Dog dishes in the pantry."

He climbed the stairs and changed into a clean uniform, then went back downstairs to find Mercy chopping up tomatoes and cucumbers for the salad she'd made.

"I found the box of produce from the farmers' association in the fridge," she said. "I hope that's okay."

"Great. I'll make omelets. Cheddar cheese okay?"

"Sure. Between the two of them, they finished off the stew." She watched as he beat eggs and poured them into a skillet.

"That's okay. I don't eat Susie Bear's stew."

Mercy frowned. "You cook for your dog but not yourself?"

He laughed as he grated the cheese and added it to the eggs. "I'm not a fan of the Crock-Pot. More of a grill guy." He flipped the omelet on a plate and placed it in front of her. Then he sat down at the table with her. "Let's hear it. From the top."

She nodded, and in between bites she told him about the Historical Society's gala and her conversation with Feinberg about Adam Wolfe and Paul-Émile Borduas and his comment about two names. "I think he was referring to the names of his two personas—Adam Wolfe and Rufus Flanigan."

"Kind of a stretch."

"Not really. Something about the bird-watcher had been bugging me. I knew I was missing something. And then it hit me. Wolves."

"Wolves." He had no idea where she was going with this.

"Adam Wolfe. Rufus Flanigan." She grinned at him. "How is your Latin?"

"Not great," he admitted. "I know that *Canis lupus familiaris* is the scientific name for dog, and *Canis lupus lupus* is the scientific name for wolf, from the Latin. Right?"

"Right."

"I still don't get it."

"*Canis lupus lupus* refers to the common wolf. But the scientific name for the red wolf is . . ." She looked at him like a patient teacher.

"*Canis lupus rufus.*"

"I looked up the etymologies of Flanigan and Adam, too. Adam is Hebrew and means 'red,' a reference to ruddy skin. Flanigan is Gaelic, a diminutive of *flann*, which means—"

"Let me guess," he interrupted her. "Red."

"Red or ruddy, yes." She hesitated. "So Adam Wolfe means 'red wolf' and Rufus Flanigan means 'red wolf red.'"

"Two reds. Like the two *lupuses*. It almost makes sense."

Mercy frowned. "I suppose it could be just some crazy coincidence, but I don't think so."

"It's not crazy." He laughed. "It's brilliant. And it sounds like the kind of thing this guy would do."

She pushed over the cell phone that Patience loaned her. "Here are the images of Adam Wolfe I found on the Internet."

He flipped through the photos of a hippie-looking long-haired dude with a full beard and mustache.

She leaned across the table. "Now picture him with a short haircut like yours—no beard, no mustache, no wild mane."

Troy tried to imagine that. He pulled his own phone out and compared the photos of the dead Rufus Flanigan and the living Adam Wolfe. "It's possible. But why two identities?"

"For his two personas. Artist and activist." Mercy pointed to each likeness in turn on the phones. "The question is, which one was murdered? And why."

"When he was murdered, he was Rufus Flanigan."

"But that doesn't mean the murderer knew him only as Rufus."

"Maybe that's the reason he was killed," said Troy between bites. "Someone found out about his double life—and didn't like it."

"We have to find this guy Max Skinner. He was in the position to know about both Wolfe and Flanigan. I'm sure he's behind the murders and Amy and Helena's disappearance."

"You know they questioned him and let him go."

"But he's the only common link," she said. "He's connected to Wolfe and the Herbert brothers and, through them, to Dr. Winters and Amy and Helena and Donald Walker."

"You could say the same thing about Amy Walker."

"You don't believe that."

"I don't know what I believe about Amy." He pushed his empty plate away and yawned. "But I know what I believe about you. You're some kind of genius to figure all this out."

"Thanks." She smiled shyly at him. "By the way, I think the jeweler who made the buckles and the pendant is a guy named Patrick O'Malley. You might want to check it out." She pointed across the room to the dogs, sleeping side by side. "I know you're exhausted, too. Go on and get some sleep. I'll clean up."

"That won't be necessary."

"It's the least I can do." She started clearing the table.

"Okay." He could really use a nap. "I meant it when I said you're brilliant. But you need to stay out of it. I'll pass all this along, but it's up to Harrington and the major crime unit."

"Harrington." She frowned. "I don't like him."

"I don't like him much, either. But he is a decent detective. It's not your job, and it's not mine. He's made it very clear that if I overstep jurisdiction again, he'll have my badge."

"Understood. Go on up. Elvis and I will let ourselves out."

"Right." He hauled himself up to his couch on the second floor and fell into it. He lay there listening as she finished up, whistled for Elvis, and left the house, closing the door.

Troy smiled. Hard to stay away from a woman like that. Even if she could get you fired.

He texted Thrasher about Rufus Flanigan's fingerprints. That was all he could do for now. Finally, finally, finally, he gave into his overwhelming urge to snore.

HE'D barely closed his eyes when his mobile beeped. It was a text from Thrasher, asking him how he knew that the dead bird-watcher Rufus Flanigan was really Adam Wolfe and telling him to phone right away. He sighed and placed the call.

Thrasher picked up. "Don't tell me. Mercy Carr."

"I went out with Susie Bear on patrol as ordered, sir. When we came home, she showed up at the house unannounced."

"She ambushed you." The captain almost sounded amused.

"She did some research and figured it out." He told him about the meaning of the two names.

"You were supposed to stay out of it."

Troy paused. "She was right, sir."

"No denying she's smart as a whip. Where is she now?"

"I told her we had to go back out on patrol and that the major crime unit would handle it. She went home."

"Make sure of that. Harrington is beside himself." The captain chuckled, then stopped mid-laugh. "It really isn't funny. I'm doing damage control, but there's a limit to my influence. Keep her—and yourself—off his radar."

"Yes, sir. Thank you, sir." He smiled as he hung up. The captain loved showing up Harrington as much as he did. And Thrasher would always save his sorry ass if he could.

But it was up to Troy to save Mercy Carr's ass.

MERCY answered the door and let him and Susie Bear in. Both dogs bounded back toward the kitchen.

"I thought you were going out on patrol."

"I thought we should check on you first." He looked around the kitchen, where a backpack sat on the counter next to bottles of water and packages of beef jerky. "You're going out?"

"Just a little walk in the woods."

"Shouldn't you be resting?"

"Elvis is a little rattled. This will calm him down." She looked at him with those bright blue eyes, all innocent concern over her dog, who seemed perfectly at ease.

"Right." He laughed. "You are a terrible liar."

She started to protest, then laughed, too. "So I've been told."

"What are you really up to?"

"Just a little walk in the woods." She grinned. "That may take us past the compound."

"We've been there; the crime-scene techs have been there."

"We didn't know who the victim was then. And it was dark. I'd like to get a look in daylight. We're missing something."

"You never give up, do you?"

"Never give up, never surrender." She was dead serious.

"Thrasher says I need to keep you out of this investigation." He was dead serious, too.

"I thought Thrasher was a good guy."

"He is," Troy said. "But Harrington is another story."

"Yeah. He's got it out for you and your boss."

"And you." Troy weighed his options. "But you were right about our victim. And we still don't know where that baby is." He was not convinced that going to the compound was a good idea, but he couldn't have her traipsing around the crime scene without him. And he had to go back out on patrol, anyway.

"Or her mother." Mercy reached over across the counter and touched his hand. "I promise I'll follow your lead."

Troy sighed. "We'd better go; it's nearly four o'clock."

"Just a little walk in the woods," she said.

Just a little walk in the woods that could get me fired, thought Troy. Or solve the case.

THE woods were quiet now. The summer sun was on its long descent toward evening. Troy pointed to the area where she'd found the victim. "We've been over all this before," he said.

"We need to go back to basics. Means, motive, opportunity."

"Let's assume for now that Max Skinner had both means and opportunity, since he was known to Wolfe and was seen here at the compound and knew the Herbert brothers, who were hunters with access to hunting knives. Which leaves motive."

"Envy. Feinberg told me that Skinner was an artist, too. But he wasn't as successful as his friend."

"So he was jealous? That wouldn't explain why Wolfe came to you as Rufus Flanigan and told you where Amy and Helena were. Or why he called in the Amber Alert in the first place."

"He must have believed Amy and Helena were in danger. Max could have been jealous of his family as well as his art."

"Or maybe Wolfe wanted Amy and Helena back and used the Amber Alert to help locate them. He came to you as the bird-watcher to find out how much you knew. He told you where they were so you'd go after them. Then once you were distracted, he bonked you on the head and left you to die."

"Only someone killed him first," she said. "Wolfe is the key to this whole thing. If we understood him better, maybe we'd understand why someone would want to kill him."

"Thrasher says the Rufus Flanigan passport is a fake—a good one, but a fake. So he definitely had something to hide. Otherwise, he wouldn't need two identities."

"The nature of duality," said Mercy. "Two identities. Two homelands. Two styles of sculpture. Two women. Two follies."

"Follies?"

She told him about the natural sculptures that Feinberg had commissioned Wolfe to create. "Maybe he wasn't trying to kill me; maybe he was just trying to keep me away from the folly."

"Why would he do that?" Troy said.

"I don't know. Let's go take a look at the folly."

They called for the dogs, and Mercy led the way. Together they went around the arched structure looking for something, anything, that might tell them something.

"See anything?" Troy asked.

"No." Mercy plopped down onto a large downed limb. "Maybe this is my folly."

"That's not true." Troy sat down next to her. "You saved the baby. You found the bones. And Donald Walker. And you figured out who Rufus Flanigan really was."

"We still don't know why Elvis alerted to explosives. And Amy and the baby are still out there somewhere."

"What you'd said, about how knowing the victim will help us figure out the motive. Well, what do we know about him?"

"We know nothing about him was as it seemed."

"Right."

"Amy told me that he was very secretive about his art."

"Looks like he was secretive about everything."

"That's true. He hid his studio on the compound, his girlfriend and his baby in a tent cabin, and his folly in the forest."

"And there's the name thing. He didn't just pick any name for his second identity; he picked one with a hidden meaning."

"A puzzle," said Mercy.

"This folly is a puzzle, too. It's constructed like a Jenga—pull out one piece and the whole thing might fall down."

"No. He's far too clever for that. He's built this to last."

"If that's true, then conceivably you could pull out a piece."

"Now that would make a good hiding place."

They looked at each other, then jumped to their feet.

"You start at one end. I'll start at the other." She went to the right-hand side of the arch and started running her fingers along the granite stones. Troy went to the other side and did the same. They'd nearly met in the middle when his thumb caught on the edge of a block. He pulled the wedge of stone out.

"Look," he said. The block was not as deep as the others.

Mercy peered up into the space. There, on a narrow ledge, was a small rectangular box, the kind used for gift cards. Carefully, she removed it. She slipped the top off and revealed the prize: a slim blue plastic card that looked much like a credit card. She presented it to Troy. "What is it, exactly?"

He held it up. "I think it's a security pass card, the kind employers issue to employees to get in and out of their offices."

"Feinberg was talking about this at the gala. He underwrote the whole thing, including new security measures. He specifically mentioned staff vetting and security."

"Art theft is often an inside job." Troy nodded. "You look to the staff first when there's a theft."

"Art theft." Mercy gave him back the box. "All that packing material we found in the steel trunks could be used to pack stolen art. Feinberg has a very valuable art collection. Wolfe knew it. He must have been planning to rob him. Max must be in on it. He killed Wolfe so he wouldn't have to share the proceeds."

"Why kill him before he got the key?"

"I don't know. But that could be what he was looking for at my house. Maybe he thought Amy had it."

"That's a lot of maybes."

"Max knows he's on your radar now." Mercy's face flushed. "He's going to make his move soon, if he hasn't already. And today is the perfect time. Everybody's in town."

"I'll let Thrasher know about the key."

She grabbed the box from him. "Not good enough." She whistled for Elvis, and he came bounding over.

"What are you doing? That's evidence."

"Evidence you'd never have found without me." She strode off down the trail that ran through the forest, Elvis on her heels. "We're going down there," she yelled over her shoulder. "Are you guys coming or what?"

Susie Bear danced in front of him, desperate to tag along with her new friends. So much for following his lead. Troy cursed under his breath and jogged after them.

Chapter 11

IN THE END Troy talked her into going back to the compound and getting his truck. They were burning sunlight, and he didn't want them wandering around the woods after dark looking for a place neither of them had ever been to before.

Troy plugged Feinberg's address into his GPS. They bounced along the back roads until they came to the three-mile drive that led to Feinberg's estate.

Two miles in, a massive black iron gate crossed the road, part of a six-foot iron fence that stretched between the trees as far as they could see in either direction. Troy spotted security cameras and pointed them out to Mercy. Before he could say anything, she was out of the truck, checking out the cameras.

"They've been disabled," she said, getting back in.

"Not good. I'm calling for backup."

"The gate is locked," she said. "We have to find another way in."

"We should wait for backup." He put in the call.

"How long will it take?"

"Hard to say. We're pretty far off the beaten path, and between the fireworks and all the big shots who need babysitting, coming to check out a possible burglary won't be a priority."

The sound of a low boom echoed down the ridge from the direction of the lodge. Elvis yelped. Susie Bear bellowed.

"Fireworks," Troy said. "Just the beginning."

"Or our thieves decided not to wait for the security pass," she said. "We need to go before they get away."

"Doesn't Feinberg have staff?"

"Yeah, but it's a big place. His bodyguards are with him in Northshire. And it's a holiday. A lot of them could be off." Mercy pursed her lips. "There's a groundskeeper, too. Feinberg told me he caught the Herbert brothers poaching on his land."

"So they know Feinberg and they know Max. There could be a lot of perps up there. More reason to wait for backup."

"We don't have time. Amy and Helena could be in there."

"Okay, okay. I'm going in for recon. You stay here."

"No way," she said, stepping out of the truck.

"You're staying here with Elvis." He got out, too, grabbing his binoculars and holstering his pistol.

"I'm going with you."

"No, you aren't," Troy said in his toughest voice. He shouldered his rifle. "Vests in the back for you and Elvis. And a shotgun. Pull the truck across the road to block the gate. Wait for backup. If there's any trouble, drive like hell out of here."

"Like that's going to happen."

"Stay out of trouble. Don't be a hero." Troy put on a vest and armored up Susie Bear. "Come on, girl."

The big dog jumped out and hit the ground running. Troy heaved himself up over the fence and landed on the drive on the other side. Susie Bear followed. They headed toward the house, keeping to the tree line, as they traced the hairpin turns up the hill.

The drive's loops ended and the woods opened up, revealing the enormous estate of Nemeton. A magnificent mountain lodge the size of a resort, made of native stone and hand-hewn logs, sat at the top of a ridge surrounded by forest. Three stories high, the home was a warren of balconies and turrets.

A grand porte cochere extended over the crescent-shaped drive that fronted the house. There was a white twelve-foot box truck parked there. Through his binoculars, Troy could see that the roll-up door on the truck was up. Two guys dressed in black and wearing ski masks and gloves came out of the house carrying rectangular objects wrapped in mover's blankets.

Paintings, thought Troy. Damn if the redhead wasn't right.

He kept a tight rein on Susie Bear's lead as they skirted the lodge, staying hidden in the maples as they made their way to the back of the property. He trained his binoculars on the colossal windows, scanning all three floors, and discovered two guys in the house, also in black, wearing ski masks and gloves.

Four in all, as far as he could see. He used the sat phone to call dispatch to confirm his report about a robbery in progress.

Then he turned to Susie Bear. "Stay."

He moved stealthily up to the three-car garage attached to the west side of the lodge. He backed up against the stone wall of the garage and inched his way around to the first door, marked SERVICE ENTRANCE. It was locked, but there was a keypad. Troy pulled the key card out of his pocket and tried it, and with a beep the door opened. Mercy Carr was right. Again.

He found himself in a mudroom lined with a wall of lockers for the employees. The mudroom led to another door, also opened only with the key card. He edged up to peek through the square window in the door. He'd located the chef's kitchen. He slipped into the room, gun at his side.

He heard the sound of a vehicle backfiring and peered out the window. Two of the masked men were rolling down the back door of the box truck. They were getting ready to leave.

He raced back through the mudroom and outside. He ran around to the porte cochere. The truck was moving forward. He waved his badge and yelled, "Stop! Game warden!"

Someone answered with a shot. Troy saw the rifle extend out of the truck window, and he dove into a small copse of birches.

The truck rumbled on, and he cursed. Now Mercy and her dog and his Ford F-150 were the only things between these thieves and freedom. Not a good scenario.

He darted back around the house to the edge of the property where Susie Bear was waiting for him. Her long black coat was rustling, her sturdy, muscular body shaking with energy.

"Come on, girl," he said, and they were off, running along the edge of the forest. He needed to get to that gate as quickly as possible. He ran harder, and Susie Bear bound ahead of him.

The truck veered out of sight as the driveway curved west. They could conceivably catch up with the thieves by forgoing the road's hairpin turns and cutting straight down through the trees. Troy and Susie Bear plowed on through the landscape.

The truck came back into view, gaining on the entrance, just around the next bend. Only five hundred yards away. Only five hundred yards from Mercy and Elvis and his Ford F-150.

Troy wanted to disable their vehicle before it got there. He was betting Skinner and company had the remote control for the gate.

Troy holstered his pistol and pulled his rifle from the case. He positioned himself behind a boulder and whistled for Susie Bear, and she circled back to him out of the line of fire. He took aim and blew out the left rear tire. The truck swerved wildly but kept on going. Troy got off another shot just as the vehicle approached the loop of the next hairpin turn. Missed.

One of the men leaned out the window and fired. The bullet splintered the trunk of a young birch several feet to Troy's left.

"Let's go," he told Susie Bear, and again they took the rough shortcut through the trees. He hoped Mercy had taken the shots as the warning they were and that she would heed that warning.

MERCY heard the gunfire and grabbed the shotgun.

"Down," she told Elvis. The shepherd was practically imploding with energy. But at least he didn't move.

She considered her options. She could leave the truck here, take cover in the trees with Elvis, and slow them down with the shotgun if Troy's truck didn't do the trick.

There might be another way. She hopped out, going around back to the bed of the truck. Everybody who drove a truck carried chain in the bed, and Troy was no exception. She dragged the chain out and ran to the gate. She could hear the roar of the thieves' vehicle in the distance growing louder and nearer.

Elvis clawed savagely at the window, scratching the pane.

Worried he'd break the glass, she let him out. "Now stay."

She wrapped the chain through both sides of the gate, looping the doors together. One loop. Two loops. Three loops.

The box truck made its final turn toward the entrance. It lurched along with an ungainly gait, and she saw that one of its tires was flat. She smiled. The game warden was a good shot.

Elvis gave a short bark, as if to say, *Time to get moving*.

"Agreed," she said. Together they abandoned the Ford F-150 and raced for the stand of trees about one hundred feet from the gate. She had the shotgun, her pack, and an extra box of ammo.

Standing behind the thick trunk of a beech, she instructed Elvis to lie down. She was a good shot, but she hadn't fired a shotgun since Afghanistan. If they were the Herbert brothers, they were experienced night hunters and poachers. Good shots.

"Steady, boy." She gave Elvis a hug for good luck. They were both going to need it. This could prove the nearest thing to a battlefield that either of them had seen since Martinez died.

Now it was a year later and she didn't know if Elvis would go crazy again. All the day hikes through the Lye Brook Wilderness, all that inhaling and exhaling on the yoga mat. Finally he seemed to be settling in with her—and then this happened.

When Elvis had gotten shot, he'd run for the barn. A sensible move, if not the correct one. If he bolted this time, she might not be able to go after him. She could only protect Martinez's dog so much. She could only protect herself so much. Life happened. Even in the woods. Maybe especially in the woods.

"We're a team now, Elvis. Like it or not." She took a few deep breaths. "We've got this." She pumped the shotgun. "'We few, we happy few, we band of brothers . . .'"

He looked up at her as if there were no doubt.

"You seem fine." She smiled. "I guess I'm the nervous one."

Shoulders squared, she pressed her cheek firmly to the side of the stock and then mounted the gun high on her chest.

Aimed. Fired. Bingo. Blew out the left rear tire.

She grinned in spite of herself. Elvis rose to his feet but did not bolt. He barked once, as if to congratulate her.

"Good boy," she whispered.

The dog was alert and poised for action but obedient. So far, so good. Maybe Martinez was his guardian angel. And hers.

A man in a ski mask, armed with a pistol, leaned out the window, while the man at the wheel struggled to control the vehicle. The gates began to open, swinging in toward the thieves.

But the two doors did not part; they only slid six inches away from each other, clanking against the chain but going nowhere.

Mercy pumped the shotgun. She could feel Elvis brace himself against her leg. She cooed "good boy" while she kept her eye on the thieves and her finger on the trigger. Where was Troy? Where was Susie Bear? Where was Thrasher?

She hated to admit it, but Troy was right: They should have waited for backup. Elvis's ears perked, and he leaned forward.

"What is it?"

She saw Troy and Susie Bear hugging the opposite edge of the road, inside the tree line of the estate, behind the gate.

If this were her operation, she'd blow out the other tires and converge on the truck. It looked like there were at least two bad guys—maybe more inside she couldn't see—but there were four good guys. Troy, herself, and the dogs. Good odds.

It was a fairly easy shot from here. She took it and hit a tire on her side of the box truck. Troy did the same on his side.

Elvis whimpered but stayed put. Just like he was supposed to do. The perfect working dog. The perfect partner. Her partner.

Pistols fired from two windows, and she dropped to the ground, taking Elvis with her. They retreated into the woods.

The truck jerked forward, straining against the chained doors, crushing it toward the F-150—a screeching of metal on metal. The fence gave way but only by a foot. Sirens sounded in the background. The driver bailed and made a run for it. He was tall but graceful for his size. Max Skinner, thought Mercy.

He leaped onto the hood of the truck and over the gate. Using the fence as cover, he ran along the metal-and-stone barricade for the woods. He was fast, and he was armed.

"Stop!" Troy stepped out of the trees but ducked when two masked men fired from the truck. They opened their doors to make their own escape but thought better of it when three police cars roared up to the gate, sirens wailing. A black Cadillac Escalade followed in their wake and parked at a discreet distance. Must be Feinberg and his bodyguards, Mercy thought.

She and Elvis kept moving, quiet as death, padding through the forest toward the point where the driver was on track to enter. The masked man approached the tree line. Almost out of sight and into the woods. Running straight for them.

"Go get him," she told Elvis, and pumped her shotgun.

"Shoot my dog," she yelled at the surprised man, "and I shoot you."

Elvis did not hesitate. For the second time in two days, the sleek shepherd took down Max Skinner.

Only it wasn't Max Skinner, after all. Surrounded by cops, the two thieves in the white box truck surrendered and joined their colleague. Unmasked, the three of them looked like brothers. The Herbert brothers.

The tallest one looked like Paul and Louis, only leaner. Their big brother in every sense of the word.

"Wayne Herbert?" Troy grinned. "Your mother will be very happy to see you. She can visit you every week in prison."

"Where are Amy and the baby?" Mercy was angry, and she turned that anger on the brothers. "Where's Max Skinner?"

"The major crime unit is in charge here, or will be shortly," said Thrasher. But he smiled at her as he said it. Maybe he liked her, after all.

"There were four of them, sir," Troy said.

Thrasher nodded at Detective Kai Harrington, who had just arrived in an unmarked car and was walking toward them with a scowl on his handsome face. "The cavalry has arrived."

"Where's Max Skinner?" repeated Mercy.

"That bastard." Louis spat on the ground.

"Shut up," warned Wayne.

"Ms. Carr," said Harrington in a voice that could freeze hell itself. "Remove yourself or I'll have you removed by force."

"Sir," said Troy.

Harrington shot him a look that said, *One more word and you're fired.*

"I'm going. No problem," said Mercy. She'd gotten poor Troy in enough trouble already. She and Elvis retreated to the perimeter, where Feinberg and his bodyguards were watching the goings-on.

"I must thank you for saving my collection," said Feinberg.

"I don't understand. I know Max Skinner was part of this."

"It does seem unlikely that those dimwitted brothers plotted all this."

Mercy thought for a moment. "Is all your missing art there?"

"I'm not sure yet. They're photographing it all now."

"I wouldn't be surprised if there's something missing. And Max Skinner has it. What's the most valuable piece?"

"Hard to say. There's the Hopper, the Pollock, the Wyeth, the Cassatt . . . but the jewel is probably the Winslow Homer."

Troy walked over to them. "You'll want to hear this."

"What about Harrington?"

Feinberg looked at them. "You're with me."

They followed him to where Harrington and the staties were interviewing the Herbert brothers. Thrasher was there, too.

Wayne was maintaining his silence, but his little brothers were talking more than enough to make up for it.

"It was all Max's idea," said Paul. "He said he could get us inside. And he did."

"And then he disappeared," said Louis.

"Shut up," said Wayne.

"Max planned it," said Paul. "Split up the rooms."

"We took the first floor," said Louis.

"Max took the upper floors," said Paul.

"And we haven't seen him since," said Louis.

Feinberg leaned in toward Mercy. "The most valuable pieces in the collection are on the upper floors."

"We're searching the perimeter," said Harrington. "But the sun's going down soon."

"The dogs can find him," said Mercy, "even in the dark."

Troy smiled and pointed to the edge of the forest.

"It's Gunnar Moe," said Feinberg. "My groundskeeper."

"With Max Skinner."

A giant of a man, with long hair the color of straw, Gunnar pushed the tall man, sans ski mask, in front of him. Skinner grimaced as he limped forward, a bloody tear in his pants.

"Found him in the woods on an ATV," said Gunnar.

"Where are Amy and Helena?" asked Mercy.

Skinner shrugged but said nothing.

"He took a shot at me," said Gunnar. "So I shot back."

"Where are they?" asked Mercy again.

Gunnar gave Skinner one last shove toward a couple of uniforms, and they cuffed him and took the tall man away. Then he shrugged off the fife case Max Skinner had carried in the parade. He handed the case to Feinberg. "He had this on him."

"Look in there," said Mercy.

"Hold on." Troy pulled plastic gloves from his pocket.

Feinberg slipped them on and opened the case. Carefully he pulled a rolled canvas out of the long cylinder. He unrolled it carefully, revealing a dark oil painting of two fishermen on a small boat in stormy waters. *"Lost on the Grand Banks."*

"Winslow Homer," said Mercy.

IT WAS after seven o'clock when Troy dropped Mercy and Elvis off at the cabin. He insisted on walking them to the door.

"We're fine," she told him.

"Elvis was great." Troy smiled at her. "You, too."

"It was a team effort."

"I loved the way Elvis took down Wayne Herbert," he said.

"And don't forget Max Skinner at the parade."

"Another great leap for canine kind." Troy grinned as he joined Mercy in spoiling the dogs with affection, scratching their ears and tummies. "It's been quite the Fourth of July."

He straightened up, and she followed suit. His sandy-brown hair had fallen across his forehead, and she reached up to brush it back. He caught her hand and held it tenderly in his own.

It felt good, but they still had work to do. She gently pulled her hand out of his grasp. "I am proud of Elvis. He was solid."

"Solid as a rock."

She rolled her eyes at him, and he laughed.

"Seriously," said Troy. "He's cured of whatever ailed him."

Mercy nodded, too moved to speak. She'd fulfilled her promise to Martinez. She'd adopted his dog and taken care of him until he was his old self again.

"Get some rest."

"We need to find Amy and the baby."

"You've done enough for one day. Everyone's on it. Local PD, the sheriff's office, the staties, us. Even Harrington."

"They don't know where to look."

"And you do? Have you been holding out on me?"

"I don't know where they are, but I feel like I should know."

"If anyone can figure it out, you can. Sleep on it."

"Okay," she said, knowing that was what he wanted to hear.

"Good night."

She and Elvis watched Troy and Susie Bear go back to the truck. Then Mercy led Elvis inside.

"We did good," she told him, scratching his head. He trotted to the sofa, settling onto his side and snoring within minutes.

She should be sleeping, too. But she was restless. There was still no word of Amy and Helena, and Skinner insisted he didn't know where the young mother and her baby were.

He admitted to shooting at Elvis and ransacking the cabin, looking for the security key, just like she'd thought. He also insisted that he didn't kill Adam Wolfe, whom he described as his "comrade in arms." But the Herbert brothers said Skinner was responsible for killing the artist and Donald Walker. Nobody seemed to know whose bones were buried in the woods.

Mercy was too restless to sit. She went to her bookshelves and stared at her collection of Shakespeare. She remembered Amy, who'd named her baby after Helena in the Bard's most popular comedy, had been reading *Othello*—a far darker reflection of "Love is blind" than *A Midsummer Night's Dream.*

She found the volume of *Othello* on the shelf. When she held it in her palms, the book fell open. Someone had folded down the corner of the page of the scene in which Emilia speaks to Desdemona about the nature of jealousy. The ink was smudged over the words *But jealous souls will not be answered so; / They are not ever jealous for the cause, / But jealous for they are jealous: 'tis a monster / Begot upon itself, born on itself.*

Mercy would never fold the corners of any pages of her books. It was Amy who had marked this page about the terrible curse that is jealousy. The distraught girl could've been drawn to this passage because of Adam's possessiveness of her.

But possessiveness was not the same thing as the sexual jealousy that drove people to murder. Amy had insisted all along that Adam was not a violent person. If that was true, then maybe Amy's marking the passage was not a reference to him but to one of his art groupies who hated her. An unhappy ex.

Like Dr. Winters.

She shut the book. Amy had never mentioned the professor specifically, but then, she hadn't appeared to take any of Adam's former paramours seriously. And she was young enough that she probably dismissed any rival over thirty out of hand.

But Dr. Winters was not the sort of woman you should dismiss out of hand. As far as Mercy knew, the professor was the only groupie still hanging around the compound. She'd gone right there after Mercy and Troy paid her that visit to question her about Adam Wolfe. Odds were she was still there when Mercy talked to the bird-watcher, aka Adam. Still there when Mercy got hit in the head. Still there when Adam died.

The professor had the means and the opportunity to kill him.

And the motive. Maybe she wasn't over Adam Wolfe, after all. Maybe all of the merger-and-acquisitions attorneys in the world couldn't make up for the genius who enshrined you in art. Maybe she was the Othello to Wolfe's Desdemona. Or the Iago to his Othello. In this scenario Amy was the Desdemona, and that meant things could go very badly for her. And the baby.

If Mercy was right, then they didn't have much time. Dr. Winters was supposedly on her way to the south of France. So she'd need to get rid of Amy and Helena before she left.

Mercy pulled her hiking boots on. "Come on, Elvis."

The shepherd jounced up, ready to go.

THIRTY minutes later she pulled the little red convertible onto the street where Dr. Winters lived, in Bennington. She'd texted Troy, but she hadn't heard back from him yet.

Mercy stared up at the intimidating Victorian pile that the professor called home. The painted lady was dark. The sun was setting now, and the place was falling into a deep gloom.

She and Elvis cased the property, but there was no vehicle in the detached garage out back and no sign of life in the house. She banged the gargoyle knocker, but no one came to the door.

She texted Troy again, and this time he called her back.

"What are you doing?" He sounded frustrated.

"I'm at Dr. Winters's house."

"You're supposed to be at home, resting. What do you think you're going to find?"

"Nothing here. The professor's gone. But I think she knows where Amy and Helena are."

"Why would she know that?"

She told him about finding the book and the quote. "She's jealous of Amy and the baby. I think they're in danger."

"I'm not sure that makes any sense."

"Think about it. She was probably still there at the compound when Adam was murdered and I was left for dead and Amy and Helena were last seen."

"True."

"I was wrong about her. She still loved Adam Wolfe. He dumped her for Amy, swapped her out for a younger Muse. That must have infuriated her."

"I can see that. But you've done enough. Let me call it in."

"Harrington won't do anything about it. He'll say it's another wild-goose chase. And by the time you convince him otherwise, it could be too late. Remember the south of France."

Troy sighed. "She does have a house on Lake St. Catherine, and anyone with a lake house spends the Fourth of July weekend there."

Lake St. Catherine was an hour north of Bennington. This time of year the lake attracted summer people and year-round residents alike for its swimming, boating, and fishing. But even with all this activity, Mercy knew many of the houses were surrounded by trees and somewhat secluded.

"Not a bad place to hide a young mother and a baby," she said. "We need to go now."

"I'll meet you there. Don't do anything on your own."

"Over and out."

Troy texted her the address.

"Come on, boy," she said to Elvis. "Let's go to the lake."

MERCY turned in at the DEAD END sign and steered the convertible slowly down Osprey Point Road. Streetlights were few and far between. It was getting late and growing dark, and the only lights out on the lake were the fireworks people were setting off from their docks and on their boats.

She parked along the street. "Come on, Elvis," she said.

They walked quietly down the dirt driveway to a little white farmhouse and approached the unlit cottage. It looked like no one was there, but Dr. Winters's SUV was parked out front. They stepped up onto the porch, and she knocked on the door.

No one answered. The house was silent.

Elvis whined and took off. She jogged after him as he raced past the SUV. He bolted down the backyard toward a wooden boathouse. Mercy scrambled down the lawn after him.

The door to the boathouse was closed, but that didn't stop the determined shepherd. He barreled down to the shore of the lake and plunged into the water. Stunned, Mercy watched as he swam over to the open end of the boathouse, the end that emptied into the lake. The dog disappeared inside.

Mercy ran to the boathouse door. It was locked. She didn't have the time to pick it, so she backed up, took a running leap, and crashed into the door with her shoulder. The jamb splintered, and the door gave way. She lurched into the dark room.

Her eyes adjusted, and she could see there was a twelve-foot bass boat in the single bay. Fireworks blazed and boomed outside, and in the light, Mercy could see Dr. Winters in the boat with Amy. The professor held a hunting knife at Amy's throat.

Amy's wrists and ankles were bound with rope. Her mouth was gagged with duct tape. The girl's eyes were bright with fear. When she saw Mercy, those eyes widened with hope.

"Let Amy go."

The baby was there in the boat, too, wrapped in a blanket and sleeping on a curl of rope.

"Why would I do that?" The professor's huge eyes were wild with spite behind her thick black glasses.

Elvis waded up to the dock. The water was shallow here, only a couple of feet deep. The shepherd leaped onto the dock.

"I loathe dogs," said Dr. Winters.

Most people who didn't like dogs were afraid of them. She didn't want Elvis scaring the woman into doing something terrible. "Come," she said. He came to sit beside her.

More fireworks exploded outside. The baby slept on.

"Why don't you put the knife down and tell me all about Adam Wolfe."

"She stole him from me." Dr. Winters did not drop the knife.

"How did she do that?"

The professor ignored her and looked down at the sleeping child. "I wanted a baby. I begged him for a baby." She kicked at the coil of rope, just missing the infant's head.

Amy jerked toward Helena, and the knife nicked her throat.

"Sit still or you'll never see your baby again."

Mercy held her breath and watched as tiny drops of blood pooled at the cut on Amy's pale neck.

"It was the art," Dr. Winters said. "His precious art. He said it came first, that his art was his baby." She glared at Helena. "And then he has this . . . this bastard child." She jostled the coil of rope with her boot. "He left me for this abomination."

Mercy edged forward, her eyes on that boot.

"Don't move." Dr. Winters's voice was thick with rage.

The baby stirred and began to wail. The dog barked furiously. Another blast of fireworks rang out like shots.

"I told you, I don't like dogs." Dr. Winters yelled over the din. "Or bastards." She turned away and reached back with her free hand to turn on the motor. The engine rumbled to life.

Mercy lunged for the knife. The professor slashed at Mercy. The weapon sliced her left shoulder, and she punched Dr. Winters in the stomach with a hard right. The professor gasped for air and grabbed for the throttle. The boat pitched forward.

"Elvis, go!" Mercy clutched at her bleeding arm.

The shepherd launched himself onto the moving vessel. Dr. Winters fell back and tumbled on top of Amy, who kicked her away and tried to curl her body around her screaming baby.

The professor righted herself to attack. But Elvis was faster. He chomped down on her wrist, and she dropped the knife.

Mercy ran after the boat as it plowed out of the boathouse. She leaped for the bow but missed. She landed in two feet of water and stumbled onto her knees. Rising to her feet, she splashed through the boathouse. The water deepened. Mercy dove forward, swimming after the boat. But her aching shoulder was still bleeding, and every stroke was an exercise in pain.

The lake was dark and choppy. But by the staccato flash and thunder of the exploding fireworks, she could spy Dr. Winters struggling with Elvis and trying to find the knife with her other hand. Amy kicked it away, and Mercy swam harder, stroke after stroke, the lines from *The Tempest* pounding in her head:

Sea-nymphs hourly ring his knell: Ding-dong
Hark! now I hear them,—Ding-dong, bell.

She saw Dr. Winters try to grab the tiller, and Elvis push his snout up to her face, barking furiously. His snarls echoed across the lake. The professor must have bumped the tiller to the side, because the boat was moving slowly in wide circles.

Ding-dong.

Mercy was getting very tired. Her limbs were heavy; her injured arm floated limply at her side while she flailed forward with her right arm. But she couldn't give up.

"Mercy! Mercy!" She heard Troy's voice calling her name over and over again, and she practically cried with relief.

"Over here," she yelled, peering across the dark night.

A torrent of red and blue and white sprays of light showered the night sky. A bellow and a splash, and she paddled around to see a black beast moving toward her with surprising speed.

"Come on, Susie Bear," Mercy shouted, and powered against the current toward the bass boat. She looked over her shoulder to make sure the Newfie mutt was following her. There, silhouetted against the exploding sky, was a canoe manned by Troy Warner, who wielded his paddle like a sword and sliced through the water like a warrior on his way to war.

Ding-dong, bell.

Mercy was in reach of the bass boat now. She lunged for starboard as it careened past her, caught the side, and held on tight. She tried to heave herself onto the boat. Failed.

"I'm going to kill you and your dog," said Dr. Winters. Elvis was holding her down against her seat, his paws on her chest, his mouth still clamped around her wrist. Whenever she tried to strike him with her free arm, he clenched harder—and she pulled back her arm, moaning with pain.

"One more word and I'll order him to break your other wrist." Mercy breathed heavily.

Amy scooted across the boat on her butt to help Mercy. Her hands and feet were still tied, and her mouth was still gagged.

She shifted her feet and lifted herself to a standing position.

The boat tipped suddenly in the wake of a speedboat passing, and Amy lost her fragile footing and pitched backward.

Mercy grabbed Amy by the shoulders as she went under, pulling her back up. Mercy took the gag out of Amy's mouth. "I'm going to turn you around. When I do, lie your head back against my chest, close your eyes, and float."

Amy moaned.

"Float," she ordered. "Float." Mercy's strength was fading, her cut arm and her concussion getting the better of her.

Where was Troy? She looked around but couldn't see anything. The dark sky was quiet now. Dr. Winters's boat lumbered on, circling them in the deep gloom. She tried to untie the girl's hands but couldn't do it and keep them both afloat at the same time. She needed help. And nearly laughed out loud when she realized Troy was right. She had to wait for backup.

She felt the big dog before she saw her. A cold nose, a wet shag rug she could hold on to for dear life.

"Good girl," she said.

Amy opened her eyes. "Big dog."

"Susie Bear," she said. "Search-and-rescue dog. We're going to be fine."

AMY closed her eyes. The fireworks started up again, and Mercy watched Troy's canoe reach Dr. Winters's boat. He climbed aboard and switched off the motor. Then he handcuffed Dr. Winters's free wrist and admonished Elvis to release her other one so he could handcuff that one, too. But Elvis was reluctant. She heard Troy say, "Drop it," two more times before the dog would relinquish his hold. But even once he'd let go, the shepherd continued to stand guard over his prisoner.

Mercy held on to Amy with one hand and Susie Bear's tail with the other as the dog swam toward the canoe. She smiled as Troy cradled little Helena and laid her carefully into the canoe. He tied the boat to the canoe and paddled over to them.

Troy helped Amy into the canoe first. He untied her feet and wrists, then stripped off his uniform shirt and wrapped it around the young mother, who was shivering with shock.

"She killed Adam. She was going to kill us."

"You're safe now."

He pulled Mercy in next. "You're hurt."

"Get Susie Bear up here first."

"We could, but it looks like she'd rather hang out with Elvis." Troy pointed to Susie Bear, swimming alongside the boat as close as possible to Elvis as he guarded the professor.

Troy paddled them quickly and expertly back to shore. As soon as they hit water shallow enough for Susie Bear to stand up in, she leaped onto the boat to join Elvis. The professor did not look pleased at the thought of two dogs guarding her now.

The dogs barked.

The professor cursed.

And the baby, happy again in her mother's arms, laughed.

FIVE DAYS LATER

Chapter 12

PATIENCE ORDERED COMPLETE REST for Mercy, and she got a people doctor and a CT scan to back her up. Not that Mercy got much rest. Patience came every day, bearing food and advice and, finally, the no-name kitten she and Elvis had rescued from the Walker place.

"Hello, kitty." She showed her grandmother into the kitchen, taking the carrier from her. Elvis leaped up and trotted over to supervise the release of their new housemate.

The cabin was crowding up. Amy and Helena had moved into the guest room. Child Protective Services had agreed that Helena could remain with her mother under two conditions: that they live with Mercy and that Amy finish her senior year.

They were in the living room, the baby playing on a blanket spread out in front of the couch, surrounded by toys.

"The kitty's good to go. But still no name." Patience started pulling out covered dishes from her tote bag. "Any ideas?"

"Not yet."

The little tiger tabby—who'd been so worn and weary the last time Mercy had seen her—leaped out of the carrier with an excess of feline energy and greeted Elvis nose-to-nose.

"She's fattened up a bit."

"Poor thing was starving." Patience shook her head.

"I tried to take care of them," said Amy. "But there were so many of them." The teenager's dark blue eyes filled with tears.

"It's okay," said Mercy. "All's well that ends well." She told Amy all about the rescue, including the magpie Munchkin and his stash of collectibles.

"What kind of jewelry?" asked Amy.

Mercy described what she could remember of the items, including the pendant with the pine trees.

"My necklace." Amy gasped, and tears rolled down her cheeks. "It was the first thing he ever gave to me. I thought Don stole it and pawned it. Do you think I could get it back?"

"I'll talk to the game warden about it," promised Mercy.

The three of them watched the baby on her blanket, mesmerized by Elvis and the cat playing together.

"Elvis is happy to see the kitty," said her grandmother.

"She's his little muse." Mercy smiled and snapped her fingers. "Her name is Muse."

"A homophone," said Patience, rolling her eyes. "A homophone pun, no less."

"More specifically, a heterograph."

"I don't get it," said Amy.

"*Mews* and *muse* are two words that sound the same but are spelled differently and have different meanings," said Mercy.

"Cute," said Amy. "I think."

"Don't encourage her." Patience frowned at Mercy.

"You are kind of a word nerd," said Amy.

Mercy laughed. "I know it's lame. But in a good way."

She excused herself to text Troy. She wanted to tell him about the necklace. And after nearly a week in the house, she was desperate to get out. She bet Elvis was, too.

"Where are you going?" Patience called her out just as she and Elvis hit the front porch.

"Two Swords K-9 Training. I thought it would be good for Elvis." The truth was, the dog was just fine. She'd spent some time on the yoga mat with him, but she'd seemed to need it more than he did.

"Uh-huh."

"I thought you liked that place."

"I do. Jake is very good."

"So we'll see you later."

"Be home in time for dinner. We have guests coming."

AT TWO Swords K-9 Training, Mercy and Elvis walked into a fenced rectangle of neatly trimmed grass the size of a football field. Happy yelping and bellowing dogs of all shapes and sizes raced around the obstacles that made up the agility course.

She spotted Troy and a good-looking, well-muscled guy with a shaved head on the sidelines, watching as a couple of assistant trainers in matching red shorts and T-shirts emblazoned with the Two Swords logo ran several dogs through their paces. She and Elvis trotted over to join them.

"Mercy Carr, meet Jake Wilder," said Troy.

"Great to meet you," said Jake, offering her a firm handshake. "This must be the famous Elvis." He held out his hand for the shepherd to sniff. "Beautiful." Elvis wagged his tail.

Susie Bear bounded over, followed by a border collie and two golden retrievers. They all sniffed Elvis, until Jake said, "Down!" in such a commanding tone that every dog on the field immediately dropped onto the grass. Even Elvis.

The dog trainers ran over, and Jake laughed. "Go on back to work." He looked at Mercy. "You can let him off the lead."

The trainers escorted all of the dogs back to the starting line, where they each took a lane and waited for their run at the course.

She watched with Troy and Jake as the border collie went first, racing through the course like an Olympic athlete.

Each dog took a turn, and all performed well. Susie Bear was up next. For her size she was surprisingly fast—even if she looked more like a sumo wrestler than a track star. But what she lacked in grace, she made up for in spirit and strength.

Now it was Elvis's turn, and Mercy held her breath.

"Sniffer dogs are typically well trained in agility," said Jake.

"It's been a while," she said. "He's retired now."

At the command—*Go!*—Elvis was off. He sailed over the hurdles, streaked through the tunnels, skimmed the seesaw, and whipped through the weave poles. Mercy couldn't take her eyes off the sleek shepherd, and she found herself tearing up.

Because it was obvious that Elvis was having fun.

Fun. The poor dog needed fun. He'd had fun with Martinez, as had she. In her grief she'd forgotten what a good time they'd all had just hanging out whenever they got a break from the battlefield. *Live a little; comfort a little; cheer thyself a little.*

Elvis finished the course with a flourish to whoops and whistles—hers loudest among them—and raced past the finish lane and right to Mercy. She petted and praised him unabashedly.

"He did great," said Troy.

"He must miss agility," said Jake.

"I don't know. I wasn't his handler. I sort of inherited him."

"A Malinois is a one-woman dog," Jake said. "Your dog."

JAKE excused himself to supervise the rest of the class, leaving Troy and Mercy alone.

"So why are you really here?" Troy asked.

Mercy smiled. "Maybe we just wanted to see you guys."

"Maybe." He waited.

"Okay, okay." She laughed. "I do have an ulterior motive. But we did really want to see you guys and meet Jake."

"Sure you did. Go on."

"Wolfe gave Amy the pendant. Did you find anything on Patrick O'Malley?"

"You were right. Patrick O'Malley, Irish jewelry designer and former IRA member, was living here in Vermont. He definitely left the area, but we've yet to confirm he's in Ireland."

"You're not going to find him in Ireland."

"Why not?"

"He's our body in the woods."

BY DINNERTIME Mercy was in the kitchen helping Patience prepare for their guests. When the doorbell rang, Elvis raced to greet them, barking until she shushed him. She ushered in Thrasher and Troy, Susie Bear on their heels.

"We thought we'd bring you up to speed on the investigation," said the captain.

Behind him Troy winked at her.

Mercy knew that their presence had as much to do with her grandmother's cooking as it did with any desire to keep her in the loop. Tonight it was chicken and dumplings.

"Come have a seat," said Patience. "You're just in time."

"Smells great." Thrasher handed Mercy two bottles of Big Barn Red and took up his place at the head of the table.

Troy held a Crock-Pot. "I brought Elvis some stew. You can keep the Crock-Pot. I've e-mailed you the recipe."

"I thank you," said Mercy, "and Elvis thanks you."

Troy grinned and joined his captain at the table.

Amy helped Mercy set the table while Troy uncorked the wine. Susie Bear and Elvis greeted one another happily, then took up their positions at either end of the baby blanket, the better to look after the infant and the kitten.

"The Herbert brothers have confessed to stealing Feinberg's art," said Thrasher. "Considering they were caught red-handed, they didn't have much choice. But they insist they had nothing to do with any murder."

"What about Wayne Herbert?"

"He lawyered up. But we contacted the Canadian authorities, who confirmed he's been living in Quebec. He's suspected of a string of art thefts there. Mostly sculpture, sold for scrap."

"What about Max Skinner?"

"Skinner knew Wayne from Quebec. But he had bigger ambitions." The captain licked his lips as Patience placed a hot casserole on the table. "As an artist, he had connections that allowed him to fence the art he stole rather than scrap it. When he realized his pal Wolfe was working for Feinberg, he recruited Wayne and his brothers to help him pull off the heist."

"We suspect that he was privately commissioned to steal the Winslow Homer painting," said Troy.

Amy fetched the baby and settled her into her seat. Thrasher pulled out a chair for Amy next to Helena.

"All set," said Patience. "Let's eat."

Thrasher spooned a large helping of chicken and dumplings onto his blue plate and passed the casserole on to Troy. "He didn't tell the Herbert brothers about the commission."

"We don't think he ever intended to share the lion's share of the proceeds with the Herbert brothers," said Troy. "That's why he told them to rob the lower floor. He knew that the most valuable pieces were on the upper floors."

"Wolfe must have told him," said Mercy.

"Adam would never have robbed Mr. Feinberg," said Amy.

Thrasher looked at Amy. "You're right. We don't think he had anything to do with the actual theft. But he had a security key because he worked for Feinberg. He must have grown suspicious and hidden the key so Skinner wouldn't find it."

"We found det cord in Skinner's pack on the ATV," said Troy. "We think the det cord was Skinner's Plan B. But he ended up getting another security key card from the girl singer in the Green Mountain Boys band."

"The sous chef?" Mercy asked.

"Good memory. Turned out she worked up at the Nemeton kitchens on a regular basis. So regular she'd a key of her own."

"So he joined the band to get to her. Skinner never cared about the Vermont Firsters at all?"

"Apparently not," said Thrasher. "Just a means to an end."

"Adam cared," said Amy. "But he'd never hurt anybody. He

regretted blowing up those logging trucks. He said he'd never do anything like that again. He said his art was his message."

"But you left him," said Mercy.

"I didn't like living off the grid. I didn't think it was good for Helena." Amy smiled at her baby. "Adam got weird. I thought that living in the woods was making him crazy. Then Adam and Max had this big fight. They thought I was asleep, but I wasn't. Adam was yelling at Max that he couldn't do it. I didn't know what he was talking about, but I knew it wasn't good. Max was mad, and when he got mad, he looked just like my stepdad. Bad news. I had to get Helena out of there."

"You were right about Skinner being dangerous," said Troy. "He killed your stepfather."

"I know. I found him dead in his chair. I saw Max driving away in his truck. I was afraid he'd kill Adam next. So I went back to the compound to warn him. He told me to hide in one of the tents until he could get me out of there. Dr. Winters came, and I told her about my stepfather. She told me to stay there with the baby. I didn't know she was crazy."

"So she knew how Skinner murdered Walker," said Troy. "That's why she killed Wolfe the same way, to throw suspicion back on Skinner."

"But why did Max kill my stepfather?"

"We believe that Donald Walker was blackmailing Skinner," said Thrasher. "He knew the Herbert brothers."

"They were hunting buddies," said Amy.

"Right," said Thrasher. "He knew them well enough to know that they'd stolen the sculpture and sold it for scrap. When he figured out that his hunting buddies were up to something bigger, he wanted in on it. But the Herbert brothers weren't in charge. Skinner was. And he wasn't having it. He tried paying Walker off, and when that didn't shut him up, he killed him."

"Paul and Louis aren't the brightest guys in the woods," said Mercy. "Did they even suspect their brother was still alive before he showed up for the robbery?"

"No," said Troy. "But I think Flo Herbert knew. That's why

she was surprised when she saw the photos of the belt buckle."

"If it wasn't Wayne Herbert, who was it?" Patience asked.

"We don't know," Thrasher said. "The DNA results could take weeks, if not months. And even then . . ."

"Go ahead, Mercy," said Troy. "Spill it."

"Patrick O'Malley."

"What?" Thrasher frowned. "The jewelry designer?"

"O'Malley made the buckles and the necklace," Mercy said.

"Then disappeared," said Troy. "Flo Herbert said he went to Ireland three years ago. About the time the victim died. But the Irish authorities confirmed today they have no record of that."

"Which gives my new theory some weight," said Mercy.

"Theories don't convict murderers," said Thrasher.

"Hear her out, Captain. She's been right about everything else," said Troy.

Mercy took a sip of wine. "Everyone who knew about this group of Vermont Firsters is dead or going to jail for art theft. Given the belt buckles and tampering of the logging trucks, I think originally Wolfe formed the group as a genuine activist organization, dedicated to preserving the best of Vermont."

"Saving trees," said Amy.

"Right," said Mercy. "If the jeweler was a believer—and given his past as an IRA supporter, he may have been sincere about supporting their work—then he may have objected to the corruption of their mission."

"And paid for it with his life."

"So which one of them killed him?" asked Patience.

"Wayne Herbert," said Mercy and Troy in unison.

Mercy laughed. "You go ahead."

"It'd explain why he went to Quebec about the same time."

"This all fits," said Thrasher. "But even if DNA tests prove it's O'Malley, short of a confession there's no way to prove it."

Troy looked at Mercy. "You thinking what I'm thinking?"

She raised her wineglass to him. "If you're thinking that we've got the bullet from the skull and a shell casing found at Donald Walker's house, then yes."

Troy raised his beer mug to her and smiled.

"Shell casing?" asked Thrasher between bites of dumpling.

"We know Donald Walker was a blackmailer," said Troy. "He could have been blackmailing Wayne, too. Maybe he was there when Wayne killed him, a hunting trip gone wrong. He found the shell casing and held on to it."

"Until the magpie Munchkin stole it and hid it," said Mercy.

"We'll have that tested right away," said Thrasher. "If you're right, it would help to find the gun that fired it. With any luck it's one of the weapons we confiscated at Feinberg's."

"What will happen to Dr. Winters?" asked Amy.

"She's going away for a very long time," said Thrasher.

"She confessed," said Troy. "She thought you were gone for good and that she'd have a chance with Wolfe again. When she saw you back at the compound, she confronted him. She told him he was an idiot and that, thanks to Max, he was going to end up dead or in jail, not in a love cottage with you. Only she could save him. He sent her home, but he realized she was right about Max. He went off to find him and ran into Mercy."

"He thought I could get Amy and Helena out of there," said Mercy, "while he stopped Max from robbing Feinberg."

"But Dr. Winters didn't go home," said Amy.

"No," said Troy. "She was in a rage. She hit Mercy on the head. When Wolfe saw Elvis alone on the trail and circled back to see what happened to Mercy, the professor killed him."

"I snuck out to see what was going on," said Amy. "I saw her hit Mercy. I wanted to help, but Adam got there first. She stabbed him." Amy's voice caught. "I just ran. I didn't try to help him."

"There's nothing you could have done," said Troy.

"I had to get Helena out of there. But she followed me and trapped us in the tent cabin. She said she'd hurt Helena if I didn't do what she said."

"Dr. Winters is capable of anything," said Mercy. "You did what you had to do."

"'Hell hath no fury like a woman scorned,'" said Thrasher.

"More Shakespeare?" Amy asked as she cleaned the baby's face and hands and took her out of the high chair.

"No," Mercy said. "It's William Congreve, from *The Mourning Bride.*" She recited: "'Heaven hath no rage like Love to Hatred turned, nor Hell a fury like a Woman scorned.'"

"She's always like this," said Amy. "Total word nerd."

"When she's not tracking down murderers." Troy laughed.

The doorbell rang, and Mercy welcomed the opportunity to escape. It was a big guy in a dark suit. One of Feinberg's bodyguards. He handed her a package. "Find the folly," he said.

"Open it," said Amy.

"Okay, okay. You can help me." Patience took the baby, and together Mercy and Amy carefully unwrapped the gift.

It was a framed sketch of a striking nude woman with a crescent in her hair, holding a bow in one hand and a staff and a quiver of arrows in the other, standing tall against a background of full-leafed trees.

"Diana," said Mercy.

"Goddess of the Hunt," said Thrasher.

"And the woods and the moon and animals and new mothers and babies," said Patience.

"Very appropriate." Troy grinned at Mercy.

"He wants me to find the other folly."

"Sounds about right," said Troy.

Mercy carried the sketch over to the fireplace and stood it on the mantelpiece. "Just until we can hang it properly."

"Perfect," said Patience. "Time for dessert."

Over her grandmother's triple-layered chocolate cake, they talked about everything from art and murder to the future of dairy farmers in Vermont. Mercy was content. Happy that there were so many people at her dining table, a prospect that would have mortified her even a month earlier.

"Other than interfering in our investigations," said Thrasher, "what is it that you actually do, Ms. Carr?"

"I've been taking some time to consider my options."

"She helps me out at the animal hospital," said Patience. "She'd make a fine vet. But her parents are pushing for her to finish her degree and go to law school. Join the family firm."

"Really." Thrasher raised an eyebrow.

Troy laughed. "The captain is not a big fan of lawyers."

"Although your parents are lovely people," Thrasher said.

Mercy smiled. "So far I've resisted that siren call."

"It would be more productive if you worked with us rather than against us," said the captain. "There's a shortage of good working dogs and dog handlers."

"We're retired," she said.

"Could have fooled me."

PATIENCE packed up the dirty casserole dishes and cake pans and promised to come back the next day with new delights. Thrasher left, and Amy settled the baby down for the night.

Mercy and Troy took Elvis and Susie Bear outside. Usually she took visitors to the back deck, but tonight she felt the need to sit out front where she could see the flag. So much had happened over the past ten days that she felt alienated from Martinez, from the life they'd shared and the life they'd planned, from his memory and what they were to each other. She didn't want to forget him or move on with her life without him. But she had a terrible feeling that was just what she was doing.

While the dogs ran around the yard, Mercy and Troy settled onto the wide front porch. She sat in her grandfather's white cedar rocking chair, and he sat in her grandmother's matching one. Patience had given them to her. "You always need a pair," her grandmother had told her. "One for you and one for your guest."

Troy was her first guest.

"Been quite a July so far," he said.

"Yeah."

"You and Elvis make a good team."

"We're working on it." She smiled as she watched Elvis bound down to the barn, Susie Bear on his heels. "He's certainly my better half."

"I'm not sure about that."

"Oh, it's true. All this time I've been so worried about taking care of him, while he's actually been the one taking care of me." For the first time, it occurred to her that maybe that was what Martinez had intended all along.

"Dogs are like that."

"I thought I was helping him get better."

"You were. He is better."

"Yes, he is."

"Maybe it's your turn now."

"Maybe." They looked out across the garden as the two dogs raced up from the barn and around the flower beds, brushing by the lavender and filling the air with its sweet scent as the sun set and the stars appeared in the dark summer sky.

"'Blessed be the man that spares these stones,'" she quoted quietly. "'And cursed be he that moves my bones.'"

"Shakespeare again. You said that in the woods when we found the bones. Which play is it from?"

"It's not from a play. It's his epitaph. The assumption is that he wrote it. No one knows for sure. I was just thinking about the bones we found in the wilderness. No epitaph for him."

"Not yet. But soon, thanks to you."

"I hope you're right. I'm sure Patrick O'Malley would prefer to spend eternity at home in Ireland."

Troy stopped rocking and turned toward her. "May I ask you a question?"

"Sure." She stopped rocking, too, but kept her eyes on the dogs.

"What's up with all the Shakespeare?"

Mercy laughed. "Amy asked me the same thing."

"What did you say?"

"I told her the truth. That reading his stories made me feel better about being human."

"Pretty heavy for an eighteen-year-old." Troy paused. "But it makes sense to me."

He leaned back in his chair. She followed suit. They sat there in silence for a moment, the only sound the panting of the dogs and the squeaking of the rockers and the hooting of the owls.

"So I guess tomorrow you'll be back out looking for people lost in the wilderness."

Troy smiled. "I've got patrols."

"Right." She smiled back. In his own way, he was a rebel.

"So I guess tomorrow you'll be back out looking for art lost in the wilderness."

"Trade you," she said.

He laughed, and she laughed with him.

THEY sat there together for a long time. Not saying anything. It seemed to Mercy that everything had been said, at least for now. Elvis and Susie Bear tired eventually and came back to the porch, curling up on either side of the rocking chairs.

It was a perfect warm summer night, filled with the deep sweep of starlight and silence. The sweet seesaw of the rocker lulled Mercy to sleep, and when she woke up, she found herself covered with a quilt, the handsome shepherd still at her feet. Troy and Susie Bear were gone.

Dawn was breaking, and she could see Orion rising over the horizon. Orion the hunter, beloved of Diana, goddess of the hunt, who was so distraught over his death that she turned him into the brightest constellation in the sky.

She gathered the quilt around her and stood up. She glanced up at the flagpole, where the flag rippled gently in the wind.

Mercy saluted. "Martinez."

She whistled, and the shepherd hustled to his feet. As the sun rose slowly over the mountains and cast the cabin in shadow, Mercy and Elvis went inside.

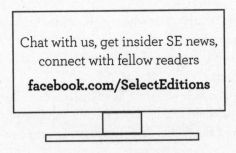

AfterWords

Paula Munier didn't set out to write a novel, much less launch a series. In fact, she was writing another book when the idea for the characters of Mercy and Elvis emerged.

A literary agent and longtime publishing professional, Munier was working on a how-to book, *The Writer's Guide to Beginnings,* and needed to write a sample first chapter of a novel to use for instructional exercises.

She had recently attended a fund-raiser for Mission K9 Rescue, an organization that rescues bomb-sniffing dogs from bad situations. She learned that many of these dogs work for defense contractors, and when they are no longer needed, they often end up in shelters. In addition, the dogs sometimes face other challenges. "I think it comes as a surprise to many that animals involved in this dangerous work may suffer from PTSD," she says. "When they retire, they need patience and love in safe forever homes."

Munier fell in love with the dogs and their handlers. She took this newfound fascination with bomb-sniffing dogs and wrote them into *The Writer's Guide to Beginnings,* never dreaming the sample chapter would become the first chapter of *A Borrowing of Bones.* She based Elvis on a Belgian Malinois that she had met at the fund-raiser and Susie Bear on her own Newfoundland-retriever mix. Her agent loved the sample chapter, and a compelling new mystery series was born.

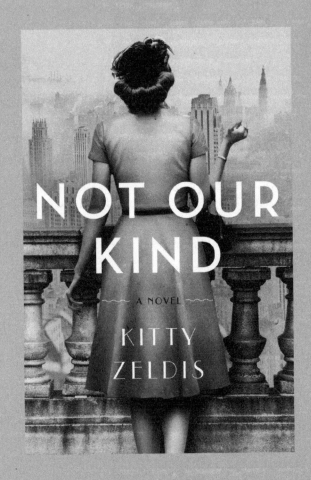

NOT OUR KIND

~ A NOVEL ~

KITTY ZELDIS

Chapter 1

THE YELLOW-AND-BLACK Checker cab nosed its way down Second Avenue in the rain. A newsboy in a sodden cap wove in and out through the slow-moving cars, hawking copies of the *New York Sun;* a man in a Plymouth exchanged coins for a newspaper as the drivers behind him honked.

Eleanor Moskowitz, perched on the edge of the backseat, didn't bother looking at her watch because she had just looked at her watch. It had been 9:29 then. It would be 9:30 now. In fifteen minutes, Eleanor had a job interview at the Markham School on Seventy-First and West End Avenue, thirteen blocks plus the width of Central Park away. It was unlikely that she was going to be on time. "Why is there so much traffic?" she asked the driver.

"Water-main break. And President Truman is in town," the driver said. "Traffic's backed up all over the East Side."

Eleanor stared at the back of the driver's neck. His hair had been shorn by a razor, like all the soldiers demobilized from the army a couple of years back. The war was a memory now, but certain images stuck.

Sweat started to pool under Eleanor's arms, and she took off the jacket of her navy crepe suit and laid it carefully across her lap so it would not crease. Her pocketbook and her umbrella—black silk with a bone handle—sat beside her. A navy hat made, like all her hats, by her mother, fit snugly on her head, but she wouldn't take it off for fear it might get crushed.

She had been so nervous about today's interview that she'd been unable to sleep the night before. Around five she finally drifted off, and then sat up with a start when she realized she'd slept through the alarm and it was eight thirty. Her mother had had an early morning appointment, and so no one had been there to rouse her. She dressed in a rush, cursed the rain that splattered against the apartment's windows, and once she was out in the street, decided to splurge on a taxi.

It was not like Eleanor to be late, especially not for something as important as a job interview. And not when she needed a job so badly. She'd turned in her resignation at the Brandon-Wythe School just two days ago, feeling her hand had been forced by the Lucinda Meriwether incident.

Lucinda had been an excellent student, yet Eleanor didn't like her. Her insights were delivered in a mocking tone, as if the class— and Eleanor—were beneath her. So when Eleanor discovered Lucinda had plagiarized a paper on Emily Dickinson, she hadn't been surprised. The girl was intellectually gifted but morally suspect. Eleanor had taken the matter to Mrs. Holcombe, the headmistress, confident of her support. She had been wrong. And she'd had no choice but to resign and scramble to find another job.

Odious as the business with Lucinda Meriwether was, its outcome had a silver lining—it gave Eleanor a reason to leave her job, a reason she could admit to. That she had another compelling reason to go, well, she didn't have to tell anyone that. Ever.

Starting back in the fall, she had allowed Ira Greenfeld, who taught physics, to slip his hands not only under the cups of her brassiere but also under the hem of her slip. The pressure of his thumb had been so intoxicating that she allowed these liberties to continue, despite the fact that they took place without the reassuring benefit of a ring on her finger.

Then, abruptly, Ira stopped calling or coming by. He also began to avoid her looks—at first wondering, then wounded—as they passed in the hallways at school. Soon the reason had become clear. Ira had turned his attention to the new teacher in the science department, the effervescent Miss Kligerman, whose blond curls looked like an electrified halo around her head and whose breasts were so enormous Eleanor wondered that she didn't topple over.

Of course everyone knew she'd been jilted. Brandon-Wythe was a small community. She had endured the humiliation, the pity, as well as her own resentment, stoically, and did not confide in her mother, who said, quite pointedly, "I haven't seen Ira lately."

"He's been busy," Eleanor said.

As much as Eleanor longed to leave her job immediately, she needed the income, and even if she were to forfeit it, she needed the recommendation from her employer, a recommendation that might not be forthcoming if she were impetuous enough to leave in the middle of the term. Then Lucinda had turned in her paper on Dickinson, and Eleanor had found a way out.

Eleanor thought of the last conversation she'd had with the Brandon-Wythe headmistress. "This incident with Lucinda is unfortunate," Mrs. Holcombe had said.

"Unfortunate?" Eleanor said, flaring. "Mrs. Holcombe, you do understand that she lifted whole sentences from Olive Thompson's *Voices in American Poetry*? There's no excuse for what she did. I've given the paper an F."

To Eleanor's surprise, Mrs. Holcombe leaned back in her chair, a wry expression on her face. "Eleanor, you are a fine, principled young woman. And an excellent teacher. But when it comes to how the world works, you're as innocent as one of our girls."

"I'm not sure I understand," said Eleanor. She was angry but did not want to antagonize Mrs. Holcombe. As one of the three Jewish teachers on staff—Ira and the despised Miss Kligerman were the others—Eleanor knew her position was not rock solid.

"Lucinda's mother and aunt were students here. The Meriwethers donate a substantial amount of money to the school, and Lucinda's father is on the board. And as surprising as it may seem to you, we need their support."

Eleanor was quiet. Could this really be the case? To her, the school had seemed replete with privilege, with resources. Still, Lucinda's behavior was wrong, and Eleanor had to say so. "But what she did—"

"Is a regrettable lapse. I'll call her into my office, and we'll explain that you are aware of what she's done, and though you're not going to do anything about it this time, others may not be so lenient in the future. We could think of this as a kind of warning."

"With all due respect, Mrs. Holcombe, that makes us as culpable as she is."

Again there was that tolerant, almost bemused smile. "As impractical and unworldly as your position is, I respect it. And I respect you. But that's not the way it's going to be, Eleanor. If you can't accept it, then I'm afraid . . ."

"That I'll have to resign." The words were out before Eleanor knew it, a challenge between them.

"Why not sleep on it and let me know in the morning. I'll accept whatever decision you make. But I'd hate to lose you, Eleanor."

"And I'd be sorry to go." That was true; there was so much about the job that Eleanor loved. Then she thought of Lucinda's smug, supercilious expression. And she thought, too, of Ira, turning away when they passed in the hallways. Out of courtesy, she would pretend to think it over for a night. But in her heart she knew: it was time to go.

And so here she was, in this yellow taxi laboriously making its way toward the Markham School on the West Side. Eleanor had resigned, and in tacit exchange for her silence about Lucinda, Mrs. Holcombe had given her a month's severance and a glowing letter of reference.

Eleanor knew her chances of landing the Markham job were slim. But she had to try because she so badly needed a job. She could have gone to work in her mother's hat shop on Second Avenue, just downstairs from their third-floor walk-up tenement apartment. As a little girl, she had loved being in the shop, with its gold-painted script spelling out HATS BY IRINA in a graceful arc across the window, loved the ribbons and bows, the veils, the silk flowers and faux fruit that made up the raw materials of her mother's craft. But her mother had adamantly refused her daughter's offer to join her. "Hats are good," her mother had said.

"Teaching is better." Irina had been nine when she came from Russia with her mother and two younger brothers; her father had been killed, and her mother was fleeing pogroms and the revolution. She'd never gone to school past the fifth grade and was determined to see her daughter surpass her. And Eleanor had. She'd gone to the prestigious Hunter College High School for Intellectually Gifted Young Ladies. After high school, she had attended Vassar on a scholarship. The job at Brandon-Wythe had been her first.

SHE'D been in this taxi for over thirty minutes, minutes during which she sat rigidly, watching the fare rise; it was now more than two dollars. "Maybe you could go down Fifth," she ventured.

"That might be even worse," the driver said. He continued on Park Avenue for a few feet, then stopped—again!—for yet another red light. Eleanor was awash in a helpless rage.

When the light changed to green, she leaned back just the slightest bit, allowing some of her tension to dissipate. But as the driver was about to make a turn, there was a sudden jolt from behind. Instantly, she was thrust forward and her face was slammed against the driver's seat. Her hands flew to her lip, which the impact had split; she tasted blood. She began to shake.

"He rammed right into me!" The driver opened his door.

Eleanor said nothing. She was trembling and kept her hands pressed over her mouth. The blood was dripping now, bright, round circles, onto her ivory silk blouse.

"Are you hurt?" the driver said, finally turning to Eleanor. "Hey, you're bleeding!"

"I'm all right," she said, removing a hand from her face to root around in her handbag for a handkerchief. "It's just my lip."

The driver's attention was elsewhere, shouting at the other driver—also a cabbie—who had inflicted the damage.

"You hit me!" the driver of Eleanor's taxi said. "Just smacked right into me."

"You didn't signal you—"

"Didn't signal? What are you—blind? Or just a moron?"

Still trembling, Eleanor remained where she sat. Outside, a

crowd had gathered. She heard someone say they were going to get a policeman from the station down the street. More shouting from the drivers, shouting that intensified when the police officer showed up. The sight of him galvanized her; she clambered out of the cab, clutching her jacket, purse, and umbrella.

"What's all the trouble?" The officer—young, with a round pink face—looked back and forth between the two cabbies.

"This guy rammed—"

"He forgot to signal—"

"All right, all right," said the officer. He pulled out a thick note-book from his pocket. "One at a time."

Eleanor stood there, the rain quickly wetting her thin—and now bloodstained—blouse. She was still clutching her jacket and umbrella but was too stunned to put on the first or open the second. She was not going to be *late* to the interview; she was going to miss it entirely. Her eyes anxiously scanned the streets, looking for a telephone booth.

"Officer, this woman has been hurt."

Eleanor turned to see that the passenger in the other cab had emerged. She looked to be in her thirties, and despite the rain, was flawless in her gray polished-cotton suit, with the kind of trim, fitted jacket and full, gathered skirt that Mr. Dior had introduced just months before.

"Are you okay, miss?" the officer said, looking away from the two cabbies. "Do you need an ambulance?"

"No ambulance," Eleanor said. "Just a telephone, please. I'm late for an appointment."

"I'll take you down to the station; you can use the phone there. But I have to finish up with these two guys first. And then I'll have to take your statement too."

Eleanor just nodded, her eyes beginning to fill. *The interview.*

"You're getting soaked," the woman said. Her gray mermaid hat, fitted close to her head and adorned with narrow white piping, was also a style endorsed by Mr. Dior. Eleanor's mother would have loved it. "Why don't you open that?"

Eleanor looked dumbly at the umbrella in her hand.

The woman regarded her indulgently. "Or, why don't you come

and stand with me?" Her hand in its net glove gestured for Eleanor to join her under her umbrella.

Eleanor walked over and stood beside her as the two men continued to offer their conflicting versions of the story while the officer grunted softly, his pencil moving rapidly across the pad.

"You're crying," the woman observed.

Was she? Eleanor touched her face. "I just want a telephone," she said. "Please!" So the woman went over to the officer; he nodded and the woman returned.

"There's a phone booth on the next corner," she said. "I told the officer you needed to make an urgent call and that we would be back as soon as you had finished."

And she took Eleanor's arm and propelled her along Park Avenue. Close up, the woman smelled of Chanel No. 5, a heady scent Eleanor could not afford to buy.

"I'll wait here," the woman said when they reached the phone booth. And she stood outside while Eleanor stepped in, dialed the number for the Markham School, and waited anxiously until someone picked up. No, the headmistress was not available now; she was in a meeting. Yes, the message would be delivered.

Eleanor hung up and looked at her watch. The crystal covering its brave little face was cracked, and the hands were frozen in place. The watch had been a gift from her father, a year or so before he died. Its loss, heaped on top of the other losses of the day, seemed too much. She began to cry in earnest. And her lip started bleeding again. She pushed the door open, desperate for air.

There stood the woman in the Dior suit. She had been waiting patiently. "Oh you poor, dear girl," she said. "We'll finish up with the police, and then you'll come straight home with me."

SHELTERING the bedraggled young woman under her umbrella, Patricia Bellamy guided her the few short blocks to her apartment building. They had each given their statements to the officer and were now free to leave, but Patricia had not wanted to let Eleanor go off by herself. Even though she had not been driving, she somehow felt responsible for the accident.

Patricia's own errand that morning—a trip to Bergdorf Goodman to pick up something for Margaux—could wait. Margaux didn't really care if her mother came home with another sweater or dress; the walking stick she was now forced to use had caused her to lose interest in new clothes and just about everything else.

As they entered the lobby, Patricia nodded to John, the doorman, and to Declan, the elevator operator. The girl, Eleanor, remained silently at her side. It was only when they reached the apartment and after Patricia had called out, "Henryka, can you get lunch started?" that she turned to her guest. "Did you want to use the telephone again?" she asked. Eleanor shook her head. "What about your interview?"

"I've missed it."

"How about freshening up a bit, then?" There was still a bit of blood on Eleanor's chin and her left cheek.

"Thank you," her guest said. She led Eleanor through the foyer, past the demilune table and the gilt-framed mirror, and the living room with its matched Louis XVI sofas, to the guest bathroom.

As the door closed quietly, Patricia realized that she had never entertained a Jew in her apartment before. She'd realized the girl was Jewish only after she'd extended the invitation, when she'd heard her give her name to the police officer. The information came as a surprise. With her fine-boned face—her nose was narrow and small, her mouth delicate—Eleanor Moskowitz did not *look* Jewish. Of course, there was the dark hair, but plenty of people of all backgrounds had dark hair. And, despite her distress about missing her interview, she had a refined way of speaking. There was that suit, a cheap, skimpy thing, no doubt bought during the war when fabric—along with just about everything else—had been rationed. But the girl's hat was a marvel—simple, but lovely. Patricia wondered whether she would have invited the girl home if she'd known that she was a Jew. But once the invitation had been given, there was simply no way she could have rescinded it.

Patricia walked into the kitchen. "Henryka, what can you bring out for lunch?" she asked her cook. "Isn't there some ham?" Yesterday she'd hosted a luncheon and knew there were leftovers, though she was vaguely aware that ham was a food a Jew might not eat. Should she ask, or would that be rude?

"There's ham. Cheese too." Henryka swiped at the counter with a rag. A stout Polish woman in her sixties with thick gray-blond braids pinned up on her head, she had worked for Patricia's mother. When Patricia married, Henryka had come to work for her. She was taciturn, and often sulky, but for Patricia, she was family.

"Do we have lemons?" Patricia asked.

"Two left," said Henryka, her thick fingers wrapped around the chrome handle of the refrigerator.

"Two should be enough," Patricia said. "Can you squeeze them and prepare three glasses of lemonade?"

"Miss Margaux eat too?" Henryka asked.

"I hope so," said Patricia. "Henryka, would you please ask her? I think she'd rather it came from you."

"All right. She like my lemonade." Henryka took the lemons out and put them on the counter.

Patricia and Eleanor were already seated at the table when Margaux lurched into the room. She introduced her daughter and exhaled silently when Margaux had crossed the room with no mishaps—there was simply no way she could move with anything approaching grace—and took her place across from their guest.

Eleanor helped herself to small portions of ham and carrots. "What are you studying in school?" she asked Margaux.

Margaux did not answer.

"Miss Moskowitz asked you a question, Margaux," Patricia said, trying not to show her displeasure. Ever since the polio, a horrid changeling had supplanted Patricia's formerly charming daughter.

"I'm not in school now," Margaux said sullenly.

"Since her illness, Margaux has had a tutor," Patricia explained. "She didn't feel comfortable—"

"Would *you?*" Margaux said angrily.

"Her father and I didn't insist. So we hired Mr. Cobb." She did not add that Margaux tormented the poor man.

"I'm hungry," Margaux said. There was a whine in her voice that would have been annoying in a child of five; in a girl of thirteen it was nearly intolerable. But Patricia ignored it, pouring herself a cup of coffee from the pot Henryka had brought in and then passing the pot to Eleanor.

"Margaux, why don't you tell Miss Moskowitz about what you've been reading with Mr. Cobb?"

"What's wrong with your lip?" asked Margaux, ignoring her mother's prompting.

"I was in an accident this morning. In a cab. I hit my face."

"There's blood on your blouse. Did you go to the hospital?" Eleanor shook her head.

"I was in the hospital for months," Margaux continued. "I had polio."

"That must have been hard."

"I felt like I was breathing through a straw," Margaux said. "It was horrible. So they put me in the iron lung. And I couldn't eat because I was afraid I would choke; the nurses had to slather my food with mayonnaise to make it go down." She stared at Eleanor. "I despise mayonnaise; I'll never, *ever* eat it again."

"I can understand why you wouldn't want to," said Eleanor.

"I was lucky. I survived. But my leg atrophied when I was sick. It will never heal." Margaux gestured to the wooden walking stick that stood propped against the table.

"You seem to get around pretty well with that," Eleanor said. "I think you have a lot of pluck."

Patricia stared at her. No one had ever posited Margaux's situation in this light before.

"Pluck," Margaux repeated, as if she were weighing the word in her mind. "Do you really think so?"

"I do," Eleanor said. "I really do."

Margaux seemed to like this, because she actually smiled. Just for a second, but still. As the smile faded, she studied their guest carefully, and then asked, "Are you from Moscow?"

"No, but one of my ancestors might have been," said Eleanor.

"Are you a Jew?" Margaux asked.

"Margaux!" said Patricia, who felt her cheeks heat with embarrassment. "You're being rude."

"No, I'm not," Margaux said.

"I don't mind her asking," Eleanor said to Patricia. "Yes, I'm Jewish. Why do you ask?"

"I've never had lunch with a Jew before," Margaux said.

"Well, you're having lunch with one now," Eleanor said.

Margaux considered this for a moment, and as she did, Patricia noticed a glimmer of her daughter's former curiosity animating her face. Faint, to be sure. But it was there.

"My father says all Jews have lots of money," Margaux said. "And that behind the scenes, they control just about everything." She looked at Eleanor, clearly assessing the modest suit, its lapels a bit shiny from wear, and added, "But I don't think you're rich."

There was a long, excruciating silence. Patricia could hardly look at their guest, let alone apologize for her daughter.

Eleanor said nothing but sat still, hands splayed and pressed flat against the table. "Some Jews are rich. Some—in fact most—aren't. But in any case, you shouldn't be promoting those old stereotypes. It's hurtful. And rude."

Margaux, who had been lolling back in her seat in a most irritating way, sat up straight. Her abrupt movement jostled the table, tipping over her glass of lemonade.

"Now look what you've done!" Patricia, released from the acute mortification that seemed to render her speechless, finally spoke. "Henryka," she called sharply in the direction of the kitchen.

As Henryka cleaned up the mess, Patricia made a show of scolding Margaux. But secretly, she was grateful for the accident and the diversion it provided. Yes, Wynn sometimes said those kinds of things about Jews but never to anyone outside their circle. Never, for heaven's sake, in *front* of them.

After everything was cleaned up, Margaux reached for her walking stick so she could rise from the table. Patricia so badly wanted to help her, but she knew the fury with which the gesture would be met, so she only watched as her child struggled until she finally gained purchase with the stick.

"It was interesting to meet you," Margaux said.

"It was interesting to meet you too." Eleanor stood.

At the door, Patricia tried to press a five-dollar bill into Eleanor's hand, but Eleanor refused to take it. "Please," Patricia insisted. "So you can take a taxi home."

"Thank you, but I live only three blocks away," her guest said.

"I'd like to apologize for Margaux. Ever since her illness, she's become so rude. Unmanageable. It's kind of unmoored her."

"Maybe if you've been through something like that you become . . . unmoored. And it takes time to find your way back," Eleanor said. "Thank you for lunch."

Patricia waited until Declan appeared with the elevator, and watched as Eleanor stepped in and the doors closed behind her. It was hours later that she noticed Eleanor's umbrella, still sitting in the umbrella stand. She could leave it with the doorman; Eleanor would no doubt remember where she'd left it and come back for it on her own. Or Patricia could contact her about it. Eleanor had mentioned that she lived on Eighty-Fourth Street, just a few short blocks east; it would be easy enough to track the girl down. Did she want to bother? She thought of the way Eleanor had handled herself during lunch. Quietly confident. Unapologetic. Altogether, an intriguing person, Jewish or not. Yes, Patricia decided. She did.

Chapter 2

ELEANOR STOOD BEFORE the mirror in her bedroom, unsuccessfully trying to camouflage her wounded lip. Even though the swelling had subsided in the past three days, there was a dark scab that face powder and lipstick did not fully cover. In the mirror's reflective surface, she saw her mother behind her in the doorway, holding a pink silk rose. "I thought this might look nice on your dress." Irina did not wait to be asked into the room. "There'll be a lot of other girls at that employment agency, and you want to stand out."

"Pretty." Eleanor took the rose.

"I don't understand why you left a perfectly good job without another one lined up," said Irina. Her English was excellent, with only a slight trace of her Russian roots.

"Are you going to bring that up *again?*" Eleanor felt she could not stand any more of her mother's inquiries; she was worried enough about being unemployed. But the wounded look that came over Irina's face made Eleanor contrite. "No one else will have such a beautiful rose," she said. "I'm glad you thought of it."

"I know," Irina said, mollified. "The color is perfect."

"Were these roses from last season's hats?"

Irina shook her head. "Next season. You're getting what's new, not what's left over."

At Forty-Second Street and Grand Central Terminal, Eleanor was disgorged from the subway car by the press of people behind her and made her way out onto Lexington Avenue toward the Chrysler Building. The bright, glittering spire was a fantastic oddity amid the buildings that surrounded it. Crescent-shaped semicircles of chrome-plated steel went up the surface, giving it the look of a stylized sunburst. Underneath, steel gargoyles of eagles' heads stared down at the city below. Her father had brought her here in 1930, when the building first opened. She missed her father, a mild, gentle man who sold men's suiting fabric for a living; he seemed free of the incessant worry that animated her mother.

The lobby of the Chrysler Building was altogether dazzling, with its burnt sienna floor, red marble walls, and decorations of onyx, blue marble, and still more steel. Eleanor darted to get into the crowded elevator before the doors—adorned with inlaid wood and enormous golden lilies—closed. By the fifteenth floor, the crowd had thinned.

When she entered the employment office, every seat in the waiting room was filled with young women.

Eleanor approached the receptionist. "I'm here to see about a job," she said. "I have an appointment."

The woman gave her a cursory once-over before handing her a printed form attached to a clipboard. "Have a seat and fill this out," she said. "Pencils are on the table."

"But there aren't any seats," Eleanor said.

"There will be," the woman said. Eleanor took a pencil and retreated to the far wall. As she completed the form, the door behind the receptionist opened and a woman walked out; another went in, and Eleanor claimed her seat. She waited for more than twenty minutes, watching as women continued to walk in and out. Finally, Eleanor heard her name called. She gave the clipboard to the receptionist and walked through the door just like she had seen the others do. Beyond the door, a seated woman motioned for Eleanor to come in and sit down. On one side of her desk was an ashtray and on the other a small sign that read RITA BURNS. She was about forty, with faintly pitted skin and cranberry lipstick.

"You can give me the form," said Miss Burns. "So you're a college graduate." She reached for a box of cigarettes from a drawer. "You studied Latin, along with English literature and typing."

"Not at the same time," Eleanor said. Rita Burns rewarded her with a smile. "My mother thought typing was a good skill for a woman to have. She said it would help me get a job."

"She's right," said Miss Burns. "But it looks like you took a teaching job instead." She inhaled on the cigarette. "Brandon-Wythe. Why did you leave?"

"I wanted to go in a different direction. Professionally, that is."

"I see," said Miss Burns, looking skeptical. "You taught English literature and composition. So maybe you'd be interested in something in publishing? Books or magazines?"

"Yes, I'd like that," she said eagerly.

"Recommendations, I presume?" She looked at Eleanor, who nodded. Mrs. Holcombe's letter was in her purse. "You'll have to take a typing test, of course."

"I'm a good typist," Eleanor said. "What kind of salary could I expect?"

Miss Burns looked her over carefully. "That depends. I might be able to get you thirty-eight, maybe even forty a week." Eleanor sat up straighter. She had only earned thirty-five at Brandon-Wythe. "But there is one thing . . ." Eleanor waited. "The name *Moskowitz* is not going to open a lot of doors. At least not the ones you want."

She pulled on the cigarette again. "You should consider changing it; Moss would be good."

Eleanor felt slapped. Should she agree? Argue? Leave?

"Don't take it the wrong way," Miss Burns was saying. "I'm only trying to help. I've seen it before—bright girl, nice education, good references, presents herself well. And goes exactly nowhere. *The position has been filled*, they say. Or, *You're not quite what we're looking for*. But after an easy little name adjustment, presto, everything changes."

"Oh," Eleanor said. "I see." And she did. She didn't like what Rita Burns was telling her, but she knew it to be true.

"No, you don't," Miss Burns said. "Not yet. But you will." She stood. "Are you ready for that typing test now?" She led Eleanor into a room that had been divided into a dozen cubicles. Each contained a desk holding a large black Remington Rand and a kitchen timer. Eleanor sat down, placed her bag near her feet, and awaited further instructions.

"The test is five minutes." Miss Burns handed her three handwritten sheets. Two were office memos, and the third was the first page of a quarterly report. "You'll start when I set the timer, and stop when it rings." Eleanor nodded. "Are you ready?"

"Ready," said Eleanor, lifting her hands over the keyboard.

"Then go." Miss Burns set the timer.

Eleanor typed as quickly as she could, hitting the carriage return with smart, efficient smacks. When she had completed the test, she waited in Miss Burns's office while the results were evaluated.

"Seventy-seven words a minute," said Miss Burns when she returned. "That's excellent. And it's all the more reason to consider the name change—"

"You already mentioned it," Eleanor said huffily.

"Yes, but you still don't get it." Miss Burns closed the door to her office. "This isn't something I say to many people. But I'm saying it to you. My name isn't Rita Burns. It's Rachel Bernstein."

So she was Jewish too. "I appreciate you telling me, but I'm not sure that changes anything for me. I don't like the idea."

"Do you think I did?" Miss Burns paused. "Just consider it, all right? I'm doing you a favor, even if you can't see it now."

On her way to the subway station, Eleanor thought about what it might mean to change her name. Hers was not an observant family, so it wasn't deep belief or daily practice she was being asked to hide. Yet there were the occasional Yiddish words that slipped from her mother's lips, the challah that she made once a year, on Rosh Hashanah; the yahrzeit candle that sat on the kitchen table on the anniversaries of the deaths of her grandparents and her father.

And there was something else, too, something that emerged only after the war. The news of the camps, the tattoos, the gas chambers. Adolf Hitler had systematically tried to annihilate her people. He hadn't succeeded, but his murderous goal made her want to ally herself more closely with those who'd survived. *Moskowitz* was the thing that announced who and what she was. By giving it up, she'd be giving up a part of herself too.

Or would she? She wouldn't change inside, no matter what she chose to call herself. And she needed to get a job. Eleanor Moss. She said the name aloud, to see how it sounded.

The uptown train came quickly, and she was able to get a seat. When she got off the train at Eighty-Sixth Street, Eleanor turned west rather than east toward her home. Yesterday she'd received a phone call from Patricia Bellamy telling her she'd left her umbrella and that she could pick it up from the doorman.

"Mrs. Bellamy left something for me," she said to the doorman, who wore a navy suit and matching cap trimmed with gold braid.

"And your name is?" he asked.

She hesitated. "Eleanor," she said finally. Something prevented her from saying Moskowitz.

"See Billy over there," he said, so Eleanor repeated her request to the uniformed man seated at the desk inside the lobby.

"Just a moment," he said, and disappeared behind a door. Eleanor looked around at the lobby while she waited; above was a six-armed brass chandelier; below, a black-and-white marble floor. Beyond an open pair of double doors, the black-and-white marble continued, only in this adjoining space it was cushioned by a thick Persian rug. A sofa sat at the far corner, and a few wing chairs dotted the perimeter; it was in one of these that Margaux Bellamy sat, walking stick propped on the arm of the chair.

"Hello there," Margaux called out. "How are you?"

Eleanor did not especially want to talk to Margaux but felt it would be rude to ignore the girl's greeting. She walked over to where Margaux sat.

"What are you doing here?" Eleanor asked.

"My mother and I are going out, only she forgot something and had to go back upstairs. Did you come to see us again?"

"No," said Eleanor. "I came for my umbrella."

"Oh." Margaux seemed disappointed. Though the day was warm, Margaux wore slacks, which Eleanor guessed was to cover her bad leg. "I wish you were coming to visit us," she said.

"Why is that?" asked Eleanor, unexpectedly touched. She sat on an upholstered chair and sank into its soft cushion.

"Because you're different. I like talking to you."

"Thank you," Eleanor said. "I like talking to you too." And at that moment, it was true.

"Would you then?"

"Would I what?"

"Come to visit us?" Margaux said. "Come to visit *me*." Eleanor was silent, and Margaux pressed on. "My mother told me you're a teacher."

"Was," Eleanor corrected. "I'm looking for a different sort of job now."

"What sort of job?"

"I might work for a book or magazine publisher."

"What if you took a job as my tutor?"

"I thought you had a tutor."

"Not anymore."

"What happened to him?" asked Eleanor.

"I made him so unhappy that he quit," Margaux said. "I tortured him. But I wouldn't do that to you."

"Why not?" asked Eleanor. She was actually warming to this girl—her candor, her intensity, and yes, even her anger.

"I told you: I like talking to you. I like *you*." Before Eleanor could answer, the uniformed man reappeared holding her umbrella,

and at the same moment, the elevator doors parted and Patricia
Bellamy stepped out. She wore a dress of wine-colored silk whose
skirt swished softly as she approached. "Hello, Miss Moskowitz."

"I was waiting here, just like you told me to," Margaux said to
her mother. "And I saw Miss Moskowitz at the front door. She was
getting her umbrella. Mother, why can't she be my tutor?"

Eleanor was silent. Tutoring this girl was the last thing she
wanted to do. Confined to an apartment, even one on Park Avenue, being at the beck and call of Patricia Bellamy and, presumably,
her husband—no, this was not for her. Yet she did not wish to hurt
Margaux, and so would humor her by pretending to consider the
position. It was unlikely that Mrs. Bellamy would actually hire her.

". . . well, I don't know," Mrs. Bellamy was saying. "We haven't
discussed it."

"No, but we could discuss it now." Eleanor finally spoke up. "The
position at the Markham School was filled, but I am an experienced teacher, and I do have references."

"You would be perfect, I know it!" Margaux burst out.

"Lower your voice please," Mrs. Bellamy said. She beckoned
to the doorman. When the umbrella was safely back in Eleanor's
hands, Mrs. Bellamy added, "I'd like to consider you for this position, Miss Moskowitz. Would you send me a copy of your résumé?
And your references? At your convenience of course."

"Certainly. I can leave a packet with the doorman."

"Thank you," Mrs. Bellamy said. "I'll look forward to receiving
it." She turned to Margaux. "Time to get going."

Despite what she'd just said, Eleanor had no intention of dropping her references off for Patricia Bellamy's consideration. She
clutched her umbrella and waited while, with some effort, Margaux
hoisted herself to her feet.

"Good-bye, Miss Moskowitz," Margaux said. "I really hope
Mother hires you and you come back."

Eleanor was about to respond with some meaningless palaver,
but when she looked at Margaux, the girl's face was filled with
such naked supplication that she could not look away. And in those
few, charged seconds, Eleanor realized that to ignore Margaux's

blatant need, her unabashed appeal, would be not only wrong but also cruel. It was a cruelty Eleanor could not bear to inflict. She would drop off the résumé and the letter, just as she had said she would. And in that moment, Eleanor decided that if Patricia Bellamy offered her the job, she was going to take it.

Chapter 3

THE RECEIVING LINE for Audrey Miles's wedding reception snaked through the opulent interior of the Metropolitan Club as the guests, a mix of elegantly attired men in tuxes and women in gowns, waited patiently to congratulate the bride.

"Why did she invite so many people?" Wynn said to Patricia. "It's a second marriage after all."

"That's no reason not to celebrate," Patricia said. But she, too, was a bit surprised by the crowd, as many members of their set had pointedly snubbed Audrey when she left her first husband. Perhaps her new husband's money had smoothed over the social awkwardness created by the divorce. "And the line *is* moving."

"No, it's not." Wynn touched the bow tie constricting his thick neck. "And why black tie when it's so damn hot, I'll never know!" He stood glaring at her as if the dress code had been up to her. But before she could answer, she heard her name being called.

"Patricia! Patricia, over here!" She turned to see Johanna Gilchrist and Tori LePage, two friends from Smith, not far ahead of them in line.

"It's so good to see you!" Patricia said, hugging them in turn.

"You'll never guess who's here," Tori said.

"Who?" Patricia demanded eagerly.

"It's Madeleine Kendricks," Tori announced.

"You're joking. Where is she?" Patricia asked. Madeleine had been the brightest star of their little group. She had looks and brains, and the self-possession to deploy both to advantage. Like Patricia, she had majored in art history. But unlike Patricia, she'd gone off to do graduate work at the Courtauld in London, then married an earl with whom she traveled the globe before settling down at his ancestral country estate and starting a family.

A discreet pressure on her elbow reminded her that Wynn had been standing there quietly all this time. "You remember my husband, don't you?" she said to Tori. Yes, of course Tori did, and Johanna too. They all chatted for a few minutes, and then the line started moving more quickly.

When they reached Audrey, Patricia leaned in to hug her. "I'm so happy for you," she said.

"Thanks, darling," Audrey said softly. "This time I got it *right*."

Patricia knew what she meant; it was rumored that Audrey's first husband was a brute—drinking too much, spending her money on other women, and on at least one particularly awful occasion, hitting her. "I hope you'll both be very happy."

Then she heard Wynn's tightly uttered, "Congratulations," to the groom, who, in addition to being several years older than Audrey, was also balding and a bit potbellied. But Audrey's face was radiant when she looked at him.

With Johanna on one side of her and Tori on the other, Patricia ran into several other friends. Better still, Wynn had happened upon an old Yale buddy, and, gin and tonics in hand, the two seemed to be having a fine time reconnecting. Patricia was relieved. Wynn's mood, so easily soured, was especially important tonight because, after reviewing Eleanor Moskowitz's impressive credentials, Patricia had hired her. Eleanor would be starting work on Monday, but Patricia had not told Wynn yet. If all went well, she would tell him later on.

Patricia went in search of Madeleine Kendricks, whom she finally found in the library.

"Tricia!" she cried. "It's been . . . decades."

"Not decades," Patricia said. "We're not all that old."

"Aren't we?" Madeleine said. "I feel old. No, ancient."

They hugged, and Patricia said, "Well, you don't look it."

They settled into green leather chairs, and Maddy told Patricia about what it was like being the wife of an earl.

"It's all very sporty," she said. "Quaint. The rituals, you know. And satisfying in its way. I have my children, my horses. And Phillip, of course. He's my rock. And now that the war is finally over, I feel like I can breathe again."

"How old are your boys?"

"Maxwell and Roger are twelve. They're twins. Charles is eight. We had another, Byron, but we lost him."

"Maddy! I didn't know." Patricia grasped her friend's hand.

"He was just four." Maddy took a deep sip of her cocktail. "A bacterial infection. He was fine one day, droopy the next, burning with fever the day after that. He was gone within the week."

"Oh God. I'm so, so sorry, Madeleine," Patricia said.

Maddy dabbed at her eyes with her napkin. "I'm all right," she said. She put a hand on Patricia's wrist. "Here I've been rambling on and not letting you get a word in edgewise. How have you been? And that brother of yours?"

"Tom is . . . well, Tom."

"You tell him I say hello, would you?" Maddy had been charmed by Tom. "Now tell me about your family."

Patricia told her about the ordeal from which Margaux had emerged alive but not unscathed.

"But she's all right then?" Maddy asked. "Over it completely?"

"Except for the leg, yes."

"What about your husband? You haven't said much about him."

"He's an attorney," Patricia said, but didn't add, *who did not make partner and who has not stopped being bitter about it for one blessed minute.* "Estate law." He'd had to switch firms after the partnership debacle, and oh, how his pride had suffered. He was certain that the reason he'd been passed over was pure spite, not because he went into work late and left early or that he'd bungled a major account.

"Does he find the work . . . rewarding?"

"I suppose so. Wynn's more interested in what he does outside the office—sailing, golf, things like that . . ." She found she did not have all that much to say about Wynn. Or rather, what she wanted to say, she couldn't. "It's just that . . . we've grown apart."

"What do you mean?"

"I hate golf only slightly less than sailing. And the only time he talks about work is to complain."

"What about your love life?"

"Well, after so many years of marriage . . ."

"Listen, Tricia. If things are all right in the bedroom, then you see all the other failings through a different lens."

"Well, there's not much I can do about it, is there?"

"Darling," Maddy said, "that is where you're dead wrong." And she proceeded to give Patricia a detailed plan for all the things she might indeed do. Both fascinated and supremely embarrassed, Patricia nonetheless drank in every word. When Maddy finished, she stood and the two women embraced. "Come and see us, why don't you? It'd be like old times."

"I'd love that." Patricia indulged in a brief fantasy: She, Wynn, and Margaux, walking through the English countryside, Margaux as nimble as a goat, no walking stick in sight.

Wynn was in a fine mood on the taxi ride home. He'd made plans to meet his Yale pal for lunch, and there had been the hint of some work being thrown his way. The meal—prime rib with *haricots verts amandine,* mashed potatoes, and gravy—had pleased him enormously, and he had considered the champagne "first rate."

The apartment was quiet and dark. Henryka and Margaux were asleep. Wynn had already started undressing when Patricia slipped into the adjoining master bath with the words, "Wait up for me." Behind the closed door, she hurriedly got out of her dress and undergarments. She undid her hair, shaking it out and running her fingers through it to give it more volume. A few sprays of perfume at certain strategic spots. Then she slipped her gold evening sandals back on and added a heavy gold chain.

Naked except for her evening shoes and necklace, she stepped into the bedroom. Wynn, stripped down to his boxer shorts, was stretched out on his side of the bed. She felt a rush of tenderness—

he loved her; he was her husband and the father of her child.

Wynn's eyes were closed, but she did not think he was sleeping because when she approached, he opened them right away.

"Tricia," he said, clearly surprised. "What's all this?"

"Do you like my outfit?" she said coyly. She felt silly; she felt excited. She'd been taught never to initiate, but to let her husband take the lead. Now here she was, breaking all the rules.

"I like it very much." He ran his hands up and down her thighs. To her surprise, she felt a thrum of the old thrill she had felt so often during their courtship but seldom during their marriage.

When it was over, he let one hand lazily caress her back while the other held a lit cigarette. Patricia was practically purring. But her work was not done; this triumph had conveniently paved the way for the next phase of her campaign.

"Darling, I wanted to talk to you about something . . ."

"Anything," he said. "Anything at all."

"I've hired a tutor for Margaux." There, she had said it.

"Please, tell me he's an improvement over Mr. Cobb."

"It's not a he. It's a she," said Patricia. "The tutor I hired is Eleanor Moskowitz. The girl whose taxicab I hit."

"Eleanor Moskowitz?" Wynn sat up.

"Yes." She knew what he was thinking. It was the name Moskowitz. It was one thing to hire a Jewish upholsterer or piano tuner, but a Jewish tutor, coming into their home every day . . . "She went to Vassar. And she excelled in everything she undertook."

"I'm sure she's very bright. They usually are. But is hiring her a good idea?"

"Why wouldn't it be? Margaux likes her already and—"

"You have a kind heart, my darling," he said. "So kind that you forget how cruel the world can be."

"I don't understand what this has to do with—"

"Doesn't Margaux have enough strikes against her? Does she need a tutor who's going to cause people to talk?"

"I don't care about all that!" Patricia burst out. It wasn't true. She did care, and she had even had the same thought. But what Margaux wanted was more important, and Margaux wanted Eleanor

Moskowitz. She could not, would not let Wynn stand in the way. Overwrought, she began to sob.

"Tricia, don't." Wynn put his arm around her. "Is it that important to you?"

"Yes! But it's even more important to Margaux, don't you see?" He was always undone by her tears.

"All right then," he said. "Hire her. Just try not to broadcast her background."

Patricia said nothing, choosing to conceal her jubilation.

ON THE Sunday night before she was to start working for the Bellamys, Eleanor stood in front of the mirror in her peach-colored slip, running her fingers through her hair to fluff it out; the hot weather had made it go limp. Behind her, on the bed, lay her outfit for tomorrow: her best black-and-white-plaid summer dress, a black straw hat adorned by a narrow white band, and a black patent leather pocketbook. She had dropped off her résumé, and she'd received a phone call from Patricia Bellamy the next day.

"I'd like to offer you a position as Margaux's tutor," Patricia had said. "Five days a week, five hours a day, at least through the end of June. In July, we go up to the country, and we'd like you to come with us. We don't expect Margaux to be doing schoolwork all day long while we're there, but she's fallen behind, and it would be good for her to keep up with her studies. If things work out, you can stay on into the fall." Patricia paused, and it sounded like she took a drag on a cigarette. "And oh—we can give you forty-five dollars a week."

Forty-five dollars a week! That was ten dollars more than she'd been making. "That would be fine," she said.

"How soon can you start? Margaux's been asking for you. Ever since her illness, she's been so angry. Since we brought her home from the hospital, she hasn't looked anyone in the eye in months. But you . . . you touched something in her."

Finally satisfied with her hair, Eleanor clipped it to one side with a barrette. The telephone in the kitchen rang, and from the sound of Irina's replies, Eleanor knew it was her friend Ruth Feingold on the phone. She'd promised to meet Ruth to head over to a social at

Congregation Orach Chaim on Lexington Avenue. But now that the appointed night was here, she was reluctant to go.

Irina appeared at the door. "Can I come in?"

"Is it Ruth?" Irina nodded. "Would you mind telling her I'm not feeling well?"

Irina gave her a look. "She already hung up. She said she'll be waiting on the corner. I told her you'd be there in a few minutes."

"Will you call her back and tell her I can't make it?"

"Why not? I thought you were looking forward to that social."

"I was," Eleanor said. "But now I'm not."

"Ellie, please. Why don't you go with Ruth? You might meet someone. Someone who will take your mind off Ira."

Eleanor turned away so her mother would not see her tears. But Irina knew anyway and gave her a hug.

"I guess I shouldn't keep Ruth waiting," Eleanor said.

Ruth chattered all the way up to the synagogue on Ninety-Fourth Street. Life behind the counter of her parents' delicatessen, her older sister's new beau, the merits of getting a permanent— these were the topics that carried them along the busy streets.

"You're quiet tonight," Ruth said at last. "Are you all right?"

"I'm fine," Eleanor said. "Just thinking about tomorrow."

"And you're not thinking about the social tonight?" She pointed to the synagogue, which they had now reached.

"That too," Eleanor said.

"Ira was a fool," Ruth said. "But some guy in there is going to thank his lucky stars because of that."

Eleanor smiled. "Let's go in." Orach Chaim was familiar ground. In the lobby, Eleanor could hear the din of voices and the strains of Ted Weems singing "Heartaches" from below. She and Ruth followed the music downstairs, and when they got there, the room was full.

"Would you look at that!" Ruth said. "All these guys. Where do you suppose Rabbi Schechter found them? They're not all from this congregation, are they?"

Eleanor shrugged. There were indeed a lot of men in the room. All were wearing yarmulkes.

"I'm thirsty," Ruth said. "Let's get something to drink." Eleanor watched her go but hung back, not wanting to force herself into that crush of people.

"Can I offer you some punch?"

Eleanor turned to see a short young man in a tan sport coat holding two cut-glass punch cups. "Thank you," she said. "How did you happen to have two?"

"It took me such a long time to get to the punch bowl, I figured I might as well take an extra. But I haven't touched either of them."

In lieu of an answer, Eleanor sipped her punch. It had a vaguely cherry flavor and was very sweet. "There's rugelach too," her new companion said, gesturing to a table that held several large plates of the fruit-filled pastries.

"Maybe later."

"I'm Harry," he said, extending his hand. "Harry Cohen."

"Eleanor Moskowitz," she said, taking his hand.

They talked for a little while. Harry was earnest and just a little bit nervous, which she actually liked. But he had a high voice and talked quickly; it was the sort of thing that soon became annoying. She would never want to kiss him, she decided, but then felt slightly shocked at her reaction. Was that *all* she thought about?

"There's my friend," Eleanor said, finally spotting Ruth. "I should go. She's been looking for me. It was nice talking to you."

"Oh," said Harry, clearly disappointed.

She turned away. "There you are!" she called to Ruth. "I thought I'd lost you."

"I saw you talking to someone," Ruth said. "Did he ask for your telephone number?"

"I escaped before he had the chance." Eleanor looked at Ruth, and Ruth looked back. Then they both burst out laughing.

"So he's not the fella who's going to help you get over Ira," Ruth said.

"No. But look, Ruthie, look at all the other fish—or *fellas*—in the sea." And with that, she moved deeper into the crowd, headed in the direction of the rugelach.

The next morning, Eleanor got up early and had coffee with her mother. It was a short walk to Park Avenue, and Eleanor had started out so early that she had plenty of time to window-shop along the way. In a store on Lexington Avenue, she saw a lovely raw silk summer dress with a full gathered skirt. As she continued down the street, she entertained a fantasy of buying the dress with her new salary. But then she tried to imagine who would be escorting her in this lovely outfit, and the fantasy collapsed.

At the synagogue mixer, after high-voiced Harry, she had talked to a stocky fellow with frizzy blond curls and another taller young man with wavy dark hair and the most adorable dimples. The stocky fellow did not do much for her, but the one with the dimples did; unfortunately, he did not reciprocate her interest and had quickly moved on. Eleanor drank another cup of punch and sampled the rugelach before finding Ruth again, this time deep in conversation with a bearlike young man who had gentle brown eyes and a nice smile. Ruth seemed effervescent in his presence and talked about him all the way home. Eleanor just nodded, all the while wishing she had met someone who made her feel that way.

As she reached Patricia Bellamy's apartment building, Eleanor hesitated for a moment before going inside. When Mrs. Bellamy had offered her the job, she told her to give her name as Moss, and not Moskowitz. "I hope you don't mind," Mrs. Bellamy had said. "It's just that the building is—"

"Restricted," Eleanor supplied.

"I know it's awkward, and of course I don't feel that way, but I'd just rather not ruffle any feathers, if you know what I mean."

"I know exactly what you mean." Ironically, Moss was the name Rita Burns had suggested.

"She's expecting you," the doorman said.

When Eleanor reached the ninth floor, Mrs. Bellamy was at the door of the apartment.

"Good morning," she said. "Margaux's been waiting for you."

"I hope I'm not late," Eleanor said. Reflexively, she looked at her wrist. The watch was not there; since the accident she hadn't had time to have the crystal replaced.

"No, not at all," Mrs. Bellamy said, stepping aside. "She's just very eager. Let's go into the study."

Eleanor followed Mrs. Bellamy down a short hallway lined with finely rendered botanical prints in thin gold frames. Eager was good, she thought. Mrs. Bellamy stopped at an open doorway.

"Here's Margaux," Mrs. Bellamy said. Margaux looked animated and alert. Her dark blond hair was held back by a black velvet headband, and she wore a pair of slacks and a blouse with a small rounded collar. A carved library table in front of her held several books, as well as a few notebooks, a pad, and some pencils.

"I've been asking Mother when you'd get here." Margaux moved over so her tutor could sit down. Her eyes—a dark, intense blue—sought out Eleanor's.

"I'm going to leave you two now," Mrs. Bellamy said. "Let me know if you need anything." She closed the door behind her.

"So tell me what you were working on with Mr. Cobb."

"Mr. Cobb was the most boring man in the world," said Margaux. "Does it really matter what we talked about?"

Margaux was right. Did Eleanor really care what the crushingly dull Mr. Cobb had said? She did not. Feeling a surge of confidence, she examined the pile of books on the table. A copy of *Romeo and Juliet*, an anthology of British poetry, *Jane Eyre*. Beneath these, several textbooks: algebra, American history, and biology. She picked up the copy of *Romeo and Juliet*. She was a good teacher, she reminded herself; she could reach this girl. "So," she said, opening the book to the first page. "Let's begin."

Three hours later, there was a knock at the door and then Mrs. Bellamy's elegantly coiffed head appeared. "Ready for lunch?"

"Is it lunchtime already?" Margaux asked.

"Yes, darling, it is," Mrs. Bellamy said. But her eyes were on Eleanor, and her look clearly said, *Whatever you're doing here, would you please keep doing it?*

Lunch was lively, with Margaux an active participant in the conversation. "Did you know that the first fourteen lines Romeo and Juliet say to each other form a sonnet?" she asked her mother. "And that Juliet is only fourteen when the play starts?"

"And you'll be fourteen next year," her mother said with pleasure. "It seems like you're really enjoying Shakespeare."

"Miss Moskowitz makes it so much fun. We've been reading some of the scenes out loud—it's like we're actors onstage."

Eleanor could feel Mrs. Bellamy beaming in her direction, but she did not let her gaze meet her employer's; she did not want Margaux to feel patronized by their reaction to her enthusiasm. She looked forward to finishing the meal and returning to the study for an afternoon session with Margaux. They were going to tackle the algebra lesson and then biology. Tomorrow she'd promised to bring along her own Latin textbook; Margaux had expressed an interest in studying it.

So after the tea and cookies were served, Eleanor and Margaux once again returned to the study and closed the door.

At three o' clock, when Mrs. Bellamy once again poked her head into the room, Margaux was aglow with her newfound understanding of the five basic concepts of biology; she insisted on enumerating them for her bemused mother: "Cell theory, gene theory, evolution, homeostasis, and the laws of thermodynamics." She turned to Eleanor. "Is that right?"

"It's perfect," said Eleanor. She was pleased with how quickly the girl caught on.

Margaux's tremulous smile was its own sweet reward, and when she asked, "You'll come back tomorrow, right?" Eleanor could answer with assurance, "Yes, I'll see you then."

Eleanor walked slowly home. She and her mother took turns making supper. Tonight was one of Eleanor's nights. She bought a cut-up chicken, which she would panfry and serve with rice. A greengrocer yielded a head of lettuce and two ripe tomatoes, along with three pounds of sweet peas for ten cents. She decided to splurge on a box of lace cookies from their favorite bakery on Eighty-Second. With their thin filling of dark chocolate sandwiched by the fretwork of pastry, they were her mother's favorites, yet she seldom bought them because of the expense. Still, tonight was a celebration of sorts—Eleanor's first day on her new job.

Her mother was already in the kitchen, setting the table.

"How was your day?" Eleanor asked as she washed her hands in the kitchen sink and put on an apron.

"Busy," her mother said as she laid out the everyday cutlery with its amber-colored Bakelite handles. "I had a bride."

"Really?" Eleanor put the rice up and began rinsing the chicken parts. Her mother's shop did not generally cater to the bridal trade.

"A second marriage," Irina explained. "She's going to be wearing a suit, and so I'm doing a little ivory toque, with silk orange blossoms and a half veil."

"Swell," Eleanor said. She patted the chicken dry gently, wondering if she would ever be a bride, even once.

"She had two bridesmaids with her," her mother continued. "They need hats too. We're doing those in periwinkle."

"Sounds elegant." Eleanor began to prepare the salad. As she sliced the tomatoes, her mother had finished setting the table and discovered the bakery box. Cutting the string to open it, Irina said, "Lace cookies. My favorite." Then she looked at her daughter. "You haven't told me about your day. Did it go well?"

"Yes," said Eleanor. "I really like the girl. Margaux."

"Well, that's a good start," her mother said. "But what about when she gets older? You'll have no security."

"I told you: I can always apply for a teaching job in a school next spring. Or the fall after that. And I'm still in touch with that Miss Burns from the employment agency. Don't worry so much."

Eleanor poured oil into a pan to heat. While waiting, she dusted the chicken parts with a mixture of flour, salt, pepper, and celery seed. When the oil started sputtering, she began laying the chicken in the pan. She thought of the day's small indignities: the slightly surly housekeeper, the cool look of the doorman when she'd given him the false name—and decided that the time spent with Margaux outweighed them all. This job was going to work, she told herself. She was going to *make* it work.

"Do you remember that dark green felt hat you made?" Eleanor asked when they were seated at the table. "It had a velvet ribbon and that one perfect faux jewel?"

"Yes!" Irina used a heel of bread to sop up juice from the chicken. "The woman who wanted to buy it asked if I could add another jewel, and another and another?"

"And you said, 'Madam, if I add one more ornament to this hat, people are going to think it's a Christmas tree!'" This was an old joke, but they both enjoyed the punch line.

Eleanor put the kettle on, and Irina fetched the new issue of *Vogue*, which they looked at while they had their tea and cookies.

"Patricia Bellamy has a dress that color." Eleanor pointed to a lovely pink dress with a full skirt and bow at the neckline.

"What kind of woman is she?"

"She seems kind. When she saw how upset I was, she brought me to her apartment to get cleaned up. She gave me lunch."

"She was probably worried you would sue her."

"Sue her? That's ridiculous. She wasn't even driving."

"You don't know what she was thinking. They're sneaky."

Eleanor didn't need to ask who "they" were—she was familiar with her mother's distrust of the Gentile world. Shaped by her past, Irina would always harbor a fear of those she considered other. But Eleanor was more curious than fearful; she wanted to find out more about Patricia, Margaux, and the world they came from. Maybe, just maybe, there would be a place for her in it.

Chapter 4

PATRICIA SAT AT THE breakfast table, sipping her coffee. Eleanor was due to arrive any minute for her second day on the job, and Margaux was already impatient. "It's after nine," she said.

"I'm sure she'll be here any minute," her mother said. She was nervous, too, about Eleanor's arrival, but for an entirely different reason—Eleanor had not yet met Wynn. Yesterday he'd gone into the office early, but today he was still in the apartment.

He finally sailed into the dining room, pausing to kiss the top of Margaux's head before sitting down at the table. Then the doorman rang to say Eleanor Moss was coming up, and Patricia saw Wynn's eyebrows go up.

"I've heard good things about you," he said when Patricia introduced them.

"That would be from me," Margaux said. "I've told Daddy everything." She patted an empty chair beside her. "Sit with me and have some breakfast? Henryka's made eggs, and they're so good."

"Thanks, I've already eaten," said Eleanor, who nevertheless sat down beside Margaux. "But some coffee would be nice."

Henryka brought the coffee and set it down a little too hard on the table. Now what? Patricia could sense Henryka was cross, but didn't know why. Was it because of Eleanor? Patricia had anticipated a problem with Wynn, but not Henryka.

"I noticed your hat as soon as you came in, Miss Moss," said Wynn. "It's very becoming."

"It is," Patricia agreed. Eleanor's hats were far nicer—and more expensive looking—than her clothes. "Where did you get it?"

"My mother made it," Eleanor said. "Maybe you know her shop? It's on Second Avenue and Eighty-Fourth Street—"

"You know, I think I *may* have heard of it," Patricia said. "But I've never been there." She was only being polite. She rarely strayed so far east. But she was intrigued. Refined, Latin-reading Eleanor had a mother who was a milliner. How had a hatmaker's daughter ended up at Vassar? Eleanor continued to surprise her.

"Second Avenue," mused Wynn. "I never get over there. Do you think I should, Miss Moss? Is there a lot to see?"

"It depends on what you're looking for." Eleanor seemed slightly uncomfortable.

"Nothing in particular," Wynn said. "I just like to . . . look."

"I doubt you'd be looking for a ladies' hat shop, Daddy," said Margaux as she buttered her toast.

"That's true," said Wynn. "I leave the hat buying to your mother. I just pay the bills." He took a forkful of his eggs and looked at Eleanor again. "My wife tells me you were at Brandon-Wythe."

"I was," said Eleanor.

"Good school. One of the best. What made you leave?"

The table seemed to go very quiet, and Patricia watched as Eleanor set down her coffee cup. "Well, I just wanted to go in a different direction and—" Before she could finish, the phone rang. It was Wynn's office, and by the time he'd finished the call, Eleanor and Margaux had left the table and gone into the study to work.

"Just stop that!" Patricia hissed when she and Wynn were alone.

"Stop what?" He gave her a wide-eyed look—the big phony.

"Stop grilling her."

"Well, aren't you curious about why she left? It can't have been easy for her to get that job. Maybe she was fired."

"I doubt it. She had a marvelous letter from the headmistress."

"That still doesn't answer the question about why she left."

"Well, maybe it was about money. We're paying her more than she was making there."

"And how do you happen to know that?" he asked.

"I asked around before I settled on a salary."

"Clever you." He patted his mouth with a damask napkin and stood. "As for Miss Moss's decision to seek out *greener* pastures, I suppose that makes sense. Looking for a financial edge."

"Aren't we all?" Patricia was annoyed by her husband's dig about Eleanor's background. But Wynn had already left the room and seconds later, the apartment. At least the first meeting between her husband and her daughter's new tutor was over.

Walking down the hallway, Patricia stopped before the closed door behind which Eleanor was cloistered with Margaux. She heard Eleanor's measured, quiet voice intercut with Margaux's higher, more insistent one. And then she heard something she had not heard in months: the sound of Margaux's laughter. What a sweet, pure delight. How long had it been since Margaux had laughed? Patricia couldn't recall. But here she was, laughing with Eleanor Moskowitz. Patricia did not care a jot why Eleanor had left her old job; nothing would turn her against the person who had wrought this little miracle.

She turned and went back down the hall. She felt almost giddy with relief and decided to get out of the apartment that had felt oppressive all morning. Stepping into her bedroom, she fetched her gloves, handbag, and hat—thinking again of that straw number Eleanor had worn—and then went into the kitchen.

"Henryka, I'm going out for a bit."

Henryka was polishing a silver pitcher. "You home for lunch?"

"Probably not," Patricia said. When she saw Henryka's wounded look, she added, "But I'll be looking forward to whatever dinner you're serving for tonight. What do you have planned?"

"Goulash, noodles, and creamed spinach. And coconut cake."

"You know I'm mad for your goulash," Patricia said. "And no one can resist your coconut cake."

"My coconut cake good," Henryka said, somewhat mollified.

"You can serve lunch to Margaux and Miss Moss at around twelve thirty."

"She will eat here every day now?"

"Would that bother you?" Henryka said nothing, so Patricia pressed on. "It seems you don't like her."

"She nice girl," Henryka said. "For a *zhid*."

Patricia recognized the slur—Polish for *Yid* and just as insulting. So that was it. "Well, Jewish or not, Margaux likes her."

"She do." Henryka's subtle defiance had softened; she cared for Margaux and had suffered along with Patricia during her illness.

"So it's important that we make her feel welcome here."

"Mr. Bellamy—he make her feel welcome?"

"He will," Patricia said firmly. "He'll get to know her better, and when he does, he'll like her as much as Margaux does."

"Oh, I think he like her right now. I think he like her just fine." She turned away and resumed her polishing.

What in the world did she mean by that? She waited a few seconds, but clearly Henryka wasn't going to elaborate. Fine. She'd had enough of this for one morning.

It was a magnificent day. The sun was streaming down on the sidewalks and on the elegant facades of Park Avenue. Instead of heading down toward Fifty-Seventh Street, or west toward Madison or Fifth as she usually did, Patricia turned east, toward Second Avenue. She had a sudden yen to see Hats by Irina. But the going was slow; the ground floors of the tightly packed brick tenements contained so many quaint and unfamiliar shops to tempt her.

German and Hungarian delicatessens where a dozen different kinds of sausage hung on hooks from the ceiling. Groceries that sold loose spices, sharp or sweet mustards, stores that offered gauzy white blouses thick with embroidery and hand-painted wooden eggs.

She kept going, only to be sidetracked by an appealingly jumbled antiques shop where her perseverance was rewarded by a crystal paperweight for Wynn and a gold ring with an oval-shaped moonstone at its center for Margaux. Then it was a secondhand bookstore that detained her. There, amid the crammed shelves and dust of the past, was a linen-bound edition of Shakespeare's sonnets illustrated with hand-tinted plates that seemed created for the sole purpose of delighting Eleanor Moskowitz. Not that Patricia had a specific reason to buy the girl a gift, she thought as the shopkeeper wrote out the receipt.

It was past two o'clock by the time she reached Eighty-Fourth Street, and there it was, Hats by Irina. Eleanor had told her that she and her mother lived in the apartment above the shop. Patricia studied the window. There was a hat very much like the one Eleanor had worn today, a pale straw cloche with a cluster of cherries on one side. There were others, too, like the wide-brimmed black straw and the tipped tricorne made entirely of feathers. All looked very well made and stylish. They would not have been out of place in the millinery department at Bergdorf Goodman.

Patricia peered inside, beyond the display. No customers were in the shop, but there was a lone woman behind the counter. Not young, but possessed of good posture. Short gray hair. Dark dress with a white lace collar. So this was Irina Moskowitz, Eleanor's mother. Patricia went in, and a bell tinkled, noting her entrance.

"May I help you?" said Irina. She had just the slightest accent.

"Do you mind if I browse?" Patricia asked, eyes roaming around the shop. Should she reveal her identity as Eleanor's employer? "I've never been in here before; you have such lovely things."

"Thank you," Irina said.

"Do you make them yourself?"

"Yes. I do." The quiet pride in that statement was evident.

"So you're Irina." Patricia gestured to the window, where the gold letters spelling out the shop's name appeared backward.

"I am. And please let me know if you'd like to try anything." Patricia nodded as she surveyed the shop. Two small oval mirrors on stands stood on either end of the glass-topped counter, and in the corner was one large cheval glass.

"Actually, there's something I'd like to try," she said to Irina. "That one, over there." Patricia pointed to a tightly fitting paisley cap shaped like a broken eggshell, with jagged points extending down and framing the face on both sides.

"You have excellent taste," Irina said approvingly. She removed it from the black lacquer stand and handed it to Patricia. "The material is a textured silk, made in Italy. Not every woman would have the confidence to carry it off."

Patricia took off her own hat and slipped on the cap, which fit perfectly. She walked over to the cheval glass. The hat was very chic, with colors—deep fuchsia, scarlet, indigo, and a surprising bit of marigold—that were at once exotic and radical. She could see this hat with a dark suit, a dinner dress, or even her mink coat.

"I'll take it," she said.

"You'll be the only woman wearing this hat," said Irina, looking pleased. "I just made one, and I won't make another." She took the hat back from Patricia and began to wrap it in black tissue paper that she pulled out from a drawer behind her. She climbed onto a stepladder and reached up, toward the shelf that ran the length of the store. On it was a row of round black hatboxes, each with a band of white bisecting its center. It was only when Irina had taken one down and packed the new purchase in it that Patricia saw the top: a series of black and white concentric circles, like a target. And in the black center, the same elegant gold script that adorned the window: HATS BY IRINA.

Thanking Irina for her help, Patricia paid six dollars in cash for the hat, which would have cost three or even four times that at Bergdorf's. She stepped out into the still glorious day. It was almost five o'clock, so she hailed a cab. As she leaned back against the seat, she looked again at the hatbox. This hat, and its maker, were two more pieces in the puzzle that was Eleanor.

The taxi dropped her off in front of her building, and the doorman hurried out as she was handing the driver a bill. She took the elevator up to her apartment and let herself in quietly. She was not sure if Eleanor was still here, but she took the precaution of going straight to her bedroom and stowing the hatbox out of sight. She'd disperse the gifts she bought at some later time. Today's outing was her secret, and it was not the only one. She had not revealed herself to Eleanor's mother, and because she hadn't, she realized that she couldn't tell Eleanor about the visit either.

On the fifth of July, Eleanor met Ruth at B. Altman, where together they scoured the sale racks. It was a successful mission: Eleanor found a lightweight dress, two skirts, a pair of summer trousers—not unlike those worn by Katharine Hepburn, one of her favorite movie stars—and a navy blue bathing suit with white polka dots and a halter neck. After they finished shopping, they stopped at Mary Elizabeth's Tea Room for lunch.

"I'll miss you this summer." Ruth drew deeply on her straw, and the iced tea in her glass subsided in response.

"I'll miss you too," said Eleanor. "But I'll write." Her new employers had already left town for Connecticut; there hadn't been room in the car for all of them, so Eleanor was taking the train up tomorrow. She was glad to be spared the ride with Henryka, who she was certain disliked her, and Mr. Bellamy, who, while never anything but polite, made her uneasy. His was the kind of civility that radiated insincerity, and she did not trust it—or him.

"Do you know what the house looks like?"

"White, with dark shutters," Eleanor said, taking a bite of her sandwich. "And there are at least two gardens."

"Imagine having all that *and* an apartment on Park Avenue."

"There's a guest cottage too; that's where I'll be staying. Two whole rooms, all to myself."

"I'll bet it's really posh," Ruth said. "Do they have a pool?"

"No, but there's one at their club."

"A club sounds dreamy." Ruth took a bite of her sandwich. "I'll bet they have dances and parties. Maybe you'll meet someone."

"None of those clubs will admit Jews," Eleanor pointed out. "I use the name Moss when I'm with the Bellamys."

"Really? What does your mother have to say about that?"

"I haven't told her," Eleanor said.

"Do you have to do it, Ellie? What if you said no?" said Ruth.

"Not possible," said Eleanor. "Not if I want this job. And I do. Working with Margaux, helping her break through that shell—I can't tell you how satisfying that's been. And there's something about Mrs. Bellamy too. I can't imagine being her friend exactly, but I wish I could get to know her better. So if I have to pretend about my name, it feels like a small price to pay." She finished her own sandwich. "Would you do it? If you were in my place?"

"No, I don't think I would," she said. "But, Ellie, that doesn't mean you shouldn't. You've always wanted something different. That's part of why you went to Vassar, isn't it? To get out of the neighborhood, meet new people?"

"It's true," Eleanor said. "But at Vassar, I was still Eleanor Moskowitz. I didn't have to pretend to be someone else."

"You'll always be Eleanor Moskowitz," said Ruth. "No matter what you call yourself."

And that, Eleanor realized, was true.

When she got home, Eleanor laid out all her new purchases on her bed; she'd show her mother when she came upstairs. Eleanor had picked up a skirt steak on the way home; she'd broil it and fry onions to go on top; scalloped potatoes would be the side dish. For dessert, she'd slice some strawberries and sprinkle them with sugar. Dinner was pleasant, even festive. Irina took out a bottle of sweet wine she'd stowed away, and they each had a glass along with their strawberries. After the dishes were done, Eleanor took her mother into her room to see the day's purchases. Irina approved of the dress, which was made of light blue eyelet. She fingered the material in a professional sort of way. "I'd like to make you a new hat before you go."

"I have plenty of hats, Mother," Eleanor said. "You work too hard as it is."

"I want to," Irina insisted. "The right hat can make any outfit."

"So you've said." Eleanor smiled. "More than once."

Irina moved the clothes aside so she could sit down on the bed. "It's not just your clothes I'm thinking about. It's everything. I'm worried. You'll be stuck up there, not knowing anyone else. No one of your own kind."

"Really, Mother, do you think that matters anymore?" Eleanor was not being truthful; she knew it mattered quite a lot. Hadn't she admitted as much to Ruth?

"Anyway, I'll miss you."

"It's not for that long. And you could always come to visit."

"No, *tochter*, I don't think so." Irina only reached for Yiddish in moments of stress or sorrow.

Eleanor began folding her new clothes. "Maybe it would be nice to have a new hat after all," she said. "Something summery."

"I can start it tomorrow." Irina brightened.

"All right," Eleanor said. "And even if no one else notices, Mrs. Bellamy will appreciate it."

"Does she wear nice hats?" Irina asked.

"Very nice. She shops at Bergdorf's and Bonwit's. Saks too. But I still think your hats are more original than theirs. That little egg-shaped one you made? From the gorgeous Italian paisley? I can see it in the pages of *Vogue* or *Harper's Bazaar*."

"Did I tell you I sold it?" Irina said. "To a very elegant woman. I'd never seen her before. She wasn't one of my regulars."

"No, you didn't tell me," Eleanor said. "Did you get her name?"

"No. I'd recognize her right away if she came in again, though. She was a little taller than you. A little older too. Blond hair in a twist. Pearl earrings. And such a beautiful dress—blue, with little satin roses on the collar and pockets."

"What color were the roses?" Eleanor stopped, a white shell sweater and matching cardigan draped over one arm.

"Magenta, I think. With dark green leaves. Why do you ask?"

"Patricia Bellamy has a dress just like that. What kind of hat was she wearing?"

Irina described it, and Eleanor said, "That was Patricia Bellamy. She came to your store, but she didn't tell you who she was?"

"Maybe she didn't realize I was your mother."

"That's not possible," Eleanor said, puzzled. "I've mentioned the shop—where it was, the name—to her. She must have known."

Why would Mrs. Bellamy conceal her identity from Irina? It made no sense. But it did suggest that Mrs. Bellamy was as curious about Eleanor's family as Eleanor was about hers.

THE guest cottage just behind the Bellamys' house in Argyle was ready; Opal, the girl from the village who did the heavy work, had scrubbed, dusted, and aired out the entire place. Then she had changed the sheets and put a stack of fresh towels next to the claw-footed tub in the bathroom. Patricia had set a white ironstone pitcher filled with wildflowers on the table, flowers that Margaux had insisted on gathering herself. The sight of her daughter, on her knees, dragging her damaged leg behind her, made Patricia want to bury her face in her hands and sob. But then she thought of Eleanor, who would no doubt have a different way of viewing the scene, Eleanor who had called Margaux plucky. How they needed Eleanor—all of them. Patricia was as glad as Margaux that Eleanor was arriving tonight, on the 5:57 from Grand Central.

Patricia was on the sunporch when Glow, a large ginger cat, jumped up to sit beside her on the wicker settee. Glow was their summer-only cat; in the off-season, she lived with Opal. Stroking the smooth orange fur, Patricia checked her watch; it was only a little before 5:00, which gave her plenty of time to change and get to the station. She'd told Henryka to hold dinner until their guests arrived. Wynn would not be coming up until tomorrow, which was a good thing—she wanted to let Eleanor settle in before she had to deal with him.

The other person she was expecting tonight was her brother, Tom, who was driving down from Maine. She wasn't sure when he'd get here, though; Tom was virtually impossible to pin down about anything. A free spirit, he held no real job, able to live on the generous inheritance their father had left him. Tom dabbled, buying paintings from his downtown artist buddies. He tried his own hand at painting, too, as well as poetry and writing plays. Wynn called him a dilettante and said he was just waiting for him to grow up. "You'll have to wait a long time," Tom had said.

But Wynn was charmed by Tom, as was everyone else. Tom

mocked everything and everyone, most of all himself. He adamantly refused to live anywhere respectable and instead inhabited a puzzling warren of rooms that he called an apartment, on Jane Street in Greenwich Village.

"Can I go with you?" Patricia looked up to see Margaux standing in the doorway, leaning on her walking stick. Her white dress was stained with grass, and her braids were loose. "To the station?"

"If you change your dress and comb your hair, yes."

"All right." Margaux turned to go back inside.

Patricia was debating whether to pour herself a gin and tonic— but she did not like to drink alone—when the front door slammed and a deep male voice called out, "Hello, hello, hello!" Tom! She stood, and the cat, whose nap had been disturbed, darted away. "Trish?" he called. "Are you home?"

"It's Uncle Tommy!" Margaux cried. Tom strode into the room, almost colliding with her.

"Margaux, my kumquat! Let me look at you!" Tom scooped her up and spun her around; the walking stick clattered to the floor.

"Uncle Tommy!" Margaux squealed.

Finally he set her down, using his arm to steady her while he reached for the walking stick and handed it to her. Then he turned to Patricia. "Your turn." And although he did not lift her off her feet, he spun her around in a tight, dizzying embrace. "How are you?" he said. He wore a linen shirt, very wrinkled, and khaki trousers. No jacket, no tie, no hat.

"I'm fine," she said. And now that he was here, she was.

"How long are you staying, Uncle Tommy?"

"I'll stay as long as your mother will have me."

"You have an open invitation," Patricia said. "Do you want to get your things from the car so Henryka can take them upstairs?"

"Oh, that's right. I've been exiled from my cottage by another, more important guest. A usurper, it would seem."

"She's not a usurper," said Margaux. "Her name is Eleanor, and she's wonderful. You'll love her; we all do. She's so smart and interesting and pretty. Even Mother thinks so. And she wears the best little hats in the world because her mother is a hatmaker."

"Well, I can't wait to meet this paragon, this tutor-with-the-best-little-hats-in-the-world," Tom said.

"You'll have your chance," Patricia said. "She'll be here soon." And then added, "Is it time for a drink?"

"Is it ever!" Tom said. "I'll just get my things."

"We'll have to make it quick; I need to change before heading over to the station," Patricia explained. "Margaux, you still need to put on a clean dress if you're coming with me."

Patricia linked her arm through Tom's as her daughter went off to her room. "It's not what you think," she said softly to her brother when they were outside.

"And what is it that I think?" Tom asked.

"That she's some ordinary little drudge. But she's not. She's really quite special. And she's worked wonders with Margaux."

"I can see that," Tom said. He pulled one valise from the backseat and another from the trunk. "In any case, she's bound to be prettier than Mr. Cobb. The man was a gargoyle."

"Tom." Patricia swatted his arm. "You're terrible." As they began walking back to the house, she added, "Eleanor *is* pretty. But you just keep your hands to yourself."

"Why, Patricia, are you implying that I'm not a gentleman?"

"She's a Jew," Patricia said, and stopped walking. "Eleanor Moskowitz. But I'm introducing her as Eleanor Moss."

"The plot thickens," said Tom. "Does Wynn know? He must. But your neighbors and pals—that's a different story, isn't it? I detect a hint of deception in the air. Yes . . . What fun."

"Tom. I'm being serious. Eleanor Moss—"

"You mean Moskowitz," he interrupted.

"*Moss*," she continued, "is the first ray of hope we've had since the doctors told us Margaux would live. If you say or do anything, and I mean *anything*, to jeopardize that—" Her eyes pooled.

"Trish," Tom said. He let his bags drop softly to the lawn and grabbed her by the shoulders. "I'm an incorrigible tease. But I would never do anything to hurt you. Or Margaux."

Back on the sunporch, Tom decided against gin and tonics; he wanted to make sweet Manhattans instead.

"Can I have a sip, Mother? Please?" Margaux asked. She was seated on one of the wicker chairs, her walking stick on the floor nearby. Patricia hesitated. Had Wynn been there, she would have said no. But he wasn't, and so she gave her daughter a taste.

"It's so good!" Margaux said, wiping her mouth crudely with the back of her hand. Really, since her illness, the girl's manners had gone straight to hell. "Like drinking silk." Patricia was mollified by the description. By the time they needed to leave for the train station, Patricia was in a very fine mood indeed.

"Come with us?" Margaux asked her uncle. She had changed into a long navy blue skirt and white blouse. Her freshly brushed hair was held in place by a headband.

"I'm going to take a shower before dinner," Tom said. "I'll be all fresh and ready to meet your new tutor when you get back. Do you think she'll make me a hat?"

"Silly!" Margaux said as he hugged her. "It's her mother who makes the hats."

As soon as Eleanor had arrived and settled in, they all sat down to a dinner of boiled lobsters, corn on the cob, and tomatoes from a farm stand down the road. Henryka passed around a stack of white dish towels, each bordered by a stripe of a different color.

"It's a bib," Tom said, seeing Eleanor's confusion. "Tuck it into your collar."

Eleanor nodded, but Patricia could see that she was even more daunted by the flushed and steaming crustacean set before her. "There's a claw cracker right by your fork," she began.

"Lobster's a down-and-dirty meal," said Tom. "You're supposed to get messy eating it. Let me show you."

He got up and, leaning over her shoulder, picked up the claw. The shell was soft enough to crack with his bare hands. Liquid squirted out and landed on the bib. "Good thing we protected you," Tom said, using the lobster fork to extract the succulent meat from the broken shell. He dipped the morsel in butter and offered her back the fork. She chewed slowly. "Delicious," she said.

"Good girl!" he said. "That's the spirit." Eleanor lifted her fork to her mouth for another piece. "Have you ever had oysters?" Tom was working on the other claw now. She shook her head. "Henryka, did you hear that?" he called out. "Miss Moss has never had oysters. We have to remedy that. Can we add your incomparable oyster stew to the menu anytime soon?"

"I make for you, Mr. Tom," Henryka said, coming in from the kitchen with a basket full of dinner rolls. "I know you like."

"Not *like*, Henryka, my love. It's my all-time, flat-out number one favorite." Tom stopped his dissection of Eleanor's lobster long enough to seize Henryka's hand and kiss it. Henryka giggled.

Patricia watched as Henryka—widowed, in her sixties, the mother of three grown daughters—basked in Tom's attention. And she was equally aware of how Eleanor, her lobster meat forgotten, was looking up at him with a similarly besotted expression.

Chapter 5

ELEANOR AND MARGAUX quickly settled into a pleasant summer routine: three mornings a week they worked on English, history, and the rudiments of Latin; the two other mornings were devoted to math, science, and French. After lunch, they engaged in some nonacademic pursuit, like drawing. Or Tom would drive them to nearby Lavender Lake, where Margaux would swim, an activity at which she still excelled. She refused to swim at the club, despite its attractive pool; to do so would mean to expose her leg to the pity and curiosity of the other members.

By contrast, the lake was deserted and quite lovely. Eleanor sat on a blanket in her polka-dot swimsuit, talking to Tom, while Margaux played by the water's edge. Tom had been to so many places, seen so many things, but it was not entirely clear to her what he *did*. Curiosity finally won out over discretion, and she asked him flat out.

"What do you mean by *do?*" he said.

"You know—for a living," she said.

"Ah, that . . ." He smiled. "Well, the fact is, I don't have to earn a living. So I'm free to do what I want."

"Which is?"

"I meet with people—artists mostly. I look at their work and talk to them about it. I give them advice—when they ask. And I help them sell their work. Or at least I try to."

"So you're a dealer of sorts."

"Not exactly," he said. "But does it matter? Do I have to be any one thing or another? Why put a label on it? Why not just live?"

"Because you do need to put a name to whatever it is that you're doing," Eleanor said earnestly. "By naming it, you're laying claim to something. To yourself."

"I never thought of it that way," he said.

"If you really were a dealer, what would you do?"

"I suppose I might rent a space and show some of the older work I've collected. And the newer work I champion."

"That sounds intriguing. Exciting even."

"You," Tom said, "are an enthusiast. Are you always such an ardent cheerleader?"

"When I like someone, yes," she said.

"I'll consider that a compliment," he said, eyes steady on her.

"It was meant as one." Her own look did not falter, but stayed locked on his.

"You take things seriously, don't you?" he said, reaching for her hand. He began to tap out a rhythm on the inside of her wrist.

"Yes, I do." The touch of his fingers against her skin was tantalizing and hypnotic; she didn't want it to stop.

They stayed later than usual that day, neither one wanting to pull away and leave. When they finally did, Eleanor felt as if she were cocooned in a soft glow, even as she was helping Margaux into the backseat of the car and then climbing in to sit beside her.

"I think you should come to live with us when we get back to New York City," Margaux said, jolting Eleanor from her thoughts.

"Live with you?" Eleanor said. The remark alarmed her.

"I'd really like that," Margaux said. "Wouldn't you?"

"Of course I would," Eleanor said. "But I don't think it would be the best thing for you."

"Why not?" Margaux asked.

"I think you need to go back to school," Eleanor said. "Not right away. But soon."

"I don't want to go back," Margaux said.

"Why not, pumpkin?" Tom spoke without turning around.

"I'll be a cripple. Everybody will make fun of me."

"Margaux, don't use that word about yourself," Eleanor said.

"Why not? Other people do. Even Daddy called me that once."

"He did?" Eleanor's eyes sought Tom's in the rearview mirror.

"Yes, when he and Mother were having an argument."

"If your father used it, he must have been upset," said Tom. "But you shouldn't use it about yourself. As for school—"

"I told you: I won't go back there."

"What about a different school?"

"You mean one for cripples?"

"Margaux!" Eleanor said. "Your uncle is right. You need friends."

"I have you," said Margaux, taking Eleanor's hand.

"Friends your own age," Eleanor said.

"I'll think about it," Margaux said in a way that clearly indicated she would do nothing of the sort. They had reached the house. She yanked open the car door and, putting her walking stick on the pebbled ground first, got out. Then she moved with impressive alacrity toward the door. Eleanor stepped out and watched her go. Tom came to stand by Eleanor. He said nothing, only placed his hand on her shoulder. Eleanor did not acknowledge the gesture, but his fingers against her bare skin were so pleasurable that she remained where she was, not ready for the sensation to end.

Two nights later, Eleanor sat alone in her room in the guest cottage, fountain pen poised over the letter she was writing to Ruth. *I think I'm in love with Tom Harrison,* she wrote in her clear, firm hand. *I love him with all my heart.* There, she'd admitted it to herself, and now to Ruth too. Then she read the words over again. What a clichéd and foolish pair of sentences. She wadded up the sheet of paper and dropped it in the wastebasket.

It was almost midnight, and she was alone in the cottage; Tom and the Bellamys had gone off to the club.

"Are you sure you wouldn't like to join us, Eleanor?" Patricia had asked before they left; just last week she had asked Eleanor to use her first name, and Patricia had stopped using Miss Moss except when introducing her. "There's plenty of room in the car, isn't there, Wynn?" Wynn had hesitated just a beat too long before saying, "Of course there is. The more the merrier."

Even if Wynn hadn't waited that telling second, Eleanor would have declined. She had gone, twice, with Patricia—for lunch and for cards. Both times she had felt self-conscious, and all too aware of the other women sizing her up. The name Moss was a poor shield against their pointed interest.

She was too restless to write or read, too restless, surely, to sleep. A light shone from upstairs in the main house across the way. Henryka. She had not warmed toward Eleanor one bit, even though Eleanor had tried to win her over. Knowing how proud Henryka was of her cooking, Eleanor had made a campaign of compliments, all sincere. It was to no avail. But oh, how that woman could bake! There had been a pie at dinner tonight, a mixed-berry pie with a flaky crust and a sweet filling. Eleanor was seized with a sudden hunger for a second slice. She walked out of the cottage and along the brick path that led to the house.

The kitchen door was unlocked, and Eleanor stepped inside, flipping the switch to illuminate the empty room. There was the pie, sitting on the counter under a glass dome.

When she went to the cupboard for a plate, she heard music; it seemed to be coming from the next room. The light was off, though; maybe Patricia had left the radio on? Thinking it would be best to turn it off, Eleanor opened the door and patted the wall for the switch. When the light came on, she gasped softly—there, as if conjured up by her imaginings, sat Tom. In one hand he held a drink, and the other propped up his chin.

"Well, hello," he said. "Another night owl."

"What are you doing here?"

"Enjoying the music." "It Had to Be You" was playing on the radio. "And the dark." He smiled.

"I thought you went to the club."

"I did. But I got bored. What a dreary crowd." Eleanor loved him for saying that. "The Talbots were leaving early, so I got a lift with them. What are *you* doing here?"

"Having another slice of Henryka's pie."

"Ah, Henryka and her pies," Tom said. "Let's drink to that." He stood and ambled over to the liquor cabinet. "What can I get you?"

"What are you drinking?"

"Scotch on the rocks. But that's not a drink for you. Let me make you something else. What about a sweet Manhattan? Patricia loves them. Margaux too."

"Patricia is letting Margaux have a drink with you?"

"Only a taste, and only when Wynn isn't around."

"She must love that." Eleanor enjoyed trying to picture it. "How's she doing anyway? With her schoolwork and all?"

"Really well. She's a bright girl. I wouldn't be surprised if she turned out to be a writer."

"Our Margaux? You think?" Tom handed her the drink.

Eleanor sipped it. It was *so* good. Or did she feel that way because Tom had made it? "Some of her compositions are first-rate. As good as any student I've ever taught. Better in fact."

"Oh, that's right. Trish said you used to be at Brandon-Wythe." Eleanor nodded. "Why'd you leave?"

Mr. Bellamy—she couldn't call him Wynn—had asked her the same question. "It was time to move on." Eleanor hoped her voice remained light and did not betray her. The song ended, and Nat King Cole's "(I Love You) For Sentimental Reasons" came on next; she jumped on the distraction, swaying her head and humming along to the music.

Tom took another sip of his drink, set it down, and grinned at her. "Shall we dance?" he said. Clearly, her ploy had worked. Pie forgotten, Eleanor set her own drink down and moved easily into his open arms. They danced without speaking for a few minutes, but the silence brimmed with sensation.

The song ended, and an announcer's unctuous voice came on, extolling the many virtues of the latest-model Chrysler. Tom let his arms remain around Eleanor, and she did not move away. When the commercial was over, Tom tilted her chin up toward him and kissed her. The kiss was long, slow, and gentle. When it finally ended, she was desperate for it to happen again.

"I've been wanting to do that since I cracked your lobster," he said. "But Trish won't like it." He traced her lips with a finger.

"Does she have to know?"

"Trish makes it her business to know everything," said Tom.

Eleanor thought about the visit Patricia had made to her mother's shop, the visit she had never mentioned. "We'll be careful," Eleanor said. She wanted him to kiss her again.

"You're such an optimistic girl," he said, and then he kissed her again. But as much as she'd wanted the kiss, she was the one to pull away first. Tom was the brother of her employer; she knew she was treading on dangerous ground. She'd already walked away from one job because of a man. Tom seemed to understand her reticence and did not press further. "Come on," he said. "I'll walk you back."

He took her elbow as they crossed the meadow separating the house from the cottage, and when she'd stepped inside, he did not kiss her again, but cupped her face in his hands. "Good night, lovely Miss Moskowitz," he said.

"Miss Moss, if you please."

"Moskowitz is just fine with me," he said. Then he turned and walked across the grass to the house.

Two nights after the party at the club, Margaux came into the living room proffering Patricia's crystal atomizer filled with Chanel No. 5. "Want me to spray you?" Eleanor wavered; she did love the scent, which Margaux had already applied to herself quite liberally. But Eleanor was afraid that Patricia would think she had helped herself without asking. She shook her head.

"Your dress is enchanting," Eleanor said, changing the subject.

Margaux looked down at her high-waisted organdy frock. "Do you really think so? It's not too babyish?"

"Not at all," Eleanor said. "It's perfect. Now I should get dressed too. It's almost eight."

Eleanor left Margaux and hurried back to the guest cottage. It was Friday night, and the Bellamys were having a party; they'd asked Eleanor to join them. She really would have preferred not to, but Margaux had been insistent.

The guest list included the Talbots, John and Dottie, from across the road; they didn't seem so bad, but some of the others had been discernibly frosty. But Tom would be there, and that would make everything better. Since that first kiss, they had not been able to find many opportunities to be alone. But they had shared two more such moments. Each kiss had been more intoxicating than the last. Maybe there would be an opportunity for another tonight.

It was this thought that buoyed her as she quickly stepped into her black taffeta skirt and pale pink silk blouse. She had a darling silk fascinator her mother had made, pink with black trim along the crown and a saucy black tassel at the back.

In the bathroom, she carefully applied her new lipstick: Dorothy Gray's Portrait Pink. She seldom wore lipstick, but the color was subtle and pretty; she hoped Tom would like it.

When Eleanor went back over to the house, several of the guests had already arrived. Tom was not among them, though. Mr. Bellamy was busy pouring drinks. "What can I get you, Miss Moss?" he asked. It seemed that he was mocking her slightly, but then, she always felt he was mocking her.

"A glass of ginger ale, please," she said.

"Ginger ale? I've seen you drink before. With Tom. Have you gone on the wagon?" He took a long sip of his own drink; Eleanor was quite sure it was not the first of the evening.

"No," she said. "I like to pace myself, that's all."

But when he returned with the ginger ale, he seemed more affable. "I added a cherry," he said. "To pep it up."

The cherry bobbed on the fizzy drink, and Eleanor pulled it out and popped it in her mouth.

"Now the cherry's gone," he said, lowering his voice suggestively. "No more cherry for Eleanor."

His crude insinuation was clear, and she didn't answer. Instead, she turned away, and as she did, she felt his hand glance off her backside. She was instantly furious and whirled back around. Over the rim of his glass, his expression was both predatory and challenging. *What are you going to do?* But then her fury was replaced by something equally primal—fear. She wanted to get away from him, as quickly as she could. She turned to look for Margaux, and when she caught sight of her, sitting by herself with a drink on the sunporch, she walked right over to join her.

"It's a Shirley Temple," Margaux said when she saw Eleanor eyeing it. "But Uncle Tommy promised me a taste of his Manhattan later. You can't tell Daddy, though!"

"I promise." The memory of his hand on her body made her feel slightly sick, and she sat down on the chintz-covered wicker sofa next to Margaux. "Are you having a good time?"

"All right, I guess," Margaux said. "I don't like how people try to look at my leg, though. Spying almost. Then they look away. Because they don't want me to see how relieved they are."

"Relieved?"

"That it's my leg that's withered. Not theirs."

Eleanor looked up to see Patricia standing in front of them; she wore a wine-colored dress of watered silk and a tight smile.

"Margaux, darling, why don't you play something for our guests?" she said, gesturing toward the walnut upright that stood in a far corner of the living room.

"I don't want to," Margaux said.

"Why not, darling? You play so well."

In actuality, Margaux was an indifferent music student possessed of only a moderately accomplished technique. But Eleanor knew that Patricia was determined to prove to her friends that despite Margaux's illness, the girl was still capable of performing parlor tricks and taking her rightful place in her mother's world.

"Eleanor, would you ask her? She seems to be in your thrall," Patricia said.

There was an edge to the remark, and Eleanor felt it immediately. She hated being drawn into this contest of wills, but there was no graceful way to refuse her employer's request. "Margaux," she began, "I'd like to hear you play something too."

"If you'll sit with me while I play," Margaux answered, and when Eleanor nodded, Margaux hoisted herself onto her walking stick. Eleanor followed her toward the piano. Patricia clapped her hands to get everyone's attention. "We're going to be treated to a little concert tonight," she said. "Margaux asked if she could play something for all of you."

Eleanor did not like hearing Patricia lie; she thought it demeaned her. But Margaux did not protest. She slid onto the bench, Eleanor beside her, where she proceeded to play a dull rendition of "Für Elise." Polite applause followed the performance, and then, mercifully, Patricia turned to one of the other guests.

"What about you, Freddy?" He seemed happy to oblige, bursting into a rousing version of "The Whiffenpoof Song."

Margaux used her walking stick to go back to the sunporch, and Eleanor followed. "Why does she do that?" Margaux asked when they were safely out of earshot.

"She worries about you. She thinks you're too isolated. She wants you to feel comfortable with people." Eleanor sat down on the wicker sofa again. Margaux flopped down next to her.

"Say, what are the two prettiest gals in the room doing way over here by themselves?" Tom strode up and yanked over a footstool so he could sit.

"We're having a little talk," Eleanor said.

"It looks very serious." He turned to Margaux. "Have you seen this one before?" His long, aristocratic fingers made a few graceful gestures near the side of his head and voilà! he'd pulled a quarter from his ear and presented it with a flourish to Margaux.

"Uncle Tommy, you're so corny," she said, but she was smiling, her gloomy mood seemingly dispelled by his sunny presence.

Freddy was still regaling the other guests with his piano playing; he had moved on to "I Get a Kick Out of You." Several people began to dance, and Tom, after glancing in their direction, turned to Eleanor. "May I have the honor?" he said.

Eleanor got up and handed Margaux her evening purse. "My

new lipstick is in there, along with a mirror. Try it if you want."

"Really?" Margaux asked as she undid the clasp and extracted the small gold cylinder.

"Very nicely done," Tom said as Eleanor moved into his arms.

"I just don't want her to feel she's been left out," she said.

"Lovely, kind, compassionate Eleanor," Tom said, spinning her adroitly. "How lucky we all are that Patricia's taxicab rammed into yours on that rainy day. And I do mean all."

She was too filled with happiness to reply.

It was after two when the party broke up. Margaux had fallen asleep on the wicker sofa; Tom and Wynn carried her to her bed. Eleanor said good night to the few remaining guests and to her employers. There had been no opportunity for a kiss tonight, but the time she and Tom had spent in each other's arms, dancing as Freddy played one tune after another, had been gift enough.

Feet slightly sore, Eleanor slipped off her shoes and walked back across the lawn to the cottage. Once inside, she felt too restless to sleep. She went to the window to look over at the house. It was dark, except for a single lighted window. Henryka still up? No, Henryka's room was on the third floor. The light was coming from the second-floor bedroom, where Tom slept.

Just knowing that Tom was awake excited her. Was he thinking of her? She continued to stare at the window, where the light was beckoning her. She wouldn't go, of course. It would be foolish. Dangerous even. She could lose her job. Besides, Tom might not like her showing up at his door—he'd think she was too forward.

But she'd had two bubbly glasses of champagne and one of Tom's expertly mixed Manhattans—*It's our drink,* he'd murmured as he handed it to her. The alcohol was weakening her resolve and fueling her desire, both at the same moment. And so, without bothering to put on her shoes, she set off back toward the house.

Tom. She had to find Tom. Treading very carefully, she ascended the stairs. Her bare feet made no noise. Once she got to the dark upstairs hallway, she waited until she had oriented herself. There, at the far end, was a thin line of light under a door. Tom's door. She moved toward it, and when she reached it, she put her hand on the knob and turned it. "Eleanor?" he said simply. He'd been reading, and an open book was splayed across his bare chest. She could make out his long form under the sheet. "I was kind of hoping you would come."

She said nothing, but felt a pleasurable heat rising up, spreading across her face.

Tom was still looking at her. "Would you come and sit by me?" He patted the space beside him.

She hesitated. "You're . . . naked under that sheet, aren't you?"

"Yes. But don't be afraid."

"I'm not afraid," she said. "Not at all. It just means I have to be naked too."

Carefully, she stepped out of her skirt and undid the buttons on her blouse. When she was completely naked, she stood there, feeling his gaze take in every visible bit of her.

"Won't you sit down?" Tom finally said, sounding oddly formal. "I promise I won't touch you unless you say it's all right."

"It's all right," she said, and gently let her weight down onto the mattress beside him. She reached out to put a hand on his chest; his skin was so warm. He caught her hand and brought it to his lips. Then he pulled her to him. They kissed slowly, tentatively, for a moment before he disengaged himself and leaned back against the pillows.

"What is it?" she said. "Did I do something wrong?"

"You're a virgin," he said.

"Does it make a difference?"

"Don't you want to save yourself? For your husband?"

"I did save myself," she said. "For you."

"But I can't be your husband," he said. "Even though I want to."

"I don't care," she replied, trying to tamp down the joy she felt at hearing these last words. "I can be your mistress instead."

He laughed, and then became serious. "No, I won't let you."

"It's not your decision. It's mine."

"Wouldn't you say that it's a decision that needs to be mutual?"

"I'm not leaving," she said finally.

"Who said anything about leaving? I never asked you to leave."

"But you said . . ."

"I said I would not deflower you. Not because I don't want to; I want to very much. But I think I would end up hurting you, and I don't want to hurt you."

"So then if you won't, I mean, you know . . ."

"There are other things we can do," he said, and he pushed her back gently on the bed. "Plenty of other things. Let me show you."

Chapter 6

WHEN PATRICIA WOKE the following morning, she felt horrible. She closed her eyes again. She'd had too much to drink at the party, and then she'd had to deal with Wynn and his *urges* when she got to bed. Their one night of mutual passion, ignited after Audrey's wedding, had never been repeated. But Wynn had changed over these last few months. Some nights he was rough with her, treating her body as something to use, rather than arouse or delight. As bad as this was, even worse were the nights that he became pleading.

A bird squawked rudely in a nearby tree, and she opened her eyes once more. She could just imagine the mess out there; she supposed she'd better go and oversee the cleanup.

To her astonishment, the room was immaculate, with no sign of last night's excesses in evidence. Glasses and plates were gone, surfaces wiped and waxed. Patricia could see the marks from the carpet sweeper crisscrossing the rug. The kitchen, too, was tidy, and she found a vase filled with early yellow mums and a pot of coffee on the stove. Had Henryka done all this? It seemed unlikely; she must have had help. But who? Patricia considered this, and then her eyes settled on the note:

> Darling, Tom and I took Margaux sailing at the club. Wanted to let you sleep in. If the weather holds, we'll be out all day.
> Love,
> Wynn

Her irritation with last night's inept fumbling was replaced by a rush of affection. Yes, Wynn had been oafish lately, especially in bed. But he was good to their daughter. He'd taught Margaux to love sailing, and she would come home from their outings, hair blown wildly around her face, eager to tell Patricia how far they'd gone, or show her a new knot Wynn had taught her to tie.

After a cup of black coffee and a hot shower, she felt significantly improved. When she came back downstairs, wearing a cotton piqué dress in a flattering shade of apricot, she was surprised to find Eleanor and Henryka together. Henryka had baked a batch of her beloved sticky buns and was pouring coffee. "Good morning, missus," she said. "You want coffee? Bun?"

The sight of the glazed pastry made Patricia's still unsettled stomach clench, but she sat down and accepted both a sticky bun and a second cup of coffee. "Thank you for cleaning up," Patricia said to Henryka. "You got everything done so quickly."

"Mr. Wynn—he help."

"He did?" Patricia was surprised. When had Wynn ever shown any interest in helping with housework? As she picked at the pastry, she reflected on her husband's dual nature: he could be such a boor, but then he'd surprise her, like he had this morning.

"Now I go change sheets," said Henryka.

After she'd gone, Eleanor remained quiet. "How would you like to drive over to Dudley with me today?" Patricia asked. She pushed the bun away. "There's a little place in town where we could go for lunch. And we might do a bit of window-shopping too."

"All right," Eleanor said.

"Finish your coffee first," Patricia said. "I'll tell Henryka we're going to be gone for lunch." Then she went into Tom's room to retrieve his keys from inside a large tarnished golf trophy that had belonged to Wynn's grandfather. Since Wynn had taken their car to the club, she would use Tom's. The room was not too untidy, though the bed had not been made. She located the keys and was about to leave when something on the pillow caught her eye. Something pink. She went over to inspect. There was a streak of lipstick on the pillowcase; *Eleanor's* new pink lipstick—she'd even let Margaux try it! Had she been in this bed, last night.

Patricia left the room. In her pocket were the car keys; in her hand was the offending pillowcase. She did not want Henryka, Opal, or anyone else to see it.

Patricia took the coastal road to Dudley, thinking the glimpses of dunes, beach, and ocean would calm her down. She was wrong. The distant waves crashing to the shore only echoed and intensified her anger. How prim the girl next to her seemed. Prim and oh so proper. But she had been in Tom's room! How could she? How dare she? Patricia rolled down the window. "Is that all right?"

"It's fine," said Eleanor. "What a perfect day for sailing."

"I detest sailing." Patricia had never actually said this aloud. "Wynn and Margaux love it. Tom too." She quickly looked over to see if Tom's name brought on a blush, a smile perhaps. It did not. "But I never took to it. It always made me seasick, and my father had no patience with anyone who got seasick. He thought it was a moral failing of some kind."

"I'd hardly call seasickness a moral failing," Eleanor said. "It's not something you have any control over at all."

Despite her simmering anger, Patricia was interested in Eleanor's point of view. "But that was my father. No babying, no coddling. I'm sure he'd think I was indulging Margaux terribly if he were here to see it."

"I don't think compassion should be confused with coddling," said Eleanor. "She's had a very hard time, and you're responding to that with love and acceptance."

The waves seemed less violent now, their ebb and flow more soothing. This was one of Eleanor's rare gifts—her ability to alter the way you thought about something.

"How does Margaux seem to you these days?" Concern about her daughter trumped her indignation over Eleanor's compromising interest in Tom—at least for the moment.

"As far as her schoolwork?" asked Eleanor. "There's no problem there, none at all. But academics aren't everything. There's still the social aspect to her development. Which is why I think she should be going back to school. She's ready, you know."

"She flat out refuses to go," Patricia said.

"It's because of her leg. She doesn't want to be made fun of or ostracized. Or pitied—she'd hate that most of all. But I've heard about a boarding school called Oakwood where every single one of the students has had polio. The headmaster's son had it, and he wouldn't go back to school either. So the father—he'd been headmaster at a school in Albany—decided to start a school for other children who'd been similarly afflicted."

"But do we really want to put her in a school for . . . cripples?"

"Don't think of it that way. Think of it as a school for survivors. Because that's who Margaux is—a survivor."

They had reached Dudley, and Patricia pulled into a space in the town center. She turned off the ignition and shifted to face Eleanor. "If we did send her there, you'd be out of a job."

"I'd be sorry about that," Eleanor said. "But it's Margaux I'm thinking about. She needs to be in school with her peers. And if her peers have suffered the way she has, all the more opportunity for her to build real friendships. I wrote asking for an application."

Patricia was stunned. Here she'd been preparing to lambaste the girl for what she'd been doing behind Patricia's back, and it turned out that one of those things was researching a school for Margaux and requesting an application to it. "Thank you," Patricia said awkwardly. Yet the business with Tom—she had to say something. But she would wait until lunch.

They got out of the car and began to walk along Old Post Road, the town's main street. Her righteous indignation had evaporated, leaving Patricia pensive. Accusing Eleanor of being promiscuous, a gold digger, or both seemed wrong now. And yet she was worried about the girl's connection to Tom. The fact that Eleanor was Jewish would make it difficult, if not impossible, for her to fit into Tom's world. Didn't he know that? Didn't she?

As she and Eleanor walked along the tree-lined main street, they passed a florist, a jeweler, and a sporting goods store, where a large sign offered 70 percent off on all ski equipment.

"Margaux used to ski," Patricia said. It went without saying that she'd never be able to do it again. "She was good too."

"That's too bad. I'd love to have gone with her sometime."

"Do you ski?" Patricia hoped her surprise was not audible.

"Ever since I was a little girl. My uncle Oscar owned a ski shop on Long Island."

They moved on until they reached a cheerful apple-green-and-white-striped awning. Beneath the awning was a familiar sign: TRACY TOLLAND, LUNCH AND TEA

"Here we are," she said, pushing open the door.

Tracy Tolland's restaurant had been serving the ladies of the area for decades. The round tables were laid with white napkins and green cloths; a bud vase holding a single white rose stood at the center of each. The hostess took them to a window seat, where a waiter held out two green-and-white-striped chairs.

"This is so charming," Eleanor said, looking around.

"It's where we've always come," Patricia said, trying to see it through Eleanor's fresh eyes. The waiter came to fill their glasses with ice water, and Eleanor drank hers down quickly.

The waiter returned to take their orders: Lobster Newburg, endive salad, and the house beverage, raspberry limeade.

"I'll talk to Wynn about the school," Patricia said when he'd gone. Eleanor was silent. Patricia could guess the reason. Henryka may have thawed toward Eleanor but Wynn had not. "I don't trust her," he'd said to Patricia. "Never did, never will."

Was Eleanor conniving, as Wynn had often said, and looking to Tom to advance her place in the world? Or was she an innocent?

The waiter appeared with a basket of rolls. Patricia took one and summoned her nerve. *Now,* she told herself, *say something now.*

"Eleanor," she began. "There's something I want to discuss with you. It's about Tom."

"What about him?" Eleanor did not look away.

"It seems to me that you two have become very friendly."

Eleanor looked uncomfortable. "Well, yes . . . Is that a problem?" She reached for a roll.

"It would be a problem only if you read too much into his behavior. If you thought that it meant more than it does."

"I don't think you're in a position to know what his behavior means." Eleanor put down the roll.

The effrontery of that reply forced Patricia to look away. The gall of her. The waiter came back, bearing their food, and so they were spared having to make conversation while it was placed on the table. When he'd gone, Patricia looked over at Eleanor again.

"I'm sorry if I offended you," Eleanor said. "But I can judge for myself whether Tom is being . . . sincere in his attentions."

"I don't think that you can," Patricia insisted. "That's the point. He's darling, he's lovable, and everyone adores him, including me. But he's not to be trusted, Eleanor." She took a bite of her food.

"How can you say those things?" Eleanor was visibly upset. "He's your brother." Her Lobster Newburg remained untouched.

"That's exactly why I can say them," Patricia said. "Because I've watched him do the same thing over and over. Someone's heart always gets broken. I don't want it to be yours."

"My heart's already been broken," Eleanor said. "I'm not as innocent as I seem."

"Evidently not," Patricia said, unable to curb the sarcasm and, yes, cruelty in her voice.

"What do you mean?" Now Eleanor looked alarmed.

"I was in Tom's room this morning," Patricia said. "I needed the car keys and knew he kept them in that golfing trophy. While I was in there, I couldn't help noticing that there was a smear of pink lipstick on his pillowcase. The exact shade of lipstick that you were wearing at the party."

"Are you saying it was mine? That I was in Tom's bed?"

"It certainly seems that way," Patricia said. When Eleanor did not respond, she went on. "I can't prove anything. But it has the look of impropriety, and given that you are acting as teacher, companion, and role model for my daughter, it poses a problem."

"You know how much I care for your daughter." Eleanor seemed to be choosing her words carefully. "And how much I've helped her. Still, if you feel I'm 'not a good influence,' you're free to let me go.

I'll be very sorry if you do. And I think Margaux will be too." Eleanor was fighting for self-composure; Patricia could see the struggle playing out on her face. "But I'm a grown woman, and I can make my own choices. I won't let you, or the *appearance of impropriety,* make those choices for me."

Patricia felt smacked. Had she *ever* been spoken to in this way by someone in her employ before? She could fire Eleanor on the spot. But what good would it do?

"Is everything all right, ladies?" Patricia looked up to see the waiter. "Everything's fine," Patricia said. The waiter retreated. Eleanor picked up her fork and probed the lobster; Patricia picked listlessly at her own. Neither woman was interested in dessert, and Patricia asked for the check. This entire enterprise had been a failure, and she could not wait to get home. They turned and walked back along the main street, toward the car.

Patricia skipped the coastal road in favor of the highway, and they arrived home very quickly.

"Thank you for lunch," Eleanor said as she got out of the car.

"My pleasure," Patricia said, mouthing the expected, rote phrase that was of course an utter lie.

Tom did not appear at dinner. After her conversation with Patricia, Eleanor wasn't going to ask where he was, but Margaux volunteered that he'd met some friends while at the club and decided, impromptu, to go off to Saratoga Springs with them.

"He didn't even come back for a change of clothes or a toothbrush," added Wynn, waving his tumbler of whiskey in the air.

"Did he say when he'd be back?" Patricia asked.

"Nope," said Wynn. He launched into an account of the day's sail, and Margaux eagerly joined in. Eleanor tried to appear interested, but she was preoccupied by Tom's sudden departure. After the night they had shared, she thought he'd have found some way to let her know his intentions. She hadn't seen him since she'd left his room just before dawn.

When dinner was over, Eleanor joined Margaux on the sunporch for checkers. She won once and Margaux twice before they decided to put the game away. "Uncle Tommy said he would teach me to play chess." Margaux dumped the red and black wooden pieces back in their box.

"Now there's a game of strategy," Eleanor said.

"Do you play chess?" Eleanor shook her head. "Maybe Uncle Tommy will teach you too," she said. "You like him, don't you?"

"Of course I do." Eleanor tried to keep her tone light.

"I mean like a boyfriend. *That* kind of like."

"We hardly know each other," Eleanor said. She was blushing, she was sure of it.

"Mother said she fell in love with Daddy right away." Margaux sounded like she was an expert on the subject. "They met at a Smith-Yale mixer. He was wearing a white dinner jacket, and as soon as he saw her, he went over and asked her to dance. She said by the time the dance had finished, she knew."

"Is that so?" Eleanor said. "How romantic."

"Maybe Tom will fall in love with you," Margaux said. She awkwardly got to her feet, gripping her walking stick. Eleanor knew better than to offer any help. "Then you could get married and be a part of our family. You'd be my aunt!"

"What an imagination you have," Eleanor said. How had Margaux seen right into her secret heart? "You'll have to start writing your ideas down. I predict you're going to be a writer someday."

"Maybe I will," said Margaux, suddenly losing her dreamy look and becoming serious. "If you're a writer, no one has to know you have a withered leg or use a stupid old walking stick."

"True," Eleanor said. "When you write, you can be . . . anyone."

BACK in the guest cottage, Eleanor felt worn out from both the lack of sleep last night and the drama of the day. A bath in the claw-footed tub was what she needed.

Immersed in the hot water, Eleanor leaned her head back and closed her eyes. Her thoughts turned to Tom. How bold she'd been. Maybe he thought she was a tramp, and that's why he'd gone off to Saratoga Springs without telling her. But Eleanor did not believe it. And she did not believe the things Patricia had said about him either. Tom *did* feel something for her; she was sure of it.

Eleanor stepped out of the tub, and swathed in one of the big, soft towels, she took out the package from her mother that had arrived earlier in the week. It contained a set of pajamas with cropped pants and a Chinese-style top. She slipped them on and, because the evening had gotten cool, added the matching wrapper. After combing out her hair, she settled into the love seat to read a little from *Great Expectations*. But she was more tired than she realized. Her eyes closed, and she let her head sink to the cushion as the book slipped unnoticed from her hand.

A loud knock woke her. Perhaps Tom had come back and was here to see her. She hurried to greet him, but no, it was Wynn Bellamy. The sleeves of his white shirt were rolled up to the elbow, and the shirt itself was untucked. His feet were bare. And he'd been drinking too; she could smell it.

"Well, hello," he said. "Aren't you going to invite me in?"

"It's late and I was going to . . ." She didn't want to say the words *go to bed* in front of him.

"Just for a little while," he said. "I promise I won't stay too long." And then, without waiting for a reply, he pushed past her and strode into the cottage, his sense of ownership clear. When he sat down on the love seat, she remained standing.

"That's a nice outfit. Does it come with a matching hat?"

"It's not an outfit. I'm wearing *pajamas*." Eleanor instinctively tightened the wrapper's sash around her waist.

"Pajamas. Of course." He looked her up and down appraisingly. How she wished she were dressed. Or that he would just leave.

"Say, would you like a drink?" And he produced a silver flask from his pocket. "It might help you to relax. Loosen up a little."

"No, thank you," she said. "I'm relaxed enough."

"You're not," he said. "You're a bundle of nerves. And you want me out of here. I can see it all over your face."

She felt the heat pricking her cheeks. "Well, I was just getting ready to go to—"

"Bed," he said. Why did that word sound so fraught? He unscrewed the top of the flask. "You don't mind if I do? Even though you're not joining me?"

She shook her head, but she did mind. What was he doing here?

Mr. Bellamy took a drink and then leaned back. "Can I ask you something, Eleanor? Something of a rather personal nature?"

"You can ask anything you like, but I might not answer."

"Clever." He took another sip. "Very clever. But then your people are clever—" He stopped himself.

Eleanor was becoming quietly frantic. If she was going to get him to leave, it had to be his idea. "Are you planning to go fishing tomorrow?" Fishing meant getting up early—a reason for him to leave the cottage now.

"Fishing? I hadn't thought about it." He raised the flask to his lips—again. "Back to my question. The one you said you might not answer. Here it is. I want to know why you don't like me."

What could she say? "Maybe I've felt that it was you who didn't like me, Mr. Bellamy."

"Wynn," he said.

"All right . . . Wynn." She had never said his first name aloud.

"Now we're getting somewhere!" He took another drink. "I wish you did like me," he said. "You seem to like everyone else around here—my daughter, my wife, my housekeeper. And my brother-in-law. *Especially* my brother-in-law. And they all like you! So much. It's always, *Eleanor says this* and *Eleanor does that*. I feel left out. It's not a good feeling, Eleanor." He took a big swig from the flask. "So I propose that we start again. Fresh. You and I. Do you think we can do that?"

Eleanor did not know what to say, but her panic receded just the slightest bit. He was drunk, but maybe he really did want to make amends. "All right," she said finally. "A fresh start."

"Splendid!" He jumped up from the love seat, surprisingly graceful for such a bulky man, and turned, as if looking for something. "Is there a radio in here?"

"Yes, but why do you—"

"I think we need to celebrate our newfound understanding. And since you won't drink with me, you can at least dance with me."

"I'm not going to dance with you." Her voice was firm.

"Why not?" He spied the radio and turned it on. "Smoke Gets in Your Eyes" was playing. "Just one little dance. How can it hurt?"

"I said no."

He crossed the room and grabbed both of her arms tightly. His face was close to hers now, much too close. And he was angry. Maybe she ought to dance with him—and then he would leave. "One dance," he pleaded.

"All right," she said. "One."

Immediately his grip relaxed, and he let one arm slide down so it was resting on her waist. "There," he said. "Isn't that better?"

Eleanor didn't answer, but concentrated on keeping her body as far from his as she possibly could. The song ended, and she stopped, but he did not release her. "You said one dance," she said.

"The song was practically over when we started," said Wynn.

"This is the last one," she said. "Really."

He said nothing but tried to draw her body nearer to his. "That's not dancing when you're so far away," he said.

The hand at her waist was rhythmically kneading her flesh and—

"Kiss me," he said softly. "Please."

Again, Eleanor stopped moving. "Mr. Bellamy, I'm not—"

"Wynn, it's Wynn—"

"Mr. Bellamy," she repeated. "You have to leave now." Panic was banging in her chest, her head. Why had she agreed to dance with him? She was a fool. He brought his mouth close to hers, but she turned her face away. "No, I won't. You can't force me—"

"Why not? What do you have against me?"

"You've had too much to drink, Mr. Bellamy." They were no longer dancing, but he hadn't let her go. "Please go."

"I'll bet you kiss other men," he said. "You kiss my wastrel brother-in-law. I've seen you. And I'll bet you two do more than kiss. Everyone knows about your people—they're hot-blooded."

"Let me go. Let me go right now!" She could scream, but then Patricia would hear—and Margaux. Unthinkable. So instead of screaming, Eleanor gave a sudden, violent twist away from him; she was unable to break free, but she'd succeeded in unbalancing him. The two of them went crashing down, her head smacking the floor. The pain was instant and enveloping.

And even worse, she was now pinned under him, his alcohol-laced breath foul in her face. "Come on," he said. "A kiss, just one little kiss." With one hand, he held her face and tried to press his mouth against hers and with the other, he reached inside the robe for the opening to her pajama top and yanked until the buttons gave way. Her panic gave her strength, and she managed to rake her nails along his forearms, drawing blood in their wake.

"What the—" He pulled away to run his fingers over the wounds, and she used the opportunity to scramble to her feet. But oh, her head hurt. Her eyes couldn't focus, and instead of one Wynn Bellamy, she saw two. Yet she still was able to grab the ironstone pitcher from its spot on the side table. "If you come any closer, I'll throw it." He hesitated, and then he was across the room and out of the cottage, door banging behind him.

She remained where she was, head throbbing, eyes still not able to focus. She touched the back of her head, where a lump was forming; there was a ringing in her ears. She began moving clumsily toward the bathroom and the tub. She wanted to wash his touch from her skin, the water as hot as she could bear. Then she vomited, a pale, foamy pool of liquid on the wooden floor.

Forget the shower. She had to get to a doctor. Where? How? Across the lawn, Tom's window was still dark but the light in Henryka's window glowed. She was still up.

She went to the closet, put on her raincoat, slid into her shoes, and picked up her purse. She was shaking, but a desperate energy propelled her through the dark, toward the house.

Once inside, she removed her shoes and found the stairs. A soft thudding noise made her freeze, and she waited, immobile, until she realized it was just the cat. She continued upstairs and down the hall until she reached Tom's room, still empty. Here were the car keys nestled at the bottom of the trophy, where Patricia had said they would be. Into her coat pocket they went. Then she climbed the staircase to the third floor—and to Henryka's room.

"Henryka," she called softly. "Henryka? It's me, Eleanor." Henryka opened the door and gasped. No wonder—Eleanor could just imagine what she looked like. "I need help. Please help me."

"What happen you?"

NOT OUR KIND | 363

"I don't want to talk here. Won't you let me in?"

Henryka stepped back. She wore a faded robe, and her hair was down around her shoulders.

"Henryka, I have to see a doctor. Now. Can you drive me?" She pulled the keys from her coat pocket and held them up. "Please, Henryka. My head hurts, and there's no one else I can ask."

All at once, Henryka's expression softened. "You wait." She stepped behind a folding screen. As she dressed, her head was still visible. "Sit down," she instructed. Eleanor sank gratefully into a chair. Henryka stepped back out from behind the screen. "Dr. Parker. He close by," she said. "Give me keys. I take you."

As they drove along the dark, quiet road, Eleanor waited for Henryka to ask her what had happened to her, but it was only when they had reached the doctor's house that she spoke. "Mr. Wynn—he do this to you." It was a statement, not a question.

Eleanor looked at her with astonishment. "How did you know?" Henryka didn't offer anything more, but the answer was suddenly so clear. "It's because he did it to you, isn't it?"

"Long time ago," said Henryka. "At Christmas party. He drunk and follow me into kitchen."

"He was drunk when he showed up at the cottage tonight. He wanted me to have a drink with him. I said no."

Henryka nodded, as if familiar with the script.

"Then he wanted to dance with me. To kiss me. But I wouldn't . . ." Eleanor hadn't cried when Mr. Bellamy was in the cottage, and she hadn't cried since. Now the tears let loose—a flood, a torrent.

"It be all right." Henryka leaned over and patted her back.

Eleanor's tears slowed. "Did you tell Patricia? Threaten to leave?"

"What I say?" Henryka asked. "Where I go?"

Eleanor knew that Henryka had been widowed young and left with three girls to raise on her own. So naturally she had stayed on at the Bellamys'. Had it happened only that one time? Or had Mr. Bellamy made a habit of it? But when she looked at Henryka, she realized that the older woman wasn't going to tell her any more. And she wasn't going to ask.

Chapter 7

ON MONDAY MORNING, Patricia woke to find Wynn packing. "Are you going somewhere?" He had planned to stay at the house this week—or so he had told her.

"I've got some business in Boston. I'll be gone for a couple of days," he said, tossing balled-up pairs of socks into the suitcase.

"All right," she said, "I just wish that—" The telephone's ring cut her short, and she went down to answer it. It was Tom, calling from Saratoga Springs.

"Where are you holed up?" she asked.

"I'm staying with Jasper Collins. He's bought this great old mansion. Eight bedrooms. Bathrooms galore. And a conservatory and a ballroom. Who has a ballroom these days?"

"It certainly sounds . . . ostentatious," she said. Patricia knew Jasper Collins. He was a very wealthy, very flamboyant character.

"You sound so disapproving, Trish. What have you got against Jasper?"

"You know what," she said. It was well known in their circle that Jasper preferred the company of men to women, including—no, *especially*—in the bedroom.

"Oh, that." Tom was dismissive. "Who cares?"

"You should care, Tom," she said. "People will talk."

"People will talk no matter what. I'm not going to live my life differently because they do. And neither should you."

Before she could reply, Henryka came into the kitchen. Patricia put a hand over the mouthpiece and said, "Could you excuse me for a moment?" Henryka left the room.

"Was that Henryka, my sweetheart, my darling? You tell her that even Jasper's fancy chef can't compete with her cooking."

"You can tell her yourself, if and when you ever come back."

"You've done nothing but scold me today. Why?"

"Eleanor," she said quietly. "Or should I say, Eleanor and you."

"Ah," said Tom. "So you know?"

"I found her lipstick on your pillowcase. I didn't tell Wynn, but he's already predicting that you're going to get her pregnant."

"Wynn believes the worst about people," Tom said. "But you don't, Trish. You never have. She's not what Wynn thinks she is."

"And what would that be?"

"Cheap. Common."

"Well, it certainly looks that way, doesn't it?"

"Forget the way it looks. Eleanor has the purest heart of anyone I've ever met."

"So why are you in Saratoga, instead of with Lady Pure Heart?"

"To tell you the truth, she scares me."

"Scares you?"

"It's that purity of hers. It's fierce. She says what she thinks. What she feels. I've never known anyone quite like her. And I feel like I'm falling in love with her. That's why I left. I don't want to be in love. Not with her, not with anyone."

"In love?" Alarm ignited inside her like a fire. It was one thing for Tom to flirt with and even seduce Eleanor. Love was another thing entirely. "What you're doing is dangerous and even cruel. Someone is going to get hurt."

She heard footsteps on the stairs; Wynn would be down any moment, and the conversation, like it or not, was over.

ELEANOR lay in bed, reluctant to get up. It had been roughly thirty-six hours since Wynn Bellamy paid her his unwelcome visit. Yesterday she had stayed in the cottage and not gone out. Late in the afternoon, she cautiously opened the door and was grateful to find a tray containing a thermos of soup and two slices of fresh bread wrapped in a kitchen towel. Henryka.

How had Henryka managed to face Wynn Bellamy since he'd done whatever it was he had done to her? And how had she faced Patricia? Eleanor was flooded with shame, guilt, but most of all, self-recrimination. Letting him in when she wasn't dressed. Agreeing to dance with him. And why hadn't she screamed? She was a fool, an idiot. She deserved what she had gotten—or at least that was what people would say if they knew. But they wouldn't know because she wasn't going to tell anyone—ever.

Eleanor forced herself to get up and to dress. She was going to go over to the house. The longer she postponed it, the worse it would be. When she reached the back door and let herself into the kitchen, she found Henryka at the stove, frying doughnuts. Oil sizzled as she set rings of dough into the pan. "You all right?"

"Yes, Henryka, I'm all right," Eleanor said.

On Saturday night, Henryka had accompanied her to Dr. Parker's house. After the exam, Eleanor followed him out to the waiting room where Henryka was sitting. "She took a bad knock on the head," he said. "She has a slight concussion, so someone will need to keep an eye on her." Henryka had nodded gravely, and although Eleanor said it wasn't necessary, Henryka spent the night at the cottage, cramming herself into the love seat as best she could.

"Everyone in there," Henryka said anxiously.

Eleanor hesitated for a few seconds; she heard Patricia's voice, and Margaux's in reply. And then . . . Wynn Bellamy. She pushed open the door, and there he was. He'd been looking down as he spooned his oatmeal, but he looked up when she came in. "Good morning, Eleanor. Henryka said you weren't feeling well. You're better, I hope?"

"I'm fine," she murmured, and took a seat. Henryka hurried in with a bowl of oatmeal.

He showed no sign of discomfort, no apparent remorse.

"Do you want another cup of coffee before I drive you to the station?" Patricia said. "Henryka's bringing out a fresh pot."

His mouth was full, so he nodded.

He was leaving. Mr. Bellamy was leaving. Eleanor's relief was enormous. Henryka appeared with the coffee and a platter of fresh doughnuts. Mr. Bellamy reached for one, and his sleeve rose up just the slightest bit. Peeking out from his crisp, white shirt cuff were a few small scratches, scabbed over and innocuous. But Eleanor stared as if they gushed fresh blood. "You'll have to excuse me."

She rose so abruptly that she knocked her chair back and it hit the floor. "I'm not well. I'll just go back to the cottage and—"

"Eleanor, what's wrong—" Patricia got up and righted the chair. Margaux cried, "Are you all right?" The only one who said nothing was Wynn Bellamy, who continued drinking his coffee.

"I'll be all right," she said, waving off Patricia's efforts to accompany her. "Please, just let me go and lie down."

Back in the cottage, she got into bed and let the trembling overtake her. Then she remembered the conversation at the table— Mr. Bellamy was leaving; *he* would be gone. She wouldn't have to see him for a few days. The trembling subsided, and she got up.

Eleanor went to the window. Tom's car was still there, but the Bellamys' car was gone, which meant Patricia and Mr. Bellamy were gone too. What a relief. She could go back over to the house. She found Margaux on the sunporch, sprawled on the sofa, listening to the radio. When she saw Eleanor, she switched it off. "How are you?" she said. "Mother was worried. So was I."

What about your father? Was he worried too? "I'm fine now," said Eleanor. "You don't need to worry."

"I told Mother you were homesick," Margaux said.

"Why did you tell her that?" Eleanor sank into the sofa.

"Because it's true," Margaux said. "I told her to let you go home for the weekend. To see your mother."

"What did she say?" Eleanor asked. This was it—the answer to her dilemma. She could go home for a few days and see Irina, maybe see Ruth. It would be just what she needed. Then she could come back and all would be as it had been before.

"She said she'd talk to you." There was the sound of a car pulling up to the house. "That's her now. You can ask her."

Patricia came in. "Eleanor!" she said. "I was just going to check on you. Maybe we ought to take a drive over to see Dr. Parker."

"No!" Eleanor said.

"Well, all right." Patricia seemed a little surprised by her reaction. "If you're sure . . ."

"I'm sorry, I just don't want you to go to any trouble. I'm fine."

"Ask her about going home," Margaux urged.

"Going home?" Patricia said.

"Yes. I wanted to visit my mother. It wouldn't be for long. I'd leave on Friday afternoon and be back on Sunday."

"You really miss her, don't you?" Patricia said.

"Yes," Eleanor said. "And she misses me, too, though she won't come out and say so."

"That's sweet," Patricia said. "I'd like to meet her sometime."

"I think you did. She said you stopped by the store one day and bought a hat from her."

"Oh, that's right." Patricia looked uncomfortable.

"You didn't introduce yourself," Eleanor said. Why was she going on about this? She knew she shouldn't.

"No? I thought I had," said Patricia.

Eleanor was angry that Patricia was lying about a visit that at this moment felt like an invasion. Another one. Then she regretted her tone. "Not that it matters. I'll just let her know I'm coming."

She followed Patricia into the kitchen and placed the call. "Your timing couldn't have been better," Irina said. "I need your help— there's been a flood."

"In the basement?" asked Eleanor. Her mother had a small storage area, and it had flooded before. " Did you lose a lot of stock?"

"There's at least six inches of water on the floor, so I haven't been able to check," said Irina.

"I'll be down on the next train." Eleanor could see her mother's familiar, worried expression, the crease between her brows. She turned to see Patricia; she had forgotten she was in the room.

"There's been a flood at the shop. I've got to get down to New York today."

"Of course," Patricia said. "I'll take you to the station myself. That's really too bad."

"I'll need to pack," Eleanor said. "It won't take me long." She left Patricia in the kitchen and walked out the door, in the direction of the cottage.

Flinging open the door, she pulled her valise out from under the bed and began to toss things inside. In went clothes, shoes, a few books. The pajamas and robe she would never wear again.

Eleanor glanced up and saw Patricia in the doorway. "I checked the schedule, and there's a train to New York in a little less than an hour. If we leave now, you can make it."

Eleanor snapped the valise shut and grabbed the handle. "I'm ready. Let's go."

They drove to the station in silence, and when they arrived, Patricia saw her off on the platform.

"I'll let you know when I'll be back," Eleanor said.

"I hope everything's all right," Patricia said. "Margaux will miss you. We all will."

Your husband too? Eleanor thought with a shudder.

On the way to New York City, Eleanor tried—and failed—to sleep. Every time she tried to lean back on the seat, she was reminded of Wynn Bellamy's assault by the tender bump at the back of her head. She'd been so naive, thinking she could come up here and, with the flimsy protection of an assumed name, meld into a pattern of life that was defined by its exclusion of people like her. She loved Margaux, and teaching her was a pleasure. She admired Patricia—her ease in the world, her polish, her graciousness—and strove to emulate her. She'd allowed herself to become smitten with Tom, and it seemed her feelings were reciprocated. Then Wynn Bellamy barged into the cottage, and everything had changed. *Not our kind*, her mother had said of the Bellamys. And as galling as it was to admit, even if only to herself, her mother had been right.

"I WISH Eleanor hadn't left," complained Margaux. There was a heat wave in Argyle, and the rising temperature, coupled with Eleanor's absence, had brought Margaux to breakfast in a snit.

"You encouraged her to go," Patricia pointed out.

"I know." Margaux sulked. "But I have nothing to do today, and I'm *bored*." Overnight, Margaux had reverted to the irritable girl she'd been before Eleanor arrived. Patricia had to do something.

"Let's go swimming," she said, and when she saw her daughter's face, she hastened to add, "Not at the club."

"Then where?"

"Lavender Lake." Patricia thought it a wretched little spot, but so what? It would be cooler, and it would give them something to do. She needed the distraction as badly as Margaux did.

They arrived at the lake to find the place deserted. Patricia did her best to jam the pointed end of the umbrella pole into the sand behind a clump of bushes; then she spread out a blanket and slipped out of her sundress. Margaux was already in the water and beckoning her to come in. Patricia waded out to join her.

The water was not murky, as she had expected, but surprisingly clear and cool. "Doesn't it feel good?" asked Margaux.

"It does," Patricia agreed. They swam companionably for a while, and then Patricia waded back to the shore. God, but it was a relief to cool off. She was seated on the blanket, wringing the water from her hair when she saw another family trooping along the pebble-strewn grass, toting their own umbrella and blanket.

"Over here," called the boy. "This is the perfect spot." Patricia watched them settle in. It was only when the boy had taken off his long-sleeved shirt—an odd choice in this heat—that she saw the shrunken arm dangling uselessly at his side. Polio.

The boy was ten or eleven. Sandy hair. Since the polio had ravaged an arm, not a leg, he was more mobile than Margaux. "I'm heading in," he called to his mother.

"Just stay where we can watch you," she said.

"You heard her, Larry," said the man. He was lighting a pipe.

"I heard, Dad," the boy said. He scampered down to the water's edge just as Margaux was emerging. She'd left her walking stick on the shore and was on both hands, propelling herself along until she reached the stick and used it to hoist herself up.

Patricia got up and hurried over to where Margaux stood, staring uncertainly at the boy. He turned in her direction.

"Patricia Bellamy," she said. "And this is Margaux." The boy's parents had joined them, and the father extended his hand. "Ray Sharp," he said, and gesturing to the woman added, "This is Pauline, and that's our boy, Larry."

"You had polio," Margaux said to Larry. Patricia's first instinct was to chastise her, but something told her to keep still.

"Yeah," Larry said, looking at Margaux's leg. "So did you."

"When?" Margaux asked.

"Three years ago. I was eight. How about you?"

"Over a year ago. It was like being in hell."

"Margaux!" Patricia couldn't contain herself any longer.

"That's all right," said Ray Sharp. "Don't worry about us."

"We understand," Pauline said. "It *was* like being in hell."

Patricia smiled in nervous relief.

"And we're the lucky ones. So many of the children on his ward didn't come home at all."

"Mother, Larry and I are going in the water," Margaux said.

"As long as you stay where we can see you."

"That's just what I told him," Ray said with a smile.

Margaux set down her stick, but instead of dropping to her knees, she took the arm Larry extended. Patricia had to make an effort not to show her surprise. It was rare that Margaux let anyone help her. For her to let someone she'd met only moments ago offer any kind of assistance was a radical departure.

"Will you join us?" Pauline said.

Ray helped Patricia relocate her blanket and umbrella, and the three of them chatted while Margaux and Larry frolicked in the water. She told them about Oakwood; Pauline said she had heard of the place and had been considering it for Larry as well.

Patricia watched the children play; how long had it been since Margaux had spent time with anyone even close to her in age? Wasn't that Eleanor's point?

She looked up to see Margaux, dripping water. Larry was standing next to her. "We're hungry," she said. "Can we have lunch now?"

"We didn't bring any sandwiches," Patricia said. "You wanted to drive into town for lunch?"

"Oh," said Margaux. "I forgot."

"If you'd like, you can join our picnic. Pauline always makes too much food, don't you?" Ray said.

Pauline nodded. "Please do. I've got peanut butter and jelly or cream cheese," said Pauline, rummaging in the basket.

"Can I please have one cream cheese and one peanut butter?" asked Margaux.

The Sharps were a welcome distraction from Patricia's own oppressive thoughts. Ray sold insurance in Hartford; Pauline had been a librarian. Like Patricia, she had wanted more children. "We tried and tried," she said. They had finished eating, and Ray was down at the water with Margaux and Larry. "But it just never happened."

"The same with us," Patricia said.

Ray, Margaux, and Larry returned to the blanket. "Mother, Larry's invited us back to his house for dinner. Mr. Sharp said it was all right with him but that we would have to ask you and Mrs. Sharp. Please will you say yes, Mother? Please?"

Patricia looked at Pauline. "We're having a cold supper. Because of the heat," said Pauline. "If you don't mind that, we'd like for you to share it with us."

"I've got a new rabbit," Larry said. "His name is Bucky. I wanted to show him to Margaux."

"Mrs. and Mr. Sharp say yes," said Margaux. "And I really do want to see Bucky."

THE Sharps' house was a perfectly acceptable, if slightly shabby, colonial set behind a massive oak on the front lawn. When they got to the door, she noticed something small attached to its frame. It had Hebrew letters and so must have been one of those things— she didn't know what to call it—that Jewish people posted on their dwellings. So they were Jews.

Margaux was smitten with Bucky, a docile gray creature with floppy ears and a twitching nose. When it was time to leave, she said, "Larry invited me to spend the night."

"We'd love to have her," Pauline said. She lowered her voice. "And it's a pleasure to see them having a good time together."

Patricia had to admit that it was. "But what about your things?" she said to Margaux. "Maybe we'd better make it another time."

"I could follow you and pick up her bag," Ray offered.

"You see?" Margaux said. "Everything's all worked out."

Patricia looked at Margaux, arms around the rabbit, face shining with hope. "All right then, if you're sure it's no trouble," Patricia said to Pauline. "I'll call Henryka and ask her to pack a bag."

"Oh, Mother, I love you!" Margaux cried. She kissed Bucky's furred gray head.

Was this all it took to make her so happy? A chance to spend some time in this dreary house with a little Jewish boy and his pet rabbit? Patricia got back in the car, while Ray followed behind. At the house, Henryka was there to meet them with Margaux's bag and a bundle of brownies wrapped in wax paper, which she handed to Ray through the open window.

"We'll take good care of her," said Ray from behind the wheel. "And I'll have her back safe and sound tomorrow."

The next day, the house felt too quiet, so Patricia went to the club, but she found the conversation—the extramarital affair of one member, the scorn-worthy new interior decorator hired by another—an unappealing mixture of spite, venom, and stupidity. Back home, she picked up a copy of the latest *New Yorker* but couldn't concentrate. Around noon, she showered—again—and dressed in a flared skirt and blouse. She was strangely lethargic, but she still forced herself to dress and primp. Then she sat down to a small salad, which, despite Henryka's protests, was all she could tolerate for lunch. "You waste away," the housekeeper fumed. Patricia just nodded, eyes straying to the clock on the kitchen wall. Margaux would be home soon, she consoled herself.

There was a sound from the front of the house—a key turning in the lock—and Patricia looked at Henryka. "Maybe it's—"

Wynn came in through the kitchen door. Patricia put her fork down as Henryka hastily retreated.

"I'm back," he said pointlessly. "We finished early, and I caught a ride down." He put his bag down and looked around the room. "The house is so quiet. Where is everyone?"

"Tom's still in Saratoga. Eleanor went home for a few days. And Margaux's staying over at the house of a family we met at Lavender Lake."

"You were at Lavender Lake? Why go to that muck-filled pond when you could go to the club?"

"You know perfectly well Margaux won't go to the club." Patricia pushed her plate away.

"So this family—they're not anyone we know?"

"No."

"And you let her stay with them overnight?"

"Yes, I did. Margaux and the boy liked each other. You *know* how impossible she can be."

"I see." He lifted his hands to loosen his tie. "I'm going to fix myself a drink. Can I make one for you?"

He said nothing as he mixed their drinks, and when he'd finished his—very quickly—he said he was going up to lie down.

Patricia sipped her own drink and let him go. When she'd finished, she felt a slight buzz, which was odd considering she'd had only one. But she hadn't finished the light lunch Henryka had served, and the afternoon was even hotter than the day before. A rest sounded like a good idea, and she went upstairs to join Wynn.

She found him stretched out and reading the newspaper on the bed, his shirt laid over a chair. "What happened to your arms?"

"Oh those," he said, looking at the scabbed-over marks. "Didn't I tell you? That damned cat—she went crazy and attacked me."

Patricia remembered that Glow had clawed her, too, for no apparent cause. They had found Glow in the woods, years ago, as a kitten. Maybe now she was returning to some feral state. She had an urge to stroke the cat and went downstairs in search of her. "Glow," she called softly. But Glow was nowhere to be found.

Chapter 8

ELEANOR SPENT THE DAY helping her mother clean up the mess in the flooded basement. She'd lost some but not all of her inventory, and the two of them brought whatever was salvageable upstairs. Irina had closed the shop while they worked.

The afternoon dwindled, and it was soon dusk. Irina hadn't

wanted to cook, so they ate cold cuts from Schaller & Weber on Second Avenue. Then Eleanor did the dishes and got her coat.

"Where are you going?" Irina asked.

"The movies. I'm meeting Ruth."

"Oh, she's not seeing her young man tonight?"

"No." She didn't want Irina to start in on why she didn't have a young man of her own. "Anyway, we won't be late."

In fact, Eleanor had no idea of what Ruth was doing tonight because she wasn't seeing her.

Instead, she headed downtown on the subway. When she emerged into the unfamiliar tangle of streets, she got lost. She hadn't been down here in years, not since her father was alive and took them all to see the neighborhood where he'd first lived when he'd come from Russia as a child. They had visited both the tenement where her father had lived and the synagogue on Eldridge Street where he'd worshipped.

But today Eleanor hurried past the synagogue. These last few days, she had not been able to tolerate the sight of her own naked body. It filled her with a sense of shame she had never known before. She felt polluted, no matter how much soap she used. Maybe there was something wrong with her, something that had drawn Wynn Bellamy to her. She had to get rid of it.

That's when she got the idea of visiting the mikvah, the Jewish ritual bath. The thought began to preoccupy her, so much so that yesterday she had walked up to Congregation Orach Chaim in search of the rabbi's wife.

"You want to go to a mikvah?" Mrs. Schechter had clearly been surprised. "Are you sure?"

"Yes," Eleanor said. "I am."

"I've rarely gone myself," said Mrs. Schechter. "The women of our congregation don't usually do that. But I can tell you where to go." She studied her carefully and then added, "If there's anything you'd like to talk about, my door is always open." The pause lengthened uncomfortably until Mrs. Schechter had finally taken a scrap of paper and written down the address, 5 Allen Street, which Eleanor was now trying her best to find.

Finally, she went up to a pair of women, both in the very obvious wigs that Orthodox women wore. "Excuse me," she said politely to the older of the two. "Can you tell me where this is?" The woman looked at the scrap of paper and up at Eleanor's face. It was obvious she did not understand why someone who looked as Eleanor did—clearly not observant—would be searching for a mikvah. But she led Eleanor down a short street, turned a corner, and indicated a brick building.

Raising her fist, Eleanor knocked. There was no answer, but when she pushed the door gently, it opened. An old woman sat at a small table, her head bent over an embroidery hoop. The woman looked up. "Can I help you?"

"I'm here for the mikvah," she said.

"You're married?" Eleanor shook her head. "Getting married?" Again, Eleanor shook her head.

The woman seemed to consider this. Finally she said, "Wait here." She then laid the embroidery hoop down on the table, shuffled through a doorway, and returned with another old woman who was carrying something folded and white. "Gittel will take care of you," she said. "Follow her." Eleanor thanked her and put a quarter in the empty jelly jar, as Mrs. Schechter had told her to do.

As they descended a flight of stairs, Eleanor saw beads of moisture on the wall. They passed several small, curtained chambers; wigs hung suspended from hooks above the piles of folded clothing. Then Gittel showed her to an empty chamber; behind its curtain was a wooden seat, two hooks, and a showerhead poking out from the ceiling. "Are you clean?" she asked.

"Excuse me?"

"Your last time of the month. When was it?"

"About two weeks ago," Eleanor said.

"And you've had no relations since then?"

Eleanor felt herself coloring. "No," she said. "I haven't."

"Good. Then you can take off your clothes and leave them here," said Gittel. Eleanor looked at the hooks; hanging from one of them was a wooden body brush with coarse bristles. "Then, you wash. Face. Body. Hair. Don't forget the hidden places." Eleanor nodded. "You brought soap?" Eleanor nodded; Mrs. Schechter had told her to bring these things. "Toothbrush too?" Again, a nod. "Good. Go to work. When you're done, call me." She handed Eleanor the white bundle she'd been carrying; it turned out to be a simple cotton robe and a rough terry cloth towel.

The water was surprisingly hot, and, as Gittel had instructed, Eleanor washed everywhere—her breasts and belly, shoulders and thighs. She washed between her toes and behind her ears and hesitated only when she got to the place between her legs. She lathered herself until the soap achieved frothy clusters before succumbing to the rushing water and disappearing down the drain. When she was done, she dried herself, donned the robe, and combed out her hair. Only then did she call for Gittel.

"Let me see your hands," Gittel said, and inspected Eleanor's nails closely. She gave a grunt of approval. "Now bend your head." She raked her fingers over Eleanor's scalp. Eleanor flinched a little when Gittel touched the sore place on her head. Gittel noticed. "I hurt you?"

"It's nothing," Eleanor said. "Just a little bump."

Gittel continued her probing. She even had her stick her tongue out. "You did a good job, especially for the first time," she said. "But first time, tenth time—it doesn't matter. The mikvah cures all ailments and washes away all sins."

"All?" Eleanor asked.

Gittel looked at her appraisingly. "Yes. The mikvah will wash you clean—no matter what you've done."

"Or what was done to me?"

"Ah." Gittel took Eleanor's hand in hers. "It will be better, *tochter*—you'll see."

Wearing just the robe, Eleanor followed the older woman along a short hall until they came to an open doorway. Six white marble steps led down to a rectangular bathing pool around six or seven feet long and lined with tiles as white as snowdrops.

"I'll take that," Gittel said, indicating the robe. Eleanor loosened the belt and shrugged the thing off. It was terrifying, standing so exposed, but she quickly stepped down into the mikvah. Her feet touched the bottom of the pool; the water came up to her shoulders.

Why had she come? What was she seeking—healing? Transformation? Or was it grace? She wasn't devout, yet here she was.

"Dunk," said Gittel. "Like this." She held her arms aloft, elbows bent. "The immersion must be complete."

Eleanor complied, then lifted her head out of the water.

"Now the prayer," said Gittel. When Eleanor looked confused, she pointed to a sign on the wall. But the letters were in Hebrew. "Just repeat after me. *Baruch ata adonai eloheinu melech ha-olam asher kid-shanu b'mitzvo-tav v'tzi-vanu al ha-tevilah.*"

Some of the words were familiar from the Passover seders she'd attended. But she intoned them fervently, and in them heard echoes of her father's voice. "Good girl," said Gittel. "Do it again."

By the third immersion, Eleanor had succumbed to the simple rhythm; dunk and bless, dunk and bless. After the last blessing, she climbed out; the robe and towel were waiting. She did not feel cleansed so much as quieted, the clamor in her head subdued. But even that small change was a relief.

THE heat had finally broken, and Patricia went for a walk after dinner in the gardens. Just as she had turned the corner, she spied a woman sitting outside. Dottie Talbot. Patricia crossed the road.

"Out for some night air?" she asked.

"I'm relieved there's been a break in the heat," said Dottie.

Patricia sat down beside her, and they chatted briefly. Then Dottie put a hand with manicured, rosebud-pink nails on Patricia's arm. "There's something I've wanted to tell you. I'm not sure if you know it already, but I know that if the situation were reversed, I'd want someone to tell me."

"Tell me what?" Patricia prayed this didn't have anything to do with Eleanor.

"It's about Henryka."

"Henryka!" said Patricia. "What about her?"

"Well, she told Colleen that she was looking for another position and asked her to keep her ears open. Colleen was supposed to keep it a secret. But she told me anyway."

"I had no idea," Patricia said.

"She's been with you a long time, hasn't she?"

"I've known her since I was a little girl." Patricia had been four or five when Henryka had come to work for her mother, and while Henryka had not been a warm presence, she'd been a constant one.

"Well, she ought to have told you first."

"Yes . . . I wonder why she didn't."

"Really, some of these people don't have a shred of loyalty. I'm sure you've been very good to her."

She was very good to me, Patricia wanted to say. When she had a cold, it was Henryka's dill-infused chicken soup that helped her mend; when she returned to Smith after a weekend, a tin of Henryka's pecan turtles went with her. Henryka had been with her and Wynn through the deaths of all their parents, and Margaux's birth and her illness. And now Henryka was planning to leave them.

"Patricia, you're so quiet. Are you all right?"

"Of course I'm all right. Honestly, she's only a cook. I'll find someone else in no time."

She got up and walked back across the road before Dottie saw the tears that brimmed in her eyes, and then began rolling slowly down her face.

PATRICIA slept fitfully and was up with the light, dressing quickly while Wynn slumbered on.

Early as it was, Henryka was already downstairs, engaged in the familiar ballet of rinsing, wiping, storing, stacking.

"Why do you want to leave us?" Patricia burst out.

Henryka stopped what she was doing to look at Patricia. "I sorry. I no want to leave. But I no can work here anymore."

"Why on earth not? Do you need a raise? I'll give it to you gladly. More time off? You can have that too."

Henryka just shook her head.

"Then what? Have I said something? Done something?"

There was a pause during which Henryka took a pan to the sink to soak. "No you," she said finally. "Mr. Wynn."

Wynn! What had he done? "Can't you tell me what's happened? Please? We've known each other such a long time and—"

She'd started to cry, and she used her napkin to blot the tears.

"Missus, I so sorry." Henryka came over and sat down across from her. "You husband—he no good. He hurt Miss Eleanor . . . I take her to doctor."

"He hurt Eleanor? I can't believe it. What did he do?"

"You ask. Maybe she tell you."

"But you don't even know if she was telling the truth."

"I know."

"How?" Patricia asked.

Henryka looked at her hands. "Long time ago, he hurt me too."

"What are you talking about?"

"At Christmas, he try kiss me. And when you were in hospital having Margaux . . ."

"What did he do while I was in the hospital?" Henryka was silent. "Please, you have to tell me. I need to know—"

"I no want say."

"But . . . You should have *told* me."

"How I tell? My girls, they little then. I need job."

Yes, of course she did, Patricia thought. She knew about Henryka's fifth-floor walk-up above a butcher on First Avenue, the three daughters she'd raised alone. "Is there anything I can do to change your mind?"

"No." Henryka placed her work-worn hand over Patricia's. "Time for me go, missus. I give notice today."

Patricia got up and went to her room. Fortunately, Wynn was in the shower, so she didn't have to face him yet. Wynn had done something to Eleanor. And to Henryka. Was there anybody else? She remembered a secretary in Wynn's office who'd left very suddenly, with no explanation. Was it because of him?

The water in the bathroom went off.

"You're up early." Wynn came in toweling off his hair.

"I had some bad news this morning," she said.

"What's happened?" He moved closer. Although he'd put on his boxers and pants, his chest was bare.

"Henryka's decided to leave us."

"Oh." He stepped back and sat in a chair to put on his socks.

"That's not exactly *bad* news, is it? Maybe she wants to retire."

"No, she's not retiring. She started looking for another job behind my back. Dottie told me."

"Really? Now that seems sneaky. Disloyal even. After all these years . . ." He tied his shoes and looked up.

"She said that she was leaving because of you. Because you did something to Eleanor. And—years ago—to her."

"What are you talking about?" His tone was truculent, but his face began to get mottled—a sure sign he was upset.

"She wouldn't give me many details, so I'm going to ask Eleanor. But I wanted to talk to you first. Did something happen between you?"

"Did she say something happened?"

"Not to me. But clearly something did, and I want to hear your side."

"This isn't going to sound good," he began. "I shouldn't have gone over there but—"

"Where? To the cottage?"

"Yes."

"Why?"

"Because I was sick of how everyone worshipped Eleanor. She makes me feel like a second-class citizen—in my own home."

"You don't like her. You never have."

"It's true. But I was sorry, and I went over to make amends."

"When?"

"One night in August—I don't remember the date."

"So you went to the cottage to offer an olive branch to Eleanor. Then what? She invited you in?"

"Yes, that's it," he said—too eagerly it seemed. "She asked me in and offered me a drink."

"A drink? Of what?"

"I don't know. Scotch, I think. Yes, that was it. Scotch."

"Eleanor kept a bottle of scotch in the cottage? I've never known her to drink scotch."

"Why are you interrogating me?"

"I'm not interrogating you. I'm just asking because Henryka accused you of something. And whatever it is, it's serious enough to make her leave us after nearly thirty years!" Tears filled her eyes, but this was no time to cry and she brushed them away. "So please, just tell me what happened."

"All right," he said. "I went over there, I had a drink, and then another one. She was drinking too. The radio was on, and she wanted to dance, so I obliged her. She wasn't really dressed . . ."

"What do you mean she wasn't dressed?"

"It was late. She was wearing some robe over her . . . pajamas, I guess. Anyway, we danced and she pressed very close to me. And I was . . . that is . . ." He looked at her imploringly. "I knew it was wrong but the feel of her was just . . . I tried to kiss her."

"Kiss her!"

"She pulled away. There was a struggle, and we fell. I think she hit her head on the floor pretty hard. I got scared and I left."

"You didn't stay to make sure she was all right?"

"No, I was ashamed. I just wanted to get out of there."

"And those scratches on your arms—Glow didn't make those. It was Eleanor." He nodded. Patricia was quiet, trying to take it all in. "How did Henryka come to know all this?"

"I don't know. Maybe Eleanor told her."

The thought of the help gossiping about them soaked her in shame. "And what about Henryka?"

"One Christmas, forever ago, I may have tried to steal a kiss under the mistletoe. But it was a joke—as if I'd go after Henryka. Obviously she's held it against me all these years."

"She also said there was something that happened a long time ago—when I was in the hospital, after Margaux was born."

He was indignant. "What, exactly, is she accusing me of?"

"I don't know. She wouldn't say anything more."

"This is an outrage. My wife, the cook who's been on my payroll for a decade, a tutor who came out of nowhere to infiltrate my home—all of you accusing me, condemning me—"

"All right," she said. "That's enough. You can stop now." He wasn't going to tell her about the other time. Neither was Henryka. But there was a chance Eleanor would tell her what had happened in the cottage—if she asked the right way.

"You'll forgive me, won't you?" he said. "What I did wasn't so terrible. No one was hurt, not really. I'm a man, and a man has urges. Sometimes it's hard to . . . tame them."

Patricia left Wynn in the bedroom and went back downstairs. Propped up beside a bowl on the counter was a letter that had come for Eleanor. She'd returned from the city late the night before last, taken Margaux out for the day, and begged off dinner, saying she was tired. Eleanor, who was blameless, and clearly the injured party. And yet Patricia found herself angry with her—had she not become part of their household, Henryka wouldn't be leaving. The feeling passed, and in its wake came remorse for having it at all. Maybe things would be better when they returned to New York. Patricia could only hope so—she was more than ready for this strange, altogether unsettling summer to be over.

Chapter 9

ELEANOR REVELED IN her return to the city. Yes, September in New York was still wretchedly hot, but she felt protected by the noise, the dirt, and the heat. She had managed to get through the remainder of her time in Argyle avoiding Wynn Bellamy, though just knowing she might encounter him kept her on the alert. Also, Tom had returned and then left abruptly and Henryka had given notice; Patricia seemed like a wire pulled taut and ready to snap. It was a fraught atmosphere and one Eleanor was glad to leave behind.

Back in New York, Eleanor regained a measure of control, at least as far as Mr. Bellamy was concerned, and she took to arriving at the Park Avenue apartment after he left for the office and leaving before he returned.

One morning after Eleanor had been back for about a week, Patricia stopped her before she went into the study. "Would you be able to join me for a drink at the Carlyle when you've finished with

Margaux today? Wynn is coming home early, and he's taking her to the theater, and I'd rather he didn't know about it."

Eleanor agreed, but she wondered—and worried—about the purpose of this meeting. Was it about Tom? She had told him he could call her apartment during the day, while Irina was in the shop; the last time they had spoken was over a week ago.

"Everything's all mixed up," he'd said. "*I'm* all mixed up. I think I just need some time away."

"Away where?" He was mixed up, but what about her?

"I haven't decided."

And then he'd gone, without telling her where he'd decided on going. This new disappearance filled her with less longing than the first time and more bitterness. He'd been using her after all—maybe not intentionally, but in the end, it didn't matter what his intentions had been. He'd made her feel cheap and disposable.

ELEANOR was the first to arrive at the Carlyle Hotel and was ushered to one of the chocolate brown leather banquettes. A waiter appeared with a menu and a glass of ice water that Eleanor sipped as she looked around at the nickel-trimmed black glass tabletops, the black granite bar, and the gold leaf that covered the ceiling. On the walls were whimsical scenes of Central Park—picnicking rabbits, ice-skating elephants, a giraffe slipping his neck between the bars of his cage. She had just glanced down at the menu—what prices on the drinks!—when Patricia appeared. "Thank you for meeting me," she said. Patricia smiled as the waiter appeared and ordered a Green Dragon for each of them.

"Is it something with Margaux?" Eleanor asked.

"Margaux is just blossoming." Patricia sipped the vividly colored drink that had just arrived. "Thanks to you. So no, it's not about her. It's about Henryka. Did you know she'd given notice? She'll be gone by the end of the month."

"Yes, I know." Eleanor had been surprised when Henryka told her. Also sorry because she had been an ally in the household. But why did this disclosure demand drinks at the Carlyle?

"Well, did you know the reason she gave for leaving?"

"No, she didn't mention—"

"She said it was because of you."

"Me? What do I have to do with it?"

"Do you remember the night she took you to the doctor in Argyle?" Patricia's fingers were holding the stem of her glass tightly.

"She told you about that?" That Patricia had known but not said anything seemed beyond understanding.

"Only what she knew—that you'd been hurt and needed to see a doctor. And that the person who hurt you was . . . Wynn."

"He didn't hurt me, not exactly; it was just that we fell, and I hit my head on the floor . . ." Eleanor couldn't finish.

"Wynn admits he came to see you," said Patricia. "He said that you invited him in, offered him a drink, and asked him to dance."

"No." Eleanor raised her eyes to look at Patricia. "It wasn't like that. You know it wasn't. I would never . . . He was your husband. And my employer."

"I don't know what to think." Patricia finished her drink and signaled to the waiter to bring two more.

Eleanor was flustered. She had never planned on sharing what had happened with Patricia, and yet Patricia had found out anyway. "I wasn't going to tell you," she said. "I wasn't going to tell anyone, not even Tom. And I didn't tell Henryka, but she guessed."

"So, what are we going to do?" Patricia was asking a question to which Eleanor did not have the answer.

"What do you want to do?"

"Well, I'm losing my cook, which grieves me more than I can say. I don't want to lose you too."

"You don't?" This was a surprise; Eleanor thought Patricia would have wanted her gone immediately.

"No," Patricia said.

"What if we never talk about it again? Pretend it didn't happen."

"Would you really agree to that? Tell no one? Not even Tom?"

"Of course," said Eleanor. She never wanted to think about that night again. Now she wouldn't have to.

"Then I think we have a plan. Can we drink to it?" She touched the rim of her glass to Eleanor's, and when the Green Dragons were gone, signaled to the waiter for the check.

IT WAS dark as Eleanor walked along East Seventy-Sixth Street toward home. Irina would want to know if she'd eaten, and if so, what and with whom. Just thinking about these questions felt oppressive. How much longer would she have to tolerate them? Ira had jilted her, and Tom had vanished—but even if he hadn't, she saw too many obstacles to imagine a life with him.

What if there were another way to live? Not with a husband, not with Irina, but—alone. The thought was terrifying. Also exhilarating. And once it had coalesced in her mind, it was followed by a rush of others. Where might she want to live? The West Side perhaps? Or downtown, in the Village, like Tom? What would her mother think? Her friends? But oh, imagine how it would feel to be answerable to no one other than herself.

In the weeks that followed, Eleanor harbored her plan in secret, adding money to her savings account faithfully every payday. Not that anyone would have been interested. Ruth had just announced her engagement to Marty Tolchin, the boy she'd met at the synagogue mixer, and was busy planning her wedding. Tom was still away, and she'd received only a folded sheet of paper with the words *Thinking of you*. The postmark was from Quebec. She looked at the note for a few minutes before ripping it in half.

By October, the weather had turned cooler, and Eleanor pulled out the black princess-style coat she'd had since college. A new coat would have been so nice, but her own apartment would be even nicer; she put the purchase on hold and hunted through Irina's trimmings for some black velvet ribbon with which she could conceal all the fraying. That, combined with black jet buttons, freshened the whole look.

"What a nice coat," Patricia said when Eleanor arrived wearing it for the first time. "The trimming just makes it."

"Thank you." Eleanor hung the coat in the hall closet and continued on to the study.

It was shortly after lunch that Eleanor heard the apartment's front door opening and then closing. "Good day to you, sir," said

Bridget, the cook who'd been hired to replace Henryka. Eleanor didn't hear the reply, but she knew it came from Wynn Bellamy; he must have been home early from the office.

"Eleanor, I asked you a question," said Margaux.

"I'm sorry. I wasn't paying attention. What did you say?" Eleanor tried to blot out the knowledge that Mr. Bellamy was here. Since that evening at the Carlyle, she'd been doing what she promised Patricia: putting the incident in Argyle out of her mind.

Still, knowing he was in the apartment unnerved her, and she had trouble keeping her mind on Margaux and their lesson. She managed to get through the rest of the afternoon, relieved when it was over. Margaux accompanied her to the foyer, where she retrieved her coat and pocketbook from the closet, anxious to leave as soon as possible. She wasn't yet out the door when Patricia, resplendent in a velvet opera cape, swept into the room.

"Mother, you look so beautiful," said Margaux.

"Thank you, darling." The cape was lined with ivory satin, visible as she moved, and her hair was gathered into a black, sequin-encrusted snood. "But I can't find my pearl drop earrings anywhere. Have you seen them?"

"No," said Margaux. "Not since the last time you wore them."

"I just can't imagine where they could have gone. I always keep them in the jewelry box right on top of my bureau."

"I hope you find them." Eleanor's hand was on the doorknob.

Patricia checked her reflection in the mirror above the demilune table. "I suppose I could do without them. But I'd still like to know where they are."

"So would I," said Wynn Bellamy as he walked in adjusting his bow tie. "They were very expensive."

Patricia said nothing, but Eleanor saw her lips compress into a thin, tight line. "I'll look for them when we get home."

"No, you should find them now."

"But I've looked everywhere."

"Maybe Bridget would know."

"She's been in the kitchen all day."

"What about you, Miss Moss?"

"What about me?" Why was he bringing her into this?

"Have you seen my wife's earrings today?"

"Not today or any other day."

"Are you sure?"

"Wynn, what's wrong with you? She said she hasn't seen them. Now really, let's go. It's getting late."

"Miss Moss, I'd like you to show me the contents of your purse—"

"Have you gone mad?" Patricia said. "She's not going to do any such thing. I don't understand why you're making such a scene—"

"It's all right," Eleanor said, though of course it wasn't. "I'd be more than willing to show you." She walked over to where he stood and snapped open the clasp of the black leather purse. She felt revolted as he pawed through its contents—leather wallet, comb, lipstick, compact, keys. "There," she said. "No earrings."

"Daddy, I don't know why you're treating Eleanor like this. She'd never, ever take anything from Mother," Margaux pleaded.

But Mr. Bellamy just said, "Your pockets. Could you please turn them inside out?"

"No, Eleanor. Don't." Patricia walked swiftly to the door. "Wynn, I am leaving right now, with or without you. I won't stand here while you insult Eleanor—"

"No, really, it's fine." Eleanor set her purse down on the table under the mirror and reached into her pockets. "Here, you can see for yourself—" From the left pocket, she pulled out a subway token, and from the right, a pair of pearl-and-diamond earrings.

It was past one a.m. when they left the party and began their walk home. Wynn seemed inebriated and was humming softly to himself, whereas despite the many drinks she'd consumed, Patricia felt disappointingly sober. The anger she'd been able to fend off all evening sifted back down over her like ash.

"Why did you plant my earrings in Eleanor's pocket?"

"Excuse me?" He stopped, a few feet from the awning to their building. Eamon, the night doorman, nodded in their direction

"Stop pretending. You put my earrings in Eleanor's pocket."

"I didn't plant them. She took them, plain and simple. I told you she was trouble—"

"That is the most preposterous thing I have ever heard." She swept past him and into their building. He followed her to the elevator, and they rode up in silence. But once they were back in the apartment, she turned to him again. "I don't believe you."

"Oh, so you believe her—a girl you picked up in the street—"

"That's hardly what happened, and anyway, she's done wonders for Margaux, you *know* that, and yet you're doing your best to undermine her at every turn. First you go barging into the cottage, drunk no doubt, trying to make a pass at her and when you fail—and I find out—you decide you'll do anything you can to discredit her, even stooping to something as obvious as to put those earrings in her coat pocket. As if she'd have done that! My God, you're not only a liar and a bully; you're an idiot—"

He was across the foyer in seconds, and his hand shot out, delivering a clean, smart slap to her face. "Never say that to me," he hissed. "Never, do you understand?"

Her own hand flew to her cheek, which was stinging and no doubt red. He'd hit her—he'd actually hit her.

"Why are you shouting?"

Patricia turned to see Margaux, leaning heavily on her walking stick and regarding them in horror.

"Darling, why don't you—" Patricia started.

"Go back to bed," Wynn said sternly. Something in his voice made her obey. Watching her retreat, Patricia moved to follow.

"Come back here," said Wynn.

"I'm through talking to you tonight."

"Come back!"

From the darkness of the hall, she turned to look back at him; he stood there, bulky and massive. "And if I don't? Are you going to hit me again?"

"Tricia, I'm sorry. I didn't mean . . . I never wanted . . . But you were goading me and—"

"I'm going in to see Margaux—God knows what she's thinking— and then I'll go into the guest room. Or you can. We can talk in the morning." And then she left him, standing alone in the light. Again, she felt that flash of anger at Eleanor, irrational as it was, for being the cause of yet another ugly quarrel.

The next morning, Patricia stoked the embers of last night's fury as she dressed. To think he had raised a hand to her, struck her . . . she would leave him. She'd take Margaux and go to Argyle. She finished buttoning her dress and gave her chignon a final pat.

But when she walked into the kitchen, there was Wynn, freshly showered. Margaux was seated very close to him, the *Times* spread out between them, and they were doing the crossword puzzle. He didn't look up when she came in, but Margaux did. "Good morning, Mother." She sounded surprisingly cheerful; did she remember the ugly scene from the night before? If so, it didn't show. "Do you want a cinnamon bun?"

"Where did those come from?" Patricia knew Bridget hadn't baked them.

"Daddy went out early and brought back a bagful. I've already had one, and they're delicious."

"That was very nice of you," Patricia said uncertainly.

Wynn looked up at her then, an apology written all over his cleanly shaved face. "I know they're Margaux's favorite," he said. "And I just want to make my girl happy."

He was trying, Patricia realized. Trying very hard. If he was making an effort, maybe she needed to make more of an effort too. "Let me try one of those buns," she said as she sat down. "They're my favorite too."

Eleanor approached the Bellamys' apartment with dread. She waited long enough to be sure Mr. Bellamy would not be home, and gave her name to the doorman, aware that this was the last time she would need to use the false moniker. Margaux was at the door to greet her with a hug. "Eleanor, I'm so sorry about what Daddy said. Mother and I know you would never have taken those earrings." Eleanor had no reply. Of course there was no question of her continuing to work for the Bellamys after what had happened. She was just here to say good-bye to Margaux.

Patricia came into the foyer. "Margaux, darling, I'd like you to go to your room. Eleanor and I need to talk—alone."

"No." Margaux planted her walking stick firmly in front of her.

"Why don't you do what your mother asks? We'll have a chance to talk later," said Eleanor.

"Promise?" Margaux asked.

"Promise," said Eleanor, and followed Patricia into the study. She sat on one of the leather chairs, and Patricia took the other.

"I'm at a loss," Patricia said. "But I do want to apologize for Wynn's behavior last night. He was entirely out of line."

"I don't know why he's so dead set against me." Eleanor chose her words carefully. "I only know that he is—and that I can't work here anymore."

"I understand," Patricia said. "It will be hard for Margaux."

"For me too. I'll miss working with her. I think you know how close we've become. But she's ready for the next step now."

"And if she won't agree to Oakwood?"

"If I'm not here, she will. It would be best for her. Really."

"I hope you're right."

"There's one more thing . . . I'd like to be able to stay in touch with Margaux. With your permission, of course."

"Of course I want you to be in touch. But right now it may be . . . problematic. I want to give Wynn a chance to settle down . . ."

"I see." Patricia was going to control her access to Margaux, and Eleanor would have to accept that. She stood up.

Patricia got to her feet as well. "I'll write you a check," she said. She went to fetch the checkbook. Margaux slipped into the study as soon as she'd gone.

"You didn't go to your room," Eleanor said.

"No," said Margaux. "You're leaving *me*."

"Don't think of it that way. I'll always care for you. Always. And we'll be able to be in touch again. Just not . . . now."

"What am I going to do without you?" Tears had formed in Margaux's eyes.

"I told your mother about a boarding school upstate."

"Boarding school? I won't go!"

"All the students have had polio. You won't feel out of place."

"I still don't want to go."

"Will you try it? For me?"

Patricia reentered the room holding a check in her hand. "Margaux, I thought you were in your room."

"We were talking about Oakwood," Eleanor said. "She's willing to give it a try. Isn't that right, Margaux?"

Margaux muttered, "Maybe. All right. If you want me to."

"I do," Eleanor said. "Because I think it's exactly the kind of place where you should be."

Margaux didn't answer, but clomped angrily out of the study.

After she had gone, Patricia said, "I'll telephone the school today." Then she handed Eleanor the check.

Eleanor looked at the sum Patricia had filled in. "This isn't right," she said. "You've given me too much money."

"Consider it severance," Patricia said.

ONCE she was back out in the chilly morning, Eleanor had to figure out what to do with her day. She felt exiled and furious—all because of Wynn Bellamy. After several minutes of indecision, she realized she was close to the Metropolitan Museum of Art, so she spent a tranquil hour looking at Etruscan statues. But even then it was only past noon; she couldn't show up at home until late in the afternoon. She thought again about the luxury of having her own apartment and the freedom it would grant her.

Maybe she could get in to see Rita Burns again. Yes, that was a good idea. She'd even save the nickel and walk downtown to the Chrysler Building.

The office was as crowded as Eleanor remembered, but she took a seat in the waiting room and stayed until it emptied out. It was five o'clock by the time she was face-to-face with Rita again.

"I remember you," Rita said. "But we didn't place you. What did you end up doing?"

"I found a position as a private tutor, but now it's ended."

"Can you get me a reference if I need it?"

Eleanor thought of Patricia. "Yes," she said. "I can."

"All right then. I'll be in touch if something comes up. Or you can stop by to check."

The next morning at breakfast, she told Irina she was no longer employed by the Bellamys.

"I thought you loved the job, or at least the girl. What happened?"

Eleanor was prepared. "They decided to send her to boarding school. She was ready."

"Just like that!" Irina exclaimed. "They didn't give you much notice, did they? I told you their kind were no good."

"She gave me a generous severance payment," Eleanor said.

"That's the least she could have done." Irina drained her coffee and stood. "Now what? You won't find another teaching job, and I won't have you helping me in the store. You'd be wasting your talents."

"I'll find something," Eleanor said.

"I hope so." Irina turned to the sink to rinse out the cup. "This is the second time you've left a job without finding another first."

In early December, Ruth called to say her cousin's husband worked at Macy's in Herald Square, and there was a position in the small appliances. "He'd hire you in a minute," Ruth said. Eleanor said no. But a week later, she decided she'd give it a try. Before she called Ruth, she would stop by Rita's office.

She settled herself in the waiting area of Rita's office and picked up a magazine. But her name was called immediately. "Are you sure?" she asked the receptionist. "I don't have an appointment, and she usually sees me late in the day."

"She told me to tell her when you showed up," said the receptionist. "I'm supposed to send you right in."

Eleanor smoothed her hair. She was sorry she hadn't had time to reapply her lipstick.

"I've been waiting for you," Rita Burns said before she even sat down. "I think I found you the perfect job."

"I'm all ears," said Eleanor.

THE next morning, Eleanor took the subway downtown to Greenwich Village, another neighborhood with which she was almost entirely unfamiliar. Her breath made little white puffs as she walked past Italian butcher shops and bakeries, as well as several intriguing little bars and cafes. It occurred to her that Tom lived somewhere down here. He'd probably walked these streets. A spike of pain went through her—best not to think of him now but to focus on the interview.

After a bit of backtracking, she finally found her way to the office of Zephyr Press, on Carmine Street. Up two flights of stairs, she walked into an open loftlike space in which papers, books, and file folders covered all available surfaces. Although she couldn't see anyone, she heard a voice call out, "Are you the girl Rita was raving about? Come on over and let's have a look at you."

Eleanor made her way through the towers of books that stood between her and the voice. When she extended her hand, a woman who looked to be in her thirties reached out to shake it. "Adriana Giacchino," she said. "And you're Eleanor Moss?"

"That's right." So Rita had used that name; well, she wasn't going to dispute it now.

"Sit down," Adriana instructed. "That is, if you can find a place. And if you can't, just make one." She had severe black bangs and bright red harlequin glasses that matched her red lips.

Eleanor moved some papers on the nearest chair to the floor.

"So tell me about yourself," Adriana instructed. "Rita says you went to Vassar. I did too—class of '37."

"I was class of '43," Eleanor said. "I majored in English."

"Did you have Professor Westinhall for Chaucer?"

"I did," said Eleanor. "She was . . . ferocious."

"So she was!" said Adriana. "I wonder if she's still there."

The interview grew even less formal as it went on. In fact, Eleanor was having such a pleasant time comparing notes on other professors, dorms, and their favorite desserts at Alumnae House that she was surprised when Adriana stood up and said, "Well, Moss, Rita was right. You're hired. You can start right now if you like."

"I am?" said Eleanor. "I can?"

"Sure, why not? You can see I need help. It's been like a three-ring circus around here." And, as if to underscore what she'd said, not one but two phone lines rang simultaneously.

Eleanor reached to answer one of them as Adriana went for the other. "Good afternoon, Zephyr Press," she said. "Give me a moment and I'll check." She put her hand over the receiver and said softly, "Ian Marshall for you."

"Heaven forfend!" Adriana mouthed as the caller on her line talked into the phone. "Tell him I'm not here."

"I'm sorry, she's stepped out," Eleanor said smoothly. "May I take a message?"

AT ZEPHYR, Eleanor typed, filed, opened mail, answered the telephone, and sifted through the unending stream of novels, stories, essays, and poems that poured in over the transom. She liked this part of the job best of all, and brought home manuscripts to read at night, when the workday was done. On the few occasions she did spot something of real merit in the avalanche of unsolicited manuscripts, she brought it to the attention of her new boss. "Good work, Moss," Adriana would say. "Keep it up."

The job was fulfilling, and Eleanor was grateful to Rita Burns for leading her to it. She did miss teaching, though. And she especially missed Margaux. But when she called Patricia to ask if she might write or call Margaux at Oakwood, Patricia said, "Let her get settled in. She needs time to adjust before she hears from you."

Soon the streets of Greenwich Village became more familiar to her, and as she walked them—easily now, and with a growing sense of ownership—she thought of Tom and wondered if she'd ever run into him down here. She knew the number of his apartment building, and she could have looked up his phone number in the telephone book or written to him. But she had her pride. He knew where he could find her.

EVER since the night when he'd slapped her, Wynn had been nothing but meek and contrite. He'd moved, by unspoken agreement, into the guest room, though he continued to take his meals with her. They spoke to each other with elaborate courtesy and formality, their conversations littered with phrases like "Could I trouble you" and "Would you please."

One evening when dinner was over, she declined dessert. "I'm awfully tired," she said. "I'm going to bed."

"Good night." He looked at her with the abject expression of a dog just scolded for chewing the master's slippers.

Patricia escaped to the privacy of the bedroom, where she undressed and slipped under the covers. She was just about to turn out the light when she heard a light tapping on the door.

"Come in," she called, and Wynn stepped into the room. It was only when he was standing there that she noticed how much weight he'd lost; the robe seemed to billow around his body.

"May I sit down?" He walked toward the bed, their bed, but instead of sitting on it, he chose the pale blue slipper chair nearby.

"Is anything the matter?"

"Yes," he said. "There is. I don't like the way we're living. Sleeping in separate rooms. Acting like acquaintances. I'm lonely, Tricia. I miss you. I miss *us*."

Despite everything, this admission touched her, yet she had no adequate response. The "us" Wynn spoke of seemed so far in the past. Too much had gotten in the way.

"Is this how it's going to be from now on?"

"I don't know," she said. She gestured beside her on the bed. "Come here. We can talk in the dark. It'll be easier that way." She switched off the light.

He sank into the space beside her. "It's her, you know. That girl. Everything was fine until she showed up."

"Everything was not fine. Our daughter was suffering. Eleanor helped her. Why did you want to drive her away?"

"I know she was good with Margaux," he said. "But hadn't her time with Margaux come to an end? Margaux couldn't stay holed up here forever. She had to start living again."

"You have a point." And it was one Eleanor had made as well. "But even so, why put those earrings in her pocket . . ."

He was silent for a moment, and then he began to cry. "Don't," she said gently. "Please don't." Her arms went around him instinctively, and he sought her throat, and then her breasts.

"No." She put her hands on his chest to stop him. "Not now." She couldn't let this happen; it was . . . unendurable.

"All right." He moved away. "Not now. But . . . when?"

"Don't make so much of it," she said. "I'm just tired, that's all."

He put a hand to her cheek—the same cheek he'd slapped. "Do you think it's too late for us to start over? I want to leave New York. I hate my job. I've hated it for years." He took his hand away. Patricia was relieved.

"I know you have."

"We don't really need the money either. Especially if we lived somewhere less expensive. Remember Uncle Walter's house?"

"Wynn, I don't want to live in Rochester," she said quietly. Rochester was so . . . provincial. And she knew no one up there.

"We'd be closer to Margaux," he continued as if she had not spoken. "It could be wonderful, finding a simpler way of life. I could devote myself to you, Trish. To you, and only you."

"Did you hear me?" she said. "I don't want to live upstate." Her tone was sharp, but she had to stay strong or else she'd succumb, and in so doing, lose herself for good.

"I just thought . . ."

"I know what you thought. And it can't be."

"What can't be?"

"Us," she said. "At least not the us we were—before." Patricia got up. "I'm not asking for a divorce." Divorce to her meant failure and unending shame. "But I won't share your bed ever again. Do you understand? Our private lives are going to be separate."

When he remained motionless, Patricia leaned over and touched his shoulder. "It's time for you to go back to your room." Because this room was hers, and hers alone.

Chapter 10

EARLY IN FEBRUARY, Eleanor received another note from Tom: *Missing you.* She ripped it up and burst into tears. How, after all these months, could he think that was enough? But she hadn't ripped up the envelope, and she checked the postmark. New York City. So he was here. She couldn't stop the swoop of her heart, though it made her angry that he still had that power over her.

The following Saturday, Eleanor went to the shop to help her mother and spent the morning attaching small red tickets to all the hats earmarked for Irina's big winter sale. When she'd finished, she took a break and went upstairs for a cup of tea. The phone rang, and it was Tom. "Why are you calling me now?" she asked.

"Because I miss you. Really. I understand if you don't believe me, though—I acted like a heel."

"I don't know what to believe." Despite her hurt and her anger, the words were a balm.

"Look, we should talk in person. Can I see you, Eleanor?" She thought about putting the phone down. Instead, the next night, she told her mother she was going to an engagement party for Ruth and that she'd be home late. Then she went downtown to meet him, walking along streets that had by now become familiar. She was even familiar with the place he'd suggested, Caffè Luigi, and when she came to it, she paused in front of the big picture window. And there was Tom. He didn't see her, so she was free to gaze at the fine blond hair and the aquiline cast of his profile. He was drinking from a tiny white cup and still wore his coat, though his scarf was draped over the empty chair—the chair that would be hers as soon as she crossed the threshold to join him.

Only she didn't. She stood outside in the cold, watching as he glanced toward the door—she stepped back so he couldn't see her—then looked at his watch. The longer she stood there, the more impossible it seemed for her to move. There was a knotted piece of her heart that wanted to hurt him as she'd been hurt. *Let him see what it's like to wait and wonder. Let him suffer too.*

Finally, Tom took his scarf and got up, leaving some money next to the empty cup on the table. As he emerged from the cafe, she hid in a doorway. He began to walk, his long strides making it hard for her to follow, but she felt pulled along in his wake.

He walked quickly, hands in his pockets, until he came to Jane Street. Then all of a sudden he whirled around and, with his long stride, doubled back so he was right in front of her. "Why are you following me—" He stopped. "Eleanor! I waited and waited—"

"I know," she said. "I was there. I saw you inside."

"So then why didn't you come in?"

"Because I didn't want to," she said.

"But you followed me." He stepped closer, as if to embrace her, but she stepped back. "It's good to see you," he said.

She nodded, but didn't know what her nod meant. That it was good to see her? Or that it was good to see him? "I live here," he said. "Please come up. We can talk in my apartment."

Should she go up with him? His key was in his hand, the same hand that had fed her that first morsel of lobster, that had touched her so deftly in so many places. "All right," she said. He unlocked the front door—no doorman for him—and let her walk in first. There was no elevator either, and they took the stairs to the second floor. Then he was ushering her in, taking her coat and hat, inviting her to sit down. "I'll be right back." She sank into a worn though elegant sofa, covered in a plum-colored velvet. The rugs were beautifully patterned but fraying and worn too.

Tom disappeared into the kitchen to make drinks, and Eleanor looked around. A carved wooden mantel but no actual fireplace. Several mismatched candlesticks lined the top of it, their white tapers in various states of molten decay. A mirror with an ornate gilt frame hung above the candlesticks. The walls were covered with paintings, drawings, and even a few photographs. More framed artwork was propped on the floor, around the perimeter of the room, sometimes two and three deep.

Tom returned with two Manhattans and joined her on the sofa. "Our drink," he said, handing her a glass. "Remember?"

Eleanor took a tiny sip. *Our drink.* There was no *our* anything. "Why did you disappear?" she said.

"You think I behaved pretty badly," he said.

"No," she replied. "I think you behaved terribly."

"I deserved that."

"What was I supposed to think? After that night we spent—"

"A night I've thought about and relived a hundred times."

"Then why did you disappear? Not once, but twice."

"I just felt our being together was . . . too complicated."

"Well, maybe it is."

"But not because of Patricia or Wynn. It was you—you scared me, Eleanor."

"*I* scared *you?*" She sat up. "Why? Because I'm . . . Jewish?"

"No, that has nothing to do with it. It was because I felt like I was falling in love with you."

Falling in love with her! "Were you planning on telling me?"

"I didn't know," he said. "I just knew I had to see you again. That's why I called you, asked you to meet me—"

"That is about the craziest thing I've ever heard," she said.

Instead of answering, he leaned over and kissed her.

Had she thought she was over him? Well, she was wrong. He continued to kiss her, and she gave herself over to it.

"I've missed you too," she said when he finally lifted his face from hers. "Even though I hated you sometimes."

"I deserve for you to hate me. Especially after what happened with Wynn."

"What are you talking about?" She moved away.

"I had a call from Margaux. She was at that school . . . What's the name of it?"

"Oakwood."

"Oakwood, right. She told me some wild story about Wynn's having planted a pair of earrings in your pocket."

"He did, and I left because of it." But she was relieved he didn't know about that night in the cottage. "I might have told you—if you'd been around."

"I was an idiot," he said. "Can you forgive me?"

"I don't know yet," she said.

He leaned over to put his arms around her, and she stiffened. She'd thought that if she didn't talk about that night Wynn Bellamy barged into the cottage, she could make herself believe it hadn't happened. Not true. He was here in this room with them. The realization made her cry.

"Can't you tell me what's wrong?" Tom asked.

"Something happened last summer. Something I didn't want to tell you, ever. But it's no good—I have to tell." She blotted her face, blew her nose, and began to speak.

"That son of a bitch!" Tom exclaimed when she finished. "He didn't . . . I mean you weren't—"

"Raped?" she said. "No."

"Why did you wait so long to tell me?"

"He was your sister's husband. I knew you'd be loyal to her. And I was afraid you'd think I encouraged him in some way."

"I would never think that," he said. "I know you too well." His face changed. "And I know *him*. Or I thought I did. He was always a little too free with his hands, but I never dreamed he'd cross the line. I'm going to have it out with him—"

"You're not going to hit him, are you?"

"Hit him? No, I wouldn't stoop to his level. I just want him to know how contemptible I find him."

"I thought it was all behind me. I was wrong."

"I'm sorry," he said. "So sorry."

He began to stroke her hair, and she wanted to give in to the feeling it stirred. Yet before she could succumb, there was something else she had to say. "Wynn took something from me that I can never have back. I don't feel the same anymore."

"He did. You are different now. That trusting quality you had—it's gone. I know it was bound to go for one reason or another. I'm just sorry it was because of my brother-in-law."

"I am less trusting. I don't even trust you." She had to look away then.

Tom put a finger under her chin to turn her face back to his. "Last summer when I told you I wouldn't let you become my mistress, it was because I knew that no matter what you said, deep down you wanted to save that part of yourself for a husband, Eleanor. To have slept with you then would have been selfish. I still want to sleep with you—I want that very much. But I'm not going to pressure you. I have to know that you want it as much as I do. And that you'll be able to wake up tomorrow with no regrets."

No regrets? How could she know that? As they continued to look at each other, she realized that she wanted to have this night with him. She leaned into him, and this time, she initiated the kiss. She saw his eyes widen a little in surprise. Then they closed as he pulled her even more tightly to him.

AFTERWARD, Eleanor lay next to Tom as he slept.

She had done it, crossed the threshold, surrendered, or rather, put aside, her virginity. Her regrets were not about what she'd done, but how she felt when she had done it. Again she traveled back to the time last summer when she'd gone up to Tom's room, and wished she could graft that night on to this one. It was like she'd told Tom—she'd already lost her innocence, and she mourned that more than anything else.

Eleanor got up quietly, feeling around for the clothes that had been tossed to the floor. Tom stirred and rolled over on his side. "Do you have to go?" he said.

"I do. My mother expects me."

"You'll come back? Soon?"

"Very soon."

"Will you be all right getting home?"

"I'll be fine. It's not even that late."

Settled in the backseat of a taxi, Eleanor looked out at the city as the Checker cab made its way uptown. The somnolent streets of the Village gave way to the liveliness of Times Square, where people were streaming out of theaters and movie houses. She wondered whether her mother would still be up and began to come up with some details about the party. The need to lie to Irina was about to end, though. She was going to get a place of her own. What had been a wish, a dream, became in this moment a certainty. She couldn't live amid the trappings of her childhood any longer; she had moved too far beyond their confines.

Three days later, Eleanor signed a lease for a small apartment on Barrow Street, not far from her office. A four-flight walk-up, it had a front room that faced the street and a back room that looked out over a tiny garden. Between the two rooms was a combination kitchen and bathroom, with a hinged-over tub that served as a counter when not in use, a hot plate, and an old-fashioned icebox. The toilet was just outside the apartment, behind a separate door.

She told her mother two days before she was set to move in, over cups of tea and the new issue of *Vogue*. "You're leaving? Why?" Irina said. "Are you so unhappy with me?"

"Not with you, Mother. But it's true that living here isn't making me happy. I need to be on my own."

"What kind of girl lives alone, without parents or a husband?"

"The kind of girl I am," said Eleanor.

"If your father were here, you wouldn't be doing this. You always loved him better."

Eleanor was stunned. This was in fact true—she had always felt closer to her father than she had to her mother—but how to reply to this without hurting Irina? "It's not that I loved him better. It was easier with him, that's all. He didn't worry so much."

"That's because he left the worrying to me," Irina said bitterly.

"You sound . . . angry about that," Eleanor ventured.

"What difference does it make now anyway?" Irina said. "Your father is dead. And you're abandoning me."

"Not abandoning you," said Eleanor. "Finding me. I want to live on my own, and I think I would want that even if Papa were here."

"I don't understand you," her mother said. "I left your grandmother to marry your father. That's what girls did."

"That was a long time ago," said Eleanor. "Things are different now. And you helped make me different. You sent me to college."

"I did even though it broke my heart. But I knew you were a smart girl. I wanted you to have chances that I didn't have."

"You see? You understand better than you think. You expected something else from me. And I expect something from myself too."

"What is that thing?" Irina no longer sounded angry. She sounded like she truly wanted to know.

"I can't say exactly," Eleanor said. "But living on my own is the only way I'm going to find out."

Irina began clearing the table. "Maybe you're right," she said finally.

There were tears on her face, and Eleanor crossed the room to hug her. "I love you," she said. "And I'll come back to see you. I'm only going to be a subway ride away."

"As often as you like." Irina wiped her eyes. "I'll be here."

PATRICIA walked quickly past the wrought iron gate, the row of painted ornamental jockeys, and through the doors of Jack & Charlie's 21 Club. During Prohibition, 21 had been a speakeasy. She'd heard all about the police raids and the clever way the owners had outwitted discovery. As soon as the raid started, a system of levers tipped the bar shelves, sweeping all the liquor bottles through a chute and into the city's sewers. Knowing this gave the place an added cachet in Patricia's eyes. Tom was less enchanted by it, but he'd still suggested that they meet here. Why?

"Good afternoon, Mrs. Bellamy," said Clyde, the maître d'. "Your table is in the Remington Room. Right this way."

When she got to the table, she saw Tom was already seated and waiting for her. Tom on time? That never happened.

"Tricia," he said, rising from the table to kiss her. "You're looking especially ravishing today."

Patricia knew her new celadon-colored suit was flattering, but he was going overboard. "Glad you approve." She sat down, and Tom ordered martinis while she perused the menu, settling on the Swedish herring and then the guinea hen.

"So why did you suggest meeting here?" she asked as soon as the drinks arrived.

"What do you mean? You love this place."

"But you don't, which makes me think you're up to something."

"You think I'm so devious?"

She swatted him with her napkin. "Come on, out with it."

"Out with what?"

"Oh, I don't know." She pretended to study the place setting on the table. "Maybe something about Eleanor?"

"I'm seeing her now. What else do you need to know?"

"The last time we talked about her, you said you were worried you might be falling in love."

Their appetizers were placed on the table, and Tom took a forkful of caviar. "I'm not worried about that anymore."

"Why not?"

"Now I know I'm in love with her. In fact, I'm going to ask her to marry me."

"Marry you! My God, Tom, are you out of your mind?"

"Not at all. Besides, she doesn't even work for you anymore, so I don't see why you have anything to say about it. I love her and—"

"That's not what I'm talking about and you know it. This isn't about love. This is about the rest of your life. Even you have to admit . . . she's . . . just not from our set."

"And what defines our set, Tricia? Are we really that bigoted, narrow-minded, incapable of seeing beyond a bunch of petty and meaningless distinctions—"

"They're not so meaningless. Have you thought about what your future would be like with Eleanor as your wife? The doors that would close, politely but firmly, in your face?"

"Maybe they're doors I don't give a damn about going through," he said a little too loudly.

"Shh," she said. "Would you please lower your voice?"

"Anyway, this is all theoretical at the moment. She hasn't said yes. Or at least not yet."

"Oh, she will," Patricia said darkly. "She's been working that angle from the very beginning."

"Is that really what you think of her? The heaven-sent girl who single-handedly saved Margaux?"

"Well, maybe not from the start but—"

"But nothing. You've been listening to Wynn for too long. Because that kind of talk isn't you. It never was."

Chastened, Patricia said nothing.

The main courses arrived.

"So when will you pop the question?"

"As soon as the moment's right."

"I can just imagine how Wynn's going to take it . . ." Patricia hadn't intended to say this aloud; the words just slipped out.

Tom looked up from his pheasant. "It's none of his business. Far from it. She told me all about that pitiful farce with the earrings."

"He was being ridiculous and I said so."

"Ridiculous? I think it was a bit more than that, don't you? I mean, what he did cost Eleanor her job."

"I didn't fire her. She was the one who chose to leave."

"Can you blame her? Wynn was out to get her."

"Maybe it was time for her to go. Margaux needed to get out of the house and start socializing with people her own age. Eleanor even said so. She's the one who told me about Oakwood, and she even telephoned the headmaster about Margaux."

"That sounds like her," he said. And smiled in a besotted way that Patricia found especially irritating.

"How's your pheasant?"

"A little dry actually. Doesn't Henryka do pheasant? I remember it was delicious. Ask her to make it again when I'm over."

"You haven't heard? Henryka's left too. She's working for a family on East Seventy-Second Street." Patricia could not meet his eyes as she disclosed this still painful bit of news.

"Henryka? Gone? But she's been with you forever. And with Mother before that. Why in the world did you let her go?"

"I didn't." And then, to her distress, she began to cry, right there in the middle of the 21 Club.

"Tricia." Tom reached out to take her hand. "What is it?"

The whole story came tumbling out. "She wouldn't say what Wynn had done to Eleanor. But whatever it was, it required a trip to Dr. Parker in the middle of the night."

"I know. Eleanor told me everything."

"She did? When?"

"Just recently. If he wasn't your husband and Margaux's father, I'd have gone after him myself . . ." He pushed his plate away. "I don't know about you, but I'm ready for dessert."

It felt better to have unburdened herself, really it did, and over the plate of profiteroles *au chocolat* that they shared, she also told him about the separate rooms and her growing disgust for Wynn.

"Why stay?" Tom asked. "Look at the kind of man he is. He went after Eleanor. And Henryka, for God's sake."

"Because I don't want to be divorced," she said. "Divorced women are outcasts. Social lepers . . . I'm not sure I could bear it."

"What about your friend Audrey?"

"It ended up all right. But at first, people shunned her."

"And so you'd live with a man who, in your words, disgusts you, a man who bullies and takes advantage of the women in his employ, because you're worried about a few invitations?"

"Think of what it would do to Margaux."

"What exactly? It would let her see that her mother had some principles and was more committed to living honestly, and with a chance at happiness instead of—"

"You may be my older brother, but in some ways, you're so young. The world isn't like you make it out to be."

"That's where you're wrong," he said. "*You* make the world you want to live in. Not the other way around."

Tom had always made his own rules and paid a price for doing so; it was a price she'd never wanted to pay.

Tom reached for the check when it came, and hugged her tightly on the sidewalk as they were about to part. "I assume you're sleeping with her," she said.

"I don't kiss and tell, sister dear." He hailed a taxi.

"Since when?"

But he only smiled and waved as she got in and the cabbie took off. Patricia waved back and settled into the seat. They had invited Audrey, her husband Harold, and another couple for dinner this evening, and she wanted to get home as soon as possible. Although it had been a relief to talk to Tom, their conversation had also stirred up disquieting feelings about Wynn. And about Eleanor. It was bad enough that Wynn had behaved so stupidly around the girl. And that her daughter kept pestering her about Eleanor.

"Why can't I see her?" Margaux had asked during their last telephone call. "Or at least write to her?"

"I just don't think it's wise," Patricia said.

"But you haven't given me one good reason. If you tell me why you don't want me to see her, maybe I could understand . . ."

"I know she was a wonderful influence on you." Patricia chose her words carefully. "And that she helped bring you out of your shell. But her role in your life ought to diminish now, not increase. You need to find other confidantes, like your friends. Or me."

Patricia had surprised herself with that. It made her sound, well, jealous of Eleanor. Which perhaps was true.

"I don't believe you," Margaux said. "I think you don't want her to be my friend because she lives on Second Avenue and she's a Jew. You and Daddy—you don't have any friends who are Jews, do you? So you don't want me to have any either."

Patricia had gone silent. Her daughter was growing more astute and more liable to lay bare motivations that Patricia would rather keep under wraps, even—no, especially—from herself.

"You need to trust that your father and I know what's best for you, and you need to listen to us."

After that, she found her feelings toward Eleanor had calcified and hardened: her name became a reminder of complexities Patricia didn't want to face. And just today, barely an hour ago, she'd learned that Eleanor might actually become her sister-in-law. The news bothered her a great deal. And it would bother Wynn too—there was no doubt about that.

To her relief, Wynn was on his absolute best behavior that evening. He told jokes, poured cocktails, flattered the men, lavished compliments on the women. Although he outpaced them all in the number of drinks he consumed—Patricia was keeping an eye on that—he seemed perfectly in control. She relaxed and began to enjoy herself. So when Audrey excused herself to "powder her nose" and Wynn stepped out of the room a moment later, Patricia didn't even think to connect the two departures.

It was only when Audrey returned looking a bit flustered that Patricia's inner alarm began a quiet but insistent bleating.

She took Audrey into the foyer, on the pretext of showing her the new chandelier she'd just had installed. "Are you all right?"

"Yes, I just need to fix my face."

Patricia saw that her lipstick was smeared. But Audrey had just gone to the bathroom, and she was holding her small evening bag. Why hadn't she reapplied her lipstick then?

"Audrey, you can tell me. You seem . . . off."

Audrey wouldn't meet her eyes at first, and when she did, her expression was pitying. "It's nothing, really. I mean, we're all used to Wynn's wandering hands; only he used to be more . . . playful about it. Now he's just getting, well, rather boorish."

Patricia was speechless. They were joined by the rotund, bespectacled, and ever jovial Harold. "Who's being boorish?"

"Oh, just Wynn got a little too familiar, that's all. I don't want to make a scene, and I'm sure he didn't mean anything by it—"

"Didn't mean anything by what?" asked Harold.

Audrey looked from her husband to Patricia, clearly deciding how much to reveal. "Wynn followed me to the bathroom, and when I came out, he tried to kiss me."

No wonder her lipstick was smudged.

"Kiss you!" Harold seemed distinctly less jovial.

"Audrey, I'm so very sorry," Patricia managed to choke out. "He's been drinking, and when he drinks he can get a little—"

"I know how he can get. But he stuck his hand right down my dress too." Audrey gestured to the bodice of her low-cut brocade that exposed a generous swath of cleavage.

"How dare he." Harold's arm went protectively around his wife. "Patricia, you don't have to see us out. And I'm sure you'll understand why we'll never come back here."

Patricia said nothing as Audrey adjusted her shawl and touched her hands to her hair, trying to envision how she could patch together the ruins of the evening. But Wynn intercepted them at the door. "Leaving so soon?" He let his hand rest lightly on Audrey's shoulder, and the disdain with which she shook him off could not have been lost on Joan and Cameron Barlow, whose seats in the dining room gave them a full view of the foyer.

"Please keep your hands off my wife," Harold said coldly.

"Excuse me, old man." Wynn retreated. "No offense meant at all. I just thought we were among friends here."

"We thought so too. But you haven't behaved like a friend. Or a gentleman. You're lucky I'm not a violent sort or I'd punch you."

Wynn's expression looked bemused, but his face was now a riot of splotchy red patches.

Harold gave Patricia a quick peck on the cheek before taking Audrey's elbow and ushering her out. Patricia stood at the door for a moment with her back to Cameron and Joan. She couldn't face them; she just couldn't—

"Whose drink can I freshen?" Wynn said loudly. No one said anything. When Patricia finally turned around, she caught the look that passed between the Barlows and within minutes they were saying how it was late and that they needed to be going.

After the Barlows had left, Wynn refilled his own glass and offered to refill hers. Patricia just shook her head. For the last fifteen or so minutes, she'd been trembling with anger, but now that she and Wynn were alone, her anger evaporated and she was left hollow and spent. "Why?" she asked.

"Oh, come on," he said. "If a woman walks around half naked like that, what can she expect?"

"That her host will have the manners and self-control not to go sticking his hand down her dress or his tongue in her mouth."

"Maybe if her host's own wife had a shred of passion for him, he might not have to resort to the charms of strangers."

"Oh, so this is my fault."

"In a way . . . yes." He downed the drink and poured another.

"You embarrassed me tonight. I'll never be able to invite them here again. And don't think they won't tell everyone we know. You'll be banned, and I'll be banned right along with you. I should file for divorce."

"You'd never do that." His voice was mocking. "Never."

"That's what you think. But I may surprise you yet."

He shook his head. "Oh no. We're done with surprising each other." He finished his drink and walked out of the room.

Chapter 11

LIVING ALONE WAS EVERYTHING Eleanor had thought it would be. Every time she turned the key and walked in, she thought, *Mine, mine, mine.* How good that felt. How right.

Ruth acted like Eleanor's decision to live alone was a temporary aberration and that Eleanor would soon assume her designated female roles: fiancée, bride, wife, mother. "Maybe you'll be next," Ruth said. "That Tom sounds like a dreamboat."

"He hasn't asked me to marry him," Eleanor said. "And even if he did, I'm not sure I'd say yes."

"But you've slept with him." Ruth looked down at her hands, where the infinitesimal diamond sparkled on her finger.

"Haven't you slept with Marty?"

"Yes, but that was after he'd proposed."

"So my sleeping with Tom means I have to marry him?" Last summer, Eleanor would have said yes to that question.

"Well, no, but, if you . . ." Ruth looked very uncomfortable.

"Sleep with a man you're not going to marry then you're a tramp?" Eleanor knew that was what Wynn Bellamy thought. And that his incorrect assumption that she was sleeping with Tom meant that she automatically would be available to him too.

"I never said *that*. I only meant that your reputation—" Ruth vainly tried to retrieve the situation.

"It's all right," Eleanor said. "Really it is. Now tell me again about the dress."

Happy to leave the topic behind, Ruth launched into the relative merits of floor versus tea length, taffeta versus moiré.

That evening, Eleanor had a date with Tom. They had dinner at his place and then strolled east, to Fourth Avenue, which was lined with secondhand bookstores. A few were still open, and they wove in and out of the shops. Tom drifted toward the art books and Eleanor toward the poetry, where she found, on a bottom shelf, a small, clothbound first edition of *A Few Figs from Thistles*—poems by Edna St. Vincent Millay. She opened it up.

> *We were very tired, we were very merry—*
> *We had gone back and forth all night on the ferry;*

Tom came up behind her and read over her shoulder. "We should do it," he said.

"Do what?"

"Ride the Staten Island Ferry. That's what inspired the poem."

"Actually I've never been on the Staten Island Ferry."

"And you call yourself a New Yorker?"

"Born and bred." She smiled.

"We have to fix that. Immediately."

"All right," she said, caught up in his sense of adventure.

They took the subway down to the terminal, where they were able to board almost immediately.

"It's such a nice night," said Tom. "Let's go stand outside."

Eleanor followed him up the wide metal stairs that led to the deck. The Manhattan skyline unfurled as the ferry slowly pulled away from the dock. Tom put his arm around Eleanor.

"I have some good news for you," he said. "I rented a gallery space. It's on Hudson Street."

"A gallery!"

"I've been talking about it for years. But you were the gadfly, Eleanor. You pushed me to do it."

"You'll organize shows? Invite people to see them?"

"When I've gotten the place together, yes." He drew her closer. "Happy?"

"Very. You?"

"Happier than I ever thought I could be."

Eleanor pressed her face against his chest; even through the light jacket and shirt, she could feel the steady pulse of his heart.

"Marry me," he said.

"What?"

"You heard me."

She moved out of his embrace, and suddenly the night, which had felt so temperate, went cold. "I don't know what to say." Last summer, she had wished to hear exactly those words. But things had changed. No—she was the one who had changed.

"Say yes."

"Can I think it over?"

"Are you serious? I thought you loved me."

"I do love you." She reached out to touch his face, and he clasped her hand in both of his. "But I've only lived alone for such a little while. And I like it so much. I'm just not ready to give that up and become a wife."

"So you're not saying *no;* you're saying *not now?*"

"Exactly." Relief washed over her. She didn't want to hurt him. Or alienate him. But as the ferry docked with a small jolt, she realized just how much she didn't want to marry him either.

They were mostly silent on the ride back to Manhattan, and when he dropped her off at her apartment, he didn't kiss her good night. Inside, she went straight to her bed, slipped off her shoes, and lay down in the dark. Tom had just asked her to marry him. She ought to have been over the moon. Wasn't this what she'd wanted? Yet she'd turned him down, and she might have been even more surprised than he was. She wasn't the same girl she'd been last summer. That girl was on a straight path: marriage, husband, children. Now she'd changed direction and didn't know where she was going. And even if she did want to get married, she didn't know how she could marry Tom. How would it feel to be living in his world—the clubs, the hotels, the apartment buildings that said no to Jews? No to *her.* He'd say he didn't care. But she cared.

Hours later, the ringing of the telephone roused her from her light, restless sleep. Maybe it was Tom. Oh, if only it was. She hadn't wanted to hurt him; she just—

"Eleanor, Eleanor, is that you?"

It wasn't Tom. The voice was drunk. "Who is this please?"

"Who is this? Why, it's Wynn Bellamy of course!" He chortled.

"Mr. Bellamy!" Eleanor switched on the lamp and looked at the clock: 3:30. "Is everything all right? Has something happened to Margaux? Or to Patricia?"

"Margaux, no, nothing's happened to her. Unless you've been poisoning her against me, just like you poisoned my wife." The chortling turned to a snarl.

"I didn't *poison* Patricia. I just told her what happened—"

"And what happened anyway? Was it so terrible that I asked for a dance? Or a kiss? Was that a reason to make such a fuss—"

"Mr. Bellamy, I don't think—"

"Now my wife despises me, and God only knows what you've told my daughter—"

"I haven't told your daughter anything. But if I ever hear from you again, in any way, shape, or form, I'll tell her. I really will. Maybe she ought to know just what kind of man her father is."

There was a short silence. "Oh no, you wouldn't, you couldn't . . . not my baby girl, no not that . . ."

He trailed off, and Eleanor realized he was crying. She listened and then put the receiver down. After a moment, she lifted it again, and when she heard the dial tone, she placed it off the hook.

THE morning after the ruined dinner party, Bridget was already in the kitchen when Patricia came in. Wynn was sleeping it off in the guest room. The coffee didn't taste nearly as good as Henryka's, but at least Bridget had made oatmeal. Patricia sipped the coffee and took tentative spoonfuls of the hot cereal.

Then she went into the library and dialed Audrey's number. She wasn't calling to talk about the night before. She was calling to get the name of the lawyer who had handled her divorce.

"So it's finally gotten to you?" Audrey asked. "I'll confess I've wondered why you haven't left him before this. But then again, I know it's not easy to go. Look at how long it took me."

"It was hard, wasn't it? Especially in the beginning?"

"Awful. All those people you thought were your friends—pitying you, judging you, ostracizing you."

"And yet you did it."

"Because staying was worse than all that. Much worse."

"That's how I feel. Or I think I do. And it will help to talk it over with a lawyer."

"His name is Theo Prescott, and he's experienced, discreet, and a gentleman. Tell him I told you to call."

Patricia took down the name and number. As they were saying good-bye, Patricia heard a subtle but audible click—someone had picked up the extension in the other room.

"Hello? I'm on the phone."

There was another click. Whoever it was had put the receiver down. Had it been Bridget? Or Wynn? She went in search of her husband and found him.

"You were listening," she said.

"And why shouldn't I? You were talking about me."

"All right then. I don't care if you know. I'm divorcing you, Wynn. You said I wouldn't do it, but you were wrong."

"Go ahead, call the lawyer. But I'll fight you, Tricia. I'll fight you with everything that's in me. And it won't be pretty."

"Are you threatening me?"

"No. I'm just telling you what to expect. You really don't want to do this. Think of Margaux, for God's sake."

"I think of her all the time. And I've decided that maybe it's time she understood what kind of man her father truly is."

Wynn visibly paled. "She's behind all this. It's her fault. She's turned you against me, and she'll do it to Margaux too."

"What are you talking about?"

"Eleanor Moskowitz. That's exactly what she said—that she'd tell Margaux what kind of man I was."

"She said that? When?"

"Last night, not that it matters . . ."

"Last night! You went to see her?"

"No. I telephoned."

"You did? What were you thinking?"

"What was I thinking? That I wanted to get my life back from the she-wolf who devoured it." There were tears in his eyes. "I want things to be the way they were before she came here."

"Can't you see it's too late for that?" But a tiny part of her wished it too.

They stood staring at each other for several seconds, seconds during which Patricia tried to absorb the enormity of what was happening. Then she turned and left the room. She dressed quickly and left the apartment. She'd go to the Colony Club. Once there, she was able to telephone Theo Prescott with privacy, and then she stayed on for lunch.

When she returned home, Bridget was waiting. "Mr. Bellamy, he asked me to give you this." She handed Patricia an envelope.

Patricia opened it. *I'm going to Argyle to sail,* he'd written. *Back Sunday night.* Finding him gone was like an unexpected gift. She gave Bridget the night off and went to 21 by herself, to see how she felt dining alone; she found the experience unfamiliar but not intolerable. Sunday dawned clear and bright, so she skipped church and took a taxi to the Claremont Riding Academy on West Eighty-Ninth Street instead. She hadn't ridden in Central Park in years, but Jester, the dark brown gelding she selected, was sure-footed and even-tempered. It was nearly seven o'clock when she took the horse back; she watched him being walked into his stall, and she wanted to say *Not yet, please, just a little longer.* But she hailed a taxi and rode uptown, pleasantly tired from her exertion.

"There's roses in your cheeks, Mrs. Bellamy," Bridget said when Patricia came through the door. Then she drew herself a bath and afterward had dinner alone, in her robe, which felt both a bit decadent and thoroughly delightful. She dreaded Wynn's return. But the evening wore on, and Wynn didn't appear.

"Were there any messages today, Bridget?" Patricia asked.

"No, ma'am," said Bridget.

So Patricia said good night. She wasn't unduly worried. There had been a couple of times when he'd stayed at the Yale Club after a quarrel. He'd come back. He always did. Fortunately, her day on horseback had worn her out, and she slept soundly.

She was still in bed on Monday morning when the telephone rang. It was Wynn's secretary, Miss Blodget.

"It's after nine thirty, and Mr. Bellamy hasn't come in yet, so I was wondering if he might be home sick," she said.

"No. He was away for the weekend," Patricia said. "He might have been delayed. I'll be sure to have him call you as soon as I hear from him."

"Thank you, Mrs. Bellamy," said Miss Blodget.

She was an older woman, and she'd been with Wynn for several years. Wynn never seemed to keep the young ones around for very long, and suddenly, the reason for that seemed obvious. Why hadn't she seen it before? Patricia got dressed and decided to call the Yale Club. No, Wynn had not checked in there.

Where could he be? Patricia vacillated between concern and irritation. Maybe talking about divorce had hurt him more than she knew. Then it occurred to her that he'd probably gotten drunk and was sleeping it off. Of course that was it—why hadn't she thought of it before? Quickly, she dialed the number of the house in Argyle, but the phone just rang and rang.

At twelve thirty, Bridget asked if Patricia wanted lunch, but Patricia told her she'd eat later. She was upset, angry, and though she'd slept well the night before, she felt utterly drained. Sleep came easily until the loud knocking on the door woke her up. "What is it?" she said crossly.

"Telephone, Mrs. Bellamy," Bridget called through the door.

"Is it my husband?" Patricia's mouth was dry, and her head hurt. So much for a nap improving things. "Or his office?"

"No, ma'am. It's a gentleman calling from Connecticut," said Bridget. "He says it's urgent."

Patricia got up, smoothed her hair, and hurried to the phone.

"Mrs. Bellamy? This is Norville Ledbetter. I'm the chief of police here in Argyle, and I'm calling to—"

"Have you found him?" she interrupted. "I do hope he hasn't caused any trouble."

"Trouble, Mrs. Bellamy? No, I wouldn't say that he's caused trouble—" Ledbetter sounded surprised.

"He's not . . . drunk, is he?"

"No, ma'am. Not drunk. You see . . . well, I'm sorry to say the truth of it is that Mr. Bellamy . . . he's dead."

THE morning after she'd gotten the call from Wynn Bellamy, Eleanor was afraid to replace the telephone receiver. That conversation had so disturbed her that she didn't want to risk hearing his voice again. But she knew she wasn't being practical. And she did want Tom to be able to reach her, so with some hesitation, she gently set it back in the cradle.

Tom didn't call, though. Not Saturday, and not Sunday either. She debated whether to call him and decided against it.

Monday was a hectic day at the office. Adriana was out with the flu, the author whose manuscript was already two weeks overdue called to say that it still wasn't ready, and there was a delay with a shipment of the linen stock used for many of the covers. Eleanor barely had time to go to the ladies' room, much less out to get lunch. And there was certainly no time to think about Tom.

On the way home, she stopped to buy eggs, coffee, and butter and allowed herself to imagine she was married to Tom and doing the marketing for the two of them. From the breakfasts they had shared, she knew he took his coffee with three sugars, that he liked his eggs any way but poached, and that he thought the meal wasn't complete without bacon, sausage, or ham. Although her family had not kept kosher, Eleanor never bought and rarely ate pork. But that was the least of it. How would she feel being married to a man for whom every day was Saturday, who spent over an hour with the newspaper every morning, who could travel on a whim?

It was past six when she reached her building, arms laden with packages, as well as a bunch of red tulips—an indulgence, but the vivid color had called out to her. Eleanor set her bundles down, fished for her key, and went upstairs. When everything was put away, she heated up a slice of meat loaf that she had left over from the weekend, and while she ate, she read a manuscript.

A loud buzz interrupted her reading. Maybe it was Tom. But he would have phoned first. She went down the stairs to see who it might be. To her utter surprise, Margaux was standing there, looking wild-eyed and distraught.

"What's the matter? Are you all right?" Eleanor ushered her in and then glanced at the narrow stairwell, which was going to be hard to navigate with the walking stick.

Following her gaze, Margaux said, "Don't worry, I can make it up. I'll just go slowly."

Eleanor went first and when they were upstairs and in her apartment asked, "How did you find me?"

"I called directory assistance."

"And your mother—does she know you're here?"

"No, I snuck out."

"She's not going to like that."

"I don't care!" And then she pressed her face to her hands and began to weep.

"Margaux, what's wrong?"

"Daddy—my father . . . he's dead. Dead!"

"What are you talking about?"

"Just what I said. He went sailing by himself. His boat capsized, and he drowned. Mother said he was drunk."

"She told you that?"

"No. But I overheard her on the telephone. She drove up to school to tell me and brought me back down here. The funeral is tomorrow—it's at the Church of Heavenly Rest."

"I can't believe it." Eleanor sat back in her chair. Wynn Bellamy had drowned. He'd seemed too powerful, too protected by his wealth for such a thing to have happened. But when he telephoned her in the middle of the night, he hadn't sounded powerful at all. He'd sounded panicked at the thought that she would expose him to his beloved daughter.

"I couldn't either. Mother is acting strangely too. She's barely cried at all." Margaux gave her a probing look. "I know he wasn't nice to you, Eleanor. So maybe you're not sorry about what happened. But I loved him. And he loved me." She began to cry again.

"Of course he did," Eleanor said. And he hadn't wanted to lose his daughter's love. If Eleanor had been kinder during that last conversation, if she hadn't made that threat, would he be alive now? The thought was highly upsetting. She despised the man—she couldn't pretend otherwise. But to feel implicated, in any way at all, in his death, was terrible. Margaux continued to cry and eventually allowed herself to be led to the sink to wash her face.

"I should call your mother. She must be worried."

"No!" Margaux sounded desperate. "Not yet."

Eleanor relented, and Margaux began to talk about her father, one memory unspooling and leading to others: Wynn taking her to the zoo in Central Park, ice skating in Rockefeller Center, and of course, sailing. "Last summer I was nervous about getting back on the boat. But Daddy encouraged me. We had the most wonderful day. I was so happy it didn't even matter that I was a cripple."

"I wish you wouldn't use that word," Eleanor said.

"I don't know why it bothers you. It's just what I am."

"Not to me," Eleanor said. "Never to me."

"To my father, though. He couldn't get used to what had happened to me. I think it did something to him."

"Really?"

"Oh yes. Before I got sick, he was much nicer—to everyone. I think he would have been nicer to you too."

"Perhaps."

"Would you come tomorrow? To the funeral?"

"Why, I don't think . . . I mean—" Why would she attend Wynn Bellamy's funeral? To spit on his grave? The grave she may have helped him into?

The telephone rang, so she was spared having to answer.

"Eleanor, it's Tom. I'm with Patricia, and something terrible has happened. Wynn drowned in a boating accident, and Margaux's disappeared and—"

"I know about the accident," said Eleanor.

"But how—"

"Margaux told me. She's here now. Tell Patricia she's safe."

"With you!" He turned away from the receiver, and she heard

him speaking rapidly to Patricia. Then he said, "Can you put Margaux on?" Eleanor handed the phone over.

"I'm sorry, Mother." She paused. "Yes, I'll stay here. I'll wait for Uncle Tom." She handed the receiver back to Eleanor.

"I'll be there as soon as I can," Tom said.

"Is Patricia all right?"

"I don't know."

Eleanor hung up. Margaux's question was still unanswered. "The funeral . . ." she said. "Your mother wouldn't want me there."

"Why not? She likes you."

"Yes," Eleanor said. "But I've been asking to see you. And every time she says no." There, it was out.

"I've asked her if I could see you too," Margaux said. "Over and over. Maybe it will be different now."

She didn't have to say, *because my father's not here anymore*, because that was something they both understood.

Eleanor switched on the radio while they waited for Tom to arrive, and sometime later, when the buzzer rang, Eleanor got up to let him in. He hugged Margaux and then Eleanor. The last time she'd seen him was the night she'd turned down his proposal. That seemed so long ago, though. Right now, he looked shaken by Wynn's death. "What was he thinking, going out alone like that? He should have known better," Tom said.

Chapter 12

HEAD BOWED, PATRICIA SAT in the first pew of the church, listening to Reverend Everett Sprinchorn eulogize her dead husband. She had been coming to this church since she was a child, and it had hosted several significant events in her life: her marriage, the funerals of her parents, Margaux's christening.

Reverend Sprinchorn had a sonorous voice, and Patricia was soothed by it as he extolled Wynn's virtues—devoted husband and father, his support of various charities, his life as an attorney. The image he painted with his words had nothing to do with the man Patricia had shared a life with in recent years, or the bloated body she'd been asked to identify at the morgue in Greenwich.

After the reverend had finished, a few other people spoke—a cousin, a colleague from the law firm, the Yale friend Wynn had reconnected with at Audrey's wedding last year. The final speaker was Margaux. Patricia watched as her daughter used her stick to ascend the two wooden stairs to the pulpit, taking the hand the reverend extended. She was wearing all black and the add-a-pearl necklace Wynn had started when she was born.

"Wynn Bellamy was different things to different people," she began. "But I was his only daughter, and so I knew him in a way no one else did." She looked drawn, but she did not cry. "He was a good father, and he used to say that I was the best part of him. So maybe there's a part of him that will live on in me. I hope so. I'll miss him for the rest of my life."

There was a murmur from the crowd as Margaux carefully descended the stairs and walked over to join her mother in the pew.

"You did that beautifully." Patricia covered Margaux's hand with her own.

But Margaux withdrew her hand. "Don't pretend you care, Mother. I know you and Daddy argued about something, and that's why he went off on the boat alone. You're probably not even sorry about what happened to him."

Patricia stared ahead, unable to meet her daughter's eyes. How could Margaux say that? The pallbearers lifted the casket and took it down the aisle to the hearse waiting outside. Patricia stood up, ready to walk down that same aisle and stand near the doors, so that the mourners could offer their condolences as they filed out of the church. Margaux and Tom were to accompany her.

They reached the end of the aisle, and Patricia turned to face the people who had begun to walk in her direction. They clasped her hands or embraced her and in muted voices offered their consoling words. She thanked them, returned the pressure of hands or the embrace. Then repeated it with the next person. This went on for a while; Wynn's funeral was well attended, and most of their friends were there, even Audrey and Harold.

When everyone had gone, Tom and Margaux would get into the car that was waiting outside and follow the hearse to the cemetery in Queens. But there was still one more person waiting to speak to her. It was Henryka. "How did you even know?" Patricia asked.

"I hear," Henryka said. "And I so sorry, missus."

"Thank you," Patricia said softly. "Thank you for coming." They hugged awkwardly. Then Patricia noticed that there was someone else standing there—Eleanor Moskowitz.

She stepped back. "You," was the only word she could summon. But it represented the fury, outrage, grief that rose in her throat and choked off all the other words she could have said. All her life, Patricia had done what was expected of her. Hiring Eleanor had been one of her very few acts of rebellion, a risk she'd taken for her daughter's sake. But where had it gotten her? To this bitter moment, filled with sorrow, reeking with disgrace. "What are you doing here?" she practically hissed.

"I invited her," Margaux said quickly.

"I'm not asking you. I'm asking her. Eleanor."

"It's true," Eleanor said. "Margaux did want me to come, and I thought I should. For her."

"For her," Patricia mocked. "That's so like you, Eleanor. So saintly. So good—good at ruining everything. Because that's what you did—you ruined my life." She had the satisfaction of seeing Eleanor's stricken face.

"Missus, you upset and don't mean what you say," said Henryka.

"That's right." Tom turned to her. "You've had a shock."

"Oh yes I do. I mean every word of it." She turned to Henryka. "It's because of Eleanor that you left, and because of her that my daughter can't abide me. Eleanor came between Wynn and me too. We argued about her constantly. It was after our last fight that he left and ended up going out on the boat and drowning."

"Mother, you have to get hold of yourself."

She ignored her daughter and brother, and spoke to Eleanor alone. "He told me he called you that night. He said you threatened to expose him to Margaux."

"No." Eleanor shook her head. "You're taking what I said out of context."

"What are you talking about?" Margaux looked from Eleanor to her mother. "Expose what?"

"Your father called me in the middle of the night shortly before he died. He'd been drinking, and he accused me of ruining his life. I told him if he ever called me again, I wasn't going to keep his secret anymore and that I would tell you about what he'd done." Eleanor seemed in control of herself, yet the tears running down her face suggested otherwise. "And your mother is right—I shouldn't have said that. But he frightened me, calling to accuse me. As if he was the injured party."

"Did my father . . . hurt you in some way?"

"Don't," Patricia broke in. "Don't you dare tell her."

Eleanor turned to Margaux. "Something did happen between your father and me last summer. But your mother is right. This isn't the time or place to discuss it."

"Stop treating me like a baby," said Margaux. "I deserve to know."

"You do," Eleanor said. "And you will. Only not now."

"I suppose I should thank you for that," Patricia said. "But I won't. You're not welcome here, and I'd like you to go."

"Trish, you need to calm down—" Tom tried to take her arm. "I think you'll regret all of this later."

"That's for me to decide," said Patricia. "Anyway, the car is waiting. Are you coming with me? Or are you going with her?" She threw her arm in Eleanor's direction.

Tom hesitated. "I'm going with you," he said finally. "But not before I apologize to Eleanor for your behavior." He looked at Eleanor, who was looking down. "Even if she won't say she's sorry, I'll say it for her. For all of us really."

Patricia was infuriated—he was patronizing her, as if she couldn't be held accountable for her words. She turned away but not before she was stabbed by the tender, maternal way Henryka's arm encircled Eleanor's shoulders and led her from the church.

The ride to the cemetery seemed fueled not by gasoline, but by Patricia's pure and unadulterated rage. Neither Tom nor Margaux spoke a word to her on the ride, and at the gravesite, they stood together on one side of the gaping hole in the ground while Patricia stood on the other. The mahogany casket was lowered carefully into the earth, and Reverend Sprinchorn delivered a final blessing. Then the gravediggers began their work. It was over.

IN THE weeks that followed, Patricia did not become the social pariah she had expected to be. Wynn's indiscretions may have offended their friends, but his death had wiped the slate clean. Invitations still filled her mailbox. There were bridge games, luncheons, and dinners. She went to some, and declined others. Those she attended were laced with a new solicitude. *How are you holding up?* And *You're so strong, Patricia.* That last was tainted with phony concern, and she hated it. What she did not hate, however, was the dawning realization that Wynn might actually have done her a favor. Divorce could have been long, drawn out, and messy, especially if Wynn had fought her. Instead, his death had cut cleanly through that morass.

In late May, before Margaux's term at school finished, Patricia decided to drive up to Argyle. She hadn't been up to the house since last year, and the thought of spending another summer there, even alone, was unbearable. She would sell the place.

The drive was traffic-snarled, slow, and hot. She put away the few groceries that she'd bought on the way, fell into bed, and did not wake until the sun was streaming through the curtains she'd neglected to close. She went into the kitchen and made herself a cup of coffee. The wicker furniture, the watercolors of lighthouses, fields of poppies, carousels—she cared about none of them. Even her clothes did not inspire any sense of ownership. There was nothing here that she wanted. But what about the books? There weren't many—a few novels, a biography of Vincent van Gogh she'd long meant to read. And the illustrated volume of Shakespeare's sonnets

she'd bought for Eleanor and never gotten around to giving her—
Henryka must have put it here.

She went onto the back porch and stared out at the cottage. That
was where all the trouble in her life had started. Right there. She
went outside and crossed the grass.

There was always a key under a flowerpot; Patricia found it and
let herself in. The cottage was warm and stuffy, the bedroom door
closed. She opened the windows in the main room and sat down on
the love seat, and ran her hand over the floral pattern. Had Wynn
sat here with Eleanor?

Unsure of what she was seeking, Patricia went into the bedroom.
She pulled the curtains apart and opened the window. The light
that poured in revealed the coating of dust on the furniture, and,
under the bed, the smallest glimpse of something red. She got
down on her hands and knees to investigate. It was the corner of
a leather case. She wiped the layer of dust that covered it with her
hand and opened it. It was filled with papers—letters, it seemed—
in various stages of completion. It belonged to Eleanor; she must
have left it behind.

Patricia sat down on the bed. These letters weren't meant for her
eyes. She ought to leave them alone—didn't she want Eleanor out
of her life and thoughts? But the temptation was too great.

> Margaux Bellamy is such a proud, angry girl. I love her for
> that, the anger as much as the pride. What happened to her
> is such a blow; she needs her anger to burn her clean so she
> can move beyond it. I'm not sure her parents understand this—
> certainly not that father of hers—but I do, and I'm glad I can be
> here for her.

Then, another page that was about . . . her.

> I admire Patricia; I really do. First of all, she is the most truly
> elegant woman I have ever met, and I mean that in terms of
> character as well as looks. She is measured, refined, and she
> thinks before she speaks. I want to be more like her. And I
> wish we could be close—friends rather than just employer and

employee. Maybe if we'd met under different circumstances that would have been possible. Instead, there are too many things that divide us. She will always look down on me a bit—daughter of an immigrant hatmaker, and a Jew besides. And I will always resent her sense of entitlement. Yet we are bound by our mutual love for Margaux, and that counts for something. Quite a lot in fact.

Eleanor could have been right—in other circumstances, they might have been friends. But they had no other circumstances. Some of the sheets were blank. Then she found one addressed to someone named Ruth. It was about her late husband.

Wynn Bellamy was here last night. I was sleeping when he showed up, and I was too afraid to ask him to leave. He'd been drinking, and he wanted to dance with me. Even though I didn't want to, I said yes because really, how could I say no? He was my employer. Margaux may love me and Patricia may like me, but in the end, Mr. Bellamy is the boss. So I agreed to the dance, and then he wanted a kiss—and who knows what else. He was holding me so tightly, and I tried to get away. We struggled, and when we fell, he landed right on top of me. He grabbed my face with one hand to kiss me, and then he tore the buttons off of my pajamas—I was frightened, Ruth. Terrified. For a moment it seemed that he might . . . rape me. But I scratched his arms and threatened him with a pitcher, and he finally left. I would never have told anyone what had happened, but I was seeing double and I'd thrown up, so I knew I needed to see a doctor. Henryka—she's the cook I told you about, the one who didn't like me—was actually kind enough to drive me. I didn't tell her what happened, but she guessed. I didn't tell that Dr. Parker either. What good would it have done?

The account of Wynn's behavior was not a surprise. But the extent of Eleanor's fear and powerlessness—these were a revelation. It wasn't just what Wynn did; it was the potential embedded in his actions. And there was something else too—this letter was never sent. Eleanor said that she had not shared the events of that night with anyone, and Patricia believed her. Yet Eleanor had needed to unburden herself, and here was the proof.

Patricia had violated Eleanor's privacy, but that violation had loosened the stubborn knot of her anger. Eleanor had loved her daughter, and Margaux loved her; she had expressed admiration for Patricia and a wish to be her friend.

Patricia left the cottage and returned to the house. She went into the bedroom she had shared with Wynn to do a more careful appraisal. She would leave most of the furnishings but began to methodically pack her summer wardrobe, as well as her toiletries and a sterling silver dresser set with her mother's monogram engraved on the hand mirror. To these things, she added the book of sonnets and the biography of van Gogh.

It started to rain as she worked, a soft, misty rain that made the air smell fresh and sweet. She kept the windows open, shutting them only right before she left. If she started out now, she could be in New York by evening. But she decided to drive up to Oakwood instead and surprise Margaux with an impromptu visit. She was on a new footing with her daughter. Margaux's anger—stubborn, implacable—had turned her into an adult almost overnight, and Patricia was almost afraid of her. But she missed her, too, especially now that she was alone, and she was going to risk the visit no matter what the outcome.

Chapter 13

IT WAS WARM FOR EARLY JUNE, a slightly muggy afternoon. Eleanor walked swiftly along Hudson Street until she came to the bottle-green door. She put down the bags filled with groceries and pressed the bell. There was a pause, and then Tom appeared. "I got everything but the wine," she said. "It was too heavy to carry."

"I didn't expect you to bring that," said Tom. "The liquor store said they would deliver it. Three cases of white, already chilled."

"Three cases!" she said. "You're expecting a big crowd."

He picked up the packages. "I've invited everyone I know."

"Including your sister?" asked Eleanor. She hadn't spoken to Patricia since the day of the funeral, and although she and Margaux had been writing to each other, she knew Margaux had not told her mother about their correspondence.

"Well, yes, but you don't have to talk to her if you don't want."

"I don't," Eleanor said. "Will Margaux be coming too?"

"She's got exams and couldn't get away. About Tricia, though— do you think you two will ever make it up?"

"Don't ask me that," she flared. "Ask her."

Tom looked hurt, and Eleanor went to lay a white cloth over the long table at one end of the gallery. Eleanor tried to calm herself as she began setting out the food. Of course Tom would invite Patricia. She would just be sure to steer clear of her. Right now, she would focus on the prospect of Tom's success, which made her very happy. It wasn't about the money. He had more than enough to cover his needs. No, she saw this gallery endeavor as a step toward maturity and adulthood that Tom was just now taking.

She arranged the thin, almost translucent slices of the prosciutto and the cheese on gold-rimmed oval platters Tom had bought expressly for this purpose at an antiques shop on East Twelfth Street. "I may not be an artist," he had said, "but I have an artist's eye. I want everything in here to reflect that."

Ever since he'd rented the space, he'd thrown himself into its transformation and had succeeded in creating an inviting environment, illuminated by an elaborate blown-glass chandelier from Venice. He painted the walls a glossy vermillion, and on them he hung the work he'd been steadily collecting for the last decade.

Eleanor put the olives, black and glistening, into a cut-glass bowl, and arranged the coin-shaped slices of sausage on the thick cutting board where she'd placed a loaf of Italian peasant bread. She looked up to see that Tom had been watching her. "I like your dress," he said. The black crepe with its georgette pleats was new, purchased just this week. "Very chic."

"Thank you." Then she noticed he had changed and was now wearing the summer-weight wool suit he'd had made in London. "You're looking pretty swanky yourself."

"You like it? I could wear it more often," he said. "In fact, there's one special occasion I'd like to wear it for very soon."

Now why had he gone and raised another sore point between them? The arrival of the wine offered a welcome distraction, and she stepped out from behind the table to direct the deliverymen. By the time she'd returned, Tom was off, attention directed elsewhere. Soon, the guests started arriving. Most of the faces were unfamiliar to Eleanor, but she did recognize a few people. So, apparently, did Tom. At one point, he pulled her over to indicate a woman in a hat with a cluster of cherries pinned to one side.

"That's Liesel Schalk. She's an art critic for the *Times*."

"Do you think she'll write about the gallery?"

"I'm going to chat her up in the hope she'll do just that."

Eleanor watched Tom for a moment before she began to circulate. And then, across the room, she saw Patricia Bellamy and she froze. Eleanor thought she looked thinner and older, yet the wistful, slightly haunted look on her face gave her beauty a depth it had not had before. She turned away before Patricia noticed her.

The gallery had grown even more crowded, and people had started to spill out into the street, the warmth of the evening an invitation. The wine ran out, and so did the food. Liesel Schalk promised a brief write-up for the next day. Tom sold three paintings, including a Jackson Pollock. Pollock's work—erratic drips and splotches of paint flung all over the canvas—did not impress Eleanor at all. Yet Tom was convinced that he was poised to become a very important and influential artist.

The last guest didn't leave until almost nine, sent off with waves and airily blown kisses. Tom was jubilant and broke into a spontaneous dance, twirling Eleanor around the gallery. "*Now* will you marry me?" he asked. "Finally? We can go to city hall tomorrow."

Eleanor stopped dancing but remained in his embrace. "No," she said, looking into his impossibly dear face. "No, Tom, I won't." It had been such a lovely evening, but now he'd gone and spoiled it.

He dropped his arms from her waist. "Damn it, why not?"

"There are so many reasons. Your sister for one. My mother for another."

"We'll talk to them. They'll come around."

"Maybe," said Eleanor. "Maybe not. There's something else too." She fell silent.

"Aren't you going to tell me?" he demanded.

"I don't know if you'll understand. But . . . it's you."

"What are you talking about?"

"I don't know if I can count on you."

"Of course you can—I love you. You know I do."

"You love me. But can I trust you? You disappear when you're scared or uncomfortable. That's not a good trait in a husband."

"If you marry me, I'll never leave you."

"You say that now," she said. "What happens when we have a fight or there's trouble?"

"You won't believe whatever I say, so why should I even try?" said Tom, his voice ragged. "If you don't trust me, loving me is useless." He dug into his pocket and fished out a set of keys, which he handed to her. "I'm leaving. Lock up before you go."

"Where are you going?" she asked.

"I don't think that's any of your business."

"Tom, I—"

But he reached the door quickly and then was gone. Eleanor surveyed the empty gallery. The crumb-littered table was covered with partially filled glasses in which cigarette butts floated. Listlessly, she began taking the glasses to the sink in the back room.

Back at Vassar, she had sensed herself on the periphery of new and unfamiliar territory, unsure if she could—or even wanted—to enter. Now Tom was offering her a passport. But even if she became Mrs. Thomas Harrison, it would change nothing. The name would be a cloak, not her true skin. She would never be one of them; she'd be dressing up, pretending. And that might end up feeling worse than simple exclusion.

The job of cleaning was too daunting; she gave up and switched off the lights before locking the door behind her. Then she began to walk, making her way along streets that were now familiar. Last year at this time she never would have dreamed that the Village would have become her neighborhood. Her decision to leave her teaching job had led to the Bellamys, and the Bellamys led her to where she was now—unmarried, unfettered, a free agent.

Even though there were many people out, Eleanor felt lonely. Alone. The thought of losing Tom was shattering. But marriage came with a particular template, one that seemed less desirable the more she examined it. Maybe there was a different way to be married, one that didn't rely so heavily on the conventions she saw around her. But if there was, she suspected she'd have to invent it.

As she approached her building, Eleanor could see a tiny red pulse in the distance—someone holding a lit cigarette. Maybe it was Tom. She felt relieved—she quickened her pace, and when she grew closer, the figure revealed itself to be not Tom, but Patricia.

"What are you doing here?" Eleanor said, not caring if she sounded rude.

"I was looking for you." Patricia put the cigarette out under the heel of her shoe.

"I thought you never wanted to talk to me again." She still felt the wounds Patricia had inflicted on the day of Wynn's funeral.

"I didn't." Patricia fingered a fold in her dress. "But I'm here now. Here to tell you I'm sorry and I hope you can forgive me."

"Sorry? You?"

"You don't believe me."

"Is there a reason I should?"

"No," Patricia said. "No reason at all. I'd just hoped . . . But maybe I shouldn't have come."

Eleanor surprised herself by saying: "You're already here. We might as well talk."

"I'd like that."

"Why don't you come upstairs? We'll be more comfortable."

"Tom tells me your apartment is very nice."

"He did?" What else had he told her?

"Yes. And he also told me that you turned him down—again. I saw him right before I came here. He seemed . . . crushed."

"Oh." Eleanor didn't like him discussing their relationship with his sister.

"He gave me something to give you." She reached into her purse and handed Eleanor a small white box and a sealed envelope. "But maybe you want to open it upstairs."

Eleanor unlocked the front door, wishing she had not extended the invitation. The stairs were steep and worn, but Patricia followed her up without comment. Once they were inside, Eleanor tried to see the place she loved through the other woman's eyes. A white voile curtain hung at the open window. Three pink peonies nodded in a cobalt vase on the table, and when she turned on the floor lamp near the armchair, the light radiated softly.

"It's lovely in here." Patricia surveyed the Ansel Adams photograph, the flowers, a needlepoint pillow Irina had made and given Eleanor as a housewarming gift.

"Thank you," said Eleanor. She hadn't realized that she wanted Patricia's approval until it had been bestowed. "Can I make you a gin and tonic?"

"That would be nice." Patricia sat down.

Eleanor got the glasses and poured. She took a sip of her drink and then another. "So why did you come?"

"I already told you: I wanted to apologize," Patricia said. "I blamed you for things that weren't your fault—they only seemed that way at the time."

Eleanor held on to the apology. She knew it wasn't easy for Patricia to offer, and like Patricia's praise, it mattered to her to have it. "How are you managing?" she asked.

"It's been difficult. But maybe not in the way you might think."

"How then?"

"I was so angry at him at first. Wynn. But I felt so guilty too."

"Guilty?"

"That last morning—we'd had a terrible quarrel, and I told him I was filing for divorce."

"You did?"

"Yes. No one knows that. Not Tom, not Margaux. I'm not sure if he believed me, but then he went off to Argyle and got on that boat with a bottle. The coroner told me he was . . . inebriated . . . when he died."

"I feel guilty too," Eleanor admitted. "In that last phone call, when I said I would tell Margaux about him . . . that upset him."

"I'm sure it did. He really loved her, you know."

"And she loved him. She always will." It was true whether she understood it or not. "I don't know if I even meant it. But that call . . . I wanted to make sure he never contacted me again. And now he never will."

"I hope, I mean, I can't stop you I suppose, but I do wish—"

"That I won't tell Margaux?" Eleanor finished the sentence. "No, I won't. Even though she's asked."

"So you've been in touch with her?"

"Yes. She's been writing me, and I write back—I'm not going to ignore her. You brought me into her life, and you can't control what happens from there. Not anymore."

"No, I can't." Patricia studied the gin and tonic in her glass.

"Does that bother you?" asked Eleanor.

"I suppose it does. But not as much as it might. Things are different between us now. Sometimes I feel that she's the mother and I'm the child."

"She's grown up a lot lately. She's had to."

"I have something else for you." Patricia reached into her bag to pull out a red leather case that she nudged across the table.

"Where did you get this?" Eleanor was a little shaken to see the case again—she'd had no idea what had become of it.

"In the cottage. You must have left it behind."

"Did you read what was in it?"

"I know I shouldn't have. But yes. Enough anyway."

"Enough for what?"

"To know that you and I—we have a bond. It began with Margaux, but it's more than that now."

"Is that what you think?"

"I do," said Patricia. "Do you?"

"I'd like to think that too . . . but I'm not sure." Eleanor wasn't going to lie to her—not here, not now.

"You know, I was wrong to ask you to hide what Wynn did to you that night. That's when it all changed. And I realize now that what he did was an attack on me too—my trust, and my faith."

"I've never thought of it that way," Eleanor said.

"When I first found out what he'd done, I had to lay the blame somewhere and I laid it on you. Reading your letters made me see it differently, though. You must have been *afraid* of him. Along with disgusted, truly afraid. But you stayed. For Margaux."

"For Margaux," Eleanor repeated.

"So tell me about you," Patricia said. "I hear there's a new job, and of course this apartment—" She gestured with her left hand, now ringless.

"I'm doing well," Eleanor said. "Things are falling into place." She glanced down at the box and note that were still on the table. Alongside those things was a flat object covered in lavender paper; was it also from Tom?

Patricia's gaze had followed hers. "That's from me," she said. "You can open it first if you like."

Eleanor loosened the paper and found inside a volume of Shakespeare's sonnets—a gift both thoughtful and beautiful—but why? "It's lovely," she said. Then she turned to what Tom had sent. Inside the box was a small silver pin in the shape of a deer. The deer was running, its front legs extended in one direction, its hind legs in the other, its neck straining forward, toward an unseen destination. No more than an inch long, it was a precious thing. Eleanor put it back in the box and set it aside while she opened the note. Written on a torn-off sheet of paper and in a hasty scrawl, it read:

> I'm sorry I stormed off, but a fellow does take a beating, asking again and again and hearing no every damn time. As for the pin, I bought it a while ago and planned to give it to you tonight, after the opening. It's not a ring, and it's not made of diamonds, so I figured you wouldn't read too much into it.

You're the deer, Eleanor. The deer in flight. And me? I'm the guy who's hoping to coax you back. To make you mine. I guess now is not the right time, though. Will it ever be? I'm willing to wait. But not forever.

Leaving my heart in your hands,

Tom

She put the note down and lifted her eyes to the woman seated across from her. One man had put a wedge between them. The other a bridge. But the choice about which path to choose—that was theirs alone.

"Do you love him?" Patricia asked.

"I do. The problem's not Tom. Or not entirely. The problem is his world. Your world really. He says it won't matter to him. Maybe he's right. Maybe not. But I know it *will* matter—to me."

"I understand. Or I think I do. Can you tell me more?"

"Yes." Eleanor placed her elbows on the table. "Yes, I can. I'd like to tell you—everything."

AfterWords

Kitty Zeldis did not always want to be a writer. In fact, for most of her youth, she aspired to be a ballerina. But after studying classical ballet for many years, in her late teens she decided her future did not lie with dance.

While at Vassar College, Zeldis studied art history. She'd always been a voracious reader, however, and found her true calling when she took a fiction-writing class while attending graduate school at Columbia University. She promptly left her graduate program to pursue writing and "never looked back."

Zeldis has always been interested in period literature, and early influences included *A Little Princess* and *A Tree Grows in Brooklyn*. Originally a short-story author, she began writing novels to appeal to a larger readership. She published her first novel at age forty-five.

In a recent interview with *Crimespree Magazine*, Zeldis describes her characters in *Not Our Kind* as struggling "against their roles and expectations. The postwar period had a lot of optimism and prosperity in this country," she says. "But Jews still suffered emotional and social hurts." According to Zeldis, the "essence of the story is about outcasts, being different," whether in terms of religion, gender, or a physical disability.

Kitty Zeldis is the author's nom de plume. An acclaimed author of books for adults and children, she lives with her family in Brooklyn, New York.

LINDA
CASTILLO

A NOVEL

A GATHERING
OF
SECRETS

Prologue

SHE DIDN'T SLEEP. Hadn't slept through the night in a long time. There was too much darkness—not the kind that was restful. At dawn, when her *mamm* peeked into her bedroom and told her it was time to feed the animals and get ready for worship, she was already awake, waiting. Ready.

Ever the obedient daughter, she pulled on her dress, tugged her hair into a bun, and covered her head with her *kapp*. Stepping into her winter tights and sneakers, she left her room and took the steps down to the living room. She avoided the kitchen, where she could hear her *mamm* frying sausage, and went out through the side door and into the cold. The morning was wet and gray. Once in the barn, she tossed hay to the horses, filled their water buckets, dumped scratch into the chicken feeder, and gathered six eggs.

She'd never lied to her parents. Not once in all of her seventeen years. But when Mamm told her to get cleaned up for worship, she complained that she'd been sick and throwing up half the night. Mamm wasn't pleased that she would miss such an important day. But what could she say?

Chores complete, she went back to her room and lay down. She stared at the ceiling and listened to the sounds of the house. The

439

voices of her younger siblings. The silence while the *gebet nach dem essen,* or prayer after meal, was recited. The slamming of the door when her *datt* went out to harness the buggy horse. The pound of feet on the floor when the little ones went out to help.

Oh, how she would miss them.

At half past seven the back door slammed. A few minutes later she heard the clip-clop of the old Standardbred's hooves against the ground. Rising, she went to the window and parted the curtains to see the buggy moving down the lane toward the road.

Time to go.

Pushing open her bedroom door, she stepped into the hall and descended the steps. She thought about her little brothers and sisters, and the pang of melancholy that assailed her nearly sent her to her knees. She'd known this would be difficult, but she also knew it was the only way. She'd asked God for guidance, after all, and He'd sent her a sign. Unlike her, He never, ever lied.

At the base of the stairs, she went left through the kitchen, trying not to notice the still warm cup of tea and dry toast her *mamm* had left. The sight of it made her smile. Dry toast and tea were her *mamm's* cure-all for everything. If only life were that simple.

I'm sorry.

The words echoed inside her head as she pushed open the back door and stepped into the early morning drizzle. She ran down the stone path to the barn. Shoving open the big sliding door, she walked into the dim interior. The stairs to the hayloft were to her left. Not giving herself time to debate, she took them to the second level. There were only two windows in the loft. But even in the semidarkness, she knew where to find what she needed.

She crossed to the mound of loose hay beneath the window. Kneeling, she raked it aside with her fingers, uncovering the coil of rope she'd hidden yesterday. Datt had bought it last summer when he'd made the swing for the boys. He'd had a few extra feet left over and stowed it in the shed for some future project.

She didn't let herself think about her family or what this would do to them as she uncoiled the rope. They wouldn't understand. But there was no recourse. God had spoken to her, and she had listened. This was the only way she could keep her secret.

The coil consisted of about ten feet of rope. She carried it to the place where the floor opened and the rafters were visible. Lying down on her belly, she looped the rope around the nearest rafter and tied a triple knot. Sitting up, she studied the other end. Her fingers shook as she formed it into a loop and tied another triple knot. A couple of quick yanks told her it would do.

Taking a deep, calming breath, she slipped the loop over her head. At some point she'd begun to cry. But she thought they were tears of relief. Mamm had always told her that death was part of God's divine plan. This morning she believed that with all her heart. She knew the Lord would welcome her with open arms. He would see her through this. Her family would just have to have faith in His wisdom. Someday they would all be together again.

Still, she trembled as she rose, trying not to notice the quiver in her stomach. She didn't think about what came next, but prayed it would be over quickly. Once it was done, she would be free.

"I forgive you," she whispered.

Closing her eyes, she stepped forward and fell into space.

Chapter 1

Six months later

HE DRESSED IN HIS English clothes. Blue jeans. Plain white T-shirt. The cowboy boots he'd laid down a boatload of money for at the Western store in Berlin.

Anticipation sizzled inside him as he left his bedroom and stepped into the darkened hall. He didn't like this secret thing he'd become. But there was no stopping it. He'd learned to live with it. Some small part of him had learned to embrace it.

His parents' bedroom door stood ajar; he could hear his *datt* snoring. The door to the room where his sisters slept was open halfway. He thought he could smell their sweet little-girl scents as he slid past. The door to his other sister's room was closed.

He wasn't unduly worried about getting caught as he started down the stairs. He was on *Rumspringa*, after all. For the last few months he'd pretty much done as he pleased; his parents pretended not to notice. He'd tasted whiskey for the first time. Bought his first car. He'd been staying out late and coming home at all hours. Of course, Mamm and Datt didn't like it, but they held their tongues. It was all part of growing up Amish. Maybe the best part.

Around him the house was silent and dark, the only light filtering in through the windows in the living room. He pulled the note from his pocket as he entered the kitchen. Pausing at the table, he plucked the tiny flashlight from his rear pocket, shined the beam on the paper, and read it for the dozenth time.

> Meet me in the barn at midnight. I'll make it worth your while. ☺

She'd written the words in purple ink. There were hearts over the *i*'s and frilly little curlicues on the tails of the *y* and the *g*. The smiley face made him grin. He couldn't believe she'd finally come around. After weeks of cajoling, he would finally have her.

He let himself out through the back door. Ahead he could just make out the silhouette of the barn, sixty yards away. His feet crunched over gravel as he traversed the driveway and went up the ramp. The big sliding door stood open about a foot. Datt always closed it to keep the foxes and coyotes away from the chickens. She's here, he thought, and a thrill raced through him.

He went through the door, the smells of horses and fresh-cut hay greeting him. The interior was pitch-black, but he knew every inch of the barn, and he knew exactly where to find the lantern—on its hook hanging from the overhead beam. He reached for it, felt around, but for some reason it wasn't there.

He pulled the flashlight from his rear pocket, flicked it on.

"Hello?" he called out. "You there?"

He listened, but there was no reply.

Puzzled, he walked past the wagon mounded with the hay he and Datt had cut last month. In the back of his mind, he wondered why the two buggy horses didn't greet him from their stalls. No matter the hour, they were always ready for a snack and never shy about asking for it. He crossed the dirt floor, sweeping the beam right and left. A grin spread across his face when he spotted the sliver of light beneath the door of the tack room.

"Come out, come out, wherever you are!" Lowering the beam, he started down the aisle.

At first he thought it odd that she would choose the tack room. But on second thought the small space was clean, with a hardwood floor that was swept daily. It was where they stored the horse blankets, halters, and harnesses. More important, the door had a lock. Datt had installed it after a halter, a saddle, and two leather harnesses were stolen a couple months ago. He knew it was the *Englischer* down the road who'd done it. Probably sold them at horse auction in Millersburg. The guy was a thief and a boozer.

Already he could feel his body responding as he drew closer to the tack room. His *datt* called it *lusht* and warned him to beware of its power. But what did an old man remember about lust? What did he remember about being eighteen years old?

Reaching the tack room, he opened the door. Her perfume filled the air. Two horse blankets had been spread out on the floor. Atop the old fifty-gallon drum a candle on a little white dish flickered. She'd even brought a bottle of wine. Two plastic glasses, the kind with stems. His smile grew into a laugh as he stepped inside.

"The only thing missing is the girl," he said, knowing she was within earshot, listening. "I wonder where she is."

He flicked off his flashlight and walked over to the blankets. The wine bottle was already open. Setting the flashlight on the drum, he sat down cross-legged, resting his hands on his knees.

"If she doesn't show up soon, I'm going to have to drink this wine all by myself," he said, louder now, expecting her to sweep into the room at any moment, giggling and ready.

He was thinking about all the things they'd do, when the tack room door creaked. A quick jump of anticipation; then the door slammed hard enough to jangle the halters hanging on the wall. Startled, he rose to his feet.

The sound of the lock snicking into place sent him to the door. "What are you doing, babes?" He tried the knob, found it locked.

"Hey!" he called out. "Baby, you are so going to pay for this!"

Sounds outside the door drew his attention. Something being dragged across the floor. Heavy things thumping against the door. Perplexed, he jiggled the knob and forced a laugh. "What are you up to?" There was an edge in his voice now.

The sounds outside the door ceased. Curious, he set his ear against the wood, listened. Nothing.

"If I have to break this door down, you're going to be sorry!" He tried to keep his voice light, but his patience was wearing thin.

He waited a beat. Thought he heard footsteps. Wood scraping against wood. *What the hell was she up to?*

Moving away slightly, he braced his shoulder and shoved against the wood, testing its strength. The door shuddered but held. Frowning, he jiggled the knob again. "Come on, baby, let me out. Whatever I did, I'll make it up to you."

When no reply came, his anger surged. Using his shoulder, he rammed the door. Another satisfying shudder. He was gearing up to do it again when the smell of smoke registered. Not from the candles or lantern. Not from a cigarette. Something was burning.

Cursing beneath his breath, he looked down and was shocked to see tendrils of smoke rising from beneath the door.

All semblance of playfulness left him. He slapped his open palms against the door. "Open up!" he shouted. "You're going to burn the damn place down, baby. Come on. This isn't funny!"

Backing up, he got a running start and slammed his shoulder against the door. Wood creaked, but it didn't give way. He set his hand against it, realized the surface was warm to the touch.

"This is a dangerous thing you're doing!" he shouted. "Stop screwing around and open the door. Now!"

He listened, heard the crackle of what sounded like fire. He stood back and landed a kick against the wood, next to the knob. Raising his leg, he kicked it again. Part of the wood jamb split. He could see the brass of the dead bolt now. Smoke was pouring in from beneath the door, black and choking and thick.

"Come on!" he screamed. "Are you nuts? Open the door!"

Coughing, he stepped back and lunged forward, his shoulder crashing against the door. The door opened an inch. He shoved it with the heels of his hands, but there was something in the way. Through the gap, flames, smoke, and heat rushed in.

Raising the crook of his arm to his face, he rushed the door, slammed his body against it. The lock had given way; he'd gained another inch. Hope leaped in his chest. But within seconds the opening ushered in a tidal wave of ferocious flames, hungry for fuel, gobbling up the dry wood, eating up the floor.

"Help me!" he screamed. "Help!"

Choking and cursing, he stumbled back. Too much heat now. Too much smoke to breathe. Lowering himself to the floor, he rolled onto his back, raised both legs and rammed his booted feet against the door. The door gave way. Wood and ash and sparks rained down on him, embers burning his chest and arms and face. Fire burst into the room, a rabid, roaring beast that came down on top of him. The full force of his predicament slammed into him. "Datt! *Datt!*" But the words were little more than muffled cries.

With a final hideous roar, the fire swept over him.

Chapter 2

WHEN YOU'RE THE CHIEF of police in a small town, a call at four a.m. is never a good thing. As I roll over and reach for my cell, I'm anticipating news of a fatality accident or, God forbid, bad news about one of my officers or my family.

"Burkholder," I rasp.

"Sorry to wake you, Chief," comes the voice of my graveyard-shift dispatcher, Mona Kurtz. "I just took a call for a barn fire out at the Gingerich place. Thought you'd want to know."

I'm familiar with the Gingerich family. Miriam and Gideon are Amish and live on a small farm a couple miles out of Painters Mill. I don't know them well. They're a nice family and lead quiet lives. Last I heard, they still have four kids at home.

I scoot up to a sitting position. "Anyone hurt?"

"Not sure yet. I talked to one of the firefighters, and he told me the family hasn't been able to account for their son, Danny."

A sense of dread sweeps over me as I throw off the quilt and set my feet on the floor. "Anyone mention the cause?"

"No one knows anything yet."

"I'm on my way."

I hit END as I rise and head to the closet for my uniform.

"What's up, Chief?"

In the light slanting out from my closet, I see my significant other, John Tomasetti, sit up and squint at the clock. His hair is mussed. Even in the dim light, I can see the overnight stubble on his jaw, concern sharp in his eyes.

"There's a fire out at the Gingerich farm," I tell him, shrugging into my shirt. "I got it covered. Go back to sleep."

"Everyone okay?"

Grabbing my trousers, I walk over to the bed and step into them. "Teenage son is unaccounted for."

He throws off the covers. "You want some company?"

Tomasetti is an agent for the Ohio Bureau of Criminal Investigation and works out of the Richfield office, half an hour to the north. Painters Mill falls within his jurisdiction, so it wouldn't be unusual for him to show up at a barn fire, especially with someone missing. I know one of these days our relationship—our living arrangement—will be discovered. This morning, with a teenager's whereabouts unknown, Tomasetti will be an invaluable resource.

Grabbing my equipment belt and .38 from the drawer, I round the foot of the bed, buckling it as I reach him. "Anyone ever tell you you're a glutton for punishment?"

"Anyone ever tell you how good you look in that thirty-eight?"

"Just you."

He lays a quick kiss on me. "Do you know the family?" he asks.

"Not well, but I've met them. They're Amish. Well thought of."

Stepping around me, he goes to the closet, yanks a shirt off a hanger. "Let's hope Junior shows up before we get there."

I TURN in to the lane of the Gingerich farm to find one side of their massive bank barn engulfed in flames. A tanker from the Holmes County Fire District rattles past as I park out of the way on the grassy shoulder. Tomasetti's Tahoe pulls up behind me as I'm getting out of my city-issue Explorer.

Embers and ash swirl like snow all around. Four fire trucks from two districts are parked haphazardly in the gravel between the house and barn, engines rumbling. Closer to the structure, several firefighters man hoses, water trained on the flames.

I'm midway to the house when Tomasetti catches up with me.

"I hope they got the livestock out," I say as we take the steps to the porch.

The door flies open before I can knock. An Amish woman rushes out, soot and panic on her face, her *kapp* askew. She looks at me, her entire body shaking. "We can't find Danny," she blurts.

"Is everyone else accounted for?" I ask.

"Yes, but Danny should be here. In his room. I can't find him anywhere." She turns and goes back inside, leaving the door open.

Tomasetti and I follow. The Amish woman leads us to the kitchen. Without speaking, she goes to the back door and steps onto the porch to stare at the burning barn.

"Danny is your son?" I ask.

"*Ja.*"

"How old is he?"

"Just turned eighteen." She turns to me, her face ravaged.

"When did you last see him?" I ask.

"Last night. He'd gone to bed. Early because he was out late the night before. He has to be at work this morning."

"You've searched the house?"

"That's the first thing we did. Looked all over for him."

"Is it possible he got up early and left without telling anyone?" I ask. "Maybe he met a friend for breakfast?"

She shakes her head. "Danny has a car he's been driving since he started *Rumspringa*. Gideon doesn't let him park it on the property, so Danny keeps it at the end of the lane. It's still there."

Vaguely, I recall seeing an old Chevy sedan parked at the mouth of the lane. The revelation doesn't bode well for her son.

"Is it possible someone picked him up?" I ask.

"I don't see why anyone would pick him up in the middle of the night. Not when he has a car and doesn't have to be at work until eight. Danny likes his sleep."

Expression anguished, she turns to look out the door. "Maybe they've found him by now. Maybe he's out there helping the firemen put out that fire."

Tomasetti touches her arm. "I'll go check."

Hope leaps into the woman's eyes. "My husband, Gideon, is out there, too. The firemen won't let him get close to the barn."

"Hang tight." Giving us a nod, Tomasetti goes through the door.

"Mamm?"

We turn to see a teenage girl come through the kitchen door, her face tear-streaked.

"Did you find Danny?" she asks.

"Not yet." The woman wrings her hands, paces from the door to the girl and then back to the door.

I make eye contact with the girl. "Danny's your brother?" I ask.

"Ja."

"When did you last see him?"

"Right before he went to bed. We had ice cream on the porch, and then he went to his room."

"What time was that?"

"Ten o'clock or so."

I keep my attention on the girl. "Let's you and I check the house one more time, okay? Can you give me a hand with that?"

It doesn't take us long to ascertain that young Danny isn't in the house. Two little girls share a small bedroom and are sleeping peacefully in their beds.

I stop the girl in the upstairs hallway. "What's your name?"

"Fannie."

"I'm Kate." I offer my hand, and she gives it a weak shake. "Does Danny have a cell phone?" I ask.

"Having a phone is against the *Ordnung*," the girl says, referring to the unwritten rules of their church district.

I press her anyway. "He was on *Rumspringa*, right? Maybe he'd gotten a phone and didn't want your parents to know?"

Fannie shakes her head. "He wouldn't."

I nod, but I know better. More than likely, an eighteen-year-old Amish boy on *Rumspringa* does, indeed, have a phone.

"*Rumspringa*" is the *Deitsh* word for "running around." It's the time in a young Amish person's life when they have the opportunity to experience the world without all those Amish rules, usually right before they become baptized and join the Church. It gives me hope that Danny slipped out in the night and didn't tell anyone.

I go to Danny's room next, open the door, and step inside. Fannie follows. Clothes are hung on wooden dowels. Shoes are lined up against the wall. I notice immediately one of the dowels is bare. A single pair of work boots is tucked beneath the bed.

I motion toward the boots. "Does he have more than one pair of shoes?"

She looks at the boots and begins to cry. "His cowboy boots are gone. He bought them with his first paycheck from his job in town. Says they drive the girls wild. He wears them everywhere."

I gently touch her arm. "Fannie, maybe he sneaked out to meet some friends or a girlfriend. Don't give up hope just yet."

The girl's expression brightens, but she doesn't look hopeful. "Luane's *mamm* and *datt* would never let her leave the house after dark, especially with a boy. Even a good boy like Danny."

"Luane is his girlfriend?"

"*Ja*. Her parents are Swartzentruber. Strict, you know. They love Danny like a son, but they still wouldn't allow such a thing."

I motion toward the stairs. "Let's go talk to your *mamm*."

A few minutes later Miriam, Fannie, and I sit at the kitchen table, trying hard to ignore the cacophony of voices, engines, and sirens outside. Miriam made coffee and set a cup in front of me. No one drinks.

"Fannie tells me Daniel has a girlfriend," I begin.

The Amish woman nods. "Luane Raber. She's a sweet girl. Only sixteen years old. I suspect they'll get married. . . ."

"Do the Rabers have a phone? Maybe he went to see his girl."

"They're Swartzentruber and have no need for a phone."

I hit the lapel mike at my shoulder and hail my third-shift officer. "T.J.? What's your twenty?"

T.J. Banks is the youngest officer in my small department and the only rookie. He usually ends up on the graveyard shift.

"I'm setting up traffic cones in front of the Gingerich place, Chief."

"I want you to run over to Mose and Sue Raber's place out on Dogleg Road. Tell them there's been a fire at the Gingerich farm and we're trying to locate Daniel. See if he's there. And find out if their daughter, Luane, is there."

"Got it."

A knock sounds on the back door. Before Miriam can get to her feet, it opens and Tomasetti enters the kitchen. He makes eye contact with me, and I see the answer in his eyes before he speaks.

Miriam stands. "Did you find him?"

Tomasetti shakes his head. "We're still looking, ma'am."

I excuse myself, and Tomasetti and I go outside. The barn is still burning, but not as ferociously now.

"Did they lose any livestock?" I ask.

"That's what I wanted to talk to you about."

I look at him, puzzled.

"I talked with Gideon Gingerich a few minutes ago. He told me at about eight p.m. he and Danny put their two buggy horses and four calves in the barn for the night."

I know what he's going to say next, and dread wells in my chest.

"We found the two horses and calves out in the pasture behind the barn," he tells me.

"Someone released the livestock," I murmur.

"Looks like it."

"One of the firefighters? Maybe one of the first responders?"

"Gingerich told me that by the time the fire department got

here, the barn was engulfed. The livestock had already been let out."

"Maybe it was Daniel," I say. "Maybe he woke up, smelled smoke. Got up to check it out and saw the fire."

"Or maybe he was pissed off about something or angry with his parents and decided to torch the barn. Maybe he couldn't bear the thought of killing those animals."

"If he took off, he would have taken his car."

"I agree. The fire chief called the fire marshal's office. They're going to take a hard look at this."

"He suspects arson?" I ask.

"He's suspicious enough so that he made the call." Tomasetti slants a look at me. "With the kid missing and those animals released, he thought the situation warranted a thorough once-over."

I nod in agreement, but I'm troubled by the possibilities.

"Any bad blood between Daniel and his parents?" he asks.

"No one has said anything, but I'll dig a little, see what I find."

My cell vibrates against my hip. I glance at the display, see T.J.'s name come up. "What do you have?" I ask.

"I'm out here at the Raber farm, Chief," he tells me. "Talked to both the parents as well as the daughter, Luane. Daniel Gingerich hasn't been here for a couple days."

"Thanks for checking."

"You bet."

I end the call and look at Tomasetti. "If Daniel Gingerich took off, not only did he leave his car behind but his girlfriend."

"Doesn't sound like something an eighteen-year-old boy would do." Tomasetti reaches for his phone and glances at the display. "I've got to go. Keep me posted, will you, Chief?"

"Thanks for coming along."

"Any time." He glances left and right, but there are too many people around for him to risk kissing me. Instead, he offers up a grin. "See you later."

IT'S NOON by the time I arrive at the police station. Before leaving the scene, I talked to the fire chief from Millersburg. I've met Fred Achin on several occasions. He's a family man, a good chief, and an experienced firefighter. The interior of the structure was still too hot for them to make entry, but Fred thought they'd be able to start sifting through the rubble this afternoon.

My uniform reeks of smoke as I slide behind my desk. I've just taken my first sip of coffee when my phone jangles. It's Fred Achin. A wave of foreboding rolls over me.

"We got a body in the barn," he tells me.

My mind spins through the repercussions. "You got ID?"

"No."

"Has anyone talked to Gideon or Miriam Gingerich?"

"No. The investigator just discovered the remains a few minutes ago. I knew you'd want to know right away."

"The fire marshal is on scene?"

"Investigator got here an hour ago." He pauses. "Look, we don't have anything official yet, but he thinks the fire is suspicious. There was an accelerant used. Gasoline."

"How do you know?"

"You can smell it."

That the fire may have been intentionally set casts an even darker shadow over an already terrible situation. "Have you called Doc Coblentz?" I ask, referring to the coroner of Holmes County.

"That's my next call."

"Fred, can you hold off a few minutes?" I pick up my keys. "I'm ten minutes away. I think it would be best if I was there to explain the situation to the family before they see the coroner's vehicle."

"Chief, I don't envy you that chore." He heaves another sigh. "I'll hold off a few minutes, but you'd better get over here quick."

I RUN my lights and make it to the Gingerich farm in record time. Fred Achin and two men I don't know are standing next to Fred's vehicle, talking. There's no sign of the coroner's van.

I park and head toward the back door. I'm midway down the sidewalk when Gideon Gingerich steps onto the porch, his expression beseeching. His wife, Miriam, stands in the doorway, looking at me as if she's about to wrench information from me by the sheer force of her stare. "Did you find him?"

I reach them, dividing my attention between them. "Can we go inside and sit down for a few minutes?" I motion toward the door.

Gideon ushers me inside, and we sit at the kitchen table.

"Mr. and Mrs. Gingerich," I begin, "let me preface by saying I do not have definitive news about your son. But you need to know that the fire chief discovered a body inside the barn."

Miriam bends away from the table. "No. *No.*"

"We do not know that it's Daniel," I say firmly. "There's been no ID. But I wanted you to know that the coroner is on his way. Once the body is recovered, we'll begin the identification process."

Gideon opens his mouth as if to speak, but he doesn't make a sound.

"An investigator from the fire marshal's office is here now. He'll be investigating the fire and will hopefully be able to find the origin and the cause."

"The . . . dead person in the barn . . ." The Amish man's words come out as a hoarse whisper. "You think it's Daniel?"

"I don't know," I say honestly.

"Who else would it be?" Miriam chokes out the words. "Our sweet Danny. I can't believe it."

Movement from the doorway snags my attention. Fannie Gingerich is standing just outside the kitchen, her hands on the shoulders of her two little sisters, about four or five years of age. Three sets of eyes flick from me to their parents and back to me.

"What happened?" the girl asks.

When no one answers, she begins to cry. The little girls look up at her and, seeing their older sibling's face, begin to cry as well.

"Hush now." Miriam opens her arms to the two little ones, who rush to her and bury their faces against her bosom. "All of this is in the hands of the Lord, and we trust Him to show us the light."

I turn my attention to Gideon. "Can I speak with you outside?"

He nods and follows me onto the back porch. We look across the driveway where two men in protective suits are inside the blackened remains of the barn. Doc Coblentz has arrived on the scene.

"Mr. Gingerich," I begin, "according to the arson investigator, there may have been an accelerant used to start the fire. He thinks it was gasoline."

The Amish man looks at me. "Are you saying someone *did* this thing? They burned our barn on purpose?"

I ask gently, "Do you keep gas in the barn?"

He shakes his head. "The *Ordnung* forbids the use of gasoline. We use only diesel for the generator."

"Can you think of anyone who might have done this?"

He shakes his head adamantly. "No."

"Have you had any disagreements with anyone? Any problems with neighbors or acquaintances? Strangers? Family members?"

"No."

I choose my next words carefully. "Mr. Gingerich, have you had any problems or disagreements with Daniel?"

"*Danny?*" He looks at me as if I've just admitted to pouring the gasoline and striking a match myself. "Never," he says, his mouth trembling. "He's a good boy."

"Has Danny—"

"Enough!" He cuts me off and then turns away, opens the door. "If you want to help us, Chief Burkholder, I suggest you get out there and find my son."

Casting a final look over his shoulder, he goes into the house, letting the door slam behind him.

TEN minutes later I'm standing outside the yellow caution tape surrounding the barn, watching two investigators wade through debris. Most of the exterior walls are still standing, but some of the rafters have collapsed, bringing down a segment of the roof.

"Good thing the fire department got here when they did or this place would have burned clean to the ground."

I glance over to see Ludwig Coblentz toddle toward me, a medical bag at his side. He's a portly man prone to bad fashion choices and the occasional fedora. He's been coroner for nearly twelve years.

"Hi, Doc." I cross to him, and we shake hands.

He sends a pointed look toward the barn. "I understand we have an as-of-yet-unidentified body."

"The homeowner's son is missing."

His expression darkens. "A child?"

"Teenager. Daniel just turned eighteen."

"Chief Burkholder?"

We turn to see one of the investigators approach, peeling off his gloves, his head covering, and the outer layer of protective clothes as he crosses the remaining distance between us.

"Bob Schoening, Department of Commerce. I'm the investigator for the state fire marshal's office."

"Any idea what happened here?" I ask.

"I just completed my initial walk-through. We've got one body. Badly burned but intact, so we'll probably be able to extract DNA if necessary. I need to get in there, thoroughly document the scene, and take my samples before I release the scene to the coroner."

I nod. "How long?"

He glances at his watch. "A few hours."

I sense there's more coming. "Look, this is all preliminary," he tells me, "but just so you know . . . I found intense localized burning outside what looks to be a tack room."

"Tack room?" I ask.

"There were halters and other equipment that's still recognizable. That's where the body is located."

"I understand there was an accelerant present."

"Plenty of it. So much that I could smell it the instant I entered the scene. I got a pour pattern right outside the tack-room door. Worse, the door appears to have been locked and barricaded with some kind of debris. Hay, maybe. It burned, of course, but the baling wire was left behind."

"So the victim was in the tack room and had possibly been trying to keep someone out?" I ask. "Some threat, maybe?"

His laugh is humorless. "It looks to me like someone locked that poor son of a bitch *in* the tack room, barricaded it with hay, some cinder blocks, and a wheelbarrow. Then they soaked all of it with gasoline, including the door, and set it on fire."

It takes a moment for the horror of the scenario to sink in. "Is there any way it could have been some kind of . . . freak accident?" I hear myself ask. "Or a prank gone wrong?"

"I suppose it could have been a prank that went south, but who would do something so dangerous and stupid?"

"Could it have been accidental? The Amish do use lanterns."

He looks around, raises an arm to blot sweat from his forehead. "Look, all I'm saying at this juncture is that either one of those scenarios is a stretch. I mean, the door was locked. It was *barricaded*. That's not to mention the presence of an accelerant."

We fall silent. "Was there any physical evidence left behind?" I ask. "Anything that might have fingerprints on it?"

"Not that I've seen, but it's a mess in there. Once we get everything photographed, we'll check everything for fingerprints—"

"Can prints survive a fire like that?" I ask.

"Interestingly, latents can survive temps up to a hundred degrees Celsius. For a few hours, anyway. It's premature to know if we'll get anything at this point, but we'll do our best."

He nods at Doc Coblentz. "I'm probably not going to have a final ruling on this for several days. That said, unofficially, there's enough evidence here for me to tell you this was no accident."

Chapter 3

NOTHING HAPPENS QUICKLY in the course of investigating a crime scene. Any evidence must be painstakingly collected, preserved, and documented, especially if there's a fatality involved. It takes a tremendous amount of time, expertise, and patience. Any cop will tell you: Waiting for results is the bane of their existence. Fingerprints. DNA. Footwear impressions. Tire-tread imprints.

Doc Coblentz and I wait for four hours while Schoening collects samples and photographs, then videotapes the entire scene. In the meantime, Doc's technician unloads a gurney, upon which a body bag and tarp have been unfolded. As soon as the scene is turned over to the coroner, the victim will be transported to the morgue.

At just before five p.m., Bob Schoening walks over to me. "We're done here for now, Chief. The coroner is free to retrieve the body."

"Are you still confident this was arson?" I ask.

He nods. "I believe the evidence will support that."

Doc Coblentz and his technician wade into the ash and debris. I watch as the technician photographs the remains. When he's finished, he and Doc Coblentz gently heft the body onto the stretcher and drape it with a blue sheet. I follow them to the van.

"Are the clothes intact, Doc?" I ask.

Doc Coblentz shakes his head. "The only thing that's recognizable is the shoes, and that's because they're leather. Boots, actually."

Something quickens inside me at the mention of leather boots. Daniel's sister had mentioned cowboy boots. . . .

I glance at the technician. "May I take a look at the shoes?"

He lifts the bottom corner of the sheet. I can make out the distinctive silhouette of a classic cowboy boot.

"Danny Gingerich's sister told me her brother's cowboy boots are missing from his room," I say.

"Good to know, Kate, but at this point I believe everyone suspects this is likely Daniel Gingerich," Doc Coblentz responds in a low voice. "That said, we still must go about the identification process, starting with dental or medical records."

"I'll check with the parents to see if Danny had any dental work or X-rays done," I say.

"That would be helpful," he tells me, and replaces the sheet.

The coroner's van is pulling away as I take the sidewalk to the back porch. The door swings open, and Gideon comes through it. His eyes are red, his mouth drawn into a grim, hard line.

"I'm sorry to bother you again," I say. "Mr. Gingerich, I need to ask you a few questions about Daniel."

He nods.

"Do you know if your son has had any dental work done? Did he ever have a broken bone? Any X-rays taken?"

Closing his eyes briefly, he nods. "He was kicked in the face by one of the cows when he was thirteen. Broke two teeth. We took him to the dentist in town. Dr. Gray, I think."

"Did Dr. Gray take X-rays?"

"I think so."

I nod. "Did Daniel ever have any broken bones?"

"When he was seven. Fell out of the hayloft and broke his arm. We took him to the emergency room at Pomerene." His mouth quivers. "I know why you're asking these questions. I cannot . . ."

Unable to finish the sentence, he lowers his face into his hands, emits a sob fraught with unbearable sadness.

I reach out and set my hand on his arm. "I'll come see you the moment I know anything, good or bad."

He nods, then walks into the house without a word.

THE Mercantile was usually silent at nine p.m. The shop closed at six, and that schedule hadn't altered since the place opened a year ago. Tonight, however, Shania Twain was belting out a song, proclaiming to the world she felt like a woman. The industrial lighting that lent so much character to the old barn buzzed with electricity.

Neva Lambright would never tell anyone, especially her *mamm*, but this was her favorite time of day. After hours, when the customers were gone, the music was blasting something that would make her *datt* frown, and it was just her and her friends, Ina Yoder and Viola Stutzman. The three girls had been best friends for so long, Neva couldn't even remember when they met. And so last year, when Neva's *mamm* and *datt* opened their Amish tourist shop, Ina and Viola were the natural choices for employees.

Tonight the three of them were at the front of the store, working on the two display windows for *Allelieweziel*, or Halloween, which was a month away. Viola had come up with the idea of displaying a few of their trick-or-treat costumes for the little ones, everything from pirates to cute Amish outfits. The second window had been fashioned to look like a *spuk haus*, or haunted house.

"Some of the Amish aren't going to like all this spooky stuff," Ina pointed out.

From her place inside the display window, Viola sprayed cobwebs onto the chair. "The *Englischers* are going to love it."

"Especially the little ones." Neva stood just off the front window, studying the display with a critical eye. "It's perfect."

"Oh, you Beachy Amish," Ina said teasingly. "Always pushing the limit of what's acceptable."

Neva took the gibe in stride. The Beachy Amish are a progressive group that allows its members to drive cars and use technology, like phones and computers, on a limited basis. Some of the Old Order don't even consider them Amish. But Neva never felt lesser in any way, especially when it came to her friends.

"Car comes in handy when it's raining," Neva said breezily.

Viola cleared her throat. "If it's all the same to you two, I'd like to finish before midnight. Let's clean up and get out of here."

While Viola and Ina gathered trash, Neva went to the café. She'd just finished wiping the table where they'd sat and drawn out their plans earlier, when the lights went out. The radio fell silent. The darkness that followed was so complete, Neva couldn't see her hand in front of her face.

"Not funny!" she called out.

"I didn't do anything" came Viola's voice.

Ina countered with "Maybe your *mamm* forgot to pay the electric bill."

Slowly Neva's eyes adjusted to the darkness. She could barely make out the front windows from where she stood.

"What do we do now?" Viola asked.

"There's a flashlight in Mamm's office," Neva called out. "I'll be right back."

Carefully, she made her way through the darkness and went into the office. Inside, she found the flashlight in the desk drawer. She was on her way to the front of the shop when a crash sounded.

Holding the flashlight beam in front of her, she ran toward her friends. "What happened?"

"The window" came Ina's voice. "It just . . . shattered."

"*What?*" Neva shifted the beam. Her friends stood near the display window, looking startled. Glass sparkled on the floor. She jerked the beam to the window. Sure enough, there was a hole the size of a basketball in the center.

"I think someone threw something," Ina said.

An instant of silence ensued. It was so quiet, Neva could hear the wind rushing through the trees outside.

"What's that?" Ina motioned toward an object the size of a soccer ball lying on the floor.

Neva shifted the beam. Recognition flashed, followed by a stab of disbelief, of revulsion. "*Mein Gott.*"

The cone of light illuminated the severed head of a hog. The smear of blood on the floor gleamed black in the semidarkness.

Gasping, Viola stepped back. "It's . . . a butchered hog."

"Someone pitched it through the window," Ina said.

"Why would someone do such a thing?" Viola whispered.

The silence that followed sent a shiver through Neva. She hadn't told her friends what was going on. Hadn't told anyone.

"It's a stupid Halloween prank is all," she said.

"It's creepy," Viola whispered.

"What do we do?" Ina asked.

Neva swept the beam over the macabre scene. She'd hoped it would stop. The threats. The intimidation. The hatred. It was the only secret she'd ever kept from her friends. She'd prayed he would find the strength to move on. To let *her* move on and forget about what she'd done. The mistake she'd made.

"Should we call the police?" Ina asked

Neva shook her head. "I'll call Mamm. She'll know what to do. She always does."

AFTER leaving the Gingerich farm yesterday afternoon, I went to see Dr. Charles Gray—the dentist who'd x-rayed Daniel Gingerich's teeth when he was thirteen years old. I let him know that Doc Coblentz would be forwarding him a set of dental X-rays for comparison and, as usual, we're anxious for results.

It's eight a.m. now, and I'm in my office thinking about a third cup of coffee, when the call finally comes. It's Dr. Gray.

"I just compared the X-rays from my archive with the films

Dr. Coblentz sent over," he tells me. "They match. The victim in that barn is indeed Daniel Gingerich."

"Damn," I mutter.

"Sorry to be the bearer of bad news. I figured you'd want to let the family know as soon as possible."

Grabbing my keys, I head for reception, catch my first-shift dispatcher just as she's finishing a call. Lois Monroe is in her mid-fifties, a mother and grandmother, and a much appreciated fixture in the department. She's coolheaded and candid; I've seen her take more than one overly cocky young cop down a notch or two.

"Lois, I need you to dig up everything you can find on Daniel Gingerich. Check for warrants. Run him through LEADS. Family members, too." LEADS is the acronym for the Law Enforcement Automated Data System, which is a statewide criminal justice database administered by the Ohio State Highway Patrol.

"You got it." Scribbling, she cocks her head. "I take it you confirmed the victim was him?"

I nod. "We're treating his death as a homicide. I need you to get a tip line set up. We're offering a five-hundred-dollar reward for information leading to the arrest and conviction of the person responsible. Get that out to all media outlets." I have no idea how I'll come up with the money, but I'll figure something out.

"You got it."

"I'm going to see the family. If you get any media inquiries, tell them we'll be sending out a press release end of day."

I ARRIVE at the Gingerich farm to find the investigator with the fire marshal's office poking around inside the remains of the barn. I park behind a buggy and offer a wave as I head toward the house.

Gideon Gingerich comes to the door as I'm about to knock. Desperate for news, but dreading it. My heart gives a hard twist.

"Is it him?" he asks.

I nod. "I'm sorry, Gideon. I'm afraid so. The dental records from Dr. Gray match the X-rays taken by the coroner."

Miriam Gingerich has come up behind him, dish towel in hand. She puts her hands over her mouth and turns away.

"May I come inside?" I ask Gideon.

He sags as if he's suddenly too exhausted to remain standing. But he straightens, opens the door wider, and trudges inside.

Miriam is standing at the sink, looking out the window. The dish towel lies on the floor at her feet. Their grief is tangible.

Gideon pulls out a chair and sinks into it. "Our boy is with God." He addresses his wife without looking at her.

"God always has a plan." She whispers the words, but her voice lacks conviction. "Sometimes we just don't know what it is."

Gideon motions to the table. "Sit down, Chief Burkholder."

I take the nearest chair. "Mr. Gingerich, the fire marshal believes the fire was arson."

"I don't understand why anyone would do such a thing."

Once again, I ask if he uses or stores gasoline. "Maybe you stored it for someone else? One of your neighbors, maybe?"

"No." He shakes his head. "The *Ordnung* allows only diesel fuel. That's all we use."

"Did you keep small square bales of hay near the tack room?"

"I keep a few bales down by the stalls for the horses."

"What about a wheelbarrow?"

"We keep it for mucking stalls." His eyes narrow. "Why are you asking me these things? What does it have to do with . . . Danny?"

I hesitate, knowing the details surrounding his son's death will upset him and his wife. But sooner or later the details will get out.

"Mr. Gingerich, the fire marshal believes Danny somehow became trapped or was locked inside the tack room. He believes some of those items may have been used to barricade the door."

Gideon's eyes widen as he realizes what I'm telling him. Vaguely, I'm aware of Miriam rushing from the room.

"Locked?" He utters the word as if it's a foreign language. "I don't see how that can be true. The door can only be locked with a key. The investigator must be mistaken."

"The lock was engaged," I tell him.

"But . . ." Grief flashes, but he pushes on. "Chief Burkholder, it was a double-cylinder dead-bolt lock. The only way to lock it is with a key. That can be done from the inside or the outside. There's no way he could have locked himself in the tack room by accident."

Which can only mean the door was locked from the outside. . . . "Do you have the key?" I ask.

"No. There are two. I keep them in the barn, tied together with a string, and hang them on a peg across the aisle. We figured if some thief came in at night, they wouldn't be able to find the keys, yet the keys would still be handy when we locked up."

"You keep the tack room locked at night?"

"Usually."

I nod. "Mr. Gingerich, can you think of anyone who was angry with Danny? Someone who may have wanted to harm him?"

"No," he whispers. "Danny was a good boy. Well liked."

"Can you think of any reason why he would've gone into that tack room at night?"

"I don't know why he would do that."

"Who knows about the keys?"

"Just me and Danny. My wife and daughter. The little ones probably, but they don't go out there much."

"Is there anyone who might be angry with you or your wife? A relative? Neighbor? Extended family? Business associate?"

"We are *Amisch*." He says the words as if that somehow explains everything. "There is no one," he tells me. *"No one."*

"What can you tell me about Luane Raber?"

"She's a good girl. Quiet. She never got caught up in all the *Rumspringa* goings-on. Danny was going to marry her."

"Who else was Danny close to?"

"His best friend is Milo Hershberger. He lives up to Millersburg now. Trains horses for the *Englischers*. He and Danny were good friends. Practically grew up together. Don't see him much anymore. But Milo is a good man. Danny thought the world of him."

We fall silent. "Mr. Gingerich, is there anything else you can tell me that might be important?"

"We had some things stolen from the barn a few months ago. A saddle. A couple of harnesses." He shrugs. "That's when we started locking the tack-room door."

I don't recall a burglary report, but I'm not surprised. More often than not, the Amish prefer to deal with problems on their own. "Do you have any idea who might've done it?"

"I know who did it. The neighbor, Chris Martino. Lives down the road in that trashy old house."

I'm familiar with Chris Martino. He's a convicted felon and did two years in Mansfield for possession with intent to sell. He rents the farmhouse next door to the Gingerich family. Martino is unemployed, divorced—and has a mean streak as wide as Lake Erie. He spends his days drinking and most weekends hawking goods at the local flea market or Amish horse auction. Two years ago I pulled him over for running a stop sign and ended up arresting him on a DUI. He became so combative, I had to call for backup.

"Did Daniel ever have any run-ins with Martino?"

"They had words over the stolen tack. Martino got mad when Danny asked him if he took it."

"Did Martino make any threats? Anything like that?"

"I don't think so, but it don't take much to set him off."

I pause, shift gears. "How was Daniel in the last week or so? Was he acting normally? Happy? Sad?"

His eyes soften. "He was the same as always. Helpful. Conscientious. Danny worked hard. He loved God. Loved his family."

"Do you mind if I take a quick look around Danny's room?"

"Why on earth do you need to do that?"

"Maybe Danny left something behind that might be helpful in some way. I don't know. A note or something."

He doesn't look happy about the request, but he's too immersed in grief to voice any reservations. "You can look if you want." He motions toward the stairs. "It's the second door on the right."

"Thank you. I won't be long." I start toward the stairs, but he calls out my name. I turn and look at him.

"He was a good young man, Chief Burkholder. I don't know who could have done this horrible thing. I just don't know."

Lowering his face into his hands, he begins to cry.

DANIEL Gingerich's bedroom is typical of a room belonging to a young Amish man. Sparsely furnished. Practical. From where I'm standing, I see a pair of socks under the bed, and it reminds me that just days ago an eighteen-year-old boy called this space home.

I turn to the mattress, kneel, and run my hands beneath it. First thing I feel is a pack of cigarettes. My fingers slide over something else. I pull out a sandwich bag into which several photos are tucked. The first is a picture of Daniel and a pretty Amish girl. I wonder if it's his girlfriend, Luane Raber. She's wearing a blue dress, a *kapp*, and a huge smile. They look carefree and happy.

I go to the next photo. It's a close-up of the girl. She's got a pretty face. A shy, sweet smile. Still wearing her *kapp*.

The last photo is of Daniel. He's shirtless, with wet hair, and he is flexing his muscles, pointing to a large brown spot on his torso. At first I think the spot is a leech he picked up while swimming, but upon closer inspection I realize it's a birthmark or mole. He's poking fun at himself, having a good time with his girlfriend. I pull a baggie from a compartment on my belt and slide the photos into it.

Daniel Gingerich was a son, a brother, a grandson, a boyfriend. According to everyone I've talked to, he was well liked and happy, a typical Amish boy anxious to start his life as an adult. Who wanted him dead, and why? What kind of monster would lock an eighteen-year-old boy inside a room and then set the barn on fire?

Chapter 4

SOME PEOPLE SAY MURDER is a senseless act. I don't agree. There's no doubt murder is a brutal act. It's a cruel act. An immoral act. Murder is an unthinkable deed. But it's rarely senseless.

As with any murder investigation, it's imperative to establish motive and develop a suspect as quickly as possible. Right now information is the name of the game.

After leaving the Gingerich farm, I swing by the station and pick up my first-shift officer. Rupert "Glock" Maddox has been with the department for about five years now. He's a former marine, a rock-solid cop with a steady personality and a boatload of common sense. I consider him not only an asset but a friend.

"Where we headed?" he says as he slides into my Explorer.

I fill him in on the turn of events surrounding the death of Daniel Gingerich. "I thought we might pay Chris Martino a visit."

"Ah. My favorite felon. Colorful guy." Then he adds, "Martino's a mean son of a bitch and dumb as a box of rocks."

"Bad combination." I make the turn onto the county road that will take us to the Martino place.

"You check for warrants?" Glock asks.

"Yup." I slow for the lane, a narrow strip that's more weed than gravel, and turn in. "None currently."

The lane wends right just as the old farmhouse looms into view. Martino rents the house from the owner, Owen Brice, who lives in Millersburg and stores his tractor and equipment in the barns and still farms the land. We take a broken sidewalk around to the front porch. Standing slightly to one side, I knock and wait.

I hear the thump of footsteps, and then the door swings open. Chris Martino is forty years old and wearing blue jeans and a plaid shirt he didn't bother buttoning. He's holding a beer in his hand.

"I was wondering when you were going to show up," he says.

"Mr. Martino, can we come in and talk to you for a second?"

He looks past me at Glock and frowns. "I reckon you ought to just stand right there and tell me what the hell this is all about."

I give him the basics of the barn fire. "Daniel Gingerich was inside. He didn't survive."

"Whoa. Man." He manages to look genuinely shocked. "I knew there was a fire. Saw all that smoke and the trucks. I didn't know the kid got burned up in it."

"I understand you had words with Daniel over some horse tack."

He blinks at me. "What are you insinuating exactly?"

"I'm not insinuating anything. I'm simply asking you if you argued with Daniel Gingerich."

"Well, if I know you cops, you're going to try and blame that fire on me 'cause you don't feel like looking for the real guy who done it. I didn't have nothing to do with it."

Glock sighs. "If you'd just answer the question, sir."

His eyes flit to Glock and back to me. "Lookit, that kid might be Amish and all that, but he ain't no angel."

"How so?" I ask.

"Well, he marched over here a couple months ago and accused me of stealing from his barn. Like I got a use for a buggy harness."

"What happened?"

"I told him I got better things to do than steal crap outta his barn."

"You were angry with him?"

"Yeah. When someone gets pushy with me, I push back."

"How exactly did you push back?" I ask.

"I told him to hit the road. I ain't going to let anyone accuse me of stealing. I don't care if he's Amish."

"Did the argument get physical?" I ask.

"No. It was just a bunch of mouth flapping, mostly."

"Where were you two nights ago?" I ask.

"Are you kidding me?" He gapes at me. "You going to try to hang that fire on me just because we had a little argument?"

Glock steps up beside me. "Why don't you just calm down and answer the question."

Martino blinks. "I went bowling with my ex–old lady; then we went down to the Brass Rail."

The Brass Rail is a bar just outside Painters Mill. Beer by the pitcher. Fights in the parking lot. One-stop shopping for any knucklehead looking for a good time or trouble or both.

I pull out my notebook. "What time did you leave?"

"We stayed till close. Two or so. Bunch of people saw us."

"Did you go straight home?"

"Yeah."

"Alone?"

"My old lady was with me."

"She stay all night?"

"Yup."

"Ex–old lady got a name?" Glock asks.

"Trisha. Last name's still Martino."

I jot it down. "Thank you for your time, Mr. Martino."

Glock and I turn away and start toward the Explorer. As we get in, Glock makes eye contact with me. "You think he did it?"

"I think he's capable. He doesn't seem like much of a planner."

"More like a punch-first-think-later kind of guy."

We smile at each other.

"When we get back, I want you to go talk to the ex-wife," I tell him. "See if she can corroborate Prince Charming's alibi."

"So we're going to keep him on the list for now."

"For now," I say.

DANIEL Gingerich's girlfriend, Luane, is just sixteen years old. She lives with her parents, Mose and Sue Raber, and six siblings on a farm seven miles south of Painters Mill. The Rabers are Swartzentruber Amish, one of the Old Order sects that maintains a vise grip on the long-standing traditions. They refuse many modern conveniences used by other Amish. Things like indoor plumbing, milk machines, and linoleum floors. Unfortunately for me, they're also known to maintain the so-called wall of silence when it comes to dealing with outsiders.

I take the sidewalk to the front door and knock. A pretty girl not yet into her teens pushes open the screen, her young face solemn.

"Sinn du eldra haymet?" I ask. Are your parents home?

Without responding, she calls out over her shoulder, *"Mir henn Englischer bsuch ghadde!"* We have a non-Amish visitor!

A heavyset Amish woman in a gray dress walks cautiously to the door and gives me a once-over. "Can I help you?"

I have my badge at the ready. "Sue Raber?"

"Ja."

"I'm looking into the fire at the Gingerich place," I tell her. "I'd like to ask you and your husband a few questions." I glance past her and see four girls standing in the shadows of the hall behind her, eyes wide. "Luane, too, if that's all right."

"We heard about the fire," she says quietly. "Sweet Danny, too. Such a terrible thing." Her eyes flick to the girls, and she motions in the general direction of the next room. *"Gay kinner hiede misse."* Go mind the children.

"Mrs. Raber," I begin, "I'm talking to everyone who knew or had contact with Daniel in the days before he died. I've been told Daniel and Luane were close. That they were planning to get married." When she raises her gaze to mine, I add, "May I come in?"

A few minutes later I'm seated at the big table in the kitchen with Mose and Sue Raber. They are polite, but one thing is clear: I'm an outsider, and the sooner I leave, the better.

From all indications the Rabers thought the world of young Daniel. They liked him as a person as well as a prospective son-in-law. They approved of his relationship with their daughter.

"Would it be possible for me to speak with Luane?" I ask.

The couple exchanges a look.

"She's been . . . *umshmeisa,*" Sue tells me. Upset.

"Ich fashtay," I tell her. I understand. "I won't keep her long."

Mose looks at his wife and shrugs.

The Amish woman rises and disappears into the living room. A minute later she returns with one of the Amish girls who'd been watching us when I first arrived.

"This is Chief Burkholder with the police," Sue tells her daughter in *Deitsh.* "They're looking into the fire over to the Gingerich place, and she wants to ask you some questions."

Luane visibly winces at the mention of the Gingerich name. She's a pretty thing with flawless skin and eyes the color of faded denim. She looks as if she's spent the last two days crying.

"I know this is a difficult time for you," I begin. "When's the last time you saw Daniel?"

"Four days ago. He helped Datt cut corn and stayed for supper."

"He was courting you, right?"

Luane blushes prettily. *"Ja."*

"How long have you known him?" I ask.

"Since I was nine or ten."

"You've been friends most of your lives, then?"

"Ja." A smile touches her mouth. "Once he stopped picking on me, anyway."

"Tell me about him."

Her smile expands, and for the first time she looks animated. "He was . . . *goot-maynich*." Kind. "Always making people laugh. We were going to get married next fall. After harvest."

Mose steps in. "Daniel was a hard worker. Put in ten hours on the farm and then went to his job down to the farm store in town."

"He's been like a son to us for years," Sue adds.

"Ate like a horse," Mose puts in with a smile.

Luane doesn't bother wiping the tears that have begun to roll down her cheeks. She doesn't look at me. "I don't know what I'm going to do without him. He was . . . everything."

"Did Daniel have any disagreements with anyone recently?" I ask. "With friends or family? A customer at the farm store, maybe?"

The three people exchange looks, their expressions perplexed and searching. Finally, Mose answers, "He wasn't the kind of young man to have an argument with anyone."

"He was easygoing," Sue adds.

Luane has remained silent. I turn my attention to her. "Luane?"

My question seems to jolt her. She lifts her gaze to mine. "Everyone loved Danny." Her eyes fill. *"Everyone."*

Someone didn't, a little voice whispers.

I wait, but no one attempts to fill the silence. "Luane, did any of the other boys want to court you before Daniel came along?"

Mose makes a sound of disapproval, letting me know he doesn't like the question. I don't take my eyes off his daughter.

"Daniel was always the one," Sue cuts in. "Always."

I maintain my focus on the girl. She can't make eye contact.

I rephrase the question. "Were any of the other young men jealous of your relationship with Daniel?"

"I don't think so," she mumbles.

"What about the girls? Were any of them jealous?"

She shakes her head. "No."

Once again her mother interjects. "The *Amisch* aren't that way, Chief Burkholder."

I nod, keep my attention focused on Luane. "Is there anything else you want to tell me?"

No one speaks. Mose makes eye contact with me. Something in his expression tells me he wants to say something in private.

I rise. "Thank you for your time."

Mose walks me to the door and follows me outside. He doesn't speak until we reach the Explorer. "Daniel had an argument with his best friend," he begins. "Milo Hershberger. Trains horses up in Millersburg now."

I recall Daniel's father mentioning Hershberger. He hadn't said anything about a quarrel. "What was the argument about?"

"What else are two young men going to argue about?" The Amish man's lips twist into an ironic smile. "A girl."

I know where this is going. "Luane?"

He glances over his shoulder toward the house and nods.

"Any idea why she didn't mention it?"

"I think it's an uncomfortable thing for her to talk about, especially with a stranger."

I nod. "How bad was the argument?"

"Bad enough. They were best friends since they were little." Grimacing, he shakes his head. "But boys grow into men. And when there's a woman involved . . ." Shrugging, he lets the words trail. "They haven't spoken since it happened. I reckon if you want the details, you ought to talk to Milo about it."

I CALL my second-shift dispatcher, Jodie, on my way to Millersburg and have her run Milo Hershberger through the various databases. He comes back clean. Not even a parking ticket.

It's nearly dusk when I pull into the gravel lane of the double-wide mobile home where he lives. It's a pleasant little ranch located in a rural area a few miles west of Millersburg. I park behind an older Ford F-250 to which a horse trailer is hitched.

A horse barn with Dutch doors is the focal point of the property. Both the front and back sliding doors are open, and I can see the silhouette of a horse standing in cross ties. Two more horses stand inside steel pipe runs. The pound of hooves draws my attention to a large pen comprised of stock panels. Within a cloud of dust, a young man in a cowboy hat is astride a rangy Appaloosa gelding.

I get out of the Explorer and walk over to the pen. "He's gorgeous," I say by way of greeting.

The young man's hat slants toward me. "And don't he know it, too," he says in a deep voice. "Whoa."

"I'm looking for Milo Hershberger."

"You found him." He gives me a thorough once-over. "You here about Danny?"

Milo Hershberger is nineteen years old and boy-next-door attractive. He's got a round face, with brown puppy-dog eyes and a full mouth. His shoulder-length hair is pulled into a short ponytail.

I nod. "Do you have a few minutes?"

"Let me get him cooled off and I'm all yours."

I follow Hershberger and his horse into the barn and watch while he untacks the animal and slips a sheet over its back.

"I heard Danny got killed in that barn fire. Is that true?" he asks.

"The coroner made a positive ID yesterday."

"Damn." He looks out over the land. Anguish flashes on his face. "Hard to believe he's gone."

I'm no schmuck when it comes to identifying phony emotions, but his seems genuine.

"I've known Danny since we were a couple of dumb Amish boys, six or seven years old. He was like a brother to me."

"You were Amish?"

"I still am, really." But he looks down at his clothes and laughs. Dusty jeans. Denim shirt. "On the inside, anyway."

"What happened?"

"Couldn't keep my nose clean. I pissed off my parents. Pissed off the bishop. I'm under the *bann* now. Haven't seen my family in almost three months."

It's an all-too-familiar scenario. I don't have to ask if he misses them; the pain of it is written all over his face.

"Why did they put you under the *bann?*"

Grinning, he motions toward the F-250. "She was the love of my life the instant I heard the purr of that engine. So they got me on the truck. We've got such an entrepreneurial spirit, you know.

I mean, the Amish. I don't know how they expect me to haul all these horses around without a truck."

"Wouldn't be easy. Unless maybe you have your clients bring them to you."

"I could, I guess." He smiles. "Sure do like that truck, though."

Despite the circumstances, I find myself liking Milo Hershberger. He's soft-spoken, with boyish charm and a kind demeanor.

He looks at me closely. "You that cop used to be Amish?"

Now it's my turn to smile. "Guilty."

"Guess that makes two of us."

"Milo, what happened between you and Daniel?" I ask.

"Girl got in the way, I guess." When I continue to stare at him, he continues. "Luane Raber. Me and Danny, we had it bad for her. I've known her most of my life, too. I was always too shy to talk to her. Then, during *Rumspringa,* the three of us—me, Danny, and Luane—went to some parties. Hung out."

I wait.

"I thought she was interested. I knew she was sort of *with* Danny, but I figured girls can change their minds, right?" He looks at me as if expecting me to confirm it, but I don't bite.

"Anyway, Luane and I went out a couple of times." He shrugs. "I liked her. A lot. But I reckon the feeling wasn't mutual, because when it was all said and done, she chose Danny. End of story."

"How did all that affect your relationship with Danny?" I ask.

"How do you think? He didn't like it much. Neither did I."

"Did you argue about it?" I ask. "Fight?"

"Both." Another shrug. "To tell you the truth, I don't know which was worse—losing him as a friend, losing Luane, or losing my family. Life's been pretty lonely without them."

"So you and Daniel came to blows?" I ask.

"Yeah," he admits. "Couple times. Danny had a hell of a left hook." When I say nothing, he flushes. "Look, it was a guy thing. We both . . . loved her. But no one got hurt. I mean, physically."

"When's the last time you saw Daniel?"

He takes a moment to search his memory. "I honestly don't

know. I saw him at the farm store a couple weeks ago. Went in to buy some stuff for my truck and he was there."

"Did you speak?"

"I would have, but he just sort of looked away."

"When's the last time you were at the Gingerich farm?"

"A few months. Maybe last fall. Used to go over all the time. I'd help Mr. Gingerich bale hay. Stayed for dinner a hundred times."

"When's the last time you saw Luane?"

"I went to worship when it was at her parents' farm a few weeks ago. She was with Danny, so . . ." He lets the words trail. "It was awkward. We didn't even speak. I haven't been to worship since."

I nod, sensing there's something else there that he's not telling me. "Where were you night before last?"

"I was here. All night. I rode until dark. I had a beer, hit the shower, and I was out like a light."

"Can anyone corroborate that?"

He grins. "That Appaloosa over there, but he ain't much on conversation." When I don't smile, he sobers. "Hey, I'm not a suspect or anything, am I?"

"At this point I'm talking to everyone who knew Daniel."

"Look, me and Danny might've had a falling-out, but there's no way I'd ever hurt him—or anyone else, for that matter."

"So what aren't you telling me?"

"I don't know what you mean."

I hold my silence.

"Look, I might've done some things that ain't very Amish-like. But I'm still one of them. I believe in God. I loved Danny like a brother, and I was raised not to speak ill of the dead. But let me tell you something. Everyone who thinks Danny was some kind of saint? Maybe they didn't know him as well as I do."

"What do you mean?"

"You want to know about Danny the Saint? I'd suggest you talk to Emma Miller." He starts to turn away and then stops as if thinking better of it. "But I reckon it's a little too late."

"What do you mean?" I ask. "Where do I find her?"

"Good luck, Chief Burkholder." Turning, he walks away.

Chapter 5

IN HOLMES COUNTY the most common Amish surname is Miller. My second-shift dispatcher, Jodie, and I spent two hours looking through the latest *Ohio Amish Directory for Holmes County and Vicinity*, an enormous tome that lists local Amish church districts and the names of their members. By the time we found Emma Miller, it was ten p.m.—too late to pay her a visit.

At eight a.m. I'm in the Explorer just east of Charm, heading north on County Road 159. A few miles down the road, I find the address I'm looking for. A sign at the end of the lane reads: BIRD-HOUSES. FEEDERS. DOGHOUSES. NO SUNDAY SALE. I make the turn.

Sam and Esther Miller live on a well-kept farm that sits atop a hill overlooking a picturesque valley. The brick farmhouse was built at the highest point on the property and offers stunning views. A massive pine tree dominates the front yard, which is enclosed by a split-rail fence. The sliding doors of the barn stand open. I see someone inside, so I pull up to the base of the ramp and get out.

I'm on my way to the door when I notice the bird feeders. Dozens of them are mounted on freestanding poles; others hang from the eaves of the barn. They're fashioned to look like mini gazebos, log cabins, buggies, and the iconic Amish-country red barn.

"Can I help you?"

I look up to see a middle-aged Amish woman approach. She's Swartzentruber—I can tell by the black bonnet and the style of her dress—but her expression is friendly and open.

"The bird feeders are lovely," I tell her. "Do you make them?"

"We make everything here." She looks around and lowers her voice conspiratorially. "We don't usually open till ten, but if you got your eye on something, I can sell it to you."

"I'm afraid this is an official call." I show her my badge and introduce myself. "I'm looking into the death of Daniel Gingerich."

Her smile falters. Something else in her eyes I can't decipher. A quick dart of apprehension. "Heard about that," she says. "Awful for that poor family." But she doesn't look too broken up about it.

"I'm looking for Emma Miller," I say. "Is she around?"

That shadow again. More pronounced this time. "Emma was my daughter," she tells me. "Passed away six months ago."

Surprise ripples through me. I find myself wishing I'd done more homework before coming here. "I'm sorry."

"Sis Gottes wille." It's God's will.

"She was just seventeen?"

The woman nods. "Left us all too soon."

"Did your daughter know Daniel Gingerich, Mrs. Miller?"

"They met a few times. Daniel did some work here at the farm for my husband last summer. Painted the old milk house down the lane. Put up a cross fence for the calves."

It's a vague answer, and in the back of my mind, I hear Milo Hershberger's parting words: *You want to know about Danny the Saint? I'd suggest you talk to Emma Miller.*

"Were Daniel and Emma friends?" I ask.

Something ugly peeks around the corner of its hidden spot. "Just to say hello."

I sense she is keeping something cached away, just out of sight, so I push a little harder. "Are you certain about that, Mrs. Miller? I was told your daughter and Daniel Gingerich knew each other."

"Someone got their information wrong," the woman says.

"Maybe they became friends and you didn't know about it."

"I knew everything about my daughter. Everything."

I try another tactic. "Did you or your husband have any problems with Daniel while he was working for you?"

She shakes her head. "Danny was a good boy. A good worker. Did his job every day, and we paid him a fair wage for his time."

"Die zeit fer is nau." The time to go is now.

I turn at the sound of the deep male voice to see a middle-aged Amish man standing in the doorway of the barn, leaning on a pitchfork, watching us. He's wearing dark trousers. Blue work shirt. Suspenders and a wide-brimmed straw hat. His expression tells me he'd been standing there for a while, listening.

"Mr. Miller?" I start toward him and identify myself.

Taking his time, he meets me halfway, his eyes sweeping over my uniform. "What are all these questions about?"

"I'm investigating the death of Daniel Gingerich."

"Daniel Gingerich? We barely knew the boy. We don't know anything about him. I don't see how we could help you."

"Your wife was just telling me Daniel did some work for you." I pause. "I understand your daughter, Emma, was friends with him."

Something that resembles a shiver runs the length of his body.

"All I know about Dan Gingerich is that he was *en faehicher schreiner.*" An able carpenter.

"Mr. Miller, did you or your wife have any problems with Daniel while he was here?" I ask.

"There were no problems," he says.

"What about—"

"We've answered enough of your questions. Our business with you is finished. You should go now."

"Mr. Miller—"

"We don't know anything. Go now. Just go."

MY ODD exchange with the Millers nags at me on the drive back to Painters Mill. There's no doubt in my mind they know more about Daniel Gingerich than they were willing to discuss; I'm even more certain that knowledge has something to do with their deceased daughter. But why are they so reluctant to discuss it?

It's after ten a.m. when I arrive back at the station. Lois is at the dispatch desk, squinting at some handwritten report. I'm not surprised to find my third-shift dispatcher, Mona Kurtz, occupied with busywork that could more than likely wait until her shift at midnight. I've talked to her about her penchant for "staying over" and my inability to pay overtime due to budget constraints. So far my concerns have fallen on deaf ears.

At twenty-four and a recent grad from the local community

college with a degree in criminology, Mona is enamored with every facet of law enforcement. When my most senior officer, Roland "Pickles" Shumaker, retires, I'm going to promote her.

Both sets of eyes land on me as I cross to the dispatch station. "Nice of you to stay late, Mona," I say easily.

She smiles a little guiltily. "Sorry, Chief. I was just helping Lois while she translates Skid's chicken scratch."

"Uh-huh." I pluck messages from my slot. "Since you're here, do you have an hour or so to spend on a special project for me?"

"Are you kidding? I mean, of course. What do you need?"

"I want you to dig up everything you can find on Emma Miller. Seventeen years old. Amish. Lived in Charm with her parents. Now deceased."

Her face lights up. "I'm all over it."

I can't help it; I grin.

I've just sat down at my desk when my phone erupts. The display tells me it's Doc Coblentz.

"Hi, Doc," I begin, hoping for information on Daniel Gingerich.

"I'm about to begin the autopsy on Daniel Gingerich. Sheriff Rasmussen is on his way. I thought you might want to be here."

"I'll be there in ten minutes." Grabbing my keys, I head toward the door.

I call Tomasetti on my way to Pomerene Hospital. "The coroner is about to begin the autopsy on Daniel Gingerich," I tell him.

"That was fast."

"We have less customers down here in Holmes County."

"They could use him up in Cuyahoga County."

"Can't have him, Tomasetti."

He sighs. "I'll be there as soon as I can."

Pomerene Hospital is a fifty-five-bed facility north of Millersburg off of Wooster Road. I nab a parking spot outside the Emergency entrance and push through the double glass doors.

I'm thinking about Daniel Gingerich as I take the elevator to the basement. From all appearances, he'd been a typical young Amish man with a bright future ahead. So why did someone see fit to lock him in that tack room and set the barn on fire?

The elevator doors whoosh open, and I step into a quiet tiled hall. I walk past a plaque that reads: MORGUE AUTHORIZED PERSONNEL. Doc Coblentz's office is to my left. I see that Sheriff Rasmussen and Tomasetti have already arrived.

"Hi, Doc." I step into his office and extend my hand.

Doc Coblentz is clad in blue scrubs covered with a transparent green gown. He's a portly man, and when he's suited up like this, he sort of resembles a glazed doughnut.

We shake, and I turn to the other two men. "Mike." I extend my hand first to the sheriff and then to Tomasetti. "Agent Tomasetti."

Tomasetti gives me his stone face, but I don't miss the slight twitch of his mouth. "Chief Burkholder."

Sheriff Rasmussen knows we're involved, though I don't believe he's aware that we're living together. Such a relationship would be frowned upon not only by the Ohio Bureau of Criminal Investigation but my own department as well. I'm pretty sure we'll be officially discovered at some point. When that happens, chances are Tomasetti will be reassigned.

Doc Coblentz is focused on the much grimmer cerebrations at hand. "There's not much left of this poor kid, Kate." Sighing, he motions toward the door. "Let's suit up and we'll get started."

The coroner leads us to the alcove off the main hall. There are shelves jammed with individually packaged gowns, masks, hair caps, latex gloves, and shoe covers. The three of us slip into protective gear, and then Doc ushers us toward the autopsy room.

The space is large and brightly lit. Stark fluorescent lighting rains down on a single stainless-steel gurney. I force my eyes to the vaguely human shape laid out atop it.

"Daniel Gingerich. Eighteen years old." The coroner pulls up his face mask. "There's no gunshot wound, sharp-force trauma, or blunt-force trauma indicated. Preliminarily speaking—and toxicology aside—in my opinion, this fire death was not the concealment of a homicide."

"He was alive when he was locked in the tack room?" I ask.

"There's soot deposition on tracheal mucosa and the dorsum of the tongue," the doctor replies, "which means he was breathing and alive at the time of the fire."

"Conscious?" Rasmussen asks.

"There's no way to know that for certain," the doctor says.

"Cause of death?" Tomasetti asks.

"I've more work to do, but preliminarily speaking, the decedent died of thermal injuries as well as smoke inhalation. Chances are, he fell unconscious due to the smoke and then he burned to death."

"Manner of death?" I ask the question all of us want to know.

"I'm still waiting for results on some of the tests I've run. More than likely I'm going to rule this one a homicide."

"Toxicology?" I ask.

"Going to be a week or so before results are in. Once they are, I'll make my official ruling," Doc Coblentz replies.

When the final questions are asked, Tomasetti, Rasmussen, and I file from the room. In the alcove we peel away our protective layers of clothing and stuff them into the biohazard receptacle.

"Who the hell does something like that to an Amish kid?" Rasmussen says.

"Any thoughts on that, Chief?" Tomasetti asks.

I tell them about the falling-out between Daniel and his former best friend, Milo Hershberger.

"You think Hershberger did it?" Tomasetti asks.

"I'm still digging," I respond vaguely.

"You talk to the girlfriend?" Rasmussen asks.

I nod. "I'm talking to everyone who came in contact with Daniel. From all indications everyone thought pretty highly of him."

"Except whoever locked him in the tack room and set the barn on fire," Rasmussen mutters.

DANIEL Gingerich not only worked on the farm full-time with his father but also held down a job at the local farm store. Quality Implement and Farm Supply is located just across the railroad tracks on the industrial side of Painters Mill. I still smell the formalin clinging to my clothes as I park and head inside.

I am immediately greeted by a petite woman with brown hair and a red Quality Implement smock. I've been in this store plenty of times over the years, and I recognize her immediately.

"Morning, Dora," I say.

"You here about Danny?" she asks.

I nod, glance toward the manager's office up on the second level mezzanine. "Is Al around?"

"He's there." She lowers her voice. "His phone's been ringing off the hook since . . . it happened."

"You knew Danny?" I ask.

"He was sort of a fixture around here. I saw him a few times a week. Nice kid."

"Thanks, Dora." I set my hand on her shoulder, give it a squeeze, and then head up to the office.

Al Shields has been the manager here since I was a kid. When I was fifteen, he caught me swiping a candy bar. Instead of calling the cops, he walked me to the cash register, pulled a dollar out of his wallet, and paid for it. I never stole anything again.

I'm midway to the steps that will take me to the office when I see Al jogging down them. "Hey, Chief."

I smile, and for a split second I know both of us are remembering that long-ago day that helped put me on the right track.

"Hell of a note about Danny Gingerich." Al gives my hand a vigorous shake. "I heard it was arson. Is that true?"

I nod. "Do you have a minute? I need to ask some questions."

"Sure." He motions toward the office. "Come on up."

I follow him up the stairs and take the chair across from his desk. "Had Danny been acting normally in the weeks before the fire?"

"I never noticed anything different. He was . . . the same. A solid worker. Always willing to lend a hand. Cheerful."

"Did Danny get along with his coworkers?"

"He got along with everyone, Kate, and that's no exaggeration. All of us—we really liked him. Sweet kid."

"What about customers? Any arguments or disagreements?"

"Customers loved him, too. I just can't figure someone doing that to such a fine young man."

"Where did Daniel work, exactly?" I ask.

"TBA." He motions toward the rear of the store.

TBA is retailspeak for tire, battery, and auto. "Was he close to any of his coworkers?"

"He used to hang out with Ralph Baker."

"Do you mind if I talk to Ralph?"

"Sure. He's there now. Just go on back." He motions toward the stairs. "I'll be here if you need anything."

I find Ralph Baker talking to a customer about a set of radials. When the customer walks away, I approach Ralph. "Mr. Baker?"

He's a big guy. Six three. Mid-thirties, with sandy blond hair. His eyes widen when he spots my uniform. "Ma'am?"

I show him my badge. "I'd like to talk to you about Daniel Gingerich if you have a minute."

"Danny. Oh, man." He blows out a whistle, looks down at the floor, then back at me. "What a bad deal that was."

"Did you know him well?"

"Sure. We worked together for almost two years. He was a heck of a guy. Knows his tires, too." He grins. "For an Amish kid."

"Did Daniel have any disputes with anyone that you know of?"

"Aw, I can't imagine Danny having a disagreement with anyone. He was real easygoing. Everyone liked him."

I go through the usual litany of questions, and I get the same answers. "Is there anything else you can tell me that might help with the investigation?"

His brows knit. "Not really. He worked until noon the day before it happened. I don't even think I told him good-bye." His eyes mist. "Jeez, I didn't know that would be the last time I saw him."

I'M IN my office poring over the preliminary autopsy report Doc Coblentz e-mailed earlier, when I glance up to see Mona cross the threshold. She's excited about something, and judging from the file in her hands, it has to do with the Gingerich case.

"That didn't take long," I say.

She's holding a purple folder in her left hand. "Did you know Emma Miller committed suicide?" she begins.

The news stops me cold. "No, but that's certainly interesting."

"She hanged herself in her parents' barn six months ago. Mother found her body when the family came home from worship."

"Any mention of suspected foul play?"

"No." She opens the file, riffles through the papers. "There was an autopsy. Girl died of cerebral hypoxia. Self-induced." She flips the page. "Lab report says no drugs or alcohol were present."

"No wonder her parents didn't want to talk about it," I murmur.

"Oh, my God."

That garners my full attention. Mona gapes at one of the papers in her hand, then looks up at me. "I'm just now seeing this, Chief. Says here Emma Miller was *pregnant*."

"Well, hell." Even as I feel that jump of cop's excitement, another part of me is saddened.

Mona passes me the file and papers.

"Her parents didn't mention either of those things when I talked to them." I look down at the autopsy report. "This explains why."

"Do you think any of this has something to do with what happened to Daniel Gingerich?" Mona asks.

"I think it opens a door worth looking into."

You want to know about Danny the Saint? I'd suggest you talk to Emma Miller.

If young Emma had a relationship with Daniel, became pregnant, and ultimately committed suicide, her father may have a motive to commit murder.

IT TAKES me half an hour to get through the file Mona amassed on Emma Miller. I am impressed not only by her thoroughness but by her creativity when it comes to mining information not necessarily found in law-enforcement databases. As I read, I'm vaguely aware of Glock arriving to start his end-of-shift reports, along with my second-shift officer, Chuck "Skid" Skidmore.

I'm engaged in my reading, trying to find some connection between Daniel Gingerich and Emma Miller. Both were in their late teens. Their deaths occurred just six months apart. Both happened in Holmes County. And, of course, Daniel did work for the Millers.

I go through the file again, this time looking for details about Emma Miller's life in the weeks and months before her suicide. There isn't much. I find a printout of a newspaper story from the *Daily Record* titled THE MERCANTILE IS CHARMED. In the second paragraph Emma Miller's name is highlighted in yellow.

I read the article with interest. It's a fluff piece written to let people know about the newest Amish-owned business in Charm, Ohio, which is about twenty minutes from Painters Mill. According to the article, the owners, Edna and Isaac Lambright, are also planning to open a café in the one-hundred-year-old round barn located on the same property. The story includes a photo of Emma, along with three other young Amish women. According to the story, she was working at the Mercantile up until the day she died.

I study the photo. Emma was a pretty girl, with big brown eyes behind wire-rimmed glasses, and a serious expression despite the smile. I go to the next photo, which is a group of four girls. All look to be in their late teens. All of them are smiling. One girl has her arm around Emma's shoulder. Her head is thrown back in laughter.

"What happened to you, Emma?" I whisper.

The only reply is silence.

Chapter 6

THE MERCANTILE IS CHOCK-FULL of personality, with massive overhead beams, reclaimed wood on three walls, and a concrete floor that's seen as many hooves as it has boots. It's a rustic-chic retail shop that beckons one to peruse—and buy.

A cowbell jingles cheerfully when I enter. To my right there's an attached silo that's been gutted and transformed into a candle-making shop. To the left of the counter is a railing, and just beyond it is a small café with bistro tables and chairs. Beyond, the store is a jungle of items Amish-country tourists and locals can't live without.

"Can I help you find something?"

I turn to find myself looking at a pretty young Amish woman. Late teens. Raven hair. Peaches-and-cream complexion. Eyes the color of cognac. She's wearing a pastel pink dress with a white organdy head covering that tells me she's Beachy Amish.

"There's more stuff in the back," she tells me. "My *mamm* makes the soap. She puts olive oil in it for soft skin."

"Tempting, but I'm actually here on official business." I show her my badge. "I'm looking into the death of Daniel Gingerich."

"Oh." Her smile falters. "What a horrible thing. Mamm said a bunch of the men from the church district are going to rebuild the barn for the family. I can't imagine losing a loved one that way."

"That's one of the things I admire about the Amish," I tell her. "When tragedy strikes, you can always count—"

"Neva! Look! I finished! And it's so pretty!"

Female voices snap my attention to the rear of the shop. Two young Amish women burst through a curtained door. They're giggling as they race around an end cap of pet supplies.

The girl in the lead draws up short at the sight of me. She's a tad shorter than the others, blond and hazel-eyed, with a round face and twenty pounds of extra weight. Her eyes go wide. "Oh. Sorry."

The second girl literally runs into the first. She's brown-haired, with a widow's peak, blue eyes, and a smattering of freckles on a turned-up nose. Tall and thin of build, she has the gangly arms and legs of a girl who hasn't quite grown into them yet.

The girls are toting a large swath of fabric that looks like a quilt. It strikes me that these are the three girls in the photo taken with Emma Miller.

"I didn't realize you were with a customer," the brown-haired girl says softly.

The blonde is staring at my uniform. "Is everything okay?" she asks.

The girl I'd been talking to sighs. She's trying hard to maintain her professional persona, but she's having a difficult time withholding a smile. "You finished the quilt?"

The blond girl glances at her sidekick and grins. "Just now."

"She cheated on stitches," says the brunette.

The blonde elbows her. "Did not."

"Go on back to the sewing room." The black-haired girl slants her eyes at me. "I'll be there in a minute and we'll take a look."

"*Ich will's sana,*" I say. I'd like to see it. "If you have a minute?"

They stare at me, surprised that I know *Deitsh*. I introduce myself and show them my badge. "I'm looking into the death of Daniel Gingerich, over in Painters Mill."

No one has anything to say about that.

I wait a beat and then ask, "What are your names?"

The black-haired woman sticks out her hand. "I'm Neva Lambright, the manager. My parents own the place."

I take her hand, and we shake.

I turn my attention to the blond girl. She's several inches shorter than me, so I have to look down to meet her gaze.

"I'm Viola Stutzman." Mimicking the older girl, she sticks out her hand. She seems to be the youngest of the group.

I turn my attention to the brunette. "Ina Yoder." She offers a smile. "We don't see too many police in here," she says as we shake.

"Evidently, they don't know what they're missing," I return. "Coffee, quilts, and pastries all under one roof."

"This old barn has been in the family for almost a hundred years," Neva tells me. "Took some doing to restore everything. Now Mamm wants to turn that old round barn out back into a café. That's going to be our next big project."

She motions toward the other two girls. "Viola and Ina work here part-time."

I let my eyes rest on Viola. "You're the quilter?"

Nodding, she offers the quilt. "It's my first."

Taking the quilt, I run my hands over the fabric. It's a sampler quilt, a mosaic of burgundy, cream, and brown. "Is it for sale?"

The girl shakes her head. "I'm giving this one to my *grossmudder*. She taught me about stitching, so I thought it only right."

"I'm sure she'll treasure it." I pass the quilt back to her, then shift the conversation to the subject at hand. "I understand Emma Miller used to work here."

The mention of their deceased coworker dims what had been a buoyant mood. Glances are exchanged, and then eyes are lowered.

"Our sweet Emma," Neva says.

"Did you know her well?" I ask.

"We were best friends." She makes eye contact with the other two women, including them. "The four of us, I mean. We were like sisters. Practically grew up together. Went to school together."

"Emma worked here part-time," Viola says.

"We all loved Emma," Ina says. "She was a gentle soul and . . ." Sighing, she looks around. "It's not the same around here without her, that's for sure. I miss her every day."

I press on. "I understand Emma knew Daniel Gingerich."

The silence that follows goes on a beat too long. Both Ina and Viola look to Neva to answer. "If I remember correctly," Neva says, "I think he did some work for her parents on their farm."

"Were they friends?" I ask.

"I think she went to a singing with him once," Viola says.

Ina wrinkles her nose. "I don't think she liked him that much."

"Why not?" I ask.

Viola gives a smile. "Emma was all about Elam Schlabach."

"Elam was Emma's beau," Ina clarifies.

"Besides, Daniel already had a girlfriend," Neva tells me.

"Oh, I almost forgot about Ruth," Viola says.

"Her name is Luane," Neva corrects.

"I think he courted Ruth Beiler for a time," Ina says.

"Daniel and Ruth went to a singing," Viola puts in.

Neva firmly overrules them. "Luane Raber was his beau and has been for as long as I can remember."

I jot the two names in my notebook. "So Daniel and Emma weren't close?"

"They were more like acquaintances," Neva replies.

"What about while Daniel was working for her parents at the farm?" I ask. "Did they see each other then? Interact?"

Ina looks at the other two girls. "I don't really know about that."

Neva shakes her head. "She never mentioned it."

"Did Emma ever have any arguments with Daniel?" I ask.

Neva laughs. "Emma never said a cross word to anyone."

"So Emma and Elam Schlabach were tight?" I make eye contact with each of the girls.

Viola blushes, looks down at the floor.

Neva holds my gaze. "Emma was crazy about Elam. He loved her, too. But she was kind of shy."

Ina chuckles. "We had to practically pry things out of her, and even then she didn't tell us much."

"Did Elam know Daniel and Emma went to a singing?" I ask.

Again, Viola and Ina look to Neva. "If he knew about it," she says, "I don't think it was a big deal for either of them. Daniel never really entered the picture."

"Is Elam the jealous type?" I ask.

"He's pretty laid back, actually," Neva tells me.

"Were any other boys interested in Emma?"

"All the boys liked her," Viola responds.

Grief flashes in Neva's eyes, followed by a wistful smile. "She had way too much common sense to go out with most boys."

"Did Emma ever have any problems with any of the guys that liked her?" I pose the question to Neva. "Were any of them too forward? Anything like that?"

"If they were, she never said. But then she wasn't a complainer, either. Emma was a good girl. She had no interest in running around. Didn't go out. Never drank beer or anything like that."

Ina has been watching the exchange with interest. She narrows her eyes on mine. "Chief Burkholder, do you think what happened to Daniel Gingerich has something to do with Emma?"

"I'm not sure," I say honestly. "I was just surprised to hear Daniel and Emma knew each other and now both of them are gone."

"The Amish community is a small one." Neva shrugs. "Everyone knows everyone. You know how it is."

I nod because I do. Still, I don't think it's happenstance that these two innocent teenagers' paths crossed—they knew each other, spent time together—and now both of them are dead.

I look from girl to girl. "Was Emma upset about anything in

particular in the days leading up to her passing? Was there something going on in her life that led up to what happened to her?"

Neva heaves a sigh that's fraught with emotion. "Her *mamm* said Emma always had a sad heart. Emma was . . ." Her voice trails. "She was innocent, and yet she had an old soul, if that makes sense. She couldn't bear the thought of hurting others."

"The silly thing." Wiping at the tears, Ina chokes out a laugh. "She worried about everything and everyone."

"Was she worried about anything in particular?" I ask.

Neva shakes her head. "I don't think it was any one thing. She was just . . . sad. And too quiet. She held things inside."

"Her *mamm* says that's what killed her," Ina whispers.

"Her heart couldn't contain all the sadness," Neva says. "The only comfort she could find was with God."

BEFORE leaving the Mercantile, I purchase three individually wrapped rosemary-and-lemon soaps, a hand-dipped candle, and a tin of cinnamon tea for my sister's birthday. I call the station as I stow everything in the back of the Explorer.

"Hey, Chief, what can I do you for?" asks Lois.

"I need an address for Elam Schlabach." I spell the last name and glance down at the time. "Get me a work address, too."

"You got it." Computer keys click on the other end of the line. "Here we go. Home address is 4139 Hogpath Road."

"Work?"

"Last place of employment . . . Buckeye Woodworks and Cabinetry on Fourth Street in Painters Mill."

I know the place. It's an Amish-owned cabinet and woodworking shop that caters to local homebuilders, remodeling companies, and DIY homeowners, both Amish and English.

"If you're going to talk to Schlabach at work, you'd best hurry," she says. "I think they close at six."

Buckeye Woodworks and Cabinetry is a large establishment set up in a metal building that faces Fourth Street. The front of the structure is adorned with rustic wood siding and two windows replete with flower boxes overflowing with bright orange mums.

All the parking spaces in front are occupied, so I pull around to the rear and park next to a loading dock and Dumpster. I get out and take the concrete stairs to a big double door that stands open.

The roar of tools—saws and drills—increases as I approach. The smell of sawdust fills the air as I go through the doors. I'm midway through the shop when a male voice rings out.

"Looking for work?"

I turn to see a white-haired Amish man approach. He's about my height, with a silver beard and a friendly, open expression.

"Actually, I'm looking for Elam Schlabach," I say.

He leads me to a workstation where a young Amish man pushes a saw blade through a piece of walnut. He glances up but takes the time to finish his cut before pushing his goggles onto his crown.

He's in his early twenties, with sandy-colored hair and green eyes. His beard is of the barely-there variety, telling me he's a newlywed.

"Elam Schlabach?" I ask.

"Yup." His eyes flash over my uniform. "Who wants to know?"

I have my badge at the ready and introduce myself. "I'm investigating the death of Daniel Gingerich."

"Heard about all that," Schlabach tells me. "Bad business."

I look at the partially finished table next to where he's standing. "That's a beautiful piece."

"Still gotta distress and stain it. I made the benches, too." I see pride in his eyes as he runs his hand over the wood.

"I know you're busy, so I won't keep you." I slide my badge back into my pocket. "I understand you knew Emma Miller."

He straightens and gives me his full attention. "I knew Emma."

"You were close?"

"What's that got to do with Dan Gingerich?"

"I was hoping you could tell me."

"I don't have anything to say about that." He turns back to his work, flips on the pneumatic saw. He lines up the board and makes the cut. I can't tell by his demeanor if I've hit on a nerve or if he's simply impatient and irritable by nature.

When he's finished with the cut, I round the bench and turn off the saw. *Du sinn heiyahra nau.* You're married now.

He gives me an annoyed look. "I reckon the *Deitsh* earns you points. You Amish or what?"

"Used to be. I left."

He's not impressed. "So what do you want with me?"

"I want to know why Emma Miller committed suicide."

Some of the attitude drains from his eyes. "She's gone. Dan Gingerich is gone. I don't see why any of it matters now."

"It matters because I don't think Daniel Gingerich got locked in that tack room all by himself."

He stares at the wood he'd been cutting, refusing to look at me.

I try another tack. "How long have you been married?"

"Three months."

"You're a newlywed."

"We got a baby on the way." He doesn't seem too happy about either of those things. One thing has become abundantly clear: Elam Schlabach is an angry and bitter young man.

"Congratulations." I wait a beat. "You and Emma were close."

"You could say that. I was going to ask her to marry me. Is that close enough for you?"

"What happened?"

"She hung herself." His voice breaks with the final word, but he covers it with a cough. "It was . . . a mess."

I give him a moment. Let him make another cut. Save face. When he's finished, I ask, "Why did she do it?"

"If I knew the answer to that, she'd still be here. I would have stopped her." He sets down the saw with a little too much force. "How does anyone even conceive something like that? If you were Amish, then you know that to take your own life is a sin."

"Sometimes people get caught up in a dark place and can't get out," I say. "Sometimes no matter how much we love them, we can't save them."

Tightening his mouth, he lifts the board and sets it atop the others he's already cut to size. "So you think someone murdered Dan Gingerich or what?"

"I do."

"I hate to disappoint you, but I didn't know him very well."

"Did Emma?"

"I wouldn't know."

"Are you sure about that, Elam?"

"Everyone says he was such a great guy." He spits out the words. "He was *maulgrischt*." A pretend Christian.

"Why do you say that?"

He leans against the bench and skewers me with a hard look. "I guess you're pretty smart for putting two and two together."

My heart jumps, wondering if he's just made some sort of bizarre confession.

He sees my reaction, and his mouth twists into an unpleasant caricature of a smile. "Wish I could make it easy for you, but . . . I didn't do it." He shrugs. "I didn't figure things out until . . . after."

"Figure what out? After what?"

"Why she did it," he says. "I blamed myself for a long time. I thought I'd put too much pressure on her." His face colors. "I wanted to . . . you know. She wouldn't until we were married. And she was . . . pure. After she died, I thought I was the reason she did it. I'd wake up in a cold sweat in the middle of the night . . ."

I wait.

"My mind would just replay all these things she'd said to me in the weeks before she died. It's like she was trying to tell me something from heaven. Or hell, maybe."

"Tell you what?"

"She never came right out and said it. So I'll never know for sure. I think Gingerich . . . I don't know. I think he did something to her. Something she didn't want him to do."

I feel myself recoil. In the back of my mind, I wonder if he knows Emma Miller was pregnant when she died.

"What did he do to her?" I ask.

He looks around as if to make sure no one is listening. "Look, Dan Gingerich did some work for the Millers a few months before Emma died. He was over there all the time. That was about the time when I noticed . . . changes."

"What kind of changes?"

"She stopped laughing. She stopped looking at me the way she had before. She, I don't know, *changed*. I'd never heard her say anything bad about anyone, but she didn't like Dan Gingerich."

"Any idea why?"

He doesn't answer.

"Elam, you know Emma was *ime familye weg* when she died, don't you?" "In the family way" is the Amish term for "pregnant."

He sucks in a breath. "Yeah, I found out about that."

"She didn't tell you?"

He shakes his head. "I don't see how she could have."

"What do you mean?"

"She was innocent. I mean, I thought . . ." His gaze meets mine. "We never"—he looks away—"you know."

"What do you think happened between Emma and Daniel?"

He picks up another board. "I don't know."

I lower my voice. "Do you think Daniel made advances toward her? Forced her to do something she didn't want to do?"

"She wouldn't talk to me. She just wouldn't say."

"Did you ask?"

"Yeah, I did."

I wait, but he doesn't elaborate, doesn't even look at me.

"Where were you two nights ago?" When he glares at me, I add, "I have to ask."

"Home with my wife. You can ask her." He swings around to face me. "Don't expect me to be sorry about Dan Gingerich being dead. Far as I'm concerned, that son of a bitch got what he deserved, especially if he's burning in hell."

CERTAIN cases take on a life of their own. When I walked into the Gingerich case, I saw Daniel as a victim. But as in most cases, the deeper you dig, the more you learn—and sometimes you realize the people you're fighting for aren't who you think they are.

If Emma Miller and Elam Schlabach were involved in a serious relationship and hadn't yet had sex, how did she end up pregnant? Was she seeing Daniel behind his back? Did her pregnancy or her death have anything to do with Gingerich's murder?

It's dusk when I arrive home. I'm about to open the back door to find Tomasetti when I hear pounding coming from the barn. The sliding door stands open, so I go up the ramp and walk inside.

"Tomasetti?"

"Back here!" comes his voice from somewhere outside.

I head toward the rear and cross to the window. I look out to see Tomasetti working on a good-sized shed of some type.

"What are you doing?" I call out.

He grins. "I think the technical term for it is busting my ass."

Laughing, I take the stairs to the lower level. Tomasetti has set up shop ten feet from the barn. The structure he's working on looks like some sort of rustic giant doghouse.

"Are we getting a dog?" I ask.

Tomasetti removes a nail from his mouth. "Two too many legs."

I think about that a moment. "We're getting a kid?"

He rises to his full height, crosses to me, and kisses me on the mouth. After a moment he motions to his project. "Give up yet?"

"I'm stumped."

Taking my hand, he starts toward the barn. "I'll show you."

We approach a small homemade pen, something Tomasetti has thrown together with quarter-inch plywood and a few nails. I hear the chirping before I see the chicks, and I feel a catch in my chest.

"You didn't," I whisper.

We reach the pen. I look down to see a couple dozen fuzzy chicks chirping and milling about. They're a few days old and about the size of my fist. "They're Buckeyes," he tells me.

I feel his gaze on me, trying to gauge my reaction.

"They're adorable," I say after a moment.

"Good layers, too. Brown eggs."

I look at him, and I can't keep what is surely a stupid grin off my face. "I love the sound of a rooster in the morning."

"They're not sexed. The breeder said there are two in there."

One of the chicks lets out a loud, distressed-sounding chirp. Grinning, I reach for it. "Gotta be the rooster."

Tomasetti chuckles. "If the beak fits . . ."

Gently I pass the chick to Tomasetti. An unexpected surge of affection moves through me. I've seen this man at his worst. I've seen him beaten down by grief and haunted by memories. But I've seen him at his best, too, and I love him more than I've ever loved anyone else in my life. More than I ever believed possible.

"I love them," I say.

I want to stop this moment. Save it for all of time, because both of us know how precious and rare this kind of happiness is.

He reaches for my hands and pulls me around so that we're facing each other. When I look into his eyes, I know something is about to change. Something solid and good and forever.

"We haven't talked about making this arrangement of ours . . . official," he says.

"You mean getting married."

"You've been skittish."

When I don't respond, he looks away, then back at me. "How do you feel about setting a date?"

I look down at the chicks, then back at him. "The Amish marry after harvest, usually in November or December. Maybe January."

"It's almost October."

"I'm a practical woman. I thought we might . . . keep it simple."

"One of about a thousand things I love about you, Chief Burkholder."

"Only a thousand?"

"And counting." He puts his arm around my shoulders, pulls me closer, and side by side we start toward the door.

Chapter 7

I ARRIVE AT THE STATION a little before eight a.m. to find Mona, Lois, and Pickles in the midst of relocating the coffee station to the corner by the window. I'm midway to my office when it occurs to me Mona shouldn't be here. She's already worked her shift, which is midnight to eight a.m. I turn and look at her. "You're still here."

She gives me a deer-in-the-headlights look. "I was on my way out the door when—"

"I could probably muster a couple hours' overtime for you this morning," I tell her. "If you're game."

She brightens. "Oh, I'm game. What you got?"

I pull out the small notebook I keep in my pocket. "See if you can come up with an address for Ruth Beiler." I spell the name. "She's Amish. Last known residence is Painters Mill."

"Coming right up." She starts for her computer.

"Mona?"

She stops and turns, her expression telling me she's afraid I'm going to lay into her for staying late yet again.

"When you find her address, I thought you and I might go speak to her."

"Seriously?" Her eyes and mouth open wide; then she catches herself. "I mean, that would be great. Experience."

"Good. Thanks."

I'm nearly to my office when I hear her let out a whoop loud enough to rattle the windows.

A FEW minutes later my phone buzzes. I glance down to see DEPT OF COMM pop up on the display. "Burkholder."

"Hi, Chief, it's Bob Schoening. I wanted to let you know about an interesting development on the Gingerich case."

"I could use some solid information about now."

"As you are aware, I collected a number of items from the scene. Among them were two mason jars located just outside the tack-room door. We suspect whoever set that fire used the jars to transport gasoline to the scene."

"Are the jars intact?"

"Unfortunately, they are not. In fact, there's nothing about them that makes them particularly unique. The most interesting item I've examined was a key. It was discovered with a metal detector a short distance from the tack room, where the body was found."

"Is it the key to the tack-room door?" I ask.

"It is. But Chief Burkholder, what's significant about the key is that we processed it for latents and we got a good print off it."

"A fingerprint survived the fire?"

"The key was beneath some wood, lying against the dirt floor. It was somewhat protected from the fire and remained cool enough for the latents to show up when we tested it."

I sit up straighter. "Do you have a name to go with the print?"

"We submitted to BCI, and they're running it through AFIS."

AFIS is the acronym for the Automated Fingerprint Identification System. "Any idea how long that might take?"

"Twenty-four hours, give or take."

"Anything else?" I ask.

"I do have a couple more items. A wine bottle was found inside the tack room. A ceramic plate. Residue from a candle."

"That's an interesting combination of items."

"I thought so, too."

"Any chance the candle started that fire?"

"I've determined that the fire started outside the tack room. That, I'm sure of."

"Keep me posted on that latent, will you?"

"You bet."

MONA is a whiz when it comes to digging up information. Not only is she adept on the law-enforcement databases, but she's also quite the sleuth when it comes to the search engine and venturing into some of the Internet's best-kept secrets.

"Would have found all this sooner, but Ruth Beiler is actually Ruth Petersheim now," Mona says from the doorway of my office. "Married Mark Petersheim about a year ago. They live up in Wilmot now. She works part-time at the Amish Door restaurant."

"Nice work." I grab my keys. "Want to run up there with me?"

Her grin is the only answer I need.

WILMOT is a pretty little village with a population of about three hundred souls thirty minutes northeast of Painters Mill. I park curbside in front of a small frame home with white paint and a crooked front porch.

"Is Ruth Petersheim Amish?" Mona asks.

"She was at some point." I remind myself this is a learning experience for her. "The main thing to remember is that Petersheim is neither a suspect nor a witness at this point. We're on a fishing expedition. The more she talks, the more fruitful this visit will be."

"Got it."

We leave the Explorer and take a narrow, buckled sidewalk to the porch. At the door, Mona looks at me. I give her a nod. Standing slightly aside, she knocks firmly.

The door opens, and I find myself looking at a young Amish woman. Early twenties. Dishwater-blond hair encased in a gauzy *kapp*. I hear a baby gaggling somewhere in the house.

She's taken aback by my uniform. "Has something happened?"

I show her my badge and introduce myself. "We're looking into the death of Daniel Gingerich," I tell her. "May we come inside for a few minutes to speak with you?"

"But . . . why?" Looking like a trapped animal, she glances from me to Mona. "I don't know anything."

She's too polite to refuse my request and steps back, ostensibly allowing us entry.

"Thank you. We won't take up too much of your time."

I'm greeted by the smells of burned toast and fresh-brewed coffee. Through a wide entryway, I see a decent-sized kitchen. A baby crib is set against the wall between the kitchen and living room.

"I don't know why you're here." Petersheim crosses to the crib and looks down at the baby before turning to us. "I don't know anything about Daniel."

"I was told you were friends," I begin.

"I don't know who told you that, but we weren't friends. I knew him. I mean, when I lived in Painters Mill with my parents. But that was a long time ago. I'm married now."

"Is your husband home, Mrs. Petersheim?"

"He's working."

I pull out my notebook. "Where does he work?"

"Obermiller Construction. He's putting in the fence out to the Inn this week."

I jot it down, giving her a chance to calm down, and then try again. "I understand you went to a singing with Daniel Gingerich."

She looks at me as if the statement makes her nauseous. "Oh, that. It was an . . . informal thing. And there were lots of other Amish there. I mean, it wasn't just the two of us."

I'm not sure why any of those things matter or why she felt the need to point them out. "So you were never close," I say easily.

"No."

"Did Daniel ever have any arguments or disagreements with anyone that you know of?" I ask.

"No, but then I didn't know him very well. Hardly at all."

The baby begins to cry. Looking grateful for the interruption, the Amish woman turns away and rushes to the crib. When her back is turned, I look at Mona and she shrugs.

Ignoring us completely, Petersheim scoops the baby into her arms. *"Wie geht's, mei lamm?"* How goes it, my little lamb?

I cross to the crib, and trying to find a way to put her at ease, I look down at the baby in her arms. *"Er is schnuck."* He's cute.

For the first time, a smile touches her mouth. *"Cannscht du Deitsh schwetze?"* Can you speak Dutch?

"I used to be Amish."

Her eyes shift to Mona. "You, too?"

"Oh, no, ma'am. I'm an *Englischer* through and through."

The three of us look down at the infant.

"What's his name?" I ask.

Smiling, she raises the baby's face to hers and rubs her nose against his. "William."

"How old is he?" Mona asks.

It's an innocent question, but Petersheim stiffens slightly. "Almost a year now."

The baby chooses that moment to spit up. Mona and I watch as Petersheim deftly slips William's soiled T-shirt over his head.

"It's just a little bit of *schmierkees*," she mutters in a baby voice, referring to the Amish version of cottage cheese. She covers his fat cheeks with a dozen kisses. "Isn't that right, *mei lamm?*"

She leaves him for a moment to grab a fresh shirt from a drawer beneath the changing table. That's when I notice the dark brown spot on the right side of the baby's tummy. It's large for such a little guy—about four inches in length and an inch wide. A birthmark, I realize, and I get the odd sense that I've seen it before. . . .

Petersheim returns and slips the fresh shirt over the baby's head. I wait until the baby is dressed before addressing her. "Ruth, can you tell me where you were Monday night?"

Her gaze jerks to mine. "I was here," she tells me. "Mothers with new babies can't just run off in the evening."

"Can your husband vouch for you?"

"Of course he can," she snaps. "He was here, too. Please, if you could just go now . . . I need to feed him."

I hesitate. "Is there anything else you can tell me about Daniel Gingerich that might help me with the investigation?" I ask.

"Like I said, I barely knew him." She motions toward the door. "That's all I've got to say."

A MINUTE later Mona and I are back in the Explorer.

"That's got to be the most uptight Amish woman I've ever met," Mona says.

"No doubt." I pull away from the curb. "The question is why."

"You think she knows something about Daniel Gingerich?"

"I think she knows *something* she doesn't want to share."

Ruth Petersheim had said her husband was working on a fence at the Amish Door Village. I make a left on Lawnford, and sure enough, I see two Amish men working on a four-rail white fence. Parked on the shoulder, an older Dodge pickup truck bakes in the sun. I pull up behind it and kill the engine.

"Since we're here, I thought we might double-check Ruth's story about where she was the night Gingerich was killed."

We get out and start toward the men. The older guy is standing next to the fence, leaning on the shovel, a collapsible cup in hand, watching us approach. The younger of the two is digging a post hole, his shirt soaked through with sweat.

"Hays genuk fa du?" I say as I approach. Hot enough for you?

Grinning, the older man motions toward the man digging

the hole. *"Hays genuk fa eem fleicht."* Hot enough for him, maybe.

I introduce myself. "I'm looking for Mark Petersheim."

The young man glances over. He's blond-haired, with a thick red beard and eyes the color of tea. "I'm Petersheim," he says.

"I'm investigating the death of Daniel Gingerich," I tell him. "Do you have a minute? I'd like to ask you a few questions."

The men exchange looks. Sighing, Petersheim tugs the post-hole digger from the hole and offers it to the other man. *"Alle daag rumhersitze mach tem faul,"* he says. Sitting all day makes one lazy. Chuckling, the older man takes the handles and gets to work.

I watch as Petersheim crosses to the truck, snaps up a collapsible cup, fills it, and drinks it down before returning to where Mona and I stand. He doesn't look pleased that we're here.

"I didn't know Gingerich," he says.

"Did you ever meet him?" I ask.

"Nope."

"Do you know of him?"

"Heard about the fire."

"I understand your wife knew him before you were married."

A brief hesitation. "I think they might've been in the same church district for a while. We're Beachy now, so . . ." He motions toward the truck and shrugs.

"Were Daniel and your wife friends?"

"Don't think so."

"She never mentioned him?" I ask.

"Not that I recall."

"We just talked to Ruth a few minutes ago," I tell him.

"I reckon you should have asked her instead of me."

Resentment simmers beneath the surface of his otherwise calm façade. Since no one I've talked to today seems inclined to talk about Daniel Gingerich, I push, hoping to find out why.

"I understand your wife and Daniel went to a singing together."

"A lot of *Amisch* go to singings. So what?"

"Would you mind telling me where you were Monday night?"

"Same place I am every night. Home. With my wife and our baby."

He glances over at the other Amish man, who has finished with the post hole, then turns back to me. "You done? I gotta get back to work."

"I appreciate your time."

He walks away without looking back.

"HE'S a font of information," Mona says when we're back inside the Explorer.

"He knows more than he's letting on," I say as I start the engine.

"Seems like no one wants to talk about Daniel Gingerich," Mona says. "I wonder why."

"Sooner or later all of these weird little secrets everyone is keeping are going to come to light." I put the vehicle in gear and pull onto the road. "When they do, we'll have our answer."

Chapter 8

IT'S AFTER NOON WHEN I PULL UP to the police station and drop Mona off. I'm thinking about Emma Miller and the possibility that her death was the result of some event linked to Daniel Gingerich in the days he worked for the Millers. Instead of going inside, I make a U-turn and head to the Miller farm.

The last time I spoke to Esther and Sam Miller, they made it clear they had no intention of opening up about their daughter. The case has evolved since then. Now that I know more about Daniel Gingerich—more about young Emma—I realize their silence may not be solely based on grief but secrets.

I take the winding lane to the house on the hill. The barn door stands open, so I park in the gravel and go inside.

"Hello?" I call out. "Mr. Miller?"

I wander toward the rear of the barn, passing a workbench loaded with several unfinished birdhouses. I'm thinking about going up to the second-level loft, when I hear footsteps behind me. I turn to find Esther Miller standing there, a bucket of paint in her hand.

"Thought I heard someone out here. You change your mind about buying one of those feeders?"

"I think I'll take the red one that looks like the Amish barn. For my sister. It's her birthday next week."

"That's a nice one." Her amicable tone belies the wariness in her eyes. "Would you like it wrapped?"

"I think she'd like that."

I watch as she sets the feeder on a newspaper and begins to wrap it. "I know Emma was *ime familye weg* when she died," I say.

The Amish woman winces as if I'd reached out and sliced her down the back with a knife.

I cross to her. "I understand how painful it must be for you and your husband to speak of her. But I need your help."

She turns and gives me her full attention. "I won't speak of her. Not to you. Not about that."

"Because she was with child?" I ask. "Or maybe you don't want to talk about her because of what happened to her."

Esther's gaze narrows. "Nothing happened. I don't know what you're talking about."

"I think you do. I think Emma went through something awful. You and your husband are either in denial or you're lying to me because you're trying to protect her."

"I don't want to discuss this," she hisses. "It's not proper."

"Mrs. Miller, I need to know what happened between Emma and Daniel Gingerich. I'll do my best to keep it confidential."

"My sweet Emma is in heaven now. She is with God. She's at peace, and I'll be with her one day. That's all that matters now."

She shoves the bird feeder at me. "Take it and go. Just . . . go and don't come back."

I don't move; I don't reach for my wallet or take the feeder. "I spoke with Elam Schlabach."

The Amish woman turns away, but not before I see the grief and shame in her eyes. "I won't discuss this."

I set my hand on her arm. "He said Emma was innocent."

She turns back to me, blinks. "Of course she was."

"We both know that doesn't make sense. She loved Elam. She was saving herself until they were married, and yet she became pregnant." I wait a beat. "What did Daniel do to her?"

She glances toward the barn door—watching for her husband, I think—and in that instant, I know she's going to tell me something that's going to change everything.

"Sam and I thought he was such a sweet boy," she tells me. "Smart. From a good Amish family. Had a good work ethic."

I wait, willing her to continue.

Pressing her hand against her stomach, she walks to the workbench. "I saw them one afternoon. Together. In the milk house. They were . . . on the floor by the stanchions. He was . . . on top of her. Her dress was . . ." Shaking her head, she doesn't finish.

I choose my next words carefully. "Was it consensual?"

She squeezes her eyes closed. "At first I didn't know. I mean, Danny was a handsome young man. And Emma was nearly a grown woman. Both were of *Rumspringa* age. I thought . . ." She breaks off, puts her hand over her mouth as if to smother a cry.

"Did he coerce her? Force her?"

She seems to pull her emotions together. "Emma came to me. Later that night. She said he'd . . . done things to her. Things she didn't want him to do. She said they were . . . of one flesh."

"He raped her?" I ask.

Tears glitter in her eyes, and within their depths I see the truth she doesn't want to face. I know she's going to shift back to the only lie that will save her from herself. From a life of self-loathing because neither she nor her husband had kept their daughter safe.

"I told her good girls don't do those kinds of things," she whispers. "I told her to pray harder. That she should have resisted him. Resisted herself. I told her God doesn't let things like that happen to good girls. She must've done something to tempt him, and for that she should seek forgiveness."

Tension grips the back of my neck. I stare at her, a violent tide of disgust rising inside me. *Your daughter came to you and you blamed her? How could you do that to a teenage girl who'd come to you for help?*

"Did it happen more than once?" I ask.

"I don't know. She didn't speak of it again, but I think maybe it did." She shrugs. "It's such a private thing—the things that happen between men and women. I thought they were, you know, beaus."

"Does your husband know what happened?"

"Enough so that he doesn't want to talk about it."

"What does that mean?" I snap. "Did you tell him? Did Emma tell him? Did he see something, too?"

"I told him."

Motive, a little voice whispers.

"How did he react?" I ask.

"He said they shouldn't tell the bishop. If the bishop found out, he would be forced to excommunicate them for six weeks." She looks down at the ground. "Chief Burkholder, I know how all of this must sound to you, what you must be thinking."

"I'm not thinking anything, Mrs. Miller."

"I was not a bad mother to Emma."

A hundred words tangle in my throat. None of them are kind, so I buckle it down and keep my mouth shut.

After a moment she closes her eyes, presses her fingers to her lids as if to keep the dam from bursting. "If God were to give me another chance, I would have stopped Daniel."

"Thank you for your time, Mrs. Miller," I say, and I walk away.

God doesn't let things like that happen to good girls. She must've done something to tempt him. . . .

I can't get the words out of my head. The thought of an Amish girl being abused in her own home is bad enough. But to know that girl went to her parents for help, only to be blamed by them fills me with outrage. Furious, I rap my hand against the steering wheel. I'm northbound on Ohio 83 when suddenly I can't get enough oxygen into my lungs. I order myself to calm down, get a grip.

Daniel Gingerich wasn't some innocent farm boy. If what I'm hearing is true, he was a rapist and a son of a bitch. I'd damn well better get used to it, because I've been charged with finding the person responsible for killing him despite the fact that some small, unacknowledged part of me believes he deserved his fate.

If Emma Miller was, indeed, raped, discovered she was pregnant, and committed suicide to escape the stigma and pain, those who loved her would have motive to seek vengeance on the perpetrator. That includes Elam Schlabach and Sam Miller. I think about her mother but dismiss the notion. Any woman who could blame her daughter for being raped possesses no sense of justice, not even the dark and twisted variety that leads to vigilantism.

It's a little after four p.m., and I'm in my office resisting the urge to beat my head against the desk, when Lois rushes in. "Tip just came in over the line we set up for the Gingerich thing."

"Go ahead. Make my day."

"Female caller says Chris Martino, the neighbor, set the fire that killed Dan Gingerich. She claims there's proof in Martino's shed."

Even without hearing the details, I experience a precipitous rise of skepticism. "Did she say what kind of proof?"

"No."

"Did she leave her name? Contact info?"

"She said she was scared and wants to remain anonymous. The call came in from the Amish pay phone out on County Roads four oh seven and fifty-eight."

A phone anyone could have used to make the call. Still, despite my doubts about its validity, I'm obliged to follow up.

"Call Judge Siebenthaler and tell him I'm on my way over," I say. "Tell him I need a warrant to search Chris Martino's home."

"You got it."

Thinking about Martino and his temper, I ask, "Who's on duty, by the way?"

"Skid came on about an hour ago."

"Tell him to get over here. I'm going to put together a quick affidavit and head over to the judge's chambers."

Two hours later I'm armed with a warrant and on my way to the home of Chris Martino. Skid rides shotgun in the passenger seat.

"This 'tip' seems a little convenient," I tell him.

"Someone with an axe to grind against Martino?" Skip says.

"Or someone who wants to divert us. It's noteworthy that the caller had no interest in the reward money."

Afternoon is giving way to evening when I pull into the driveway of the Martino place. There's only one vehicle—Martino's old pickup truck—so I pull up behind it and park adjacent to the shed. It's a small building, about the size of a single-car garage.

Plucking the warrant from the console, I get out. The windows of the house are open, and chain-saw rock blares from inside.

We take the sidewalk to the house. Standing slightly to one side, I knock firmly. "Mr. Martino?" I call out. "Painters Mill Police Department. Can you come out here and talk to us a moment?"

Through the screen, I see someone approach. An instant later the interior door swings open and Chris Martino appears.

"What's this about?" The big man steps onto the porch. I can smell the alcohol on his breath from where I stand.

I hand him the neatly folded document. "This is a warrant, Chris. We have permission to conduct a search."

"A *search?*" He stares down at the warrant, then raises his gaze to mine. "Just out of curiosity, what the hell are you looking for?"

"Everything you need to know is in the warrant."

Skid and I wait while he reads. After a full minute he looks up at me and smiles nastily. "Nazi cops."

"Thank you, Mr. Martino." I step back. We're going to take a look in that shed; then we'll get out of your hair."

"Knock your socks off," he says. "You ain't going to find anything unless you plant it."

Skid and I start toward the shed. My heart sinks when I get my first look. The small space is jam-packed with every imaginable variety of junk. An old car is parked in the center of the mess. An old door that's being used as a workbench is covered with engine parts. Cinder-block-and-board shelving lines the far wall.

"Doesn't look like anyone's been here in a while," Skid mutters.

He's right. Again, I wonder about the veracity of the tip.

I work my way over to the car and glance at the door handle—it's an old chrome thing with a thumb button—and I notice a smudge in the dust. I look down; there's a mark on the concrete floor where the dust has been disturbed. A heel print, I realize; someone has been here. I reach for the handle. The hinges groan when I open it. I shine my light on the floor and do a double take when I spot the mason jars. Two of them, filled with clear amber liquid.

"Skid, I've got something."

He rounds the hood and comes up behind me. I motion toward the two jars. "They haven't been here long."

"Looks like gas." He whistles. "Didn't the fire marshal find a couple of broken mason jars at the scene?"

"Yep." I lean into the car and sniff. "It's definitely gas."

"What's that sticking out from beneath the jar?"

I push the jar aside. "It's a key."

"Looks new."

"The dead bolt on the tack-room door over at the Gingerich place was only a couple of months old." I glance up at Skid. "There were two keys. One was found at the scene."

"Maybe this is the other one. State boys pick up latents?"

"They did. Haven't heard back on the ID yet," I tell him.

"Easy enough to figure out if the key fits the lock."

My uneasy sense of skepticism mushrooms into cold, hard suspicion. "Skid, why would someone who was questioned by the police about an arson hide something like this on his property?"

"That's a stretch even for Chris Martino. You think someone planted it?" he asks.

I nod. "The big question is who."

I glance toward the door to see Chris Martino standing in the doorway, looking in.

I lower my voice. "Call BCI and get a CSU out here. We need those mason jars and that key processed for latents."

"You got it."

We start toward the door. Martino is standing a few feet away, one hand in his pocket, the other holding a beer.

I cross to him. "When's the last time you were in that shed?"

"Been so long I don't remember. Two or three months, maybe."

"We found the mason jars," I say quietly, watching him.

"Mason jars? What? Do I look like I can tomatoes?"

I say nothing.

"Look," he says, "whatever crap's in that shed don't belong to me. That ain't my car. Ain't my junk. It belongs to the landlord."

I think about asking him about the key, decide to keep that bit of information to myself. "Do you keep gasoline on your property?"

The nasty smile falters. "I got a gas can on the back porch for my lawn mower. Mower's broke, and I think the can's empty." For the first time, he looks worried. "What's this all about?"

"Has anyone been in that shed, Mr. Martino?"

"No one," he tells me.

"Has anyone been on the property? Visitors?"

"No. What did you find in there? A dead body?"

"Look, we're going to tape off this area. We've got a crime-scene unit coming out here to take a closer look at the shed."

"Crime-scene unit, huh?" He laughs. "You people better not be aiming to hang anything on me."

"The only way you're going to get anything hung on you is if your prints turn up on those mason jars. Do you understand?"

"Yeah, I got it."

"I may want to talk to you again, Mr. Martino, so if you have to leave town for any reason, you need to let me know."

"I ain't going anywhere." Taking a final, disgusted look at me, he sighs and heads back toward the house.

Chapter 9

THE *GRAABHOF* IS LOCATED on the township road west of Painters Mill. It's nearly ten a.m., and as I make the turn, I spot a convoy of black buggies headed toward the cemetery. Daniel Gingerich was well thought of among his brethren, and they've shown up in force to pay their final respects.

The actual funeral was held earlier at the Gingerich home. I contemplated stopping in but decided not to. Because the service was in an Amish home, I wouldn't have been welcomed. Following that service, friends of the Gingeriches, other family members, and the hearse traveled to the *graabhof* where Daniel will be laid to rest. This is the rite I can attend without intruding.

I drive through the gate and park in the shade of the *bois d'arc* tree that's guarded this entrance since I was a kid. I try not to think of the other funerals I've attended here, my own parents' included.

I hang back until the coffin is removed from the hearse. Leaving the Explorer, I enter the cemetery as the casket is carried by pallbearers, using two stout hickory poles. I reach the crowd as the casket is placed over the open grave.

Miriam and Gideon Gingerich and their three children stand nearest the grave, heads bowed in silent prayer. Luane Raber, her siblings, and her parents are on the other side of the grave. I spot the three girls I met at the Mercantile yesterday, standing together instead of with their respective families. Even Milo Hershberger has shown up. There's no sign of Esther and Sam Miller.

Once the casket is in the grave, one of the Amish ministers reads a hymn. A silent prayer follows, and then the four pallbearers begin to shovel dirt into the grave.

"Chief Burkholder?"

I turn, surprised to see Ralph Baker, from the farm store, approach. "Hi, Mr. Baker."

He draws up next to me. "After talking with you the other day, I remembered something that might be important. About Danny."

Realizing we're standing too close to the mourners to discuss the case, I motion toward the Explorer. "Sure."

"Anyway," he says as we start that way, "I didn't think anything about it at the time, but the day before Danny was killed, we took our supper break together, went out for burgers. He was all pumped up about some woman. Said she'd left him a note and he was going to hook up with her that night."

My interest jumps. "Did he mention a name?"

He shakes his head. "No. He talked like he was going to get lucky. He'd been wanting to hook up with her for some time."

I think about that a moment. "Is it possible the note was from Luane? Maybe she was going to surprise him?"

"Seems like it was kind of an illicit thing, you know?"

"Did he say where they were meeting?"

"No, ma'am."

"Did he say when?"

"Well, he got the note the day before he was killed in that fire. I assumed it was that night," he tells me. "The night he was killed."

"Did you see the note, Mr. Baker?"

"Caught a glimpse of it. He was laughing and waving it around. I gave him the cold shoulder because I didn't think it was right."

"Do you remember anything specific about the note?" I ask. "The kind of paper? Was it handwritten?"

"I think it was just regular notebook paper." Brows knit, he rubs his chin. "I think it was colored ink. Pink or purple. The writing was kind of girlish, with swirls and hearts and stuff like that."

"Any idea what happened to the note?"

He shakes his head. "Never saw it again. Me and Al went through Danny's locker at the store, but there wasn't anything in there. Just an old cap and his work gloves."

"Had he ever mentioned this mystery woman before?"

"Well, you know, he was a young guy. He liked girls." Ralph Baker ducks his head. "Talked about 'getting some' all the time. I figured he was lying, like the rest of us. Now I'm not so sure."

ARSON is a particularly difficult crime to solve. Mainly because much of the evidence left at the scene is often destroyed by the intense heat or by the efforts of the firefighters. Despite my growing suspicions about Daniel Gingerich, the notion of someone getting away with such an insidious crime doesn't sit well.

Pulling out a legal pad, I go to a fresh page and write down the things I know about the case so far.

Note? Unknown individual lured Daniel Gingerich to the barn. A woman?

Suspects: The neighbor, Chris Martino. Felon. Ex-con. Argument over stolen horse tack. Temper.

Early on, Martino was a viable suspect, but no more. Now the question in my mind is who left the mason jars and key in his shed—and why.

Milo Hershberger. Jealousy over Luane Raber?

Emma Miller's parents, Sam and Esther Miller. Daughter was pregnant. Had she been raped by Daniel Gingerich?

Elam Schlabach. Did he find out something happened between Daniel and his girlfriend and decide to mete out a little revenge?

Luane? Did she know her husband-to-be was cheating on her?

Did Mose and Sue Raber know their daughter was planning to marry a serial seducer—or worse? Did they murder Daniel to prevent her from making a mistake?

What about Ruth Petersheim? Nervous. Evasive. Mark Petersheim? Connection?

Frustrated by my lack of progress, I go back to the file. I come across the photos I found in Daniel's bedroom, and something pricks at my memory. I go back to the one in which Daniel is without a shirt. That's when I realize the thing that's bothering me is the birthmark on his abdomen. I've seen it before. But how is that possible? I'd never met Daniel. . . .

The baby.

The memory strikes me like a blow. Ruth Petersheim's baby. The day Mona and I went to see her, Ruth had changed his shirt, exposing the exact same mole on his abdomen.

"My God," I whisper. "Is Daniel Gingerich the father?"

No wonder Ruth Petersheim had been so nervous, so standoffish. I'd assumed it was because she'd become pregnant out of wedlock. She fudged on the date and didn't want anyone to do the math. Having grown up Amish, I understand that. This is different, especially if she was pregnant by another man and passed off the child as her husband's.

I find myself thinking about Mark Petersheim. If I'm right about the birthmark, does he know the baby isn't his? Did Ruth tell him? If Daniel is the baby's father, did he and Ruth have a consensual relationship? If there was a sexual assault involved, does Mark Petersheim know about it? Did he decide to do something about it?

A glance at my computer tells me it's too late to pay Ruth Petersheim a visit tonight. Probably best to catch her when her husband is at work, anyway; she'll be more apt to speak openly, especially if Mark Petersheim doesn't know the child he's raising as his own was fathered by Daniel Gingerich.

THE next day, I roll up to Ruth and Mark Petersheim's house just before noon and park curbside. I take the narrow sidewalk to the porch and knock. Ruth Petersheim peers out at me, eyes darting.

"Hi, Ruth. Do you have a minute to talk?"

A dozen excuses scroll across her face, but she acquiesces.

The small house smells of bacon and coffee, with the lingering redolence of dirty diapers. There's a can of furniture polish with a raggedy dishcloth on the end table.

The Amish woman stops in the center of the living room and turns to face me. "Like I said, I barely knew Daniel Gingerich."

"Your husband is at work?" I ask.

"Of course he is."

"I've heard a lot of things about Daniel Gingerich in the last few days," I begin. "Since I last spoke with you. I'm not sure he was the upstanding young man everyone seemed to think he was."

No response.

I pull the photograph of Daniel Gingerich from my pocket. It's the one in which he's without a shirt, showing off his muscles to his girlfriend. I hold it out so that Ruth can see it.

She stares at the photo as if it's a bloody, violent thing that's about to jump off the paper and tear her to shreds.

"The other day when I was here," I say, "I couldn't help but notice the birthmark on William's abdomen."

"He doesn't have a birthmark."

"I saw it," I say gently.

Her mouth opens. She raises her hand and steps back. "I think you should go," she says. "I don't want to talk to you anymore."

I hold my ground, hold her stare. "I did a little research on moles and birthmarks." I flick the photograph with my finger. "This type of mole is hereditary. It's passed down from parent to child. The mole on your son's abdomen is identical to Daniel's."

"Sell is nix as baeffzes." That's nothing but trifling talk. She takes another step back. But she knows there's no escape.

"I need you to level with me about your relationship with Daniel Gingerich," I tell her.

Her eyes fill with tears. "I can't talk about that."

"Did you have a relationship with Daniel?"

"No. Never."

"Is Daniel William's father?"

A brief hesitation and then, "No."

"Did you have a sexual relationship with Daniel Gingerich?"

"No." For the first time, anger resonates in her voice. "What kind of question is that? How could you ask such a thing?"

"Tell me," I say quietly. "Please."

Ruth chokes out a sound and begins to cry. "My husband doesn't know. No one knows. They cannot find out."

"What doesn't he know?"

"He doesn't know William is . . ." She closes her eyes as if uttering the words aloud is too painful, too shameful. "Mark doesn't know. Please don't tell him. He loves little William so much."

For a full minute she stands there, head down, sobbing.

"Ruth, I'm not trying to hurt you or your husband or that sweet little boy. But I need to know what happened."

The statement seems to calm her, and she regains control of her emotions. She takes a moment to wipe her eyes and blow her nose.

"Is Daniel Gingerich William's father?" I ask.

Closing her eyes against fresh tears, she jerks her head. "Yes."

"You had a relationship with him?"

"No." She opens her eyes. "Not a relationship. Never."

I wait.

As if resigning herself, she sags, her shoulders coming forward. "I met him a few times over the last few years. Daniel was . . . nice. Hardworking." Her mouth twists. "He was handsome, too. All the girls liked him.

"I'd just met Mark, and we'd gone out a few times, but we weren't that serious yet. And so when Danny asked me if I was going to be at the singing over to the Schwartz farm after worship, I told him I'd be there. I figured there'd be no harm in it."

An Amish "singing" usually takes place on Sunday evening, after worship. It's an occasion in which Amish youths from different church districts can get together, sing hymns, and visit. It usually ends around ten or eleven p.m.

"You have to understand, Chief Burkholder. Daniel was from a good family. He had a good job. Those are important things when you're a seventeen-year-old Amish girl."

"You met him at the Schwartz farm for the singing?"

"I did, and he was a perfect gentleman. Afterward he offered to drive me home. He had a car, you know, and the thought of riding in it was such a thrill. So I went."

She looks at me, eyes shimmering. "We listened to the radio, and it was . . . wonderful. We parked and listened to music and drank tequila right out of the bottle."

Her mouth tightens. "It was the first time I ever drank alcohol, and I couldn't handle it. At first it was fun, but then . . . I told him I wanted to go home. I thought it was going to be okay.

"Chief Burkholder, something happened to him when we were parked out there on that back road." She says the words so quietly, I have to move closer to hear. "It was like he turned into another person," she whispers. "He . . . dragged me from the car, threw me on the ground, and he forced me." The words tumble out of her.

"Did he rape you?"

She jerks her head. A single, devastating nod. A sob escapes her. "It was my fault. I shouldn't have gone with him. I shouldn't have drank the alcohol. Worst of all, I was already seeing my husband. But that's what I get, isn't it?"

"It wasn't your fault," I tell her. "No one deserves that."

Her eyes go hard. "I'd never . . . you know. I mean, before that night. A few weeks later I knew I was *ime familye weg*."

I stare at her, feeling more than is prudent. "What did you do?"

"I lied. To everyone. I let Mark court me. I . . . you know, with him as quickly as I could manage." She closes her eyes, seems to struggle with something. "Mamm told me that those kinds of little white lies are okay as long as they protect tender feelings."

"You told your mother what happened?"

"She found the blood from that night. You know . . . on my underwear." She takes a shuddery breath. "I told her nothing happened. That it was just my monthly. But I think she knew. She was in an awful hurry to get me married." She looks down at the floor.

"Does your *datt* know what happened?"

"I don't think my *mamm* told him."

"Did you see Daniel or speak to him after that night?"

"No."

"Did you write to him? Or leave him a note or letter?"

"No." Her brows knit in confusion. "Why would I?"

"Did you ask him to meet you in the barn the night of the fire?"

"What?" She shakes her head. "Why would I do such a thing?"

"You tell me."

"Chief Burkholder, I haven't seen him since . . . that night. I couldn't face him. I can barely face myself. Some days I can't even look at my innocent little child." Pain contorts her features, and she begins to cry. "I don't mean that."

I let her cry, let the silence and the weight of the words that have passed between us ride.

"I've prayed for forgiveness," she tells me. "I've forgiven myself. I've forgiven *them*. I've moved on with my—"

I've forgiven them. The statement stops me cold. "What did you say?"

She shoots me a blank look. "I said I've moved on—"

"You said 'them,'" I cut in. "Who are you talking about? Was there someone else there?"

Shame clouds her face. Something else she didn't want me to know. "Daniel's friend was there. Milo Hershberger."

"Milo was there the night Daniel assaulted you?"

"He needed a ride home after the singing. Daniel said he'd drive him. But instead of going to Milo's house, we started drinking. Ended up parking on that back road."

"Did Milo—"

"No." She shakes her head adamantly. "*No.* He got out of the car." Her visage turns sullen. "I do recall Milo being angry afterward. I mean, with Daniel. They had words."

"Daniel and Milo argued?" I ask.

"Milo was upset about what Daniel had done."

"Did the argument become physical?"

Another shake of her head. "I don't know. I was so . . . ashamed and upset. My whole world just sort of fell apart that night."

The cry of a baby sounds from the bedroom at the rear of the house. Ruth looks over her shoulder, her eyes not meeting mine.

"Please, can you just go now? I've told you everything. I just want to forget it ever happened."

THERE are some topics that are so taboo among the Amish that they won't even acknowledge they exist. Sexual violence is one of them. Daniel Gingerich was a monster in disguise. The more I learn about him, the more I detest him. It's not a good mind-set for a cop who's been charged with solving his murder.

My exchange with Ruth Petersheim haunts me during the drive to Millersburg. I almost can't get my mind around the casual violence of it and the fact that the ordeal was swept under the rug.

I was wrong about Milo Hershberger. I'd liked him. I'd been moved by the fact that he'd been shunned by his Amish brethren. I'd identified with him, believed him. Rookie mistakes all.

I pull into the driveway of Hershberger's double-wide to find a hodgepodge of cars and two buggies parked haphazardly. A couple dozen young men mill about the front yard. Every one of them is holding either a beer or a plastic cup full of some concoction.

"Terrific," I mutter as I get out of the Explorer.

My uniform draws plenty of stares; everyone gives me a wide berth as I make my way to the house. I'm about to knock, when the screen flies open and two young men stumble out, laughing.

One of them looks me up and down and grins. "Is that uniform for real?"

"I'm looking for Milo," I say.

"In the kitchen." He opens the door for me. "Beer's in the fridge. Help yourself, and then come on out and enjoy the party."

The house smells of cigarette smoke. In the kitchen two young men help themselves to whatever's in the pitcher. Milo stands in the doorway, grinning. He jolts upon spotting me.

"Hello, Milo," I say as I cross to him.

"Chief Burkholder?" He's smoking a cigarette, holding a can of beer in his left hand. "Uh, I didn't know you were coming over."

"Is there someplace quiet we can talk?"

"We can go to the barn if you want. Quieter there, probably."

Nodding, I cross back through the living room, go out the door, and head to the barn. Midway there Milo falls into step beside me. "What's going on?" he asks.

I don't respond. I'm too angry. I need to calm down.

We reach the barn. He opens the door. I walk midway down the aisle, then turn to face him. "Close the door behind you."

He blinks, then slides the door shut. "What?"

"You lied to me," I tell him.

"About what?"

"Don't play dumb." I stalk over to him. "Lying to the police is against the law. I could arrest you right now for failure to report a crime. It may not stick once you get to court, but I also would be within my rights to arrest you as an accomplice to sexual assault."

"I don't know what you're talking about," he says.

"I know about Ruth Petersheim. All of it."

His face pales. He stares at me, blinking, mouth open.

"You were there," I say.

He starts to turn away, but I grasp his arm and stop him. He yanks it away. "Get your hands off me."

I let my hand slide off him, take a moment to pull myself back from a place I know better than to venture into.

He walks to the sliding door but doesn't open it. Instead, he shoves his hands into his pockets and then turns to face me.

"I didn't do anything wrong," he says.

"For God's sake, Milo. You witnessed a sexual assault. You didn't help her. Didn't stop it. Didn't report it."

"I didn't know!"

"You're a liar." Calmer now, I cross to him. "I'm in the midst of a murder investigation, and you withheld information."

"I didn't have anything to do with what happened to Danny."

"You expect me to believe anything that comes out of your mouth now?"

He shakes his head angrily, looks away.

"Milo, I'm an inch away from arresting you for the sole reason that you are a lying son of a bitch. You had better start talking."

"That Danny," he says after a moment. "I always knew there was something wrong with him. Didn't figure out what it was until that night."

I wait, saying nothing.

"Danny was a charmer, and boy did he love his women. If we went out drinking or whatever and he found a chick he wanted to be with, he could really turn it on. Most of the time it worked. I mean, the girls were crazy about him. How ironic is that?

"But there were a few times when he got turned down, and let me tell you, it pissed him off. He was like Jekyll and Hyde."

"What happened with Ruth Petersheim?"

"Amish girls are a little different; they're not as wild, but then that didn't matter to Danny. He always said he liked a challenge."

I stare at him, saying nothing, giving him nothing.

"Danny knew Ruth was seeing the guy she eventually married. He didn't care. He went after her. Turned on the charm, and she fell for it." He blows out a breath. "The night it happened, we went to a singing out to the Schwartz place. Ruth was there with one of her friends. That Beachy chick that works at the Mercantile."

"Neva Lambright?" I wonder why Neva didn't mention it when I'd specifically asked about Daniel Gingerich.

"Yeah. Her. Anyway, around ten o'clock or so Danny asked Ruth if he could drive her home. She balked at first, but her friend told her to go ahead. 'Hey, he's fine. Go for it!' So Ruth agreed.

"All I needed was a ride home. Danny said he'd take me, so I went with them. I figured he'd drop me off first." He rubs his eyes with his thumb and forefinger. "It was the three of us. Danny broke out a bottle of tequila. We started passing it around. All the while, I'm thinking three's a crowd, but it didn't stop Danny boy."

"What did he do?"

"We were on some back road. Everyone's drunk. I got out to take a leak. When I get back in, Danny and Ruth are in the backseat, sort of . . . going at it. So I get out. Next thing I know, the car door flies open and they spill out onto the asphalt. They were fighting. Danny was pissed. Ruth was crying. It was . . . ugly."

He turns his gaze on me. "Look, I tried to intervene, but . . . I'd had too much to drink. I wasn't thinking straight." He shrugs. "We came to blows right there in the middle of the road. He broke my nose. It was pretty much the end of our friendship, and we'd been best friends since we were like six years old."

"What did you do?"

"I got the hell out of there. Ended up walking home."

"So you just left her there with him?"

He looks away, but not before I see shame in his eyes.

"I'm not proud of it," he says.

"You must have been angry."

"Yeah, I was pissed."

"Pissed enough to lure Daniel into the barn, lock him in that tack room, and start the fire?"

"Oh, I wanted to kill him plenty of times. Especially after I realized what he was. But I'm no killer. I didn't do it."

"Who else knows about what happened that night?"

"Far as I know, just me, Danny, and Ruth."

"What about Mark Petersheim?"

He hesitates, looks away. "I don't know if she told him. Sometimes Danny would sort of hint around about things. He'd brag about his conquests or whatever." He shrugs. "Word gets around."

"So it's possible Mark Petersheim knows?"

"I'm betting he probably knows *something* happened. I doubt if he knows how ugly it got. Mark may be Amish, but he's not the kind of guy who'd put up with any kind of infidelity."

"That wasn't infidelity," I snap.

"All I'm saying is, he's not the kind of guy who'd swallow something like that happening behind his back. To his woman. He cares about what the Amish think."

I find myself thinking about Ruth Petersheim and how an insecure husband might react to rumors that his wife had betrayed him or that his child belonged to another man.

"Were there other women he assaulted?" I ask.

He winces. "I don't know. Danny was . . . You couldn't believe half of what he said. I mean, when it came to women. He was always hinting around that he'd been with someone."

"I need names."

"The only one that stands out now is this young Amish girl."

"What's her name?"

"I don't know. He used to go up to that little shop in Charm all the time to see those girls. Had his eye on all of them, I guess."

"The Mercantile?"

He nods. "It was like he was . . . stalking them. But after all that happened with Ruth, I cut ties with him. We stopped talking."

"Is it possible Daniel bragged about things that didn't really happen?" I ask.

"I'm sure he did. But I think something happened with the girl from the Mercantile. I don't know about any others."

I pull out my card, write my cell number on the back, and pass it to him. "If you have to leave town, you need to let me know."

He takes the card, looks down at it. "All right."

"Stay away from Ruth Petersheim," I tell him. "If you try to make contact with her, I will come after you. Are we clear?"

"I got it." He shakes his head. "I tried to do the right thing that night, Chief Burkholder."

"Evidently you didn't try hard enough." Turning away, I start toward the door.

"Chief Burkholder. Wait."

I turn to him and fix him with a hard look.

"I should have stepped in that night. That I didn't . . . it kept me up nights. Still does. If I could, I'd make it right. I mean that."

"We don't get do-overs, Milo."

Chapter 10

MY EXCHANGE WITH MILO Hershberger weighs on me the rest of the evening. Daniel Gingerich was a sexual predator, and there's no doubt in my mind that someone killed him for it. The questions now are how many women did he rape and who knew about it?

It's after nine p.m. I'm in my office, various reports from the case spread out on my desk. My cell phone chirps, and DEPT OF COMM pops up in the window. I snatch up the phone.

"Hi Kate, it's Bob Schoening. I hope I'm not calling too late. I figured you'd want to hear this as soon as possible."

"You have my undivided attention."

"A couple of things. First of all, the latent recovered from the key at the Gingerich fire? We ran it through AFIS and struck out."

"So they're not in the system."

"Correct. I also wanted to let you know that key you found at the home of Christopher Martino is indeed a match to the lock we recovered at the Gingerich fire."

I sit up straighter. "Were the mason jars the same as the jars found at the Gingerich place?"

"No way to tell. The only thing I *can* tell you is that they're made by the same manufacturer."

"Did you pick up any latents?"

"We got a single decent print off one of the mason jars. As with the key, we're running it through AFIS now."

"Twenty-four hours?"

"Give or take."

"What about the key found at the Gingerich scene? The one with the print. Was it an original key? Or a duplicate?"

"The key recovered at the fire showed slight signs of wear. More than likely it's one of the original keys that came with the dead bolt Gideon Gingerich purchased a few months ago. The key found in Martino's shed was made by a different manufacturer and showed no discernible sign of wear, which means it's a duplicate."

My mind churns through the implications. "Did Gideon Gingerich or anyone else in the family make a copy of the key?"

"He claims he did not."

"Is there any way I can get my hands on the duplicate key?"

"The lab guys have gone over it." He pauses. "You going to try and figure out where it was made and who made it?"

"You never know when you might get lucky."

"I'll have it couriered over to you first thing in the morning," he says. "One more thing of interest with regard to the keys. The dead bolt that Gingerich purchased came with two original keys, and so far no one has been able to locate the second one. Gideon Gingerich says he always left both keys on the hook in the barn."

"Tied together with a string," I say, recalling my conversation with him. "Lost in the fire maybe?"

"It's possible we missed it, but not likely."

I thank him and end the call. If I get the key tomorrow, I'll have Mona check area hardware stores. If we can find out where it was duplicated, we might be able to find out who had it made.

Now, however, I need to get home to Tomasetti and my life. I'm in the process of locking my office when Jodie calls out my name.

"You still back there, Chief?"

"Right here," I say as I enter reception.

"I just took a call from a motorist out on Hogpath Road. Says he hit a deer and it busted his windshield. Vehicle's in the ditch."

My heart sinks. "Where's Skid?"

"He just responded to a fight call out at the Brass Rail."

Thinking of Tomasetti, I sigh. "I'll take it. Give that motorist a call back and see if he needs medical attention or a wrecker."

"Will do."

"Where on Hogpath Road?"

"Just past the Painters Creek Bridge."

"Got it." I go through the door and into the night.

HOGPATH ROAD IS A NARROW strip of asphalt banked by corn-fields on both sides. The farms are both Amish and English, but they're large and some of the houses are more than a mile apart. The Painters Creek Bridge is about two miles south of Painters Mill.

I spot headlights in the distance as I approach the bridge. They cut through the dark at an odd angle, telling me the vehicle isn't level. Flipping on my emergency lights, I idle across the bridge and park on the shoulder, about thirty feet from where the vehicle faces me from its place in the ditch.

"I'm ten-twenty-three," I say into my lapel mike.

"Everyone okay out there, Chief?"

"Not sure just yet. No sign of the driver. I'm going to take a look." I slide my Maglite out of its pocket.

Leaving my headlights and emergency lights on, I get out and look around. The other vehicle's lights are blinding; I can't make out the make or model. The driver is nowhere in sight.

"Painters Mill Police Department!" I call out. "Everyone okay?"

"I hit a deer!" comes a male voice.

"Hang tight, sir," I tell him. "I'll be right there."

Using my Maglite, I start toward the vehicle. "Sir, are you injured? Do you need an ambulance?"

"I'm okay. Just shook up."

I catch a glimpse of a silhouette. The driver is still behind the wheel, fiddling around with something on the seat. No passenger. "Could you step out here, please," I call out.

No response.

I shine my beam on the vehicle. It's a pickup truck, not in the ditch but parked at a steep angle a few feet off the shoulder. The truck is an extended cab with a long bed. Dark blue or maybe black. That's when I notice the missing front license plate.

I stop walking and sweep the beam to where I'd last seen the driver, but he's gone.

"Sir? Can you step out here and talk to me."

No answer. The hairs at my nape stand up. *Where did he go?*

I hit my shoulder mike. "Ten-seven-eight. Get Skid out here. Expedite."

Never taking my eyes from the vehicle, I walk backward toward my Explorer. "Driver! Show yourself!"

My hand slides down to my service revolver. I thumb off the leather strap, tug it out. All the while, I'm keenly aware that I have no cover. That I'm visible in the headlight beams.

The crack of a gunshot splits the air. I hear it ping into the Explorer behind me. Every nerve in my body jerks taut.

I turn, run headlong toward the Explorer. I hit my lapel mike. "Shots fired! Shots fired! Shots fired!"

I'm scant feet from my vehicle when a second gunshot rings out. Then a third. I reach the Explorer, my hand against the hood. I'm midway to the rear when something slams into my left forearm. Pain zings down my arm. I go down hard, land on my hip. I lose my grip on the Maglite and watch as it rolls out of reach.

Clutching my .38, I crawl to the rear of the Explorer. I'm panting when I grapple for my mike. "Shots fired! Hogpath Road!"

Two more shots clang against the Explorer. My nerves jump like electrical wires. I scramble to the passenger side, peer out. I see someone pass in front of the headlights of the truck. A male. Six feet tall. A hundred seventy-five pounds. Rifle in hand. Ten yards away. I fire two shots in quick succession.

"I'm a police officer!" I scream. "Drop your weapon!"

I hear a car door slam. The truck's engine revs, and I know the driver is coming for me. I fire two shots, but my aim is off. Panic hovers at the fringe of my brain. "Easy," I whisper. "Easy."

Engine screaming, the driver does an abrupt U-turn. Tires sliding, the vehicle spins and I know he's going to run. Gravel flies, pings against the Explorer. Through the rise of dust, I see the red of taillights. Taking aim, I fire my last two rounds.

"You son of a bitch!" I grapple for my shoulder mike. "Suspect is eastbound on Hogpath Road! Pickup truck. Extended cab. Blue or black. Long bed. Male driver is armed!"

I hear sirens in the distance. I need an ambulance, but I don't make the call. Instead, I lean against the Explorer's front fender. I holster my .38 and tug out my phone. I let gravity take me down to a squatting position. Using my uninjured hand, I reach for my lapel mike.

It's over.

THERE'S something about getting shot that conjures a whole new perspective. Not only about being a cop but about life in general. It makes you think about the things that really matter.

Four hours have passed since someone did his utmost to kill me. I spent the first hour sitting in the backseat of Skid's cruiser while officials from three different law-enforcement agencies took turns questioning me. Tomasetti drove me to the emergency department of Pomerene Hospital, where my left forearm was x-rayed—no broken bones—and my "minor" gunshot wound was treated.

It's one a.m. now, and I'm home safe with the man I love. I'm lying in our bed, propped against pillows, my laptop in front of me. The pain in my forearm has faded to a dull ache. I wish the knot of foreboding in my stomach could be so easily banished.

"You're still awake."

I look up from my laptop to see Tomasetti stride into the room. "Any word on the shooter?" I ask.

"I talked to Rasmussen," he says. "Every agency in the four-county area is out in force. Nothing yet."

"Were they able to get tire-tread impressions? Any brass?"

"They got brass." Tossing me a frown, he slides into bed beside me. "Not sure about impressions."

"This wasn't random," I say. "This is about the Gingerich case."

He sighs. "You got someone in mind?"

"No, but I know it circles back to Daniel Gingerich. Someone thinks I'm getting too close to the truth."

"They want you to back off."

"Evidently they don't know me very well."

"They have no idea," he mutters, and then reaches over, closes my laptop, and slides it onto the night table beside him. "Didn't the doc tell you to take the rest of the night off?"

He's said and done all the right things since arriving at the scene on Hogpath Road a few hours ago. But I'll never forget the look on his face as he'd run to me. The way his eyes swept over me, as if looking for some catastrophic injury I wouldn't survive. I knew exactly the thoughts that were running through his mind. I'd hated doing that to him, and yet I don't know how to make it right.

I turn slightly and face him. "One more thing we need to cover."

"I'm not in trouble, am I?" The lightheartedness of the statement doesn't match the gravity in his eyes.

Still, I smile. "I'm careful when I'm on duty. I don't take chances. What happened tonight was . . . bad. But I'm good at what I do. I want you to understand . . . you don't have to worry about me."

He turns to me. "I'm not going to lie to you. When I got the call, it scared the hell out of me. But Kate, that fear was tempered by the knowledge that you're a good cop. I mean that."

"I don't know what to say," I tell him.

"You don't have to tiptoe around me. I'm a big boy, Kate. Good or bad or somewhere in between, I can handle it."

I set my hand over his, find my voice. "I do have one concern."

"Yeah?" He scoots closer to me. "Shoot."

I smack his shoulder for the poor word choice, and then I nestle closer, lay my head on his shoulder. "I'm not sure how people will adjust to calling me Chief Tomasetti."

"It's got a nice ring."

"You think?"

"I think you don't have a thing to worry about."

DESPITE my best efforts, it's ten a.m. by the time I hobble into the station. Lois is standing at the front desk when I walk in the door. As expected, I find Mona sitting on the floor behind the desk. They're both looking at me with a little too much concern.

"I'm fine," I say as I cross to the desk.

"Heard things got dicey out on Hogpath Road last night," Lois says as she hands me my messages. "Any word on the shooter?"

"Not yet," I tell her. "We'll get him."

"Oh. Before I forget." Mona plucks an envelope from my message slot and hands it to me. "Someone left this for you."

I take the envelope. "Any idea who it's from?"

She shakes her head. "T.J. found it taped to the door when he brought in breakfast burritos at six a.m."

In my office I open the envelope and read:

Mark Petersheim killed Daniel Gingerich.

Rising, I leave my office and go back to reception. Both women watch in silence as I cross to the front door where the note was found, open it, and peer out across Main Street.

"Mona?" I say without looking at her.

"Yeah?" She comes up beside me, and we look across the street at Dawdy Haus, an Amish tourist shop.

I motion toward one of the security cameras next to the striped awning that shades the sidewalk. "If I'm not mistaken, that security camera will capture the front of the police station."

Mona looks at me, her eyes widening. "The note."

"Might be worth a shot."

A few minutes later Mona and I are in the small office at the rear of Dawdy Haus. The manager, Jenna Fourman, sits at the computer, tapping keys. "Heard what happened to you last night, Chief Burkholder. This have something to do with it?"

"I'm not sure yet," I say vaguely.

She presses the down-arrow key a dozen times. "This particular tape runs from six p.m. last night through six a.m. this morning."

"That's the time frame we're looking for. Is it possible to fast-forward through it?"

"Sure."

The buzzer on the outer door sounds, telling us a customer has arrived. Jenna glances at the door and rises. "I gotta get that." She motions toward the computer. "You guys can mouse through pretty quickly. Just drag that little blinking line from left to right."

"Got it." I motion Mona into her chair. "Thanks, Jenna."

At the 12:45 a.m. mark, we both see the shadowed figure and lean closer to the monitor.

"It's a woman," Mona murmurs.

"Looks Amish," I say, squinting because the resolution is grainy and dark. "Run it again."

The woman enters from the left, or south, side of the police station, walks directly up to the outer door, looks both ways, reaches into her pocket, and slaps the note onto the glass.

"Too dark to see her face," Mona comments.

"Or make out the details of her clothes. Definitely wearing a dress and *kapp*, though. Average build. Not too tall. She's sticking to the shadows."

Mona sighs. "At least we know the culprit is a woman."

"And Amish. That's significant."

"What's next?"

"I thought we might borrow this tape and see if we can get some stills." Even as I say the words, I'm not optimistic that an image will be helpful. "Once we get the images, I want you to courier this tape up to BCI to see if they can enhance it."

"I'm on it."

"Thanks." I start toward the door. Midway there I stop. "Did Bob Schoening with the fire marshal's office send that key over?"

"It came in this morning."

"On your way home I want you to hit the two hardware stores in Painters Mill to see if they can tell us if they made that duplicate."

Mona looks after me, her face broadcasting how pleased she is to be part of this. "Anything else, Chief?"

"You might want to squeeze in a few hours of sleep."

We grin at each other, and then I turn and go through the door.

BY THE time I get my hands on a decent image of the mysterious woman who left the note, the morning is gone. I'd been entertaining the notion of picking up Mark Petersheim and bringing him to the station. But I'm not convinced the note is legitimate. I opt instead to talk to the three Amish girls at the Mercantile.

According to Milo Hershberger, Neva Lambright was at the singing with Ruth Petersheim the night she was assaulted. Why didn't Neva mention it when I talked to her? Honest oversight? Was she simply trying to protect her friend's privacy? Or does she know more about what happened that night than she's letting on?

I push through the antique door of the Mercantile. A middle-aged

Amish woman operates the register. The type and color of her dress tells me she's Beachy Amish, and I wonder if she's Neva's mother, the owner of the shop. I go to the aisle where the candles are displayed, select a pillar, and take it to the register.

"That bergamot-and-sweet-rosemary combination is a lovely scent," the woman says. "Is it a gift?"

She's about fifty years old, with a stout build and a ruddy complexion. Dishwater-blond hair just starting to go gray is tucked neatly into her *kapp*.

"It's my sister's birthday." I look around the store as she rings up the sale. "Is Neva around?"

"In the back, I think." Lifting a brow, she gives my uniform a once-over. "Anything I can help you with?"

I show her my badge and identify myself. "I'm looking into the death of Daniel Gingerich, over in Painters Mill."

"I read about that." Clucking, she assumes a somber expression. "Such a terrible thing, losing a young one like that. Some of our men are going up there tomorrow to rebuild the barn for them."

"The Gingerich family will appreciate that," I tell her in *Deitsh*.

If she's surprised by my fluency, she doesn't show it. When she's finished with the sale, she offers her hand. "I'm Edna Lambright, by the way. My husband and I own the shop."

We shake over the counter. "You've done a nice job with the place. I understand you're going to open a restaurant in the old round barn in the back."

"Well, it's a work in progress. Place is older than the hills, and there are some structural issues." Her eyes sharpen on mine. "What do you need to speak with my daughter about?"

"I know Emma Miller used to work here. I understand she knew Daniel Gingerich." I try to keep my answers vague. "I'm hoping Neva might be able to offer some insights on their relationship."

"Well, the Amish are a tight-knit bunch. Everyone knows just about everyone else. Let me call her up here for you."

She picks up the phone and presses a button. "Neva, come to the front please," she says over the intercom system.

A moment later the sound of female chatter draws my attention.

I turn to see Ina Yoder and Viola Stutzman coming down an aisle, dresses swishing, arms loaded with this evening's projects.

"Hi, girls," I say.

Viola's stride falters. "Oh, hi, Chief Burkholder."

I look past her to see Neva Lambright striding toward us from the rear of the store.

"I need a few minutes of your time," I tell them. "Is there a place where we can sit and chat?"

Edna Lambright looks up from the quarters she's counting. "You can use the break room in the back."

"In the meantime"—I pull out the photo of the woman who left the note on the police station door and set it on the counter—"do any of you recognize her?"

Edna slides glasses onto her nose and looks down at the photo. The girls set their bags on the floor and gather around the counter.

"She's Amish," Edna says.

"Not a Beachy dress," Neva adds.

"Looks like gray fabric," Viola says to no one in particular.

I watch the four women as they scrutinize the still. They're bent over the counter, expressions serious, brows knit.

"Can't really see her face," Ina says.

"I'm sorry we can't be more helpful." Edna's eyes flick past me to a customer who's approached with a shopping basket laden with kitchen towels. *"Zrikk zu verk,"* she mumbles. Back to work.

A few minutes later Ina, Neva, Viola, and I are seated at a small oak table in a room that's not much bigger than a walk-in closet. Viola can't seem to keep her eyes off the bandage on my forearm. "We heard what happened to you," she says solemnly.

"It must have been scary," Ina says. "Are you okay?"

"I'm fine," I tell them. I pause a moment before continuing. "You know I'm working on the Daniel Gingerich case," I say.

Three heads bob in unison.

I focus my attention on Neva. "I know you were close friends with Emma Miller, and I understand your loyalty to her. But I need you to be honest with me. Do you understand?"

Neva stares at me, eyes wide. Ina and Viola are looking down.

"I know what happened to Emma," I say, hoping they'll fill in the blanks. "I need you to tell me what you know."

I wait, but no one speaks, so I add, "Emma deserves that."

Just when I think no one is going to respond, Viola makes a sound. I glance over at her. She's staring at the tabletop, crying.

"We have to tell her," the girl whispers.

"Viola," Neva snaps, a warning in her voice.

"Emma wouldn't want anyone to know," Ina says.

I say, "You can trust me with the information. I'll do everything in my power to keep it confidential. You have my word."

Neva raises her gaze to mine. "How did you find out?"

"I can't tell you," I say. "But I need to know what happened."

"We all noticed something different about her," Neva says. "She'd lost weight. Grown quiet. A few weeks before she died, she came to me after work. She was just . . . broken inside."

"What did Emma tell you?"

"It was about Daniel. When he was working for her parents. At first she said he'd been . . . looking at her funny. I mean, she'd mentioned it before, and we just kind of laughed it off. But this was different. Serious. It had been happening the whole time he was there, working for her parents. Emma told her *mamm*, but Mrs. Miller . . . wouldn't listen. Emma was so sweet. Innocent. And in love with Elam. She didn't want anyone to know."

I make eye contact with each girl. "Daniel raped her?" I ask.

Neva nods. "He trapped her out in the milk house. She was . . . so ashamed. Blamed herself."

"We told her it wasn't her fault," Viola whispers.

Neva shakes her head. "She didn't listen. It was incredibly sad."

"She'd been saving herself for Elam," Ina says. "All she wanted was to marry him and have children."

"Do you think that's why Emma killed herself?" I ask.

Neva nods. "I do."

"She felt guilty about it, even though she had no reason to blame herself," says Viola.

"And she couldn't get away from him," Ina adds.

I tamp down a rise of outrage. "Her parents didn't protect her?" I pose the question, but I already know.

Neva shakes her head. "They were . . . old-fashioned that way. I mean, about . . . you know, men and women."

Nodding, I move on. "Did Emma tell Elam what happened?"

Neva gives the question a good bit of thought and shakes her head. "She didn't say, but I don't think she would have told him."

"She wouldn't have risked hurting him," Viola adds.

"Was Elam protective of Emma?" I ask.

The silence that follows goes on a beat too long. "Sometimes," Ina says.

"Does he have a temper?" I ask.

"He didn't . . . I mean, before Emma died," Neva says.

"And after she died?" I ask.

Neva slants a look at the other two women and nods. "He . . . changed after he lost her. All that pain, I guess."

"Can't blame him," Viola says.

Neva looks me in the eye. "Elam Schlabach is one of the most decent young Amish men we know, Chief Burkholder. There's no way he would hurt anyone."

Nodding, I rise. "I appreciate your answering my questions and talking about something so painful."

The three girls are subdued as they rise and push in their chairs. I linger as they shuffle from the room. I'm thinking about Ruth Petersheim now, and Neva is the girl I need to talk to. Alone.

"Neva?" I say as she goes through the door.

The Amish woman looks at me over her shoulder. "Yes?"

"One more thing." I motion toward the table and chairs. "Do you have a minute?"

Ina and Viola exchange wary looks. They don't want to leave her. Neva sends a smile to her friends. "Go on. I'll be out in a sec."

I pull out one of the chairs. She returns to the break room and sinks into it. I take the chair opposite her.

"Why didn't you tell me you went to the singing with Ruth Petersheim the night she met up with Daniel Gingerich?" I ask.

Her shoulders stiffen. "I didn't think it was important."

I let the statement hang. Both of us know it's not true.

"How well do you know Ruth?" I ask.

"I've known her since I was a kid, but we were never close."

"You rode together the night of the singing at the Schwartz place?"

"Yes."

"Did anything unusual happen that evening, Neva?"

"Not that I know of."

"Who did Ruth ride home with?"

A too-long pause. "I think you already know the answer to that."

"Why did you lie to me?"

"I didn't lie. I just didn't realize it was important."

"It's called lying by omission, Neva. I asked you about Daniel Gingerich, and you didn't see fit to tell me about that night?"

She narrows her eyes. "Did something happen to Ruthie?"

"You tell me."

She stares at me for a long time. "If something happened to her, she never mentioned it. That's the truth."

"Did you hear any rumors? Anything like that?"

She shakes her head. "I would have told you. Especially after what happened to Emma. I've no reason to hold anything back."

"Is there anything else I need to know about?" I ask.

Her brows go together, and she considers the question. Finally, as if she's come to some firm conclusion, she gives a nod. "I think that's about it."

Chapter 11

AFTER LEAVING THE MERCANTILE, I head north toward Wilmot. I've just pulled onto the highway when my phone chimes. I glance at the display to see HOLMES CNTY SHERIFF, and I snatch it up.

"Kate, it's Mike Rasmussen. How's the arm?"

"An ID on the shooter would ease the pain," I tell him.

"Wish I could oblige. I figured you'd want an update, good or bad. I got a little of both."

"Lay it on me."

"We retrieved four cartridges at the scene."

"You get prints?"

"We did. Unfortunately, we didn't get a match."

"So he's not in the system." I sigh. "Caliber?"

"Caliber is three-oh-eight. Common hunting rifle."

"Were you guys able to pick up tire-tread imprints?"

"We got a partial. Lab's looking at it now."

"You're making my day with all this good news."

He doesn't laugh. "You still think it's related to Gingerich?"

"I do."

A thoughtful silence and then, "Do me a favor and be careful out there, will you?"

"You got it."

I MAKE a right on Milton and park in front of the Petersheim house. I'm thinking about the note and the questions I need to ask as I take the narrow sidewalk to the front door. I knock and wait. When no one comes to the door, I go around to the back and knock on the screen door, but there's no reply.

That's when I hear the baby crying. Not merely cries, but screaming. I knock again, this time using the heel of my hand. "Mr. and Mrs. Petersheim? It's Kate Burkholder," I call out.

I wait, but there's no response. Just the continuous screaming of an unhappy infant. I remind myself Ruth could be in the shower. But there's something in the tone of that cry that's worrisome.

I open the screen door and rap on the glass. "Mr. and Mrs. Petersheim! Kate Burkholder! Can you open the door please!" I wait, but the only sound I hear is the howling cries of the child.

There's a window to my left. I leave the porch and approach it, stand on my tiptoes to see inside. At first all I see is a typical kitchen. Yellow countertops. White cabinets. Out of the corner of my eye, I see a cat in the window. I don't pay much attention. Then the cat raises its paw and leaves a red smear on the glass.

Grabbing a terra-cotta pot from the step, I go to the door and break the glass. I reach through and yank it open.

Then I'm in the kitchen. The scream of the baby echoes throughout the house. I follow the sound down a dimly lit hall.

"Mark! Ruth! Are you okay? It's Kate Burkholder!"

I tug my .38 from my holster. Ahead a door is cracked open a few inches. The hardwood floors are mottled with bloody paw prints. All the while the baby screams.

"Mark? Ruth?" Pistol leading the way, I sidle to the end of the hall, push open the door with my left hand.

A gasp escapes me when I see them. Mark and Ruth Petersheim lie side by side atop a cream-colored quilt, surrounded by an ocean of blood. I know immediately they're dead.

For a moment I can't move. Can't speak. Can barely think.

The crying of the baby snaps me back. Giving myself a hard mental shake, I go to the crib and scoop the child into my arms. I look down at his angel's face. I see tears in eyes the color of a summer sky, and I want to cry for him.

"It's okay, little guy," I whisper. "I've got you now. I've got you. Everything's going to be okay."

Little William looks up at me and begins to wail.

THE next hours are a blur of questions from a flurry of law enforcement. I spend most of that first hour trying to balance my need to know what happened to the Petersheims and caring for a hungry and dirty infant whose future has been forever altered.

It takes an hour for the social worker from Children Services to arrive. A red Camry parks on the street two cars down from mine. A woman in a maroon suit gets out and starts toward me.

"Chief Burkholder? I'm Deb Cooke with Children Services."

"Hi." I cross to her and, shifting William, offer my hand.

She looks at the baby, sleeping in my arms. "What a cutie."

"Yes, he is." I send a nod toward the house. "I think he's been alone for some time. His parents are inside, deceased."

Sighing, she shakes her head. "I've been in contact with a foster family. They're a sweet couple about fifteen minutes away."

William's body is warm and soft against me as I carry him to the social worker's car. I press a kiss to the little boy's cheek and set him in her arms. "Take care of yourself, little William."

She lifts the child and, bending, places him in a car seat. Straightening, she looks at me, tilts her head, and digs into her bag for a card. "If you want to check on him later, give me a call."

"Thank you." After taking the card, I watch her get into the car and drive away. For a moment I feel . . . bereft.

"Chief Burkholder?"

I turn to see a man striding toward me. He's about fifty years old, with a receding hairline, wire-rimmed glasses, and the beginnings of a paunch. He's got cop written all over him.

"I'm Jim Hawkins with the investigations unit." He sticks out his hand, and we shake. "Hell of a thing for you to walk into."

I nod. "What's your take?"

"Got all the hallmarks of a murder-suicide. Looks like there was a struggle. He got her on the bed, shot her in the back. He got into the bed beside her, put the muzzle in his mouth, and pulled the trigger with that rifle. I'm glad he didn't take that baby with him."

"Any idea how long they've been dead?" I ask.

"Coroner thinks eight to twelve hours." His eyes narrow. "Wilmot is a hike from Painters Mill. You know these people?"

I shake my head. "I talked to them a couple of times." I give him the condensed version of the Gingerich case.

"Heard about all that. You think Mark Petersheim set that fire?"

"I think it's possible."

"If he did, it could be a precursor to all this." He motions toward the house and shrugs. "If he thought he was going to jail for what he did to Gingerich, he might've decided to just call it a day."

"Maybe."

"In light of your ongoing case, we'll take a close look at this."

"I appreciate it. Let me know if I can help in any way."

"Will do."

It's FULLY DARK BY THE TIME I arrive home. I'm thinking about little William as I let myself in through the back door. I find Tomasetti standing at the counter eating ice cream from the carton.

"You get that baby taken care of?" he asks.

"Handed him off to the social worker an hour ago."

"Tough break for the kid." He kisses the top of my head.

Over rum raisin we discuss how the day's developments might affect the Gingerich case. "I'll get with Stark County and have them send Petersheim's fingerprints," he says. "We'll do a comp and see if they match anything we got from the Gingerich scene." His brows go together. "Petersheim had a rifle?"

My mind's eye flashes back to the rifle lying on the bedroom floor. I know where Tomasetti is going with this.

"You think he's the one who shot at me?" I ask.

"Gingerich raped his wife. Got her pregnant. She didn't tell Petersheim. She married him and passed the baby off as his." He shrugs. "If he didn't want that coming to light . . ." His voice trails.

I think for a moment, trying to get a handle on what isn't settling in my gut. "I never figured Petersheim for killing Gingerich."

His eyes find mine. "The person who killed Gingerich may not be the person who took a shot at you last night."

I toss him a frown. "I thought of that."

"Who else are you looking at?"

"Elam Schlabach."

"The dead girl's boyfriend."

I nod. "And Milo Hershberger. The best friend."

"I don't have to tell you to keep your eyes in the back of your head open, do I?"

"Don't worry. I'm going to be looking over my shoulder for a long time."

ASIDE from a loose-hog incident in which Skid and I spent two hours chasing a boar down Dogleg Road, the next morning is uneventful. I finished my report on the Petersheims. When I spoke with the chief deputy, he told me all indications pointed to murder-suicide. I also called the social worker to check on little William and learned he will be placed with family members later today.

Yesterday's events placed Mark Petersheim squarely at the top of my suspect list in the murder of Daniel Gingerich. Chances are, he's also the person who tried to kill me. He knew he would be caught, so he murdered his young wife and ended it.

So why aren't I convinced he's my killer?

"Because I don't think he did it," I say, glad there's no one around to hear me talking to myself.

I page through the Gingerich file for the hundredth time. I stare down at the autopsy photos of Daniel Gingerich, the remains of what had once been an eighteen-year-old Amish boy with his own secrets. "Did Mark Petersheim do that to you?" I whisper.

"Chief?"

I look up to see Lois standing in the doorway of my office. "Everyone's here," she tells me.

"Thanks." I close the file, shift gears.

Just this morning the mayor came through, authorizing me to hire an additional patrol officer. I didn't waste any time; I called Mona into my office and promoted her on the spot. It's the first time I've seen her speechless. The first time I've seen her cry.

"You got the card?" I ask.

Lois presents a yellow envelope containing the congratulations card all of us signed for Mona. I take it out and scribble my name.

"I've never seen her this nervous," Lois says under her breath.

"In that case," I say as I rise, "let's not keep her waiting."

I step into the meeting room to find my team assembled. I take my place behind the podium, clear my throat. "As most of you know, our department is understaffed and has been for quite some time. I'm pleased to report Mayor Brock has increased our budget and Mona Kurtz is now Painters Mill's first female officer."

I leave the podium and stride toward Mona, my hand extended. "Congratulations, Officer Kurtz."

We shake, and I can't help but notice how incredibly happy she looks, despite the sheen of tears. "Thanks, Chief," she whispers, and then pulls me into an embrace.

Next to her Skid rises and high-fives her.

"About damn time," Pickles mutters.

Jodie squeals. "I'm so happy for you!" Joining hands, she and Lois dance in a circle.

Glock smacks Mona on the back before wrapping her in a bear hug. "Welcome aboard, rookie."

T.J. crosses to her. "I guess this means I'm off graveyard shift."

I pause at the door and watch the scene, putting it to memory, knowing it's one of those moments that will stay with me.

IT'S four thirty p.m. when I get the call from Tomasetti.

"The lab supervisor of the latent-print unit just called. The latent on the casing left at the scene the night you were shot belongs to Mark Petersheim. He was your shooter."

I let out a breath. "Do his prints match the latent lifted off the key found at the Gingerich scene?"

"It's not a match," he tells me. "We've fingerprinted everyone in the Gingerich family. Those comps should be done soon."

"Okay."

"Interestingly, the latent on the mason jar found at Chris Martino's house doesn't belong to Petersheim, either."

"So my arsonist is still out there."

"This is where the plot thickens. The print found on the key retrieved from the Gingerich scene *matches* the print found on the mason jar."

"So whoever handled the key at the Gingerich farm also handled the mason jars found in Martino's garage. The information swirls in my head. "What about the tire-tread imprint?" I ask, referring to the one taken the night of the shooting.

"Still working on the comp. Probably going to match the tires on Petersheim's truck." Tomasetti sighs. "Wish I had better news. I know you were hoping to close the case."

"At least the shooter was identified."

"One threat down." He pauses. "You coming home soon?"

"I thought I might talk to Elam Schlabach before I call it a day."

"The Amish boyfriend of the girl who killed herself."

I give him my impressions of Schlabach. "He's twenty-three

years old and newly married, with a baby on the way. And yet the only emotion I got out of him when I talked to him is rage."

"Give me a call if you need anything."

"Bet on it."

It's nearly five p.m. when I swing by Buckeye Woodworks and Cabinetry on Fourth Street, only to be told that Elam Schlabach has already left for the day. I drive out to his home on Dogleg Road. His wife tells me he's working late.

I stand in the driveway and wonder: *Where the hell are you?*

In a small town like Painters Mill, that question isn't always difficult to answer. There are three drinking establishments in the area. The Brass Rail is too rowdy. McNarie's is too . . . bikerish. That leaves Miller's Tavern. Most of the patrons are local business owners and shopkeepers. Just the kind of place a young Amish man might frequent when he doesn't want to go home.

Back in the Explorer, I head toward town.

There are no buggies parked in front of Miller's Tavern, so I idle around to the alley at the rear. Sure enough, there's a nice-looking bay gelding hitched to a lone buggy, snoozing. I park next to it and then enter the bar via the back door.

Elam Schlabach sits in a booth, a mug of beer in front of him, watching me. I hold his gaze as I make my way over to him.

"Mind if I join you?"

"Do I have a choice?"

"Nope." I slide onto the seat opposite him.

He lifts his beer, takes a long pull. "So is this about Danny Gingerich or what?"

I give him a long, assessing look. "Did you have anything to do with the barn fire that killed Daniel Gingerich?"

"No. That's not to say I didn't think about it. I did. Hate to disappoint you, but I never mustered the grit."

"I know what he was," I say.

"I doubt it."

I hold his gaze. "I know what he did to Emma. And others."

"Look, Chief Burkholder, I know you think I killed Danny. But if you know what he was, then you've probably realized I'm not the only one who isn't exactly mourning his death."

"Do you have someone in mind?"

"Even if I did, I wouldn't say." He looks away, shrugs. "Far as I'm concerned, he did the world a favor."

"How many other women did he rape?" I ask.

He shrugs. "I heard he did Mark Petersheim's wife." His expression distorts into something acerbic. "Heard what happened to him, too, by the way. They were a nice couple. Gingerich ruined the lives of a lot of good people."

"Who else did Daniel Gingerich hurt?" I ask.

A full minute passes without an answer. I'm thinking about hauling his ass down to the station, when he finally responds.

"I heard he done one of them other girls Emma used to hang with. The one worked with her at that shop in Charm."

I go still, my heart giving a kick. Milo Hershberger's words float through my mind. . . . *He used to go up to that shop in Charm all the time just to see those girls. Had his eye on all of them. . . .*

"I need a name," I say.

"I don't know." He shakes his head. "Look, if you want to know about Danny's escapades, talk to Milo Hershberger. They were best friends. I suspect Milo would be the moron he'd brag to."

"Are you and Milo friends?"

His laugh is bitter. "Not even close."

He looks away, and for the first time, I see a chink in his armor. A glimpse of the man he must have been before the woman he loved committed suicide.

"So are you going to arrest me or what?" he asks.

"You'll be the first to know." I pluck my card from a compartment on my belt as I rise and hold it out for him. "If you think of anything else, call me. And don't even think about leaving town."

He takes the card and tosses it onto the tabletop.

DUSK has fallen by the time I pull into the farm where my sister and her husband live. Despite my best intentions, I missed her birthday. I've been carrying around the gift-wrapped candles and teas I bought for her at the Mercantile for a couple of days now.

I take the sidewalk to the back door. The barn door is open, and I see her husband, William, inside grooming a Standardbred. I raise my hand in greeting. He waves back, but the gesture is half-hearted. My brother-in-law doesn't approve of my leaving the fold.

The door opens. "Katie! What a nice surprise. Come in!"

I'm trying to remember the last time I saw her. It's been a while. Sarah is two years older than me. Blond and pretty, with the kind of sweet smile I never quite mastered. She's wearing a light blue dress with a white apron and *kapp*.

She leads me into a big kitchen that smells of something delicious. My little niece, Hannah, who has somehow grown into a toddler, is standing in the doorway clutching an obese cat.

"Hi, Hannah," I say. "That's a pretty *bussli* you've got there."

The little girl grins and hefts the cat. "Sammy!" she proclaims.

"Er fett e faul." He's fat and lazy. My sister sends her child a sideways glance. "Say hello to Aunt Katie, Hannah."

The little girl obeys, but her expression lets me know that I'm a stranger to her, a fact that hurts more than I want it to.

I take a chair at the table. "Happy birthday." I set the bag containing the gifts on the table. "Sorry it's late."

She rattles the bag. "I'm just glad you're here. You don't come over enough, you know."

She delivers the admonition in her gentle way, which somehow makes the sting more powerful. I came here to spend a few minutes with my sister. Remind my niece she has an aunt. Despite all the years that have passed, there's still a part of me that craves the approval of my family. Maybe even the Amish community as a whole.

"I have news." She sets her hand protectively over her abdomen. "I'm *ime familye weg.*"

I'm out of the chair, bending to her, hugging her close. For an instant I think about telling her that Tomasetti and I have set a date for our wedding, but the timing doesn't seem right. This is her moment. I'll fill her in next time I see her.

I motion toward the gift. "It's not going to open itself."

Grinning, she digs in. "A candle! From the Mercantile! Katie, that's my favorite store these days. They make the best candles."

"Best everything." I glance at the gift bag. "There's more."

"Well, my goodness, Katie." She pulls out the soaps and tin of tea. "Did those sweet Amish girls make all of this?"

"They made the candles. I think the owner made the soap."

"Edna," she says.

"You know them?"

"I was just there last week. Had keys made for the new gates."

"Keys?"

"*Ja.* Someone opened the gate in that back pasture last week. Let all of our goats out. We're keeping all the gates locked now. William wanted extra keys, so I had duplicates made."

"You had keys made at the Mercantile?"

"Edna made them." Smiling conspiratorially, she leans close. "William thinks I'm quite the dutiful wife. Little did he know the only reason I went there was for the shopping."

Chapter 12

IT'S EIGHT A.M. and I've been sitting in the parking lot of the Mercantile for half an hour when a buggy stops outside the big antique door. I watch Ina Yoder and Viola Stutzman climb down. Viola turns and waves to the driver as the buggy drives away. Ina pulls a wad of keys from her pocket and starts toward the door.

I reach them as Ina unlocks the door. *"Guder mariye."*

Viola startles upon hearing my voice. "Oh, Chief Burkholder! Didn't hear you drive up. *Guder mariye* to you, too."

Ina opens the door and ushers us inside. "We're not quite open yet, but you're welcome to coffee while we get the register running."

"I appreciate that. Is Neva here yet?" I ask.

"She always gets here early to make coffee," Viola tells me.

"She drives a car, so the drive doesn't take her quite as long," Ina says with a hint of petulance.

"I heard that."

The three of us look ahead to see Neva standing next to the customer service counter. She's wearing a dusty pink dress and a pair of Keds that are a little too stylish for most Amish. She makes eye contact with me. "Is everything all right, Chief Burkholder?"

"Everything's fine," I tell her. "I just need to speak with the three of you if you can spare a few minutes."

Ina nods. "We don't open until nine, so we have some time."

"Coffee's made," Neva says. "Would you like to sit?"

A few minutes later the four of us are seated in the café. I pull the key from the plastic bag and slide it to the center of the table. "Can any of you tell me if this duplicate key was made here?"

The three girls stare at the key.

"I don't know if there's any way to tell." Neva starts to reach for the key but hesitates. "Can I look?"

"Sure."

She picks it up and glances at Ina. "Is this one of ours?"

Ina shakes her head. "I don't know how to run the machine."

Viola leans close for a better look. "I told Mrs. Lambright I want to learn how to make the keys. She hasn't shown me yet."

"Probably need to check with Mamm on that," Neva tells me.

"I will." I take the key and drop it into the bag.

I look from face to face. "You heard about Ruth Petersheim?"

"We heard," Ina mumbles.

"I heard little William is going to live with his *grossmudder*," Viola says, referring to the baby's grandmother.

"*Ruth's* grossmudder," Neva says.

Ina whispers, "Word is, Mark may not have been the father."

"That's just cruel gossip if you ask me," Viola snaps.

"Well, people are talking," Neva points out.

Viola's gaze finds mine. "Do you think what happened to them has something to do with Daniel Gingerich?"

"I do." I take a sip of coffee, aware of a new tension zinging among us. "I know Daniel used to come in here on occasion."

"I think he only came in a few times," Neva says dismissively.

Viola slurps hot chocolate. "It was a long time ago."

The girls begin to chatter among themselves, so I smack my hand on the tabletop to get their attention. "Stop lying to me."

Startled looks are exchanged. Neva sets down her cup. Ina looks away. Viola scoots her chair closer to the table.

"I'm not the enemy here," I say softly.

"We know that," Neva says.

"You didn't tell me that Daniel used to come in here bothering the three of you."

"He didn't," Neva blurts.

I give her a look that lets her know I'm not happy with the answers I'm getting. "I think he did a lot more than bother you. What else haven't you told me?"

"Why are you being so pushy?" Ina snaps.

"I think you know more than you're telling me," I snap back.

The three young women stare at me, eyes wide.

"Daniel came into the Mercantile a few times," Neva says quietly. "He'd always pretend that he was looking for something, but it was about us." She trades looks with the other girls. "All of us."

I'm debating the wisdom of pushing for more, when the tinkle of keys draws my attention. I glance over to see Edna Lambright approach the café. I hadn't heard her come in.

"Looks like you girls are having a productive morning." She reaches the railing. Narrowed eyes flick from Neva to me and back to Neva. She holds out two pies. "These custards need to be sliced, put on plates, and wrapped."

Chairs clatter as the girls rise. Quickly they scatter.

Edna is taking it all in, watching me. "What brings you here this morning?" she asks.

"I'm trying to find out where this duplicate key was made." I pull the key from the bag as I leave the café area. "Any chance it was made here at the Mercantile?"

She squints at the key. "It's possible we made it here, but there's no way to tell. Is that what you were talking to the girls about?"

"I was told Daniel Gingerich used to come in here."

"Lots of people come in here. All kinds of boys skulking around to get a look at those girls. They don't think too much about it."

I stare at her, wondering how much she knows about Emma Miller. "Are you sure?"

"I'm quite sure. Sorry we couldn't be more help."

I drop the key into the bag.

"This have something to do with the fire?" she asks.

"Yes, it does."

"How does that key play into all that?"

"I'm not sure, but I think I'm going to get it figured out soon." I stuff the bag into my pocket. "Thanks for the coffee."

THE police station is quiet on a weeknight at seven p.m. Skid left for patrol a couple hours ago, and everyone except Jodie and me has gone home. I'm sliding my laptop into its case, when my cell phone vibrates. Expecting Tomasetti, I snatch it up. "Hey."

"Chief Burkholder? It's Edna Lambright." Her tone is frantic. "It's Neva. She's . . . gone. I can't find her. She left a . . . note."

"She's missing?"

"Yes. I haven't seen her since five. I found the note half an hour ago. It says she doesn't want to be on this earth anymore. I'm afraid she's going to hurt herself."

"Have you searched for her?"

"Isaac checked the barn. He walked our whole property. I looked in the house, even the attic and root cellar. She's not here."

"Is there someplace she might've gone? A friend's, maybe?"

"She's close with Ina Yoder, of course. Little Viola. I'm in the car on my way to the Yoders' now."

"Can you think of anyplace else she might've gone?"

"Isaac is on his way to the Stutzman place. If I don't find her at the Yoders' . . . I don't know. She might've gone to the shop." She makes a strangled sound. "I'm scared, Chief Burkholder."

"Do you know what she's upset about?" I ask.

"I don't know. She barely said a word all day."

I pause, wondering if it has anything to do with my visit earlier, and ask, "Edna, do you think Neva is suicidal?"

I hear a quick intake of breath on the other end and then a sob. "I don't know. I just . . . The note scared me."

"Does Neva have a car, Edna? Or is she on foot?"

"She has that old car Isaac gave her."

"What's the make and model of the car?"

"It's white. A Ford Taurus. Old. Two thousand five, I think. Chief Burkholder, would you mind driving over to the Mercantile to see if she's there?"

"I can be there in fifteen minutes."

"Oh, thank you. I'll meet you there as soon as I talk to the Yoders. They're only ten minutes from the shop."

"Don't worry. We'll find her."

I hang up and call Skid with a quick summary of the situation. "She's eighteen years old and might be on her way to the Yoder farm out on County Road Twenty-Four."

"I know the place," he says. "I'll swing by, do a welfare check."

"I'm on my way over to the Mercantile. Keep me posted."

I LET Jodie know where I'm going as I go through reception; then I dash into the pouring rain. I run the Explorer over the speed limit and make it to the Mercantile in twelve minutes. As I pull into the lot, my headlights glint off the darkened windows. There are no cars. No lights inside. I pick up my radio. "I'm ten-twenty-three," I say to let Skid and dispatch know I've arrived on scene.

I rack my mike and scan the front of the shop, the rain pounding on the roof of my vehicle. "Come on, Neva," I whisper. "You're too smart to do something like this. Where are you?"

I idle past, keeping my eye on the windows for movement or light. I reach the end of the building and peer into the side lot. Lightning flashes with blinding intensity. An instant later thunder cracks like a cannon shot. I pull around to the side and creep toward the rear, where the old round barn is being renovated.

Hitting my high beams, I squint to see through the rain-streaked windshield. The round barn is a huge structure, half of which is surrounded by scaffolding. There's a massive cupola at the peak. A small, square window stares down at me like a dead, blank eye.

I'm in the process of turning around to wait for Edna Lambright when I see a flicker of light near the front door of the barn. I run my spotlight over the façade, but there's no one there; the door is closed. No light in the window. There's no vehicle. No buggy. Still, I'm certain I saw a light. So where the hell did it come from?

"Only one way to find out."

Resigned to getting wet, I shut down the engine, grab my Maglite, and hightail it to the door. When I twist, the door creaks open. The interior is dark. The rain on the roof is deafening.

"Hello?" I call out. "Neva? Are you here?"

I listen, but no response comes. Stepping inside, I shine the beam around the interior. It's a large area with a wood-plank floor. The remnants of a dilapidated silo stand in the center. Several stanchions on a raised concrete slab are still recognizable. Two full-sized stalls to my right. Curved stairs run along the wall to a second-level loft and down to the ground level. To my left I see a scaffolding set up against the wall.

I walk to the center of the space. "Neva!"

Ducking between the stall rails, I cross to the stanchions and peer into the silo. The dirt floor is ten feet down. I'm midway to the stairs when I notice a faint dome of light coming from a niche ahead. Moving quickly, I start toward it. My beam illuminates a small battery-powered lantern atop a wood crate. There's a spiral-bound notebook. A pen. A cell phone. A brown prescription bottle.

"Oh, no," I mutter, and then, "Neva! It's Kate Burkholder! Come out here and talk to me."

The floor is covered with a drop cloth or tarp. The kind a painter might use. I'm midway to the alcove when a loud crack! sounds. The floor gives way beneath my feet. Then I'm falling into space.

I land hard, feetfirst, dust and debris flying. My knees buckle on impact. The ground isn't level, and I fall sideways, my shoulder and head slamming against the ground.

Groaning, I roll onto my back, blink dust from my eyes. Darkness all around. Flashlight nowhere in sight.

Bad move, Burkholder, a little voice chides.

I lie still, wait for my head to clear, taking physical stock. Aside from some scrapes and bruises, I think I'm okay.

"Chief Burkholder?"

Relief sweeps through me at the sound of Edna Lambright's voice. I push myself to a sitting position. "Down here," I call out.

"You've taken quite a fall. Are you all right?"

A flashlight beam appears to my left. I glance over to see the Amish woman making her way down rickety steps. "Guess I should have taken the stairs," I say, trying not to feel foolish.

"I should have warned you about that floor. We're having it replaced. Are you hurt?" she asks as she reaches the ground level.

"I'm fine." I make it to my knees. "Any sign of Neva?"

"No." She blinds me with the flashlight beam. "She's never done anything like this before."

I'm still shaken. "Can you get that light off me?" I say.

"Sorry." She reaches me and stops. "Let me help you."

Her light shifts. I can see the outline of her dress. She's fiddling with something in her right hand. I hear the rip-tear of Velcro, and she bends toward me. Something hard is jabbed against my back.

"What are you doing?" I start to get up.

A loud crack! snaps through the air. Pain explodes through my body. The next thing I know, I'm laid out on the ground. For an instant I think I've been shot. But I know that sound. *Stun gun.*

Edna Lambright stands over me. No emotion on her face. Squatting, she yanks my radio from my belt. I try to stop her, but she hits my arm with the stunner, and another jolt zips from my shoulder to my fingers. She slides my .38 from its nest.

"What the hell are you doing?" I rasp.

She sets her hands on me, digs into my pockets, yanks out my phone. "Danny Gingerich was a devil in disguise," the Amish woman says. "He was a monster."

I don't know if she's speaking to me or talking to herself. The one thing I do know is that I'm in trouble.

"That boy hurt everyone he came into contact with," Edna tells me. "Man like him has no place on this earth. God struck him down is what He did. I just helped Him get the job done."

I flop onto my side. My brain is beginning to clear.

"Where's Neva?" I ask.

"Don't worry about her."

I try to get up, but my arms and legs fail. I get my first good look at the stun gun as she thrusts it at me. "Don't!" I shout.

The electrodes snap. She stabs it hard against my back. Agony streaks up my spine, leaving me twitching and helpless.

"You know what he was," she says. "You should've looked the other way. Let it be so we could all be done with it."

My brain is misfiring. "People know where I am," I manage.

"Nothing I can do about that."

She starts toward the stairs. I'm aware of the hiss and bark of my radio as she carries it away. Skid trying to get me on the horn. I think of him walking into this. She's armed with my .38.

"You would have gotten away with it, Edna. Why do this now?"

She stops, turns to me, blinds me with the flashlight. "I did what I had to do. There was no pleasure in it. He had to be stopped."

I try another tactic "You're right about Daniel. Let me go and I won't say a word."

"I don't believe you. I know your kind."

For an instant I think she's going to level the .38 and empty the cylinder into my body. Instead, she starts toward the stairs.

I struggle to my hands and knees, scramble to my feet. She's midway up the stairs; there's no way I can catch her. "I'm a cop, Edna. People know where I am. They'll be looking for me."

I stumble toward her, my coordination returning. I dash to the base of the stairs, look up to see her go through the door at the top. I clamber up the steps, using my hands, as fast as I can manage. I'm halfway there when the door slams. The lock snicks into place.

"Edna!" I reach the door, grab the knob, and twist, but it's locked. "Open the door!" I shout. "Open it! Now!"

Nothing.

Turning, I face the darkness, wonder if there's another way out. I feel my way down the stairs and get my bearings. I'd had my flashlight in my hand when I fell. Did it come down with me? Or did Edna take it? It had been on; I should be able to see the beam.

I make my way over to the place I landed and kick away some of the wood and debris. Sure enough, I spot the beam and snatch up the flashlight. I get my first good look at my dungeon. The space is about thirty feet wide, with a low ceiling comprised of wood support beams and planks, all of it held up by massive columns resting on concrete piers. The floor is dirt. The exterior wall is a mosaic of wood siding set atop an ancient stone foundation. There are no windows on this level. Just the staircase to my left.

A noise from above quiets my thoughts. I hear footsteps, movement, something being dragged across the floor. The next thing I know, something heavy lands a few feet away from me. Flicking on the light, I realize Edna tossed a wood pallet through the opening. I shift the beam upward in time to see a wooden crate tumble down. A second crate follows, busting on impact.

I'm about to call out to her when I discern the unmistakable smell of gasoline. Fear lands a punch in my chest.

"Edna!" I shout. "Unlock that door and let me out!"

Several more boards fly down through the hole. The smell of gasoline intensifies, and I realize she's dousing the wood with gas.

I hasten to the staircase, take the steps two at a time to the top. I try the knob again. No go. I check for hinges, thinking I might be able to tap out the pins, but they're on the other side of the door.

I step back, raise my leg, and kick the wood next to the knob hard enough to jolt my bones. Once. Twice. The door holds solid.

"Edna! Don't do anything stupid." Grinding out the words between gritted teeth, I take the steps back down to ground level. My eyes scan the area, looking for something I can use to bust down the door. I spot a T-post, rush to it. I'm bending to pick it up when I hear a tremendous whoosh! A fireball the size of a car flares above and then plummets downward.

A gust of intense heat shoves me backward. Turning away, I sprint to the stairs. At the base I glance over my shoulder to see the pile of wood ignite.

"Edna!" I scream. "Open the door!"

Smoke rises and expands along the ceiling, pouring out through the opening from which I fell. I dart to the T-post I saw earlier, snatch it up. I rush back to the stairs, take them two at a time to the top. Using the post like a battering ram, I slam it into the door as hard as I can. The impact jars my body. But the door holds.

Setting down the T-post, I snatch the flashlight from my waistband and descend the stairs. I see that the fire has doubled in size.

"Help me!" I scream.

Smoke scorches my throat. My shirt is still damp from the rain. I rip it off my shoulders and tear off one of the sleeves. I wrap the sleeve around my head, cover my nose and mouth, and tie it at my nape. I put what's left of my shirt back on and jog to the wall farthest from the fire. The stone-and-concrete foundation is a couple of feet high. I run my hands over the wood siding, looking for loose boards, but there's nothing.

Disbelief swamps me. I can't believe my life is going to end this way. I think of the people I'll leave behind. But it's John Tomasetti that dominates my thoughts. The intensity of my love for him. Even if I die here today, I know that will live on.

A crash shakes the building. In my peripheral vision I see sparks raining down, and I know the ceiling is starting to cave. If I don't get out now, I'll either be crushed to death or burned alive.

"Tomasetti . . ." I scoot closer to the foundation. Nowhere else to go. No air to breathe. Just fire and heat and smoke.

A cool puff hits my face. Then I smell rain. The flashlight is still in my right hand. The beam illuminates nothing but dirt and stone, all of it obscured by smoke. Then I spot the gap where the mortar has crumbled. Water seeping in from the outside.

I roll onto my back, set my feet against the stone foundation, and I stomp as hard as I can. Hope leaps when the stones shift. I reposition myself, mule-kick with all my might.

Another surge of hope when I feel movement. Lifting both legs, I stomp the stone again and again. It slides a couple of inches. Finger-size chunks of mortar fall toward me. I scream and kick and choke in a frenzy of panic and resolve.

The stone gives way. The one above it shifts down. Mortar crumbles. Lungs burning, I kick it. Once. Twice. And it's gone.

Twisting, I sit up, set my face against the rush of cool, clean air. I thrust my hands and arms and head through the hole. Digging my toes into the dirt, I shove my torso and hips through. Drizzle and cool night air greet me. I grab handfuls of weeds and grass and mud and pull myself free of the hole.

Then I'm outside, gulping fresh air, coughing. Rain cools my heated skin. I roll onto my back, look up at the night sky. For an instant I can't move. I don't know whether to laugh or cry.

A crash from inside the barn snaps me from my stupor. I struggle to my feet. I'd been so focused on escape, I hadn't considered the possibility that Edna Lambright is still around. That she's got my .38. I make my way toward the Explorer to radio for help.

I'M MIDWAY to the Explorer when I see the flash of emergency lights. Skid's cruiser pulls up next to my vehicle.

He jumps out and jogs toward me. "Chief!"

I break into a run. "Edna Lambright is armed!" I call out. "She locked me in the barn. Set it on fire."

He speaks into his lapel mike. "Ten-thirty-five," he says, putting out the code for a major crime alert.

"She's in a 2005 Taurus," I tell him. "We need to stop her." I reach him, aware that he's staring at me with concern.

"You okay, Chief? You need an ambulance?"

I yank open the door of his cruiser. "I'm fine. Let's go get her."

I slide into the passenger seat. Gravel flies from beneath the tires as he turns around and starts toward the road. "She's probably on her way to her farm."

He makes a right and floors the accelerator.

"Skid, she's got my gun," I tell him. "You got an extra?"

"Just that shotgun in the trunk."

"That'll do."

The radio lights up with activity as the alert goes out to dispatch and the Holmes County Sheriff's Department. Skid's driving fast, eyes scanning left and right as he passes dark country roads, fields, and lanes obscured by trees.

Taillights appear ahead. "There," I say.

"Looks like our vehicle."

Skid pulls up close behind the car. For a second I think she's going to run. Then the turn signal flicks on; she pulls onto the shoulder and stops. Skid stops. "I'm going to get her out."

"Armed-driver protocol," I say. "Pop the trunk."

"Yep." He draws his weapon. The trunk mechanism clicks.

Opening his door, he grabs the mike for his loudspeaker. "Driver! Turn off the engine! Roll down your window and let me see your hands!"

I open my door and, staying low, slink around to the trunk. I lift the trunk and unseat the Remington 870 from its mount.

"Driver!" Skid's out of the car now, his weapon trained on the vehicle. "Show me your hands now!"

Two hands appear through the driver's-side window.

"Open your door and step out of the vehicle!"

The driver's-side door opens. The Amish woman sets her feet on the ground and slides out of the vehicle.

"Get your hands up! Turn away from me! Face the other way!"

I raise the shotgun, praying I don't have to use it.

Edna Lambright stands quietly with her back to us, her hands raised to shoulder level.

"Walk backward!" Skid shouts the command twice.

When she's a few yards away, he orders her to stop. "Get down on your knees! Keep your hands up."

Skid's .38 is aimed at the woman, center mass. I move forward, round the front right quarter panel, shotgun at the ready. In the light of his headlights, I see him remove the handcuffs from his belt. Cautiously, he approaches her.

"Where's the gun?" he asks.

"I don't know," she cries. "I dropped it. In the car."

He's a few feet away from her. He's reaching out to cuff her left wrist, when her right hand drops. Skid sees it at the same time I do. "Get your hand up!" he shouts.

As if in slow motion, Edna Lambright turns, still on her knees. In the glare of the headlights, I see a black weapon in her right hand. Coming up. Her eyes on Skid.

"Drop it!" I scream. "Drop the weapon! Drop it!"

Skid is too close to her for me to fire the shotgun. I see his gun hand move upward.

"Drop it!" he shouts.

The gunshot freezes everything in place: I see a tremor pass through Skid; the Amish woman on her knees, twisting around, facing him, her right arm straight, the weapon pointed at him.

Two more shots in quick succession. Edna Lambright pitches forward, falls facedown on the asphalt.

"Skid! *Skid!*" I lower the shotgun, dart over to him.

He backs up a couple of steps, nearly runs into me. I set my hand on his shoulder. "Are you hit?"

"No." He shakes his head. "I don't think so."

I kneel next to Edna Lambright. She's lying prone, with her head turned. She's alive, her eyes open and blinking. She's not moving, but I can see the rise and fall of her back as she breathes. There's blood on her dress. A hole in the fabric where the bullet struck her.

I touch her shoulder. "An ambulance is on the way, Edna."

"Neva," she whispers.

"Neva will be fine," I say. "You, too. Just hang on."

She closes her eyes. "I set the fire."

"I know. We'll deal with that later."

"No. The Gingerich fire. I set it. I did it."

I look at Skid. He heard it, too. I look down at her, but the Amish woman is gone.

Chapter 13

NEVER DOUBT IN THE DARK what God has shown you in the light. The words were one of my *mamm's* favorite sayings, especially in the face of tragedy, and I heard it often growing up. When my *grossmudder* passed away. When a neighbor was killed in a buggy accident. The axiom reflects the Amish tenet of maintaining faith in times of heartbreak. One of many reasons I never fit in.

Edna Lambright was pronounced dead at the scene a little after ten p.m. It took the fire department an hour to extinguish the blaze. Because the incident included an officer-involved shooting, I called Tomasetti. Somehow he made the thirty-minute drive from Wooster in under twenty. At that point, BCI assumed control of the scene. Sheriff Mike Rasmussen showed up a short time later, along with the BCI crime-scene unit truck. Later Bob Schoening with the fire marshal's office arrived, and I spent another half an hour or so answering questions.

I stuck with Skid throughout. We stayed on scene until the coroner pulled up. That's when Tomasetti offered us a ride to the police station. We accepted the offer.

Once we arrived at the station, we were separated. Tomasetti interviewed Skid. He collected Skid's revolver, which will be tested and later—once he's off administrative leave—returned to him. I gave my statement to one of the other BCI agents. He was decent enough to do a welfare check on Neva, who was safe at home and hadn't left the house all evening.

As chief, one of the responsibilities I take very seriously is the death notification to the deceased's next of kin. I disliked the idea of sending T.J. to break the horrific news to Edna's husband, Isaac, and Neva. But because I was personally involved in the shooting, I couldn't do it myself.

"Go to Bishop Troyer's house first," I told him as he headed out. "Tell him what happened and ask him to go with you."

"You got it, Chief."

I know T.J. will be kind but straightforward. Still, it's a difficult assignment and I hated to put it on his shoulders.

It's now two a.m. I'm sitting at my desk, a cold cup of coffee in front of me. I'm wondering if Tomasetti is still around—if they're finished with me for the night—when Skid walks in.

"You're looking a little worse for wear," I say.

"You, too."

558 | Linda Castillo

"Figured." I motion to the chair opposite my desk. "They done with you?"

"I think so." He looks down at his uniform. "I feel kind of naked without my gun."

"You'll get it back in a week or so."

He takes the chair and grimaces. "Chief, an Amish woman? Why the hell did she pull that gun? I mean, we had her. . . . She had to have known it wouldn't end well. For any of us."

I shake my head. "You heard her last words, right?"

"Yep. You think that's why she did it?" he asks. "She figured her life was over anyway and she decided to go death by cop?"

There's a bitterness to his voice I don't like. "Maybe. I don't know. Skid, the most important thing for you to remember right now is that we get to walk away from this. Because you did your job. You stuck to your training. You did everything right."

"I killed an Amish woman." He scrubs his hands over his face. "That's so nuts I can't even get my head around it."

"I know. Me, too. She didn't leave you any choice."

A soft tap at the door draws my attention. I look up to see Glock and Pickles standing in the doorway, Mona behind them.

"I hope we're not interrupting," Glock says.

I stand, drawing their attention, giving Skid a moment to shore up. "I probably don't have to point out it's after two in the morning."

That's one of the things I love about my team. Not only are they good cops but they're good people. When one of their own is in trouble, they drop everything and show up in force to support them. Skid might be resilient, but he doesn't have family here in Painters Mill. Tonight he shouldn't be alone.

I notice the brown paper bag Glock's holding at his side.

"Jack Daniel's comes to the rescue," Pickles says.

"He's in good hands," Glock assures me.

"We're professionals, Chief," Pickles adds.

I nod and turn my attention to Skid. "You're off for a few days, Skidmore. Protocol for an officer-involved shooting. I'll keep you posted and let you know if we need anything."

"Great." He rises. "Appreciate it, Chief."

I let my gaze connect with Glock's and then Pickles's. "If it's not too much to ask, stay out of trouble."

"We got this, Chief," Pickles says, and they usher Skid through the door.

It's not until I'm home that I realize what an absolute wreck I am. I reek of smoke and sweat and singed hair. The bathroom mirror reveals a face and neck that are smudged with soot and dirt.

Tomasetti was with another BCI agent when I left. I caught his eye as I headed toward the door. I could tell he didn't want me to leave without him. But I needed to get out of there.

It's only when I'm in the shower that I examine my own emotions—and relive the horrific moments I was locked inside the barn. The sense of being trapped. The terrifying thought of being burned alive. The all-encompassing panic and disbelief.

When I close my eyes, I see Edna Lambright as she lay dying on the ground. Her face when she'd spoken her final words.

The Gingerich fire. I set it. . . .

I rush through the shower, scrubbing myself clean, my hair and face and hands, wishing I could scrub away the images.

I'm sitting at the kitchen table in my old sweatpants and a T-shirt when Tomasetti comes in the back door. I can tell he's concerned.

He kisses the top of my head. "You're shaking."

"I'm okay. Hair didn't fare so well."

Spotting the tumbler of whiskey in front of me, he growls low in his throat. "You hate whiskey."

"It'll do in a pinch." I look over at him. "Want one?"

He pours two fingers of eighty-proof into a glass. He takes the chair across from me, sets the glass on the table, and reaches for my hands. "You scared the hell out of me."

"I know. I'm sorry. I—"

"Don't apologize. It's okay. I just . . . when I got the call . . ." He turns my hands over in his, looks down at the smattering of blisters on my palm, and frowns. "You're burned."

"I don't think they're bad."

"Uh-huh." He leaves the kitchen and returns with the first-aid kit. "Let's have a look."

Neither of us speaks as he tears open a roll of sterile gauze, wraps it loosely around my hand, and tapes it.

For a moment he doesn't say anything. Then he raises his gaze to mine. "Kate, this isn't official yet, but I thought you should know. The crime-scene technician found several rounds in the console and on the floor of Edna Lambright's car. When he checked your thirty-eight . . . the cylinder was empty."

"*What?* But . . . that doesn't make sense. She drew her weapon."

"It looks like she emptied the cylinder," he says.

"Why would she do that?"

He shakes his head. "I don't know."

I pick up the glass and sip. "You know she confessed to setting the fire that killed Daniel Gingerich."

"I read your statement." He swirls his whiskey. "Hard to figure."

I shake my head. "Tomasetti, suicide by cop?"

"We've seen crazier things. With her being Amish, maybe the guilt was too much."

"She knew what Gingerich was."

"Even so. Maybe she couldn't handle what she'd done and decided to end her life without having to do the dirty work herself."

"It doesn't make sense."

Even as I say the words, I realize it does, but in a way that's so twisted, I'm not sure I'll ever be able to get my head around it.

THEY say criminals always return to the scene of the crime. Sometimes cops do, too. Drizzle falls from a Teflon-gray sky when I pull into the parking lot of the Mercantile. For five days I've debated whether to come back. I haven't been able to stop thinking about the three young Amish women whose lives intersected with mine in the course of the Gingerich case.

Today is the first day the shop has been open since Edna Lambright's death. The community has come out in force to support the Lambright family. Inside, customers stand in line at the cash register, which is being manned by Ina Yoder. I wave when I walk in, but Ina doesn't notice. I start toward the rear of the store.

I'm midway through the candle section when I spot Viola Stutzman in the next row. I start toward her. She's been crying at some point. Her eyes are puffy; the tip of her nose is red and chapped. If I'm not mistaken, she's lost a couple of pounds.

There's no hostility in her eyes when she looks at me, no blame. "Chief Burkholder. I'm . . . I'm glad you're okay."

"I hope you're okay with my being here. If not, I can take off."

"I'm okay with it. I just . . ." She lets the words trail. "What a terrible tragedy."

"I'm sorry about Edna," I tell her.

Pain flashes across her face. "Thank you."

"How are you holding up?"

"I'm okay. Sad for Neva, mostly. She took it hard."

I glance around the shop. "How is she?"

"Her heart is broken. First Emma and now her *mamm*. I told her not to come in today. It's too soon. I caught her crying back in the break room twice. I don't think she's going to be able to stay."

I nod. "I'd like to offer my condolences. Do you think she'd talk to me?"

"She doesn't blame you for what happened. She's just . . . sad and confused. If you want to see her, she's in the break room."

I reach out and squeeze her hand. "I won't keep her long."

I make my way to the break room and find Neva sitting at the table, unmoving. For an instant I consider leaving.

Then she raises her head. Her eyes meet mine and widen. Surprise flashes, but it's overshadowed by the grief I see etched into her every feature. "Chief Burkholder."

"Hi, Neva."

She starts to rise. "I didn't think you'd—"

"Don't get up," I tell her. "I can't stay. I just wanted to . . . see you. See how you're doing."

She lowers herself back into the chair. "I'm okay."

We both know the words couldn't be further from the truth.

"I'm sorry about your *mamm*," I say quietly.

Bowing her head, she chokes out a sob and begins to cry.

I put my arms around her shoulders, give a brief embrace.

"If you want me to leave, I'll understand," I say quietly.

Pulling away slightly, she raises her head. "Don't go." She blows her nose. "I know it wasn't your fault."

I tug out the chair next to her and sit. "I didn't think you'd be back at work so soon."

"I couldn't stay away. Mamm loved this place so much."

"Sometimes work is good therapy," I tell her. "And it helps to be around people who love you."

"I don't know how I'd have gotten through the last few days without Ina and Viola. Even the customers have been sweet."

"I know what happened is painful. If you want to talk about it, I'm here. If you prefer not to talk about it, that's okay, too."

She gives me a grateful look. "I don't know what could have compelled her to do such things. To Daniel Gingerich. To *you*." She chokes out a sound of pure anguish. "What could she possibly have been thinking?"

I think about the final minutes I spent with Edna Lambright in the barn. The things she said. The things she knew.

Danny Gingerich was a devil in disguise. . . .

"Your *mamm* knew what Daniel Gingerich was," I tell her. "She knew what he did to Emma. I think she knew he wouldn't stop. Maybe she handled it the only way she knew how."

Neva stares at me. "Mamm loved Emma like a daughter."

I nod, wishing there was something I could say to ease her pain.

"None of that explains what she did to you." Her whisper is hoarse, her words barely audible.

"I was a threat." I shrug. "We'll probably never know all of it."

She struggles for a moment, then raises shimmering eyes to mine. "I'm sorry for what she did. To you. To Daniel, even. I don't know how to make any of it right. I'm so . . . ashamed."

"It wasn't your fault."

"I love her. I'll always love her. And I miss her desperately. But I'm *angry* with her, too."

We fall silent, and for the first time, she looks uncomfortable. Time to go, I realize. Let this be. Let all of it go and move on.

"I've got to get back to the station," I tell her as I rise. "I just wanted to stop in and see how you were doing."

She wipes her eyes, takes a deep breath, and composes herself. "It must have been hard for you. Thank you."

Before I can respond, she rises and throws her arms around me, burying her face against my shoulder. "I'm glad you're okay."

Pulling away, she gives me a sad smile, and then she's gone.

I start toward the front of the store. I'm nearly to the door when I walk past the old-fashioned bulletin board affixed to a column. A piece of card stock tacked to the cork catches my eye. My eyes are drawn to a handwritten announcement.

Candle-making class! Tuesday evening 6:30 to 7:30 p.m.
Just $15. Open to the public.
Sign up at the customer service desk. ☺

The advertisement is written on a five- by eight-inch index card in purple ink. Someone has drawn in a smiley face in the lower right-hand corner. There's nothing particularly unusual about it. Nothing that should have given me pause. And yet . . .

Around me the sounds of the shop fade. My vision tunnels on the handwriting. It's cursive, embellished with ornate swirls and curlicues. There are five *i*'s; each one is dotted with a little heart.

I snatch the card from the board and take it to the customer service desk, where a Mennonite woman is helping a customer with a return. I show her the card. "Do you know who wrote this?"

"That's Viola's handwriting," she says. "I can sign you up for the class, but you'll need to get in line and wait your turn."

For an instant I stand there, feeling as if I've been suckerpunched. Sliding the card into the back pocket of my trousers, I back away from her and head for the door.

TWENTY minutes later I pull into the parking lot of Quality Implement. Hoping I'm wrong, I tug out the card as I walk inside. I find Ralph Baker sitting on the top rung of a stepladder in the windshield-wiper aisle, jotting SKU numbers onto a clipboard.

"Mr. Baker?"

He glances up. "Oh, hi, Chief Burkholder." Smiling, he rises. "What can I help you with today?"

I show him the card. "Do you recognize this handwriting?"

"Huh? Well . . . let me see." He tilts his head back to look at it. "What am I looking at here, exactly? I mean, what is this?"

I rephrase my question. "Is there anything about this handwriting that's familiar to you?"

Again, he looks at the handwriting. "I don't know that I've ever seen it before. But I'm not sure where you're coming from here."

"Mr. Baker, when you came to me about the note Daniel Gingerich received shortly before his death, you described it as a 'girlie' style of handwriting. You mentioned little hearts over the *i*'s. Is that correct?"

"Oh! I'd forgotten all about that. Sheesh." He takes another look at the index card. "Gosh, Chief, I only saw that note for a second, but this sure looks like the same writing. Same little hearts over the *i*'s, just like what's on that card there. Same color ink, too."

"Do you think it's the same handwriting?"

"Well, I can't say for sure, but it sure looks like it."

QUESTIONS bombard me as I walk back to the Explorer. Is it possible Viola Stutzman wrote the note that lured Daniel Gingerich to the barn the night he was killed? Was she involved? Or did she simply write the note for Edna Lambright? If that's the case, why didn't she mention it when I talked to her about it?

Thoughts racing, I call Tomasetti. "Do the latent prints on the key found at the scene of the Gingerich fire belong to Edna Lambright?" I hear the high-wire tension in my voice. I'm pretty sure Tomasetti hears it, too, because he takes his time responding.

"I thought you were about to close the case."

"I thought so, too." I tell him about finding the card at the Mercantile and my conversation with Ralph Baker.

"He thinks it's the same handwriting?"

"He only got a glimpse, but he remembers the little hearts above the I's and the purple ink."

"Viola Stutzman probably isn't the only teenage girl who writes that way or uses colored ink."

"I know. And I know it's a tenuous connection."

"That's not to mention you don't have the note for comparison."

"The note was never found. I assumed it was destroyed in the fire." I take a breath. "Tomasetti, I don't think I can ignore this."

I hear computer keys clicking on the other end of the line, and I know he's accessing the information on the latents. He makes a sound low in his throat, telling me he found what he was looking for—and he doesn't like what he sees.

"Because of the cause and manner of Edna Lambright's death, fingerprints were obtained at the time of autopsy." A few more clicks sound, and then, "That comparative analysis was never done, because Edna Lambright confessed."

"Can you get that for me?"

"Let me make some calls." But he pauses. "Kate, Edna Lambright confessed. She tried to murder you. We can't ignore that."

"Tomasetti, what if she was trying to protect someone?"

"Viola Stutzman? Were they that close?"

Mamm loved Emma like a daughter.

I close my eyes. "Look, if you could check on those latents for me. I need to check a couple of things on my end."

"What are you going to do?"

"I'm going to go back to the Mercantile."

It's nearly six p.m.—a few minutes before closing at the Mercantile. I'm sitting in my Explorer in the side parking lot. I'm feeling more than is prudent, wishing I could walk away from this.

I didn't hear back from Tomasetti until nearly four p.m. The news wasn't what I wanted to hear. The latent prints found on the mason jar that was discovered in Chris Martino's garage and the prints lifted from the key found at the scene of the Gingerich barn fire did not belong to Edna Lambright.

I get out of the Explorer and walk into the shop. Neva Lambright stands at the cash register, ringing up a sale. I head toward an aisle jam-packed with kitchen décor: glass pitchers, vases, votives, and other appealing items that draw tourists from as far away as Pennsylvania. I grab four votives. They're about two inches tall and made of smoked glass. I tug a tissue from my pocket, wipe each of the votives clean, and start toward the front of the store.

Neva Lambright gives me a double take on spotting me and offers a poor imitation of a smile. "You're back."

"I forgot to buy these when I stopped in earlier." I set three of the votives on the counter, hand the remaining one to her.

She takes the votive, turns it over in her hand. "I love these." Her smile is sad. "For your sister?"

"These are for me." I watch as she upends the votive and enters the SKU number and amount into the cash register.

"Would you like a gift box?"

"Yes, I would. Thank you."

She carefully wraps each of the votives.

"Are Ina and Viola around?" I ask.

"You missed them by about twenty minutes. Left early today."

I'd been hoping to catch the other girls, too. I'm going to have to settle for what I've got—and hope to hell I'm wrong.

"Thanks." I reach across the counter and touch her arm. "Take care of yourself," I tell her, and head for the door.

Once I'm in the Explorer, I call Tomasetti. "Where are you?"

"I'm standing in our kitchen trying to decide on the Brie or Manchego and letting this nice Spanish Rioja breathe."

"Will it keep?" I ask.

"That depends. What do you have?"

"Fingerprints. I need to process them for a comparison with the latents found on the mason jars and the key."

"You've been busy."

"Tomasetti, I don't want to be right about this."

"You mean about Viola Stutzman?"

"I mean about any of them."

He sighs. "I know the lab supervisor in the latent-print unit in Richfield. Let me give her a call. Can you meet me up there?"

"I'm on my way," I tell him, and disconnect.

AFTER leaving the Mercantile, I met Tomasetti at the BCI field office in Richfield, where he works. He got me through security, and we met with the supervisor of the latent-print section of the lab. Margaret Brooks is a certified latent-print examiner. I don't know how Tomasetti did it, but she agreed to process and extract the prints from the votives, do the comparison, and get back to us.

It's nearly five a.m. now. I'm sitting at the table in my kitchen waiting for Margaret Brooks's call, a cold cup of coffee in front of me. I have a sinking feeling I'm facing a busy morning.

"Kate."

I look toward the door to see Tomasetti come through and squint at me. Despite my mood, the sight of him conjures a smile. Mussed hair. Scruffy whiskers. Sweatpants and a faded T-shirt.

"You get any sleep?" he asks.

"A little."

"Uh-huh." He knows better.

I motion toward the coffee maker. He pads to the counter and pours, then carries his cup to the table and sits across from me. "Daniel Gingerich was a serial sexual predator." I say the words without looking up. "He ruined countless lives. If I'm right about this, if I follow through, where is the justice?"

He sets down his cup. "We've been around the block enough times to know that Lady Justice doesn't always get it right."

"Those girls are barely out of their teens. They've got their entire lives ahead of them."

"They should have thought of that before they locked that son of a bitch in the barn and burned him to death."

"Gingerich was a threat. If he'd escalated—"

"He was not an imminent threat. We don't get to judge, Kate. We enforce the law. The rest is up to the courts."

I rub my hands over my face, realizing I'm too tired to think clearly.

After a moment he reaches for my hand. "Look, if you're right, if it goes to court and those girls are put in front of a jury . . ." He shrugs. "There's such a thing as extenuating circumstances. If other women—other victims—come forward." Another shrug. "Furthermore, even if those girls are convicted, they may not draw long sentences. They may not do time. We don't know."

I jump when my cell phone chirps. I snatch it up. "Burkholder."

"Kate, hi. It's Margaret Brooks. I didn't wake you, did I?"

"No. I've been expecting your call."

"Figured as much." She sighs. "Look, I know this is important, so I did dual comparisons. One with the computer. And a side-by-side visual comparison using the ACE-V method. It is my determination that those prints came from the same source. Of course, I'll still need to have my findings verified by another . . ."

It is my determination that those prints came from the same source.

"Chief Burkholder? Are you there?"

"I'm here," I hear myself say. "Margaret, thank you so much for doing this. For staying up all night. I appreciate it."

"Yeah, well, you're welcome, Kate. Just tell that Tomasetti character he owes me big-time."

"Will do."

I drop the phone into my pocket and take a moment to shore up, slip back into my cop persona. I rise and look at Tomasetti. "The prints on the key and the mason jar belong to Neva Lambright."

"It's enough." He rises, too. "You got her."

I look at the clock on the wall. Not yet six a.m. "I'm going to grab a shower and head that way."

I start to turn, but he reaches out and stops me. "You want me to go with you? Or meet you there?"

I think about that a moment. "I'll call you."

"You know where to find me."

Chapter 14

THE MERCANTILE DOESN'T OPEN until nine a.m., but when I roll into the parking lot a little after eight, I spot Neva Lambright's car parked between the burned-out shell of the round barn and the shop. It's not until I get out of the Explorer that I spot Viola inside the barn. As I draw closer, I see the other two girls standing together on what's left of the steps.

Sighing, I step into the building. "Good morning," I say.

Viola and Ina spin toward me, their expressions surprised. Neva blinks upon recognizing me.

"Hi, Chief Burkholder," says Ina.

"Didn't expect to see you here this morning," Viola adds.

I look from girl to girl, my gaze lingering on Neva. There's so much misery there. But there's guilt, too.

"You're not here to buy something, are you?" Viola asks.

"Actually, I'm here to see the three of you."

Looks are exchanged, but no one speaks.

"So much of life is about the decisions we make," I say to no one in particular. "I've made my share of bad ones. I live with them every day. What do you do when there's no way to make it right?"

Viola takes a step back. Ina stares at me, eyes wide. Neva raises her gaze to mine. In the depths of her eyes, I see the things I don't want to see. Realization. A sense of betrayal. And fear.

"I need to talk to you about Daniel Gingerich," I tell them.

"We've already talked to you about him," Neva says.

"I always wondered," I say slowly, "what kind of killer lets the livestock out of the barn to keep them safe?"

Something unsettling flickers in Ina's eyes. "We have no idea what you're talking about."

I don't relent. "I know what you did. I know what all of you did. I have the fingerprints to prove it."

My gaze settles on Neva. Her face is colorless now.

"Your fingerprints were on the mason jar you planted at Chris Martino's house," I tell her.

"But . . . that's not possible," she says. "I didn't go there. It's not mine. It can't be."

Viola sets her hand on a crossbeam and leans. "We didn't do anything wrong." But her voice has gone hoarse.

"Where does it end?" I ask.

A sob bursts from Neva's throat. "My *mamm* put those jars there!"

she cries. "I must have . . . touched them or something when they were in the cellar. That's all."

"I only mentioned one jar. How did you know there were two?"

Her eyes dart to her friends, begging for help. "I don't know what you're talking about. Jar. Jars. What does it matter?"

"Your fingerprints are also on the key we found in the Gingerich barn." I divide my attention among the three of them. "You were there, and you lied to me."

"The Amish community is a small one, Chief Burkholder," Viola tells me. "Maybe we made the key for him. Maybe—"

"Stop lying to me," I snap. "Just . . . stop."

The girls fall silent.

I look at the three of them. "Hate and shame are powerful emotions. The kind that can make good people do bad things."

"We didn't do anything wrong," Viola whispers.

"You should have gone to the police after what he did to Emma," I say. "Instead, you took things into your own hands."

"We did nothing," Ina says.

"Which of you did he rape?" When no one answers, I focus my attention on Neva. "Was it you?"

She raises her hands, sets them against her face. Bending, she lets out a wail so filled with agony that I feel it echo all the way to my bones. "Stop saying that! You've no right to say it!"

Ina rushes forward, grasps her friend's shoulders. "You're wrong, Chief Burkholder. She didn't do anything. None of us did."

I push harder. "He raped Emma. He got her pregnant. And she committed suicide. Then it was Neva. The three of you knew what he was, and you knew he wouldn't stop. So you came up with a plan." I look at Viola. "You wrote the note. Purple ink. Little hearts and swirls." I look at the other two. "Then you lured him to the barn, locked him in the tack room, and set the place on fire."

Viola's face is contorted and red. "He was a monster! He was . . . *da Deivel!*" The Devil. "I hated him. *Hated him!*"

"That doesn't give you the right to murder him."

Viola takes a step back. "I thought you cared about us. How could you betray us like this?"

"Because I don't have a choice," I tell her. "Because life isn't fair. Because you didn't do the right thing, and I have a job to do."

Neva straightens. "I thought you were our friend."

"Don't do this," Ina cries. "Please don't make us—"

I cut her off. "I know he was a monster. I know what he did. And I know Emma and her unborn child weren't his only victims." I can hear myself breathing. I rein in my emotions. "You can't do what you did. You can't do that. Even if he *deserved* it."

For a full minute no one speaks. I'm aware that Neva is crying openly, choking back sobs. Ina is standing next to Neva; she's shaking so violently, I see her dress quivering.

"Please don't tell," Viola whispers.

"I do not have a choice." I look at each of them. "You should have done the right thing. You should have gone to the police."

Neva sobs hysterically, her entire body quaking. "Emma would have been shamed. She was *ime familye weg*. Everyone would have assumed she'd given in to Elam. The bishop would have put her under the *bann*." Her voice is strangled, the words running together. "She didn't do anything wrong. Daniel did that to her. He treated her like an animal. Made her want to die!"

I struggle for calm. "Which one of you lured Daniel to the barn that night?" When no one answers, I turn to Neva. "Was it you?" I turn my attention to Ina. "I know you used the guise of a meet-up to get him into the tack room. Then all you had to do was lock the door and set the fire."

"I did it," Neva cries. "It was me. Just me. They had no part."

Viola shoots her a warning look. "I wrote the note. I gave it to him, told him I wanted to meet him in the barn. That I was ready."

"He was so stupid and predictable," Ina hisses. "We knew he would come. He couldn't stop himself. He deserved what he got!"

I divide my attention among them. "Who was in the barn with him the night he was killed?"

"All of us," Ina says, her voice breathless and shaking.

"Who set the fire?" I ask.

"I bought the gas." Viola looks from girl to girl.

"I closed the door, locked it." This from Neva. "Then I poured from the can."

"We piled some things against the door," Ina adds. "All of us. The cinder blocks. That old wheelbarrow and hay."

"I threw the matches," Ina tells me.

Viola starts to cry. "He was pounding on the door."

"We wanted to let him out." Neva sobs the words. "But the fire got too big too fast. And then we couldn't."

"So we just . . . ran," Ina finishes.

I stare at them. I should be pondering the question of how they could do something so monstrous. But I already know.

"What about Edna?" I ask. "How much did she know?"

Neva looks at me as if I just thrust a knife into her belly. "My *mamm* was only trying to protect us."

Ina puts her arm around her friend's shoulders. "Edna knew what he was."

"We didn't tell her," Viola puts in. "She figured things out."

"She was smart that way," Ina adds.

"And the night she was killed?" I ask.

"She did it for us," Neva tells me. "For Emma. For all of us."

THE Amish believe that every day is a gift from God. It's the Amish way. Be thankful for what you have, even in the face of adversity. Especially in the face of adversity. It's one of many Amish tenets I could never quite subscribe to. There are certain days I wish I could erase from my life. Today is one of them.

It's dusk now, and I'm at the farm sitting on the dock, looking out across the pond. I've got my jeans rolled up to my knees, my feet in the water, and a cold bottle of Killian's Red beside me.

"I thought I might find you out here."

I look over my shoulder to see Tomasetti approaching from the house. He's holding a Killian's Red in his right hand. He sits down beside me and lowers his feet into the water. For the span of several minutes, neither of us speaks.

"Rasmussen booked the three girls into the county jail," he tells me. "They'll be arraigned and formally charged in the morning."

I close my eyes against a tangle of emotions I don't want to feel. Remorse. Guilt. Loss.

"Their lives are ruined," I say.

"Changed, to be sure." He shrugs. "Maybe not ruined entirely."

"I talked to the prosecutor," I tell him. "He's talking about second-degree homicide."

"That could change."

I slant him a look.

"Neva Lambright told Rasmussen that Mark Petersheim had been threatening her."

"Did she explain why?"

"According to her, he blamed her for his wife getting into the car with Gingerich the night she was raped. He was afraid Neva was going to talk about it and the Amish community would find out. There was a certain level of intimidation occurring." He shrugs. "Prosecutor might be a little more willing to cut a deal."

"Tomasetti, what they did was wrong. I mean that. But they're not sociopaths. I don't believe they're a danger to society."

"If you want to help them, I suggest you get the other women who were victimized by Gingerich to come forward."

I find myself thinking about Milo Hershberger and our final conversation. *If I could, I swear I'd make it right.* He isn't the only one with regrets. Emma Miller's mother remained silent, and her daughter died. I don't think she'll make the same mistake twice.

"I've got a couple of people in mind who'll step up," I tell him.

Leaning closer, he puts his arm around my shoulders and presses a kiss to my temple. "Is there anything I can do?"

I rest my head on his shoulder. "Just be you."

"Now there's a scary thought."

I laugh, and it feels good. It reminds me that life goes on. That it's good. That I'm a lucky woman with a lot to be thankful for.

"What do you say we swing by the barn on our way back inside?" he says. "Check on those chicks?"

"I'm game." I get to my feet, brush dust from the seat of my pants. Tomasetti rises, too, and for a moment we stand there looking out over the water. I think of the man standing beside me, and

I acknowledge how much we have to look forward to in the future.

"That water looks nice," he says after a moment.

I nod. "Nice on the feet."

"You know what we haven't done yet?"

I slant him a look. "Had dinner?"

He grins. "Christen the pond."

I grin, step away from him. "You wouldn't."

"You know I would."

"John Tomasetti, you're so not going to—"

He reaches for my hands, pulls me against him, crushes his mouth to mine. The next thing I know, we're falling. His body is warm against mine, then the slap of cold as the water envelops me.

The water isn't deep, about four feet. We come up sputtering. His hair is sticking up on one side. He's got moss on his forehead.

We burst into laughter.

"I thought that might cheer you up," he says after a moment.

"That speck of moss above your eyebrow helped."

"Small sacrifices and all that."

Leaning into him, I put my arms around him. "Seeing those chicks probably would have done the job."

"Now you tell me," he says with a laugh.

Hand in hand we wade to the bank and start toward the barn.

AfterWords

After ten installments of the Kate Burkholder series, *New York Times* bestselling author Linda Castillo is still finding new ways to develop her lead character. "She's got a lot of layers," Castillo says of the small-town police chief in an interview with criminalelement .com. "She's imperfect—and human. Even after ten books, I'm still peeling away some of those layers and learning new things about her."

To research her novels, Castillo travels to Ohio's Amish country every year to spend one-on-one time with members of the community. It's important to Castillo to portray Amish culture in an "honest and respectful way," without stereotypes. While Amish country may be an unusual backdrop for a crime series, Castillo believes that the peaceful rural setting of Painter's Mill adds dramatic tension to her novels. "One of the elements I love most about setting a thriller series among the Amish," she says, "is the juxtaposition of the bucolic countryside with the evil introduced into it."

Castillo's work has been nominated for various awards, and her debut thriller, *Sworn to Silence*, was adapted into an original movie starring Neve Campbell as Kate Burkholder. In addition to writing, Castillo's other passion is horses. Originally from Ohio, she currently lives in Texas with her husband, two rescued blue heelers, and two Appaloosa horses.

Library of Congress Catalog Card Number: 98-640138
ISSN: 1541-0900

Printed in the United States of America

ACKNOWLEDGMENTS

Page 149: Jesse Neider. Page 295: Lynne Wayne. Page 575: © Pam Lary.
Jacket and title page image: Mimadeo/Shutterstock.

The original editions of the books in this volume are published and copyrighted as follows:

The Last Time I Lied, published at $26.00 by Dutton,
an imprint of Penguin Random House LLC
© 2018 by Todd Ritter

A Borrowing of Bones, published at $26.99 by Minotaur Books,
an imprint of St. Martin's Press, LLC
© 2018 by Paula Munier

Not Our Kind, published at $26.99 by Harper,
an imprint of HarperCollins Publishers
© 2018 by Kitty Zeldis

A Gathering of Secrets, published at $26.99 by Minotaur Books,
an imprint of St. Martin's Press, LLC
© 2018 by Linda Castillo

The volumes in this series are issued every two months.
Readers may receive this service by contacting us by mail, email, or company website.

In the United States:
Reader's Digest Select Editions
PO Box 50005, Prescott, AZ 86304-5005
bookservices@rd.com
rd.com

In Canada:
Reader's Digest Select Editions
PO Box 970 Stn Main, Markham, ON L3P 0K2
bookservices@rd.com
rd.ca

Some of the titles in this volume are also available in large-print format.
For information about Select Editions Large Type, contact us at
PO Box 433031, Palm Coast, FL 32143-3031 or selt@emailcustomerservice.com.